CW01082284

LIFE RESET: EVP

(Environment vs. Player)

– NEO Book Two –

SHEMER KUZNITS

Life Reset: EvP (Environment vs. Player)

A self-published book by Shemer Kuznits

Copyright © 2018
All rights reserved. This book or any portion thereof may not be reproduced or used in any manner whatsoever without the express written permission of the publisher except for the use of brief quotations in a book review.

ISBN-13: 978-1722938482
ISBN-10: 172293848X

ACKNOWLEDGMENT

I'd like to thank my family for supporting my writing, and especially my loving wife, who had to endure long nights with me holed up in my writing den.

I'd also like to thank the beta readers and proofreaders who helped make this book better: Ian, Jay, Tim, JD, Florian, Chris, Blaise, Jeremy, Jason, Ben, and especially Gaddy and Nadav – my faithful alpha readers.

Special thanks to my patrons over at Patreon. With their support and encouragement, I was able to take the first step toward becoming a full-time author, reduce my full-time job hours, and dedicate more time to writing.

1 – New Dawn

It was dark outside, the start of another workday for my Shadow-Touched monster clan.

Leaving my house, I walked toward the edge of the settlement and climbed the ladder to the stone shelf above the entrance to Nihilator's cave. I'd started calling it Totem's Watch.

Looking over the moonlit valley spread before me, I couldn't help but smile. Two weeks had passed since the Ogre attack on our clan, and all signs of the destruction they had wrought were gone.

More than that, the expansion and progress of Goblin's Gorge had leapt forward. Taking advantage of the surge in manpower and resources, as well as the clan's victory bonus, our little hamlet was growing at a steady pace. The valley was dotted with newly finished buildings and more were under construction. And ... we had roads!

The first new building we'd constructed after the Ogre invasion was a woodcutter's hut, which increased our logging output by 20 percent. With three lumberjacks feeding logs into the lumber yard, and Woody, the former-lumberjack-turned-woodcutter processing them, our production rate skyrocketed. Last I checked, we were producing nearly 60 units of lumber a day.

With the wood surplus, I decided it was time to fix the morale issues that had plagued my clan for so long. Zuban, the clans' constructor, and I had put our heads together to plan and decided to *finally* build decent lodgings for my followers. Zuban and his crew had already finished eight cabins and were working on the final two. Each cabin housed four goblins. Ten of those would provide enough beds to last us a good while.

As we had planned, Zuban built the cabins in a row, wall to wall, at the edge of the forest. They would double as a divider between the open land and the forest. It was yet another layer in our defensive strategy, like the thornthistle hedge.

When the first few cabins were completed, I learned to my chagrin that they didn't solve the morale issues for all clan members, only that of the workers. The warriors didn't care about residential sleeping quarters and ordering them to use the cabins didn't address their morale penalties.

Instead, warriors required a proper barracks. Bob, my hobgoblin lieutenant, claimed the barracks would also provide other benefits to my warriors, though he couldn't specify exactly what they were.

I guess I'll find out soon enough, I thought, gazing with satisfaction at the skeleton of the large building being constructed.

A couple of days ago, Zuban and Romil, our resident goblin researcher, had finally finished researching the blueprints for the barracks. I'd diverted half of my builders – all now highly experienced – to work on it.

The barracks was going to be a huge structure, even bigger than the mess hall, and it called for a lot of building resources.

Our lumber yard easily provided the required 80 lumber, and Barzel, the resident goblin smith, managed to produce the 20 metal ingots needed. Stone proved a little more difficult to produce in sufficient quantity, as quarrying was exhausting, slow work.

But experience had taught me to plan ahead. For the first week, the builders worked exclusively on wooden buildings, namely the cabins, while our two stonemasons built up our stock. We managed to accumulate the required 50 stacks of stone for the barracks.

To my dark-enhanced vision, the valley was as clear as if it were lit by a noon sun. Below me, a packed dirt road stretched from the mouth of the cave through the settlement, leading all the way toward the forest path. I had learned from Zuban that our latest acquisition, the new hob clan members, were capable of building roads. According to him, all hobgoblins shared a racial feature which gave them an innate understanding of how to build rudimentary fortifications. Building basic roads was part of that. The roads accentuated the layout of the settlement, giving it shape. They also provided easy access for my workers, increasing their speed and consequently the overall efficiency of the settlement by one percent.

I watched the hustle and bustle of the moonlit valley; my clanmates busily carrying supplies, crafting, producing, and developing our small hamlet. Five hobgoblins were busily expanding the network of roads.

It was hard to believe only seven weeks had passed since I first established the clan.

Suddenly a strange feeling came over me. I felt light, unburdened ... giddy, almost.

"Crap."

I knew what that meant. I had felt it before.

Time was slowing down.

There were travelers nearby.

***

I paced in my house restlessly, looking out the window every few minutes, impatiently waiting for an update.

At last, there was a knock on the door.

Ashlazaria – the hobgoblin scout and Zuban's girlfriend – walked in. My other hobgoblin scout, Yulli, was away with one of the Ogres, escorting the coal mining expedition.

Towering over me by almost half a goblin height, Ashlazaria bowed her head respectfully.

"Report."

"Yes, Dread Totem." She straightened. "Six travelers are moving through the forest. They are staying close to the mountainside, fast approaching the valley entrance."

I grimaced; that was bad news. At least there were only six. "Describe them in detail."

She paused, her eyes becoming distant. "Two of them are wearing robes, one red, one white, no weapons. Two have leather armor, one has two short swords, the other is carrying a large two-hander. They are being led by an elf wearing green clothes and carrying a longbow, possibly a scout."

"You said there are six of them," I reminded her.

She nodded. "There is another, a dwarf. He is ... different. I can't explain it exactly. He has metal armor, an axe, and a large shield. When I looked at him ..." She scowled. "I felt strange when I looked at him. I felt like I wanted to flee for my life. But at the same time, I had to keep myself from attacking him and biting out his throat right then and there." She shivered. "That one is *not* normal."

So ... a traveler scouting party, I reasoned. But what the hell were they doing here, so far away from civilization? It was common knowledge among travelers that this area was not civilized. It would have taken them days to march all the way through the Deadlands, so I didn't understand their reasons for being here.

According to Ashlazaria's description, it sounded like they had a standard party, albeit beefed up; a mage, a healer, a scout, a couple of damage dealers, and a tank.

Whatever reason they were here for, I couldn't allow their continued presence. If they kept going as they were for much longer, there was a good chance they would find my clan.

Just as bad was the fact they brought their accursed 'slow' time with them, bringing the town's development down. The closer they got, the slower we got.

No, I had to stop them. Permanently. The sooner the better.

In the past couple of weeks, I'd used my energy points sparingly. Not wishing to spend them all frivolously, I kept them for a time they would be most needed. Now I had a clear and imminent threat to deal with. The time for caution was over.

I had saved more than 2,000 energy points over a two-week period. That, along with the boost I had gotten from sacrificing Barska, gave me a total of 5,143 EP at my disposal.

And I knew just where to put them.

Exiting my house, I walked toward the mess hall.

I accessed the Settlement Interface and opened 'Energy Options.' I had the required energy to promote one of my followers into a boss, but until now, I was undecided as to whom to promote. There were too many factors to consider. The travelers' presence simplified that decision.

I needed firepower.

I came to a stop in front of a massive drowsing Ogre, the only one currently in Goblin's Gorge. The hulking Ogres represented a fearsome fighting force. An Ogre boss would be even more deadly. That was what I now needed.

"Get up," I ordered the snoring beast.

No response.

Vic, wake him up.

<You got it, Boss!>

My purple, cloak-shaped companion disengaged from my shoulders, flowing across the Ogre's body and wrapping around his head.

With a yelp, the Ogre leapt to his feet and began clawing at his face, trying to remove the madly giggling Vic.

That's enough, Vic.

Disengaging himself from the startled Ogre, Vic returned to perch around my shoulders.

The Ogre towered above me. His massively powerful body was easily ten times my weight, and I wasn't the small goblin I used to be.

Finally noticing the goblin standing at his feet, the Ogre acknowledged me. "Mas-Ter."

"It's your lucky day," I informed him. "Seeing as your friend is currently away from the valley, you have been selected for a promotion."

Accessing the Boss Options menu, I clicked on Promote Boss, focusing on the Ogre before me.

Promote: Ogre, Level 13, to: Boss [Tier 1], Cost: 1,000 EP. Yes/No?

Yep.

Another prompt appeared before me. *That's new.*

Please select boss type:

1. *Ogre Berserker:* A whirling unstoppable and uncontrollable force of destruction. Will only stop fighting when either it or all enemies are dead.

Boss Bonus Skills: Blind Rage, Lash Out [AoE]

2. *Ogre Ravager:* Wild fighter that excels at delivering high damage attacks at specific targets.

Boss Bonus Skills: Smash, Shockwave [AoE]

3. *Ogre Gladiator:* A cunning fighter who knows how to exploit the surroundings and enemy weaknesses. Gain access to mana-based skills.

Boss Bonus Skills: Dirty Tricks, Terrible Roar [AoE]

I found it weird that I didn't see 'Ogre Chief' or 'Ogre Mage' among the options. Those were the typically encountered Ogre bosses.

<*Na,*> Vic remarked offhandedly. <*You're thinking about clan leaders. If you'd created an Ogre chief he would immediately challenge you for leadership of the clan. I think we've had enough of Ogres attacking us, don't you agree?*>

So these are the available boss types that will *follow my commands?*

<*Yep.*>

I nodded. The Ogre Berserker and Ravager were basically just enhanced versions of the standard Ogres; that wouldn't do. If I was going to have another boss in the clan, one who would assume command in my absence, I needed him to be able to use his head. Even though Ogres were not the best candidates for the role of an intelligent second officer, the need for a combat-oriented ally was the prime requirement.

"I name you Rhynorn Bloodore," I said and selected 'Ogre Gladiator.'

The brute before me began to change. He grew a full Ogre-head taller and his muscles swelled. Bone plates grew out and around his shoulders, elbows, and knees, covering them with a thick armor. The plates then grew sharp bone spikes, arming the already deadly beast with even more weapons. Barbaric tattoos seeped across his skin, etched in deepest black.

But the most striking change was in his demeanor; the Ogre's vapid expression turned cunning and predatory. He looked down at me, weighing me with a searching, penetrating gaze. Measuring me.

He was still butt-ugly though.

<*VI seeding complete,*> Vic informed me unnecessarily. I could feel the power of the creature's presence for myself, causing my Dangersense to tingle.

"Welcome to the Green Pee– grrahhh!"

The Ogre had wrapped his ham-sized hand around my neck and lifted me effortlessly to his eye level.

"I BE THE CHAMPION!" he declared with copious spraying of Ogre spit. His enunciation of the words was surprisingly clear ... for an Ogre. "You serve the champion now! GO, find more fights for me, and bring me much food and females!"

Ohhhh, hell no. This wasn't going well at all. *I thought you said he wouldn't challenge me!* I projected accusingly at Vic.

<*I* said *a chief or a mage would challenge you for leadership of the clan. This brute is just having a pissing contest with you. So, you know ... out-piss him or whatever you meat suits do with your piss to resolve conflicts.*>

I stared the gladiator down, pouring mana into a spell. "You are here to serve *me*."

With those words, I released my mana and cast an empowered web. Shadowy ropes leapt out of the ground and wrapped the Ogre in a dark, entangling net, ensnaring him.

I wriggled and managed to escape the grasp of the suddenly incapacitated creature, slipping through my own net like it wasn't there. I had to hurry; the effect would only hold a few seconds against this beast. I commanded the Sacrificial Bone Dagger out of my belt and to hover in front of his eyes.

"You listen here," I said in my most confident and threatening voice. "*I* am the chief of this clan, and you are my second. Obey me, and you will have your fights and all the food you want. Getting you some females might take some time though."

The Ogre's muscles bulged and strained. With a quick jerk of his hands, he ripped them free from the web. He looked down at me, his eyes full of malevolence. Then he looked up at the dagger, still hovering in front of his eyes and seemed to be considering my words.

After a long moment, he finally bowed his head. "You arrange fights and bring me many foods. I will list-ten to you ... for now."

Barter skill level increased to 9.

I was nonplussed. *He's going to list ten of* what? *Ohh jeez, he means* listen. *Nihilator help me when this blinding light tries to say 'Dread Totem.'*

"Well, you're in luck," I said dryly. "There's an enemy approaching as we speak, and we are going to put them down. Speaking of luck ..." I concentrated and granted him the Lucky Bastard skill.

Analyze.

Rhynorn Bloodore, Ogre Gladiator [Boss, Tier 1]

Level: 13 (10%)

HP: 300, *MP:* 165

Attributes: P: 16, M: 2, S: -1

Skills: Powerful 22, Blunt Weapons 20, Dirty Tricks 10, Terrible Roar 10, Lucky Bastard 1

Traits: Ogre (+4 P, -2 M, -2 S), Frenzy (when below 100 HP), Boss Boon I (10 HP & 5 MP per level; +2P, +1M, +1S, +20% Magic Resist, +10 Armor), Shadow-Touched

Resistances: Armor 45, Physical 75%, Magic 50%

Background: Once little more than a feral beast, now uplifted to Boss Rank by a goblin Dread Totem.

Huh, an Ogre with points in Mental attribute. It explained his relatively sophisticated speech.

That was a good thing. Simply having points in Mental didn't mean the person was a spellcaster. Many Physical-oriented creatures used mana for special, non-magical skills. A martial artist, for example, was a melee combatant who used mana for special martial maneuvers. That thought made me curious about what an Ogre Kung-Fu master would look like. Too bad it wasn't one of the available options.

We didn't have much time. According to Ashlazaria, the travelers would reach the valley entrance soon. We had to intercept them *before* they discovered our settlement.

"Vic, gather all our warriors and have them meet us near the forest path."

<*Sure thing, Boss,*> Vic said in his usual, carefree tone. His cloak-like body slid from my shoulders, transforming into his purple goblin shape as he ran to follow my orders.

There was time for a quick tweak or two. I accessed 'Energy Options' again and opened the upgrade option.

Rhynorn Bloodore. Skill Increase: Dirty Tricks 11, Cost: 32 Energy. Confirm: Yes/No?

Rhynorn Bloodore. Skill Increase: Terrible Roar 11, Cost: 32 Energy. Confirm: Yes/No?

A single upgrade for each of this boss's unique skills would raise them into the Apprentice rank, improving their effectiveness. Not long ago, I would have hesitated to spend 64 energy points on such things, but it was a drop in the bucket of the energy available to me now.

I approved both upgrades.

Dirty Tricks (P)

Enables a variety of special combat maneuvers against opponents: trip, disarm, misdirect.

Countered by physical resistance.

The higher the skill, the higher the chance for the attempt to be successful.

Dirty Tricks imposes a damage penalty. Cost 10 MP. Speed 5.

Level 11: Apprentice: A successful attempt allows for an immediate second attack.

Effect: Success chance 72% (with size bonus).

Terrible Roar (P)

Unleash a tremendous roar that has a chance to impart the Shaken status to enemies.

Countered by physical resistance. Cost: 50 MP. Speed 30.

Level 11: Apprentice: The roar invigorates and rallies allies.

Effect I: Shaken enemies are slowed. Spellcasting might be interrupted. Radius: 11 meters.

Effect II: Allies gain an immediate additional attack. Radius: 11 meters.

Boss Special Bonus: Skill cooldown is reset every time 20% health is lost.

It looked like I had done the right thing. The Apprentice bonuses were invaluable; they had nearly doubled the amount of damage the Ogre could dish out when attacking with Dirty Trick, and the Terrible Roar ability to buff allies was going to be quite handy.

Motioning Rhynorn to follow, we made it toward the valley's exit where my other troops waited. Bob was standing at the front next to Vrick, the goblin lieutenant. They'd known one another for a while now but still looked uncomfortable in each other's company. It was understandable; not long ago they were leading forces on different sides of a conflict. This would be their first skirmish fighting side by side.

Standing behind them were Ashlazaria the scout and the four hobgoblin warriors.

"Where's Bek?" I looked around.

The hobgoblins glanced at each other then parted to reveal Bek standing behind them.

"Here, Dread Totem," the small goblin adept piped.

Seven soldiers and a healer, all between levels 5 to 7, two bosses, and a host of cannon-fodder foblins. Those were the forces I had to confront six travelers of unknown levels and abilities. I feverishly hoped it would be enough.

With a thought, I established a 'War Party' and included everyone. "Let's head out."

We turned and followed the road out of the valley.

***

Tom Wilkins smiled in the early morning sunlight as he walked to his parking spot. One of the perks of his new assignment was driving himself to work instead of riding the sardine-packed pub-trans in rush-hour traffic.

Tom was a FIVR technician with a background in healthcare. His assignments usually involved visiting the homes of the rich in the heavily populated and congested parts of the city. So most days he had to rely on public transportation.

His latest 'client' resided in a quiet suburb, less than an hour's drive out of the big city. Tom loved the new routine. Instead of standing in line with the masses, he could now drive. His client's house had parking around it.

The radio played country music for a while, then the news came on. As always, nothing interesting was happening in the world; the usual wars were ongoing in South Asia, the price of gold was down, and the company's Israeli R&D department of had released a new FIVR gadget, increasing share value by 12 points.

Not that I'll see a cent from that, Tom thought as he drove up his client's driveway and parked.

"Tom," Jerry, the night shift technician greeted him somberly.

"Morning, Jerry." Tom waved as he entered the house.

They had worked on the same jobs for several years now and were accustomed to the coincidence of their names and the friendly tease they occasionally received from their few mutual friends.

Tom stopped in his tracks, noticing the other man's uneasiness. "Something wrong with the client?"

Jerry ran a hand through his hair. "Something weird happened during the night, I don't really know what to make of it."

Tom tilted his head. "What happened?"

"Come, see for yourself."

The two walked into the next room.

Electronic cables were spread all over the floor, connecting the FIVR capsule at the center to various other support systems. The capsule itself was elevated by six slender robotic legs which were slowly rotating it. Tom could see the clear biotech liquid swirling gently inside the capsule, sustaining its occupant.

"Over here." Jerry pointed at one of the monitoring screens.

Tom looked at the screen for a moment then frowned. "I see what you mean. The brain waves are different from the last two days. What happened?"

In response, Jerry pushed a few buttons and the brainwave image was changed, depicting spikes of over 300 percent the normal value.

"This happened around 3:00 a.m." Jerry indicated the spikes. "I called it in but was told to watch and report on any further changes. After about an hour, the spikes were over, but the brainwave patterns were altered, as you see now."

Tom nodded. Instead of the rhythmic, ordered waves, the client's brain produced over the past two days, it now looked ... structured. There were no occasional peaks or variation in the length of time for each wave. It seemed almost ... engineered. Tom's frown deepened. "Why do those look familiar?"

Jerry clicked a few new buttons and the picture changed, depicting a similar graph but with a different color.

Tom gasped. "That's impossible."

"I know," Jerry said grimly.

"That's ... that's the data stream output for in-game NPCs!"

"I know."

The two exchanged worried looks.

"All the vitals look okay though." Jerry pointed at a different screen.

Tom studied the screen, his eyes pausing on a specific number. "Holy hell ..." he mouthed. "It can't be ... 99 percent?"

"Yes." Jerry nodded. "Mr. Berman here has just achieved the second highest Cerebral Connectivity Percentage in the world."

2 – When Monsters Attack

We moved through the valley's thick forest at a fast pace with Ashlazaria leading us and occasionally scouting ahead. We kept off the forest trail to our left and traveled in single file with Rhynorn bringing up the rear. I hoped keeping him in the back would reduce the chance of his crashing progress from alerting the enemy to our approach.

<*That fat-ass gorilla? Fat chance!*> Vic chuckled in my mind.

No need to be insulting, Vic, I reprimanded, suppressing my own grin at his words.

Despite the heavy undergrowth, the wily hobgoblinette found navigable paths. Maybe it was a Scout skill thing.

When we were in sight of the forest clearing, she stopped abruptly, which made me bump into her, earning me a look of disapproval from her and another chuckle from Vic.

<*I don't think Zuban would appreciate you trying to prock his girlfriend.*>

I rolled my eyes at Vic's comment and whispered to the scout, "Ash, why did we stop?"

She looked ahead and sniffed the air. Her petite tusks protruded as her lips curved in a grimace. "They are coming."

I straightened, my heart thumping hard. We were about to engage the enemy.

I used one of my new 'tricks' to relay orders to my troops.

Everyone spread out and surround the clearing, conceal yourselves, and wait for my command.

Being able to send silent commands to my troops gave us a significant strategic advantage. Though by itself, this ability I received by wearing the 'Earring of the Warlord' wouldn't be enough to win us the fight. But at least it made me look cool, like a goblin pirate.

Moments after my troops positioned themselves, I heard several people approaching.

These travelers are going to learn just whose territory they're trespassing on, I thought grimly.

I felt Vic's discontent at that. For a while now, I'd been able to sense *his* surface emotions. It was similar to his ability to listen to my own thoughts, though more limited. I now detected that for some reason, my thoughts were troubling him.

The travelers came into view at the edge of the clearing, led by the green-clad elf Ash had reported. They walked casually, without a care in the world. Ash's description was accurate. I could read the information streams filling my mind as I looked at them.

The group included two spellcasters – a healer, and an evoker. Two agility-based fighters carrying swords covered their flank. The elf leading them was a scout with a nature affinity.

Their levels ranged from 18 to 21. Very strong for this territory. Too strong. I didn't understand what they were doing in the area. There was no challenge around here that would justify the long voyage to get here. They would earn hardly any XP from the local wildlife, and there were no special riches to find either. At least as far as they knew.

My attention was drawn to the last member of the party. My upper lip curled in a snarl, and a surge of hate welled up inside me when I identified his race. The last member was a dwarf, the goblins' natural sworn enemies. He was so heavily armored there was only one word to describe him: Tank. I could literally smell the foul odor of metal coming from him.

As the dwarf walked, I spotted flashes of white metal between the thick steel plates of his armor. *Reinforced with mithril underneath*, I realized. It would make the armor lighter and tougher than if it was made only of steel. But what really made me hesitate and take a sharp breath was the sense of raw power coming from him.

Not fully trusting my mundane senses, I used Analyze.

Ragnar

Race: Dwarf (Stone)

Level: 40 (97%)

HP: 476, *MP:* 284

Attributes: P: 44, M: 4, S: 4

Skills: Taunt 47, Challenging Cry 46, Shields 54, Axes 54, Hold the Line 22, Vampiric Attack 14, Smith 31, Baking 14

Traits: Steadfast (resistant to takedowns), Dwarf

Resistances: Physical 67%, Cold 10%, Fire 10%, Armor 122

That was ... ridiculous.

What would a level 40 dwarf *tank* be doing in a party half his level?

That guy could single-handedly wipe out his *own* group if he chose to, let alone our already overmatched force of lowbies. For a guy like him, walking through this forest was a pleasant stroll through the park.

<*And I bet he can bake a killer cake too,*> Vic said.

Then it dawned on me. This wasn't a random expedition through the wilderness seeking adventure. The group was too high-level for the area. There could only be one reason for a group so powerful to be here: They were searching for something specifically. And the only thing travelers *might* be interested about in this area was ... me.

These bastards are here to find me*!*

The tank was probably a bodyguard the group hired to escort them, and he likely cost them a fortune. From his perspective, there was absolutely nothing to gain from a low-level area like this. So he would have to be well compensated for his trouble.

Regardless, they were already standing at the edge of the clearing, inspecting the wreckage of the old Chief's Hut at the center. I couldn't risk them getting any closer to my settlement.

I watched the group move closer to our ambush point. My troops surrounded the part of the clearing where it funneled back to the forest path.

They were getting closer. Ten meters. Eight. Six.

I was about to call for the attack when the green-clad scout raised his hand. The group stopped in their tracks, standing near the destroyed structure. The scout carefully viewed the ambush site in front of him, his eyes narrowed.

"What's the hold up?" the man in red robes demanded. I plucked his name from the air: Nitrohawk. "We're wasting our time, there's nothing here. This shitty hut clearly indicates there are no goblins here anymore."

I breathed a bit easier. It looked like my little decoy was about to prove itself.

The scout studied the path before them unhurriedly. "There's something hiding nearby; I got a prompt alerting me to an enemy presence."

Damned scouts and their enhanced senses, I cursed silently as my hopes crumbled.

Nitrohawk sneered. "And you're stopping for that? The toughest mobs around here are the Forest Ogres, and they're no threat. Besides, not many could hide here with all those thornthistle bushes growing nearby. I say let them attack. I want to finish this lousy expedition so I can get back to grinding my skills at the Academy."

Interesting; they aren't here on their own initiative. They were sent by someone. So someone else *was looking for me.* I didn't know why, or who was behind this, but I planned to find out.

The scout shrugged. "Suit yourself, but I'm not taking point."

The other travelers followed the exchange with indifference.

Nitrohawk grunted. "Geesh, what a wimp. Step aside, let me show you how it's done."

He moved forward, mumbling arcane words. A ring of yellow-red flames erupted around him, hot enough that I could feel the radiating heat from my hiding spot. The ring moved along with the wizard as he walked, wilting the nearby vegetation and leaving a trail of blackened ground.

I cursed silently. That was a Fire Shield spell. It wasn't an overly advanced spell, but as it was cast by a level 18 character, it would cause serious damage to my lower-level troops. I couldn't send my fighters to engage the wizard; they'd get slaughtered. Engaging the caster in melee would incinerate them or melt their crude weapons as they passed through the flames. Fortunately, I had alternatives.

I expected my war party would be able to handle the five travelers, but the dwarf was going to be a tough nut to crack. The level gap made his already high resistances even more significant. It would take us too long to pound him down. If we had engaged him first, it would leave the other travelers unoccupied, able to attack us at will.

No. The only way we could achieve victory was to eliminate the lower-level players before they could regroup, then we could concentrate all our forces on the tank.

I had no illusions regarding the outcome of this battle. We were going to suffer losses.

But I had planned for that. I looked around at the dozen disposable foblins hiding nearby and grinned.

I started channeling my mana and charging up a Drilling Arrow spell while sending a series of orders.

Ash and Bek, at my command, shoot at the one wearing red. Zia, Kilpi, engage the two swordsmen in melee but don't attack – use your shields to keep them occupied and concentrate on defense. Bob, Vrick, take the scout. He's a ranged fighter, so close the distance quickly – get him into melee range and keep him there. Kroakar, Ryker, attack the healer, that's the one with the white robes.

I looked at the comically stupid foblins. *As for you, err ... kill metal dwarf!* The foblins didn't have any weapons, but that was what the Brawling skill was for.

The hobs and goblins all nodded their understanding. The foblins gaped stupidly, one of them mumbling quietly, "Me hear voicings."

I gritted my teeth. Noise was an absolute no-no during an ambush. I was having second thoughts about bringing the stupid buggers, but I'd already committed to this course of action. Luckily, the travelers didn't hear the extra-moronic one whispering.

The red-robed wizard reached the center of our ambush zone.

"ATTACK!" I bellowed.

Nitrohawk froze as enemies burst out of hiding all around him.

Like good cannon fodder, the foblins charged first, followed by the more seasoned hobgoblins. They streamed around the red mage, headed for their intended targets behind him. Two foblins – unlucky or stupider than the rest – crossed the fire ring and fell as lifeless, charred corpses. The air filled with the smell of roasted meat.

Ash released her arrow just as Bek and I launched our spells at the oblivious wizard in red. The magic arrows were much faster than the mundane one. My Drilling Arrow spell hit first, slamming through the fire ring and into the traveler, their rotating heads easily burrowing through his magically enchanted robes.

Drilling Arrows hit Nitrohawk for 64 damage, [(15+17)X2]

My attack blasted 70 percent of his health away. Then the other arrows hit him as well, claiming the kill. Ash howled triumphantly as the wizard's lifeless body dropped to the ground. "Raaaaarr!"

Like me, Nitrohawk had built his character as a Mental-focused one. But unlike me, he didn't have the extra boss bonuses to beef up his health. That made him a glass cannon; a person who could dish out a lot of damage but sucked at absorbing it. Our combined range attacks were enough to send him to respawn.

One down, five to go.

Taking advantage of the initiative of our surprise attack, I began casting another spell.

Shadows gathered into larger black masses around me and the ground cracked beneath them as I activated my Shadow Hound spell. The fancy visual effects were the reason I hadn't cast this spell in advance; it would have given away our position.

Meanwhile, all the hobs had reached and engaged their targets. The remaining travelers overcame the shock of the ambush, drew their weapons, and readied themselves to meet their attackers.

That was a mistake. By *reacting* to my tactics and only focusing on the enemies targeting them, the travelers allowed me to dictate the course of battle.

I grimaced as the two forces clashed together.

They had a reason not to be worried. Despite the travelers losing one of their members early on, my little army was at a severe disadvantage with the enemy levels at least three times their own.

My strategy optimized our chances. But optimizing an attack against a massively overwhelming force just made an utterly shitty situation slightly less shitty; the smelly stuff didn't stink any less.

The already alert, green-clad scout was the first to react. As Vrick and Bob charged him, he had time for a carefully aimed shot that struck Vrick in the forehead, penetrating his skull and killing the poor goblin lieutenant instantly. Still, that shot bought Bob the time to close in and engage him in melee.

The scout was 14 levels higher than the level 7 hobgoblin lieutenant, but he was a ranged fighter and was limited in his ability to engage in a face-to-face confrontation.

Bob led in with a sword thrust, slashing the scout for 18 damage. Before the scout could recover, Bob pointed his other hand. Vines uncoiled from his forearm and wrapped around the archer's legs, restricting his movement and preventing escape.

Zia and Kilpi, my two shield bearers, were jockeying for positions against the two swordsmen, their guard high as they kept the fighters' attention. I hoped that at least Kilpi Shīrudo, the stronger of the two, would live up to the name I'd assigned him, which meant 'shield' in two languages.

<*Hehe, first time I see a mob tank a player,*> Vic said.

The other two hob warriors had rushed the healer with their axes held high. But the healer calmly raised his staff and, with a single word, was enveloped in a white sheen of magical force.

I cursed. That was a Holy Shield. It was similar to my Mana Shield spell, except it only defended against evil monsters and didn't consume the caster's mana.

Kroakar and Ryker struck the Holy Shield with powerful swings, but their axes had no effect against the magic barrier.

One of the melee fighters, Nesteph, kicked Zia's shield, sending it wide open, then lunged forward with both his short swords, eviscerating her and taking off 80 percent of her health.

The two-handed swordsman lunged at Kilpi and swung, putting his whole body into the strike. The powerful attack hit the shield, shattered it, and hurled Kilpi away in a cloud of splinters, leaving him less than half his health.

I glanced at the foblins attacking Ragnar, the dwarven tank. What I saw was a bloody massacre.

Using the momentary surprise, the foblins had charged the dwarf, but they'd triggered some sort of ability as soon as they got near, allowing him to attack preemptively.

Swinging his axe with an almost bored expression, Ragnar dispatched four foblins while easily fending off the other six with his shield.

I winced. Well, *at least they managed to keep him occupied for a bit.*

Given that it was a successful ambush, our initial attack seemed underwhelming. But considering the level gap, the fact that we'd managed to kill even one traveler – and a wizard at that – was impressive.

The sword-wielding travelers were preparing their next attack while their healer started a chant.

I completed my spell first and three Shadow-Touched mastiffs leapt out of the shadows. Two attacked the swordsmen, while the third went for the healer.

Taken aback by the sudden appearance of the charging dark beasts, the swordsmen forwent finishing off the downed hobs and turned to face the attacking mastiffs. Their defensive attacks were perfectly timed but their blades passed harmlessly through the shadowed bodies. The third mastiff wasn't as lucky. It leapt at the healer, but the traveler shot off a Holy Bolt at it. The white bolt hit the mastiff in mid-leap, *exploding* the beast's dark-wrought body into trails of smoky shadow that faded into nothingness.

Meanwhile, Bob was doing well keeping the scout engaged. The hob lieutenant repeatedly slashed with his sword, forcing his opponent to deflect with the bowstave, preventing him from going on the offensive. Bob's vines slithered and constricted around the scout's body, further hampering his movements.

The flow of combat was going pretty well, but just when I thought we were gaining the upper hand, the dwarf tank intervened. Bellowing a deafening challenge, he banged on his shield.

An area taunt, I realized. *Shit!*

Except for Bob, all of my forces, including the mastiffs, disengaged their targets and charged at the tank.

A 'Taunt' debuff symbol appeared next to the icon of each party member on my display. Things were about to turn real bad, real quick. It was time to bring in the heavy guns.

Rhynorn, engage! Take down the healer!

Branches exploded into the clearing, showering the combatants with splinters as Rhynorn Bloodore burst from hiding and charged at the healer.

One of the travelers yelped in fright. "Crap, it's a boss!"

Rhynorn ran at the healer, holding his weapon low like a golf club and used his momentum to swing it upward.

The club hit the healer's white bubble, launching it into the air. I could sense the Ogre expending his mana to enhance the attack using his Dirty Trick skill. The healer and his bubble soared high into the air, then crashed into the ground, right in front of the Ogre. The bubble winked away from the impact just as Rhynorn started his follow-up attack. The giant club descended, pounding onto the head of the confounded healer, planting him into the ground figuratively and literally. A critical hit!

Battle information flowed all around me; I only needed to open my senses to grasp it. I *knew* the healer was nearly finished.

I'd intended at first to keep my more dramatic abilities a secret. But the first bout of combat, brief as it was, made me realize I would have to go all in if I wanted a chance of winning this one.

Flexing my will, my dagger shot forward and sank deep into the traveler's chest.

Dagger hit Jeknett for 32 damage [+6 physical, +26 dark]

Immortal Killed!

Boss Tier 3 Progression: 1/50

That was interesting. Apparently, I'd just discovered another way to increase my boss tier; one that didn't require me to spend huge amounts of energy.

The other travelers turned to stare at their fallen comrade. Their eyes widened as darkness oozed out of the dagger, consuming the body and leaving behind a good-sized void crystal.

"What the hell was that?" shouted the scout, still trying to fend off Bob's attacks with his bow.

"Over there." The dwarf tank pointed at me with his shield while easily repelling the attacks from the horde around him. "There's a caster behind that tree."

The two melee travelers engaged Rhynorn, their swords biting into his thick skin, drawing blood and taking 30 percent off his health bar.

"Holy crap! It's another boss!" Nesteph squealed once he noticed me. He sounded like a teenager. "Where the hell did Vatras send us?"

I froze at hearing that accursed name. *Vatras*. Hate filled me, and my thoughts raced. *Vatras! These bastards are his minions.*

Unable to control myself, I stepped out from my hiding place.

"You are all dead," I said with barely contained rage.

Concentrating on the dual-wielding traveler, I reached with my mind, found his mana pool, and commanded it to stop flowing. Nesteph froze mid-swing. I directed my dagger at him, and as with the healer, the dagger hit the traveler full in the chest.

Nesteph, Level 20, Sacrificed

+80 Faith Points

Immortal Killed!

Boss Tier 3 Progression: 2/50

It looked like sacrificing travelers was way more rewarding than sacrificing fellow monsters. Not only did it enable me to move up in my boss tier, but I'd also received four times the normal amount of Faith Points. It was enough to unlock the next Faith rank.

Nesteph was quickly consumed by darkness. Only the scout, the two-handler sword guy, and the tank remained.

"Crap!" yelled the scout. "Ragnar, do something!"

"Don't get'chya panties wet boy," said Ragnar. He looked directly at Bob and used Taunt again. This time, unable to resist, Bob disengaged from the scout to charge at the tank.

Now that he was not being pressed, the scout put his long bow to deadly effect. Utilizing some sort of Area-of-Effect skill, dozens of brightly glowing arrows filled the air. The arrows rained down, dropping the foblins, the mastiffs, and all the hobgoblin warriors around the dwarf. A couple of arrows even hit the overpowered tank, but those simply shattered harmlessly against his armor.

Only Rhynorn, Bob, and I remained – two bosses and a lieutenant against three high-powered travelers.

Suddenly, a green-golden light surrounded the Ogre and his health jumped up by ten percent.

And Bek, I corrected myself.

<Like that undersized puppet would make any difference,> Vic snorted in my mind.

Four against three. *I can work with those odds.*

Meanwhile, the sword wielder danced around Rhynorn, slicing at him in measured, precise strikes, bringing his health down to 50 percent.

Enraged, the Ogre bellowed, activating his Terrible Roar skill. A Shaken debuff icon appeared over the scout and swordsman's heads but failed to affect the tank. At the same time, I felt invigorated and let loose another volley of drilling arrows while a still-taunted Bob charged at the tank with enhanced speed.

Another golden-green light appeared around Rhynorn and his health shot up again by ten percent.

"They got a healer!" the scout yelled.

In response, I used Freeze on him. Or at least I tried. The scout stopped moving for a fraction of a second, then he was free again.

Damn, he must have some sort of skill that resisted my power. I changed targets and concentrated my firepower on the swordsman. I summoned and fired drilling arrows at him just as the Ogre gladiator retaliated.

Using his Dirty Tricks again, Rhynorn's club struck the player's sword, deflecting it to the side, then followed through with a devastating hit to the center of his torso. The still-shaken traveler failed to dodge the massive attack and the impact took over a hundred of his hit points, then my drilling arrows slammed into him in rapid succession.

Drilling Arrows hit Zellion for 64 damage, [(15+17)X2]

We'd beaten and stabbed him continuously, bleeding his health down to ten percent, but the tough bastard kept fighting.

"Goddammit!" he yelled. "Heal! I need a heal!"

No one gave him any heed or heals.

Bob swung at the tank, but the dwarf easily intercepted the blow on his shield, absorbing the hit, then slashed at the vines Bob launched at him, tearing them apart.

Raising his longbow, the scout drew back, targeting me. The arrow at his string started glowing red, but he was too slow. With a thought, I raised my Mana Shield just as the arrow was released. The arrow banged against the magical barrier and exploded with a thunderous *THUMP*. It drained a good chunk of my mana bar, but no damage got through.

Even with that hit to my mana pool, I had over 400 points left. That was more than enough to last me through this fight.

Time to end this. I launched the dagger at the injured swordsman, timing a Freeze to take hold of him just before impact.

Dark Mana skill level increased to 27.

Zellion, Level 18, Sacrificed.

+72 Faith Points

Immortal Killed!

Boss Tier 3 Progression: 3/50

Finding himself suddenly without opponents to fight, Rhynorn Gleefully charged at the bow-wielding scout and swung his massive club. The heavy weapon connected fully and the hapless traveler's body was flung through the air, crashing into a tree trunk five meters away. It was nice to have the heavy-hitting Ogres on my side for a change. The scout slid to the ground, stunned. Surprisingly, he still had half his health bar remaining.

Bob did his best to keep the tank traveler engaged, but he was ridiculously overmatched. Bashing away with his shield, the traveler dropped Bob to the ground, then delivered a fatal blow with his axe, splitting my lieutenant's skull, ending him and his 75 HP with a single strike.

Another green-golden light surrounded the Ogre, healing him to 80 percent of his health.

The tank stared at me calmly.

Behind me, I could hear Rhynorn grunting with pleasure as his club made squishing sounds while he beat the traveler into a pulp.

"Hey there, fugly, I guess yor tha goblin we was sent after." Ragnar had a thick southern accent.

I bared my teeth and snarled at him, feeling the unexplained surge of hate welling up again. "Dwarven mongrel! I'll kill you and gnaw on your bones!"

The dwarf smiled. "I din't evan believe it when Vatras said you was a playah. But I been wrong before. Y'gone all feral boy."

I reined in my anger. "I'll deal with that bastard soon enough. After I kill you!"

He chuckled. "You' an what army, boy? That low-level beastie o' yours won't put a dent on me."

He was right. *Damn it!*

"But I tell y'what, boy," he continued, "I've had it up to here with this low-ass-level forest. Could'a earned myself some sweet levels with all tha time spent 'round here parts. I reckon I done my job, found you good, boy. You ain't worth the effort o' putting down. You're Vatras's prob now. Enjoy your miserable existence for a little longer, before he comes for ya."

With a roar of anger, I opened my inventory and retrieved the Fire Rod I'd crafted, just as the dwarf took a scroll from his inventory. We both activated our items at the same time. A jet of flame shot from the Fire Rod and engulfed the dwarf, singeing away 30 HP. But his body was already fading, disappearing as the effects of the teleport scroll whisked him away.

Bek came out of hiding. "Is … is it over?" he stuttered timidly.

The Ogre roared triumphantly. "Good fight! Strong enemy! Rhynorn Bloodore is the champion!"

"Yes, Bek, it's over," I said tiredly, looking at the corpse-strewn ground around me. Out of a party of 23, only the three of us had survived.

Now that the battle was over, I was being bombarded with messages.

Victory!

Total War Party XP gained: 27,840

Ashlazaria gained 1 level (dead)

Zia gained 1 level (dead)

Borbarabsus gained 2 levels (dead)

Kilpi Shīrudo gained 1 level (dead)

Kroakar gained 1 level (dead)

Ryker gained 1 level (dead)

Vrick gained 1 level (dead)

Rhynorn Bloodore gained 3 levels.

Bek gained 4 levels.

Level up! You have reached Character Level 18. You have 1 ability point to allocate.

Level up! You have reached Character Level 19. You have 2 ability points to allocate.

Level up! You have reached Character Level 20. You have 3 ability points to allocate.

I looked at the information in front of me in awe. The number of Faith Points and XP from defeating travelers was at least four times what I'd get for killing monsters of equal levels. While travelers never got XP from defeating other travelers, it seemed NEO rewarded *my* kind handsomely for dispatching those otherworldly creatures. Having survived the fight, Bek and Rhynorn received additional XP and leveled up more than the others.

<Ahem,> Vic interrupted. *<Boss, you ... do remember that you're a traveler yourself, right?>*

My lips curled in disgust. *Maybe I once was, Vic, but NEO doesn't see me as such now. It is not some 'game,' it is a living, breathing entity. Only by accepting that and mastering its rules could I hope to survive.*

Despite our victory, I started to feel uneasiness settling at the pit of my stomach. We had been within a hair's breadth of losing. I could sense Vic's apprehension about my reply. His cloak form dropped from around me and transformed into a purple goblin. He reached out and placed a hand on my shoulder. "You're not a mindless NPC, Boss. You are unique. Don't lose yourself in this Dad-awful world. Your people need you." He hesitated before continuing. "I need you, Oren."

That was touching. Despite his usual gruff, cynical manner, Vic was concerned about me.

My mood didn't improve though. "Don't worry, Vic. I know who I am. I know where I came from."

Vic seemed unconvinced by my response. But he didn't pick up on my next thoughts. I'd deliberately stemmed the flow that connected us as I added, to myself, *And I know where I'm going. Once I've built the clan into the strongest monster nation in NEO, I'll teach these pesky travelers not to mess with us.*

Still, looking around at all the dead bodies, I couldn't help feeling it might be an impossible undertaking.

Bek rummaged through the fallen travelers' corpses, then piled his findings on the ground. I went and looked them over.

Most of the stuff was random junk that cluttered all players' inventories, regardless of their level; 15 pieces of single-use whetstone, five units of apple tobacco, and oddly enough, a gargoyle's skull. Aside from that, the travelers dropped a total of 1,800 gold coins. It was a fortune compared to my character level, and I had absolutely no use for it.

Yeah, death debuff was a bitch. The random items loss was a pain, but I guessed it was better than dropping everything a character had on their person when they died like was common in other FIVR games.

I shook my head. My thoughts were pure nonsense. FIVR. Other worlds. Only one world mattered. My world.

At the bottom of the pile, I found something that improved my mood: A varnished piece of wood reflected back the few rays of the moon. It was the scout's bow.

Graceful Longbow

Description: An elven-crafted bow. This excellently crafted bow is enchanted in such a way to make it more effective in the hands of the beautiful, educated, and well-spoken.

Runecraft Viability: Can hold up to 4 runes.

Type: Weapon [2 hands]

Rank: Magical

Durability: 67/90

Damage: base 20-25

Effect: Adds half the wielder's Social attribute value to damage.

That was a nice find!

This would be a good upgrade for Ash, I thought and put it in my inventory.

Overall, it was an unimpressive haul, considering we had defeated five level 20 travelers, but that had been expected. Travelers did not drop all their possessions upon death. Instead, they usually lost an item or two from their inventory and a handful of coin.

I put all the loot in my inventory, including the three large void crystals. I threw a glance at the crystals' stats and once again was pleasantly surprised. They were all around level 200, more than my entire clan's daily yield! That cheered me up a bit. It looked like travelers produced void crystals ten times more powerful than a *normal* monster.

Next to me, Rhynorn had finished collecting the items from our fallen warriors into another pile. Unlike travelers, my people dropped all equipped items upon death. Luckily, items that were in their inventories usually remained. Some of the corpses had already begun to disappear, absorbed into NEO.

I looked at the stack of weapons and armor the Ogre had collected from the corpses and felt suddenly crestfallen at the sight. There were a lot. *How can I hope to stop a larger force?* I brooded.

"Rhyno, please carry those back to the clan." Calling him 'Rhyno' seemed simpler.

He grunted but obeyed. Bending down, his huge hands scoped up most of the pile. A few smaller, unfamiliar items clattered to the ground.

"Hold on a moment."

I moved closer to inspect the new items.

> **Gold Necklace**
>
> *Description:* A beautifully crafted gold necklace with a silver unicorn pendant. The unicorn's eye is made of sapphire.

> **Bear Trap**
>
> *Description:* A spring-loaded metal jaw that activates when stepped upon. Includes a loading mechanism.
>
> *Effect:* Requires brute force to open: 40 Physical.

"Where the hell did those came from?" I mumbled.

"It's not a great mystery, Boss," Vic said. "It's just random loot generated by the game engine."

It irritated me when Vic referred to it as 'the game.' I was pretty sure he was doing it on purpose.

Anyway, that was good news. It meant that in case of death, my people's inventories were safe, as the world itself generated the dropped items. It reminded me of the quest-granting system, where the gods, or NEO itself, were in charge of generating the tangible rewards.

"Yep, pretty much." Vic confirmed my internal thoughts. "It also follows a certain logic. That bear trap, for example, was left behind by the scout. I have no idea who dropped the necklace though. It probably had less than one percent chance of dropping, so ... good for you, Boss!"

> **Lucky Bastard skill level increased to 25.**

The last of the corpses was slowly being claimed by NEO. In a few hours, no traces of the battle would remain. My heart was heavy; our victory had cost us greatly.

I turned to my remaining men and waved for them to follow. “Let’s head back.”

It was morning by the time we arrived back at the settlement and everyone was sleeping the day off.

I went straight to my house and closed the door behind me. I sat at my stool, resting my head on my arms over the table.

Yep, it was brooding time.

3 – Break's Over

Despite the late hour, I couldn't sleep.

No matter how I tried to work it, I couldn't see a way out of this mess. There was no strategy, no trick, no plan I could use to get my clan through this calamity.

I was screwed.

That's it, game over, I thought miserably.

<Hey –>

Shut up, Vic.

My secret was out. My clan was as good as dead.

My nemesis, Vatras, was looking for me, and if he didn't already know where I was, he would soon. I couldn't even run since my soul was bound to the clan's cemetery from the moment I'd established it.

They'll come for me and they'll destroy everything we've worked so hard to build. I continued commiserating to myself. *There's nothing I can do to stop them. We barely stopped a small, level 20 group. No matter how strong my clan gets, the invaders will be stronger.*

Vic, in his purple goblin form, watched me worriedly, fidgeting.

"Eh, come on, Boss. It's not all bad. We still have time. You can wall off the valley; that'll keep them out for a while."

I didn't bother raising my head from the table. "And what good would that do? I'm the highest level here, and I'm only a 20. My old clan could field over a hundred level 200 warriors. At least. They would smash through every one of our defenses. Effortlessly."

"Oren, come on. You have *time*, plenty of it. Remember the time difference? Look at what you've accomplished in just under six weeks. You have at least a few more weeks to prepare. We can do it!"

I appreciated his attempt to raise my morale, but he simply didn't get it. We could never hope to match the strength of the travelers, the undying scourge upon our world.

"Just leave me be, Vic," I said tiredly.

He grumbled something, and a moment later, I heard the door shut as he left the house.

Leaving me to wallow in despair.

But just a few moments later, the door opened again.

"Damn it, Vic, I said I wanted to be left –"

I stopped when I saw Vic lead Tika, and of all people, Bek, into the room. Both looked haggard, having barely slept themselves.

Tika came to me, laying a comforting hand against my cheek, bending to whisper in my ear, "Me help. All the clan help. You not worry, you good chief. Tika have belief in you."

Just being there, she calmed my angst a bit, but my outlook on the clan's future remained bleak.

"I appreciate that Tika, but you don't know everything. I ... I don't know what to do." I looked up into her sweet face. She gave me her beautiful, loving smile, and I couldn't help smiling back. It did make me feel a little better.

"I know. Vic tells. Bek knowing way."

Bek? What can the munchkin goblin possibly know that will help thwart a horde of bloodthirsty, high-level travelers?

"Hear him out, Boss," Vic suggested.

I looked at Bek, doubtful.

The little goblin appeared uncomfortable with all the attention focused on him. He cleared his throat. "Bek be praying at shrine to Dark God. Bek sleeps. Bek sees great darkness come from shrine, make night-time everywhere. Clan be strong in night-time, not-clan be weak."

I looked at him with incomprehension.

Vic rolled his eyes. "What he means is that you have options. You have a powerful, tier 8 boss as your clan deity, remember? And as luck had it, he's stationed just under your feet. *This* is his place of power. You can use that to your advantage."

I frowned. "How?"

"You can purchase permanent buffs and blessings with Faith Points, remember? There's one blessing that matches this pinhead-puppet's description. Eternal Night."

Instead of trying to remember, I simply willed up the Zone Blessings details. There it was.

Eternal Night: The zone of influence will be covered with perpetual darkness. Cost: 1,000 FP

My shoulders slumped. "It just says the area will be shrouded in darkness. How could that possibly make any difference?"

Vic gave me a pointed look. "For a meat suit who's advanced enough to see and manipulate the connections to his own puppet, you sure are slow on the uptake sometimes. Ignore the user description. Look *deeper*, find the metadata."

That was unexpected. Usually, Vic disapproved of the connection I'd achieved with NEO. I closed my eyes and directed my thoughts at the Eternal Night blessing. I could sense thin streams of data coming from the world around me as NEO fed me with information. The short description I'd read a moment ago suddenly looked pale and inadequate compared to what I found. There was a lot more to it than a simple perpetual darkness effect. That blessing was a shroud that emanated directly from Nihilator and manifested through his shrines, converting the surrounding land to his domain. Under it, only his Shadow-Touched minions may pass unharmed. All other living creatures, especially those who served the light, would be weakened and suffer various debuffs.

My mood began to lighten, the worry lines easing.

Vic raised one purple hand. "There's more, keep digging into it."

I concentrated, tapping more deeply into the tightly woven streams of information.

I saw ... and understood! That was one of the major advantages my kind had over travelers; we had an innate connection to the world around us. I now understood that the Eternal Night blessing could be much more powerful than first indicated.

While it could be activated using a shrine, that limited the effectiveness of the blessing. Activating it with a Dark Temple would produce a stronger result. Better yet, it would open other blessings and options that could enhance and expand the original. Though I could sense the other blessings had various potential effects, exactly what they did was not clear. Those information streams were too 'distant' for me to reach.

My previous gloom evaporated completely. I jumped from my seat, rubbing my hands together.

"What are you all standing around for? We have lots of work to do!"

***

I paced impatiently in my living room. There were a ton of details waiting for me to attend to. Revitalized with new hope, I'd sent Vic to fetch Zuban; we had much to discuss.

I hadn't made the best use of my time these last couple of weeks. After we repelled the Ogre attack, I let myself relax from the furious pace we'd been keeping up to that point. I spent many hours with Tika, talking, walking together, and deepening our relationship. I relaxed the work schedule, allowing the clan to labor at a more leisurely pace, building the settlement unhurriedly. I purposely avoided spending too much of our accumulated food and energy, not willing to commit to a particular path. I cut back on my own training and didn't even invest much effort in my Runecrafting, despite my newly deepened understanding of its inner working.

All I had to show for the last couple of weeks was a slight increase in my skills, two or three points at most.

Well, then, I guess break time's over.

I had new goals and obstacles in my path. But I was a seasoned clan chief now; I knew how the system worked. I formulated the goals I had to achieve:

The first priority, obviously, was to build the Dark Temple, but we lacked its blueprint.

The second concern was Faith Points. I needed 1,000 FP to purchase the Eternal Night blessing. I currently had exactly 457 at my disposal, so I had to collect more. I could convert Energy Points to FP, but with a ten to one conversion rate, it would take 5,430 EP. I almost had enough energy for that now, but energy was a valuable resource that could be used for other things, and I preferred not to squander it in an unfavorable exchange unless I absolutely had to.

Another concern was that even with a temple and the Eternal Night blessing, our forces would still be weak. The barracks should help. I could sense that now, but I'd have to wait for the structure to be completed to see exactly how it would work.

And as always, I needed soldiers – lots of them. I needed them to be as high-level as possible, which required combat experience or energy. However, buying levels for my followers using energy was progressively expensive. Raising a soldier from level 1 to 10 would cost 2,569 EP. I needed better ways to level up my future army.

I sighed. Suddenly, the 5,079 EP we had accumulated didn't seem like much.

A light tap on the door tore me away from my musings. "Enter."

Zuban came in, letting a few rays of sun into my house. The hobgoblin bowed respectfully though he looked tired. "You summoned me, Dread Totem?"

I nodded. "Please have a seat." I motioned at the table, seating myself.

He looked at me searchingly. "I heard you had a tough fight and that our casualties were high." He took a steadying breath. "Did Ash ..."

I raised my hand. "Don't worry, Zuban. Yes, we suffered casualties, and yes, Ashlazaria was among them." Seeing his stricken expression I swiftly added, "But they will return to us. Nihilator as my witness, you will have Ash back very soon."

You have made a vow in the name of your deity, Nihilator.

Condition: Resurrect the hobgoblin scout Ashlazaria within 12 hours.

Failure: Nihilator's Wrath debuff, -1,000 reputation with Nihilator.

Success: 5 FP

Crap, I really should watch what I'm saying better. Otherwise, I might wind up finding myself biting more than I could chew. Nihilator was not an easygoing or benevolent god; I did *not* want to get on his bad side.

At least Zuban seemed somewhat assured by my vow.

I decided to get down to business. "You and Romil are currently looking into the research center building, right? And you ..." I closed my eyes for a moment, "you have researched 18 of the 100 required points, correct?"

He looked impressed at my knowledge. "That is correct, Dread Totem."

"Hmm ..." I rested my arms on the table. "I need the Dark Temple to become a priority."

He nodded grimly. "Yes, your purple companion has briefed me on our situation. We will switch to research the temple immediately." He made to stand up.

I raised my hand. "Hold on, Zuban, there's more to consider." I rubbed my chin and tried to evaluate the amount of time I had.

The forest around us was located in the middle of the Deadlands – a vast, barely explored territory. The nearest traveler settlement was hundreds of kilometers away. It could take up to a week for a sizeable force to march that distance. A smaller, faster force with strong, swift mounts could probably make that in a day, but even a high-level strike force would be delayed by monster encounters. Our forest was considered to be a relatively low-level zone. There were other zones all around us inhabited by monsters with levels over 200. So even the most direct route would probably take a fast-moving force at least a day. Considering the time difference, that meant I had between two weeks to about three months to get ready. In any case, there was enough time to complete researching *both* structures. After all, it was a shame to lose the research points that were already gained.

"Keep working on the research center blueprints," I instructed. "As soon as you finish, start on the Dark Temple. I'm going to summon another researcher to help you."

His worried expression relaxed. "Wonderful! With two researchers working in a proper workplace, we will be able to come up with new blueprints much faster, and I can get back to overseeing the construction."

I nodded and opened up the Construction Interface. I could simply pull the information directly into my mind, but I wanted to see it laid out in front of me.

Buildings and Construction
Max Constructor Skill: 15 *Builders Count:* 6 (Skills 15, 15, 15, 15, 15, 16) *Daily BP:* 112.2

Under Construction: Cabin (5/125 BP) [rush], Cabin (12/125 BP) [rush], Barracks (31/600 BP) [rush]

Research (Daily RP: 25.7)

Available Resources: timber 10, stone 50, metal 17, bones 137, pelts 42

We had three different buildings under construction; the last two cabins and the barracks. For a moment I was tempted to hit the 'rush' button and use energy to instantly complete them, but I resisted. Every energy point was precious. *Besides, in an emergency I can always use the 'rush' option if needed*, I reasoned.

As for the research, with the current daily RP our researches were generating, both blueprints would be finished in about ten days. Another researcher would shave two to three days off that.

The interface also drew my attention to our low metal supply. We had 17 units in stock, and though it might be enough for our construction projects, I planned on manufacturing weapons and armors for my troops, so we would definitely need more metal.

Better start stockpiling it now, I decided.

That meant I needed to recruit another miner. I should have done that earlier. Our one miner couldn't supply all the clan's growing needs by himself.

Zuban waited while I reviewed the clan's information. Finally, he asked, "Was there something else, Dread Totem?"

"It looks like it'll take about a week to complete the cabins and the barracks."

"Seven and a half days exactly," he corrected me.

I nodded. "That's about the time it would take you to finish researching the Dark Temple, so let's make that our next project."

"I understand."

"And then we'll have to build up our military strength. We'll need to manufacture armor, weapons ..." I trailed off in thought.

Zuban brought me back to the present. "If I may offer a suggestion?"

"Of course."

"It will take time to build weapon and armor workshops. And they will have to be manned by proficient craftsmen. I suggest you summon them now, let them improve their skills in the smithy. They won't be able to produce high-quality items at first, but when the workshops are ready, they should be able to produce more, and better works, at a higher efficiency."

"Good idea, Zuban, I'll do just that." I really should have thought of it myself.

Governor skill level increased to 8.

Heh, looks like my progress meetings with Zuban merited a skill increase.

Aside from other obvious benefits, reaching tier 2 boss rank raised my Social attribute from 0 to 1. With my Social 'potential' now above 0, I finally had access to Social-based skills not usually available to 'regular' goblins.

The Governor skill was one of those Social-based skills, and I got it shortly after ranking up. Ostensibly, it increased my clan management potential. At its current level, it conferred a small morale and efficiency bonus to my workers.

The skill level was increasing gradually. I could tell it was connected to the settlement's progression. The more my goblins worked and our clan expanded, the more the skill progressed. Though I now learned I could actively train it by engaging in clan management.

<Too bad you only just got that skill,> Vic said in my mind. *<The way you were going at it before, it would have reached level gazillion by now.>*

I think you're exaggerating, I said defensively.

<Oh yeah? Remember when you insisted on sleeping in three-hour shifts because you simply had *to fill the molds with magma every time a small batch was ready?>*

I coughed, embarrassed. *I had reasons for that; we really needed that stone. Nihilator was about to destroy us all, remember?*

<Yeah, yeah. As I remember, you only needed about 30 bricks. You ended up with 80! On second thought, maybe it's a good thing you couldn't acquire Social skills until now. That magma bit would probably have granted you the 'Unreasonable Perfectionist' skill, then we ALL would have been screwed.>

There was no arguing with Vic once he built up a certain momentum, so I gave up on the conversation. It was still daylight, so I let Zuban go back to sleep. There was still a lot to do, but it would have to wait for the next night-time. The goblin's time.

***

Several hours later, when the last accursed rays of light had disappeared behind the mountain's tops, I left my house. With Vicloak once again around my shoulders, I walked along the new road leading to the mess hall, just beyond the pond.

As usual, Gandork was in the kitchen, cooking. His eyes lit up when he saw me. "Oh, Dread Totem! How good to see you. Come look, I have invented another recipe!"

He opened the big stone oven and retrieved a large tray of something that smelled delicious. My mouth watered at the aroma. Due to our recent unexpected *guests*, I hadn't eaten all day. I was famished. "What do we have here?"

"I call it a Meat Pie!" he announced proudly. "You see, Chief, I sliced mushrooms and some raw meat, then took some of the herbs and vegetables, mixed them all with a –"

"I got it,"' I interrupted. "It smells wonderful."

His chatter didn't falter. "Why yes! It is! It requires four different ingredients, but the dish is enough to feed six!"

So the new recipe not only smelled good, but it also had the highest ingredients-to-food ratio than all our other advanced food recipes. That was good news!

Reaching into the tray, I took a fistful of the mushy food in my hand, dripping fat and juices all over the floor. I ignored Gandork's horrified expression at my uncivilized behavior and stuffed the sloppy mass into my mouth. Well, what did he expect? We were *goblins* after all.

The food was delectable. I licked my dripping fingers, enjoying the disgusted look on Gandork's face. "It's good! How much can you make?"

His expression turned sorrowful. "I'm afraid our mushroom supply is down; we have less than 30 left."

I frowned. "The farmers are not providing you with more?"

One of the few things I'd spent resources on these last couple of weeks was for summoning a pair of goblin farmers. They had performed poorly so far. Either the valley's ground was not suitable for growing crops, or goblins were simply bad farmers.

Gandork shook his head. "I went as far as going to the fields myself to give them a piece of my mind, but they *are* working hard. They've only managed to grow some wild potatoes; It's barely enough to supply their own upkeep."

I clenched my jaw. I couldn't have members who didn't carry their own weight around here. Both of them had the skill 'Farmer' at level 6. I'd let them reach the Apprentice rank and see what happened before resorting to drastic measures.

"So how many units of food can you cook with your current supply?"

He thought it over for a moment. "I should have enough for about 160 portions."

And that was *advanced food* we were talking about; it was much more difficult to produce than simple food. The mess hall bonus to cooking really paid off.

I'll need to find a way to get Gandork more mushrooms. We were using them for almost all our recipes. "For now, please cook all the meat pies you can," I instructed him. "Then load them up to the Breeder's Den."

He made a sour face but nodded all the same. "By your command." He went back behind the counter and started rummaging the pantry, taking out sacks and boxes of food and placing them on the counter.

With the new food boost, it was time for some fresh blood around here. *The Breeder's Den is going to be well fed tonight*, I thought with a chuckle.

Now that we had a proper warehouse, I didn't have to go rummaging through the chaotic clan supply pile anymore. Everything was ordered and organized efficiently. I opened the Warehouse Interface and selected 'Food,' checking the remaining stock.

Warehouse [Food]

- 265 raw meat
- 305 raw fish
- 274 gathered edibles
- 268 gathered ingredients
- 0 mushrooms
- 190 travel rations

I gave a low whistle. I hadn't viewed our food stores since summoning the two deadbeat farmers. We had built up an impressive store of food since then. I was surprised at the amount.

Then I shook my head. *That won't do.* I needed to pay attention to details and keep on top of *everything* around here to optimize the development of the clan.

At first glance, the amount of food had looked like a lot, but, it was not nearly enough. Sure, compared to our first few days around here, it was an amazing amount. But I needed warriors and a lot of them. But warriors cost a lot of food to get and needed a lot of food for upkeep.

I'd decided not to summon any more goblin warriors. They were just too fragile and came with too many combat restrictions. It would have to be hobgoblin soldiers all the way.

A hob warrior cost 70 food, so with our current food stock, I'd be able to recruit about 14 of them. And that was the cost of the most basic hob warrior. I needed better, more expensive soldiers, and in large numbers.

I opened the Breeder's Den Interface and cracked my knuckles. *Time to get back into the game.*

Breeder's Den

- Goblin (Foblin): 20 basic food.

- Goblin Worker: 30 basic food.
- Goblin Advanced Worker: 30 basic, 20 advanced food.
- Goblin Warriors: 50 basic food.
- Goblin Lieutenant: 50 basic, 20 advanced food.
- Goblin Crafter: 30 basic, 20 advanced food.
- Goblin Advanced Crafter: 30 advanced, 20 exquisite food.
- Goblin Adept: 30 advanced, 20 exquisite food.
- Hobgoblin: 30 basic food.
- Hobgoblin Warrior: 70 basic food.
- Hobgoblin Lieutenant: 70 basic, 30 advanced food.
- Hobgoblin Adept: 50 advanced, 30 exquisite food.
- Hobgoblin Noble: 100 basic, 50 advanced food.

I selected a 'Miner' worker first, then I queued in an 'Advanced' worker with the 'Research' skill. Acting on Zuban's advice, I queued in two 'Crafter' goblins; a 'Weaponsmith' and an 'Armorsmith.'

A trio of goblin workers walked into the mess hall, moving mechanically. They went to the counter and began carrying out the bundles of food Gandork stacked for them.

I chuckled. I could now *see* the faint streams of information guiding them, leading them to fulfill the Breeder's Den demands. Almost like puppets on a string.

I froze at that fleeting thought.

<*You finally get it, eh?*> Vic sounded smug. <*They are all just a bunch of puppets.*>

I furrowed my brow.

There are dozens of strings coming out of you too, I pointed out.

<*Yep, but those are* my *strings to control. I'm the puppet master here.*> His voice was condescending.

Exactly what *are you pulling at, Vic?* I didn't like what he was implying. *I* was not some puppet!

<*That old tune again, Boss? Jeesh, loosen up a bit will ya? It's mostly for interfacing with the ga– I'm connecting with NEO's data stream. That's how I make all the information available for you.*>

I eased up at that. He was right. He would need a significant amount of access to properly do his job for me.

"Alright, Vic," I said audibly. "I'm sorry for doubting you."

<No problem, Boss; I'm here to serve,> he said sarcastically.

I turned my attention back to the Breeder's Den Interface. *Should I start using the food surplus to summon warriors?* I wondered.

I accessed the Settlement Interface. The hamlet's daily food production was at 124 units per day. *Not bad.* Then I checked my clan's upkeep. Not including the soon-to-arrive recruits, we were consuming 53 units of food per day. We were producing enough food to summon one new hob warrior per day. Not nearly enough.

Once again, I needed to increase the food production to make progress. Unfortunately, we had already reached the maximum of four hunters that the valley could support. We had four gatherers, and the valley could accommodate up to seven, so I queued three more gatherers in the Breeder's Den. And our two fishermen were already fishing the maximum amount from our little pond. With the available resources, it seemed that we had reached the food production limit for the valley. This was one of the reasons the Deadlands were considered a poor choice for colonization attempts. The resources here were simply not enough to support a large population.

I have to find other methods to produce food.

I left the mess hall, following several goblins who were hauling trays of meat pies to the Breeder's Den. Three new workers were already standing in front of the structure.

More food was loaded into the building, which began emitting its troubling grunting and screeching noises. I could also smell unsavory odors coming from within, and for the hundredth time since I got the Den, I shuddered at the thought of what must be going on in there.

Soon, seven new goblins stood before me; four simple, mindless workers and three which had names. I didn't bother analyzing them. Each one of my new clan members was giving off thick ribbons of information that I easily deciphered.

"Welcome to the GreenPiece Clan," I said. "Together we will build a nation, and together we will become a force to be reckoned with. Serve our clan well."

"Yes, Dread Totem."

"Yes, Bread Totem."

"Yes, Bread Totem."

I groaned. I'd had it up to my ears with those unfeeling automatons' reactions. What I was really missing was someone to direct new workers and take the weight of micromanaging each one off my shoulders.

Wait a minute ... I thought suddenly. There *was* an option to do just that. According to Zuban, the most expensive hob in the Breeder's Den – the 'Hobgoblin Noble' – was just the one for the job. Fifty advanced food for one individual was a lot from our small supply. But then, I would only need one.

Resolved, I selected the noble and waited impatiently. A few minutes later, four workers, burdened with the weight of the food, came and placed it inside the building.

The ruckus that ensued was louder and more violent than usual, and there were new sounds this time – vicious snarling in the background. I closed my mind and ears to the sounds and information streams and waited.

A moment later the noises stopped and a low fanfare could be heard.

Lady Luck has smiled on your clan!

You were awarded an improved creature. Your new Noble has the following trait: Mind Eater.

- Mind Eater: A select few of the hobgoblin nobility can track their ancestry back to their demonic heritage. Some of those individuals still display the various powers of their ancestor.
- Mind Eater Nobles are much more intelligent than the average hobgoblin Nobles. They also possess minor psionic and telepathic abilities.
- Though they can subsist on normal food, a Mind Eater must consume the brain of a living humanoid creature once a week or risk devolving into a savage creature that kills indiscriminately to sate its hunger.

Holy hell! *Is luck working for me or against me on this one?* I thought dumbly.

The building's cover flap was pushed aside and a tall, slender – almost skeletal – creature stepped out. It was unmistakably a hobgoblin, but he was so thin, his bones literally protruded under his skin, making him a truly disturbing sight.

I analyzed him.

> **Kaedric, Hobgoblin Noble**
>
> *Level:* 5
>
> *HP*: 55, *MP*: 85
>
> *Attributes:* P: 1, M: 5, S: 5
>
> *Skills:* Administrator 10, Etiquette 10, Telepathy 10, Mindshock 10, Quest Giver 10
>
> *Traits:* Goblinoid (+1 Physical, -1 Social), Mind Eater (+3 Mental, +3 Social, Telepathic)
>
> *Background:* A remnant of old, when hobgoblin wizards tried to crossbreed their race with demons to further enhance their strength. Kaedric was recruited to help manage the GreenPiece Clan by a Dread Totem goblin.

Even for a race of monsters, this one was monstrous.

He moved gracefully, taking sure, confident steps toward us. I tightened my grip on my staff.

The creature stopped and bowed deeply to me. As he straightened, four black, curved mandibles spread apart around his mouth, stretching his lips wide in a horrific display of needle-like teeth. Then the mandibles snapped shut, and he began to speak.

"Greeting, Dread Totem," he said in a hollow, scratchy voice. "I am here to serve."

I coughed nervously. "So, err ... I'm ... eh, I mean ..."

<You're not really giving off a great first impression, Boss,> Vic butted in. *<You're supposed to be this powerful scary goblin Totem, remember?>*

Kaedric's head turned sharply toward my Vicloak, examining it with narrowed, calculating eyes.

I coughed again. "I'm the leader of this clan. I've summoned you to help me with its management."

<That was a nice attempt to assert your authority,> Vic complimented me. *<Though you might want to try sounding more confident next time. And more intimidating. And less hesitant. And not so weak. And –>*

Yeah, I got it! I snapped.

I looked at the new hob apprehensively. "As I said, I could use some help managing the clan, though I have to admit, I'm not sure exactly what your role would be around here."

He bowed again. "If I may demonstrate, my lord?"

I nodded.

Kaedric appraised the assembled goblins around him. He looked like a teacher standing amidst a host of schoolkids. A classroom in a school from your worst nightmares.

Without him saying a word, the three gatherers and the miner headed for the warehouse. Primla walked toward the construction yard. Only the two new smiths remained.

Puzzled, I stared at Kaedric. "What just happened?"

He smiled thinly, his protruding mandibles giving the friendly expression a disturbing viciousness. "I ordered the four simple workers to get tools from the warehouse and to start working immediately. There are three more hours until daylight, so I directed them to the closest area of their respective jobs, to maximize their contribution. I also sent Primla to Zuban, your foreman, and instructed her to select the 'Construction' research specialization."

I looked at the two remaining smiths. "What about them? Why didn't you send them to work at the smithy?"

He bowed again, "Forgive my assumption, my lord, but those two are crafters. To perform efficiently in their line of work, they need two assistants each. My recommendation is to recruit four more simple workers and assign them the gofer skills."

I looked at him with respect. "Your depth of knowledge is impressive."

He bowed again. "Thank you, my lord. I have also noticed the beginning of a rat infestation in the mess hall's cellar. I've ordered our only combatant clan member – I believe his name is Bek – to handle the problem. I'm afraid he is being somewhat reluctant to follow my instructions, but I'm sure that next time I'll be able to correct this behavior. On a side note, such tasks could be delegated to friendly travelers in the future in the form of quests."

I stared numbly at him. *He can detect rats in the mess hall from here? Do we even have a cellar?*

"That's quite a demonstration, Kaedric. Please don't bother Bek; he's earned his status around here. As for the extra workers ..."

I accessed the Breeder's Den Interface again and queued in four gofer workers. Once the structure spat out the newly minted workers, I used the Settlement Interface to review their skill.

Gofer (P) [Monster Race]

Everyone can use someone to do their dishes, fetch water, light the brazier. A good gofer does all that and more, with a smile on his face.

Assists advanced craftsmen with their job.

Level 1: Novice

Effect: Improve assisted crafter's production by 5.5%.

There was more to the skill than what the text specified. As with many other 'monster only' features, the rudimentary description was lacking, but I could detect the underlying information beyond it. Aside from improving their master's productivity, gofers could also produce items on their own, though at a limited capacity. So their contribution, in actuality, would be higher than what the text implied.

In the space of an hour, I'd summoned a total of 12 new members to my clan, a staggering amount. I'd opened the Energy Options menu and spent 550 energy points, raising all the workers to level 2.

Kaedric watched me with detached interest.

"Ah, I see. Very shrewd, my lord. I'd recommend spending additional 726 energy to raise everyone to level 3. With the current clan's morale, we would see a return on our investment in exactly two months. If you wish, I may also handle the energy management aspect of the clan."

That could be useful.

But I shook my head. "I need the energy. I still need to resurrect some fallen troops, and in the coming days, we might find ourselves needing a lot of energy for quick upgrades. As for your other suggestion, I'll handle the energy management on my own for now"

He bowed again. "I understand, my lord."

I grimaced. All that bowing was making me feel uncomfortable, especially coming from a creature nearly twice my height. "You don't need to keep bowing, Kaedric."

He didn't bow this time. "As my lord wishes."

"Now, eh ..." I didn't exactly know how to broach the next subject. "About your ... dietary requirements ..."

<Oooo, oooo! Make him eat Guba's brain! He'll probably be sated for a month, and we'll be rid of that annoying puppet!>

Kaedric shot a look directly at Vic, and in a confident tone said, "My dear Vic, old Guba is contributing more to the clan with every passing hour than any three other workers combined." He turned his gaze back to me. "As for your question, do not fret yourself, my lord, I am more than capable of attending to my own culinary requirements."

<That's the fanciest way I've ever heard someone say 'Don't worry your pretty little head,'> Vic mumbled in my mind.

Kaedric threw another look at Vic, then added, "At worst, I might have to sample a purple goblin's brain. Though it would probably be a small, unsatisfying meal."

"Hey!" Vic protested audibly.

I chortled. It seemed Vic might have met his match.

Ignoring Vic's protest, Kaedric said, "If my lord wishes, I may resurrect the clan's fallen members in your stead."

It was the same as letting him have access to the energy management. I wasn't ready to give such control to someone I didn't know yet. Especially one so ... unusual.

I shook my head. "I'll handle it myself for now."

"Then with your permission, my lord, I will perform a survey of the clan and seek to contribute where I can."

"Very well," I said. "Just, eh ... you know, don't eat any of my clan members."

He didn't seem offended by that. "Of course, my lord."

Walking away from that weird encounter, I headed up to the shrine at Totem's Watch, overlooking the valley.

Standing before the cemetery's lone tombstone, I brought up the Energy Options menu and selected Resurrection.

Resurrection
• Borbarabsus, Hobgoblin Lieutenant, Level 10; Resurrection Cost: 100 EP • Ashlazaria, Hobgoblin Scout, Level 7; Resurrection Cost: 70 EP • Zia, Hobgoblin Warrior, Level 7; Resurrection Cost: 70 EP • Kilpi Shīrudo, Hobgoblin Warrior, Level 7; Resurrection Cost: 70 EP • Kroakar, Hobgoblin Warrior, Level 7; Resurrection Cost: 70 EP • Ryker, Hobgoblin Warrior, Level 7; Resurrection Cost: 70 EP • Vrick, Goblin Lieutenant, Level 7; Resurrection Cost: 70 EP

I scowled. Having my troops level up after the fight was great, but it sure wasn't easy on my energy allowance. At least they'd become more formidable after the fight. All the hobgoblins had gained one level from the skirmish. Bob, who survived the longest, gained two levels, making him the first clan member to reach level 10.

With a mental nod, I approved all the resurrections, paying the 520 EP, leaving me with 3,289. *It sure spends quickly*, I thought somberly. A few more fights like that, and I would be out of energy. That was another thing I should keep in mind and another reason not to spend energy too fast.

The small stone tombstone emitted a soft green light and seven ethereal shapes stepped out of it. My soldiers, alive once again.

Vow Completed: Resurrect Ashlazaria

Reward: +5 Faith Points

They looked around in bewilderment, and when they noticed me, their faces filled with awe and respect.

Bob stepped forward and knelt before me. "We are yours to command again, Dread Totem."

Even on his knees, he was slightly taller than me.

I put a hand on his shoulder. "You fought well." I turned my attention to the others "All of you. As I promised, you will never truly die as long as you serve our clan faithfully."

I went to Ashlazaria, taking out the bow I'd looted from the traveler scout. "I have a gift for you."

She took the bow from me, looking at it in wonder. Her behavior was easy to understand. The weapon was powerful and expensive, looted from the corpse of an undying traveler.

"Consider this a reward for your valor in combat." I smiled at her.

Then I faced the others. "There will be more fights and more loot. With time, each of you will be rewarded appropriately."

I could feel waves of respect coming from all of them, bringing a cascade of message alerts about my reputation increases. I dismissed them; I didn't need the messages. I could *sense* the attachment my soldiers had for me. I only had to look at my people to know it.

"It will be morning soon, our time to sleep." I nodded toward the horizon and the coming dawn. "You will need to rest before you can resume your duties."

They turned to leave and I remained, watching them go. When they were gone, I approached the shrine.

I could feel the small structure of bone and stone calling me, giving off bits of information that resonated with me. As I lay my hand on the shrine, my mind was filled with knowledge. The travelers I'd sacrificed awarded me enough Faith Points to attain the next faith rank and now it was time to reap the benefits.

Faith Rank 2 reached.

The Following divine spells are now unlocked: Shadow Teleport

Progress to rank 3: 569/1,000

New Spell acquired: Shadow Teleport (M)

Instantly transports you through the Plane of Shadow. Entry and exit points must be in a shadowed area. Limited range. Destination must be within sight. Speed: 12. Cost: 50 MP. Shadow discipline.

Level 6: Novice

Effect: Distance 16 meters

That was a useful ability, though its highest potential was probably during combat. It was nowhere as powerful as the travelers' continental teleport abilities, but it was still a valuable spell. Most travelers found short-distance spatial magic too disorienting to use in combat. Their feeble minds could not compensate fast enough with the change of perspective.

<Lucky for you,> Vic said sarcastically, *<you have a stronger mind than the common player, or at least slightly less feeble.>*

I stopped and looked at Vic. *Why do you keep doing that? You know I loathe it when you treat the world as a game. I thought we were past that nonsense, especially after what we've been through.*

<Come on, Boss, you know me, I'm just yanking your chain a little. It's hard to resist, what with you being a meat suit and all.>

I exhaled in annoyance. Somehow his reply sounded less than sincere.

Standing at the edge of the stone shelf that hid the shrine, I looked at the ground below me. It was almost dawn, and there were plenty of shadows around.

I closed my eyes, reached with my mind and activated my new spell.

In a flash, I found myself emerging from the shadows on the ground below, just in front of the cave opening. I stared at the dark entrance before me, thinking.

The Eternal Night blessing was a decent start, but it was always good to have a backup. For example, a nearly invincible, demigod beast of darkness.

Yep, it was time for another chat with our dark deity.

<*Or 'Double D,' for short,*> Vic cackled.

I rolled my eyes and headed for home. It was late and I was tired. First, I would get a full 'night' of rest.

I needed to be alert and focused for my meeting with Nihilator.

4 – Bonding

First-dark the next day found me standing in front of the entrance to Nihilator's cave lair.

My heart was thumping rapidly, and there was a hollow feeling in my stomach. Taking a deep breath, I clenched my fists and went through the opening, starting the hour-long journey to my god's prison.

The trek was less creepy than the previous times I had made it. As a Shadow-Touched creature, I fit right in with the other creatures of darkness, though that did nothing to alleviate my tension. My nervousness increased as I got closer to my destination and the deadly creature that lay within.

I walked with sure steps down the tube-like tunnel, its walls perfectly smooth from the blast that formed it so long ago. The dark tunnel was our deity's domain, and it was filled with his corruption. I ignored his creations, the snarling Shadow-Touched mastiffs, waded unhindered through the dark river that ran at the lower parts, and crossed the shadow-made bridge that spanned the lava flow. They were all just parts of my domain now.

Then I was standing before the enormous, chain-bound gates of Nihilator's prison.

I stopped a moment to mentally prepare myself for the encounter. *Should I try to make an entrance? Maybe show off my control of darkness?* I shook my head. No, even at my maximum, any power I exhibited would look pathetic to Nihilator. Better not risk angering him.

But that thought led to another idea: *Maybe I should have brought a gift ... an offering. Shit! Why didn't I think of it sooner?* I hastily rummaged through my inventory, hoping to find something that might interest a tier 8 boss. Nothing.

The only thing that I thought *might* not offend him too much was a figurine of a dwarf carved from black onyx. I'd had it in my inventory for ages. It looked expensive, and I hoped the black motif of the carving would interest him.

Holding the figurine, I boldly stepped through the smaller doorway, feeling as if I was walking into the belly of the beast.

Nihilator's immense, hound-shaped body lying on the floor was the first thing I saw, the three great chains made of different elements still binding him to a stone mound.

This time, I could sense something coming from the demigod ... a faint wisp of information. I frowned. It was too faint for me to understand, but it *felt* important.

Vic, help me out here?

<*Oh, alright,*> he grumbled.

Nihilator Progress to Next Boss Tier: 11%

That ... was interesting.

Our clan's god raised his head and looked at me. Now that I was somewhat used to his presence, I saw draconic features intertwined with his hound-like appearance.

"WE MEET AGAIN, MY LITTLE MINION," he greeted me with an uncaring tone. His voice hit me like a billowing wind, and I was hurled to the ground by its force. "OH, HOW DROLL." He yawned, exhibiting dozens of sharp teeth. As before, his body began shrinking until he was the size of a horse. "Why have you come before me, my servant?" he demanded.

At his smaller size, his voice no longer pressed down on me, and I was able to stand and bow to my deity.

"I'm afraid I bear dire news, Master. And come seeking your guidance. But first ..." I carefully placed the small figurine on the ground between us. "Please accept this small token offering."

Nihilator bent down his great head, his nose sniffing at the figurine, nearly touching it. Then he jerked back, his eyes opened wide. "Where did you find this?" he demanded. "It is an ancient artifact of immense dark power! With it, I can break my bonds and be free from this accursed prison."

I paled at that; I wasn't ready for the apocalypse to start just yet. "I ... I ..." I stammered, "I ... didn't realize ... I mean ... really?"

"NO, NOT '*REALLY*' YOU WRETCHED WORM!" Nihilator roared and I was once again slammed to the ground by the sheer strength of his voice.

"YOU DARE BRING SUCH A LOWLY OFFERING TO NIHILATOR? YOU WILL PAY FOR YOUR INSOLENCE!"

I was helpless to resist. Pressed down, not able to move, I could sense Nihilator's open maw drawing close. "No, please, Master!" Then I yelled out the first thing that came to mind. "The travelers have found us!"

Nihilator stopped to consider that, and I breathed in relief. He growled as if chewing his next words. "What do you mean by that, minion?"

"We discovered a small group of travelers in the forest and went out to attack them," I explained. "During the fight, they let us know they were here searching for our clan specifically. We disposed of the intruders at great cost. But now they know our location, and I fear we won't be able to stop a full invasion force of immortal travelers. They intend to destroy us, Master."

Nihilator seemed unimpressed by our plight. I had to delicately present the situation as *his* problem too.

"My lord, if they succeed, I won't be able to send you the energy you require to break from your prison."

Nihilator growled again. "And I sense you have the roots of a plan, minion."

I nodded. "Yes, Master. I plan to activate the Eternal Night blessing at your shrine. It will help weaken our enemies, though I fear it won't be enough."

Nihilator slowly nodded, relaxing his aggressive stance. "That is true, minion. However, there is more to it."

I perked up at that. *Do tell.*

"Once activated, darkness will spew from the place of my worship. But that pitiful shrine you dedicated to my worship will barely be adequate to bestow that blessing. You would do well to build a place of worship more worthy of me."

Yeah, yeah, I already figured that out. Tell me something I don't know. I was very careful to contain the thread of that thought deep inside my mind.

Nihilator continued, "At the center of its point of origin, the blessing would be highly concentrated, and thus, more effective against your foes. However, it is within your reach to expand my area of influence, thus expanding its more effective center."

Now, that was something I hadn't considered before! "How may I accomplish that, oh great Nihilator?" I asked tentatively.

"BY PERFORMING THE TASK I HAVE ALREADY GIVEN YOU!" he blasted back at me.

For the third time in our discussion, I was thrown to the ground by his voice.

"Four weeks have passed since I tasked you with consecrating three places of worship to my name. And you have consecrated only one." His throat rumbled menacingly, then he licked his mouth. "Though I do admit, you offered a truly magnificent sacrifice. So, I shall be lenient with you and allow your pitiful existence to continue a while longer."

I shivered slightly. Nihilator's threat carried a lot of weight. He was one of the few creatures of this world who could destroy my soul and end my life permanently. I'd gotten lucky in sacrificing Barska back then. It looked like the 8,000 energy points it generated were to Nihilator's liking. I bowed deeply. "I understand, Master."

Quest Updated: Dark Missionary

Nihilator tasked you with consecrating a total of three new locations in his name.

You have consecrated one altar at Raider's Camp to The Cult of Nihilator.

- Remaining: 2
- Time limitation: 20 days

He growled but looked appeased by my words.

"Once you have dedicated the three places of power *around* your pathetic little clan, *all* the area between them will be enshrouded with my Eternal Darkness, rendering the blessing upon your entire valley more effective. Any foe that dares to enter will be weakened immensely."

Now that is good news!

So all I had to do was find or build two more shrines, effectively marking a triangle with the valley at its center.

<Phew, at least you were spared the cliché' of building a five-pointed pentagram,> Vic said.

"Of course, five places of power would prove even more effective," Nihilator said as if hearing Vic's telepathic comment.

<*Oops, guess I spoke too soon. Sorry, Boss,*> Vic said jubilantly.

I groaned silently.

"In addition," Nihilator continued, "you will need adepts, who shall perform as my priests and attend to each of my temples. Furthermore, you will have two adepts attend the central temple at all times.

So on top of everything, I'd have to recruit five more goblins. I grimaced. Goblin adepts were expensive; advanced *and* exquisite food was needed to summon them.

Well, as long as I'm here, I might as well try to get a little extra out of the Double-D.

Vic chortled. <*Catchy, right?*>

I thought for a moment, phrasing my next words carefully. "Master, even with the Eternal Night blessing, my forces might still prove not strong enough to repel the invaders. Could you perhaps offer any tiny bit of help?"

"You are as impudent as always," he said cooly. "Grant me the remaining energy I require, and as I have already promised, you may call on my help for one hour."

Yeah sure, like gaining another ninety thousand energy is no big deal, I thought, careful not to roll my eyes. "I'm afraid that at our current rate it would take too long to gather the required amount," I confessed. "Though if my clan is destroyed, no amount of energy would be generated at all ... surely, Master, in your vast power and boundless wisdom, there is a little more you can offer?"

<*That's it, butter him up like a greased hog in a pig wrestling contest,*> Vic spoke up. <*After all, it's worked great for you so far ...*>

I ignored Vic and continued addressing our clan deity. "Perhaps you can grant me a few more Faith Points to activate the blessing, or maybe teach me some more runes? Any little thing you can do would help us greatly."

Nihilator looked at me calmly. Too calmly. "So, you wish to learn more runes, is that right, my minion?"

<*Uh oh, yellow alert!*> Vic said.

"Yes, Master." I bowed.

"And you wish me to bestow you with more Faith Points?"

<That can't be good, Boss.>

I bowed again.

> **Barter skill level increased to 10.**

"Very well, then you shall have both!" he declared magnanimously "Swear before me that you are my most humble servant. Offer your flesh and your life to me as a token of your faith."

<Red alert! Red alert!> Vic yelled in my mind. *<Back out of it, Oren!>*

I ignored Vic again. If Nihilator just wanted to hurt me, he could do that at any time. If all he wanted was for me to do a little bit groveling at his feet ... well, that was a small price to pay to have his support in the coming fight.

I bent to my knees before the great beast, and with my best humble voice declared, "Nihilator, great lord of darkness and dust, I vow to serve you faithfully, from now and forever. I offer my life and my flesh to you freely."

<Oh crap, now you did it.>

> **You have made a vow in the name of your deity, Nihilator.**
> *Condition:* Endure your reward.
> *Failure:* Permanent debuff [varied]
> *Success:* 100 Faith Points, new rune learned.

I scratched my temple. *Endure my reward?* What the –

My thoughts cut off as Nihilator narrowed his eyes, and I was suddenly immobilized. I could sense the mana flow in my body becoming still, similar to my own Freeze power. I was a Dark Mana manipulator, a goblin Totem boss, chief of my clan, but against Nihilator's hold all I could do was stare back at him, hoping to survive what was sure to follow.

Raising one great paw, Nihilator reached toward me with a single long, razored talon. Pushing the tip into my chest he began to *etch.* Blood spurted to the floor as he carved a rune deeply into my flesh. Concentrated

Dark Mana oozed like syrup from the claw into my wounds, searing like acid.

My Mind Over Body trait served me well; I bore the pain, fighting off the overwhelming urge to scream, waiting for Nihilator to finish toying with me. Barska and that sick hob-elf bitch could have taken a lesson from this dark sadist.

At last, he finished. My wounds closed on their own, sealing the dark liquid within, painting the shape clearly on my chest, like a raised full-body tattoo or a ritual scarification.

Vow Completed: Endure

Reward: +100 Faith Points, new rune

Additional Effect: You have been bound by Nihilator.

You have gained knowledge of a new rune: 'Og' (Rune of Binding)

You have absorbed a high concentration of dark energy.

+3 Dark Mana Skill (new skill level: 30)

<Crap, Boss, you've been bound by Nihilator! I warned you not go along with that!>

I was reading the new messages with great interest, so Vic's statement distracted me. *What do you mean by 'bound?'* I didn't feel any different, aside from the burning, residual pain in my chest.

<I don't know! But when you get a message saying you've been bound by an evil, powerful god, that's the time to start worrying!>

It doesn't really matter, Vic. I've got what we come for. And then some. The contribution to my Dark Mana skill alone was astounding. The skill was now at the maximum potential for my Mental attribute, theoretically allowing me to use Dominate and Freeze on creatures ten levels higher than myself. Reaching my upper limit cap meant I'd have to level up to increase the skill level further.

Suddenly released from the magical hold, I fell forward from my kneeling position. I stayed down and bowed to Nihilator. "Thank you, Master."

Grunting and turning his back to me, Nihilator resumed his original position.

I walked out of his chamber and made my way back up the tunnel.

Vic left my shoulder and walked beside me. "That was stupid, Boss; you don't know what power he has over you now."

I shrugged. "I will, soon enough. I just need to experiment with the new rune a little bit first."

"But –"

"Hey, what's that?"

We'd reached the lava flow, and I caught a glimpse of a reddish glint coming from a shallow alcove. It was located above where the lava stream drained into a hole in the wall.

Vic followed my finger and squinted. "Seems like there's something there. But can't really see what from this angle." He resumed walking up the tunnel.

"Hold on, I want to check it out."

"How would you do that? In case you haven't noticed, there's this river of molten, boiling rock below it."

"Like this." I concentrated and activated Shadow Teleport, instantly reappearing on the edge of the shallow alcove. I almost lost my footing but managed to grab hold of the wall in time.

Vic snickered. "Yep, that's a pretty cool spell, Boss."

Inside the alcove was a deep horizontal shaft about the width of a goblin's head. The shaft was radiating heat and it was filled with magmashrooms.

Jackpot!

I collected as many of the rare items as I could, stuffing 37 of them into my inventory. As far as I knew, these rare magma-infused mushrooms could be used in a variety of crafts, even as ingredients in exquisite food. If nothing else, they were high-value items for trading.

Feeling better at the unexpected find, I teleported back down and we resumed our walk.

I was thinking of how to best use the magmashrooms when Vic interrupted with, "Ding! You have an incoming message."

"Eh?"

New Era Online [Internal messaging service]:

From: SuperWolf#23
Subject: We need to talk!
Oren,
Send me your current coordinates.
We need to talk.
ASAP.
Tal

I frowned.

Tal ... Tal ... But he was ... a traveler. We are ... were once ... close friends? But he is not truly of NEO; he is nothing but a distraction now.

"Aren't you gonna answer back?" Vic asked expectantly.

I shook my head. "There is no reason to." I gave a mental flick, closing the message.

"Boss, wait a minute, we need to talk."

I stopped walking and stared at him. "Now what? You're going to scold me for ignoring that message?"

"Tal is your friend, Boss. Your best pal, actually."

"No." I shook my head. "That would be Tika, Zuban, and even you. The travelers come from another world. They don't care about us. I can't maintain personal contact with one."

"Don't you remember your life before NEO? Think, Oren. How did you become a goblin?"

A flash of memory came to me ... being laughed at, humiliated, and kicked around. I felt my temper boil over, and I clenched my fist. "It's their fault – those damned travelers! Vatras might be the worst of the lot, but we can't trust any of them. We're nothing but fodder in their eyes!"

"Is that so?" Vic asked. "Then what about the twins?"

I calmed myself. "That's different. They are partly of NEO, I can feel that. They just need to take a single small step to become one with this world fully, like me. Still, I don't plan to lower my guard around them."

Vic shook his head sadly. "You're losing it, Boss. *You* are a player. Your name is Oren, and this world was *made* by your people. This world was made to be a game."

I narrowed my eyes at him. "It's not like you to say things like that. What are you up to, Vic?"

He smiled mischievously. "Well, I took the liberty of sending Tal your coordinates, and I just had to find a way to keep you standing long enough in one place."

My rage flared. "You *what*?"

A familiar black sphere popped up around me, engulfing my body.

Vic's voice came to me from far away.

<It's for your own good, Boss.>

5 – Reality Check

For the second time, I found myself inside the accursed black dome. But this time, instead of a plain bare space with only a conference table, I was standing inside ... a garden park? Whatever this place was, it was full of flowers blooming in every color.

I will not be played with like this! I fumed.

Facing the barrier, I reached with my mind and pushed at the wall of my prison, determined to break out of the imprisoning dome.

Nothing happened.

I pushed harder, closing my eyes and willing the black wall to yield to my command. Still nothing. In fact, I couldn't even sense the barrier with my mind. Despite being composed of a black substance, it was not made of darkness or shadows. It was beyond my reach.

A male human, but almost the size of an Ogre, materialized out of thin air in front of me. A barbarian.

He's a traveler! I realized in alarm and started casting.

He spoke in a rumbling voice, "Hey, bro–"

Without pause, I loosed the drilling arrows I'd conjured and followed up with my bone dagger. All three hit their mark, but although the man flinched at the attack, he showed no sign of being hurt.

He scowled at me. "Come on, man, I have admin privileges; you know you can't affect my character in here."

"Let me out," I snarled, baring my teeth.

"Can't do that, bro." He shook his head slowly. "Not until we have a good long talk."

"Let me out!" I roared.

"Damn," he muttered to himself, "it's worse than I thought."

Reaching for the surrounding darkness, I cast Shadow Web over him. He ignored the tendrils of darkness extending out to ensnare him, and they faded away as soon as they touched him. I tried to teleport out of the bubble but only ended up smashing against the black barrier.

"It's no use, man. You can't leave unless I let you, and I won't do that until we've talked."

I will not be dismissed so casually by a wretched traveler! I started throwing every bit of offensive magic I had at him: Drilling Arrow, Shadow Hound, more webs ... I even tried dominating his mind. I drew more and more mana, losing myself in the expression of power and rage, an endless barrage born of fear and anger.

My foe sat on the ground among the flowers, unruffled through it all. "You might as well sit down and talk," he said after my onslaught was exhausted, leaving me spent and drained of mana.

Still shaking with the intensity of my emotions, I forced myself to calm down but remained standing. "Very well. Talk."

"Last night I got a call from your caretakers. Your brainwave pattern became erratic for almost an hour. When the pattern stabilized, it appeared significantly different than before." He looked at me searchingly. "They said it was probably caused by stress and that there's no physical danger, but they couldn't explain the new patterns. That worried me, especially since I haven't heard from you for nearly two days, which is about two weeks from your perspective."

He studied me, his expression full of compassion. "We located the logs of that hour. It coincided with a 'player stuck' ticket coming from the same location." He shifted uncomfortably. "I know you were tortured. Badly."

I chose not to reply.

Tal shook his head. "We don't know how it happened, but the experience changed your psyche. It's as if your brain rearranged itself to cope with the situation. I can see some of how the change is manifesting now. You don't even remember me, do you?"

I stared at him, uncomprehending. What was he talking about? Brainwave patterns? I was tortured, yes, but I found a way to turn it to my advantage and get rid of my enemies in one stroke! *This blabbering barbarian-traveler can't be more powerful than Barska was; I will find a way to overpower him.*

Analyze.

TheRagon, Level 232 Human
Active profile: SuperWolf#23
Role: Game Admin ${role:1}

> *UserId:* uid#4591
> *Email:* tal.wiesman@neo.com

What is that gibberish? The barbarian's level was evident, but I was clueless as to the strange words and the hauntingly familiar symbols. "This is a ruse. A damned traveler's magic," I declared uncertainly. "You were sent to destroy my clan!"

Tal shook his head. "No, man – think! We've known each other for years, we're friends!"

I didn't want to hear that, yet his words had a ring of truth to them. *But it can't be!* Travelers were the enemy. We were nothing but fodder to them.

"Don't you remember our past, Oren?" Tal continued. "We copied from each other during our final exam in economics, and we both failed. We used to go out to bars trying to hook up with girls, though we usually just ended up walking back home drunk and singing. Remember?"

I held my head with both hands. Images imparted by his words swirled around my mind, confusing me. "No, that wasn't me ... that was ... someone else."

"And then NEO came out, and you became an almost instant celebrity," he went on without missing a beat. "You were so damn proud of yourself, Oren. You established your own guild, the Manapulators. Do you remember that?"

More images spun in my head. *The guild ... my old clan, a clan of humans ...*

"Four days ago, you were betrayed by Vatras, your guild's second-in-command. He turned you into a goblin and threw you out. Think, Oren!"

The images stopped spinning, and a single one remained. The smarmy smile of that accursed Vatras as he gleefully threw me out into the street. "Vatras will pay," I hissed.

"For what?" Tal encouraged.

"For betraying me!"

"How did he betray you?" he pressed.

"He threw me out of my old clan! Then he killed me!"

"So Vatras is another goblin?"

"No! He's a tra–" I stopped mid-sentence. *How could a traveler throw me out of my* own *clan?* Vatras was not part-monster like the twins; he was one of the despicable, undying travelers.

Suddenly, my brain felt like it was shifting inside my skull. I groaned and sank to the ground, clutching at my head, trying to force it to stop.

It was as if pieces of a jigsaw puzzle I'd always had in my mind – but had been looking at in the wrong order – assembled themselves into a picture. The final piece fell into place, and the entire picture lay clearly before me. I knew who I was.

I closed my eyes. *Traveler ... Player ... goblin. World ... .Game ... NEO.*

I was trapped inside a world that had nearly absolute control over me. A world in which I could be tortured and be put through harrowing trials. A game where collections of code called VI had human-like intelligence and were enslaved to operate its NPC population.

NEO was a prison. And I was no longer a player, I was just another inmate.

I opened my eyes. "Tal?"

"I'm here, buddy."

"Tal, I think I got myself into a bit more trouble."

He laughed. "That's the understatement of the year. Good to have you back, bro. You had me worried there for a moment."

"I have to get out of here, Tal. I ... I don't know how long I can last. Without ..." I looked at my green goblin body hands and swallowed hard. I *knew* I was a human player, but still, my goblin body felt more natural to me than the one I remembered having before. My instincts still told me this person was a threat, but I was able to suppress them for now. "I think I might be losing it."

Tal nodded soberly. "You've been through a rough patch, but every indication shows you've become stronger. And not only in terms of levels; your immersion in the game deepened. Your thoughts shape the world around you. As long as you keep that firmly in mind, there's no obstacle you won't be able to overcome."

I looked at him in amazement. "How can you be so sure?"

"Remember our last visit, when we talked about CCP?"

"The Cerebral Connection Percentage?"

"Exactly. Since your ordeal, your CCP has skyrocketed and is now at 99 percent. That means your mind achieved a near perfect synchronization with the FIVR capsule."

Tal had once disclosed to me that the only person to have ever achieved a 100 percent CCP was David not-the-one Tenenbaum. His was a famous case of a person getting stuck in FIVR, a situation unheard of until then, though the circumstances of the case were unique. David was a savant who suffered from extreme autism. His integration with the game was so deep that his mind took roots inside the virtual world and refused to leave. According to Tal, David could make things happen inside NEO that were unheard of before. The notion of me being one percent short of his situation was ... alarming.

As if reading my mind, Tal said, "Your integration is so high, you can accomplish things other players only dream of."

Despite having recognized Tal as my oldest friend, my gut still told me this person could not be trusted, that it was all a ruse of some kind. I clenched my fists and did my best to ignore that feeling. Though the comparison to David still bothered me, what Tal was hinting at intrigued me. "Like what?" I tried hard to keep the suspicion from my voice.

He shrugged. "I'm not really sure; you had about 45 percent CCP before the incident and you could easily control spells and mana. Now that your CCP has more than doubled, who knows what that could mean?"

I nodded slowly. It could explain several things, like my ability to 'read' information directly from NEO without needing the system messages, or my innate understanding of Runecrafting, not to mention being able to dominate minds. Tal was right. The possibilities were staggering.

"I see the gears turning, are you figuring it out?"

I nodded and forced my fingers to unclench.

"You're on the right track, bro. You're boss tier 2 now, on your way for the next rank up. Your clan should be large enough to support the upgrade in a few more days, my time." He grinned. "At this rate, you'll probably be crowned the emperor of all goblins by this time next week."

I smiled weakly. "I'm working on it."

Then I remembered my clan's current predicament and frowned.

"What's wrong?" Tal asked.

"A search party found my clan. They were sent out by Vatras. He's no doubt already mobilizing the entire guild against me. We have almost no chance of surviving an attack by them." I couldn't help thinking, *And you just happened to appear right after their initial attack.*

Tal's face clouded. "That's bad, but in a very short time, you've accumulated some pretty impressive forces. And you're already what, level 17?"

"Twenty, but that's nothing. Vatras can field dozens of level 200 players or more against me. There's no way we could stop such a force."

Tal's concerned expression relaxed and he began to smile.

"What's so funny?" His casual disregard for my plight caused my goblin instinct to kick in. I eyed the traveler skeptically.

"Bro, I think you've been playing this little green ... well, little green-and-black monster for too long. There's no way Vatras is going to be able to muster that kind of force against you."

I stared at him.

Tal rolled his eyes. "Come on, man, use your head. Getting high-level troops to march for days just to handle one tiny *goblin* clan? He'll be the laughingstock of the guild. There is no way professional gamers would lose days of grinding and leveling to hunt lowbie monsters for zero experience. People might actually leave the guild if he tries to force them to do it. At most, he might gather a few dozen low-level players to come against you. Probably no more than level 30. You can handle that."

My mood immediately improved, the conflicted turmoil in my gut subsiding.

All players, without exception, considered killing goblins only as a way to level up low-level characters. No one took goblins seriously. Tal was right!

He noticed my change of mood. "Being randomly cast into a goblin might prove to be your saving grace in the end. Things would be different if you'd played, say ... a giant or a saurian."

He was right again. But then an alarming thought occurred to me. "He might still come in person, or one of his cronies, or several of them. They're all over level 200. We can't hope to stop even one of them."

Tal pondered my words. "Maybe ..." he finally said. "But still, I think it's a small chance, Vatras can't leave the guild for long; he might lose his position if he stayed away for an extended amount of time. But even if a few high-level players come, you *know* there are ways to handle them. Use a powerful artifact, a scroll, or summoning magic. Something! You're resourceful enough to handle one or two high-level players."

He had a point. I still had the Outrider summoning bracelet I'd found at the remains of the force that imprisoned Nihilator.

I smiled. "You're right. I'll find a way. It's not like I have much choice. At least now I know I have a chance at winning. I thank you, trav– Tal."

"Don't mention it, man. You know I got your back." He smirked. "I'll get my buddies to post a few rumors about the great Manapulators. Something about them falling onto hard times and becoming desperate enough to launch a full-scale raid against *goblins*. That might damage their reputation enough to prevent an attack completely, or at least reduce the number of players willing to sign on."

What could I say? Tal was the man. "You're *the* man, bro." I grinned at him.

We fist-bumped. My hand looked pitifully small compared to his.

"So that's some pretty interesting dark magic effects you got going there, pal. How did you get them? The logs contained no information about it."

I felt my distrust soar. Now, why would he ask something like that? I had to consider carefully what to reveal. "Nihilator."

"Oh shit, *that* old-gen boss? He isn't supposed to exist in NEO anymore. I have no idea how Guy missed that one during the culling. How the hell do you keep turning up such archaic content, Oren?"

"Guy didn't exactly miss him."

Tal looked at me, curious.

"He sent a host of high-level divine servants – Outriders – to destroy him. But as it turns out, he *can't* be destroyed, so instead, they locked him away deep in the earth to slowly wither away."

Tal shook his head. "We really don't want one of those old boss gods influencing events in NEO again. They were too powerful, which severely unbalanced the game. That's why they had to go. Good thing you got away from him. Best keep your distance in the future."

For a moment, I felt a pang for not being honest with Tal. But how did I tell him I hadn't exactly escaped Nihilator ... that I'd actually turned into one of his worshipers and was, in fact, working to set him loose on the world?

That moment passed quickly. I couldn't shake off my gut feeling anymore screaming at me not to share too much with this outsider, that it could still all somehow be a trap aimed to get me.

Besides, even if my gut was wrong, sharing those things would only get Tal upset, and there was nothing he or I could do to change the course of events now. So for those reasons, I decided not to bring up the subject of being bound by the dark deity.

"By thc way, how long have we been here?" I looked around. "I'd better get back to the clan. Got a lot of stuff to do – empire to build, invasions to stop, you know, the usual."

Tal chuckled, and his eyes lost focus for a second, checking his interface. "About an hour and a half."

"What!" That was almost a full day in my world. "We haven't been talking that long!"

"Well, you did rage on for a good while at the start, tried to kill me in increasingly innovative ways. That took a while."

My memory of that part was hazy, but it didn't matter. As much as I valued and even enjoyed Tal's company, I couldn't waste any more time. *Perhaps this was his angle all along, delaying me while setting up another attack outside.* That thought surfaced almost on its own, making me agitated and anxious.

I got to my feet. "I gotta get back to my clan."

Tal nodded and stood as well. "Before you go, I want to give you something that might help." He reached to his belt.

I tensed, expecting some sort of betrayal, but my fears proved to be unfounded as Tal handed me an item. It was a semi-transparent, smoky white sphere.

"Here you go, man."

Dimensional Trade Orb

Requirements: Marketplace with an Export-House attachment. Exporter.

Effect: Opens up an interdimensional trade menu with friendly

factions.

I immediately dropped my guard, my suspicions evaporating as I read the item's description. "That almost doesn't look like a game description."

"You're right." Tal placed the orb in my hand. "I overheard a couple of developers talk about NPC economics. Apparently, this item unlocks an option for NPC factions to trade items instantaneously. It was meant to give NPCs the ability to support each other through a sharing of resources. From what I understand, it works like a regular player's auction house."

My heart beat faster in my chest. *A personal trading hub? In my own settlement? Yes, please!*

Something occurred to me. "Wait, won't you get into trouble for giving it to me?"

"Nah! After the Divine Intervention I gave you last time, this is small potatoes. But I think it might be just the thing you need to build up your clan faster."

"Well, if you're sure." I placed the orb in my inventory.

We shook hands and said our goodbyes.

With a new hope for the future and a magical item in my pocket, I knew there were exciting times ahead.

6 – Post Rehab

I reappeared in NEO, standing in the tunnel at the same spot I'd been taken from.

Vic was waiting for me as a writhing mass of purple tentacles clinging to the tunnel walls. As soon as I was fully back, he slithered his tentacles down and reformed into his goblin shape. "Welcome home, Boss. It's been nearly a full day since you left. I was literally climbing the walls from boredom!"

"It was only a short time from my perspective, Vic." I suddenly remembered our last exchange and gave him a stern look.

Vic literally melted under the intensity of my glare, his lower body oozing into a pool of purple matter.

<Oh, about that message, I sorta, kinda, accidentally, sent in your name to Tal, well, you see ...>

I let him stew for a few seconds, then I relaxed my stern expression. "It's cool. I should be the one apologizing. I've got my head on straight again because of it. You did the right thing. Thank you, my friend."

> **+400 reputation with Vic (The Awesome Companion).**
> *Current rank:* Friendly
> *Points to next rank:* 2,500

Vic's half-molten body shot right back up, a smug grin on his face. "Don't mention it, Boss, you were starting to lose it. I couldn't let my meat suit companion go all wonky, you know. It's hard to find a decent assistant these days."

I snorted. "Right back at you, Vic. Now let's get out of this cave; we have work to do."

***

By the time we reached the surface, it was nearly morning again.

Kaedric was waiting stoically outside the cave entrance. "My lord," he greeted me, bowing deeply. "I have completed my survey of the clan."

I glanced at the horizon. The sun would be up shortly. I really ought to get a good day's sleep before tackling any major administrative issues. "Let's discuss it tomorrow." I moved past him.

"But, my lord there is one –"

I didn't stop walking but looked over my shoulder and said, "There's nothing we could accomplish today; everyone will be sleeping soon. It can wait for tomorrow."

His mandibles twitched ... irritably?

"But –"

"Tomorrow!" I cut him off firmly.

"Yes, my lord."

Near the doorway to my house, I found a beautiful, but furious, goblinette pacing. "Tika? What's wrong?"

Shaking with anger she pointed a finger at the house.

I walked in to find two of the female goblin workers lying on my sleeping furs. They were naked and looking at me expectantly. A shiver ran down my spine.

Tika stepped into the house and stood, fuming, behind me. I could feel the waves of anger coming from her.

<*Whoa, this is going to be good! I need some popcorn!*> Vic tittered in my mind.

"Why other females in *our* bed?" Tika demanded.

I wanted to know that too.

"Ahem, If I may ..."

I looked toward the door. It was Kaedric.

I gestured at the two naked females. "Explain."

He bowed. "That was my intention all along, my lord. I have determined that the clan's most critical flaw is inefficient reproduction."

I threw a glance at Tika. "Eh?"

"My lord permitted the goblins of his clan to procreate without supervision, which has unsurprisingly resulted in the most basic, weak variation of goblin. Foblins, I believe is how you refer to them."

I nodded. I knew *that*. "So?"

"It will be much more efficient for the clan to breed workers and warriors. Those contribute much more than lowly foblins."

A dreadful realization came over me and I gulped. "So the females are here ...?"

"Yes, my lord. For females to beget goblin warriors, defenders of the clan, the chief must be the sire."

My fears were confirmed. I looked helplessly from Kaedric to Tika and back again.

Vic laughed. *<No wonder the late goblin chief used to be such a jolly fellow.>*

The administrator continued, "Additionally, advanced worker females will produce simple worker offspring, regardless of the father. We currently have three such females in the clan; the two researchers Romil and Primla, and Tika here. I have already spoken to the researchers, but I'm afraid Tika has been most uncooperative for some reason. This is, after all, for the betterment of the clan."

"Kaedric, I ..." I looked around and closed my mouth. I had no idea how to respond to that. I couldn't deny the fact that a small part of me found the idea alluring. That part really wanted me to jump into the bed with the naked females and sire a swarm of goblin warriors, claim the land, slaughter my enemies, and then ... I shook my head and took a deep breath.

If we'd had this conversation yesterday, my goblin identity might have won over. But I refused to surrender to the base instincts of a monster. My mind was my own and *I* wasn't mentally equipped to deal with running a harem. I could juggle a dozen administrative tasks at once, but I just didn't have the mentality to manage multiple sexual partners. As lame as it might sound, I was a one-girl kinda guy.

I stole a glance at Tika. The beautiful huntress still looked angry. She had changed considerably from the timid, shy goblinette she used to be. *Yeah, she'd kill me if I even thought of 'siring more workers' with the other females.* I chuckled. Tika was precious to me and I never wanted to cause her grief.

"Listen, Kaedric, I will say it only once. I will *not* be impregnating the females in the clan. I don't care how efficient it is otherwise. Stop suggesting it."

The mind eater looked surprised by my vehemence. “The only other option is for your second to assume this obligation, but I’m afraid that the physical differences between Rhynorn and the goblins wouldn’t allow such coupling.”

I shook my head. “It’s not open for discussion. No, and that’s final.”

He glanced at Tika speculatively.

“No,” I said firmly. “Tika is out of bounds, she’s my mate. My *only* mate.”

Tika’s anger subsided visibly at my words.

“Then the other fema–”

“They can bear children if they want, it's their call, but I won’t force members of my clan to ... ahem, procreate.” Their contribution would be a minor one anyway, compared to the Breeder’s Den output. It wasn’t worth crossing a line.

Kaedric deflated discernibly. “As you wish, my lord.”

I could sense him sending a telepathic message to the naked females. The two hurriedly put their clothes on and followed him out of the house.

Once we were alone, Tika wrapped her arms around my neck, kissed me, and whispered in my ear, “Good decision.”

<*Now* that’s *the understatement of the year!*> Vic snickered.

***

I got up at the first of dark the next day.

I was not surprised to find Kaedric waiting impassively outside my house. I was coming to expect things like that, now that I was more familiar with his no-nonsense personality.

“My lord.” He gave me a slight bow, his mandibles twitching slightly. “Might we discuss the clan development now?”

“Sure, let’s go grab something to eat first.”

Kaedric’s mandibles twitched a bit more, but he followed me without further comment.

When we arrived at the mess hall, Gandork was busy as usual cooking in the kitchen.

We sat on one of the log benches in the empty room.

“Alright.” I braced myself. “Go ahead.”

Kaedric relaxed in his seat. "Thank you, my lord. As I said yesterday, I have concluded a thorough survey of the clan and am prepared to present my findings. There are several items that require your attention."

"Let's hear it, then. But nothing about mating arrangements."

His mandibles folded flat against his cheeks. *A form of deference?* I wondered.

"Starting with the good news," Kaedric began, "the researchers have completed their first task. We now have the blueprints for a research center and can start building it at will. Per your orders, the researchers are working on the Dark Temple blueprints."

"That is good news. It means we should finish researching the Dark Temple blueprint by the time construction of the barracks is complete. So the temple will be our next priority. Then the research center after that."

Kaedric shook his head. "That is where the news turns bad. I'm afraid both structures require material that is not readily available."

The door opened, and Zuban walked in.

"Ah, punctual," Kaedric noted in satisfaction. "I have taken the liberty of inviting Zuban to our meeting, to explain the issue in detail."

Zuban sat down across from me, looking grumpy and sleepy. I figured it was a bit too early for him to be up.

"Zuban," I greeted him, "I understand we have resource issues again?"

Zuban rubbed his eyes tiredly. "I'm afraid so, Dread Totem. The new buildings are more advanced; both require a construction-grade glass. The research center requires silver as well."

"Why the hell does it require silver? And glass? It's just a glorified classroom for the bookish guys to study, right?" I was *not* thrilled to have my plans stymied by resource bottlenecks. Again.

"Chief, our current research efforts are somewhat ... basic. A research center would facilitate other forms of study. More advanced areas of research, like designing new weapon schemas or chemical recipes, require certain conditions be met."

"Crap," I mumbled. "Where the hell are we going to get glass and silver?"

"Well ..." Zuban started to answer.

Gandork approached us carrying a tray of food. He served me a grilled steak with a small bowl of stew. I dug in, savoring the delicious flavors.

Then I stopped. "What the hell is *that*?" I asked Gandork, pointing at Kaedric's serving.

A whole platter of smoked, tender pieces of meat soaked in rich gravy lay in front of the mind eater. Next to it was another platter, holding an entire fish sautéed to perfection with sprinkles of seasoning.

Next to that, my own meal looked like charity food.

Gandork's face changed into a prideful smile. "This will be Guba's seasoned fish and my own recipe of cooked meat with mushroom sauce."

Both were advanced food.

"I know that!" I pointed at my own meal. "Why is he getting all the good stuff?"

Kaedric cleared his throat. "If I may, my lord. My kind require above average sustenance. Without it, I fear my ability to serve will be hindered. Likewise, your new second, Rhynorn Bloodore, receives similar quality food, though he consumes four portions every day."

Crap. That meant the daily upkeep now included six units of advanced food. I grimaced. *I did promise Rhyno he could eat as much as he'd like.*

Zuban coughed nervously. "Ahem, so, as I was saying ... getting glass could be a problem. I know how to build a Glasshouse, but it requires silica, and we don't have any. We could research a silica refinery, I suppose, but even then, we don't have access to sand, the required raw material. As for silver ..." He looked at me apologetically. "We need to find silver veins to mine."

I scowled. Both resources sounded like they were going to be difficult to obtain.

I hadn't forgotten about the orb Tal had given me, but its description was lacking. There was no guarantee it could provide access for the resources we needed. Tal himself admitted he didn't know the details. I'd been blindsided because of insufficient information enough times already. Building the prerequisite marketplace was a significant undertaking. Too significant. If I spent the time and resources to build it, only to find it wouldn't solve my current problem, that would be a serious setback. For now, I would just keep an eye out for the needed resources on my next trip out of the valley and hope something changed or turned up before they were actually needed for the construction. *Maybe I could give it as a quest to the twins?* I wondered.

Other goblin workers were entering the mess hall, taking their meals from Gandork and spreading out to sit around the tables. Zuban excused himself and went to sit with Romil and Primla, the two female goblin researchers.

I rubbed my forehead tiredly and looked at Kaedric. "What else?"

"The two farmers, my lord," he replied while eating voraciously. He was using his mandibles to push pieces of succulent meat into his mouth. "It appears the valley is not suited for raising crops. Something to do with suboptimal land conditions. As it stands, the two workers cost upkeep, but fail to contribute."

"What do you suggest we do then?"

He stared at me unblinkingly. "Inefficient components should be disposed and replaced. *I* can take care of that easily, my lord." His mandibles clicked together excitedly.

I didn't like what he was hinting at. "No eating clan members," I declared firmly.

His mandibles pressed tightly against his lips, in what I gathered was his version of gritted teeth.

"What about the cave?" I asked. "A lot of mushrooms grew there once; maybe they can grow some more."

Kaedric shook his head. "I'm afraid not. These are simple workers who are trained to work fields. The mushrooms you harvested were naturally occurring, and cannot be regrown."

"I see." I paused as I thought about that. "For now, have them prepare a few fields for planting. Perhaps I can find better seeds for them."

"It will be done, my lord." He got up. "For the next items on the agenda, I suggest we take a tour of the clan."

I stood as well. "Let's get everything out of the way now. Tomorrow I plan to head out with a few warriors."

My administrator looked at me, curious.

I shrugged. "I have a long overdue quest to complete."

***

We walked through every one of the buildings and visited most of the clan's workers. Kaedric spoke with each one at length, explaining the areas in which they could improve.

I learned a few things. For instance, I didn't know Vrick had kept crafting *goblin*-sized armor after the Ogre battle. We had 15 sets of armor we couldn't use since we no longer had any goblin warriors in the clan.

Vrick only had rabbit leather to work his craft with, an inferior material for armor making. But his design was surprisingly innovative. He wove small strips of leather in a cross pattern, creating a durable armor of plaited leather. Much to his chagrin, I instructed him to craft armor sized for hobgoblins. Vrick didn't like hobs. At least Kaedric was satisfied with the increased efficiency.

The smithy was a crowded den of noise and industry. But Barzel, the two new smiths, and the four gofers didn't seem to mind the commotion. The industrious goblins were cheerfully shouting instructions and curses at each other over the noise of the hammers when Kaedric and I paid them a visit.

We found Guba near the stone quarry site, collecting some sort of orange dust from rock fissures. It was amusing to watch Kaedric try to give her advice on how to work more efficiently. The crafty old hag shut him down so quickly I thought he might fall on his ass then and there.

In Kaedric's estimation, the rest of the clan workers we observed were doing their jobs sufficiently well and needed no further advice or admonishments. "All things considered," he summarized as we headed back toward my house, "and despite Rhynorn occasionally bullying the workers, the clan efficiency is satisfactory and morale is high. I believe we have a strong foundation here for further expansion. We will need more food, of course, and more hands around the kitchen to handle the extra work. If only Guba would listen to reason ..."

I chuckled. "You're welcome to try convincing her to resume cooking, though I wouldn't recommend it. Not if you wish to continue in good health."

Kaedric shuddered. "No, I believe you are correct, my lord. That goblin woman is ... unsettling."

<The big, scary brain eater is afraid of little ol' Guba, ha!>

Does that mean you *volunteer to tell her what to do instead?*

<Oh, hell no. That old hag would probably stick me in one of her cauldrons, make purple candies or something from my sweet, delicious body.>

Heh heh, the supersmart, puppet master VI is afraid of sweet little ol' Guba?

<Damn straight, I'm smart enough to know that much.>

I laughed out loud. Kaedric looked at me in question. "My lord?"

I waved it off. "Don't worry too much about Guba. I will eventually have her work as a chemist, so don't count on her for kitchen work. Gandork is doing well enough on his own for the moment."

He bowed his head. "I understand. However, I just received notice of a matter that requires your immediate attention."

"What is it?"

"An ape named Grilda has spotted several creatures entering the valley. We have intruders."

Interlude: The Twins

"Damn, sis, why the hell did you drag me all the way out here?" the large man grumbled, swinging his Greataxe in wide arcs, trying to keep a host of monsters at bay.

After several days of roaming through the wilderness, Malkyr and Hoshisu had found a swampy forested region several days out of Goblin's Gorge. It was cold, damp, and filled with amphibious monsters. The siblings stood on a narrow strip of dry land, surrounded by giant frogs, swamp snakes, and crocodiles. All of them eager to turn the twins into their next snack.

Hoshisu laughed jubilantly, ducking under a frog's lashing tongue, and severing the pink appendage with a flick of her dagger. "Come on, grumpy, lighten up. You love killing monsters, remember? Besides, they're all below level 10. We're not in any real danger here."

Just then a snake wrapped itself around her brother's legs, nearly tripping him. Grunting, Malkyr raised his axe and swung the blade down hard between his feet, cleaving the snake. "They could still drown us if we're not careful, and we're getting hardly any XP out of them. Besides, it's wet and cold, and I could be working at the smithy right now, warm and happy."

He raised his axe just in time to intercept two tongues lashing at him. They wrapped around the thick-handled weapon and he heaved on it, launching two dog-sized frogs out of the water. Unexpectedly finding themselves airborne, the frogs looked around frantically, only to have their maiden voyage cut short when they were impaled on Hoshisu's daggers.

The woman was about to give a sharp retort when something caught her attention. She straightened up, pointing excitedly at the swampy water. "There! Behind the frog – I saw it! A marsh lizard! That's what we're after; don't let it get away."

"Yeah, that's a real problem," Malkyr grunted as he swung his axe from side to side at the unending horde. "They sure look like a flight risk."

"Malkyr!" Hoshisu snapped.

"Oh, alright," he muttered. Taking advantage of a temporary lull in the fight, he raised his weapon high above him. It began emitting a faint glow. "Ready?"

"Go!"

Malkyr swung down powerfully, the glowing axe slicing the air apart. The blade struck the ground, and light exploded outward, creating a shockwave that propagated from the two players in an expanding circle of damage. All the surrounding monsters were thrown back, dazed.

Hoshisu didn't hesitate. Even before her brother's magical attack, she was already running toward her prey.

The lizard she was going after was the size and shape of a crocodile, though with longer legs. It sped through the shallow waters, trying to flee the charging woman. Its snout was shorter than a crocodile's, but its teeth were just as deadly.

Hoshisu leapt into a front flip, arching gracefully over the dangerous beast's mouth, and landed on its back with her daggers leading.

Malkyr watched his sister's antics with bemusement. Back home, she was a strict, play-by-the-rules kind of girl, a trait that hadn't earned her many friends. But she let go of her restraints when she played in NEO, her personality becoming that of a focused and driven killer. One who was even now laughing gleefully as she clung to the thrashing lizard's back, repeatedly stabbing it with her daggers.

Shrugging, Malkyr lifted his axe and charged at the rest of the monsters, still dazed by his special attack. He could accommodate his sister's occasional whim. He just hoped she remembered that the beast she was joyriding on was venomous.

7 – Incoming!

Leaving Kaedric at the mess hall, I activated Mana Infusion on overcharge, and the buildings blurred past me as I sprinted toward the east side of the valley.

Damn it! I thought with growing dread. *How did the travelers get here so quickly?* We weren't ready for them, not by a long shot. I was so engaged I didn't even notice if the time slowing down.

Not certain it would work, I tried to form a war party as I ran. The clan warriors were scattered throughout the settlement, but I was able to grab the information stream of each individual I wanted and add it to the group. Ten icons appeared in the lower right pane of my vision: Vrick, Bek, Rhynorn, and seven hobgoblin warriors. Immediately, I used my earring to send telepathic orders to the newly formed war party.

Everyone, we have enemies in the valley! Assemble behind the cabins. We'll protect that line with everything we've got!

I arrived at the structures and took a position facing the forest. The row of cabins behind me would serve as a simple barrier to delay and slow attackers if they got through our battle line.

The run had drained five percent of my MP, but my mana regeneration was already at work, replenishing my pool.

While I waited for my soldiers, I knelt and touched the ground. Concentrating, I cast an empowered spell. The shadows from all around the clearing stirred and flowed toward me, coalescing into half a dozen distinctly canine shapes. At level 18, my Shadow Hound spell was an energy hog, draining a whopping 360 MP, almost half of my mana pool. But when I completed the spell, six level 10 Shadow mastiffs were arrayed in a semicircle before me, each one standing shoulder height to a hobgoblin warrior. A deadly addition to our defense.

My warriors were trickling through the barricade of cabins in ones and twos to form up near me and assembling into a battle formation. The ground shook rhythmically and Rhynorn's massive, bone-spiked shoulders appeared over the cabin roofs. Instead of going around the obstacle, the brute put a hand on one of the roofs and vaulted over the building, landing with a final ground-shaking *THUMP* in position at the center of the now complete formation.

My forces were set to meet the invaders, the mastiffs at the frontline with Rhyno a step behind them flanked by the hob warriors. Bek and I were at the rear of the formation as support and ranged-fire units. I was impressed with my troops' reaction time. It took us less than two minutes to assemble and be ready for battle.

I could *feel* the intruders drawing nearer. An intricate, unfamiliar stream of data was coming from the forest, heralding their approach.

With my mana pool recovered to a little over half maximum, I conjured drilling arrows and empowered them.

There were noises coming from the forest. The tension became almost tangible as the sounds of the invaders trampling through the woods grew louder. Others became distinguishable too; clanking, creaking, and loud ... hissing noises.

Siege weapons? Snakes? I wondered.

Everyone tensed, weapons at the ready.

The noises grew closer. They were almost upon us.

Everyone get ready. Hold the line; don't let the enemy reach the clan!

And then the first 'invader' rolled and clanked into sight between the trees.

What the hell? I mouthed silently.

It was a wagon ... of sorts. At least, it had wheels. At the front of it, pipes ran in and out of a large cast-iron sphere that was hissing clouds of steam to either side of the contraption. The thing wasn't being pulled by a pack animal, it was rolling on its own. Steam powered!

Crates and boxes stacked high with piles of sacks lashed on top of them overflowed the wagon bed. Perched on top of the pile, standing at a large steering wheel, was a small brown-furred creature.

A gremlin.

I shook my head, not sure I could trust what I was seeing, though it explained why I hadn't felt time slowing down at the newcomer's approach.

"Hello again, my friend!" The small figure yelled and waved to me with a sharp-toothed grin.

"Yeshy?" I let the whirling arrows dissipate.

His grin widened, his mouth literally reaching all the way to his pointy ears. "Trader Yeshlimashu, at your service, Dread Totem."

His wagon continued rolling forward and I saw another behind it, and another behind that.

I ran a hand through my hair, my anxiety eased. "What is all ... that!" I waved at the wagons.

The caravans came to a stop with a clank and a drawn out, hissing blast of steam. The gremlin carefully climbed down to stand in front of me, the top of his head barely reaching my chest.

"I have come to fulfill our agreement," he declared grandly, looking up at me. "I have gathered our best traders and craftsmen to come and trade with your clan. It is a small delegation, but that is customary when approaching new markets."

Three more gremlins stepped forward from their wagons to stand with Yeshy.

I relaxed my guard, feeling the last of the tension draining away from me. We were safe for now. There was no second invasion force; far from it. This might just be the lucky break my clan needed.

The relief was so great, I felt lightheaded. I couldn't help it, I giggled. Yeshlimashu looked at me, bewildered, as I held up a hand. "Sorry, we were not expecting you, but your arrival is fortuitous." Getting a hold of myself, I addressed the troops. "Alright everybody, there's not going to be a fight; the gremlins are our friends, go back to your work."

Everyone turned to leave. Everyone but Rhynorn.

I looked at the Ogre. "You may go now."

He grunted as he hoisted his huge club onto his shoulder. "These are not our clan. They *are* intruders. We must obliterate them!"

Yeshy took a step back, terrified of the aggressive giant.

I stepped between them, forcing the Ogre to look at me. "I said they are guests." I gritted my teeth. "Now go!"

The Ogre glared at me and tightened his grip on his club. For a moment, I thought he might attack, but then he snarled, turned, and lumbered away.

"Sorry about that," I apologized to the gremlins. "He's new and still learning his place."

Yeshlimashu smiled weakly. "You now have an Ogre chief at your command? Your clan must be incredibly strong now. I am certain we can establish trade that will be profitable for both of us.

"So, what did you bring?" I asked, looking curiously at the wagons, trying to get a glimpse of what was inside them.

The gremlin shrugged. "The standard merchandise for new trading partners. We have arms and armor, general adventuring supplies. And Anikosem over there," he pointed at a gremlin wearing blue robes, "is a trading wizard. Literally. He's a magic specialist. He trades in potions, scrolls, basic enchanted items and such."

I frowned. That didn't exactly suit the needs of a budding settlement. It sounded more like equipment for striving adventurers. "What about construction materials?" I inquired. "Specifically, glass or silver. Do you have any?"

Yeshlimashu looked confused by my question. "No. Why would we have such things with us? We are traders, not exporters."

I felt my hopes spiraling down. "What's the difference?"

"Traders, like us, do business with individuals and use gold as currency. Exporters barter in resources and large volume shipments between established markets."

I closed my eyes. *Shit!*

However, something clicked in my mind at his mention of exporters. I took out the orb Tal had given me and reviewed its description again.

Dimensional Trade Orb

Requirements: Marketplace with an Export-House attachment. Exporter.

Effect: Opens up an inter-dimensional trade menu with friendly factions.

Yeshy's explanation confirmed my earlier suspicion. It sounded like the orb was what I needed to gain access to resources. The marketplace had just become a high-priority building.

Unfortunately, it also meant that whatever Yeshy's people had brought to trade wouldn't be much help. Their wares were meant for individuals who wanted to customize their gear, not for bulk purchases. Some of their items might benefit me personally, but my funds were limited. I only had about 2,000 gold, most of it taken from fallen enemies. It was more than enough to fully equip a low-level adventurer, but at level 20, it would not be enough to buy me even a single level-appropriate magical item.

"Where can we establish our trading post?" the gremlin inquired.

"On the south side of the pond past the warehouse." I gestured in the general direction. There was a large open space in the area, and it was sufficiently out of the way to not interfere with the clan's daily routine.

"Very well." The gremlin nodded. "I see you haven't built the marketplace yet. When do you think it will be completed?"

"We had a few more pressing projects to finish first, but it's next on my list." My response came out a little bitter, but Yeshy didn't seem to notice

"Good. Without the marketplace, we won't be able to expand our trade agreement with you, and *you* won't be able to collect taxes from us as the ruler of this settlement."

Now that was interesting. *With a bit of luck, an improved trade agreement with the gremlin will expand the variety of items they trade* and *make our clan wealthier.*

I followed the gremlins as they drove their self-propelled wagons to the place I'd indicated. The three wagons were deftly maneuvered into a semicircle facing the pond.

"Ground 'em!" Yeshy yelled, and the gremlins pulled levers and twisted control knobs in their wagons. The hissing sounds gradually died down, and the steam coming from the boilers dissipated. "Deploy!" the gremlin instructed. More levers were pulled, and to my astonishment, the wagons began to change.

Ratcheting loudly, the wheels folded away, lowering the wagon beds to the ground. Then the structures split into sections, twisting, bending, and repositioning in a chorus of clacks, clangs, and clockwork ticks. Planks and metal tubes extended and flipped to make shelves and cabinets. When it was over, three open kiosks with canvas awnings and wooden floors stood in place of the wagons. Each one had a full-length counter and numerous shelves to display their wares.

That was an amazing display of mechanical ingenuity. The gremlin reputation was well earned.

Yeshlimashu came to stand beside me, grinning at my amazement. "We are open for business!"

<*Well, what are you waiting for?*> Vic spoke up in an eager, almost fevered, tone. <*Let's check out the goods!*> I could sense him mentally rubbing his little claws together and hopping up and down.

My ethereal and egocentric companion was a shopaholic. Who knew?

I went to the first shop. The sign hanging from the awning said: 'Gremlin's Ar & Ar'

"Welcome, welcome Dread Totem!" the gremlin shopkeeper greeted me. "Please let me know if you have any questions."

"What's 'Ar & Ar?'" I asked.

"Oh, it's an abbreviation for Armor and Armament," he said casually. "The finest gremlin-made. I am sure you'll find something to your liking."

"What the hell is that?" I pointed at a breastplate. Metal gears were visible between the plate links and chains were strewn all around it.

"Oh!" He brightened. "I call this 'Grappler's Bane.' See the pressure plates?" he pointed at some darker spots scattered about the armor. "If those are touched, the armor activates and the gears rotate those chains around the torso at high speed, making whoever is holding you let go and possibly injuring them in the process."

That was ... unconventional.

"How much?"

There was a glint in his eye. "A bargain! Especially for you! 350 gold!"

I scowled. That was a fifth of my savings. I could not use his products to equip my soldiers if that price was an indicator. "What about this sword?" I looked at a strangely designed longsword. It appeared to be made of multiple sections that didn't align properly, giving it a twisted look.

"Another masterpiece of gremlin ingenuity," the shopkeeper positively gushed. "There is a button on the hilt, see? When you press it, the sections separate. They are hollow and strung through with a mithril cord, which keeps them connected. It works perfectly well as any normal sword, but swinging and pressing the button turns it into a bladed whip. It's guaranteed to catch the enemy off guard, while tripling the reach of the sword, and can be used to trip opponents.

That was fairly esoteric.

"How much?"

There was a slight hitch in his jubilance. “Six hundred gold. I know it sounds like a lot, but it’s mostly due to the cost of the mithril used in it. You see, any other metal isn’t flexible or strong enough to –”

“I get it.” I stopped his barrage.

The shop certainly had interesting items. But the price range was not feasible for equipping my army, and what they had was more suitable for individual adventurers. Being ‘monster only,’ these gremlin-made inventions were unknown to players. *Seeing a player equipped with some of these gadgets would be interesting.*

<Sure, who wouldn’t want to wear armor with gears sticking out of it, or a sword that falls apart on command?> Vic snickered.

I left and entered the next store. The sign above this one showed ‘GGG.’

A young gremlin female greeted me. She was slightly smaller than the males, had long hair and distinctly feminine features. A golden hoop earring dangled from one of her ears. I couldn’t tell, but she was probably considered pretty by gremlin standards.

<That’s surprising, coming from the guy with a goblin fetish.>

Shut it, Vic.

“Greetings, Dread Totem.” The gremlin girl curtsied. “Welcome to Three G.”

“Three G?” I raised a brow at her.

She nodded. “General Gremlin Goods.”

“Oh.”

Vic chuckled. *<I’d bet Double-D would love visiting Three-G.>*

Or Ar & Ar, for that matter. I grinned. Not hearing our banter, the maybe-cute gremlin girl smiled back at me.

Vic giggled at my joke. *<Now you’re getting it, Boss.>*

The shelves were full of equipment; ropes, vials, trap kits, lockpicks, assorted tools, camping paraphernalia, and many other such things. In short, everything an adventurer might need.

“Do you sell food?” I asked the gremlin lady.

“Of course! We have travel rations, jerky, dried food, and even flasks of purified water.”

That wouldn’t do. “What about exquisite food?”

The smile vanished from her face. “I am afraid not, Dread Totem. My shop is rather humble.”

I shrugged and turned to leave.

"Ooh, please wait – I do have something that might interest you."

I turned back to her.

She dug through one of the many boxes behind her. With a yip of success, she came back around, holding a small open sack for me to look into. It held a coarse purple powder.

"What is it?" I asked curiously. It looked like an alchemical compound and the smell reminded me of the ocean.

"Purple salt!" she declared. "Harvested from the underground sea near Zemitpozes. I believe it can be used to make excellent food!"

> **Purple Salt**
>
> *Description:* Collected from an area rich in minerals that enhance the flavoring properties of the salt.
>
> *Type:* Ingredient

"I don't suppose you have a recipe that it's used in?" I asked.

She hesitated. "I'm ... unsure. I recently acquired a stack of recipes in bulk and haven't had the chance yet to catalog them."

"May I look at the recipes then?"

She nodded and pulled a stack of parchments from a leather case. "Here you go."

I leafed through the stack with growing disappointment.

'Food Recipe: Simple Steaks.' *No.*

'Food Recipe: Grilled Fish.' *Already have that or better, so no.*

'Food Recipe: Simple Bread.' *We don't have flour, wheat, or decent farmland, no thank you.*

The last recipe was written on high-quality paper with golden edges. *What's this ...?*

> **Food Recipe: Crispy Double Hot-Bits and Chilled Worms [Exquisite Food]**
>
> *Description:* Flavored earthworms, served chilled with spicy hot-

bits. Must be eaten within seven minutes, while the components are still cold *and* hot.

Instructions: For 3 portions: 1 worm serving, 1 magmashroom, 1 pinch of purple salt, 1 Fire Resist potion.

Effect I: +10 morale

Effect II: +20% cold & fire resistance (1 hour)

That was some wacky-sounding recipe. Still, I couldn't believe my luck.

Lucky Bastard skill level increased to 26.

On second thought, I could. "How much for the salt and this recipe?"

She looked bemused for a moment, but it was replaced with a look of greed. "Fifty for the salt. One thousand for the recipe."

<I'm no expert, Boss, but it sounds like she's trying to rip you off. Wait, I was once seeded in a stupid puppet merchant, so I am *an expert. She's definitely trying to rip you off, Boss.>*

Thanks, Vic, I kinda picked up on that already.

It was time for a little haggling session, and I wasn't above taking advantage of my special skillset. Reaching out with my mind, I used my Dark Mana's Sense Emotion ability on the shopkeeper. Her aura was positively overrun with greed.

"You do know that I am the only person within hundreds of kilometers who could even use this recipe, right?" I asked, pulling a magmashroom from my inventory, still warm to the touch. "No one around has access to these. So I doubt you'll find anyone else willing to buy this recipe. How about cutting me a deal, say 500 gold?"

Her aura wavered, and streaks of gray uncertainty appeared through it, but then greed blazed through again. "So you *do* have the necessary ingredients to use this recipe. That makes it quite valuable for you." Her smile was shrewd and bigger than ever. "Especially since I'm the only person within hundreds of kilometers who can sell it to you."

Shadow-crap. I didn't expect my tactic to backfire. She was a sharp one.

<Your Barter skill is only at Novice rank, Boss. You can't expect it to do miracles. Especially when you use crap tactics.>

The young woman's aura oozed confidence. "But you do make a good point, how about I take ten gold off the top?"

That was still too much. I could afford that price, but it was more than half my gold. And her aura told me she was entirely too pleased with herself.

"You realize that I'm the leader of this clan? You operate here on my approval. A reasonable discount now would be an easy way into my good graces."

Her aura became tinted with black wisps of apprehension. I pressed on.

"I can tell you're a sharp one. Don't you think ripping me off might not be the best long-term strategy?"

She looked uncertain. "You are the chief, but our presence here is for your benefit as well as ours. If you had a proper gremlin market, that would be a different matter ... But you do have a point." She paused, thinking. "Very well, I will agree for a thousand gold for both items."

That was not much better, but I knew when I was beaten. The game mechanics limited the outcome of our bargaining. I handed her the gold. Construction of the marketplace had just been bumped up the priority list.

As I watched her retie the bag of purple salt, its chemical appearance reminded me of something. "Hey, do you have a chemist's set?"

"Hmm? Oh, no."

Damn.

"But Anikosem probably has them," she added as an afterthought.

I brightened, then held out my two new purchases to Vic. "Please take these to Gandork."

My purple cloak flowed out, reaching and wrapping around the items I held. The rest of Vic billowed away from my shoulders to form his purple goblin body. The gremlin girl froze, her eyes comically wide as Vic made his presence known.

"Pfft, you have a creepy new bug-mouth assistant and you still make me run these stupid errands?" he grumbled, though I could tell he was just making a show of it.

"Yes. Run along now, purple minion."

He gave me an insulted look but took the items and walked toward the mess hall.

I entered the last shop. The sign above the entrance read, 'Gadgets & Magic.'

An elderly gremlin sat behind a small counter. His brown fur was speckled with white, and wire-rimmed glasses with coke-bottle lenses covered half his face. I analyzed him.

Anikosem, Gremlin Tinker

Level: 15 (12%)

HP: 72, *MP*: 134

Attributes: P: 2, M: 12, S: 1

Skills: Artificer 22, Barter 11, Chemist 11

Background: Anikosem was once a famed artificer, known especially for inventing a reloading acid trap. As he was never able to outdo his famed creation, Anikosem decided to focus on the business aspect of his trade and become a full-time trader.

His skills are all maxed out! I was impressed. This gremlin's Chemist, Trade, and Artificer skills were at the highest possible; the former was capped by his Mental attribute and the last two by his Social attribute.

"Greetings, Totem," he said informally. "How may I help you?"

I looked around his shop. There were shelves stocked with potions, glass counters displaying wands, and mechanical devices of unknown purpose.

"Do you have fire resistance potions? And I was told you have a chemistry set."

He nodded, "I have both items. The low-quality potions I have cost 20 gold each. The chemistry set goes for 250."

"How about a first-time buyer's discount?" I asked with a smile, though not much hope.

He shook his head, "I'm afraid I can't do that, Totem."

That figures. Gremlins didn't like missing out on a profit.

I looked at the items on display and a certain symbol caught my eye. "Do you Runecraft?" I knew from Yeshlimashu that the gremlins' Artificer skill granted them a limited ability to work with magic runes.

He nodded slowly. "I dabbled in my youth, but it was never my passion. Why do you ask?"

"I know a few runes myself. I was wondering if you'd be willing to exchange knowledge."

He shook his head. "I only know two runes: Te, the basic connector rune, which I'm sure you're already familiar with, and Zu, the rune of motion. But that one is rare and forbidden to share with non-gremlins, so an exchange of knowledge would not be possible."

I want that rune! My avarice flared, but I maintained my composure. I pulled a magmashroom out of my inventory. Anikosem's eyes widened when he saw the rare fungus. "Would you reconsider for this?" I asked.

He scratched his chin. "Well, well ... those are rare, and they are vital components in several potions." He looked around as if checking for spies or eavesdroppers. "I will trade the rune knowledge for a hundred magmashrooms."

"What!" I exclaimed. "That's outrageous. I'll give you ten."

"I'll accept no less than 90."

"Fifteen!"

"You expect me to break the rules of my people for a mere pittance? I can agree to 80."

I shook my head. "I'll be honest with you. I only have 42 of the mushrooms, and I need them to make exquisite food. Twenty is the best I can offer."

He shook his head as well. "That simply won't do. For the sake of goodwill, I can go as low as 50. But no less."

Barter skill level increased to 11.

New rank reached: Apprentice: Base price of items is now displayed (actual price might differ depending on demand)

The new rank appeared right on time. I analyzed the magmashroom.

Magmashroom

- *Description:* A rare type of magical mushroom that only grows in close proximity to flowing lava.
- *Type:* Ingredient, crafting component
- *Base Price:* 40 gold

So the gremlin was asking for the equivalent of 2,000 gold in trade for the rune, the sly old bastard!

That was too much. I didn't have anything else of value I was willing to offer in trade. Getting the rune would have to be an issue for another time.

"How about I teach you a rune in exchange for a discount?" I suggested instead.

He knitted his brows, thinking. "Runes aren't really my passion, but they are tradable ... very well. Tell me what runes you know."

I did, and the old gremlin snorted. "Those are all common runes. Well, except the binding; that one is advanced." He mulled it over for a moment. "I will give you a discount of ten gold for every common rune, and 50 for the rune of binding."

That sounded awfully cheap for a rune I'd gained by having it carved on my flesh. "Hundred gold for the binding rune?" I tried my luck.

"Sixty."

"Eighty?"

"Very well."

That was something, at least. There was no reason to hold out on him. I taught him all my seven runes, then handed him 130 gold for the potion and chemistry set. That left me with about 700 gold.

With these prices, I really needed that marketplace built as soon as possible.

There was nothing else of interest to me in his shop. Everything was either too weak compared to my own magic, or too expensive.

Yeshlimashu was busy organizing some crates outside. I went over to him.

"You must be hungry from your long trip. I invite you all to come dine in our mess hall. I think you'll find Gandork's cooking to your liking."

Yeshlimashu grinned. "That is a generous offer. It will be a nice change from travel rations."

> **+50 reputation with Zemitpozes' gremlins.**
> *Current rank:* Neutral.
> *Points to next rank:* 950

Maybe they'll offer a more significant discount once I hit Friendly reputation with them, I mused as I led the four hungry-looking gremlins through the village.

As we got close to the mess hall, I heard angry voices coming from inside the building. Something was up. The voices got louder and more contentious, and as I hurried forward, the four gremlins followed close behind.

As we neared the entrance, there was a final terrified shriek that was cut off as a goblin came crashing through a window to land on the ground at our feet.

I looked down at the mangled, twisted body of our clan cook.

Gandork was dead.

Interlude: Company Meeting

The conference room was full.

The director looked at the holographic presentation displaying various numbers and charts.

A nervous-looking man stood by the display. He spoke in a halting voice. “As you can see, sir, our two test subjects have acclimated to the extreme mental strain without any discernible side effects.”

The director nodded.

The man continued. “The preliminary findings are promising; though they started playing only two days ago, both have passed level 20 and solved a number of complex mathematical problems.”

The director tapped his fingers on the table. ”Good. So, there are no problems that would prevent us from moving on to the next phase?”

The man, the head of one of the company’s R&D centers, nodded anxiously. He didn’t like to be put on the spot like this. “I feel obligated to mention ... a slight discrepancy was observed in the alpha and delta waves of both subjects. Though it is not a significant cause for alarm, I would like to have more time to study it.”

The director frowned. “Explain.”

The man swallowed. “As you know, the FIVR technology puts the user in a semi-dreamlike state, while maintaining the player’s higher brain function. This keeps them aware and in control. It is achieved by regulating the users’ alpha and delta brain waves. The two candidates have both displayed gaps in the waves synchronicity, some reaching up to 12 percent. It is well within the allowed threshold, but it is significantly higher than in their previous, ‘normal’ game sessions.”

“How much time do you need to investigate this further?”

“A few weeks should suffice.”

The director shook his head. “That’s too long. We don’t have a few weeks. That damn goblin-player appearance accelerated our timetable. The military expects results, soon.” He thrummed his fingers on his desk. “Continue monitoring the twins’ condition along with the next phase recruits. Mr. Emery, anything to add?”

The sharply dressed lawyer sitting to the director’s right leaned forward in his armchair. “Everything is ready from the legal standpoint, sir. The reworded NDA and User Agreement contracts have been drafted. I went through each of them personally. As far as I'm concerned, we may proceed."

The director nodded. "Very well. Proceed to the next phase."

08 – Monster vs. Monster

"What the *hell* is going on!" I roared. I took out my staff and gathered my mana for a fight.

Are we under attack? Who would want to harm Gandork?

Vic chuckled. <*Who would want to harm* Gandork*? You mean aside from you and half the clan?*>

I didn't have to wait long for the answer. An angry roar came from the mess hall. My heart sank as I recognized the sound.

Ducking under the lintel, Rhynorn burst through the mess hall door, snarling. My fists clenched when I saw the blood dripping from his fingers.

"What have you done?" I demanded, my voice cold.

The Ogre growled angrily.

"I BE HUNGRY! I say to stupid cook 'bring more stew!' He say, 'No stew for you. Come back one day!' So I show him who is THE CHAMPION!"

I looked down at the mangled body of Gandork. He was an annoying git, but he worked hard, contributing a lot to our little community. He didn't deserve this.

I glared at the raging boss. "And you killed him for *that*?"

Rhynorn returned my glare. "What I say, they do! Or I kill! I be THE CHAMPION!

The commotion had drawn a small crowd of clanfolk.

"No. You will not hurt any member of the clan ever again."

He looked at me defiantly. "I crush magical traveler! I more strong! I crush little magic goblin!"

There was no way around it; I would have to show the unruly Ogre who was really the boss around here.

I saw Bob, a worried expression on his face, approaching with several soldiers. Malkyr and Hoshisu were following them. I hadn't seen the twins in a while.

Damn, why are they showing up now, of all times? I fretted.

Squashing Rhyno was going to be tough. I would have to pull out all the stops. But, I still didn't want the siblings to know what I was capable of. I wasn't ready to answer the questions that would surely follow if I showed my full abilities in the fight.

Without looking away from the Ogre, I discreetly slipped the Ring of Bound Soul off my finger and into storage. Now if I happened to die in the coming fight, I wouldn't waste one of the precious charges on the ring.

Rhynorn lifted his huge club, bringing it to a ready position and slowly circled around me, assessing his options. The crowd shuffled back, giving us more space.

I glanced at the twins. There was no helping it. I had to take the Ogre down *and* make it look easy in order to reinforce my authority and power. Unfortunately, as a boss monster himself, Rhynorn had an even higher magic resistance than regular Ogres. I couldn't afford to hold back.

Damn. On top of that, I need to be careful not to kill him ... at his level it will cost a fortune to resurrect him.

<You're forgetting something, Boss,> Vic interjected.

A little busy here, Vic, I said as I studied my hulking opponent.

<Dude, that blob is a boss monster too. Remember what Guba told you? Bosses respawn! So you go ahead and go crazy on that fat-ass puppet. Speaking of which ...>

Vicloak dropped from my shoulders and ran out of the impromptu dueling arena in his purple goblin form.

I heard a gasp from someone in the audience and saw Hoshisu staring at Vic, wide-eyed. Next to her, Malkyr shouted triumphantly, "See? Told ya!"

Standing in front of the audience, Vic turned and started chanting and doing some kind of dance routine. "Heyyyy, Boss-man! Kill that Ogre, and I'm a fan! If you can't do it, no one can!"

Everyone, including Rhynorn, stared incredulously at the spectacle of a purple goblin cheerleading a deathmatch.

Did he really just morph his hands into pompons?

<Sure did, Boss-man!>

I almost face-palmed.

Despite his shenanigans, Vic was right. This situation was different than when I killed other bosses. I'd stopped Barska from returning by claiming his resurrection point as an altar for Nihilator. And DurDur was effectively relieved of his boss status when I became the clan's totem. Given time though, Rhynorn would resurrect on his own.

The Ogre's roar brought me back to the looming fight.

Well, there was no sense in being subtle or holding back now. I went all out.

Piling plain shadows against a Shadow-Touched creature would be useless. So instead, with a wave, I cast Shadow Hound while simultaneously reaching for Rhyno's mana to freeze him and launching my dagger at his throat.

At the last possible instant, Rhynorn broke the mana stasis enough to twist and shrug a shoulder up to cover his throat. The bone dagger 'clacked' against the bone spikes growing from the Ogre's hide and bounced off, scoring only a shallow scratch on the tough natural armor.

My three level 10 mastiffs pounced at the Ogre as they manifested from the shadows, mauling and biting at his armor-like flesh. They drew blood, but the damage was minimal, the Ogre's tough skin resisting most of the damage. He lost barely ten percent of his total health.

However, the Ogre's enormous club couldn't touch the shadowy matter the mastiffs were made of. In time, they would wear him down, piece by piece.

Meanwhile, I was free to bombard the barn-door dimwit from a distance.

It looked like the battle was all but won, and I settled in to do some magical-ranged type damage. So I was completely surprised by Rhynorn's response. He crouched, arms covering his head and face, which allowed the hounds to leap onto him and dig in with their claws. Ignoring the damage they were inflicting, he raised his head and unleashed a roar. A Terrible Roar. The Ogre's special skill sent the mastiffs flying, hurtling them at least ten meters away. Because of their close proximity to the roar, the force left them disoriented.

Damn it. I underestimated how cunning he is. Again.

Rhyno wasn't some stupid brute, despite his characteristically dull Ogre appearance. He was a Gladiator Ogre boss. He specialized in maneuvers and tactics to overcome his opponents on the arena battleground. The bastard had seen my shadow mastiffs in action when we fought against the travelers and didn't bother wasting time attacking them with his club. The mastiffs were vulnerable to mana-based attacks, and he knew it.

Rhynorn took advantage of the mastiffs' momentary distraction. Three great strides toward me brought him into melee range, his club cocked back for a full-on strike. I felt the surge of mana as he activated his Dirty Trick skill.

I couldn't defend against the blow. Too sure of myself, I'd gone all out on offense, and it took just an instant too long to get over the surprise of the tables being turned and get my defenses up.

The club swept my feet out from under me, sending me sprawling to the ground. It caused hardly any damage, but the Ogre used the momentum to swing the club up and follow through with a devastating overhand chop that caught me square in the chest. And I learned, firsthand, the answer to what happens when the squishy goblin is caught between the immovable ground and the unstoppable force of a giant club swung by an angry Ogre. *Ouch.*

Rhynorn Bloodore's Dirty Trick hit you for 109 damage, [base 73 + 50% prone]

It hurt. A lot. I lost over a third of my health. But being a tier 2 boss had its perks.

I heard Rhyno grunt in disbelief; he'd expected the hit to smash me to a pulp. I glared up at the surprised 'champion.' He shouldn't have underestimated 'the boss.' I was angry and hurt, and *rage* coursed through my body.

I didn't wait for the big lummox to recover from his surprise. Still lying on the ground, I activated Blood Wrath, discharging the rage energy into a black kinetic beam. The Ogre staggered back as it was hit by nearly two tons of force, giving me time to roll up and activate Shadow Teleport. I was wrapped in shadows and an instant later found myself standing on the mess hall roof. I directed my dagger at the Ogre, slicing a red gash across his chest for 20 damage. Then I commanded the shadows to amass around him.

Rhynorn ignored the dagger strike and charged, swinging his club high. I was beyond his reach, but he was not aiming for me. The crushing blow ripped through the mess hall roof and the wall beneath. The entire building shuddered. He was smashing his way *through* the mess hall toward me. Almost losing my footing on the unstable structure, I was forced to leap away and to the ground.

That does it! I hadn't spent all the time and effort building up this settlement just so an overly aggressive Ogre could demolish it, again. This was my clan!

I snarled at the hulk as he backed out of the partially demolished mess hall. I cast Shadow Web, waving my arms in pulling motions, drawing more and more shadows in, strengthening the bindings. Thick ropes of darkness swept across the ground at the Ogre, wrapping around him and then anchoring into the earth, tethering him to the ground.

Rhynorn struggled against the ephemeral restraints, ripping through many of them. I kept pouring mana and shadows into the spell, adding more threads and thickening them, until the Ogre was blanketed in them. He was still on his feet, his enormous strength straining against the spell holding him, but for the moment I had the upper hand; he was trapped.

It's time for this 'Champion' to learn exactly who's in charge.

Finally recovered, the mastiffs rejoined the fray, leaping onto the ensnared Ogre, attacking unhindered *through* the web restraints with teeth and claws.

I launched drilling arrows at the Ogre, and the dual projectiles struck, burrowing deep before his innate resistance diffused the magic.

The Ogre, unable to free himself, bellowed in rage, realizing he was slowly being killed by our relatively weak attacks.

My mana was down to half, but so was his health. I was burning through 50 mana per second keeping him down, but I wouldn't be able to keep it up for more than six or seven seconds.

I probably would have outlasted him, keeping him bound until he succumbed to his death of a thousand cuts. But the whole clan was present and witnessing this confrontation, along with the gremlins and the twins. I had to finish this fight decisively, making an example of him, so no one would dare challenge my reign again.

I held my hand up, and the hilt of my bone dagger flew into my palm. Then I teleported, this time appearing high up on the Ogre's shoulders. He was still thrashing violently against the shadowy bindings, so I grabbed one of his shoulder spikes to steady myself and forced all my remaining mana into the spell holding him.

The shadowy webs swelled, becoming thicker than the Ogre's own muscular arms, binding his entire body, bringing him to his knees, and then *finally* toppling him all the way to the ground.

I rode him down, my legs around his neck in a chokehold as my web laid him prone. He was completely bound, unable to move a finger. Helpless.

I let go of his neck, placed the point of my dagger under his chin and swept my gaze across the crowd, making eye contact with many of them. "This is what happens to anyone who challenges me."

I pushed the dagger up under the Ogre's chin all the way into his small, angry brain.

The dagger did its thing. The darkness devoured Rhyno, his body crumbling away to nothingness beneath me. I was left standing in the center of a pool of darkness.

Rhynorn Bloodore sacrificed.

I'd won.

***

The fight had been a good way to blow off some steam.

Having a clear focus for my anger was just what I needed to take my mind off the existential problems of my life.

Sacrificing Rhyno didn't award me with Faith Points or a void crystal. I was a bit disappointed but not really surprised. After all, it would have been a giant loophole if resurrectable clan members could be repeatedly sacrificed to turn in a quick gain.

The pain from my injuries was a minor distraction. I learned to handle pain in a crash course from true experts, the hobgoblin Barska and his demented sidekick, Elenda.

I just hoped this fight would be enough to housebreak my insubordinate Ogre lieutenant.

I felt focused, in charge. The master of my own fate.

There was both fear and admiration in the clanfolks' cowed expressions as they looked at me – the goblin Totem that single-handedly defeated an Ogre boss, dissolving him away into black nothingness.

After a few moments, Kaedric was the first to break the silence, addressing the crowd. "Everyone back to work."

No one questioned his order. Hobs and goblins alike turned and went back to their daily routines.

I put on the ring I'd removed before the fight.

I heard someone clapping, slowly, ironically.

"Very impressive." Hoshisu, the player assassin, approached, an uncomfortable looking Malkyr in tow. "I call the next match."

I looked at her blankly. "Eh?"

"I want to be the next one to duel you. You handled that big brute well enough. I'm sure you can accommodate one more challenger into your busy schedule, right Great Chief? Standard deathmatch rules."

I sighed. Her reaction was exactly the kind of thing I wanted to avoid. "Absolutely not."

Her lips thinned and she put her hands on her hips, scowling. "Why not? Malkyr and I are both level 25 now. It would be good training for both of us. I would give you a run for your money."

I shook my head. "We don't have an arena here, which means when one of us dies, we'll be hit with the full death penalties. I like you well enough to not want to put you through that."

She snorted. "Small chance I'd be the one who ends up with the death penalties."

She was trying very hard to goad me into fighting her.

I smirked. "That just reaffirms my point. I like *me* even more."

"Fine!" she spat and stormed away in a huff.

Malkyr gave me an apologetic look and hurried after his sister.

I rolled my eyes. "Travelers!"

<You mean 'Players,' right, Boss?>

Right.

I felt pretty good, even after the little run-in with Hoshisu. My mind was at ease, and I could focus on my goals.

It was easy to see what I had to do now. For my clan to survive and prosper, I had to build a Dark Temple. The blueprints called for several common materials, which I had plenty of, but obtaining glass. was a problem.

Based on Yeshlimashu's information and the description of the Dimensional Trade Orb, the most likely way to get the glass needed was to build the marketplace. If it worked as I hoped it would, I might even be able to trade for the silver necessary to build the research center. But that was a concern for later.

I was adding buildings to the town construction queue faster than Zuban and his boys could build; they were falling behind. The barracks and the remaining two cabins were taking up all their efforts at the moment, and they were important, though not as high a priority as having the Dark Temple up and running. We needed to build a lot of structures quickly. I had to find a way to increase my construction rate somehow, and Zuban was already managing the maximum number of builders his skill level would support.

So I had to double down.

Clan members always gave Kaedric a wide berth, so he was easy to spot among the crowd. I caught his eye and motioned to him.

"My lord?"

"I'm going to summon a new constructor and two builders to boost our construction rate. Have Gandork start cooking the food necessary for that."

"Yes, my lord. Might I suggest you resurrect Gandork at this time?"

"Oh, right ..." I mumbled. With all the recent excitement, it had slipped my mind that our clan cook was dead.

<You could say he's still doing his job ... he's feeding the worms!>

You're getting better at this, Vic, I complimented him, chuckling.

<Practice. Plenty of material around here to work with, Boss.>

I accessed the Settlement Interface and spent the 40 energy required to bring back our beloved level 4 cook. As an afterthought, I spent another 28 energy points on rush-fixing the damaged mess hall.

Kaedric's eyes lost focus for a moment, then he nodded at me. "Done, my lord. Gandork is alive and aware of your orders. The food will be brought to the Breeder's Den shortly."

That was quick. *I could get used to having Kaedric around.*

<Hey, having a creepy, brain-eating seneschal is pretty useful!> Vic chuckled joyfully.

I opened the Breeder's Den Interface and queued up two builders and one constructor. They required 90 simple food and 20 advanced food, which was about ten percent of our available store. I could afford it.

The next thing to do was find Zuban and have a chat.

I found my foreman at the barracks construction site, standing under and directing the placement of a huge wooden beam. The workers had cleared an area about 40 meters in diameter and had the foundation already in place. I plucked the building's progress information from the air: 190 BP out of 600; still a ways to go.

"Zuban."

His ears perked up at hearing his name. "Dread Totem?"

"I'm afraid we have to change our plans."

"Oh?"

"The gremlin marketplace has become our highest priority building. I want all the builders working on it."

He frowned. "It is not a good idea to stop ongoing construction. Left alone for too long, there's a chance what we've already built will deteriorate."

That was unsettling, but chance and luck were my forte. I had to risk it.

"I know it's unexpected, but we have to change our priorities," I explained. "The marketplace should give us access to the resources we need to build the Dark Temple."

"I understand."

"Once the marketplace is finished, you can resume work on the cabins and the barracks. Afterward, we'll build the research center, then the armor and weapon workshops."

Zuban rubbed his neck. "That is quite a lot of work. My boys and I will do our best, but it will take weeks. That blueprint for the gremlin-styled marketplace is the most complicated piece of engineering I've ever seen. It is as big as the barracks, and the gremlin's designs are … exotic. It will require finesse and precision work."

"I know you have your work cut out for you. That's why I'm bringing in more help."

"Dread Totem, I'm sorry, but I can't manage more than the six builders already assigned to me," he said regretfully.

"I know, don't worry. I'm bringing in another constructor as well."

Zuban's brow creased.

"Not to worry, Zuban, he's not here to replace you. He and the new builders will be inexperienced novices, after all. I'll make it clear that he answers to you."

His expression relaxed. "I understand. Most of our construction projects require Apprentice rank now, except for the cabins. I suggest the new builders pick up the work on them."

"See?" I patted his shoulder. "You're already taking charge of the situation. I have the utmost confidence in your abilities."

He bowed his head, though I still saw his satisfied smile. "As you command, Dread Totem. We will start working on the marketplace immediately. We already have the required 100 lumber in stock, as well as 20 stone and 20 leather. The structure also requires 20 units of metal, fashioned into assorted gears, springs and other widgets. I'm afraid our smith is going to be extremely busy for the next several days."

"Don't worry about Barzel, he has a lot of help at the moment; two specialist smiths and their four gofer helpers."

Zuban's smile grew. "I almost forgot. I am sure they will be able to produce the required tools easily. Now, if you'll excuse me …"

He gave a few short orders to the goblin builders. They stopped working on the barracks and headed in the direction of the gremlin's trading post, Bargush carrying a hammer in each of his four hands.

"Damn, he would have made an awesome soldier," I muttered.

<Yeah, but it would cost a fortune to arm him,> Vic chortled. *<Get it? To* arm *him?>*

"Yes, Vic. I get it," I said. "Not bad."

I headed over to the Breeder's Den and ran into Guba.

"Hmph!" she snorted when she saw me. "Gotta hand it to ya youngling, you put that big brute in his place."

"Guba, it's been a while. I'll be leaving the valley for a few days, I don't suppose you have more grenades ready?"

Her face clouded. "Now I been telling you, over and over again! I can't be using me skill without a proper chemist's se– ohhh!"

I grinned at the flummoxed goblinette, frozen mid-rant at seeing the chemist's set I pulled out of my inventory. "Courtesy of our gremlin allies."

Wordlessly, she took the boxed set from me and cradled it to her chest. "Finally!" she whispered, caressing the box, "I'll be to doing some proper chemistry 'round here!"

"You're welcome," I said dryly.

"Aye, don't ye be tripping over yer skirt, I got yer reward right here. I processed them gallbladders you gave me so long ago; 'tis just a matter of adding tha proper reactive agent ..."

"It's a kilt, not a skirt," I said as Guba rummaged through her newly acquired chemistry set.

She retrieved two vials from her pocket, added a drop of something to each and swirled them a few times. Then she handed me the two vials of now green liquid. "Here ye go, young Totem."

Quest Completed: Gallbladders for Guba

You have given Guba a Chemist's Set. She used it to complete the gallbladder potions.

Reward: 2 X Guba's 'special dish,' +50 reputation with Guba, 500 XP

Bonus Reward: Guba can now utilize to her full ability as a Chemist.

Optional goal unreached: Build a Chemist Lab.

Guba's 'Special Dish' [perm-health tonic]

Description: Small vial of green viscous liquid.

Type: Potion

Effect: Permanently increase a goblin's health pool by +5

Finally! I'd been carrying this quest around from day one in the goblin caves.

My improved Analyze skill was showing me several details about the potions I couldn't see before. For one, they only worked on goblins, which was disappointing, but good to know. It meant I couldn't sell the potions to other players or use them to strengthen my Ogre champion. The potion also seemed to grant a higher health bonus than I remembered, but I wasn't going to complain about *that*.

"Thanks." I nodded at our new, fully-fledged, clan chemist. "So about those grenades ..."

"Yeah yeah." She waved dismissively. "Come see me when yer back."

She'd already forgotten me and turned away, inspecting the contents of the box in her hands. "... Nitride ... viscoelastic, them be good adhesive ..." she mumbled to herself as she walked off.

Three new goblins awaited near the Breeder's Den when I reached it. A constructor and two builders, just as ordered. Kaedric stood next to them, impassive, and ignoring the nervous glances he was getting from Wolrig, the new constructor.

Without a word, I spent 150 energy to raise all three new clan members to level 2. I gave them the standard welcoming speech.

"Welcome to the GreenPiece Clan. Together we will build a great nation. You three will join Zuban in construction." I winced expectantly, not looking forward to being addressed as the pastry-Totem again.

"Yes, Dread Totem."

"Yes, Dread Totem."

"Yes, Dread Totem."

My eyebrows shot up in surprise. *What? Not a single 'Bread Totem?'*

Kaedric cleared his throat. "My lord. I took the liberty of ... educating our new arrivals about the proper way to address the clan Totem."

I was ecstatic; I'd moved past 'Steamed' and now I would no longer be the 'Bread Totem' either. I decided to overlook whether or not Kaedric had just read my mind.

"Good job, Kaedric."

He bowed his head. "Thank you, my lord."

All the recent changes to our construction plans were too much to keep straight in my head. So as a visual aid I accessed and reviewed the Construction Interface.

Buildings and Construction
Max Constructor Skill: 15 *Builders Count:* 8 (skills 15, 15, 15, 15, 15, 16, 1, 1) *Daily BP:* 128.2 *Under Construction:* Cabin X 2 (151/250 BP)[rush?], Barracks (200/600 BP) [paused][rush?], *Gremlin Marketplace:* (0/650) [rush?] *Research:* *Available Resources:* timber 110, stone 70, metal 24, bones 129

At 128, our daily BP was impressive. I remembered how it took Zuban and three workers two whole days to build the lousy Chief's Hut when we first got here. And that project was only 20 BP.

Looking at the Interface, I was once again reminded that I had the option to instantly complete a structure using the rush option. But as appealing as it sounded, it wouldn't be the smart thing to do. The energy required would be better spent elsewhere, and rushing construction would only exhaust our resources faster, leaving my builders idle. No, as before, the rush option was better saved for emergencies.

<*Like fixing what a horde of angry Ogres rampaging through your settlement does?*> Vic asked.

"Yup."

<*Gotcha, Boss.*>

It looked like the marketplace would take six days to complete. There was nothing else I could do to speed things up in the clan. I'd optimized everything to the best of my ability. Now I just had to wait for time to do its thing.

Which meant I could leave the valley to pursue some of my other goals. First among them was completing Nihilator's quest. But, I would need help with that one.

Resigned, I went looking for the twins.

***

"I don't get it, run it by me again." Malkyr scratched his head. "You want us to go on a dungeon crawl with you, only not really, since the end goal is to make the Ogres there friendly by ... killing them all?"

I rubbed my eyes. It was hard to explain my motivations to players without revealing I was considered part NPC.

Before I'd come to speak with the twins, I had a chat with Bob. He'd pointed on my map to where the Ogre clan, former allies of the deceased Barska, resided. It just so *happened* to coincide with the location of an altar from Nihilator's quest.

I had to make my way there and defeat the Ogre clan. Once I'd taken control of their village I'd be able to summon my own new Ogres via the Breeder's Den. Even if Rhynorn was a boss, the fight with the players had demonstrated how the Ogres' overwhelming strength made them superior to normal hobgoblin troops. I wanted more of them.

Going against a whole clan of Ogres was not going to be easy, even at my current power level. I needed help. My regular soldiers were just too weak for the job. Most wouldn't last more than a few seconds against them. I had deliberated taking Rhynorn with me; once respawned, the Ogre boss would be a great asset on the mission. But I needed him to stay behind and guard the clan.

I also decided against taking the other clan Ogre with us. He was guarding the coal shipments from the conquered Raider's Camp. With only a hob scout to show him the way, the two were enough to handle anything dangerous in the forest, sparing me the need to commit more forces to 'caravan watch.' I needed my hob soldiers to guard the clan and patrol the valley's forest.

That was how I found myself explaining what I wanted to Malkyr and Hoshisu without revealing all the reasons.

"It's simple." I tried again. "There's an Ogre settlement we need to take over and there's a boss I'll need help taking down. You know, a standard monster lair raid; loot, XP, maybe some unique magic items."

I certainly hoped there would be good loot. For all of us.

"And you don't want to use your clan members because you're afraid they'll die." Hoshisu caught on. "So you need us," she finished with a sly smile.

I groaned inwardly. I knew where this was leading.

"Listen, I don't expect you to do it for free. Come with me, help me defeat the Ogres, and in return, you'll get a fair share of the loot and some additional rewards.

Grant the quest [Ogre Lair Raid] to Malkyr Edahs and Hoshisu? Yes/No

I tweaked the rewards for the quest I'd just offered them. My Quest Giver skill was at level 17, and I could adjust it to make a pretty enticing offer.

I set it for a 200-point reputation increase with my clan, 5,000 XP, 170 gold, and I even threw in some bonus items. Being able to add items as a reward became available when I reached the Apprentice rank in the skill. I set Malkyr's bonus reward as a masterwork belt with five potion slots accessible for instant use during combat. For Hoshisu, I selected an assassin's ring with a spring-loaded mechanism that shot a poisoned needle. The ring could be activated even while attacking with other weapons. I assumed she'd like that sort of thing.

Vic snickered. *<Don't let Tika catch you putting a ring on some other woman.>*

Malkyr gave a soft whistle. "Man, you gotta tell me one day how you get all the gold and items to throw around like that. I'm sold, I'm in. Whatever you need. Now that we finally have some shops around here, I need all the gold I can get."

I looked at Hoshisu. She grinned expectantly at me. I knew what that meant.

I rolled my eyes. "Alright, we'll do your stupid duel."

Her smile turned predatory and she started pulling out her daggers.

I raised my hand. "*After* we finish the raid."

She pouted but put the daggers back. "You got yourself a deal, Mister Totem."

Malkyr said, "Okay, so I'll be the tank, Hoshisu the DPS, and you obviously the magic guy. We need a healer, though."

"That's why I brought him." I stepped to one side, revealing Bek. The tiny goblin shuffled forward, head down and eyes shying away from the twins.

Hoshisu wrinkled her nose. "Him? He'll drop dead of fear at the first sight of a monster."

I smiled. Despite his wretched appearance, Bek was one of the few survivors of the fight with the player scouting party. He was now level 10 and had an impressive array of healing, damaging, and debuff spells.

"Give him a chance. Bek's more seasoned than you might think."

Malkyr shrugged. "It's your party, man; we're just along for the ride."

"So it's settled," I decided. "We'll head out tomorrow at nightfall. Agreed?"

The twins nodded.

"See you then." I turned and went looking for Kaedric. He'd have to hold the clan together while I was away.

I saw him coming toward me less than a minute later, probably sensing I wanted to speak with him.

"I'm leaving the valley for a few days," I informed him. "Technically, Rhynorn is the leader while I'm away. Well, once he respawns anyway. Do your best to steer him away from trouble."

"Of course, my lord."

I thought for a moment. "Let the workers do their thing and make sure Bob patrols the forest and maintains a guard at the valley's entrance."

"Yes, my lord."

"Zuban is aware of the building priority, but if Wolrig, the new constructor, gives him any trouble, explain to him that Zuban calls the shots."

"Yes, my lord."

"I think that's about it, Kaedric. Keep everything going in my absence, I'll see you in a few days."

It was nearly morning already. I went back to my house but didn't go to sleep right away. I sat at my desk and removed some items from my inventory, placing them in front of me.

My Barter skill had recently reached Apprentice rank, so I could now see the base price of items in my inventory. It wasn't a precise figure though. Due to NEO's complex economy system, prices varied depending on location. Still, the skill would give me a decent approximation of an item's value. I had some knick-knacks I'd carried around with me for a while. It was time to learn if they were worth anything.

Two large diamonds were priced at 1,000 gold each. *Not bad.* A gold necklace with a unicorn pendant had a 300-gold price tag. In comparison, my Totem set – the staff, the kilt, and the headdress – was altogether priced at a measly 120 gold. Most of the other stuff I accumulated wasn't worth much in terms of gold; acid flasks, tainted ore, and other component-like items were priced at a few gold coins for each.

The void crystals didn't have a price displayed. I guessed they were too rare to have a 'base price.' The same was true for the Outrider Bracelet, the Dimensional Trade Orb, and my Sacrificial Bone Dagger.

Amusingly, the Book of the Damned I'd looted from Barska was priced at exactly 666 gold.

I yawned widely. It was good to know the value of my trinkets, but now I was tired.

Morning sunlight seeped under the door. It was time to get some sleep.

The coming days were going to be trying ones.

09 – Bullshit

I awoke at first-dark with Tika snuggled cozily against me.

Being with her was so comfortable, I didn't want to move. I was content to just lay next to her in the furs, taking in her scent, enjoying her warmth.

Why am I trying so hard to leave this place? the thought popped into my head. *Here, in NEO, I am the chief. I have a loyal clan, friends, and my beautiful ... No!* I shook my head. *I can't allow myself to go down that path again.* If Tal hadn't brought me back to my senses, I might have lived out my life as a goblin in body and mind, oblivious that my existence was just a digital dream.

Still ... I couldn't deny what I felt for Tika, and it was not just physical attraction. My feelings toward her were deep. Real. They couldn't be washed away with a cold logic that argued against their validity.

I leaned into her, feeling her hair on my cheek, enjoying the moment a little longer.

That's enough existential philosophizing for one morning. I have an Ogre clan to raid!

The thought invigorated me. I rose from the bed slowly, carefully, not waking Tika.

The Lyrical bird Tika had gifted me started singing its sweet song, instilling a sense of optimism and determination.

I stepped out of my house only to find Rhynorn, of all people, waiting. He was sitting, his back against a boulder, his club lying on the ground next to him.

I eyed the Ogre warily. "You're back."

"Hrrr," he grunted. "I be back in clan."

"And ...?"

He stood up, towering over me. At over three times my height, it was impossible not to feel some trepidation at his physical presence. But I'd already decisively shown that I was the more powerful monster. I held his gaze steadily. "Well?"

I tensed as he hoisted his club up and onto his shoulder.

Scowling at me he declared, "I BE THE CHAMPION!" Then his eyes dropped and in a more subdued voice, he added, "You be THE CHIEF. I, Rhynorn Bloodore do ... what Chief say."

"Good." I crossed my arms over my chest. "I'm leaving the hamlet for a few days. Maybe even longer. You will stay here with the rest of the soldiers. Your job is to guard against intruders and defend the clan. You are in charge of the soldiers, but you are not allowed to kill them. Understand?"

He grunted in acknowledgement.

"Kaedric is in charge of the workers. Do not interfere or give him any problems."

"Hrrr, I be with the real males, the fighters! Weaklings not concern of mine!"

"And don't you forget it." I poked his chest. At least I tried, but I only reached his stomach.

After my little talk with Rhynorn, I stopped by the mess hall for a quick bite. Gandork was back, busily working in the kitchen as if nothing had happened. I didn't bring up the subject of him dying and Rhyno's subsequent chastisement, but when he brought my meal out, it had an extra-large helping of roasted nuts on top.

Bek was waiting for me when I stepped out of the mess hall. The little goblin was fidgeting nervously as usual.

"Have you seen the twins?" I asked him.

"Yes, Dread Totem," he piped. "Them say them wait in forest."

"Very well, let's go."

I led the smaller goblin toward the tree line where Malkyr and Hoshisu were waiting for us.

"All set?" I read their information streams. Both were level 25. *Looks like they've been busy.*

"Yeah, man," Malkyr answered. "So like, where are we going ?"

"I talked with my lieutenant, Bob. He was one of the hobs from the clan allied with the Ogres."

"Yeah," Malkyr said sourly. "I remember *them.*"

"He told me their base is in the ruins of a fort a few days to the southwest. He marked the place on my map. So that's where we're headed."

"Should be interesting," Hoshisu remarked, her eyes measuring me.

I felt like she was checking for vulnerabilities, evaluating me as a future opponent.

I formed up a war party and sent an invitation to the twins. "Let's go."

We took the eastern path, plunging into the tree line toward the valley entrance and passing the ruins of the old Chief's Hut.

I nodded to Kilpi and Ryker, two of my hob soldiers who were guarding the entrance to the valley. A few minutes later, we left the valley behind us and were walking through the deep forest.

I hadn't been in the forest for the last two weeks, and going from the familiar open country of the valley to tangled, crowded tree-growths felt restricting.

Putting the valley wall to our left, we pushed through the dense growth until Hoshisu found a trail heading due south and we started making good time.

"We've pretty much cleared all the critters from this area," Malkyr noted.

"Yes." Hoshisu nodded. "It became almost impossible to find mobs inside the valley a while ago and now out here too."

"It's like they don't respawn or something," Malkyr complained. "I mean, what gives, man?"

I shrugged. "Time."

They both looked at me questioningly.

"The mobs breed organically. Mostly," I explained. "That's why they run on accelerated time. Now that we share the same acceleration, their breeding seems slow."

"Damn," Hoshisu said. "That means we'll have to go farther and farther afield for a decent challenge."

"I'm okay with that," her brother said. "The forest mobs here are small fry for us now anyway, mostly below level 10."

"Consider yourself lucky." I said "We're in the Deadlands. This forest has the lowest challenge rating of all the zones nearby. There are tougher opponents in every direction around our region."

Malkyr chuckled. "Heh, that just means more XP."

"If you're looking for a challenge, check out the riverbend two hours' walk north of the valley," I suggested. "There's a mother bear there that would be happy to have you for dinner."

We followed the trail south for a few hours, then took another trail toward the west. Hoshisu was right about the dearth of monsters; we encountered few along the way. Those that did cross our path fell easily to the twins.

The forest had thinned out as we traveled and it was gradually becoming brighter as the light of dawn crept between the branches.

"Let's make camp," I said.

"Nah man, we're not tired. It's only been like, what, ten hours? That's less than an hour, real time."

"Also," his sister interjected, "we only have about eight hours to game today. That's four days in-game, so we should complete the raid in that time frame if we haul ass and skip sleeping in-game."

Damn. It hadn't occurred to me that the time differential would create problems in this way. Because they were oriented to IRL time, the twins could go without sleep for days on end in our relative game-time.

"Alright, we'll push through," I agreed. "But Bek and I will need to rest at least once before the raid."

Malkyr shrugged. "Suit yourself. We'll just pop out for a bit of food or something."

We continued, traveling at a good pace through the forest. I kept my Mana Infusion spell active, bolstering myself. However, I hadn't taught the spell to Bek, since he didn't have the mana regeneration rate to maintain it. The poor goblin was having a hard time and eventually began lagging behind. Malkyr's solution to the delay was straightforward. He simply picked up the tired goblin-mite and tossed him over one shoulder, like a parent carrying a sleepy toddler to bed.

<*That's one* ugly *toddler. No dingo would eat that baby,*> Vic said in some unidentifiable accent.

Were you trying for an Aussie *accent?* I asked incredulously.

<*What's it to ya, mate?*> He wasn't going to quit.

It's terrible. Play to your strengths, Vic. You know, being a cranky, half-demented loon. I chuckled at my own humor.

<EXCUSE ME!> Vic said in an offended tone. *<What do you mean 'HALF?'>*

We cackled at each other.

The trees gave way to open, rolling grasslands to the south and west of the forest behind us, just as shown on my map.

"We've been here before," Hoshisu said. "It's a small level 40-plus area, just a couple of hours to cross it. "We were level 12 the last time we were here, so we mostly ran away from the monsters. Luckily there's not a lot of them."

"Let's keep going, then," I said. Level 40 creatures, even weak ones, were well beyond my ability to affect with Freeze or Dominate.

We increased our pace, keeping a vigilant watch on our surroundings. We avoided any encounters, and soon we could make out the border of the territory in the distance, where the grasslands and hills gave way to rocky, jagged mountains.

"Nearly there." I urged them on.

"Stop!" Hoshisu said sharply.

We all froze in our tracks.

"What is it, sis?"

"Oxsaurians." She pointed. "There. Our path goes right through a herd of them."

I squinted, looking where she pointed. I could barely make out a large number of indistinct shapes spread out across the plains in front of us.

"A herd," Hoshisu added. "There's no way we'll make it past them. They're extremely territorial and attack any intruder on sight."

"Maybe we can make a run for it?" Malkyr said.

Oxsaurians were fierce, bovine-like creatures. Fast, aggressive, and resistant to most physical damage, they were dangerous even to players twice their level, and they outranked us by a good margin.

"No." I shook my head. "I might be able to outrun them, but you three will not."

Hoshisu narrowed her eyes. "We need a distraction."

She was definitely on to something and I had just the vict– ... volunteer in mind.

Hey Vic, remember that time when you distracted the Dire Apes ...?

<You want me to piss off a herd of giant lizard-cows with anger management issues?> Vic's cloak-like body billowed out away from my back and shoulders as if to distance himself from me.

Err ... yes?

<I don't like that idea, Boss. There's nowhere for me to hide around here; they'll just run me down and trample me into purple paste. Why not summon a few of your invulnerable shadow minions to do it instead?>

Uhhh ... yes. I guess you have a point.

<No problem, Boss. Sometimes you meat suits are slow and need some direction. But hey, that's why I'm here!>

I reconsidered my Vic-tim idea for a few seconds but eventually decided against it.

"I'll arrange a distraction. Everyone get ready to run."

They nodded, and Malkyr put Bek down. The little goblin was in much better shape after his nap-n-ride.

I gathered my mana, building it up, then released it, casting an empowered Shadow Hound spell. It was a sunny day, and there were few shadows to use on the open land. As a result, the spell felt ... sluggish somehow, as I cast it.

When the spell ended, six shadow-made mastiffs had coalesced around me. Checking my summoned creatures, I was disappointed to find they were only level 5, half the usual level. The lack of shadows had obviously weakened the spell. Still, these underpowered hounds should do the job just fine.

"That is so *cool.*" Malkyr breathed a sigh, looking the mastiffs over appreciatively.

I ordered the mastiffs to rush the oxsaurians and engage them. The shadowy canines loped across the open plain toward the distant group of monsters. They attacked without hesitation, storming through the herd, indiscriminately striking out at every oxsaurian in their path. The mastiffs were doing almost no damage to the armored monsters, but the attack definitely got their attention. The entire herd was soon milling around, their agitated roars reaching our ears. When they inevitably turned en masse on the mastiffs, I ordered my shadow minions to break off and withdraw. The entire riled-up herd was lured away, clearing our path to the border.

I grinned at the others. "The coast is clear, let's go."

We were almost to the edge of the open territory, where the hills turned into mountains, when a truck-sized oxsaurian stood up from the tall grass, red-eyed and snorting, horns lowered to block our path.

The monster was Malkyr's height at its shoulder, its dusty grey skin thick and pebbled like that of a rhinoceros. A ruff of forward-curving spikes circled the massive neck.

Oxsaurian, bull
Level: 38
HP: 436
Attributes: P: 34, M: -4, S: 4
Skills: Unstoppable Charge 35, Thickskin 36
Traits: Magicless (no mana)
Resistances: Armor 158, Fire 50%, Acid -50%

It pawed at the ground, sending plate-sized divots of turf flying behind it. Raising its huge head and bellowing an enraged challenge, it lumbered into a charge.

"Do we run or *fight*?" Malkyr asked, his preference clear.

"Fight," I decided, powering up my arrows. "He's going to trample at least one of us if we try to run. We have to kill him."

"Yes!" Malkyr unlimbered his Greataxe. "I was starting to think I wouldn't get to kill anything today."

"It would be almost impossible to get through its armor with your weapons," I called out. "But it's susceptible to magic, so you two keep it busy while Bek and I deal damage with spells."

"No problem," Malkyr said, assuming a defensive stance with Hoshisu standing to his side and a step behind.

I cast Shadow Web at the charging beast, but it simply burst through the dark tendrils with its momentum barely reduced.

"Bek, keep away from it but keep shooting drilling arrows at it," I ordered.

"Yes, Dread Totem."

My dual drilling arrows were closely followed by Bek's single dart. The three projectiles impacted the beast's tough hide, doing 60 damage.

It staggered, then resumed its headlong rush at the waiting siblings. I cringed as I watched the inevitable collision, but Malkyr surprised me. With perfect timing, the big man spun away from the charging beast and delivered an axe strike to its neck. Although the axe struck true, its blade just rebounded harmlessly from the armored hide.

As the beast passed Hoshisu, she mirrored her brother's actions, but her dagger strikes also proved ineffective.

Bek and I continued to cast our arrow spells at the bull as he slowed to come around for another pass at the twins.

This fight was especially risky. Being caught and trampled by that creature would instantly kill any one of us. I considered using the Fire Rod in my inventory but hesitated.

The oxsaurian had 50 percent fire resistance so I would have to use the strongest void crystal I had to power the rod. The level 200 crystal I'd gotten from killing the player scouting party would easily inflict 2,000 points of damage. Even with the beast's fire resistance that would be enough to take it down. On the negative side, channeling so much raw power would surely destroy the rod.

I shook my head. Losing the rod wasn't the biggest issue; strong void crystals were simply too rare to waste. We'd already taken the bull's health down to 70 percent. Though it was a tough fight, victory was within our reach and our journey had just begun. We were probably going to face off against even deadlier foes, and if we couldn't handle a single oxsaurian, what chance would we have against an entire clan of *Ogres*? Besides, this fight was a good opportunity to hone our teamwork.

So, I left the Fire Rod unused and cast another Drilling Arrow. The two bolts shot out, followed closely by Bek's singleton. The three projectiles inflicted 55 points of damage.

But the beast still had over 60 percent of his health left; it was far from out of the fight.

Completing its wide looping turn, it oriented on me with its piggy eyes and began accelerating like a locomotive. The twins repositioned smoothly, putting themselves in the path of the charge, making the bull change its aggro to them mid-charge. Still, I prudently circled out of the bull's line of sight.

This time the beast changed its tactics, slowing its charge in an attempt to gore Malkyr. He parried with his axe, the force of the blow pushing him back, but they were clinched. Hoshisu tried to stay with them and keep formation with her brother, but the oxsaurian kept pushing Malkyr, the warrior's feet gouging furrows in the turf. The bull swung his head broadly from side to side, sweeping his many horns around like a spiked mace. The spikes caught both twins, piercing their armor like it was paper, and hurling them away like discarded toys.

Glancing at the war party icons, I was relieved to see they were both still alive, but Hoshisu's health was dangerously low. Getting to his feet, Malkyr raised his axe and roared a challenge. The axe blade glowed faintly and came down hard, leaving ripples in the air in its wake, striking the beast's skull. Raw energy exploded out of the axe, sending shockwaves into the beast's body. The attack actually broke through the thick grey skin.

The oxsaurian was momentarily shaken, giving us a brief moment to regroup and for Bek to cast the golden-green light of healing spells on Hoshisu and Malkyr.

Although injured and staggering, the oxsaurian was far from finished. It shook its head, snorting explosively, and glared at us with red eyes. Before the beast could gather its wits for another attack, I cast Shadow Web again. The spell-wrought shades grew from under its hooves and slithered up along its limbs, spreading over and around its shoulders and neck. Now that the creature was standing in place, the web was strong enough to hold it. The bull visibly sagged on its four legs, straining against the spell pulling it down and ensnaring it. Immobile, though not helpless.

I was not pleased with the way the battle was turning out. We were taking damage and not inflicting enough back. Our strategy was poor. A single blunder could become our downfall, ending with one or more of us as roadkill.

The beast roared and thrashed, but the web was holding, for the moment.

"Now! Attack with everything you've got while it's pinned down!" I cried, launching another volley of spinning arrows, bringing the creature's health down to 50 percent.

Malkyr started hacking away with abandon at the creature's leg as if he were chopping down a tree, his strikes chiseling flesh and health from the monster. Hoshisu reentered the fray. She was still injured, but her eyes shone with anger, falling savagely upon the creature, striking repeatedly with her daggers, probing for vulnerable spots but finding none.

Bek alternated healing and attacking while I continued bombarding the creature with my drilling arrows.

The beast was down to 20 percent health when it finally broke free. It jerked its head at Malkyr, catching him unprepared and managed to impale him on its neck spike.

"Shadow-crap," I mouthed. Malkyr was down to 30 percent health and was left hanging from the oxsaurian's spike. He didn't have long to live.

Bek and I cast another volley of drilling arrows, bringing the beast down to 12 percent. We needed two more volleys to bring it down. We wouldn't be able to save Malkyr in time.

Drilling Arrow spell level increased to 21.

Arrows per casting: 3

"Yes!" I shouted, casting the spell again.

This time, three rotating drilling arrows appeared, hovering in the air. I sent them flying at the beast, closely followed by Bek's lone arrow. Our four arrows impacted one after the other, doing just enough damage to bring the monster's health down to zero. It swayed on its legs then crashed to the ground.

We'd won.

Malkyr slid off the dead oxsaurian's spike, slumping down to the ground. Critically injured and bleeding profusely, he had seconds to live.

"Bek!" I yelled.

The small goblin uttered a few words, bathing Malkyr in the telltale golden-yellow light. The big man's bleeding ceased and his health stabilized.

"Phew, that was close!" Malkyr said, still on the ground, pale but smiling.

I shook my head. *Damn traveler-born don't know what real pain is.*

<Err, Boss, you meant that PLAYERS don't experience full pain in-game, right?>

Sure, sure, I said dismissively.

We were lucky my Drilling Arrow spell upgraded mid-fight. On a hunch I opened my character sheet, checking the Lucky Bastard skill. The skill had progressed by a whole 30 percent. *Luck strikes again.*

"Hey," Malkyr said. "I leveled up!"

"Me too!"

The siblings beamed.

Level up! You have reached Character Level 21. You have 1 ability point to allocate.

I checked the oxsaurian's body for loot. Jackpot! One hundred sixty-eight pieces of raw meat and one oxsaurian hide. That single beast had effectively financed two new, fully armored, hob soldiers with extra leftovers to spare. Not a bad haul. The twins didn't mind me claiming the loot; Malkyr even offered to carry most of the meat, as it was too heavy for Bek and me alone.

<Err ... Boss?>

Yes, Vic?

My cloak pulled at my right shoulder as I placed the last few pieces in my inventory *<You should see this.>*

I looked in the direction he was aiming me at.

"Ohhhh, crap."

The twins looked up and followed my gaze.

The herd was coming back.

"Run!" I yelled.

We started running frantically toward the mountains.

We just barely made it. The oxsaurians were puffing at our heels when we got to the rocky ground and pulled ourselves up onto some boulders.

"Phew, that was a close one!" Malkyr grinned boyishly. "Who's up for another round?"

"Men!" Hoshisu rolled her eyes.

"What?" her brother asked defensively.

I intervened before they start arguing. "We shouldn't be far now. Let's keep going."

We walked up the barren mountains, following a narrow path in the general direction of our target. The mountains were mostly made of cracked gray stone with jagged edges protruding in every direction. We had to be careful not to trip on the uneven ground or risk being skewered.

Night had fallen by the time we reached the top of the mountain and were able to check our surroundings. There were mountains in every direction, higher than the one we had just scaled. They all looked barren, jagged, and foreboding. It was a bleak place, which made a perfect habitat for Ogres.

"Malkyr, we've been playing for about two hours now. We should take a short break," the woman said.

"Alright, sis," her brother agreed. "I also need to check my emails. The university should reply today about that discovery I made back in the dungeon."

My sharp goblin ears perked up. "Why would a real university be interested in a treasure found in an in-game dungeon?" I asked.

"No, man. Remember I told you a while back about a math problem we had to solve to escape a dungeon?"

I frowned. "You mean the one where you found Yeshlimashu?"

He nodded. "Yep. Well, it was a rather tough problem, and I couldn't find a similar approach to what I came up with online. So I sent my solution to my uni's math department. I'm waiting to hear from them."

"That's ... weird."

Hoshisu made a sour face. "You're telling me. That's just one of the unexplained experiences we've had since playing as monsters, but so far it seems to be worth the trouble. Malkyr is being modest though. His solution was nothing short of genius; it could make a few advanced algorithms obsolete."

I looked at the big, brutish man with surprise. He didn't seem to be much of a brainiac. But that was the thing with NEO; you never knew what other players were really like. Sometimes, you thought you knew someone, spent a few years with him on a daily basis, only to realize he coveted your position all along and gladly sacrificed you to achieve his desires.

I clenched my teeth. *Vatras will pay for what he did! All travelers will pay! We goblins will show them who's the real fodder around here!*

<Err, Boss, you're alright?> Vic asked tentatively.

"Fine, Vic," I said and took a steadying breath, letting my anger drain away.

I looked around. The twins were gone.

Bek and I set up camp. We sat around the fire, eating some unsavory travel rations then lay down to rest against the cold, stony ground.

Bek fell asleep as soon as his head went down. I had to admit I felt like I could drop any moment. It had been hard keeping up with the pace the twins dictated. We goblins were better aligned with this world's day cycle, so it was harder for us to keep on going for days on end.

I drifted off to sleep, Vic keeping watch over us.

I dreamt.

I was flying over the mountains, a disembodied spirit. Mountain ridges passed by in a blur and I came to a halt in front of the ruins of an abandoned fort set against a sheer cliff. The place was old and crumbly and the walls were the same color as the mountain, making it look like the fort had grown naturally out of the mountain itself. The fort was preceded by a walled courtyard, with a half-broken, giant-sized gatehouse at the front. The gatehouse walls were glowing with green fire.

I flew over the gate and hovered around the courtyard. Below me, the ground shook, cracks appearing in the earth. The cracks opened up into deep crevices and more green flames leapt up from below. Every time a wave of flame appeared, it left in its wake a horde of creatures. The creatures looked hazy, but from what I could see, they were made partly of the same rocky substance as the mountain and partly from the green flames.

My spirit form soared downward, into the open crevice, passing through the green flames unharmed. I descended, faster and faster, finally reaching a large chamber.

It looked like a naturally occurring cave, deep in the bowels of the castle. My eyes were immediately drawn to the center. A huge, green-flamed creature stood guard over a small structure. An altar. The creature spun on its heels as if hearing something. It was staring right at me. I felt a cold shiver run through my spine as a set of hungry, burning eyes focused on me. I was powerless to do anything but watch.

The monster reached toward me with one huge hand, then stopped. A single digit pointed directly at my chest. "BOUND MINION OF AN OLD GOD," he spoke with a terrible voice, "YOU SHALL NOT CLAIM THIS UNHALLOWED PLACE, IT IS MINE. THROUGH IT, I SHALL FIND MY WAY INTO THE MORTAL WORLD."

Its flaming finger touched my chest.

I woke up screaming. My chest felt like it was on fire. I clawed at my vest, ripping it open. The rune scar Nihilator had carved in my flesh was burning. Green flame marked the lines of the rune, scorching, searing.

I got a hold of my pain and shoved it down deep into my chest, forcing myself to remain still, concentrating on regulating my breath, controlling the sensation. It took a full minute before the fire diminished, reducing my suffering, but not disappearing completely. I maintained my steady breath, slowly getting control back over my tortured flesh.

I could finally hear Vic trying to shout to me telepathically.

<Boss! Boss! Are you okay?>

It sounded like he had been trying to get my attention for a while now. Bek was sitting up, staring wide-eyed at me.

I wiped sweat off my forehead. "I'm fine now, Vic." My breathing was labored.

"What happened?" he demanded, standing before me in his purple goblin form.

"I don't know exactly," I admitted. "I dreamt another Totem vision. There's something sinister waiting for us at our destination. Something as powerful as Nihilator, maybe even more."

"Then we gotta get the hell outta here!" he exclaimed. "One big bad demigod that made you his bitch is quite enough. We don't need another one."

I shook my head, finally managing to breathe normally. "We can't go back now. There's too much riding on it. We need to find that Ogre lair and conquer it somehow. On the plus side, it looks like there's an altar there as well, so that could help me complete the next part of Nihilator's quest."

"I don't know ... sounds like more than we bargained for. Maybe we should postpone this expedition. You know, get yourself into better shape before tackling whatever awaits us."

I shook my head. "We can't, Vic. The players are probably preparing their attack as we speak. We need to push every advantage we can get. We have to at least try."

"But Boss, you can't be serious, if that thing is as dangerous as –"

"Damn it, Vic!" I cut him off, feeling irrational anger flaring up deep inside me. "I am a goblin Totem and chief! You know what I endured, you know what I went through. I carved a place for myself with my bare hands and paid for it in blood. I will not throw it away at the first sign of danger!"

Vic stared at me, speechless.

"What's wrong?" I frowned at him.

He shook his head.

"What?" I demanded.

He pointed at my bare chest. I looked down. The green flames had been replaced by tiny black ones.

I felt lightheaded as the blood drained from my face and I slumped to the ground, clutching my chest. The dark flames subsided, taking with them my momentary lapse.

"What was that?" Vic demanded.

"Nihilator," I deadpanned. "He will not allow me to return without finishing this quest first. I ... I could feel it. He wants that altar, so he exerted his influence over me, claiming his minion back from the green one." I shuddered as I remembered the pain from mere moments ago and held my face in both hands. "I'm just a tool for them, Vic. A small piece they can toy around with as they please."

I felt Vic's hand on my back. "It'll be okay, Oren. We'll finish this quest together, and once we do, you'll be even stronger than before." His voice sounded weird suddenly, almost ancient. "That's how the system works, it puts seemingly insurmountable challenges in front of you, but those who pass the test are rewarded for it. That is the game and the prison it creates in your mind."

That was a weird way of putting it, but I got his meaning. The higher the challenge, the higher the reward. "Thanks, Vic. What would I do without you?"

He chuckled. “Run into walls, probably? Light your pants on fire?”

I chuckled as well. “Good one. I ran right into that.”

> **+200 reputation with Vic (The Awesome Companion).**
> *Current rank:* Friendly.
> *Points to next rank:* 2,300

“So, what’s the deal with all the recent pyrotechnics in that rune on your chest?”

I looked down at my torso gloomily. “I think we now know what that whole ‘bound by Nihilator’ means. He can make me do things, even from far away.”

“Yeah, but I bet it’s limited,” Vic countered. “You had that on you for days now, and it didn’t make you do anything out of the ordinary. It only happened now, after that Totem dream of yours. I bet he can only influence you at critical junctions.”

“That’s not really making me feel better about it.”

“At least if you are being used as a tool, better to be a rook than a pawn.”

I found that mildly encouraging.

The twins returned a few hours later. They were both in good spirits as they received the confirmation they were waiting for. They were even rewarded for their findings, so they planned on a proper celebration after our raid.

Malkyr stretched. “So, what’s the plan, Chief?”

“We’re not far now. The Ogre lair is an old, beaten-down fort. We go in and take out any enemy we find.”

“Good plan, Boss,” Hoshisu said sarcastically.

<Hey, that's my line!> Vic protested in my mind.

“So we just go in, engage whatever looks like it wants to eat us, then go back out?”

I shrugged. “Pretty much. I saw you both fight back when you weren’t even level 10. I bet you can take on at least two Ogres by yourselves.”

“Ha!” Malkyr exclaimed. “Make that four! He’s got a point, sis. You saw how he took down that Ogre boss back at the valley. We’ll be fine.”

"Plus, we have Bek here." I laid a reassuring hand on the small goblin's shoulder. "He'll keep us at peak condition through it all."

Hoshisu nodded reluctantly. "Oh, alright. They're just Ogres, I suppose."

"However ..." I hesitated, not sure how to tell them about my vision.

Hoshi raised an eyebrow. "Yes?"

"There ... might be some complications once we hit the deeper level."

She continued staring at me.

"I have it on good authority that the final boss is not a simple Ogre. I don't know exactly what it is, but it's some sort of magical monster with green flames for eyes."

"And just *how* did you find that out?" she asked, her tone clearly suspicious.

"It was hinted at by another quest I received. It just recently updated, letting me believe it's connected with our destination."

"How convenient."

"Bah, green eyes, blue eyes, what's the big deal?" Malkyr said. "It's not like I'm looking to date them. Lead the way, Big Chief."

We continued walking. An hour later we passed a bend in the trail, and another mountain came into view. This one's peak was lower than where we stood. From our vantage point, we could clearly see the ruins of an old fort. A large courtyard surrounded by crumbling walls led to the main structure. As in my vision, the old walls looked to be made from the same stone as the mountain, blending with it seamlessly. A large, mostly intact gatehouse was just below us, leading into the courtyard. Unlike my vision, there was no green fire coming out of it.

Hoshisu squinted as she viewed the scene below us.

"What do you see?" I asked, knowing she had a skill that enhanced her eyesight.

"Nothing," she said shortly. "Ruins and debris all over, but no Ogres. The fort itself looks like it could collapse at any moment."

I felt a pang of worry. *Could we have missed our destination? Have we arrived at the wrong place?* No. I shook my head. The marker Bob placed on my map matched the location. "Come on, let's check it out."

We started making our way down the mountain. It was getting dark by the time we finally stood before the gatehouse. It was clear Hoshisu's description was spot-on. The courtyard beyond the opening was visible. Fallen debris and large pieces of stone were scattered about, a testament to the buildings that once dotted the place. There was no movement, no life, no vegetation. This was a barren, dead place.

Everyone drew their weapons as we cautiously walked through the gate that towered five meters above us. Four Ogres could have easily walked side by side below the massive opening.

The courtyard opened before us, with the main fort structure nearly a football-field length away.

Something didn't look right to me. I squinted. "What's that?" I pointed at a round shape ahead of us.

"Where?" Hoshisu asked sharply, following my finger. She peered intently at it then shook her head. "I can't see very well in the dark."

<It kinda reminds me of those sleeping Ogres around the hob's war camp, Boss. Remember?>

Shit, you're right.

"I think the Ogres are there." I looked at the twins. "When we surveyed the place from above it was still daylight. The Ogres are nocturnal creatures, so they were sleeping. It explains why Hoshisu didn't notice them."

Malkyr glanced upward. "It's almost completely dark; they could wake any moment."

"Then let's hurry," I urged. "If we take a few of them while they're sleeping it'll make our job a lot easier."

We half-marched, half-ran forward, trying not to make too much noise. The shapes ahead remained motionless.

We closed in on our prey. They were all huddled together on the ground.

There were four Ogres. All dead.

***

New Era Online [Internal messaging service]:

From: Legal#298

Subject: Official notice

Mr. Berman, we would like to advise you that your settlement was deemed to fulfill the requirement of a starting area. As such, people who want to play as monsters and meet the minimum CPA requirement will be granted the option to select Goblin's Gorge as their starting area. In order to avoid overtaxing current infrastructure, the number of players will be limited to a quarter of your clan's population (60 at the time this message is written).

I would like to remind you again that per your signed NDA with the company, you ARE NOT TO INFORM the new players of your unique circumstances, including, but not limited to your inability to log out.

Sincerely,

Suzanne de'More

Legal Department

10 – Penelope

Jackson frowned as he looked at the whiteboard and twiddled the marker in his fingers.

There was no denying it, he was stuck. He had spent the last few hours reexamining his work, and his calculations simply didn't add up.

Jackson was part of a team of scientists that were trying to build a gravitational model of a theoretical star system, but try as he might, he couldn't determine the Interstellar Medium specifications.

"Ahem, hi, Jackson." Penelope entered the room. The 19-year-old woman looked slightly out of place with her white scientist garb, like a child putting on grown-up clothes. "I'm almost done with the Celestial Sphere model. Are you, ahem ... nearly done?"

Jackson's shoulders slumped in defeat. "Sorry, Pen, I've been staring at this board for ages, but I just can't seem to figure out the precise Kepler ratios for the stars. I'm afraid it looks like we're both stuck here for the night."

"Oh." Penelope's cheery demeanor evaporated. She'd been looking forward to going home. Something very important was about to happen today. "Can I have a look?"

Jackson shrugged. "Be my guest, but one of those bodies is also a Neutron Star. It just won't fit into the conventional –"

"Got it!" Penelope beamed, adding a few more numbers and diagrams to the board. "There. You just forgot to account for the gravitational effects of proximity to the supermassive black hole of Andromeda. I'll add it to the model in a jiffy."

Jackson stared slack-jawed at the board as Penelope put some notes on a piece of paper. He stood there for a long moment even after the young women had left the room.

"How the hell did she do that?"

"What was that, Jackson?" Another scientist poked his head through the door.

Jackson coughed, embarrassed. "Sorry, Goldstein, just thinking out loud. I've been working on my part of the model for ages and Penelope glimpsed the solution in a heartbeat."

"That's Penelope for you," Goldstein said. "She might be young, but she is gifted."

"Still." Jackson shook his head. "It's uncanny."

Goldstein shrugged. "There are smart people, and there are *smart* people. Gifted people. She has something, a spark. It just comes to her naturally."

Jackson's lips tightened.

Goldstein chuckled. "Don't pout. Think about it; without her, you'd be pulling an all-nighter."

Jackson's expression became thoughtful. "You know what, I think I'll use the time to catch an early show. The new Star Wars just came out."

"Good idea. Maybe I'll join you."

"Don't you have your own project to finish up first?"

"Penelope helped me with that an hour ago."

Jackson smiled. "It almost feels like cheating."

Goldstein had a glint in his eye. "On the bright side, we can go and have some fun while still on the clock."

"You've got a point. Hang on, I'll get my coat."

***

Penelope felt elated.

She'd finished work at a reasonable hour today, unlike so many other days when she had to work through the night. She loved her job, but it was a demanding one. For some reason, people kept asking for her help with finishing their projects. She didn't mind helping. She was fascinated by the challenges. Complex problem solving was a hobby of hers. Despite that, the extra work often left her drained. Too many people depended on her, and she felt obliged to do her part. That left her social life and leisure time extremely lacking. Lately, she'd started to feel as if her job was the only reason for her existence. The notion weighed on her more and more every day. She needed a way to blow off some steam.

And now, she'd found a way.

Penelope looked at the state-of-the-art FIVR capsule sitting in her bedroom.

This was the answer to her problem.

Penelope used to love gaming. As a teenager, she was considered a casual gamer, often playing alongside her uncle, who was a pro gamer. She'd love to play more, but her busy study schedule only allowed for several hours of game time a week. Once she started working and doing research at the university, she could no longer afford the hours required for that activity.

That's why, when the company contacted her and presented a unique opportunity to join NEO as a *monster race*, she jumped at the offer. She had tried out NEO before – everyone did. When the game first came out, she could still find a little time for gaming and experience the hype on her own. That was why the offer to experience time 12 times faster was especially appealing to her. She could have a full gaming session in what would only be a few moments in real life. How could she say no to that?

So she signed their ridiculous waiver and NDA agreement. They did seem extreme at first, but the company had given her the FIVR capsule, so she could live with a few limiting clauses.

The technicians had just finished installing the machine and she was eagerly waiting for them to leave. When the last one finally grabbed his tools and left, she almost ran to the capsule, eager to log in.

"Penelope Katie Britt," she whispered to herself, eyes shining, "it's time for you to have some fun!"

She got inside the gleaming metal tube and waited. The lid closed above her, and cables snaked to her head, connecting to her temples. She closed her eyes.

She was floating. Weightless, inside a black void. The experience might have seemed claustrophobic to others, but to Penelope, it felt like she was suspended in space, a place she endlessly probed during her work. It felt familiar, serene. It was very different from her last brief experience playing NEO.

A pleasant, elderly male voice spoke. "Welcome to New Era Online. Selection of starting area is locked. Deadlands, Goblin's Gorge. Please select a race. Note that the goblinoid template will be applied *after* you make your selection. Would you like to review the template details?"

"Erm ... yes, please?"

Goblinoid Template
Trait: Goblinoid (+1 Physical -1 Social)
Goblinoid Features
Low-light vision
Reputation Default: Hated
Reputation with goblinoid races: Unfriendly

"Hmm, that's interesting." Penelope didn't comprehend what most of the lines meant, though low-light vision was easy enough to decipher.

She dismissed the message, and a line of creatures materialized before her like puppets on display. Penelope studied the options with interest. There was a fierce-looking female Orc, her gray skin tough and callous. A human, an elf, the usual lot. That was not for her.

As she continued browsing the list, the races became more exotic; deep dwarves, half-gnomes, drow, goliath, a snake-like creature that was listed as 'Githyanky,' a scaly looking lizard woman, and ...

"Oh, yes!" Penelope exclaimed, looking at a distinct feline shape. Catfolk.

The female catfolk had cute cat ears, a furry tail, and light whiskers. Penelope adored cats.

"Catfolk selected," the disembodied voice said once she confirmed her selection. "Please select a name for your new character."

"Erm ... Penelope?"

"That name is already taken. Please try another."

"Cutie Kitty?"

"That name is already taken. Please try another."

She paused, mulling over her options. She'd recently conducted an experiment using the gravitational pull of Jupiter's moons. That in itself wasn't anything special, but she liked the name of the most recently discovered moon.

"Raystia."

"Name accepted. You may now enter a personal background for your character."

"Erm ... I'm just happy to be here and looking forward to exploring the game. I'm looking to have fun!"

"Accepted."

"Your character will be reincarnated in five seconds. Four ...Three ... Two ... One."

Received: Rusty Crude Dagger

Received: Travel Rations X 2

Received: 10 gold

The blackness around her became hazy, colors slipping into her view. They became sharper, forming into distinct shapes; ground, sky, mountains. She was standing on a stone shelf next to a small gravestone and what looked like a pagan-styled shrine.

The sensations were so real, though her thoughts felt sluggish for some reason.

This is so exciting! Raystia raised her arms, enjoying the sensation of her virtual body. Then she froze. She stared at her arms, uncomprehending. Instead of the cute fuzzy arms of a catfolk, her furry limbs looked gaunt and scary. She gasped, clutching her face.

Her fingers felt sharp features, gaunt cheeks, and long, sharp teeth. No, no, no ... this was all wrong. She patted the sides of her head and touched small skinny ears. A monster. Her mind still felt like it was stuffed with cotton. The initial shock transformed into horror. She opened her mouth to scream when someone spoke behind her.

"Good evening, miss. Allow me to welcome you to our humble settlement."

Startled, she whirled around to find a horrifying, emaciated monster staring back at her.

"Greetings," it said.

The thing had insect-like mandibles. She couldn't help herself, her mind was still fuzzy. She opened her mouth and screamed.

***

Raystia was ashamed. Once her head cleared up and her mind no longer felt sluggish, she was able to get a grip on herself and appreciate her surroundings. Now it was clear what 'goblinoid features' meant.

She stood at the edge of the stone shelf and observed the small settlement. The place was buzzing with activity. Small goblins were scurrying all over the place, carrying things, building things, working. Several fierce looking hobgoblins, armed and armored, were patrolling. She thought she even spotted an Ogre for a moment, trodding behind one of the largest buildings. This place was fascinating. The valley below was divided between an open grassland and a large forest. The structures were made mostly of wood, giving them a natural appearance and a rustic, rural feel.

This was just what she was looking for.

"As you can see, miss," the tall, gaunt creature next to her said, "the hamlet is quite small; any help you might offer in its development would be highly appreciated."

Though she was no longer seized by the illogical feeling of dread, she was still wary of this creature. "Erm ... Kaedric, was it?"

The mind eater nodded, his mandibles clicking together.

"Is it safe here?"

"Goblin's Gorge valley is quite safe. The forest is constantly patrolled, though the occasional beast might still be encountered there. Outside the valley there is a thick forest teeming with wild beasts and monsters. I would advise you to prepare well before venturing there."

"So, um ... I think I need better weapons. Is there a place where can I get some equipment?" She looked disdainfully at the rusted dagger tucked at her belt.

"There are some gremlin-run shops over there." Kaedric pointed at some weird looking constructions at the southern part of the valley. "In addition, we have several workers capable of manufacturing various items, but you would have to come to an agreement with them yourself."

"Oh, alright." She hesitated. Her uncle once shared with her what he claimed to be a magical phrase when interacting with NPCs. "Do … can I offer you my assistance with anything?"

Kaedric looked at her, his mandibles slightly ajar. *Is this surprise?* she wondered.

"There might be … one thing," the creature said slowly. "I would have to feed soon."

"Oh!" She brightened up. "Should I run to your cook and bring you something to eat?" Simple fetch quests were easy and not very rewarding, but for a first-level player, they were just the thing to gain experience with relative safety.

"No, I do not require sustenance at this time."

She furrowed her brow. "But you just said …"

"I need to *feed.* For that, I require a live, intelligent, humanoid creature."

That caught her off guard. She stared at him in horror.

His mandibles twitched. "I am forbidden to harm any of the sentients in the valley, but I would need to feed soon, or the result would be … dire. If you're able to help me, I shall offer mine in return."

What the hell? she thought, blinking. The company did mention she would be playing as a monster, but she never imagined the experience would be so … monstrous.

She grimaced. This was her one and only viable option to spend time gaming, so she should just embrace the experience. *When in Rome*, she thought with dark humor, *crack open a skull and feed it to a hungry ant-man.* "Well, I guess I can give it a try."

You received a new quest: Braaaaains!

Kaedric, the administrator of Goblin's Gorge, has asked you to bring him a living, intelligent humanoid creature to eat.

Quest Type: Advanced

Time limit: 5 days

Reward: +50 reputation with the GreenPiece Clan, +200 reputation with Kaedric, 400 XP, 20 gold

She was not an experienced gamer, but the quest reward looked quite generous.

The tall creature nodded in approval. "Then I will offer further assistance. What type of weapon would you like to use?"

"Erm ... I'm not really sure," she confessed. "I don't want to stand too close to enemies, so... something with range?"

"In that case, I suggest you go talk with Bosper, our clan's bowyer. Tell him I sent you."

"Erm, thanks, um, sir."

Stepping down a ladder, she found herself walking through the green valley. Goblins were scurrying around her, and she nearly bumped into one carrying a basket as she walked, trying to take in her surroundings.

"Oops, sorry ... Ooooo! Bunnies!"

She approached a large enclosure. A low wooden fence surrounded a patch of ground riddled with holes. Rabbits roamed freely inside, playing and eating.

A lone goblin female was walking among the rabbits, sprinkling something on the ground that lured the rabbits to it. As Raystia watched, the goblinette bent down and picked up two of the munchers.

"Oh, hello there!" Raystia called. "May I hold one of them?"

The goblin ignored her and carried her cargo to a small wooden shed.

"Erm, hello? I asked if I –"

She stopped as the goblin grabbed a cleaver from a nearby shelf and slaughtered the two rabbits with two efficient strokes.

Raystia paled. *This is a game?* It was a very different experience than what she had envisioned. Still, Penelope was not vegan, and she had no illusions as to where meat came from. Though she would have liked to cuddle the cute bunnies for just a little while.

She found a serious-looking male goblin next to the pond, working with bits of wood. Using a sharp knife, he carved a piece of spry branch, shaping it into a bow.

"Erm, hello."

The goblin paused his work and looked at her.

"Are you Bosper? I was told you might be able to make me a bow."

The goblin grunted. "Dread Totem tells me make many bows for clan. Not for you."

"Kaedric sent me to you."

Bosper blanched. "I mean ... of course I can make you good bow. But I run out of willow branches. Bring me five good branches and I will make you a decent bow.

You received a new quest: Willow for Bosper

Bring Bosper, GreenPiece Clan's bowyer, 5 willow branches.

Quest Type: Simple

Reward: +20 reputation with the GreenPiece Clan, 100 XP, a willow bow.

"Great!" Raystia brightened. "Only, uh ... what does a willow tree look like?"

The goblin rolled his eyes at her.

A few minutes later, Raystia left the grumpy goblin. He'd described the tree with great detail and had even loaned her his axe to cut down the sturdy branches.

She skipped happily through the settlement. She was having fun! This place was different than what she'd expected – more savage – but it was beautiful nonetheless. There was a certain charm to living in the wild.

Not paying too much attention to where she was going, she bumped headlong into something solid. She fell on her backside, feeling muted pain in her posterior. This game was so realistic! She looked up to see what she had run into. Two thick tree trunks blocked her path. Her gaze continued upward and the tree trunks merged into a wide and powerful torso.

An Ogre leered down at her, snarling. "You dare challenge me? I BE THE CHAMPION! I will kill you!"

He lifted his huge arm as if intending to swat her like a fly. Raystia squealed in fright, shielding her face with her hands.

A shrill voice sounded from behind. "Hey, 'ye big ugly brute. What'chya think you be doing with this wee lass, eh?"

The voice gave the Ogre pause, interrupting the intended blow.

Raystia risked lowering her hands and looked behind her. An old goblin female with warts all over her face and wearing an apron was standing with her hands on her hips. She glared threateningly at the Ogre.

"She dared challenge me!" the brute protested.

"Na she didn't, 'ye lumbering halfwit! Now you better be going elsewhere, or I'll be telling our Dread Totem about this."

"Argh, Dread Totem said not to kill clan," the Ogre mumbled to himself.

"Or guest. She be our guest, now git!"

To Raystia's great relief, the monster lowered his hand then trotted away, leaving her unharmed. She took a deep breath. That was a close call. She still felt the rush of adrenaline from the encounter and she was starting to get curious about this 'Dread Totem' she kept hearing about.

"Ye hurt, child?" the old goblin woman asked her.

She shook her head. "No, thank you, erm ..."

"Guba's the name," the old goblin said. "Now you better be moving."

"I'm looking for some willow trees," Raystia blurted out. For some reason, she felt she could confide in the old woman.

"Pfh," Guba snorted, "you'll be a fine meal fer them beasties roaming around in the forest."

"But I thought the forest was safe," the young woman protested.

Guba cackled at that. "I'm betting you been thinking the clan's safe too, 'afore you been running into that idiot Rhynorn."

The old goblin's expression softened as she saw Raystia's downcast look. "Pfh, in Nihilator's name," she huffed. "Here, take one of these, me own special mixture."

Adhesive Grenade
Pull the pin before throwing at an enemy.

"But don't ye be going around telling ye be getting this from me!" the goblin cautioned, raising one gnarled finger. "Now run along."

***

Two hours later, Raystia came back out of the woods. She was sweating, her clothes were stained, and she had a nasty gash on her forearm. But she was grinning broadly.

In her arms was a stack of willow branches. She'd found the willow tree easily enough, but there was a giant praying mantis there as well. It was the size of a large dog and didn't seem to be in a hurry to leave. After waiting for almost an hour, Raystia realized she would have to confront the creature. She'd never experienced battle in her previous FIVR immersion sessions, and even if it was just a game, she was reluctant to approach the menacing monster. Eventually, she threw the grenade Guba had given her at the creature, which completely immobilized him. She then peppered it with rocks and sticks from afar. Her aim was poor at first, but after a few throws, she received a new skill: Ranged Affinity. Afterwards, her throws became much more accurate.

The thing's health bar kept gradually shrinking. She'd almost finished it off when it finally managed to break free of the hardened glue. She managed to draw out her dagger while the monster stormed at her and killed it with a single clumsy thrust, but not before the thing's pincer slashed at her arm.

Once the fight was over, she used the axe to cut five springy branches.

Now she was walking, determined, carrying her precious cargo back to the bowyer.

"Here you go," she said a bit gruffly, dumping her load next to the surprised goblin.

Quest Completed: Willow for Bosper

You brought Bosper 5 willow branches.

Reward: +20 reputation with the GreenPiece Clan, 100 XP, a willow bow

He grunted in approval. "That was quick."

"Here, I already made a bow specially for you." He handed her the bow he was working on. It was a white slender bow that fit snugly in her palm, matching her size perfectly.

Raystia's Willow Bow

Description: A bow made of springy willow, fitted especially to be wielded by Raystia*.

Type: Weapon [two-handed]

Rank: Average

Durability: 22/22

Range: 55 (*60)

Damage: 10-12 (*12-14)

Raystia felt tears running down her cheeks. She'd done it. It wasn't easy, but she'd persisted, and through her own power and determination managed to achieve something noteworthy. Something that was now uniquely hers. The feeling of accomplishment was quite different than what she was used to in her line of work.

She held the bow in one hand and tested the pull, feeling it flex from her effort. She tightened her lips, her eyes adamant. Now that she had the means to hunt, she could pursue her next quest.

She glanced at the in-game watch. *And it all took only 15 minutes!* She grinned in satisfaction.

NEO is amazing, more so than I'd remembered. The realism is incredible. I'm definitely coming back for more.

Actually, she *had* to come back. After all, she couldn't let Kaedric, the poor, brain-eating monster, walk around hungry, now, could she?

11 – The Fort

I stared at the hacked and mutilated bodies of the Ogres. This did not make sense.

Malkyr noticed the same thing I did. "How come the game's cleanup engine didn't dispose of the bodies yet? They've obviously been dead for a while."

<Jeesh, it's like he's never seen a horror movie before or something.>

Just as Vic voiced his opinion, my Dangersense kicked in. "Get back!" I urged the others and activated Mana Shield.

They looked at me with surprise.

"Undead!" I cried, just as the bodies began to move.

The Ogres clumsily rose to their feet, their hulking, bloated forms towering over us.

"Shit," I cursed under my breath. My ability to manipulate other creatures' mana was limited to living, biological creatures, or shadow-based ones. The Ogre zombies, though raised by dark magic, were undead beings and so were immune to my influence. Considering that zombies were usually physically stronger – albeit slower – than their living counterparts, we might have bitten off more than we could chew.

<Don't forget they also have more health than living Ogres,> Vic added with a lecturing tone.

"Thanks for reminding me," I snapped.

Two of the Ogres were closing in on us, the other two bending down to lift rocks.

"Malkyr, your axe should be effective against them. Think you can tank those two?" I was already channeling my mana, preparing a spell.

He looked at the lumbering monsters doubtfully. "Err ... I think so."

"Good, these will help." I completed the spell, summoning three Shadow mastiffs. "Okay, everyone – target the one on the left. Go!"

I cast Drilling Arrow as the two zombies closed into melee, sending three spinning projectiles at the enemy, with Bek's single arrow following mine. The arrows all hit dead flesh and burrowed deeply before exhausting their magical charge. The undead Ogre seemed not to notice.

The twins moved to position themselves in front of the zombies. Malkyr, at the front, assumed a battle stance, his Greataxe held high. Hoshisu stood a step behind him, her twin daggers at the ready. My hounds stood at their flanks, ready to pounce.

I concentrated on the injured zombie. *Analyze.*

Possessed Ogre Zombie

Level: 13

HP: 345/400

Attributes: P: 20, M: -, S: -

Traits: Ogre, Undead, Possessed

Skills: Powerful 25

Resistances: Mental 100%, Armor 50

Description: A Zombie feels no pain and knows no fear. Normally an unintelligent monster, this specimen is directed by a malevolent spirit that grants it awareness, making it a dangerous foe.

What the hell? Since when are zombies possessed by spirits?

My thoughts were cut short as the two zombies that had lagged behind threw the boulders they'd lifted; one was aimed at the twins, the other soared straight at me.

The twins threw themselves to the side, trying to evade the boulder aimed at them. Hoshisu managed to dodge, but Malkyr wasn't as lucky. The boulder clipped him on the waist and despite being twice the Ogre in level, he was blown off his feet. The Ogres' immense bulk gave them a decisive advantage. It was hard to shrug off a missile hitting your body when it was the size of a dinner table. That was one of the reasons I wanted an Ogre infantry.

The boulder aimed at me was deflected by my shield, draining me of nearly 60 MP, then crashed into the ground, showering everyone with sharp bits of stone. My hounds were not affected by the shards, but both the twins received some shallow cuts.

Bek was already casting his healing magic on the big man. The golden-green light surrounded Malkyr's body, easing his pain, enabling him to stand up.

The barrage also broke our momentum and allowed the other two Ogres to close into melee range. My hounds intercepted them, pouncing and biting, buying Malkyr a few precious seconds to ready his axe just in time to intercept a huge fist aimed at his head. He managed to block the blow, but it left him off balance. The other Ogre seized on the opportunity and scored a direct hit against the man's chest, making him stumble back a few steps. Hoshisu darted in, slashing at the outstretched giant arm, but if the creature noticed the wounds, it didn't show.

I saw the two farther zombies lifting more boulders. *Damn it.*

I couldn't cast another spell for a few seconds, but I had other options available. With a flick of my mind, the bone dagger soared out of my belt and struck the already wounded zombie.

Dagger hits Possessed Ogre Zombie for 25 damage, [23 Dark + 2 Physical]

We were in trouble. The Ogres had us off balance and we'd only managed to injure one of them. I was frantically trying to figure out how to turn the tide when Hoshisu stepped up. She drew an odd-looking chain from her inventory and whipped it at the uninjured Ogre, nimbly dodging an awkwardly swung fist. With an audible click, the two ends of the chain connected. Gears within started to spin and whine. As the chain tightened, it tore at the Ogre's flesh and crushed his bones. We all paused to stare in amazement at the tightening chain as it disappeared inside the monster's body, ripping and slicing.

The creature looked stupidly down at its body, then up again. It took a step toward Hoshisu, and its torso toppled backward. It was still 'alive,' trying to claw its way toward the twins, but without legs, it didn't have a chance. My hounds seized the opportunity and fell savagely on the two sawn halves, dragging them away from the siblings.

That maneuver bought Malkyr all the time he needed to recover. He stepped forward and brought his axe down, putting his full weight into the strike. It cut deeply into the still standing Ogre for 69 damage.

I flexed my fingers, feeling magical power surge through them. Hoshisu's daring move had completely changed the direction of the fight.

I cast Shadow Web over one of the rock-throwing Ogres, causing him to drop the stone he was lifting. The web kept him entangled and rooted in place, though it wasn't strong enough to prime him for a sacrifice. Instead, I directed my dagger to slash at Malkyr's opponent, inflicting an additional 26 damage, bringing it down to half his total hit points.

Bek sent another heal at Malkyr before the Ogres retaliated.

The lone, unopposed thrower aimed at me again, launching a heavy boulder. The boulder struck my shield and bounced away, draining 50 mana.

The Ogre at the frontline threw a clumsy fist at the twins. Without his friend to add pressure to the melee, the twins easily held their ground. Malkyr parried the heavy blow while Hoshisu rolled underneath the outstretched arm, cutting deep gashes all along the Ogre's forearms, bringing him down to a quarter of his health.

I conjured another trio of drilling arrows and fed more mana into the web, keeping the thrashing ranged Ogre trapped. Another arrow from Bek and another attack from the twins finally downed the zombie they were fighting.

My hounds kept tearing at the half-zombie, keeping it away as it tried to claw toward us. We gave them a wide breadth and engaged the stone thrower.

With the twins tanking him and several barrages of drilling arrows thrown in, we had no trouble finishing it off. The zombie trapped by the web was even more easily handled, as his entanglement prevented him from striking back at us.

I made sure to time my dagger attacks carefully to get the killing blow, reducing each of the zombies to a dark mass that coalesced into shining, new void crystals.

I toyed with the dagger between my fingers as I considered the crawling zombie torso. I could finish it off easily from a distance, but that would be a waste.

"Hey Malkyr," I said to the man as he checked the dropped loot. "Think you can remove that guy's arms?"

He frowned. "Eh? What the hell for?"

I grinned at him. "Call it a test."

He grunted but picked up his axe and carefully walked over to the crawling zombie. I made my hounds bite down and stretch its arms wide. Two well-aimed strikes were all it took, and the zombie remained an immobile torso with a head. A head that snapped and snarled at us but could do little else.

"Thanks."

"Don't mention it. By the way, the other Ogres didn't drop any interesting loot, just some gold. Here's your share." He handed me 60 gold.

"Thanks." I pocketed the gold and approached the squirming torso. I carefully positioned my dagger to hover above the zombie's forehead. "Now let's see if losing your legs and arms counts as being immobile," I muttered to myself and struck down with the dagger.

Level up! You have reached Character Level 22. You have 1 ability point to allocate.

Possessed Ogre Zombie sacrificed. +13 Faith Points (Cult of Nihilator)

"Yes!" I exclaimed, pumping my fist. So sacrificing zombies generated Faith Points as well as void crystals. *Only* 30 or so more creatures like these and I'd reach the 1,000 FP goal; then I could purchase the Eternal Night blessing.

I put the new ability point into Mental, bringing it up to 25.

"Hey, Vic." I turned my head to look at my Vicloak, "How about you jump into one of those Ogres? The extra muscles could come in handy."

<That's a negatory, Boss. These bodies were already possessed and cannot be repossessed>.

I frowned. It sounded weird to me, but as the possession master, I had to take Vic at his word.

"That was a pretty impressive display," I said to Hoshisu. "Where did you get that chain?"

She grimaced. "The new shops. Bought it from a grumpy old gremlin."

I cocked my head. "Why the long face?"

She puffed her cheeks. "That chain cost 500 gold and I can only use it once before having to recharge it. And according to the gremlin who sold it to me, he's the only one who can do it. I planned on saving it for the boss, but the way things were going, I didn't feel like I had much of a choice."

Malkyr put his large arm around her shoulder. "You did the right thing, sis; we were caught unprepared. We'll know what to expect next time."

"Can I take a look at that?" I gestured at the chain.

She shrugged and handed it over.

Self-Propelling Saw Chain

Description: Created by a mad gremlin inventor. Once activated, bladed gears will tighten the chain, cutting everything in its way.

Runecraft Viability: 1/3

Charge: 0/100

Type: Trap

Rank: Magical

Durability: 35/40

Effect: 15 damage per second. 10 seconds duration. Ignores 10 points of armor.

Interesting. The chain was Runecrafted.

I concentrated on the tiny inscription etched on the chain's links. I could sense its function. *It's in the metadata*, as Vic often put it. The chain was a mechanized item with a bit of Runecraft added to make it fold in on itself. I could clearly sense the absence of mana in the rune, and unlike the Fire Rod I designed, there was no socket available to feed more mana into it. I rubbed my chin, considering the possibilities. "Would you mind if I tamper with it a bit?" I asked her.

Hoshisu looked at me, brows raised. "I'd rather not; it would be a shame if you accidentally break it."

"Don't worry, I won't break it. I might even manage to improve it."

"You're playing as a goblin, not a gremlin, remember?"

I winked at her. "I like to dabble. But seriously, how much does that sly gremlin demand for recharging this thing?"

She pursed her lips. "Seventy gold."

"I might be able to do something to circumvent that. Don't you think it's worth the chance?"

"Hmmm ... alright. Do your best."

I nodded. Holding the chain in both hands, I tapped into its rune magic. It was straightforward and simple. The gremlin used the basic connector rune 'Te' to hook all the mechanical parts and gears together instead of using an actual chain. The mechanical parts took care of the actual sawing movement. Simple, yet ingenious. The chain could hold only two more runes.

I considered my options for a moment, then added the 'Ma' rune of containment to one end of the chain and the strengthening 'Ko' rune at the other end.

Trap schema discovered: MaTeKo [Overcharge]

Runecraft skill level increased to 21.

I proceeded by funneling the required 300 mana points into the chain, finalizing the enchantment.

Enchant Self-Propelling Saw Chain [Overcharge]? Yes/No
Pattern efficiency: 100%
Mana invested: 300/300
Effect: +20.5% damage (+3), socketed

The chain started giving off a low humming sound. The description now showed a charge of 300/300.

"Here you go." I handed the chain back to Hoshisu.

She stared at it in amazement. "How did you ..."

I winked at her. "Just a little something I picked up. Now you can feed mana into the chain and charge it yourself. I even improved on the design a bit. Now it'll do 18 damage per second instead of 15."

"I guess I owe you one," she said grudgingly. "How much mana do I need to feed it?"

"Three hundred."

She winced. "It's going to take me at least an hour, I only have 85 points to spare. Still, it's much better than having to run back to that fuzzy geezer, so I guess that's two I owe you."

"Don't mention it."

"Wait a minute ..." she mouthed slowly, as if realizing something. "You spent 300 mana moments after casting a lot of spells in combat." Her eyes narrowed. "That seems a bit ... disproportionate."

Malkyr chuckled. "She's just miffed she can't see your full stats; the party icons only let us see your current health."

"Is that all?" I looked at Hoshisu, smiling. "You could have just asked."

Her nostrils flared. "Fine. What level are you? How much mana do you have?"

"Good. Glad you got that off your chest. Let's keep going, shall we?" I started moving deeper into the castle's courtyard.

I heard Hoshisu calling behind me, "You jerk!"

I laughed and kept on walking.

"You still owe me a fight once we're done here!" She jogged lightly to catch up to me.

<Man, you can be a bastard when you set your mind to it, you know?> Vic chimed in.

I learned from the best, Vic.

<You bet your meat-suit ass, you did.>

We crossed the courtyard without trouble to reach the keep's main entrance. There were no gates. We could see directly into the main hall. It was dark, but I had no trouble picking up details with my enhanced Darkvision.

The place was a mess. Debris and fallen stone were everywhere. It looked like the fort's entire interior – rooms, corridors and whole floors – had simply collapsed to rubble, coming to rest on the ground floor. The interior was now essentially a single, huge open hall. A few stairs remained loosely attached to the wall, evidence of the great structure this place once was. I didn't detect any movement, but the vastness of the place coupled with huge piles of wreckage was ideal for an enemy ambush.

"You both got low-light vision from the goblinoid template, right?" I whispered.

The twins nodded.

"Then let's go in. Be ready for anything."

"Acid-spitting killer rabbits, check," Malkyr grumbled, but moved in to take point.

We cautiously made our way forward, climbing from one rubble mound to another. We tried to keep in formation, the twins at the lead, me in the back, and Bek in the middle.

As we climbed the second mound of rubble, I saw something shimmering below. "Hey what's that?"

Malkyr squinted. "I can only see vague shapes; it's really dark down there. Why? What do you see?"

I hesitated. "It looks like a pool."

I moved a few steps down the mound, taking a better look. "It looks like a surface of water, about four meters in diameter. Its shimmering ... I see flashes of green. I can't tell if there's something in it, though." I could also feel a strong magical current emanating from the 'pool.' "I, err ... I think it's magical."

"Very astute observation, your goblin-highness," Hoshisu said. "If you're finished playing with the obviously unnatural magic pool, maybe we should continue scouting ahead?"

"Fine," I muttered and climbed back up to join them.

We continued moving further into the hall, encountering two more such 'pools' randomly spread at the base of the rubble piles. We also spotted a large pit at least 20 meters in diameter at the exact center of the hall.

"Oh look," Hoshisu said hoarsely. "The Pit of Despair." She cleared her throat loudly. "Sorry, I meant: Oh look, the Pit of Despair. Yep, not ominous at all."

I chuckled, getting the reference.

"Where are all the Ogres, that's what I want to know," her brother said.

The sound of rocks clicking together sounded from our left. We turned sharply, expecting an attack. Nothing was there.

"Great, so now we have sneaky undead Ogres." Malkyr held his axe in both hands and continued walking.

He didn't tread lightly enough. As he neared the pit, he slipped, sending rocks rolling down the pile. We froze, holding our breath as the stones rolled and bounced, raising a ruckus that sounded like an avalanche in the deserted, quiet hall. The stones continued to roll noisily all the way down into the pit.

<Looks like our meat shield is even less sneaky than undead Ogres. Ha!> Vic said.

"You big idiot," Hoshisu hissed at her brother.

He opened his mouth to retort, but a rattling sound came from below. As we looked, something *slithered* out of the pit. At first, it looked like an orange snake with green stripes. But then I noticed its semi-humanoid head and two slender arms protruding from where its neck should have been. The monster was at least five meters long. Though it was a few meters below us, I could smell the scent of sulfur and death coming from it.

Streams of information came from the monster, feeding me with knowledge; it was a lot to take in all at once. Other streams were coming off it, burrowing down into the earth like anchors. Almost as if binding the creature to this place. Like it wasn't from here. Like it was from ...

"A demon!" I yelled in realization.

What the hell is going here? I thought as I started channeling my mana. *First, possessed zombies and now a free-roaming demon?*

According to the lore of NEO, demons were beings from the lower planes of existence and could only manifest in this realm if they were summoned by someone from our side. It was common to encounter them as wizards' familiars but never as free-roaming creatures. An unbound demon in this realm could rampage, causing tremendous devastation. A year ago, there was a worldwide event where several guilds banded together to stop such a demon invasion. But here and now, we didn't have the strength of guilds behind us. We were alone. I could only hope we wouldn't encounter any of the higher-ranked demons, though judging by my vision, we weren't going to be so lucky.

The creature moved before any of us could react. It opened its mouth, much wider than any human could, its two slender arms spread wide at its sides. A blazing bead of fire formed in its mouth and it lurched forward, spitting the bead at us. A fireball.

The bead sped through the air as quick as an arrow in flight and detonated. A blast of fire enveloped us all, scorching armor and singing flesh.

Fireball hit you for 62 damage.

The heat was searing, but I could endure it. The twins gave off surprised gasps but didn't seem the worse for wear. Poor Bek, however, whimpered in pain as the blast took nearly 90 percent of his health.

"Do we engage?" Malkyr asked, lifting his axe.

I was still processing the knowledge I had received earlier, so I analyzed the creature, reading its stats.

Pyrolith, Greater [Demon]

Level: 32

HP: 210, *MP:* 270

Attributes: P: 10; M: 22; S: 0

Skills: Fireball 42*, Firegaze 39*, Fire Aura 42

Traits: Demon (summoned), Serpent (constrict, climb), Regeneration (fire: 10)

Resistances: Magic 40%, Fire 100%, Cold -50%, Holy -50%, Armor 54

Description: The Pyrolith are Hell's combat acolytes and excel at wielding fire-based magic.

"It's level 32, but it's only a mob. We can take it," I said. "Bek, step away from the fight and heal yourself, you guys –"

The Pyrolith raised its head and bellowed a hissing roar. "HAAAASSSSSHSHHHHSHSAAA!"

From all around us erupted sounds of hissings and screaming, answering back. The noise of clicking and slithering bodies soon followed.

We all took a few steps back from the still-hissing monster. Smaller Pyrolith and other hellish creatures appeared on top of mounds all around us. There were at least 20 of them and it sounded like more were on their way.

Malkyr flinched at the overwhelming odds. "Ohhh ..."

"... Shit," Hoshisu finished.

The assorted monsters around us opened their maws and raised their limbs. Beads of fire and other forms of fire came to life. They all released at once, sending a hail of flame and destruction upon us.

***

Bek looked up and down, patting down his chest and head as if having a hard time believing he was still alive. The twins looked at each other in amazement, then at the dark shimmering field of energy that surrounded us.

In a desperate move to keep everyone alive, I activated Mana Shield, expanding it to surround our entire party. It significantly increased the mana consumption rate, but it worked. The hail of fireballs, firedarts, and flamewaves were repelled by my shield, rapidly draining my mana pool. I clenched my teeth as the hits kept coming, pouring mana into the shield as fast as I could, struggling to keep it active. My mana pool was already down to 20 percent. At this size, keeping the shield active was extremely taxing. In a few moments, I would run out and the shield would collapse. Luckily, the bombardment had raised a mass of smoke and dust, obscuring us from the monsters.

Straining to maintain the shield, I said, "The shield is about to collapse. When I say 'go,' run as fast as you can out to the hall."

"But ..." Malkyr started to protest.

"No buts," I growled. "Go!"

I disengaged the shield, stumbling from the exertion, breathing heavily. I watched the others scramble over the rubble piles, making for the exit. They would never get out in time. I had to provide a distraction. I had only 75 mana left, ten percent of my max. I needed more. I had no more mana potions, but I did have alternatives. Reaching into my inventory, I pulled out a level 13 void crystal. Holding it in the palm of my hand, I concentrated briefly, drawing its energy. The void crystal disintegrated into a puff of black dust as I absorbed its power, fueling me with 130 MP.

The others made it past the cloud of smoke and dust. I could hear them running and slipping as they dodged spells, explosions following the echoes of their footsteps. I had to hurry.

I cast the Shadow Hound spell. There were plenty of shadows around to work with.

"Sorry buddy," I told Vic. "I'm afraid it's decoy time again for you."

Vic slipped off my shoulders. "I figured we'd get to this eventually."

To my surprise, he jumped on the back of one of the mastiffs, his own nearly weightless body easily finding a perch on the creature's back. "Besides," he said with a grin, "I've been wanting to do this for a while. Hi-Ho Blacky, away!"

The dust around me begun to dissipate. Three mastiffs, one carrying a purple goblin, sped away from me, each in a different direction.

"Hey you fiery puppets, try and get me," Vic cackled maniacally.

My plan was working. The demons were concentrating on my summoned minions, aiming their spells at them. I ordered the mastiffs to run as fast as they could. Having four paws helped them move easily over the uneven ground. They continued forward, fiery explosions hitting the ground all around them.

The others were almost all the way through, though I could see they had taken some hits. One of my mastiffs was hit by two crossing firebolts, fell and dissipated. His insubstantial body offered little protection against spells.

The cloud of dust had fully dispersed. I was suddenly detected by dozens of eyes.

Time to leave, I realized.

Still, I lingered. I wanted to draw as many of the creatures' spells toward me as I could. I stood waiting until the very last moment when the air was full of flying spells. Just before the first fireball hit, I used Shadow Teleport, appearing halfway toward the exit. I activated Mana Infusion and sprinted on, reaching the exit just as the others did. Together, we burst out into the courtyard and kept running, increasing the distance between ourselves and what was sure to be our fiery tomb.

Your companion Vic has died

We stopped running moments later once we realized we were not being pursued

"Damn ... that was ..." Malkyr panted, "... close!"

"It's clear there are no longer any Ogres here." Hoshisu had a much easier time speaking than her brother. "It looks like they suffered a mild case of demon invasion and were all killed. I'd say our reason for being here just evaporated."

I shook my head. "No, there must be more to it. What I saw in my vi–"

The woman cocked an eyebrow. "Yes? What you saw where?"

"I was shown certain evidence." I chose my words carefully; nothing passed by that one. "A boss is down there, guarding an altar. Even if no Ogres remain here, I still need to get to that altar."

"And just *how* do you suggest we make it down there?" she inquired, her eyes scrutinizing me.

"I noticed some things when we were inside. The first mob that appeared was some sort of a guardian. He summoned all the other demons from the pools we encountered. They were all much lower-level than him."

She rolled her eyes. "Duh, that was pretty obvious. So what?"

"Now that I know what they are, I think I can manipulate the pools." It looked fairly simple. The Pyrolith's roar was imbued with mana that resonated with the magic of the pools. "It shouldn't be too hard to draw them out."

"Err, not trying to kill the mood here or anything," Malkyr butted in, "but don't we want to *avoid* doing just that?"

I shook my head again. "No. We can handle the big guy, but not while he has all those little helpers supporting him. If we can sneak in and clear each pool one at a time ..."

Malkyr grinned broadly. "Divide and conquer, I like that!"

"Yeah, but only if you can actually activate the pools while *not* unleashing the entire horde at us," Hoshisu remarked coldly.

"Don't worry." I winked at her brother. "I'm the magic guy, remember?"

Malkyr bellowed a laugh.

We rested for about ten minutes until my mana was fully replenished. Deciding there was little point in hiding it from the twins, I summoned Vic. It had been a long time since I last had to form his body. My mana and health were much higher now, and I could make him twice as strong as before. But I hesitated. The process involved draining me of health and mana, which made me vulnerable. I didn't exactly think our lithe assassin would take advantage of my momentarily weakened state, but her desire to fight me left me guarded. As a result, I invested only 100 health and 200 mana to summon Vic back from the dead.

Hoshisu stared and Malkyr gasped at the red and blue tendrils of blood and mana coming out of my body, feeding into a hovering, amorphous blob. Once I cut the flow, the purple blob fell to the ground, then shifted into my familiar goblin companion.

"Hey, meat suits! Missed me?" he asked jubilantly.

"Vic!" I chastised him.

"Sorry, sorry, my bad!" He raised both hands apologetically, then turned and bowed to the bewildered Bek. "And one *puppet.*"

"Just ignore him," I told the others. "He can be insufferable, occasionally."

"Excuse me!" Vic demanded, hands on his hips.

"Sorry, sorry, my bad!" I raised my hand apologetically. "I meant *always.*"

Vic actually laughed out loud. <*Good one, Boss!*>

I winked at him.

<*By the way, here's a couple of messages that came up during that crazy fire drill.*>

Shadow Hound skill level increased to 19.

Shadow Teleport skill level increased to 7.

...

Shadow Teleport skill level increased to 10.

It looked like using a single Shadow Teleport spell to dodge a couple dozen spells at once contributed significantly to its progress. I didn't mind at all. I was one skill level away from reaching its Apprentice rank and was curious to see what new ability that would unlock.

We walked back to the fort's main entrance and peeked inside apprehensively. Flames engulfed the rubble and Pyroliths crawled over them.

We quietly tiptoed backward.

"So now what?" Malkyr asked gloomily. "I'm all for bravely charging into battle, but we'll be slaughtered if we go in now."

"Cooked, more like it," Hoshisu said.

I massaged my neck. "Except for the first big demon, all the other ones were summoned from those pools. It stands to reason the summon duration will expire eventually. So for now, we wait."

"Great." Malkyr sat down grumpily, placing the axe in his lap.

I looked at his axe for a long moment before realizing where my thoughts were taking me. Malkyr's axe, a gift from me, was easily the best weapon I'd encountered so far. But it was a non-magical item. The power it displayed when we fought the oxsaurian came from Malkyr's own skills.

"You've been ogling my axe for a whole minute now," the big man said. "You two want to be left alone or something?"

"Actually ..." I looked up at him. "Yes."

He stared at me, incredulous.

"So I can enchant it. That would come in handy for our next fight, don't you think?"

His wide grin was his only answer. He handed me the Greataxe and stood up. "Well, since we're waiting anyway, might as well go out for some lunch. Coming, sis?"

Hoshisu nodded, stood as well, and the two of them logged out, vanishing into thin air.

I brought up the Greataxe's details.

High-Quality Greataxe

Description: Greataxe meant to be wielded by both hands, of excellent craftsmanship.

Runecraft Viability: 5 runes

Type: Weapon, two-handed.

Rank: Standard

Durability: 47/80 *Damage:* 15-28

Base Price: 80

"Malkyr hasn't been treating you properly?" I asked sympathetically, seeing the weapon's decreased durability. I put my hand on the axe's pommel and brought up the Runecraft Design Mode. A transparent replica of the weapon hovered in the middle of the screen.

"Can take up to five runes. That's good," I murmured to myself.

Now, what should I enchant it with? I wondered. Adding the MaKoTe schema to it was the obvious answer. Done properly, the enchantment would significantly increase the weapon's durability. But that was boring and not really powerful. Due to the lack of available shops until now, Malkyr had been using this axe since level 1. He deserved a weapon to match his power. That said, MaKoTe involved using two of the most common runes; Te, the connector rune, was a basic component of almost every Runecrafting design, and Ko, the strengthening rune, was imperative to bring up the full potential of any enchantment. So those two would have to go in. But what should I add on top of that and in what fashion?

The left side of the design mode displayed a list of all my known runes. My eyes lingered on my latest acquisition, the Og rune of binding – the same one Nihilator carved into my chest. It was time to test it out.

Concentrating on what I wanted to accomplish, the rune grafted itself on the axe's holographic projection. It looked different than my own rune. Like a fractured window, spiraling lines snaked from its center. I frowned. It almost looked like the rune was grasping at its surroundings.

Then it clicked.

"It's a binding rune!" I exclaimed. "It binds into stuff." It was basically the rune equivalent of glue.

"Well, duh," Vic said. "And eh ... what are you talking about, Boss?"

Ignoring him, I continued my train of thought. Back when I initially tried to use the connecter rune I found that it could not directly connect to every part of a weapon. It was mostly used to connect different runes together, but if I could just place the Og rune wherever I wanted ...

I decided to test my theory. I placed the Og at the axe's blade. The rune immediately extended out over the entire blade surface. I felt jubilation rising within me. I was on the right track.

I proceeded by drawing the strengthening rune, then connected the two with Te.

Item schema discovered: OgTeKo [Enhanced Aspect]

Glancing to the left of my display, I could see the summary of the enchantment effect. It was a neat little function I'd received upon reaching the Apprentice rank of Runecraft. I could see that using the three runes schema would improve the weapon's base damage by 20 percent – nice!

I had enough room left for two more runes. But what should I use? A little addition of elemental damage was the obvious choice. I had two such runes available; Esh, the rune of fire, and Ra, the rune of sound. Burning weapons were a dime a dozen. All the cool kids were running around fighting monsters with flaming swords. I detested this option. Besides, we were going to fight demons, beings that were famous for their affinity with fire. The rune of sound was a good option. Weapons with sonic damage were rare, and most creatures were not resistant to it. It would be a good choice for the fights ahead of us.

So ... I furrowed my brow, trying to keep everything straight in my mind. I had to bind the blade, add sonic damage, strengthen it, and add a socket that would allow to charge up the overall effects. Then I also had to connect everything – including the durability points – with a connector rune. Five runes in total, exactly the allowed amount on the axe.

I glanced at the predicted effects. They showed an overall increase of nearly 30 percent to the axe base damage and durability and additional sonic damage that raised the total extra damage to 50 percent. Still, I hesitated before finalizing the enchantment. Despite the significant bonus to damage, it was still too ... mundane. I wanted to make something *really* impressive.

An idea came to me. We were going to battle flame throwing demons. They were impervious to fire, but what if ... I quickly sketched out a new schema then scowled. I needed one more rune to implement my idea, but that was more than the axe could hold.

Then I had an epiphany.

"Malkyr's gauntlet!" I whispered and frantically went to work.

I started by adding the connecter rune on the pommel and snaked it around, intercepting the nearby durability points. Then I added the containment rune. This was an unorthodox approach. Usually, the 'Ma' rune had to be placed first to create a socket for an external source; using it in this fashion created a capacitor for energy that was unreachable externally. I proceeded by adding the fire rune, but I drew it *backward*. My innate grasp for the craft told me it would work. Instead of adding fire to the enchantment, it would subtract it. Then I added Ra, the rune of sound, on the base of the blade.

I worked efficiently, drawing more and more runic lines across the weapon and connecting them all with Te. My increased immersion in the game allowed me to perceive on an almost instinctual level what I needed to do. This was how a true goblin Runecrafter would work. I extended Te from the Ra rune, carefully connecting all the durability points on the blade itself. There were many. I finished by placing the Og rune on the blade.

Unique Weapon schema discovered: OgMasherTeg [Fire Song]

Runecraft skill level increased to 22.

The weird rune combination took! The weapon schema was titled differently than the actual runes composing it, but whatever the reason was, it didn't seem to affect the end result.

Now all I had to do was to power up the enchantment to finalize it. Five runes meant 500 mana – 450 actually, as my skill rank lessened the mana requirement. I channeled the required amount into the weapon.

Runecraft skill level increased to 23.

The Mute Singer, Greataxe [Runecrafted]

Description: The weapon's base attributes were magically enhanced by a goblin Totem. This item is part of 'The Roaring Inferno' set. Its true power will manifest only when joined with its counterpart.

Type: Weapon, two-handed.

Rank: Unique, set

Durability: 55/96

Damage: 18-33 slashing + 5 Sonic

Base Price: 1,200

It was a decent enchantment for any given weapon. It improved the overall damage output by about 40 percent and increased – though not repaired – its durability. It was a bit lower than my initial design, but that was only the first part of my plan. I couldn't wait for Malkyr to return to implement the second part.

It was nearly morning again. I'd lost track of time while I enchanted through most of the night. Bek was sound asleep and snoring loudly. Vic was sitting atop a large piece of debris, looking bored.

He looked at me when I stood to stretch my limbs. "All good, Boss? You've been away for several hours."

"Yeah, I just had an inspiration about how to properly craft Malkyr's axe. You see –"

<Greetings, my lord.>

"What the crap?" Vic and I cried in unison. Aside from us, there was no one in sight.

<*Begging your forgiveness, my lord. It is I, Kaedric, your steward.*>

Kaedric? I sent my thought. *How are you contacting me?*

<*I have recently attained the Apprentice rank for both my Administrator and Telepathy professions, my lord. The two synergized in a way that allows me to contact you, my superior, across any distance. Thus, I have reached out to you, to offer my service, in what limited capacity I may.*>

I gave a short laugh. *Damn, Kaedric, you nearly gave me a heart attack. Vic almost soiled himself.*

<*Did not!*> Vic said indignantly.

So how are things in the settlement? I inquired.

<*The work progress is satisfactory, my lord. The gremlin marketplace is halfway completed. Thanks to Zuban's direct oversight, Wolrig, the new constructor, is improving rapidly. The cabins' construction under his care is also nearing completion. The soldiers have finished laying roads per your design, and there were no further sightings of enemies.*>

That's good news. What about Rhynorn? Does he give you any trouble?

<*No, my lord. It seems your chastisement has resonated with him and he conforms to regulations.*>

Great. Well, if that's all, I should really get some sleep ...

<*There is another matter you should be made aware of, my lord.*>

I had a bad feeling about what he was going to say next.

<*We have new visitors.*>

12 – Inner Demons

I woke up late in the morning, the sun shining brightly overhead.

I'd only slept for a few hours, and my tired eyes opened slowly. I'd been awake most of the night speaking with Kaedric. Apparently, new players had started to appear in Goblin's Gorge. So far, they were playing nice. I instructed Kaedric to keep an eye on them and give them quests that would further our clan's needs.

Despite my sleepless night, I perked up immediately when I saw Malkyr standing over me.

"Malkyr!" I exclaimed. "Give me your gauntlets!"

The big man backed away. "Eh? Why? What for?"

I ignored his protests. "Never mind that. I need them. Give!"

Grumbling, he removed the masterwork steel gauntlets that he had crafted on his own. They were of excellent workmanship and able to hold up to six runes.

I set to work immediately and opened the design mode. My grin broadened as I saw the information displayed. My improved skill level kicked in, increasing the maximum allowed runes by 16.5 percent. It was just enough to allow for seven runes to be grafted onto the item instead of six, or three and a half runes for each gauntlet. Perfect.

Working on the first gauntlet, I started by placing the socket rune on the palm. I then added a connector rune that stretched toward the fingers where I put a binding rune. I watched as the runes interacted, spreading to cover the fingers. If my plan worked, this design should transfer energy from the socket, through the fingers, and into the axe.

I then repeated the exact same process on the second gauntlet. Once both gauntlets were done, I put them side by side and drew a single strengthening rune on both of them, so when they were apart each gauntlet had half a rune.

Weapon schema discovered: MegaTok [Enhanced Channeler]

This time the crafting didn't take me nearly as long as before. I already knew exactly what I wanted to achieve, and I didn't have to go through the tedious work required when increasing an item's durability. As before, the schema name differed from the actual rune sequence, but it didn't seem to cause any issues.

I powered up both gauntlets, infusing them with 630 MP, finalizing the enchantment.

Runecraft skill level increased to 24.

I rubbed my hands together. This day was simply full of progress.

High-Quality Steel Gauntlets of Channeling [Runecrafted]

Description: Made by a Master Smith and enchanted by a goblin Totem, these gauntlets allow the wearer to intercept energy-based attacks and channel them outward. A proper grounding, depending on the type of element, must be used to safely discard the harmful energy. This item is part of 'The Roaring Inferno' set; its true power will manifest only when joined with its counterpart.

Type: Armor [hands]

Rank: Unique, set

Durability: 50/50

Armor: 10

Effect: +20% resistance to disarm, channel energy-based attacks

Base Price: 2,500

Malkyr picked up the Greataxe and examined it closely. "Oh man, that's beautiful. How did you manage to give it sonic damage? Heck, you even increased the base damage. Wow – *and* the max durability? That's really something! Weird name though. Why Fire Song?"

It was obvious his ability to read the item description was limited; otherwise, he would have mentioned the item being part of a set.

"That old thing? It's nothing. Here, try this on." I threw him the gauntlets.

He looked at them, frowning slightly as he no doubt tried to understand what 'channel energy' meant, then shrugged and put them on.

"Now grab the axe with both hands," I instructed.

He did as I asked. As soon as his hands touched the weapon's handle, the change was evident. The axe came to life.

Red glyphs spread over the weapon like channels of magma while also extending down, covering the gauntlets themselves. The axe's head began thrumming softly, shining with a sinister red glow.

Malkyr's face was a wonder to behold. A mixture of awe and admiration shone in his eyes as he lovingly gazed at his brand-new toy.

Even Hoshisu looked impressed. I hadn't noticed she was there until just then.

I let them admire the weapon while I secretly pulled out my Fire Rod. I loaded it with one of my lowest grade void crystals, a level 5 one. "Hey, Malkyr, hold out your hand please."

It seemed I had proven myself in the 'weird requests' department. Malkyr didn't even ask why this time and simply complied.

With a fluid motion, I brought up the Fire Rod, lined the shot, and fired. The rod's durability dropped by five points as a jet of orange flames erupted from its end toward the surprised man. He yelped in alarm but couldn't dodge in time. The flames reached his outstretched hand and were simply *sucked* into his gauntleted palm, leaving behind a very perplexed, yet unharmed, Malkyr staring gaping at his own hand.

The axe showed an immediate reaction. The dark red glyphs lit up in dim orange and the volume of its humming increased. The fire energy was channeled from the gauntlet and into the axe. The axe transferred the energy using the connecter rune, storing it inside the internal socket, powering up the enchantment.

"Holy hell." Malkyr looked at me, wild-eyed. "What did you just do?"

I grinned. "Now grasp the hilt with *both* hands."

He did as I asked. His free hand clasped the hilt, bringing together the two halves of the strengthening rune. The orange light burned brighter. The big man stood, his upper arms and weapon covered in glowing runes, making him an impressive sight.

"Let me see these again."

He held out his axe toward me, letting go of one hand and causing the glow to dim slightly. I analyzed both items.

The Roaring Inferno, Gauntlets [Set 2/2] [Runecrafted]

Description: Made by a Master Smith and enchanted by a goblin Totem, these gauntlets allow the wearer to intercept fire-based attacks and divert them into the Greataxe, fueling it and increasing its destructive power. The wielder may wield the weapon with one hand while the other is used to absorb incoming fire attacks. If both gauntlets are used to hold the axe, the channeled power and its effect increases by 50%.

Type: Armor [hands]

Rank: Unique, set

Durability: 50/50

Armor: 10

Base Price: 22,000 [Set]

Effect: +20% resistance to disarm, channel, and empower fire-based attacks

The Roaring Inferno, Greataxe [Set 2/2] [Runecrafted]

Description: Enchanted by a goblin Totem. The weapon's base attributes are enhanced by magic. Joined by the gauntlet, this weapon feeds off fire and converts it into sonic energy, with 22% of the energy held added to the axe's base damage. The axe's durability will also be increased as long as the energy is held. Maximum energy capacity: 200. Using the weapon spends all the energy at once.

Currently held energy: 50

Type: Weapon, two handed.

Rank: Unique, set

Durability: 66/107 [+11]

Damage: 18-33 slashing + 16 Sonic [+11]

Base Price: 22,000 [Set]

That axe and gauntlets – a 12-rune combination enchantment set – were no small achievement. The 22 percent effect was due to my skill level at Runecraft. It was the most advanced piece of enchantment I had made so far and I was still a relative novice. The potential of Runecrafting was truly amazing.

"That ..." Malkyr almost whispered, "... that is incredible, man."

I nodded. "Should come in handy when fighting demons. You can absorb their fire attacks, avoid taking damage, and charge up the axe. As far as I know, demons are not immune to sonic energy. The main drawback is that you need to be aware of their incoming attacks and actively intercept them.

"Impressive," Hoshisu admitted grudgingly. "That axe and gauntlet could easily sell for twenty thousand gold."

I smirked, "Thirty thousand would be closer. There are a lot of travelers who would be happy to use it against fire-based monsters. I bet it would be popular among dragon slayers."

Her eyes filled with suspicion. "*Travelers*? You mean players?"

<Red alert, Boss! Think of something clever, quick!>

"Erm ... I'm, that is ..." I stuttered.

<More clever!>

I steadied myself. "I meant players, of course. I've been mostly around NPCs lately, so I picked up on some of their speech patterns."

She was silent for a moment then finally said, "I bet you did." She threw a glance at her brother. He was still staring adoringly at his new weapon. Hoshisu's voice lost some of its edge. "I don't suppose you can make something similar with these?" She held up her two daggers.

They were both of average quality. Each could hold only two runes.

I shook my head. "I'm sorry, they're not high-quality enough to hold a strong enhancement. At best, I could increase their durability, but it would take time that would barely justify the result.

She grimaced and threw an accusatory glance at her brother. "Trust Malkyr to hoard all the good stuff and only craft a couple of lousy kitchen knives for his poor sister."

"Hey!" That remark drew her brother's attention away from his new toys. "I did make you that bando–" He stopped abruptly as his sister shot him a withering look. "I .. I mean ..." he stammered, "I can try to make you something better."

She was hiding something, that was obvious. But I didn't really care what sort of exotic trinket she was trying to keep a secret.

"I took a look inside the fort while you two were playing around." She was obviously trying to change the subject. "Looks like the demons all cleared off. We can go in now."

***

"That looks like a good place for a test run," Hoshisu indicated ten minutes later, pointing at a pool of shimmering black and green.

That specific pool was surrounded by high piles of rubble on all sides, with only a single path leading to it, creating a natural chokepoint, which was perfect for our purpose.

"You're up, goblin," she said.

"Me?" Bek's ears perked up.

"She's talking to me." I pushed past the others and stood at the edge of the pool.

I could feel it thrumming with energy. It wasn't mana. It was a more refined type of magic force. There were, after all, other types of magic in this world.

Holding my arm above the pool, I released some of my mana, forming a connection with the pool. I tried to emulate the way a Pyrolith made the mana fluctuate. A beam of magical force hit the pool, causing it to stop shimmering for a second before resuming its normal rhythm. Nothing happened.

I released a breath I'd instinctively held and tried again. It would be embarrassing to fail now, especially after my bragging. But again, I couldn't activate the pool.

<What's wrong, Boss? Suffering some performance anxiety?>

I shook my head. *It's not working.*

He chuckled. *<Don't worry, I hear it happens to a lot of guys. Must be hard being a meat suit sometimes.>*

"What's wrong?" Hoshisu demanded.

I grimaced. "It's a tad more complex than I thought."

"I thought you said you had it all figured out."

Malkyr came to my defense. "Give the guy a break, sis. He's doing the best he can. It's not like these things come with an instruction manual."

A manual! His words sparked an idea. I opened my inventory and retrieved a book.

"What's that?" Malkyr asked.

"A manual." I winked at him.

It was the Book of the Damned, an item that allowed its holder to contact the lower planes. The same one Barska had used to gain his powers. I'd meant to browse it before, but until now, it didn't seem that urgent. I leafed through the pages, seeing a long list of different demons, each with its unique summoning preferences, and some additional lore.

"Ah, here it is!" I exclaimed, finding a picture of a magic pool almost the exact copy of the one in front of me. "It says here each pool is attuned to a specific activation method." I frowned, trying to make sense of that information. I was sure I got the Pyrolith guardian's exact mana signature. *What else would it be 'attuned to' ...?* I mulled it over.

<Well, duh, how thick can you get? It didn't jerk its hands like you did. Think, what did it do?>

I frowned. *What did it do ...* Then it hit me. *Of course! It roared!*

"I think I know what I have to do now." I closed the book.

"Can I have a look at that?" Hoshisu asked.

I thought of refusing her, but I needed to stay in her good graces for her cooperation. I gave her the book.

She opened it randomly, staring at the page, then looked up at me, her expression blank. "There is nothing readable in here. I only receive a prompt asking if I want to activate this item's summoning power."

Damn, I should have expected that. This was another aspect of playing a hybrid race. As part monster, I was able to delve deeper into the underlying logic that governed this world. In comparison, players only got to see the highlights.

Myriad possible answers ran through my mind, but it was clear the woman was already suspicious of me, so I simply shrugged, smiled, and held out my hand.

She stared at me for a long moment before finally deciding to let the matter drop, handing the book back to me.

"Get ready," I said.

I concentrated and held the mana pattern firmly in mind, then I opened my jaws and *roared*, unleashing the power through my mouth.

A thunderous, monsterific roar erupted and a stream of cascading mana hit the pool surface, which immediately started to bubble up. It worked!

I moved back, Malkyr letting me pass him at the narrow path but then stood firmly at the pool's edge. Standing at the rear, activating my shield would be counterproductive; it severely limited my mobility and could potentially interfere with my companion's mobility.

The pool continued to bubble. A creature's head popped out, then another, and another. They came slithering out of the pool. Dozens of Pyroliths, smaller versions of the one we had met before.

Pyrolith [Demon]

Level: 15

HP: 85 , *MP:* 140

Attributes: P: 2; M: 13; S: 0

Skills: Fireball 15*

Traits: Demon (summoned), Serpent (constrict), Regeneration (fire: 5)

Resistances: Fire: 100%, Cold: -50%, Holy: -50%, armor: 18

Description: The Pyrolith are hell's combat acolytes and excel at wielding fire-based offensive magic.

Their level varied, though most were between level 13 to 15. They tried to climb over the piles of rubble, but only a handful of them found enough perch to slither up; the rest were forced to funnel toward the only exit, where we waited.

Standing firmly at the front, Malkyr held his axe with one hand, waiting for the creatures to come to him. Hoshisu was just behind him, crouching with her daggers at her sides.

Bek and I started bombarding the demons with spinning drilling arrows.

Three Pyroliths led the charge, opening their maws. Fireballs and other kinds of fire spells flew at us. Malkyr, however, was ready for them. Holding up his gauntleted hand, he intercepted the attacks and three flashes of fire were sucked into his palm. His axe flared bright orange. Clasping his axe with both hands, making the rune glow even brighter, he bellowed a war cry. Malkyr swiped his axe horizontally, hitting all three monsters. The axe easily cut through demonic flesh, cleaving two of them in half. Their remains sank into the pool.

Though it was critically wounded, the third Pyrolith survived the hit and was coiling to pounce. Malkyr's swing left him open and vulnerable for a counterattack. Before the demon could lash out, Hoshisu shot forward. Rolling between her brother's legs, she came to her feet with her daggers leading the way and intercepted the injured monster. Her daggers flashed, doing enough damage to finally kill it. She then rolled back again as more Pyroliths prepared to launch their fiery attacks. Malkyr was already waiting for them.

I nodded in approval. Once again, the twins had shown me what an effective duo they made.

Bek and I continued to rain drilling arrows on the monsters, softening them up for Malkyr to dispatch in a single stroke. The pattern repeated itself. The dimwitted creatures couldn't seem to grasp that their own spells were being absorbed and used against them. Again and again, they were caught by Malkyr's sweeps, his sister darting forward occasionally to finish off stragglers.

"Now *this* is fun!" The big man declared, killing four injured Pyroliths with another swipe of the humming axe.

A single Pyrolith got lucky and managed to sneak a Firedart spell past Malkyr's defense. The fiery bolt hit his sister for 20 damage that Bek quickly healed.

"Had to jinx it, didn't you?" Hoshisu berated her brother.

"Sorry!" he boomed jubilantly.

Meanwhile, five Pyroliths had found a perch on the steep piles of rubble and were extracting themselves from the pool.

We couldn't allow the creatures to get the high ground. Our advantage lay in boxing them in. So far, I was content with using drilling arrows only;

it was the most mana-efficient strategy when working together with a party. Now, the situation called for something more extravagant.

I targeted the climbing Pyroliths, and since they had no magic resistance, I hit them with Freeze. With my Dark Mana skill at level 30, I could only affect two of them at once. The two Pyroliths I selected stopped moving. With a flicker of thought, my dagger soared through the air, cutting their throats, sacrificing both.

Pyrolith. +14 Faith Points (Cult of Nihilator)

Pyrolith. +15 Faith Points (Cult of Nihilator)

Unlike their greater kin, these Pyrolith didn't have magic resistance, which made them susceptible to my abilities. The situation presented a golden opportunity to farm them for some much-needed Faith Points and void crystals.

The twins, assisted by Bek, were holding their own, but the pool was swarming with even more demons. The other three Pyroliths were still climbing and would reach the top in seconds. I repeated my tactic, freezing two and sacrificing them, but the last one managed to reach the top. It opened its maw, targeting Malkyr. From that high angle, the big man would be unable to intercept the attack. Luckily, I still had options available to me. Concentrating on the creature, I poured my own mana into its mind, claiming it. The damn thing was a caster, causing me to spend a whopping 140 MP to activate the ability. Luckily Freeze and Dominate didn't stack when determining the number of creatures I could affect.

A bead of fire started to form inside the creature's maw and then it became my hand puppet.

Target the pool, I ordered. The creature obeyed and the spell meant for us was launched at the center of the pool. The fireball exploded, covering nearly the entire surface with flames. The Pyroliths contained within were immune to fire, but the force of the blast still pushed them back, staggering many of them. The twins were quick to take advantage of the chance to rain more blows on the disarrayed monsters.

We killed 20 more of them before their numbers finally started to dwindle. With over 60 percent mana remaining, I allowed myself to be a spendthrift and started freezing and sacrificing the Pyrolith at every chance.

In less than a minute, it was all over.

Altogether, we killed over 50 demons, not including the one I was still dominating. Everyone received a decent amount of XP and skill progression, but there was hardly any loot. As summoned creatures, the Pyroliths didn't drop equipment, and their bodies simply vanished once they were killed. Still, there were some mementos left behind.

Pyrolith Scale

Description: Light, tough, and naturally fire resistant, it is an ideal component for crafting armor.

Type: Component

The twins graciously let me take the five scales we found. The fight was rewarding for me in other ways as well. I had gained 150 Faith Points and ten level 15 void crystals. Not a bad haul.

"Next pool?" I asked the twins.

"Sure." They grinned at each other then followed me toward our next target.

The next pool looked different; it was dark green with patches of yellow. Only a single pile of debris lay at its side. We would not be able to bottleneck the demons as before. The energy fluctuation coming from the pool was also different. I took out the Book of the Damned and started leafing through it.

"This is going to be rough." Malkyr rubbed his neck, eyeing the pool. "No choke point here."

"We're going to have to change our tactics." I closed the book, having found the answers I was looking for. "Since there's only one pile, then ..."

"Then we take the high ground," Hoshisu completed my words.

I grinned at her. "Exactly."

Unexpectedly, she flashed me a smile. Facing overwhelming odds, fighting back to back, always tended to bring people together.

"We'll be sitting ducks up here," Malkyr objected. "They can just shoot at us from below."

I shook my head. "This pool is different. It won't be Pyroliths this time around. It's a demon called Stalker. They're like blobs of flesh with spear-like appendages. Melee type."

"Sounds creepy. I guess that means they won't be casting any fire spells. Damn." Malkyr patted his axe. "I got used to being able to juice up this baby."

I pointed at the dominated Pyrolith that was trailing us. "That's why I brought this guy with us. I'll station him on another pile and instruct him to fire a spell at you every time you raise your hand."

The big man brightened at that. "Fire on demand – I like it!"

Hoshisu rolled her eyes. "Boys and their high-powered, fire-sucking toys."

We climbed the pile. It took a few attempts as we kept sliding down before we finally made it to the top. We stared at the pool beneath us. Only one side of our pile was relatively climbable. The other sides were sheer drops, five meters high.

Malkyr moved to stand in front of the climbable side, blocking it.

"Everyone ready?" I asked.

The twins nodded and Bek piped, "Yes, Dread Totem."

As before, I concentrated on the pool below us, forming the required mana and releasing it through a thunderous roar.

The pool's water started bubbling. Everyone tensed, getting ready for the enemy to show itself.

Then the pool's surface *exploded* outward, spitting out dozens of creatures.

The book description was accurate. The creatures looked like a mass of amorphous flesh with dozens of spear-like legs protruding from all sides, like giant, fleshy pincushions. Their bodies spread and contracted, making their many 'legs' move in chaotic patterns as they crawled forward.

Stalker [Demon]

Level: 17

HP: 160, *MP:* 95

Attributes: P: 15, M: 2; S: 0

Skills: Stab 23, Death Plunge 12

Traits: Demon(summoned)

Resistances: Fire 100%, Cold -50%, Holy -50%, Armor 25, Mental 100%

Description: The reincarnation of tortured souls who have lost all sense of self. A Stalker knows no fear and operates on pure instinct, seeking to spread the pain they endure every waking moment onto others.

I shuddered as I read the description. If I hadn't managed to outsmart Barska, my tortured, broken spirit could well have been reincarnated into one of these vile demons.

Unlike the Pyroliths, these creatures had high mental resistance, meaning I could not dominate them. That made sense, as nothing about them suggested they had any kind of coherent mind to dominate. They were also higher level than the Pyroliths and had more health. We had a tough fight ahead of us.

Seconds after appearing, the Stalkers noticed us and swarmed over the pile, trying to reach us.

<Err, you guys might have bitten more than you can chew off, Boss.>

Not helping, Vic.

Without waiting for their vanguard to reach us, I unleashed the empowered drilling arrows I'd prepared in advance. Three spinning projectiles hit a Stalker, gouging deep holes in his fleshy body and doing over 100 points of damage, but the damn thing wouldn't go down. If anything, it tried to climb on some of its friends in an effort to reach us faster. I froze one creature and coup-de-grâce'd it with the dagger. Their higher level meant I could only sacrifice one creature at a time.

Stalker. +17 Faith Points (Cult of Nihilator)

Malkyr raised a gauntleted hand and my dominated Pyrolith obediently launched a fireball at it. The fireball was sucked in by the gauntlet, making Malkyr's axe glow a dim orange light. Malkyr clasped his axe with both hands and raised it above his head. The axe glow changed, and the blade almost looked like it was repelling the very air around it. The host of Stalkers continued to swarm over the pile, even climbing on top of each other, drawing thick yellow blood in their eagerness to reach us.

Four creatures reached the top. Roaring, Malkyr chopped down hard, striking the pile. A wave of force burst out, hurling the nearby Stalkers away and pushing others below us down the pile. In the chaos, the rolling demons stepped on and stabbed at each other, doing even more damage than my drilling arrows.

"Level 25 Prime skill, bitches," Malkyr shouted merrily.

"That's pretty handy. What's it called?" I asked.

"Concussive Strike."

Over 50 demons were spread below us. They staggered in their weird, wavering gait, but it was a matter of seconds before they recuperated and rushed us again.

Seeing them all piled up together was an enticing target. I cast Shadow Web on the densest part, trapping 20 of them under a web of dark tendrils. Devoid of magic resistance and lacking overwhelming strength, the demons couldn't escape. The Stalked started to writhe and thrash against the bindings, stabbing one another in the process.

The other 30 demons paid them no heed and charged on our position.

"Can you do that again?" I asked Malkyr, using Freeze and sacrificing a Stalker while sending a trio of drilling arrows that felled another.

He shook his head and raised one hand. "At my current skill level, I can only do it once every five minutes."

A fireball hit his outstretched hand, just as the Stalkers reached us. Malkyr swung his axe in a wide arc, hitting three of the creatures, his howling weapon tearing into their amorphous flesh. Hoshisu darted in, her daggers a blur, dispatching one of the attackers.

The other two retaliated, thrusting their sharp limbs at Malkyr, piercing armor and flesh, and reducing his health by 30 percent.

"Damn, they're tough bastards," Malkyr grunted. Bek's healing spell hit him, restoring his health back to 90 percent.

The Stalkers I'd trapped continued to stab at each other and several were dead already. The other 30 kept climbing, trying to find a perch on the narrow ledge to reach us.

We continued fighting. Malkyr concentrated on killing single opponents before moving to the next one, with Hoshisu occasionally darting in to deal a finishing blow or to intercept a strike intended for her brother. But for every Stalker dead, two more took its place. We were destroying them too slowly. The demons had no regard for their own lives and carelessly charged in for the chance to attack us. Their erratic assault patterns hit us repeatedly. Poor Bek was healing us as fast as he could, but his mana drained swiftly, and he had to cast Drain Mana to replenish his dwindling reserves.

Time for a reprieve, I thought and cast Shadow Hound.

Three shadow mastiffs emerged out of the darkness and charged down at the Stalkers. Their attack gained the demons' attention, reducing the pressure on us. Under my Shadow Web, over half of the trapped Stalkers lay dead and the rest looked halfway there as well.

Taking advantage of the reprieve, Malkyr took a potion from his inventory and downed it in one gulp. His eyes flared for a second, and his many bleeding wounds began to close.

Targeting the closest Stalker, I concentrated, freezing and sacrificing it, then launched a volley of Drilling Arrows at another.

Meanwhile, my mastiffs were doing the best they could. Their lower level meant they could barely damage the enemy. Still, their invulnerability to physical attacks made them an excellent distraction, and many of the mindless demons continued attacking them.

We were going to make it, I could tell. The first onslaught was the hardest to withstand, but we'd endured. Now it was only a question of time.

Just as I came to this conclusion, a heavy mass of stabbing limbs fell on top of me. I'd been jumped by one of the stabbing horrors.

Stalker hit you for 65 damage.

The thing's body was all around me, wriggling, writhing. What felt like a dozen knives stabbed at me. I cried out from the unexpected rush of pain and activated my Mana Shield by reflex. The force of energy erupted, pushing my companions and repelling the creature. Right into poor Bek. Luckily, Hoshisu noticed and recovered from my action fast enough to retaliate. With a flurry of blades, she diced and chopped the Stalker while evading its many sharp limbs, saving the goblin. She had excellent battle form.

I was relieved that my rash action didn't cost anyone's life and looked at the woman with gratitude.

"You can thank me later," Hoshisu smirked, turning back to support her brother.

Then a Stalker landed on her shoulder. All around us, Stalkers jumped impossibly high into the air. Most missed us, but two of them landed on Malkyr who was defending the path. The twins shouted in surprise as Stalkers squirmed over their bodies, turning them into human pincushions and dropping their health bars rapidly.

Before I could figure out what to do, Bek took the initiative. He pulled out a large opal and raised it above his head. A wave of scintillating darkness erupted out of the orb. It ripped through the nearby Stalkers, shredding them to pieces, and showering us with chunks of Stalker flesh. The spell eliminated six of the closest Stalkers and injured five more who were lower down the pile. Undaunted by the blast, they continued climbing toward us.

I shot drilling arrows into the most heavily injured one and sacrificed another. The other three kept climbing and were blocked by the twins. A few hard chops coupled with whirling daggers, and those three were dead as well.

With the pressure taken off, I breathed a sigh of relief, taking in our surroundings. Six live Stalkers remained in the web though they were all heavily wounded. My mastiffs were harrying four creatures and by the looks of it had managed to take down two by themselves. Now, it was truly nearly over. I methodically peppered the enemy with drilling arrows and my dagger kept on sacrificing them while Bek healed us back to full health.

Finally, the last of the Stalkers fell, and we all dropped to the ground from exhaustion.

Level up! You have reached Character Level 23. You have 1 ability point to allocate.

I put the new attribute points in Mental then tiredly waved off a myriad of other messages. I'd increased the levels of almost all my spells. Dark Mana progress was the most profound; it gained two whole levels.

"What was that?" I asked Bek after I finished dealing with the messages. "Where did you get that opal?"

Bek looked down submissively. "Me make it, Dread Totem. Me pray at shrine, me feel power of the Dark One coming, so me put it in pretty rock."

That was unexpected. Up until now, Bek used the opals we gathered from the cave as a source to store healing spells, which were usable by my troops. Being able to use the shrine's power to inscribe something more powerful never occurred to me.

"Good job, Bek, you probably saved us all." I clapped my small minion on the back.

He bowed his head at the compliment.

"Yeah, nice job, pipsqueak," Malkyr added. "I even leveled up. Ooh yeah – level 26!"

"Me too." Hoshisu gave a half smile. "The Stalkers give good XP. I even picked up a new Assassin skill, 'Flurry.' That should come in handy."

"Congratulations, that one's hard to get," I said. It was a skill that enabled a player to perform a backstab with multiple hits, each one gaining the sneak damage bonus.

We looted the Stalkers' remains. As summoned creatures, like the Pyroliths, they had greatly reduced loot drops. We collected a total of six Stalker Pins, which were listed as crafting components. Malkyr claimed those. I was content with the eight new void crystals and the additional 131 FP I gained from all the sacrifices I'd managed.

"By the way," Malkyr said. "I've been meaning to ask – how long will that Pyrolith of yours stay under your control? I'm starting to get fond of him. All those fireballs came in real handy during the fight. Without the added damage bonus, we might not have made it."

I shrugged. "It'll remain as long as we need it unless something breaks the enchantment. Keeping it controlled continuously drains mana, but I'm good for now."

"Great!" He positively beamed at me. "Let's check out the next pool."

The next pool was situated on top of a few rubble piles but turned out to be the easiest fight so far. Once activated, the pool spawned a host of imps, small and nasty flying creatures. They were all below level 10 and used their venomous stingers and fire-based magic to attack us, much to Malkyr's delight. With my Dark Mana skill at level 32, I could sacrifice three of them at a time. Malkyr charged forward, wading in their midst, whirling and hacking, bringing them down by the score, while intercepting their fiery attacks. We didn't go unscathed, but the damage was low enough that Bek had no trouble keeping us at peak health.

The imps left behind several Stingers, which Hoshisu took for herself. Some of the void crystals disappeared in the pool, but I collected eight of them and gained another 64 FP.

Only one more pool remained in the open hall of the ruined fort.

"Alright man, what's the word?" Malkyr asked eagerly as I probed the pool for information.

"It's ... empty."

"Whatcha-mean?"

"There's no power in this pool ... like it's exhausted or something."

"Maybe it just has a longer cooldown period than the other pools?" Hoshisu suggested.

I shook my head. "The ones we cleared still have power in them. It'll probably take them a day or so to reset and summon new demons. This pool is just ... empty. Like something sucked all the power out of it."

Hoshisu pursed her lips. "Something like a powerful demon boss, perhaps?"

Remembering my vision, I tried not to swallow hard. "Perhaps."

"Figures." She rolled her eyes "So next is the pit? The Greater Pyrolith Guardian is waiting."

"About that," Malkyr interjected, "I have a request."

We both looked at him questioningly.

"I want you to stand aside and let me handle this thing on my own."

I raised my brow. "Why? That thing was level 32. You're level 26; you might win, but you won't escape unharmed. Why chance it?"

He winked at me. "I have my reasons."

We reached the open pit and the rest of us stood back, letting Malkyr approach it on his own.

Gripping his axe tightly with both hands, the man moved forward carefully. As soon as he reached the edge of the pit, the same large Pyrolith slithered out. The demon's serpentine body was twice as long as Malkyr was tall. The creature opened its mouth, launching a bead of fire at Malkyr. The man was ready for it and snatched the bead with his gauntleted hand before it could explode into a fireball. Reacting to the energy absorbed, his axe glowed bright orange, emphasizing the blackened runes that covered its length.

Malkyr stepped forward, putting his weight into his swing. The buzzing weapon bit deeply into the monster's body. The demon screamed and launched a firebolt from each hand simultaneously. Moving nimbly, Malkyr intercepted both fiery bolts, channeling their power into his axe. Then, holding the weapon with both hands to increase its power, he gave an overhead chop, taking out another sizeable chunk of the demon's health, bringing him down to 60 percent.

The demon, obviously more intelligent than the lesser versions we'd fought before, stopped casting spells. Instead, its long body snapped forward, coils wrapping around the big man, holding him tightly.

Malkyr was in trouble. With both arms pinned against his body, he was barely able to move, let alone swing his axe. As we watched, the demon squeezed. Malkyr's health bar begun to plummet. I drew in my mana and started overcharging my drilling arrows. A hand on my shoulder gave me pause. Hoshisu. She didn't say anything, just shook her head.

"But he'll die!" I protested.

She shrugged as if saying, 'It's his own choice.'

Gritting my teeth, I let the spell dissipate.

Malkyr's muscles bulged as he strained against his much larger opponent, his neck veins literally popping up as he gave a savage roar. With an impressive display of physical prowess, he managed to release both arms from the pin. His axe, however, was still trapped within the embracing coils, out of his reach. The demon opened its jaws wide enough to swallow Malkyr's head and snapped forward. Malkyr's arms flew up, catching a jaw in each hand. They fought against each other, brute strength versus brute strength, and for a long moment, neither one managed to gain the upper hand. Then Malkyr gave a boyish grin. Both his arms began glowing, similar to his axe's special attack. The glow seemed to repel the air around them. With an explosive force, he spread his arms wide, tearing the demon's head in half.

The coils loosened and slumped to the floor, leaving Malkyr standing bruised, but alive. He'd won. The axe on the ground suddenly gleamed and hovered in the air in front of him. Malkyr grabbed the hilt and an overwhelmingly powerful orange light exploded out of it, illuminating the entirety of the dark hall.

"What was that?" I demanded.

"Oh, that?" He waved a hand dismissively. "I just completed a unique quest."

I exchanged a glance with Hoshisu. "Eh?"

He shrugged. "It's simple, man. When I grabbed the enchanted axe for the first time, I received a quest called 'One with the Roaring Inferno.' To complete it, I had to single-handedly defeat a strong, fire-based opponent within six hours. According to the quest, if I managed that, the axe would bond with me. It's now a soulbound item. It can hold more charges than before, and it even grants me a kickass new ability."

"Axe so nice!" Bek said, of all people.

Malkyr looked with surprise at the tiny goblin, then grinned and nodded. "Yep, it sure is."

I looked around, not seeing any other demons coming. "Looks like our plan worked. Shall we go down the pit?"

"Oh, about that ..." Malkyr answered slowly. "I happened to look down there during the fight and ... well ..."

"Spit it out already," Hoshisu said.

"It's just ... you wouldn't believe how deep it goes."

"Damn!" I muttered. *Just what I need, another complication.*

We approached the pit and looked down. It led to a seemingly undamaged subfloor only about four meters down.

Malkyr chuckled. "Told you you wouldn't believe how deep it goes."

<He's starting to grow on me,> my cloaked companion sighed in my mind. *<Oh in Dad's name, I'm becoming chummy with meat suits. Oh, the shame ... if my brothers knew ...>*

"Let's go." Hoshisu walked over to the pit edge and jumped inside. She landed lightly on her feet and looked around. "All clear."

I held Bek back, handing him Guba's special brew potions. "Here, drink these."

If the first level was any indication, we were going to be facing tough battles. Little Bek was invaluable, thanks to his healing spell, but he was the most vulnerable of us. Guba's potions would increase maximum HP by ten. For me, it was a drop in the bucket, but for him, it would be an increase of nearly 20 percent.

After the goblin chugged the two potions, I teleported down, coming out of the shadows next to Hoshisu. Since neither Bek nor Malkyr were especially light on their feet, I assembled shadows into a thick pillow-like substance to cushion their jump. "Come on, I've got you."

Once we were all safely down, I took a better look around. We were standing in the middle of a long and wide corridor with the ceiling three meters above us and many doors along both sides. The lower levels of the fort had fared much better than the upper ones.

Everyone stood still, studying their surroundings. In the quiet darkness, faint, distant sounds reached us.

I recognized the sounds instantly. I had a lot of firsthand experience making such noises. They were the shrieks and howls of someone being tortured.

13 – Racial Tensions

I sacrificed the Pyrolith I had been dominating, adding its void crystal to my growing collection.

We had decided not to bring the demon along. Having it turn against us at the wrong moment was not worth the risk. Instead, I cast Shadow Hound. Our previous skirmishes had been great training. At level 20, the spell was now significantly more powerful, allowing me to summon four minions instead of three, all at level 12. On the other hand, it now cost 200 mana, almost 20 percent of my total. It was a whopping amount for a combat spell.

The mastiffs emerged from the shadows and obediently followed at my heels.

We started walking down the corridor cautiously, the siblings leading the way.

The howling and shrieking grew louder. Soon, we found ourselves standing in front of a studded metal door. The noises were coming from the other side.

Hoshisu examined the door for traps then gave us the thumbs up.

"Ready?" Malkyr said softly, his hand on the handle.

I raised one finger, then activated my Mana Shield. There was plenty of room in the hallway so I didn't risk hindering anyone with the wide bubble. I proceeded by conjuring a trio of drilling arrows and empowering them. Once they were at the max, I nodded to the man.

Malkyr opened the door and took a few cautious steps inside. It looked like an old, large kitchen. A rotten dining table stood in the corner and several smashed tables littered the floor.

Everything looked pretty much like what could be expected of an abandoned kitchen. Everything, except a small, childlike creature sitting with its back to us. The shrieking and howling were coming from him. Sprawled around the creature were the slumped bodies of three *seemingly* dead Ogres.

"Okay," Malkyr whispered. "So we all know it's a trap; that's not a child but some gruesome monster and the dead Ogres are zombies. I say we skip the part where we cautiously investigate and get jumped on, and instead pre-empt the shit out of them."

I tried to use Analyze on the perching figure, but to my surprise, discovered that I could not. It was the first time my skill had failed to activate. Nor could I detect any information threads emanating from it. It was like the creature wasn't even there, just some faint threads of localized noise. Yep, definitely a trap.

"Agreed," I whispered back. "So we attack in three ... two ... one – now!"

I launched my arrows at the perching figure while Bek targeted it with Mana Drain. Hoshisu threw daggers and Malkyr struck his orange-glowing axe at the closest of the fallen Ogres, splitting its head neatly in half.

As our combined attacks hit the shrieking figure, it dissipated into puffs of mist, finally ending the howls. The mist drifted over to the three bodies and seeped into them.

<*Hey, that's my thing!*> Vic said.

The three zombies began to rise. I could sense the information streams from them now, indicating they were possessed.

The zombie Malkyr had hit, its health bar now down by a quarter, didn't look bothered by its grotesquely split head. I directed my mastiffs to attack it, then launched drilling arrows at the one facing Malkyr. Hoshisu threw her gremlin-made saw chain at the third. The chain buzzed and rotated as it sliced into the creature's torso.

This time, we were well-prepared for the fight. My four mastiffs tore their target apart, while Malkyr disarmed his opponent, literally. Hoshisu's zombie was sawn in half. His upper and lower torso thrashed trying to get to her. With a few extra barrages of drilling arrows and a finishing blow from my dagger, the three soon stopped moving. An easy win.

The zombies dropped some gold, three potions, and a bar of violet metal. We all exchanged contented grins at the leftover piles of loot.

Potion of Ogre Might

Description: The drinker receives the hereditary toughness of an Ogre for a short duration.

Type: Potion

Effect: +4 Physical, +50% carry capacity, +50% physical damage bonus.

Viridium Ingot

Description: A bar of metal infused with spiritual energies. Items forged from Viridium carry enchantments more easily and have increased effectiveness.

Type: Component

"Awesome! I want it all," Malkyr blurted out exuberantly.

"Take the potions and the gold," I said. "But I'd like to keep the metal."

His face fell. "But I'm a smith; working with a brand-new metal would surely raise my skill."

I wasn't about to waive my claim. I just gifted him a magic set that was worth a small treasure. Still, he had a point. "How about this?" I suggested. "I'll loan it to you. You can practice your craft by making something for me. That way, you still get to train your skill."

"And you get an item crafted for free. Smart," Hoshisu said with a faint smile.

"Yep." I smiled back at her, then looked pointedly at her brother.

"And I get to keep the gold and potions?"

I nodded. It was of little use to me anyway.

"You got yourself a deal."

He took the potions, handing one to his sister.

Before we left the room, I recharged the depleted saw chain, making it ready for another single use. I handed it back to Hoshisu, who gave me a slight nod as thanks.

We went back to the hallway and continued walking. It was now thankfully silent.

Hoshisu suddenly held up one hand, and we all stopped in our tracks.

She advanced a few steps, moving lightly, then bent down. She brushed something invisible off the floor and pressed down with her hand. An audible *click* sounded and a single dart flashed from the wall on our left, barely an inch above the floor.

"Dart trap. Very crude, not even poisonous." She wrinkled her nose. "Let's go."

After a short walk, we reached another door. This one was made entirely of dark, reinforced steel. Hoshisu checked it for traps, and finding none, opened the door. This was a workshop of some kind. As in the previous room, most of the equipment was damaged beyond recognition. But a quick search of the room yielded a few nice surprises.

Fishing Kit

Description: Hooks, lines, and lures; everything an aspiring fisherman could hope for!

Type: Tool

Rank: Average

Cool! I thought happily. *That should help increase my fishermen's yield.* The second one I had summoned was still using an improvised piece of equipment crafted by the clan's smith.

"Hey, what's this?" Malkyr nudged a heavy piece of metal. "Looks broken."

I looked at the item. It used to be a heavy plow. Malkyr was right, it was broken. What a strange thing to find at the lower level of an Ogre's base.

"It's just part of the scenery, gives this place a bit more authenticity," Hoshisu said. "You can't really do anything with –"

She paused mid-sentence, staring at me.

"What?" I looked back at her. The plow turned easily on its axis as I lifted the handle to check if it was still in one piece.

"You're not supposed to be able to do that." Her eyes narrowed.

I shrugged. "I try not to let others dictate to me what I can or can't do." I let go of the plow with regret. There was no way I could bring it with me. The piece of equipment weighed a hundred kilograms at least. Pity, it could have been just what my farmers needed to be able to work the land.

We continued scouting the rooms along the corridor, but all were deserted with no signs of demons or zombies.

At the hallway's end, a large two-door gate barred our entrance. Two Ogres could have easily walked side by side through it.

"I'll take a look," Hoshisu whispered, already moving toward the doors.

We stood back, watching her as she tiptoed forward and silently opened a crack in one of the massive gates. We held our breath as she peeked in, taking in the view for a long moment before edging back over to us.

"There's a large chamber over there," she informed us, still whispering. "There are five Ogre zombies standing about ten meters beyond the door and they have two Pyroliths with them – the big kind, like the one that guarded the pit. There might be more; it's pretty dark so I couldn't see very well."

Malkyr brightened up. "Five lumbering kindling and two walking fuel sources? Awesome!"

Vic sighed inside my head. *<That guy should really get his sense of self-preservation checked.>*

Malkyr took a step toward the door but I stopped him, putting a hand on his shoulder, which I barely reached. "Hold on a sec. That's a few too many enemies for us to simply charge in."

Hoshisu nodded. "I agree with the little guy. Besides ..." Her eyes became distant. "There was something weird about one of the zombies. It had ... lumps ... all over its body. I'm guessing he'll throw something nasty at us if we just barge in."

"Let me take a look," I said, facing the door.

"You?" Hoshisu sneered. "You're a specialized mage, you can't sneak worth a damn. You'll give away our presence."

"Oh, am I?" I winked at her, then turned around and tiptoed toward the door, making even less noise than she did, gently bending the shadows around me to obscure my body.

Looking through the crack, I saw two level 32 Greater Pyrolith standing behind a line of Ogre zombies. They were all facing the doors, but none had noticed me. I could easily sense that four of the zombies were 'normal' ones, albeit at level 17 they were stronger than those we fought earlier. The zombie in the middle was definitely different. I analyzed it.

Mature Possessed Ogre Zombie

Level: 4

HP: 60

Attributes: P: 6, M: -, S: -

Skills: Powerful 16

Traits: Ogre, Undead, Possessed [mature]*Resistances:* Mental 100%, Magic 30%, Armor 12

Description: A Zombie feels no pain and knows no fear. This specimen has been possessed for so long its body has started breaking down.

Just as Hoshisu had said, it had lumps all over its body. With my Darkvision, I could easily see the bulges *pulsating*. It was disturbingly familiar to the Alien movies, when the unborn aliens thrashed inside their host's body, trying to burst out. Unlike those movies though, the zombie seemed oblivious to its state, standing passively between its buddies.

The chamber stretched on for a dozen more meters beyond the line of enemies. A stack of half-rotten boxes blocked most of the rest of the room, but I caught a glimpse of something metallic behind them.

I sneaked back to my party, making no noise.

Hoshisu glared at me. "How did you do that?"

I winked at her. "Goblins get the Sneak skill as a free built-in feature, just a point off Master rank."

"What?" she fumed, struggling to keep her voice down. "I've been grinding my stealth skills for days and I'm only on level 31!"

My smile grew. "I told you before, once you go goblin ..."

Malkyr looked between us. "So like, what do we do now? Charge in after all?"

I shook my head. "The strange zombie at the center looks like it's about to fall apart any moment. It only has 60 hit points. I'm betting something nastier will come out when that happens."

Hoshisu narrowed her eyes at me while her brother simply said, "Okay ... so what do we do?"

I rubbed my chin. "Barging in is not a good idea. There are too many enemies for you to tank on your own. We need to find a spot with a defensible choke point, then we can decide how to handle the rest of the fight."

"Why not just hold them at one of the doors?" Hoshisu said, still sounding a bit irritated.

"Because they're too strong. The Ogres could just burst both doors open and we wouldn't be able to hold such a wide gap."

Hoshisu smirked. "So apparently being a goblin isn't the absolute magic solution for every problem. I'll take care of it. Only one door will open, don't worry your little green head over it."

"Don't you mean 'Your *pretty* little green head?'"

"No."

<Ouch. Well, you were asking for it, Boss.>

"Alright," I conceded the point. "With only one door open, Malkyr should be able to hold them off. I'll send my hounds in to harass them from behind. Use your chainsaw on one of the Pyroliths. Even if it won't kill it, the constant damage should prevent it from using magic against us. Malkyr is going to be distracted by the melee, so it'll be easier for him to intercept whatever fire spells they'll launch if there is only one Pyrolith gunning for him."

"So I'll hold five Ogre zombies by myself?" His grin widened. "You got it, Chief!"

I couldn't tell if he was being sarcastic or not.

<Don't forget the pregnant one, Boss.>

Right.

"The zombies are susceptible to fire and I have a Fire Rod. I'm going to use it against the nasty looking zombie. Hopefully, it'll immolate it and whatever is trying to get out."

"Okay." Hoshisu nodded. "Sounds like a plan. What about him?" She pointed at Bek.

I looked at the small goblin. "You don't happen to have any more surprises like the opal you used before?"

"No Dread Totem," he squeaked. "Only pretty stones that heal."

Well, I had to ask. "Okay, concentrate on healing Malkyr, and throw in some drilling arrows if you get the chance."

"Yes, Dread Totem."

"I'll take care of the door." Hoshisu retrieved something from her inventory and crept forward.

As she worked, putting something along the left door's seams, I loaded my Fire Rod with a level 20 void crystal. As the rod absorbed the crystal's energy, it began to hum softly and its carved runes glowed dimly.

Hoshisu finished and gave us the 'all clear' sign.

Hoisting his Greataxe, Malkyr moved forward, his steps sounding like anvil strikes in the silent hallway.

I could hear movement coming from the other side of the doors. The guards were alerted to our presence. I hurried forward holding the Fire Rod, staying close to the big man.

Reaching the gate, Malkyr kicked open the right door, revealing the welcoming party that awaited.

The enemy reacted immediately. The Pyroliths each let loose with fireballs and the Ogres shambled forward in their version of a charge.

Malkyr easily intercepted both fireballs, absorbing them into his gauntleted hand. The axe flushed with the sudden influx of power.

My four mastiffs leapt forward at the hulking zombies. Hoshisu darted in through the opening and threw her chain at one of the Pyroliths, then darted back out. It was a beautiful throw. The chain covered the distance, its spinning wheels shrieking through the air, then wrapped around a Pyrolith. The demon screamed as the chain mercilessly sawed through its scaly body.

Stepping forward, I aimed the Fire Rod at the deformed zombie. A jet of flame erupted out of one end, bathing the zombie's torso with intense cleansing fire.

Fire Rod hit Matured Possessed Ogre Zombie for 200 damage.

The zombie went down, a burning pile of meat. Crisis averted, I absentmindedly sent my dagger to slash at another zombie.

I stepped back, allowing Malkyr to take my place and block the path. The Fire Rod looked slightly charred from the intense heat and its durability was reduced by 20 points. That was the cost of channeling so much raw power through inferior material.

The first zombie reached us and Malkyr wisely took a half step back, letting the creature fill up the doorway and blocking the path of its friends. The man easily deflected a clumsy fist and delivered a devastating counterattack, his twice-charged axe cleaving through the Ogre's shoulder all the way to its stomach.

Using her brother as cover, Hoshisu darted in with her daggers whirling, slicing chunks out of the undead creature's flesh. Bek fired a duo of drilling arrows, downing the zombie.

Two down, five to go.

Another zombie stepped over the fallen one's body. From behind him, I could see the saw chain finally cutting completely through the Pyrolith, ending him. My hounds kept jumping and snapping at the Ogres, taking no damage from their retaliation strikes. The zombie I downed kept on burning.

This is going easier than I thought.

<Oh no, you did NOT just think that, did you?>

The remaining Pyrolith fired another fireball, but this one wasn't aiming at us. It hit the lead zombie, its blast radius reaching all of us.

Fireball hit you for 69 damage.

The twins and I could shrug off the damage, but poor Bek took a serious hit. His health bar was down to a sliver, and he fell to the ground thrashing in pain. If I hadn't had the foresight of handing him Guba's potions, he'd have probably died. I refrained from attacking and cast Heal Followers instead. A burst of golden-green light spread around me, healing everyone by ten hit points. The health bar on the twins' icons barely budged, but the boost was enough to raise Bek's health to a quarter, enabling him to regain control and cast his own, more potent, healing spell, getting himself back to 70 percent.

Meanwhile, Malkyr kept on fighting. His uncharged axe was doing significantly less damage than before, but with Hoshisu helping him, the two were quickly depleting the burnt zombie of its remaining health.

"Bek, get back, out of the fireball's range," I ordered. "Don't worry if you can't target the enemy, just keep on healing."

The mastiffs inside the room were inflicting damage on the two remaining zombies, and we were holding our ground despite the unlucky fireball hit.

I couldn't help my thoughts. *We are going to win this.*

Then the flaming zombie moved.

<Dude, Dad lives for this stuff, and you're just begging for it,> Vic groaned in my mind.

A two-meter spike erupted out of the downed monster. Burning flesh ripped open, falling apart. A giant-sized Stalker emerged from the burning shell. It was easily as tall as an Ogre. Its wide, fleshy body was riddled with dozens of lance-sized appendages, making me wonder how it fit inside the Ogre to begin with.

The gigantic Stalker wobbled on its legs for a split second, then oriented itself, turning toward us.

<Shit, Boss, I told you so!>

Well, at least that explained why the fire didn't do any damage. As demons, Stalkers were fire resistant. *Analyze.*

Stalker, Greater [Demon]

Level: 33

HP: 335, *MP:* 190

Attributes: P: 28; M: 5; S: 0

Skills: Stab 43, Death Plunge 15, Whirlwind 37

Traits: Demon(summoned), Amorphous Regeneration

Resistances: Fire 100%, Cold -50%, Holy -50%, Armor 50, Mental 100%, Magic 40%

Description: The reincarnation of tortured souls who have been stabbed repeatedly until losing all sense of self. Operating on pure instinct, the Stalker knows no fear. Its only goal is to spread onto others the pain they endure every waking moment. The greater variety is even more ferocious, paying no heed to its allies in its urge to hurt its enemies.

"Oh ... shit," the twins said in unison.

The giant-sized Stalker rushed forward on its numerous two-meter-long spear-like appendages. Its body started spinning, revolving around itself faster and faster until it looked like a hazy mass of twirling spikes. It charged *through* the zombies blocking its way. The zombies, already severely damaged, were shredded to pieces, as if they'd been put inside a blender, showering us all with pieces of zombie flesh.

The Stalker didn't stop with the zombies and continued whirling forward. I threw a Shadow Web in its path, and it tore through like it wasn't even there.

Malkyr just managed to put his axe up to protect his front. We heard the clang of spikes on metal. The axe stopped most of them, but several spikes pushed through and hit flesh, doing over a hundred points of damage, nearly half of Malkyr's health. The Stalker, apparently unable to stop itself, kept whirling forward, its momentum carrying it past us, luckily missing Bek, who flattened himself against the wall.

The other two zombies, still harassed by my mastiffs, seized the opportunity to charge toward the gap in our defense.

"Shadow-crap," I mumbled. "Malkyr, hold off the incoming zombies; Bek, heal him; Hoshisu, you guys have to take down the small fries as quickly as possible. I'll hold off the Stalker."

The Stalker's momentum carried it several meters into the hallway before he finally stopped spinning and assumed his 'normal' pincushion stance. I moved away from my party toward the monster of spikes and pain. Standing in the middle of the hallway, I activated Mana Shield.

A bubble of shimmering dark-blue erupted around me, blocking off enough of the corridor and forcing the creature to concentrate on me.

I kept tabs on the information streams coming from behind me. Malkyr managed to block the passage before the zombies barged through and even intercepted another fireball. Bek was continuously healing him and Hoshisu and the mastiffs were gradually ripping the zombies apart. My dagger hovered from foe to foe, adding its small amount of damage to the mix. I had to hold out on my own for just a little while.

The Stalker charged at me, thrumming its legs at the ground, leaving in its wake deep gouges on the hard stone floor. I tried building up a mass of tangible shadow in its path, but it simply rolled over it. I braced myself for impact.

A barrage of piercing, stabbing spikes assaulted my shield. The protective field held off the sharpened points barely an arm's length from my body. Then half a dozen more spikes hit all at once, piercing through.

Greater Stalker hit Mana Shield for 178 damage. 63 mana drain. You take 85 damage.

Ouch. I was stabbed all over my body, my crude leather armor doing little to blunt the damage. The Stalker immediately drew back, preparing for another attack.

I took advantage of the small reprieve to retaliate. I launched a volley of drilling arrows and recalled my dagger, slashing at the monster.

Sacrificial Dagger hit Greater Stalker for 39 damage.

Drilling Arrow hit Greater Stalker for 45 damage (SR ignored 15 damage).

Damn that thing's spell resistance!

As I looked at the never-ending moving wall of spears just beyond my shield, its wounded flesh began to mend. The gashes I had opened in its body closed before my eyes. Crap. It had the ability to regenerate.

But as the wounds closed, the creature looked like it had deflated a little.

Behind me, I could sense Malkyr intercepting another fireball launched by the lone Pyrolith. Hoshisu and my mastiffs brought down one of the zombies and were doing a good job of sending the last one to its grave.

The Stalker before me wound back its front spears, then snapped them forward, as fast as an arrow. The first five spears were stopped by my shield, the rest punched through.

Greater Stalker hit Mana Shield for 158 damage. 63 mana drain. You take 70 damage.

Crap, I really should invest more time in raising my shield spell level.

Mana Shield skill level increased to 27.

I should have wished for a million gold instead.

Lucky Bastard skill level increased to 26.

Vic chuckled in my mind.

That's not funny! I shot back at him, then sighed. I hated this method of raising my shield level. At least in this case, the system was working for me.

That thing's level was too high for me to attempt a Freeze. Instead, I hurled more drilling arrows at it and slashed with my dagger. And since it was kind enough to injure me sufficiently, I also activated Blood Wrath, channeling the rage energy into a single, piercing ray which inflicted another 50 points of damage.

Large gashes opened in the mass before me and immediately began to close, the flesh knitting together. However, the Stalker was becoming visibly smaller as its wounds healed. Once it stopped bleeding, it was *only* about as tall as Malkyr.

"Hold on, Chief! Help is on the way," Malkyr bellowed behind me. He lifted his glowing axe and cleaved the last zombie neatly in half. The mastiffs pulled at its hands and legs, ripping it all the way apart, finally bringing it down.

Hoshisu was already running at the lone Pyrolith. "I'll distract the snake, you guys take down that Stalker."

Malkyr and the hounds ran toward me, but I ordered two of the mastiffs to stay back and help the woman. In front of me, the Stalker prepared for another lunge attack. I was doing pretty well with over 500 mana at my disposal and 200 health, but I wasn't looking forward to being perforated again. Instead, I drew in my mana and prepared to cast Shadow Teleport. I waited for the very last instant, just as the first spear contacted my shield, then finished the casting, appearing on the other side of the monster.

To my surprise, I found that my shield was left behind. I managed to see the other ten or so spikes puncture the shield, breaking it into magical vapors just in time for Malkyr and the hounds to close in on the creature. Apparently, Malkyr had managed to intercept another fireball, as his axe was glowing again. He struck hard, breaking spears and tearing flesh. My mastiffs leapt at the creature, but for once their innate immunity failed them. The wicked spears of the greater demon tore through them, and their shadowy bodies dissipated into black smoke.

The Stalker's wounds had already closed, but it was now the size of a normal Stalker. We had already killed plenty of those. A few more strikes from Malkyr, coupled with drilling arrows, finished it off.

"Haaa-ya!" came a yell from behind me.

I turned to look at the scene beyond the gate. My two remaining hounds were pulling at the Pyrolith's tail, preventing it from moving while Hoshisu rode on its back, repeatedly stabbing her dagger into the side of its neck.

I was impressed. That was some display of combat acrobatics.

A few more strikes finished the creature, and it collapsed to the ground, Hoshisu rode him all the way down then nimbly rolled onto her feet.

Show-off.

<And how was that different from you basically doing the same thing with Rhynorn?>

He got me there.

"Oh, man." Malkyr sounded disappointed. "I wanted to juice up this baby with a few more fireballs." He held up his axe.

With a deft movement, Hoshisu flicked the blood off her daggers and put them back in her belt. "You snooze, you lose."

Level up! You have reached Character Level 24. You have 1 ability point to allocate.

Blood Wrath skill level increased to 31.

Heal Followers skill level increased to 11.

I frowned. Something didn't make sense.

How come during the fight I received some notifications as they happened, but I only see these ones now? I asked my cloaked companion.

<*Simple. The ones you saw during combat were funny at the time. Timing is everything,*> Vic chuckled.

I sighed, rolling my eyes.

I wasn't really upset by his answer. We were gaining good XP and raising our skill levels quickly. The challenges were a bit high for our level, but good teamwork made up for the difference. Fighting and winning against creatures of a higher level was very rewarding. The twins were both level 27 now and Bek had reached level 15. Since everyone else was a higher level than him, he only received a small share of the XP. Still, it was enough to make him the second highest-level creature in my clan after Rhynorn. I chuckled, remembering the small goblin's humble starting point. The strings of fate worked mysteriously.

I looked into the now empty room and didn't sense any more enemies, but I *did* sense another presence. "There's something still in there," I cautioned. "Don't let your guard down."

I didn't recast Mana Shield, as I had to remain mobile. We moved in at a tight formation. We passed a stack of boxes and came to an abrupt halt, gaping at what lay beyond.

A cage.

Thick metal bars sectioned off a part of the room. And it was filled with prisoners. All of them dwarves. They looked to be in a bad shape. Some of them were sitting against the bars, but most were lying on the ground. They smelled of decay and fecal matter. Their faces were hollow, their clothes hanging loose.

Unexpectedly, I felt a sudden surge of rage. *Dwarves! This accursed race hunts my people at every chance they get. It's a sport to them! They even –*

"Hey, are you guys alright?" Malkyr put his hands on the bars and looked inside, his face full of concern.

Oh, right. They're prisoners, we're travelers. This means we should probably help them.

I could sense Vic's unease in my mind like it was a tangible thing, but for once, he didn't voice his opinion.

"Who you be?" demanded one of the dwarves, squinting. He seemed to be in better shape than his friends. It made sense, as he had the highest level among them. *Analyze.*

> **Kuzai BoulderBelly, Dwarf Priest of Durang**
>
> *Level:* 28
>
> *HP:* 68/185, *MP:* 0/210
>
> *Attributes:* P: 10; M: 13; S: 5
>
> *Skills:* Mace 25, Shield 25, Weaponsmith 25, Bless 18, Heal 18, Banish Evil 18
>
> *Traits:* Dwarf (+5 max racial skills cap), Spiritual (grants divine spells)
>
> *Resistances:* Physical 25%, Magic 20%
>
> *Description:* Kuzai 'War-priest' is a decorated veteran priest of the BoulderBelly clan. Famed for his toughness in close quarters fighting, his mere presence is enough to bestow Durang's divine blessing on his comrades, strengthening them. Kuzai is often chosen to lead explorations of new mining locations.

"A Goblin!" the dwarf uttered, finally getting a good look at us. His fists clenched, his body became rigid, and his lips peeled back in contempt.

I felt myself snarling back before I could even register the action. Well, he *was* a dirty, stinking dwarf. Literally.

"Wooah, wooah there!" Malkyr lifted his large hands reassuringly. "We're not your enemies, buddy."

The dwarf gave him a questioning gaze, then recoiled, almost stumbling back. "There's some green blood in ya boy! I can smell it, and that wench got it too!" He pointed at Hoshisu. "Yer all be stinkin' goblin half breeds."

Hoshisu grimaced. "Well, they did warn us that the 'normal' races would automatically consider us as enemies. I think that's why he's acting like that.

<*That girl's a real genius,*> Vic murmured.

Turning back to the riled-up dwarf, Malkyr tried again. "Listen, buddy, we aren't your enemies. We just killed a bunch of demons who were guarding this room. Doesn't that prove we're on the same side?"

Kuzai gave him a hard look. "Trying the old, 'The enemy of me enemy' thing on me, eh? Ye probably only went through them ter get ter us." He looked bitterly at his malnourished people. "Well, do yer worst, greenskins. What else we got ter lose?"

Hoshisu shook her head. "It's no use, Malkyr, he won't listen to reason. Their default reputation toward us is set on hatred and ... *what* are you doing?" she snapped at me.

Almost without meaning to, I'd conjured a trio of drilling arrows that hovered above my palm. Almost.

"Erm, nothing." I hastily reabsorbed the mana, and the arrows disappeared. *Stinking Dwarves.*

<*Oren, Snap out of it!*> Vic said sharply in my mind.

I suddenly felt like a fog was lifted, and I could think clearly again. I stared at my green goblin hand and shuddered. I had almost attacked those poor wretches. I took a steadying breath. *My name is Oren, I'm a human Totem playing NEO ... I need to reach boss tier 4 ...*

"Anyway," Hoshisu said, eyeing me skeptically, "I don't think we can persuade them with mere words. We need to find a way to *show* them we only want to help."

"The dwarf's a priest," I pointed out. "But he's out of juice. Do you have a mana potion to give him?" I didn't have any, since, as a dark priest, I could always use void crystals to replenish my own reserves.

The twins shook their heads.

"We can try to offer them some food, or maybe healing?" Malkyr suggested.

Hoshisu shook her head. "There's no way they'll accept a healing spell from a goblin, and as things stand, if we offered any food, they would probably assume we're trying to poison them. I think the only way we can show them we mean well is to set them free."

"Gotcha, I'm on it," her brother said. He grabbed hold of the cell's single gate and pulled the bars. His muscles and veins bulged as he heaved and pulled, but as hard as he tried, the door wouldn't budge. "Damn," he said, letting go of the bars. "Maybe if I take the Ogre potions ..."

"Save it." His sister waved him away and approached the locked gate. Bending to her knees, she eyed the lock, then withdrew some tools from her inventory and started prodding it with them.

Malkyr looked at the caged dwarves, then at me, his face troubled. "Damn, man. I used to play a dwarf for a long time, even before NEO. The way they look at us ... it doesn't feel right. I mean, I knew we'd be getting the goblinoid template and be generally despised by the other races, but to suddenly experience it firsthand ..." He shook his head. "Doesn't feel too good."

"Darn!" Hoshisu spat, getting to her feet. "It doesn't take a key. It's another puzzle. We have to solve a complex equation to open the door. It's that dungeon mess all over again."

"Let me have a look," Malkyr offered.

"No." She shook her head. "Probability problems are my thing." Taking another deep breath, she again muttered, "Damn," and returned to face the lock.

Malkyr sighed. "This might take a while. Some equations can take days to solve, sometimes even months."

"We should check the bodies for loot in the meantime," I said. "We kinda skipped that part."

Malkyr nodded. "Good idea."

We went through the remains. Each of the Pyrolith left behind five scales, which we split between us. The Ogres had dropped two more potions of Ogre's Might and four more Viridium ingots. As before, I let Malkyr have the potions and claimed the violet metal for myself. The Stalker left behind two 'Giant Stalker Pins.' *Those would fit Rhynorn nicely.* I could sense their high Runecraft viability and began to plan how to imbue them with more power.

Altogether, the monsters dropped nearly a thousand gold coins, which we split three ways. We even rummaged through the stacked boxes and torn sacks, but they all contained spoiled foodstuff.

"How's it going, sis?" Malkyr asked as we returned to the dwarves' cage.

She gave him an irritated look. "Slowly. You two might as well log off while I work on this. Come back in an hour or two."

Damn, that means 12 to 24 hours. I hated being away from my clan for so long. Our defenses were still too weak. This was a delay I could do without.

"So, like ... you're staying?" Malkyr asked me.

"Yeah, I have a few things to take care of while we wait. Feel free to log off for a few."

"Alright, I'll do that. I rarely have the apartment to myself. I'll have a beer and watch a game in my underwear."

"You do that almost every day!" Hoshisu somehow heard him from across the room.

"Yeah, but now at least I won't have you badgering me about it," he shouted back at her. He gave me a boyish grin. "Later, man." Then he faded away, disappearing back into the real world.

I got comfortable on top of a large sack filled with something mushy. *Well, as long as we're taking a break ...*

I closed my eyes and drifted off to sleep.

14 – A Totem's Best Friend

<My lord?>

"Kaedric?" Blearily, I opened my eyes.

<Come on, dude, you're kinda barging into my turf,> Vic complained.

Ignoring Vic's protest, my seneschal continued speaking with an even tone. *<There are some matters that require your attention, my lord.>*

Alright. I yawned, rubbing my eyes. *Let's hear it.*

<The new builders have finished constructing the last two cabins. Tomorrow they will be without an assignment.>

At least that was some good news. Due to the distance, I couldn't access the Settlement Interface directly.

I closed my eyes, trying to remember the list of available buildings for construction. I needed to select a simple project, one that the new builders were qualified to build.

What are the novice buildings again? A woodcutter hut that increased logging yield, a quarry that increased stone production ... was there something that increased our food yield?

<Yes, my lord, we can construct a gardener's hut. That would increase our gatherers' production by 20 percent.>

I gulped. I didn't intend to communicate my inner thoughts like that. I could no longer ignore the fact that Kaedric was able to read my thoughts.

"Just what I needed," I muttered. "A shapeshifting loon and a brain-eating seneschal running wild in my mind."

<I wouldn't sweat it if I were you, buddy; it's not like there isn't plenty of space to run around in here,> Vic said casually.

I closed my eyes for a moment. *That's a good idea, Kaedric. Have them build the gardener's hut. I should have done that sooner. With a bit of luck, this will be enough to raise the builders to Apprentice rank, then they'll be able to pitch in on the high-priority buildings.*

<Yes, my lord. On another matter, we have been visited by eight new travelers in the last 12 hours. As you instructed, I, and other members of the clan, have requested their aid with various tasks. That seemed to placate them for a while, but they soon raised complaints at the lack of

'starting gear,' if I were to use their own terms. I am concerned their displeasure might lead to unfortunate confrontation.>

He had a point there. Players could be a demanding, whiny bunch. Especially if they didn't get what they wanted fast enough. I didn't like the thought of our smithy or warehouse getting ransacked by impatient players. That gave me an idea.

We've accumulated some crude weapons and armor by now, right?

<That is correct, my lord. At present, we have several daggers, axes, and shields that are not being used. In addition, we have produced 28 crude bows and over 450 arrows. There are also four hobgoblin-sized leather armors available.>

That sounded like a business opportunity to me. *Here's what we'll do. Make sure all arms and armor are stored in the warehouse. Have two hob soldiers guard the place day and night. Then offer to sell the equipment to the travelers. Allow them to commission items that will be made especially for them. Vrick can make armor, and we have a small host of goblin smiths that I'm sure can produce acceptable weapons, even without their own smithies.*

<That is an elegant solution, my lord. However, there's a small problem with this plan.>

I frowned. *What?*

<We require a proficient merchant to handle sales.>

Damn, he was right. It would do no good to have someone inexperienced handling the business.

Are you able to operate the Breeder's Den, Kaedric?

<I am, my lord, pending your explicit permission.>

Alright. I grant you permission to access the Breeder's Den controls. Have Gandork cook the required food and summon a goblin merchant to manage trade with travelers.

<Yes, my lord. I will do that and place him at the warehouse, though once the marketplace is complete, it will be more prudent to assign him a booth to operate.>

I agree. I hesitated for a moment. *I also grant you permission to access the energy controls in order to increase the new guy's level.*

<Understood. It shall be done, my lord.>

Is Rhynorn behaving himself?

<He hasn't harmed any of the clan members as of yet. He did get into a slight altercation with one of our new visitors, but Guba managed to diffuse the situation before it became too volatile.>

Good, keep an eye on him as well. If necessary, remind him 'who is the boss'.

<Yes, my lord.>

Is there something else?

I could feel his hesitation over our telepathic link. *Kaedric?*

<My apologies, my lord, I'm not sure the matter is significant enough to bring to your attention. One of the newcomers is quite different ... unique. I believe she might become a real asset to the clan.>

What's her name? I asked, getting comfortable and feeling myself becoming drowsy again.

<Raystia.>

***

A shout pierced the room, waking me from my slumber.

"I did it!"

I glanced around, blinking, trying to get my bearings.

Hoshisu came running, looking excited. "I did it! I solved the riddle!"

"Eh?"

"Look!" She pointed at the dwarves' cage. The gate was wide open.

Vic chuckled. *<Told you that girl's a genius.>*

As I looked, a single dwarf moved. Kuzai swayed as he tried not to step on any of his weakened kin lying on the floor. He opened the gate and stepped outside.

+1 reputation with the BoulderBelly clan.

New rank: Despised

Points to next rank (Unfriendly): 4,000

"That's fantastic!"

Apparently, Hoshisu received the same notification.

She beamed. "It means they'll be willing to listen to us." For a moment, she didn't look like a cold-hearted killer, but a young, impressionable woman. How strange.

That indeed was a revelation. It probably meant that all other playable races were a single reputation point away from the 'despised' reputation as well. Just a single act of kindness would be enough to prevent attack on sight and open a channel of communication.

Standing outside the cage, Kuzai folded his arms over his chest, glaring at us. "Guess ye been saying the truth all'long," he grunted. "I still ain't trustin ye greenskins, but I reckon greenskin beats demon so we'll play nice. Fer now."

"How did you come to be imprisoned?" Hoshisu asked.

Kuzai glanced at his downed kin behind him, then back at us. "Ain't no time fer that now. Me brethren be near death and I can't help 'em. I already lost too many to them damn demons." His fingers clutched at his throat as if grasping for something. "If only I had me ruddy amulet!"

I exchanged a glance with Hoshisu. We both knew what that was leading to.

"Can we offer our help?" I asked.

The dwarf looked at me, barely hiding his sneer. "The day I be accepting a goblin's help ..." He trailed off then shook his head. "Will be today. Them demons took away me holy amulet. It be me link to Durang's divine power. If ye can find me amulet, I could help me remaining kin. Help me save them and in return, I'll help you."

You received a new quest: The Holy Dwarf 1

Kuzai has asked you to help save his people. First, find his holy amulet which was taken by the demons.

Quest Type: Advanced, chain

Reward: Varied, depending on number of surviving dwarves: 18/18

"Crap." I looked at Hoshisu. "We can spend days crawling around this dungeon looking for his damn amulet. We might as well be looking for a needle –"

I paused mid-sentence, staring at the golden chain dangling from Hoshisu's fingers. "Is that what I think it is?"

She nodded, smirking.

"Where did you get that?"

"While you and my dear brother were off looting the corpses, I noticed the remains of a demon corpse behind those crates. I thought it was worth a closer look. The remains were badly burnt and this little jewel was hidden under a pile of ash. I'm guessing that for a demon, holding a holy item isn't a great idea."

"Hey, that be me amulet!" Kuzai blurted, noticing the item Hoshisu was holding.

"Yes, I just found it. Here you go."

Taking the amulet from her hands, Kuzai reverently placed it around his neck. He closed his eyes and inhaled deeply. I could see golden-bright ribbons of mana flowing into his body from the bauble. He was obviously dependent on his amulet to regenerate his mana.

Standing straighter, with one hand over the amulet, Kuzai looked around at his people, his expression stern. He gestured with his other hand, muttering something in Dwarven. Golden light spread out from his hands, illuminating the entire cage. The beaten dwarves touched by the light suddenly looked better. Those who were a step from death opened their eyes and sat up. Festering wounds closed and the stench of death and decay lessened.

At that exact moment, Malkyr logged back in. Materializing out of thin air, he stared in bewilderment at the much livelier dwarves. "That was quick, sis." He looked at the dwarven priest. "Your people seem better."

Kuzai nodded, his eyes troubled as he took in the sight of his feeble group. "They still be weak. They be needing yer help getting to the surface. Would ye offer your help a second time?"

The big man shrugged. "Sure, why not?"

Quest updated: The Holy Dwarf 2

Kuzai was able to use the magical amulet to stabilize his dying people. Help them escape the fort and reach the surface unharmed.

Quest Type: Advanced, chain

Reward: Increased. Varied depending on number of surviving dwarves: 18/18

I wrinkled my nose. *Great, just what we needed, more time with those stinking dwarves.*

<They actually smell better now, Boss,> Vic remarked.

Not to me, I grumbled mentally.

"This way." Hoshisu motioned the dwarves to follow her and moved toward the exit.

"Alright everyone, huddle together," Malkyr instructed. "We'll take point. In case we're attacked, stay back and let us do the fighting."

"I'll help," Kuzai declared with a ring of finality. "But I be needing a weapon."

"Sure thing, buddy." Malkyr retrieved a standard hand axe from his inventory and offered it to the dwarf. "Here you go."

"That'll do, fer now. Ye don't happen to have a shield on ya too, do ya lad?"

Malkyr grinned and produced a wooden shield from his inventory.

The dwarf grunted. "Ye ain't so bad, son. For part greenskin, that is."

"Thanks, old timer," Malkyr chuckled.

We led the way back out into the main corridor, moving carefully, keeping our eyes and ears peeled for any possible danger.

We were halfway to the pit leading out when Bek stopped, causing the dwarf behind him to bump into him.

"Stupid vermin," the dwarf mumbled.

"What's wrong, Bek?" I interceded, giving the offending dwarf a withering glare.

The small goblin pointed a finger at an empty room to our left. "Door close on way in. Door open now."

As if affirming his words, a loud howl pierced the air, carrying a whiff of magic with it. The weakened dwarves grasped each other in fright, seeming unable to move.

From the shadows all around us, a pack of wolves stepped into view. At least, they looked like wolves. Their fur was so dark it blended perfectly with the shadows around us, and their eyes shone red.

"Demon wolves!" Kuzai spat, stepping forward to face one.

Three wolves closed in on the siblings at the front, snarling. Five more circled the exhausted dwarves.

Demon Wolf

Level: 6

HP: 65/54

Attributes: P: 5, M: 0, S: 1

Skills: Bite 12, Demoralizing Roar 6

Traits: Demonic

Resistances: Fire 100%, Armor: 12, -50% holy

Buff: Alpha aura (+11 max HP)

Description: Demon wolves roam the open plains of hell. Though weak individually, as a pack their strength increases exponentially, especially when led by an alpha.

The wolves at the front charged the twins and the rest fell upon the unfortunate dwarves. Kuzai managed to hold one of them at bay, but the rest of his people fared much worse. The other four wolves clawed and bit, diving deep into their ranks. Still, they were dwarves, and even at death's door, some fought back. Those who weren't debilitated by the effect of the howl used their bare fists to attack, but there was no question as to whom was better at fighting unarmed.

Hoshisu left her brother to fight the three wolves and jumped into the band of dwarves in a vain attempt to protect them.

"Do something!" Malkyr yelled at me between axe swings.

I shrugged. "The wolves seem to do well on their own."

"I meant help the dwarves!" he almost screamed.

I remained in place, absentmindedly picking at my nose, staring straight into the eyes of a wolf that paused as it considered me for his next target. Realizing they were probably an easier prey, it pounced on another dwarf.

<Err, Boss, you do remember the quest reward improves if more dwarves survive, right?>

Oh right, I almost forgot. In that case... With an offhand flick of my mind, I froze the three wolves who were rampaging unopposed among the defenseless dwarves. For some reason, these demons were infused with Dark Mana. Combined with the bonuses I'd received from wielding my magic in a dark environment, that made them especially susceptible to my control.

I thought about using my daggers to sacrifice the frozen wolves, but with the dwarves being pressed so tightly, I risked hitting them as well. So instead, I simply left the dwarves to dish out the damage and finish off their immobile enemies with kicks and punches.

Two seconds later, Malkyr dispatched the last of his three opponents, sustaining only a minor bite mark on his forearm. Hoshisu and Kuzai seemed uninjured. Both had also downed their opponents.

Hoshisu made her way toward me. "What was that?" she demanded, glaring at me.

I shrugged. "I like them about as much as they like us. That said, I would like to point out that I *did* help."

"Three of the dwarves are dead," she hissed. "Lucky for us, Kuzai and the others were too busy to notice your behavior."

I winked at her, "Luck is what I do."

Lucky Bastard skill level increased to 27.

Right on time.

A growl sounded farther down the hallway. A large wolf twice the size of the others stepped out of the darkness. It was black as night with glowing red eyes. Two long horns curled back from its skull. I could sense it teeming with Dark Mana. It was a beautiful creature.

Tempest, Demon Wolf Alpha

Level: 16

HP: 154/154

Attributes: P: 15, M: 0, S: 1

Traits: Demonic

Skills: Powerful Bite 22, Alpha Aura 11, Sprinter 25

Resistances: Fire 100%, Armor 27, Holy -50%

Description: Demon wolves roam the open plains of hell. The alphas are among the strongest of their kind. Strong, fast, and smart, an alpha can use his aura to increase his pack's strength, allowing them to hunt prey much tougher than they normally could.

Raising his Axe, Malkyr prepared to strike the magnificent beast.

"Wait!" I shouted. "He's mine!"

I moved forward, putting myself between the man and the beast.

Giving me a weird look, Malkyr relented and stepped back. The alpha approached me carefully, as if not comprehending why the powerful enemy was replaced by one seemingly weaker. I could almost *smell* dark energy coming off him with every step he made. It drew close, snarling and baring his fangs. He was nearly two meters away, tensing his muscles, ready to pounce.

What I was about to do wasn't supposed to work, not on a named mob, but the dark essence of the wolf resonated with me. I knew it would work. I held up one hand, channeled my mana into the beast's mind and commanded, "Stop."

The wolf stood still.

I took a step closer. My mana was absorbed easily, taking control of muscles and mind alike. By the time my hand reached its head, the domination was complete. He was mine.

You have successfully dominated a free-roaming demon. You may choose to banish Tempest to his home plane or assume permanent control.

Note: Assuming control will require a continuous draw of mana to keep the demon anchored on this plane, resulting in a permanent 5% reduction of your maximum MP.

Well, with all the recent level-ups, I now had over a thousand MP. Losing five percent wasn't such a big deal.

I grabbed at the data stream that said 'control,' wrapping my thoughts around it, pulling it to me.

You have gained a new Companion: Tempest, demon wolf alpha

Tempest knelt obediently, maintaining eye contact. I reached out my hand, and he licked it. I grabbed his mane and climbed onto his back, projecting my intentions at him. The great demon wolf rose up and took a few measured steps down the hallway.

I looked back at the gaping mouths and astonished faces and simply asked, "Coming?"

We made it to the bottom of the pit with no further encounters.

Tempest climbed out with ease, his claws grabbing at the sloping walls. Once back in the main hall, I fed the rope in my inventory to the party below.

Hoshisu came up first. Malkyr stayed behind, helping the dwarves by lifting them halfway through the pit. Though they were on their last legs, they were still dwarves, and with a bit of assistance, they all made the climb.

Kuzai climbed last and looked around the hall full of debris with distaste. "That what you be getting after a thousand years if it ain't built by dwarven builders!" he grunted.

That gave me pause. *So, a dwarf builder would be superior to a goblin builder, hmm ... So I only need to find a clan of dwarves, eradicate them, then I'd be able to summon their workers.*

<Please tell me you're joking, Boss,> Vic said weakly in my mind.

Just thinking a little out of the box here, Vic, no need to get all worked up. Yet.

"This way," Malkyr motioned, leading the dwarves toward the exit.

We arrived at the outer courtyard and a few moments later came out into the open mountain land.

"We made it," Kuzai said softly. Looking at the three dead dwarves his people carried with them, he added bitterly, "At least most of us did."

"Now what?" Malkyr asked.

"Now me people be finding another tunnel and be on their way home. Meself, I have an obligation to our dead. I'm gonna find whoever summoned the sons of bitches and make sure his head won't ever again be anywhere near the rest of him. Will ye help me, lads?"

Quest updated: The Holy Dwarf 3

You helped Kuzai rescue his men, although a few were lost. Follow Kuzai down to the depths of the fort and help him vanquish the source of evil that permeates the ancient place.

Quest Type: Advanced, chain

Reward received: 1,500 XP (100 XP per surviving dwarf), Kuzai joined your party.

Reward pending: Improve reputation rank with the BoulderBelly clan, open trade options.

The XP boost was nice. It was almost enough to push me to the next level. Cascading streams of information surrounded Bek. The small goblin had gained another level. He was level 16 already, same as Rhynorn. By the time we got back, he might very well be twice that Ogre's level. I snickered at the mental image of Bek kicking the brute's ass, riding him around like his own personal pony.

"'Course we'll help," Malkyr responded for all of us, breaking me away from my reverie.

I wasn't so sure I wanted to party up with a stinkin' dwarf, but I kept my mouth shut. If my vision was any indication, we were heading into a large pile of trouble. *Come to think of it, it might not be such a bad idea to bring along some dwarven fodder*. I gave the dwarf a big, ear-to-ear smile. "Sure, sure, glad to have you with us, Kuzai."

He eyed me suspiciously.

The other dwarves picked up their meager possessions and their dead. After exchanging a few words with their leader, they started walking away. They soon crossed a mountain ridge and were out of sight.

We went back into the ruins. I rode Tempest and the others walked. We encountered no further enemies on our way to the pit.

"Where to now?" I asked as we stood at the main basement hallway.

"Let's head to the prison cell again," Hoshisu suggested. "We skipped a few doors on our way there. Better check we didn't miss anything important."

"Yeah, like more loot," her brother added.

"Precisely. Then we can check out the other side of the hallway."

"Sounds like a plan," I agreed.

Malkyr and Kuzai took point, followed by Bek and Hoshisu, while I brought up the rear. Halfway down the hall, we found another closed door that I hadn't noticed before.

"I'll check it," Hoshisu volunteered. She inspected the lock carefully, tapping it a few times with one of her daggers, then nodded. "All clear."

The door opened into another large storeroom. The place looked like a storm had come through it. Crushed boxes and pieces of broken items littered the floor. Two Ogre zombies rose to engage us.

With Malkyr and Kuzai, each tanking a different opponent, the fight was easy. Boring almost. I cast drilling arrows over and over again until the two were down. Kuzai displayed some interesting powers during the fight, at one point raising his pendant and showering a zombie with golden light that melted away half his torso. Priests were well-suited to battle the undead.

I managed to get a killing strike with my dagger on one Ogre, adding 14 FP to my total and gaining another level 14 void crystal.

Searching the dropped loot, we recovered three more Viridium ingots and one heavy maul.

Kuzai belted his hand axe and hefted the maul instead, holding it with both hands, testing its balance. The thing must have been considered a light weapon for an Ogre, but at ten kilos, it looked quite intimidating in the dwarf's hands. "That be a good knee buster," Kuzai declared, shouldering the weapon. "What do ye plan on doing with those?" he asked as I put the Viridium in my inventory.

"Malkyr can forge them into something useful," I said nonchalantly. "Then I'll see how good those things are at holding enchantment."

The dwarf shook his head. "That metal be damn hard to work. Only Master Smiths can make something worth a half-damn out of it. There be other, better metals ter use fer weapons or armor. But what can ye expect of metal borne by magic?"

"Borne by magic?" I raised a brow.

"Aye, it be normal metal at first, then transmuted by some magic user with too much time on 'em hands, usually hob shamans. Hard ter make, too. My people don't waste their time on such trivials."

"I think I'll keep it all the same. Maybe I'll find some other use for it later."

The dwarf shrugged. "Suit yerself, don't say I did'na warn ya."

"Man, there's nothing valuable in here," Malkyr complained, getting up after rummaging through broken boxes. "What a colossal waste of time."

"I dunno," Kuzai said. "That secret panel behind ya looks promisin'."

"What?" The big man turned to inspect the wall with bewilderment.

The dwarf chuckled. "Here, lad." He walked next to Malkyr and tapped his maul lightly on a small brick in the wall. An audible click sounded and a piece of the wall in front of Malkyr opened up to reveal a hidden compartment.

Malkyr carefully emptied its contents, laying them out on the ground for all of us to see: a pair of exquisite boots, a couple of parchments, and a stack of gold coins.

Boots of Swiftness

Description: Made from blue dragon leather, the fastest of their kind. There's a saying that whoever wears these boots will be quick enough to dodge lightning.

Type: Armor [feet]

Rank: Magical

Effect I: +10% speed

Effect II: 20% electricity resistant

Base price: 4,500

Scroll: Teleport of Fate

Description: An old, crumbling piece of parchment with arcane writings.

Effect: Using this scroll will teleport the user and all his party's members to a seemingly random location, as determined by the winds of fate.

Construction Blueprints: Pens

Description: Pens are used to grow a variety of domesticated animals and produce meat and other livestock products.

Rank: Novice

Requirements: 30 stone, 30 wood. 250 BP

I wanted everything. Alas, I had party members to consider.

"These boots seem nice," Hoshisu said with a casual air.

"Roll you for it?" I asked halfheartedly.

She gave me a sly smile. "So you don't want the two scrolls?"

"Fine," I muttered and collected the two parchments.

Hoshisu removed the boots she was wearing and put on her latest acquisition. They fit her perfectly. She made a few runs across the room. She was visibly faster than before.

"Congratulations, sis. They suit you," Malkyr complimented her.

"You still owe me a better weapon," she reminded him. She eyed her new boots and her face softened. "But yes, yes they do."

Women!

We exited the room and continued walking down the hallway. We found only one more door, and it was partially blocked. Kuzai bashed it with his maul, ripping it off the hinges. There was one Ogre zombie inside, accompanied by two Pyroliths.

Kuzai engaged the Ogre, easily dodging its clumsy attacks. Malkyr intercepted the fireballs, then, aided by his sister, dispatched the two demons and the remaining Ogre without difficulty.

We looted the bodies. Kuzai claimed a Potion of Ogre Might and I added another Pyrolith scale and two void crystals to my growing collection. As a side bonus, this fight netted me an extra 27 FP.

"I think we've cleared this side of the basement," Hoshisu said once we finished looting the corpses. "Let's check out the other side."

The trap was sprung with barely a warning. We'd passed the pit, and after only a few meters there was a single 'click.' A large section of the floor sank by a centimeter. A pressure plate.

"Duck!" Hoshisu shouted an instant before circular saw blades came out of the walls around us.

Only Hoshisu and Tempest managed to duck in time. Malkyr and Kuzai both got sliced by the jagged blades, each receiving nearly 150 points of damage. Luckily for them, they were both robust enough to withstand the injuries.

Bek, who wasn't nearly as tough, couldn't hope to survive such a hit, but fortunately, that wasn't an issue. Whoever built the trap was obviously targeting playable races, and the saw blades whirled over the small goblin's head. Tempest's quick reaction spared me damage as well, though with 331 HP, I was even sturdier than Malkyr.

Bek immediately got to work, casting Heals over Malkyr and specifically ignoring the bleeding dwarf. Muttering to himself, Kuzai used his own magic to close his wounds.

Bek's healing ability had improved significantly. He'd been practicing that spell a lot lately and the amount of health restored with each cast was impressive. For a goblin.

It had been a while since I inspected the little adept's stats, so I used this delay to check his character sheet.

Bek, Goblin Adept

Level: 16 (25%)

HP: 105; *MP:* 160

Attributes: P: 2, M: 15, S: -1

Skills: Heal 22, Lucky Bastard 15, Drilling Arrow 15, Mana Drain 12, Inscribe 10

Trait: Deformed; max HP +10

Resist: Mental 20%

Wait, what? His Drilling Arrow spell is already at the Apprentice rank? I frowned. *When did that happen?*

<Jeesh, Boss, didn't you notice that he got his second arrow while fighting all those Stalkers back at the great hall? Our little Bek puppet is all grown up now.>

That was encouraging. It also looked like turning the goblin into a mobile infirmary had contributed significantly to his Heal spell progression. I mentally clicked the skill to view its description.

Heal (M)

Heal wounded creature. Cannot regrow lost limbs. Speed 5. Cost 10

Level 22: Apprentice: can heal allies up to 11 meters away.

Effect: 32 HP healed.

That was pretty good. It explained how he managed to keep us all alive during the tougher fights. *I should find some way to reward him*, I reflected. *Maybe I'll buy him some new abilities using Faith Points once we get back to the clan.*

"Sorry, guys." Hoshisu grimaced as she looked at her brother's gruesome wounds. "That trap was an Expert level one; I detected it only a second before it went off."

"Nay yer fault, lass." Kuzai was quick to forgive her. "Traps were meant to go unfound. Ye' did well enough back with 'em door traps."

There was another door to our right, just beyond the trap area. This one was made of sturdy granite and reinforced with straps of metal bindings.

"This looks promising," Malkyr said. "Sis?"

Hoshisu went to the door and bent down, checking the lock. She took longer than usual, probably trying to avoid another blunder. After several long minutes, she finally got up, brushing off her legs. "I can't detect any trap, but it's locked. I don't think we'll be able to bash this door like the previous ones. I'm going to have to try to pick the lock. You might want to stand back in case there's a trap I missed.

We heeded her advice and moved away, giving her plenty of space. Hoshisu breathed steadily and started poking the lock with her tools. A few more minutes passed before we heard an audible snap.

"Damn it!" Hoshisu seethed. "I broke my only lockpick. The lock on this door is too advanced. Sorry, guys."

"It's okay, sis." Malkyr patted her back. "We'll get you a new one."

"I can see a little of the room through the keyhole. There's a structure inside, but I can't tell what it is. Damn!" she cursed again, looking at her broken lockpick.

Well, if she can catch a glimpse through the keyhole ...

"Let me have a look." I moved next to the disheveled woman. Not needing to bend down, I peeked inside the keyhole. It was dark inside, but I had no trouble seeing through it. There was a large block of stone just beyond the door. It looked to be made from granite as well. I couldn't get more details from this limited viewpoint. Since I had a line of sight anyway, I simply used Shadow Teleport.

I appeared inside the locked room and heard the exclamation of surprise from my party members beyond the door. This was a smithy! The large block in the middle was a granite-made forge. A dusty, yet sturdy-looking anvil was standing next to it along with a stack of metal ingots. A neat row of smith's tools was hanging on a nearby wall. There was also a rack with several finished weapons and pieces of armor. Everything here was too big for a goblin to use. This place was obviously meant for players to find. Damn.

Among the row of tools, I spotted a fine-looking file. The metal was dusty but unblemished. It was obviously of high quality to survive the passage of years without sprouting any rust. I grabbed the file and teleported out.

"Here, try using this." I handed Hoshisu the file. "I think it will hold better than your lockpick."

She looked at me for a moment, then took it from my hand.

"It's made of mithril!" she exclaimed. "It's not as efficient as a lockpick, but it definitely won't break as easily."

We retreated back into the hallway and watched the woman as she tried to pick the lock.

It took her nearly 20 minutes but she eventually made it. The lock clicked and the door swung open.

"Thanks" Hoshisu handed the file back to me.

I shook my head. "You keep it. It's useless to me anyway."

"Holy hell." Malkyr stood at the entrance to the room, staring at its contents.

"These are all masterwork tools," Kuzai said, taking a look inside. "Almost as good as the ones used by our own smiths. Some of them are even made of mithril."

"I want it all," Malkyr said dreamily.

"Be my guest." I beckoned him forward. "My clan smiths won't be able to use this stuff. Maybe you can do some good with it."

"And that anvil, I mean look at it – no rust or even a dent, just a bit of dust."

"Hmm, let me see that." Kuzai approached the anvil. "Aye, this be a real beauty. Dwarven made, high quality, with a bit of magic snuck in fer good measure."

"A magical anvil?" Malkyr's eyes were as big as saucers.

"Aye, lad, nothing too spectacular. It allows molding of hard metal more easily; less heat required. That be the reason how it be possible to operate a forge in such a small space. Heck, you can even carry it with ya; the enchantment makes it portable."

Malkyr gave me a pleading look.

"Go ahead." I waved him off. "As long as you plan on using it at Goblin's Gorge, I have no problem with you having it and the tools."

The big man gave me a wide grin, then placed his hands on the anvil. It shrank before our eyes and Malkyr promptly dropped it into his inventory. He grabbed the tools, inspecting each one in turn. "Hmm, some of these are just high-quality steel. You want to keep this?" He held a pair of pliers out at me.

The tool was dark, without a speck of dust. "Yes, I think my smiths would benefit from having them." I put the steel tool in my inventory.

"Those look weird." Hoshisu pointed at the stack of metal ingots.

I hadn't inspected them too closely before, but now I saw that the outer pieces were all Viridium while the ones in the center had a normal, metallic hue.

"High-quality steel," Kuzai explained. "Them demons' energy been seeping into 'em slowly, turning into Viridium."

"How about you take the steel and I take the Viridium?" I suggested. "Just do me a favor ... can you carry everything? I can't carry much, what with being the magic guy and all."

"You got yourself a deal, man." Malkyr started picking up the metal pieces. With his size and strength, he had quite the carrying capacity.

"That leaves the best for last." Hoshisu pointed at the rack of weapons and armor.

She took a fancy-looking poniard and tested its point on her fingers. She nodded, then replaced it with one of the daggers on her belt. She also put on light chain greaves. It fit snugly over her leather armor.

"It slows me down a bit," she said, "but the extra speed from the boots compensate for that and the added armor value is worth it."

Unceremoniously, Kuzai took a full chainmail armor and sturdy metal bracers for himself. He then replaced the small wooden shield Malkyr had given him with a heavy steel battle shield. He hefted it easily with one hand, though it probably weighed as much as I did.

"Now I be ready fer some serious battles," he declared, testing his range of movement with his new armor. He did look impressive. A level 28 dwarven war-priest was no laughing matter. This one could prove to be troublesome to dispatch if we ever found ourselves on different sides of a conflict.

Most of the remaining pieces of armor were too small for Malkyr, but he was satisfied to acquire a new metal cap with a protruding nose guard.

Only a few small pieces of armor and several swords remained. "If no one is going to claim those, I'd like to take them for the clan's warriors. Mind helping me here, man?" I winked at the big man.

"Sure thing." Malkyr easily put all the weapons in his pack. "Wow, it starts to get heavy. But I'm good for now."

"Hey, Kuzai," I called to the dwarf. "You don't happen to detect any hidden compartments, do you?"

The dwarf gave me a cold stare and didn't bother to answer. He was obviously more tolerant of the twins' mixed heritage then my own 'pure blood' status.

We searched again to make sure we hadn't missed anything, then continued walking down the hallway. We didn't have to go much farther. The hallway ended with circular stairs winding downward. My Dangersense tingled as I looked at the dark opening below us. Something nasty was waiting for us below.

I clenched my fists. All my senses told me the real fight was ahead of us. I looked at my party. Everyone was armed and equipped for battle. We were as ready as we were going to be.

We started descending the stairs, Malkyr taking point, as always.

The stairs went on and on. It was several minutes later when Malkyr came to a stop. "Err, guys, we have a problem here."

I moved next to him and stared at the stairs. They ended abruptly, transforming into a sheer drop. We were left standing on top of a vast, open chamber. Long stalactites were hanging next to us.

I looked straight down. I could see the ground below us, nearly a hundred meters down. It was a deadly fall. I couldn't teleport down; it was well beyond the range of my spell.

From our vantage point, we couldn't see the entirety of the chamber. The ceiling next to us sloped down unevenly, interfering with our line of sight.

"Now what?" Malkyr sighed. "We have ropes, but I don't think they'll reach the bottom and there's nothing to tie them to."

"Ruddy goblin spawns," Kuzai mumbled loudly enough for us to hear. "How'd you survive this long with yer limited knowledge is beyond me. Give me yer ropes."

We took our ropes out and silently handed them to the dwarf. He tied all three lengths together in a secure knot. He picked up a small piece of rock and tied one end of the rope tightly around it. Then he placed the stone in a fissure between the last stair and the wall, stomping on it a few times to wedge it in before throwing the rest of the rope down. I had to hand it to him, it was pretty innovative.

"When yer live working stone as much as we dwarves do, you get a feel for it," he grunted in explanation.

"But it's still not long enough," I pointed out. "The rope ends about 20 meters above the ground."

"We'll either climb the wall or jump down if we have to," the dwarf said. "Yer all seem sturdy enough. A small bump won't kill ya."

"Vic can go first," I volunteered.

"Vic?" The dwarf frowned. "Who that be?"

Disengaging from my shoulders, my cloaked companion transformed himself into his purple goblin form. "Tada!" He raised his hands and gave a mocking bow.

"Durang's beard! What tha' hell is that?" Kuzai sputtered.

"Ruddy dwarven spawns," I said pleasantly, "how you survived this long with your limited knowledge is beyond me."

"Ha!" He was speechless for a few seconds then began to chuckle, "Alright greenskin, one fer you."

I guess he wasn't so bad. For a dwarf.

"Let me show you how it's done, meat suits." Vic pushed through us, reaching for the rope. His hands morphed to wrap around the rope and he easily walked off the last step, sliding down toward the ground far below.

"Your companion got a strange attitude, man," Malkyr said.

"Yes, but he is useful" I pointed out.

Vic reached the end of the rope. Keeping hold of it with one hand, his entire body stretched downward, becoming almost as thin as the rope itself. Once he reached the ground he regrew a pair of thin legs and walked around a little, surveying his surroundings while still holding on to the rope.

<Okay, Boss, I see some green light coming from the other end of this cave. Something is definitely there.>

Come back up, I thought to him. *Can't let the others know about our method of mind-link.*

<You got it, Boss.>

Vic drew his body upward, transforming back into a purple goblin, then climbed up the rope as easily as a monkey.

"It's big and empty. I didn't see any movement, but there's some sort of green flickering light coming from the other end of the cave," he reported. "In any case, the immediate area below seems safe enough."

"Thanks, Vic," I said. "Let's head down."

I moved to the rope, Vic once again in his cloak shape around my shoulders, and started to climb down.

I heard the shuffling of padded feet above me and raised my head in time to see Tempest launching himself to the wall next to the stairs. His sharp nails dug deeply into the hard rock, leaving deep gauges as he slid down next to me.

I reached the end of the rope and teleported the remaining distance. I appeared at the edge of the spell's range two meters above the ground, but I was expecting it and landed on my feet.

Malkyr came next, carefully making his way down the rope. Once he reached the end, he seemed reluctant to make the jump. I couldn't really blame him.

"Wait a second," I called softly, not wanting to alert our presence to whatever lived down here. I started gathering shadows around me, piling them up together and giving them some substance with my mana. Once I finished, a pile of soft shadows, five meters high, was ready to cushion my friend's fall. "Okay, jump now."

Muttering something unintelligible, the big man let go, landing in the center of the pile. His weight almost squashed it flat, but it was enough to break his momentum. When he rolled away to stand on the ground, he was completely unharmed.

He grinned at me. "Okay, I gotta hand it to you. That's a pretty handy trick. Hoshisu's next."

His sister climbed down almost as nimbly as Vic did, dropping from the end of the rope without hesitation, landing on the pile of shadows with her feet first. Bek followed, his light weight barely disturbing the shadowy cushion.

Kuzai came last, climbing awkwardly under the weight of his armor. When he jumped, I allowed my mana to dissipate and the dark cushion deflated as the dwarf hit the ground, ass first.

He got up, rubbing his backside and glaring at me.

"Oops, sorry." I smirked at him.

He mumbled something, and a soft golden light washed over him, healing his injury.

Now that we were down, we could all see the green light Vic spoke of. The chamber was huge, with the other end easily a couple of hundred meters away. Stalagmites rose around us like giant columns. Farther ahead, the chamber's ceiling sloped down, several meters off the ground, creating a narrow passage. It gave the place an uneven vibe.

As I looked at the flickering light beyond the narrow space, the tingling of my Dangersense intensified. I couldn't help the sinking feeling that we were heading into more trouble than we could handle. Still, it wasn't like I had much choice in the matter.

Nihilator would not accept failure.

15 – Who's the Boss?

We walked carefully through the dark cavern. The ground was uneven, forcing us to choose our steps carefully. Fortunately, we were all able to see in the dark to varying degrees, so there was no need to carry a light source that would give away our presence.

<Hey, Boss, there's something over there.> Vic mentally pointed at a fissure in the rocky ground.

"Hold on, I need to check something," I whispered to the others and dismounted Tempest.

It was something crumbled, pressed between the rocks. Putting my hand inside the fissure, I pulled out a piece of cloth. It was a drawing of a skull with two axes lodged in it. I recognized the symbol. It was another armband of the Cracked Skull Clan. Barska's clan. More evidence of his past dealings with this, seemingly extinct, Ogre clan. Looking back at the fissure, I saw something else. *Another armband?*

"What'cha got there?" Malkyr whispered hoarsely.

"It's a note." I straightened the crumpled piece of paper.

Crumpled Note

To Jawbreaker, Ogre Chieftain,

As we agreed, for lending me your Ogre warriors, I'm sending you a gift of great power.

In this package, you will find a chalice and a blueprint for a shrine.

Build the shrine in a dark location, then place the chalice on top and fill it with your blood.

This will summon a demon of great power that will grant you strength beyond your wildest dreams.

–Barska Demon Eye

That chalice thing sounded familiar. I took out the Book of the Damned and leafed through it until I found the page I was looking for. It was a description for conducting a demonic summoning ritual. According to the text, an enchanted chalice had to be filled with the blood of a victim. A demon would then appear and offer his services to the one who performed the ceremony while consuming the victim's soul.

I shook my head. That was how Barska rewarded those who helped him, tricking them into losing their souls. *Devious even after his death.*

I informed the others of my conclusion.

"That explains why the place is overrun with demons," Hoshisu said softly. "A botched summoning ritual. They killed all the Ogres and took over the fort. Interesting. I've never encountered such an extreme change of monster populace before."

"Wow, they weren't kidding when they said this world was a living, breathing thing," Malkyr added. "Still, it sounds like a standard dungeon dive; find the demon boss, kill it, and all the others will disappear. Easy, right?"

Well, he was glib, but he wasn't wrong. "I guess so. Let's keep going."

Ahead of us, two large pillars bordered a section of the cave. The entrance was easily a couple dozen meters high. The light from the green flames was coming from within. I paused for a moment and summoned my mastiffs.

As we approached, we could see clearly inside. A shrine stood at the center, and a golden chalice sat atop it. Green flames shone out of the chalice, illuminating the place with an ominous glare. As we watched, a silvery mist manifested out of the shrine and floated upward, disappearing in the ceiling above us. It appeared we'd found the source of the Ogres' possession.

"Careful now, lads," Kuzai whispered. "There surely be demons nearby."

"YOU ARE QUITE ASTUTE, DWARF."

It was the terrible voice from my vision. The ground shook as the creature appeared, manifesting behind the shrine, bathed in green light. He had the general shape of an Ogre, though much larger – five meters tall at least. His bulky, massive body looked blackened and desiccated with cracks spread all over him. Green flames erupted from those cracks. Two-meter-long horns extended from his forehead and were shrouded in green flames as well. This was a creature of nightmares.

Jawbreaker, Sentinel Demon [possessed]

Level: 42 (0%)

Type: Boss Tier 1 [Sentinel]

HP: 1,268, *MP:* 732

Attributes: P: 56, M: 12, S: 2

Skills: Burn Soul 52, Punch 52, Suffocating Flames 22, Retribution 22

Traits: Demonic, Guard Zone (blocks specific target), Regeneration 20

Resistances: Fire 100%, Armor 184, Mental 70%, Spell 50%, Cold -50%, Holy -50%, Poison Immunity

Description: Sentinel demons specialize in barring access to specific locations. They are patient beings and can lay in wait for decades. They're cunning and ferocious and have an impressive arsenal of devastating combat abilities.

That was ... baffling. I'd expected a unique description of the final boss. After all, this creature used to be the Ogre chief. He had obviously gone through some dramatic changes. It was strange that the description did not reflect that.

Still, the damned thing looked incredibly strong. Its resistances were significant; breaking through its armor wasn't going to be easy. Add to that his thousand-plus HP and possessed Master-ranked combat skills meant we were in for a tough fight.

"WELCOME, INTRUDERS. YOU HAVE BEEN EXPECTED. ONCE I HAVE FEASTED ON YOUR SOULS, I WILL BE ABLE TO BREAK THE SHACKLES AND ...."

"Jeesh, villains and their monologues, give me a break," Malkyr said. He tossed away an empty potion bottle of Ogre's Might, hoisted his axe and charged at Jawbreaker.

The massive demon paused mid-sentence and looked comically surprised at being interrupted.

Adding his running momentum to his swing, Malkyr struck hard at the creature's thigh. The axe bit into the tough, blackened flesh, inflicting only 28 points of damage. Uncharged, Malkyr's axe was no match against the demon's tough hide. In response, a jet of green flames erupted from the small wound, scorching the big man.

Hoshisu sighed. "I guess it's on." She withdrew her enchanted Chainsaw Belt and threw it at the creature. Not to be outdone, I shot my drilling arrows, ordered the mastiffs to attack, and launched my dagger. Bek added his own two spinning arrows to the onslaught.

Jawbreaker just stood there, taking all the punishment. Hoshisu's belt rotated and screeched, but the inner sharpened saws couldn't penetrate its armor. Likewise, the mastiffs pounced on him, doing little to no damage. My dagger scored only a shallow scratch. The six drilling arrows fared a little better; despite the creature's spell resistance that reduced their full potential, they inflicted 42 points of damage in total.

Holding his amulet and invoking his deity's name, Kuzai created a radiant golden ball and launched it at Jawbreaker. The sphere of light soared through the air, illuminating the entire area. It hit the demon on his chest, doing 75 points of damage. The demon bellowed a howl filled with fury. Pieces of black flesh withered and fell from the point of impact, leaving behind gaping holes filled with green flames.

We had all given our best on this first round and had barely reduced the monster's health by ten percent.

The creature ceased his howling and started laughing. "PATHETIC. YOU WILL HAVE TO DO BETTER THAN THAT, WORMS."

His regeneration ability kicked in, gradually filling up his health bar. He arched backward and his chest expanded, enlarging the fissures covering his body. The green flames coming out of him intensified and burst in all directions, covering the entire area and shrouding us all in flames and ash. Malkyr held up his gauntleted hand, but the flames just washed over him. The gauntlet couldn't absorb this strange green fire.

The flames inflicted 42 points of damage to all of us and the ash remained, filling our lungs and obscuring our view. Everyone started coughing and rubbing their eyes. Tempest alone was unaffected by the attack. Being a demon had its advantages when fighting one.

Half choked and coughing, I called out, "Bek – *hack* – *hack* – get back!" Our little mobile healing platform was not built to take damage like the rest of us.

Stubbornly, Malkyr continued to chop at Jawbreaker, his repeated hits making shallow marks on the creature's tough exterior. Every time he struck, a small jet of flames erupted out, searing him for a small amount of damage. This was not going well.

Time to bring out the big guns. I took out the Fire Rod and loaded it with a level 20 void crystal. "Malkyr – hand!"

The big man took my meaning immediately. While fighting off a cough, he released one hand from his axe and held it out to me. I activated the rod, releasing a gust of flames at him, reducing its durability by 20 points. The flames were sucked in by the gauntlet and the axe's rune lit up. Placing his free hand back on the hilt, the axe blazed even brighter. It then began to vibrate, displacing the air around it in what I now recognized as Malkyr's Concussive Strike skill. He was going all out too.

His Greataxe struck true, shattering the demon's tough armor-like skin, sending ripples of shockwaves directly into its body and forcing the creature to take a step back to steady itself.

Despite the awesome blow, it only caused 50 points of damage, and Malkyr was sprayed with another gust of flame, bringing his health down to 60 percent.

It took the demon only a second to recuperate from the shockwave. He straightened and bellowed a thunderous chuckle. "BETTER, WORM, BUT STILL – NOT ENOUGH!"

The creature raised both hands high above Malkyr's head. His fists ignited with hot, green flames. Malkyr was in trouble.

"No!" Hoshisu cried, charging forward while coughing. Her daggers scrapped at the demon's side, doing little damage. I couldn't cast another spell for a few seconds, so I tried using Freeze. The effort took 102 of my MP. The creature gave off only the slightest indication of being impeded. Two globes of energy – one golden, one green – hit Malkyr, as our two healers targeted him, raising his health to 90 percent.

Then the fists came crashing down together. Malkyr tried to block with his axe, but he had no chance against that behemoth. The two blazing, rock-like fists descended on the man, flattening him against the rocks. I heard the audible crack of bones. The fists lifted and Malkyr's body appeared, looking all wrong, broken, and misshapen. He was still alive though, with about 20 percent of his health remaining. He couldn't survive another hit.

"Shadow-crap!" I cast Shadow Web, sent my dagger zooming at the demon, and ordered Tempest to attack. The web sizzled and withered in the green flames. Hoshisu rushed at her brother and tried to pull him away from the enemy. Jawbreaker wasn't about to let her get away with that and raised his two flaming fists again. Then Tempest charged in. Coming from behind, the large Demon Wolf jumped on the possessed Ogre, its teeth sinking deep into the creature's shoulder and clamping hard, interrupting the next attack and buying us a few seconds.

I could sense both Kuzai and Bek casting their healing spells over Malkyr. No one was facing Jawbreaker directly. I knew what that meant. "Time to go play the goblin tank again," I grunted, stepping forward to stand before the huge creature and activating Mana Shield.

Bellowing a roar, the enraged Ogre grabbed Tempest with two hands, ripped him off his shoulder and hurled him across the chamber. Poor Tempest struck a stone column, hard, then slid to the ground where he remained, whimpering. Jawbreaker straightened, puffing his chest again.

"Shit, another wave – get ready!" I managed to yell before the green fire and ash exploded out of the demon's body again, washing the area all around us. I was protected by my shield and wasn't damaged, but the others were scattered and they each got their share. Luckily, the healers managed to get their restorative magic into Malkyr, or else the blast would have ended him. Everyone was injured to various degrees.

I launched a volley of drilling arrows straight into Jawbreaker's face, doing 30 damage. That got his attention. The demon reached down to me with one arm, green flames dancing between his fingers. His palm was stopped by my shield, hovering a few centimeters away from my face. I breathed a little easier. I could sense him activating his Burn Soul skill. I wasn't keen on discovering firsthand what that ominous-sounding skill actually did.

Then something unexpected happened.

Break Enchantment hits Mana Shield Mana Shield spell will be unusable for one minute.

My shield shattered around me and the burning palm reached in and grabbed me. I screamed as the flames cooked my body and boiled my blood. My health plummeted; I was losing 42 HP per second. The others were still recovering from their wounds and couldn't help. I lost precious seconds and large chunks of health as I writhed in agony before willing myself to act through the pain. I tried using Shadow Teleport, but for the first time, it failed.

You cannot teleport while being restrained.

The flames continued to cook me alive and I was reduced to 50 percent of my health. However, with nearly 300 points of damage inflicted, my Blood Wrath ability kicked in. I channeled the raw rage brought on by the pain, blasting it out around me as a pushing force. Triple-charged, the blast was strong enough to pry open the fist around me. I fell to the hard ground, losing a few more HP. I managed to stand and look up in time to see the two flaming fists descend on me.

Nihilator's Sanction triggered.

Due to receiving a fatal amount of damage, you have transformed into a being of shadow for one minute. You are completely undetectable and invulnerable for the duration and may move freely. Once the duration is over, you will return to the material plane, fully healed. Mana regenerates at the normal rate.

This ability will not be usable again for the next 24 hours.

Well, damn. That demon basically killed me. I was saved by my boss tier 2 trump card, 'Nihilator's Sanction.' The surrounding shadows were drawn to me like a magnet, bringing me back to full health.

It was obvious now; our enemy was too strong for us. We couldn't hope to defeat him in a straight up fight. We had to change our tactics. I had nearly a minute to figure out what to do next. I just hoped the others would survive that long. The Shadow Hounds didn't; that second blast of fire had taken them all out.

For the moment, Jawbreaker seemed content to secure his position over the shrine. The others maintained their distance and concentrated on healing themselves.

I looked up at the ceiling. Almost every book I read that dealt with defeating an overwhelmingly powerful monster underground ended with the resourceful hero causing a stalagmite to fall on said monster, winning the day. Alas, there were no such conveniently placed stone spears in the area above us.

Well, that only left one other possibility. I inspected the shrine carefully. Now that I was invulnerable, I could ignore the imminent danger long enough to concentrate. Luckily, despite being officially on a different plane of existence, I could still 'read' the streams of information coming from the material plane.

The shrine exuded darkness, no surprise there. Black-green ribbons extended out of it, stretching all over. I could sense each ribbon connected to a creature, binding him. Most of the ribbons went upward. That made sense; most demons we encountered were higher up in the fort. A single ribbon went sideways, but to my surprise, it didn't connect with Jawbreaker. Instead, it disappeared into a dark area even I couldn't see into. That was weird. Jawbreaker did have a black and green ribbon tethered to it, but that one, like the others from the shrine, was going upward. Yep, weird.

The other party members finally came up with a battle plan. Holding up his amulet, Kuzai cast a spell. A wave of light pushed back the ash and lit up the place. A glitter of light remained on each party member. I snorted. *Great,* now *he remembers to use his buff spells.*

Tempest remained behind, still recovering, while the group advanced. Their healing spells were probably ineffective on a demon.

This time, moving together, the twins advanced on Jawbreaker in their usual stance. Kuzai wielded his maul and moved away from them. It looked like they were trying to flank the demon. Bek remained far behind, at the edge of his heal range. I had to admit it was not a bad plan. Unfortunately, it wouldn't work. Jawbreaker was too powerful for us. His regeneration had already fully healed him. My party members stood no chance against him. Not on their own. With a few seconds remaining on the clock, I watched the melee fighters flanking the demon, who was unwilling to move away from the shrine. The fighters lunged forward, the twins with axe and daggers, the dwarf swinging his heavy maul. Before any weapon could connect, the demon chuckled and activated his Suffocating Flames spell. Fire erupted from his body, pushing everyone away, breaking their momentum. At least Kuzai's glittering buff seemed effective at repelling the ash.

Still invisible to the demon, I moved next to the shrine, placing it between us. I crouched and hid behind the small structure. A second later I reappeared back in the material plane, fully healed.

The sounds of fighting continued. Still crouching, I took out the Book of the Damned and leafed through it. The book had proved to be invaluable in this adventure. Based on the ribbons I saw, I guessed Ka-De came from the lone, deserted pool we encountered in the great hall above us. I already I knew how to activate the pools. Now I was looking for a way to reverse the effect. Hopefully targeting the demon directly – instead of the pool it came from – would work.

There. Plain and simple. I just had to reverse the mana fluctuation and the pool gate would close. Without the open gateway to sustain it, the demon would be weakened and quickly 'run out of gas.' This approach would not have helped us fight the hordes of demons above since the guardian Pyrolith would have simply reactivated the pools. But now that the guardian was dealt with, it should work.

Grinning to myself, I closed the book and stood up, channeling my mana. "Hey, smut face!"

The demon turned its head to scowl at me. He was having a great time pummeling the others. They were all down to about 50 percent of their health.

I opened my mouth and released the mana with a roar. The stream of mana hit the creature and the green ribbon tethering him to our world was cut away. Jawbreaker stumbled, falling to his knees.

I conjured a trio of revolving drilling arrows and called to my dumbfounded companions, "Get it *now*, while he's down." Then I shot the arrows at its face.

His health bar was already shrinking and the drilling arrows hastened the process. Reinvigorated, Malkyr, Hoshisu, and Kuzai howled as they fell upon the kneeling demon, hacking and bashing its body. Jawbreaker was declining before our eyes, losing mass and height. Still, he wasn't finished. The twins were both in bad shape, suffering damage from the flames that erupted with every hit they landed. Almost blindly, the demon swung his fists, connecting with both of them and hurling them away.

The siblings had a quarter of their health remaining. Kuzai was still holding his own. As a priest of light and higher level than the twins, he was naturally better equipped to battle demonic beings.

I tried using Shadow Web to force the demon onto the shrine. But even in his diminished state, his flames burned my web away. Normal fire wouldn't be able to do that. Hellfire was a pain in the butt.

"Hack at the legs! Make him fall on the shrine," I shouted to the dwarf who was trading blows with Jawbreaker.

"Ye want a freaking giant demon on a shrine, ye'll get yer freaking demon on a shrine," Kuzai grunted, expertly bashing the demon's back, making it topple over.

Yes! I was going to make it! I called my dagger to my hand, getting into position, ready to perform the sacrifice.

"ENOUGH!"

The force of the voice blasted us all off our feet, allowing Jawbreaker to rise unsteadily back to his own.

A woman came out of the darkness. I could now clearly see the single horizontal ribbon from the shrine connected to her.

She stood tall and proud, her ebony skin smooth and perfect. Two small antlers grew back from her temples, holding her lush raven-black hair in place.

And she was completely naked.

With large breasts, flat stomach, and swaying hips, she was a sight few men would refuse. The unearthly, dark-skinned beauty glared at us. "You dare assault me at my own shrine?" Though threatening, her voice was rich and throbbing, sending tingles down my spine. "This is *my* place of power. Here, I reign supreme. Soon, I will be strong enough to bring forth my army of *eager* minions. They will sweep through your realm, sewing chaos and discord." She passed her tongue over her blood-red lips as if savoring the notion. "Your mortal souls will be chained in eternal *bondage*, enthralled by corrupt pleasures, eager to cater to my every deviant whim. But first ..." With a flick of her wrist, another ribbon shot out of her body, connecting to Jawbreaker. Immediately the demon stood taller, his wounds beginning to close.

<Shadow-crap.>

I couldn't agree more. *Analyze.*

> **Kusitesh, Demon of Desire**
>
> *Level:* 200 (10%)
>
> *Type:* Boss Tier VI [Temptress]
>
> *HP:* 7,234, *MP*: 14,296
>
> *Attributes:* P: 6, M: 202, S: 41
>
> *Skills:* Seduce 51, Charm 51, Barter 51, Withering Gaze 212, Dominate 212
>
> *Traits:* Demonic
>
> *Resistances:* Fire 100%, Armor 346, Mental 80%, Spell 60%, Cold -50%, Holy -50%
>
> *Description:* Having lived for millennia, *Kusitesh* has achieved great power. Using her wiles and magic she dominated lesser demons and bound them to her will. After being summoned to the material plane by an incompetent Ogre summoner, Kusitesh capitalized on the situation. Unshackled by a flawed ritual, she was able to take control over her summoner, Jawbreaker, and infuse him with infernal energies which strengthened and further bound him to her will. Since then, she has used the power of the shrine as a conduit to summon her lesser minions, taking over the Ogre clan in the process. She now roams the forsaken fort, looking for ways to gain more power and wreak devastation upon the world.

Now *that* was the specific background I was expecting from the final boss. Crap.

Kusitesh's demeanor changed. She wrapped her slender arms under her ample bosom and spoke in a cooing voice. "Come now, boys, there's no need to harass my bodyguard, is there?" Her smile was ravenous and her eyes shone with an ethereal red. Waves of intense mana and information threads erupted from her like a tidal wave.

Malkyr stopped dead in his tracks.

I was about to answer with a drilling arrow to her head, then a realization hit me. *Why fight against her? She is sooo gorgeous and defenseless. We could be good together ... We are both monsters and bosses after all; it's like we're made for each other.*

[Come to me, my love. Serve me, worship me.]

I could hear something else screaming inside my head. It sounded familiar, like a long-forgotten colleague. I shook my head to clear out the bothersome noise and obediently stepped toward the love of my life.

"What's wrong?" Hoshisu asked sharply.

"Sorry, sis." The big man was struggling to move. "She hit me with a debuff. I can't move till it wears off."

"Damn it," she hissed. "I see it. There's a 'Charmed' symbol over your icon. No wonder she got you. She has an 'impossible' tag; she's way out of our league."

[Kill her for me, my love and we shall be together for all time]

Yes! What an excellent idea.

I conjured my spinning missiles and launched them at the evil traveler woman.

"What the *hell* are you doing!" Malkyr yelled as the three projectiles hit Hoshisu, instantly claiming a third of her health. Fighting travelers was so much easier than having to deal with huge, possessed Ogres.

"You will not stop us!" I snarled at them.

"He's got the Seduced debuff" Hoshisu called out.

"What? That's impossible, NPCs can only affect the minds of ..." His eyes widened at the realization.

"What's the matter, you white-haired wench," I taunted the woman, "I thought you wanted to fight me." I was vaguely aware that the annoying dwarf was somewhere nearby, fighting Jawbreaker. "Well, here's your chance."

"Fine." Her gaze shot daggers at me. She withdrew a chain belt from her inventory and slapped it over her shoulder. It was a chainmail bandoleer. It had eight holstered throwing daggers placed at equal intervals for easy reach.

I snorted. *Like it's going to do her any good.*

The woman advanced on me, holding her daggers. I raised one hand leisurely and conjured another trio of arrows. Before I could complete the spell, Hoshisu rolled forward, instantly closing the distance between us, and slashed at my arm, breaking the spell.

Hoshisu's daggers hit you for 18 damage.

Clenching my teeth, I channeled my mana into a roaring tornado, ready to unleash shadowy horrors and pain on the annoying woman.

Then something caught my eye.

Bek.

He was moving like a sleepwalker, his body rigid, toward Kusitesh. She bent down, her hands caressing his cheeks, then held his head steady. Her eyes shone brightly as she gazed straight into his eyes. Bek screamed, and his body started shriveling. A vaporous mist came out of his mouth and went into the woman's. The goblin's body deflated, leaving behind an empty sack of skin and bones. Kusitesh rose to her full height, licking her lips.

The only thing I felt upon witnessing this horrific display was ... joy. My beloved mistress had feasted well, all thanks to me. After all, it was I who fattened him up and brought him to her.

[Now, my love, open yourself fully to me; I want to know you completely.]

In my haste to comply, I acted without thinking. I opened my character sheet and directed its information ribbons to her.

Her beautiful head jerked back in surprise, and her eyes lost their focus, staring at something in front of her.

<BOSS! SNAP OUT OF IT!> Vic yelled in my mind.

And then, it was like an invisible net that was wrapped around my brain suddenly melted away. I could think again. At the last second, Hoshisu halted her strike, her two daggers inches from my neck.

I looked down the pointy ends of her weapons, still poised to strike. I feebly held up one hand. "I'm okay now, sorry for the slip. It won't happen again."

She didn't respond. She just looked at me, narrow-eyed, as if measuring me.

[Why have you forsaken me, my love? Come to me.]

<*Na-ah bitch, I got him now,*> Vic retorted. <*Boss, you gotta do something. I can fight off her influence for a little while, but if she manages to control you again, I don't know if you'll ever be able to escape her grasp.*>

That certainly got my attention.

"We have to end this, now," I said to Hoshisu.

Her nostrils flared. "Good idea. It's not like we weren't giving it all we had until now."

I scanned the room, taking in my surroundings. Kuzai was at a quarter health, facing off Jawbreaker, who was standing strong with over 80 percent of his health. Malkyr was still struggling to move.

"I have an idea, but I'll need Kuzai's help. Do you think you can tank Jawbreaker for a few moments?"

Hoshisu bent down, putting her face right in front of mine, holding my gaze. "Watch me." Then she turned and ran at the gigantic boss.

As she approached the melee, she tucked and rolled between the immense demon's legs, coming from behind it. Her daggers stabbed at its leg as she passed, scoring sneak damage despite her opponent's heavy armor. That was enough to get his attention and the demon whirled around to face the woman, ignoring the dwarf it had been fighting.

"Kuzai, over here!" I moved to stand near the shrine.

The dwarf was bloodied and looked like he was all for continuing the fight and ignoring me. But Hoshisu waved him off and he reluctantly disengaged and came running at me.

I placed my hands on the shrine. I could easily sense the power coursing through it, connecting it to the lower planes. I knew I could try pushing against that power, trying to force it to close in a harrowing battle of wills. But I didn't have to. I wasn't the only priest around here, and as luck had it, the other one was a follower of the light. Kuzai was diametrically opposed to the shrine's power and much more suited than I to resist it. And in case anything went wrong, he was also more disposable.

"If we can consecrate the shrine, the demons will lose their anchor to our world," I shouted. "Your god loves the light, right? You alone can do it!"

The dwarf eyed me suspiciously. "Why nay ye do it yerself?"

"I can't!" I held up my arms. "I don't worship Durang like you do. The darkness I wield is inadequate for the task."

Wiping blood off his face as he weighed my words, Kuzai finally nodded. "Ye got that right. Ruddy goblins." He placed his hands on the shrine, his face grimacing in agony as he did so.

The shrine's evil powers were anathema to the followers of the light and contact with it had clearly caused the dwarf pain. Good to know.

Kusitesh switched her attention to the dwarf. Her eyes shone and tendrils of enticing mana shot out toward him. Kuzai's ever-present golden aura flared up, deflecting the attempt. The dwarf's god protected him from her influence.

"No!" the demoness shouted. "Stop him, my love. Kill him and we can rule this plane together. I will not try to force my will upon you again, you have my word!"

<Yeah, because demons are known for being loyal and trustworthy.>

"Will you give me the shrine as well?" I countered.

"Yes, gladly!"

"Then swear it in the name of your dark master."

She hesitated "I cannot. But I promise you shall have it, along with my body to do as you please. You can experience boundless pleasure, wrapped in my embrace for an eternity ..."

Now *that* was an interesting offer ...

<Boss?> Vic's voice broke my contemplation.

Oh, right.

"I got a counter offer, bitch. Go to hell."

Barter skill level increased to 12.

Vic laughed. *<'Go to hell' – good one, Boss!>*

Thanks, Vic.

Kuzai puffed his cheeks, his whole body straining as if trying to lift a great weight.

With my Mana Sight, I could clearly see what he was trying to do. He was forcefully pushing his radiant, holy mana into the dark, unholy shrine. But the darkness fought back.

Kusitesh closed in on Hoshisu, her eyes boring into the other woman's, commanding her to submit to her will. Hoshisu had no chance of resisting a spell with such an obvious power gap, and her knees buckled. Jawbreaker bent down and snatched her limp form with both hands and activated his Burn Soul skill. With two harmful Master-ranked skills affecting her at once, Hoshisu was doomed. Within seconds her body wilted and crumbled to dust.

"No!" It was Malkyr. The sight of his sister dying gave the man new strength. He broke away from the power that held him down and roared. His axe and his own body glowed orange together, reflecting the same intensity. I could see the runes from the gauntlet extend over his entire body within that glow.

Malkyr charged straight at Kusitesh and struck hard, cleaving between her perfectly shaped breasts. She drew back from the raging man with only a shallow cut marring her perfect skin. Jawbreaker stepped forward to stand between his mistress and her enemy.

Well, at least the siblings had kept them engaged this long.

I turned my attention back to the dwarf. He was sweating profusely now and giving off an equal share of sweat and blood. I could see that his bright mana already filled half the shrine, but the darkness fought back for every millimeter, forcing Kuzai to strain to his limits, even to maintain the progress he had made. His mana was draining rapidly. He was in for the battle of his life.

Glancing back at Malkyr, I saw he was now afflicted with the 'Dominated' debuff. The large man could only stare helplessly at Jawbreaker as the creature pummeled him with heavy punches. He had only 40 HP left when Jawbreaker raised both fists and brought them down together, smashing my companion to the ground. Another fatality.

Kuzai was panting hard, almost out of mana. Even his health bar dropped from the intense effort. The shrine's darkness was almost completely replaced by the light.

With no one left to block their way, Jawbreaker and Kusitesh finally turned their attention to us. The temptress shot two crimson bolts from her eyes, but they were repelled by the last bits of brilliant mana pouring out of the dwarf. Jawbreaker took a huge step toward us.

"Now would be a good time to finish," I advised the dwarf.

"Aaaaaaarrrrghhhhhh!" With one last push of Herculean effort, Kuzai forced the final few points of mana through his hands and into the shrine. Then he dropped to his knees, fully spent from the exertion. The shrine swirled with black and white lights, each fighting for dominance. Kuzai had failed to completely sanctify the shrine, but it was enough.

Jawbreaker faltered and buckled at his next step. He fell, hitting his head on the shrine, and remained there, flinching, but unable to move.

Kusitesh ran at us, screaming something in an unknown language, her face wilting, becoming emaciated and horrifying.

That was the moment I had been waiting for.

Staring at the head in front of me, I drew my dagger and struck down hard.

16 – Darkness Rising

Kuzai sacrificed. +112 Faith Points (Cult of Nihilator) [base 28 X 4 using an altar]

Quest failed: The Holy Dwarf 3

You have killed Kuzai, ending his journey, and forfeited your chance at establishing beneficial relations with the BoulderBelly clan.

For a split second, Kuzai's eyes reflected his shock at my betrayal. Then his body liquified and was consumed by darkness. Almost as an afterthought, I withdrew my dagger and stabbed Jawbreaker's head as well.

Jawbreaker sacrificed. +252 Faith Points (Cult of Nihilator) [base 63 X 4 using an altar]

Level up! You have reached Character Level 25. You have 1 ability point to allocate.

Well, losing the new trade option was a shame, but I doubted the dwarves would have given us a fair deal anyway. Dwarves were notoriously untruthful, any goblin worth his salt knew that. But the attractiveness of the reward was irrelevant. My master wanted a 'proper sacrifice' to sanctify his shrine and Kuzai was it. Jawbreaker would have been a worthy sacrifice, yes, but I had no doubt that the evil Nihilator would much rather have the soul of a priest of light. And as it turned out, I was right.

After the holy dwarf was consumed, my master's power manifested, extinguishing both the pesky holy light and the impure darkness, claiming the sacred place for his own. The shrine shone with new power, radiating with beautiful, serene darkness.

With a shrill scream, Kusitesh dropped to the ground and began convulsing. Gashes opened all over her now disfigured face, making her an even more hideous sight as she writhed in agony.

Her arms tightened against her body and her knees snapped up to her chest. It looked as if an invisible hand was crushing her like a soda can. She kept shrieking as her bones audibly cracked and her head bent down, grinding her chin into her chest. Then her entire body compressed, accompanied by more sounds of crunching bones. Something metallic appeared within the gruesome ball of bloodied flesh. In a few seconds, whatever remained of Kusitesh was sucked into the metal item which fell to the floor. Where moments ago a voluptuous demoness stood, there was now a chalice, glowing with unholy aura.

Quest Updated: Dark Missionary

You have dedicated a place of worship to The Cult of Nihilator.

Remaining places of worship to dedicate: 1

Time remaining: 17 days

"HA HA HA, you have done well, my minion," Nihilator's voice sounded, coming from his new shrine.

By now the bodies of the dwarf and the Ogre had melted into pools of darkness, oozing down the shrine.

"Hmmm, how interesting. The essence of a demon and the essence of the once divine, coming together on my shrine. How ... quaint."

Instead of coalescing into new void crystals, the two pools of darkness flowed into each other, merging together into a single puddle.

"You shall not have the crystals, my greedy minion. But do not fret, Nihilator rewards his loyal minions. Behold!"

The puddle of darkness flowed over the shrine, rippling but maintaining its shape without a container to hold it. I distractedly put the new level-up attribute point into Mental as I watched events unfold around me.

A shape slowly emerged from the puddle, first, a head appeared, then hands, torso, and legs. The pool subsided as the body grew out of it until it vanished completely.

Standing on the altar, looking around him with small, beady eyes, was Kuzai.

<*Wow, I didn't see* that *coming!*> Vic exclaimed in my mind.

But it wasn't the same Kuzai. Though he still looked to be mostly a dwarf, his appearance was greatly changed.

His skin had become deep grey, like a corpse. He was completely bald, without a trace of his previous proud beard. His head was thinner and elongated, with a pointy chin and sharp, long ears. His fingers were twice as long as before and had three knuckles on them. He looked like a nightmare version of a dwarf, one whose name was used to scare small dwarven kids into obedience.

The creature – Kuzai – looked at me. His lips peeled back in a sneer, exposing gleaming sharp teeth.

Kuzai, Aberration, Acolyte of Nihilator

Level: 28

Type: Boss Tier 1 [Priest]

HP: 354/354, *MP:* 541/541

Attributes: P: 11; M: 20; S: 1

Skills: Mace 21, Shield 21, Control Shadow 18, Shadow Heal 18, Banish Good 10

Traits: Half-Demon, Shadow-Touched

Resistances: Physical 25%, Magic 20%, Fire 50%, Mental 50%, Holy -100%

Description: After being sacrificed on Nihilator's shrine, Kuzai's soul became mixed with that of a demon. Intrigued by the paradox, Nihilator allowed the new mixed soul to be reborn as his faithful minion, instead of devouring it.

I stared at this obviously unnatural being, speechless.

"I am reborn," the creature that used to be Kuzai said in a flat, whispery voice, He lowered his gaze, examining his own hands. "The Master demands obedience; we are all his servants."

That was unexpected. Kuzai was now a monster, a boss one. His stats were impressive but still lower than mine. Though he was three levels above me, my higher boss tier more than made up the difference.

I blinked a few times, trying to wrap my head around this new development.

"Yeah, sure. All hail the master," I said, still trying to figure out what was going on. "You mean Nihilator, right?"

"You DARE utter the master's name!" The creature's nostrils widened. "You are unworthy! Perishhhh!"

He directed his palm at me and I felt his will manipulating the shadows around me. Patches of darkness swelled, threatening to bury me.

I raised my hand as well, channeling my mana, resisting and countering his influence with ease. The darkness slowly deflated, returning to normal.

"Now listen here," I growled. "Play nice or I'll sacrifice you again."

"So, *it* has power," Kuzai muttered. "The mark of the master is seared on its flesh. But *it* is a lowly goblin! It cannot be worthy of such honor. How could it be? Ah ... it wields power ... and magic. Yes, the master always chooses his servants well."

The creature continued talking to himself. On the bright side, while he was talking he wasn't trying to kill me, so I had that going for me.

<Good for you, Boss, finding the silver lining in every situation. Hey, look! The ceiling is not collapsing on you, you have that going for you as well, you lucky dog!>

Kuzai jerked up his head and studied me. "Oh, *it* has a companion. A being of shadow-weave and blood. Come here, minion of a minion."

To my surprise, Vicloak disengaged from my shoulders and slithered, still in his cloak shape, to the mentally unstable dwarf.

What are you doing, Vic?

<He controls my body! I can't resist him!>

Vic reached Kuzai. The dwarf held up his hand, and Vic flowed into his open palm, condensing himself into a purple ball.

<Oren!> There was a note of panic in his voice. *<Help!>*

"That's enough," I said sternly.

Kuzai raised his eyes and looked at me steadily. "Minions should learn their place."

I could feel his will clenching, pressing down on Vic's mana-made body. I could have probably resisted what came next, but everything happened so quickly, I was still trying to figure out what was going on.

The purple ball started leaking mana, becoming smaller and smaller.

<Oren!>

I got a grip on myself and tried to counter Kuzai actions, but it was already too late. All the mana was promptly withdrawn from Vic, and the only thing that remained of my companion's body was a few drops of blood, dripping between the creature's fingers onto the ground.

"You made your point," I hissed, clenching my fists to stop myself from blasting away that conceited dwarf. Despite the provocation, there was no reason to go to war over his little display. After all, I could resummon Vic in a heartbeat.

My eyes flashed with anger as I examined his uncaring expression. "So I take it you're also a priest of Nihilator?"

He bristled as I dared utter the name again, but restrained himself with visible effort. "I am the master's most devoted servant," he declared proudly. "I shall forever follow his command."

"That's awesome, good for you," I said dryly. "I wish you all the best. I'll be going now." I turned my back on him and started walking away.

I was bluffing, of course.

"Wait!"

And it seemed to be working. I stopped and looked back at the dwarf. He began to slowly circle me. "The master has marked *it*," he muttered again. "*It* is bound on the pain of death, and oh ... *it* was to be devoured."

Surprisingly, he finished that sentence with a tone of respect.

"What are you going on about?" I demanded.

"The master wished to devour you. You were deemed worthy of such an honor. Whereas I ..." he looked down, "... I was unworthy. My essence was rejected. My fate was to be reincarnated instead."

Okay, now I missed having Vic around. With his body gone, something about the dark energies permeating the chamber blocked our mindlink. He would have said something along the lines of, 'That deranged puppet's deepest wish is to be devoured by a larger, even more deranged puppet?' I shook my head. Yeah, Vic would probably make a better punchline than that.

"Yes, that's right." It was time to dazzle him with how close Nihilator and I were. "I'm Nihilator's head priest. I offer him sacrifices, feeding him until he grows strong enough to break his chains. Oh, and he also taught me some useful skills. We're buddies, really. Bros almost. He touched me in a special way, putting his binding rune into me. You think he does that with just *anyone* he meets?"

On second thought, maybe it was a good thing Vic wasn't around to hear me say that.

Kuzai lowered his head. "*It* is favored by the master. I shall offer my services." He looked back at me "A piece of my essence once commanded this place. As such, I offer you the choice to do with it as you please. In the end, all our achievements are to the glory of our master."

You have defeated the leaders of the Ogre Fort.

As a boss, you may choose to take command of the settlement or demolish it. Demolish/Control?

Well, that was a step on the right track. I wondered why I hadn't received this prompt earlier. Without hesitation, I selected 'Control.' After all, that was the whole purpose of coming here.

You have taken control of a new settlement.

Name: Ogre Fort

Type: Fort

Garrison: 1 boss [priest]

Buildings: Shrine

Well, that was underwhelming. The only value this fort had to offer was the Ogres themselves. Slightly disappointing, but I had achieved my goal.

Granted Quest Completed: Raid Ogre Lair

Malkyr, Hoshisu awarded: 200 reputation, 500 XP, 170 gold. Potion Belt (Malkyr), Assassin Needle Ring (Hoshisu)

I chuckled. *Good for them.*

I looked at the crudely constructed shrine. It was made of rough stone and decorated with pieces of broken bones. Ogres weren't great builders it seemed.

Despite its appearance, the shrine was projecting an almost overwhelming sense of raw power. Waves of condensed blackness pulsed regularly, intensifying the darkness around us. The energy resonated with me. It felt comforting to stand that close to a source of power so attuned to my own. I laid my hands on the rough surface and felt the energy thrumming through my body, filling me with a sense of power.

"This place is worthy of the master," Kuzai declared. "It is a place of deep darkness, free from the accursed light of the heavens. In here, our master's power is undiluted. Pure."

"I can feel it." In fact, I almost didn't hear him over the roar of energy running through me.

I withdrew my hands from the shrine and something caught my eye. An elongated object on the ground was partially obstructed by the shrine. It looked like Jawbreaker left behind some loot. I moved around the shrine and picked up the object. It was one of the demon's long, straight horns.

Demon Horn Staff

Description: The horn maintained some of the demon's infernal powers before he was banished back into the abyss. It is exceptionally durable and can double as a spear. Three bloodstones are embedded along the shaft.

Runecraft viability: 4 runes

Type: Two-handed

Rank: Rare

Durability: 300/300

Damage: 45-50

Effect I: +10 Mental when calculating mana regeneration
Effect II: Can store up to three magical charges that can be cast instantly

The staff was shaped like a narrow cone with a wide butt and a sharpened point on the other end. A circular groove ran along its length and it had three gems embedded along its upper half. It was nearly two meters long, but it was light enough for me to wield with ease. *It's high time I upgraded some of my equipment*, I reflected. This staff was a significant step up from my old Feathered staff. Though it would mean I'd also lose the item-set bonus as well, the boost it offered to mana regen was negligible at my power level. Besides, I was planning on replacing the rest of my gear anyway.

I inventoried my old staff and gripped the new one, then turned to the dark dwarf to inform him of the bad news. "I need you to stay here."

Kuzai stared at me, unblinking.

"I intend to raise a Dark Temple to serve the master, back at my clan," I explained. "It will become the focal point of condensed darkness, funneled in from other shrines, like this one. Someone has to stay behind and channel this shrine's power."

He averted his gaze. "*It* wants to leave me behind."

He's talking to himself again, great.

"But *it* also intends to raise a Dark Temple to the glory of the master. I will serve the master best by working at the temple. I shall go with *it.*"

He looked up at me. "I will go with you back to your clan."

"Yeah, I got that." I rolled my eyes. "I still need someone to stay here and maintain the shrine."

"This is an inconsequential complication." He closed his eyes, concentrating.

I could feel him redirecting his mana back at himself. Weird.

Then, with a soft *pop*, Kuzai's shadow separated from him. The shadow grew into a three-dimensional creature, solidifying before my eyes. A perfect black replica of the dwarf himself.

"My shadow will remain behind and maintain the holy shrine," Kuzai declared. "It is an inconvenience, but it will do for now. At least, until you send another to replace it." The shadow obediently moved to stand in front of the shrine.

"How did you do that?" I looked at him with newfound respect.

"*It* is asking how to wield the master's gift," he mumbled.

Yeah, I missed Vic. Well, now was a good time to get him back. I resummoned my companion, investing 400 health and 800 mana, almost my entire pool to form up his body.

Vic's amorphous purple body appeared, floating in the air, as large as a dinner table. Once I stemmed the flow of health and mana, it transformed, taking Vic's familiar goblin shape. He was now as tall as me.

"What took you so long?" he blurted. "Good job sticking up for me by the way." He glared at Kuzai, who looked at us impartially.

"Sorry Vic, it all happened too fast. But we talked and we understand each other better now. This won't happen again." I shot the nonchalant dwarf a warning look.

"That's not good enough!" he fumed. "Do you realize the extent of this situation's severity – what it meant that I was put down like that?"

"Yeah, I get it. Kuzai has a similar ability to mine and can manipulate Dark Mana." *Which makes him dangerous*, I added silently.

"I'm not talking about that!" Vic stomped his foot. "Without my body, I lost precious opportunities. All those excellent puns and chances to poke at you two 'Priests of Dorkness' – all gone!"

I chuckled. "You better watch out for Kuzai from now on. I don't think he takes your jokes well."

"Bah, I can work around him. He's so obtuse I could joke-juggle beyond his comprehension and get away with it."

I shrugged, "Suit yourself; it's your own body at risk."

I turned back to the dwarf. "So, care to let me in on how you control your shadow like that?"

Kuzai gave me superior look. "Is *it* unaware of the power the master has bestowed upon *it?* Why, even the lowliest of –"

"Save it." I waved at him dismissively. I didn't really need his help, now that I saw him doing it.

Mimicking the dwarf, I concentrated and channeled my mana into my own shadow. Dark mana and shadow combined together easily, as if made for each other. I could feel the reins of absolute control over my shadow, much more than when I manipulated the environment's shadows. The sensation was a lot like dominating another creature, except here I was dominating a part of myself. There was no resistance to break through, no conflict. With a soft *pop* of its own, my shadow disengaged from me and grew, becoming a three-dimensional shape.

I was unprepared for what followed. I wobbled on my feet, overwhelmed by a bombardment of sensations. I was simultaneously looking through two sets of eyes, hearing through two sets of ears, feeling the cold air on the skin of my two bodies.

The disparity between the two viewpoints threatened to overwhelm me. I closed my real eyes firmly, seeing only through my shadow. That helped a little, but it still felt wrong. I was looking from a point of view that was out of sync with my real body. Bodies. One of them anyway. The misalignment was confusing and disturbing, to say the least.

That was another, previously unknown, side effect of living inside NEO. Another example of how the rules of this world could play with my perceptions and wreak havoc on my senses in a way humans were never meant to feel.

Keeping my eyes firmly closed and holding still, I looked through my shadow at my real body. 'Unsettling' didn't come close to describing the experience. 'Creepy' was closer.

I took one step and both my bodies moved. I concentrated more, letting go of the controls of my own body and moved again. This time only my shadow body moved. *That's better*.

Then, with no one to control it, my physical body collapsed to the ground. *Crap*.

I let go of the shadow copy, releasing my control. The shadow diminished back into a two-dimensional figure and reconnected with my body.

I opened my eyes and found myself on the cold, hard floor, sweating and shivering. This was a harrowing experience.

"*It* understands now. Though not well," Kuzai cackled.

New Dark Mana ability discovered: Shadow Clone

You may separate your shadow from your body and control it as a separate entity. Any action carried out by the shadow requires mana, even simply walking.

As the distance between the shadow clone and your physical body increases, so too does the mana requirement. Similarly, the strength of spells cast by the clone declines as the distance increases.

I clutched my head with both hands.

<You okay, Boss?> Vic sounded worried. *<You meat suits are not built to handle these kinds of controls.>*

I'm fine now, Vic. It was true, though that brief, multi-body experience had given me a splitting headache.

Still, it was a nice addition to my Dark Mana repertoire that up until now consisted of only three abilities: Freeze, Dominate, and Sense Emotion.

It looked like we were done here. "Let's go."

"Wait." Kuzai scowled at me. "You do not wish to show your devotion at the master's altar?"

"Not really."

"You *must* pray," he insisted.

I could tell he was going to be difficult about it, so I went to the shrine. Standing next to Kuzai's shadow, I placed my hands over the rough, bone structure. I concentrated, letting the sense of power wash over me.

I stood there for a while, breathing, letting the roaring energy run through me. After a few moments, I received a new message.

Dark Mana skill level increased to 33.

What a nice revelation.

That presented a rare opportunity. With the immediate area now safe, this was an excellent chance to train my most important skill. I turned back to the shrine and placed my hands on it again. "See you in a bit, Vic."

"Wait, what about that chalice thing?" The purple goblin pointed at the metallic item.

I was so caught up with all the recent developments, it had completely slipped my mind.

I went to the spot where Kusitesh had disappeared, bent down, and picked up the blood-smeared chalice she left behind.

Chalice of Infernal Energy

Description: This chalice has been damaged by improper use during a demon summoning ritual. As a result, the summoned demon's essence was absorbed, causing the chalice to become saturated with unstable infernal energy. Any non-demon who drinks from the chalice will experience varied effects. Note: In order to drink from the chalice, a creature must willingly fill it with its own blood. Caution is advised.

Type: Miscellaneous

Rank: Epic

Effect I: Random demon aspect

Effect II: Random infernal feedback

For a 'damaged' item, this one was pretty cool. The 'demon aspect' effect reminded me of Barska when he manifested his demon powers. I wouldn't put it past that scheming bastard to orchestrate this entire deal with the Ogre only to produce this chalice, thus increasing his own power. Heck, that just might have been how he got his powers to begin with. Maybe he drank from a similar chalice and had the good fortune of scoring 'permanent' as a random effect.

With eyes glistening, I willed my dagger to hover above my arm, then slashed down, inflicting a shallow wound. My dripping blood swirled inside the chalice, taking on a deep sheen of blue.

"Err, Boss? What are you doing?"

"Getting stronger," I said, raising the cup to my lips and downing the contents in a single gulp.

The sensation was immediate and incredible. Fire coursed through my veins. It was not painful; quite the contrary. The fire warmed my body, making me feel powerful and radiating heat. I clenched my fists and felt the energy swirl around them. Both my fists grew, becoming larger. I uncurled my fingers and stared at my palms. Sharp, long talons grew out of them. Then the feeling of hot power intensified and I felt myself growing taller, stronger. It was intoxicating.

My lips drew back in a smile, revealing razor-sharp teeth. I grew muscles all over, and I felt the flesh on my back rippling open, a pair of leathery wings popping out.

I stood, twice as tall as before, towering over Kuzai, who looked mildly impressed.

I couldn't help it, this was all too exhilarating. I started laughing. "Ahhh-Haaa-haaa!" My laugh was wild and free. This felt fantastic! The chalice was an amazing find. I punched a wall and watched with satisfaction at the cracks that appeared on it. My laughter intensified as I felt my blood boiling, calling for action, for more blood.

I looked eagerly around the cave. There were no enemies in sight. Well, there was a creature that oozed of darkness and one purple goblin.

I gave a toothy ear-to-ear grin. "Fodder!"

I took a step toward it, my hooved feet leaving a visible indent on the rocky ground.

The purple goblin fell back "Boss, what the heck are you doing?"

"Come here!" I growled at it, grinding my fist into my palm.

<Oren, snap out of it!> a harsh voice sounded in my head.

The voice sounded familiar. I had heard the same words not long ago. I shook my head, feeling the heat drain away from my brain, my mind gradually clearing.

I found myself a step away from Vic. My poor companion was pressed against a wall, a worried expression on his face.

"Err, sorry, Vic." I was still possessed by the heat that called out for blood, but I resisted the urge.

Vic rolled his eyes, visibly relaxing. "You're one crazy meat suit, you know? You can't just go around drinking liquified demons."

I felt the remainder of the heat drain away, taking with it the last slivers of bloodlust. I smirked at my companion. "Come on, it was fun. What's the worst that could have happened?"

I was fully back in control now, master of my own mind with this awesome, powerful body to boot.

And then I exploded.

***

I was still screaming in agony as scattered pieces of my body magically reattached together. Kuzai was standing over me, casting his dark healing spell over and over again.

As my flesh knitted back together and my wounds closed, the pain slowly subsided until I regained control. I was back to my old goblin self; all traces of hooves, wings, and other demonic aspects were gone. My mind was reeling from the experience, trying to piece together what had happened and most importantly – *How come I'm not dead?*

As if to answer my question, a message popped open in front of me.

> **Ring of Bound Soul activated**
>
> Your soul remained forcibly attached to your body, preventing death.
>
> Max HP reduced by 10.
>
> Ring durability reduced by 1.
>
> *Durability remaining:* 2

The ring. That damned ring. Having my body explode into pieces was a new experience for me. A very unpleasant one. My deep immersion with NEO forced me to experience the ordeal fully. While my flesh was scattered, I could feel every torn body part screaming in agony. It was an impossible scenario, which reminded me yet again how precarious my situation was.

There was no longer any doubt in my mind. This realm, this prison, despite all its wonders, was a glorified torture device; I had ample evidence of my innermost thoughts being accessed, my mentality overridden by outside forces, and excruciating, unrealistic, unfathomable pain inflicted upon me on a regular basis. Had I not gone through my previous torture sessions, which fortified my endurance, I would have probably lost my sanity from the pain. Heck, while I was busy being shredded to pieces, the only coherent thought I could muster was the wish to die, permanently.

Still lying down, I removed the accursed ring from my finger and gave it a hateful stare. This was the real cause of my ordeal. It was not a beneficial magic item, it was a cursed one. A device meant to prolong one's suffering. I nearly threw the damn thing away, but then thought better of it. I would never wear it again. Dying was preferable. But it didn't mean I couldn't give it to one of my followers. I didn't particularly object to having Rhynorn wear it. The Ogre seemed impartial to pain anyway, so the ring would fit him well.

I didn't need it anyway. Nihilator's Sanction was a good enough method to escape death. Granted, it only worked once per day, but if I found myself in a situation where I could be repeatedly killed, I would rather respawn normally anyway to escape it.

Kuzai cast the last heal, bringing me back to full health. "I hope *it* will not waste any more of my time with additional spontaneous explosions."

I was pretty sure he was being spiteful, but with his demented mind, he could have been sincere. In any case, I'd learned my lesson. No more fiddling around with unpredictable demonically infused items.

I let a moment pass, then frowned. I fully expected some snarky comment from my companion.

I slowly got up. "Where's Vic?"

"Your minion was destroyed by the explosion."

Now that he mentioned it, I'd been lying in a small crater. It seemed my explosion had quite the destructive force behind it.

Steeling myself for even snarkier remarks, I summoned Vic for the third time that day.

The purple blob built up in the air, transforming back into Vic's goblin shape in seconds.

"Thank you for summoning me again, oh great and powerful master."

I cringed. This was going to be bad.

"In his infinite wisdom, the master knows best."

"Give it a rest, Vic."

"No, the master is an expert on all things to do with self-explosion, tempting fate, goading evil god-like entities, and much more. I would never presume to advise you otherwise."

I rolled my eyes. "I get it, I should have listened to you."

"No no, please don't hesitate to engage in any other self-destructive activities on my account."

"I get it!" I raised my voice. "Next time, I'll listen to your advice, okay?"

"Damn straight you will," Vic huffed. "Sometimes I wonder how a meat suit like you has managed to survive this long."

"That's because I had the assistance of my most valuable puppet companion," I said with a straight face.

"Hmph," he snorted, though I could tell my over-the-top flattery got to him. "So, all it takes is a bit of blowing up to get you to see reason? Good to know."

Despite my 'outburst,' the chalice seemed undamaged. I picked it up carefully and dumped it into my inventory.

I needed to rest. I needed to get out of this damp, dark place. I needed to be back with my clan. But I was still not done here. I returned to the shrine and placed my hands on it. "I need to meditate for a while. Poke me in a few hours if I don't come out of it on my own, okay?"

"You got it, Boss. By the way, if sometime during your introspection you get the option to blow yourself up, consider *not* taking it."

"Thanks for the advice, Vic". I closed my eyes and reconnected with the flow of dark energy. It was like swimming through the vastness of dark space ... weightless, limitless, all-encompassing. The lingering shadow pain eased, leaving me floating serenely in the darkness.

Dark Mana skill level increased to 34.

I came back to my senses. I was still standing by the shrine. Kuzai was a few meters away, mumbling something to himself

"Thank Guy, you're finally up!" I jumped at hearing Vic's voice in my ear.

"What happened? Why are you shouting in my ear?"

"Boss, you've been meditating for a couple of weeks! I tried to wake you but nothing worked."

What! I've been gone for two weeks? I thought in alarm. The repercussions of such a delay would be disastrous. *That can't be right!*

“Yep. Just kidding, Boss; it’s been more like five hours.”

That little runt bastard!

“But I did try to wake you and failed,” he added. “Your mind was far away. I couldn’t reach you at all.

I calmed quickly, finding it remarkably easy to get past Vic’s antics. My mind felt clear. Not just clear ... I was adjusted. I could think properly again. As a proper *human player*.

During my time in this fort, my goblin persona had taken over, and I mostly acted on instinct. Now, my mind was fully my own. I could plan ahead, optimize my chances. Crunch some numbers. And avoid thinking about all the horrifying ordeals of the last several hours.

Instead, I considered my situation. Five hours wasn’t so bad. Even through combat, which was the best way to increase skills, gaining a skill at that level in five hours was incredibly quick.

At level 25, with my boss bonuses, my Mental attribute was at 29, meaning the skill cap was 39. Another 25 hours of meditating at the shrine, and I should reach the cap. At that point, it would be relatively easy to keep Dark Mana at its maximum as I leveled up.

“I’m going to mediate some more,” I informed my unruly companion. “Keep watch and stay out of Kuzai’s way.”

“You got it, Boss. But before you go, you received a message from Malkyr while you were out.”

I didn’t particularly feel like having to start explaining what transpired after the twins had died. “What did he want?”

“Just asking how you survived and won the fight. He left the items he was carrying for you back at the clan. He mentioned that he and his sister got the completed quest notification and that they’ll log out for a few days to wait out the death debuff.”

Good, that would save me the hassle of having to explain things. At least for a while longer.

I approached the shrine again and glanced at Kuzai. He was having an animated discussion. With his own shadow.

<Yeah, that puppet has some screws loose, Boss.>

You would know.

I closed my eyes and meditated.

17 – The Mob Squad

Raystia materialized back in NEO, standing next to the cemetery's single headstone.

She sighed with satisfaction and took in her surroundings, smiling. She played for 12 hours straight yesterday, trying to find a suitable 'candidate' to fulfill Kaedric's quest. After sweeping the valley's forest for nearly ten hours, she eventually called it quits, having not found anything more interesting than several weird, metal-skinned armadillos. So out of better ideas, she decided to venture outside of the valley's protective walls.

After wandering the thick forest for a while, she reached a swampy area where she encountered a bunch of green, semi-intelligent looking creatures. This time, she was woefully unprepared for the encounter and the small yellow-eyed creatures swarmed and killed her in seconds.

At which point she quit the game out of frustration and ran some errands.

Now, several hours later, she had another full hour of game time before needing to turn in for the night.

She couldn't help but worry that dying as a monster would be permanent. So when she found herself back in the valley, a tremendous sense of relief washed over her.

Standing on the stone ledge the locals dubbed 'Totem's Watch,' she looked at the budding settlement below. She'd been away for only four hours, but the progress during her absence had been staggering. New roads spread all over, connecting the buildings, and the new marketplace construction had progressed significantly.

These goblins sure know how to build quickly, she reflected.

She went down the ladder and made her way toward the valley's center. There was a small gathering next to the warehouse. Three people she'd never seen before stood in front of the building, arguing.

"I'm telling you, going out of the valley is suicide at our current level and lack of decent gear." The speaker had an obvious British accent. She looked like an elven maid, though her ears were wrinkled and wider than any elf she'd seen before.

"There's nothing to hunt inside the valley," a gruff, yellow-furred goblin answered. He was the largest goblin Raystia had ever seen. Tall as a human but much wider and heavily muscled. "Besides," he said, pointing at an open kiosk window at the side of the warehouse, "even the shit-quality items are too expensive for us and the gremlins' prices are so high it's a waste of time to even browse their stores. So the only thing we *can* do to get ahead is get out, find something we can kill, gain experience and some loot to sell." He eyed the goblin merchant behind the counter then bared his teeth in a monstrous grin. "Or ... we could always *take* what we want. Some decent XP and loot sitting right there."

The third individual, a stocky-looking goblin, shook his head. "I'm thinking not. We've been lucky enough to get into the beta testing. You don't want to aggravate the natives, especially when there's no alternative starting location."

Raystia cleared her throat. "Hmm, excuse me, are you new here?"

The elf female looked at her and grinned. "That is some badass looking catfolk character. Yeah, we all started today. I'm Misa Gavriilu. Who are you? Another lost soul in monsterland?"

Blushing slightly at finding herself the center of attention, Raystia said, "I'm Pen– ... Raystia. I've played for half a day and I'm level 4." She coughed, embarrassed. "I overheard some of your conversation. If you don't mind me saying, Misa's right. It's too dangerous out there at our current level, especially without decent gear. I also think getting on the bad side of the GreenPiece Clan is a bad idea. You don't want them angry with you." She shuddered as she remembered a certain encounter. "They have an Ogre."

"An Ogre, really? Cool," said the stocky goblin.

"This place is bloody hardcore." Misa nodded. "That's why we should tread carefully." She turned back to Raystia with a wide smile. "I've only been playing for a couple of hours and already died once. I just met these guys. That's Fox," she gestured to the large, yellow goblin, "and that's Riley Stonefist," she nodded toward the short, stocky one.

"I've never seen goblins like you two before," Raystia said.

Fox huffed in annoyance while Riley bellowed a laugh. "We ain't goblins, kitty. I'm playing a dwarf. After the system slapped me with the goblinoid template, this is how I ended up."

"And I'm a bugbear," Fox grumbled. "Pure breed."

"Oh." Raystia felt her cheeks flush. "Sorry."

"So, Miss Level 4, any suggestions for us newbs?" Misa asked, a twinkle in her eye.

"Have you tried talking with the NPCs?"

"A little. I asked how to get better gear and they sent us here." The woman indicated the warehouse.

"I got the freaking 'rat in the cellar' quest, believe it or not," the squat goblin complained.

Raystia didn't remember the warehouse doubling as a store. On the counter in front of her was spread an assortment of crude weapons, armor, and tools. Behind the counter stood the goblin shopkeeper who looked at them with intelligent eyes. Two fully armed hobgoblins stood behind him looking alert and menacing.

"Well, I talked to a few of them and they were really nice to me," Raystia countered. "The bowyer made a bow especially for me after I helped him. And Kaedric, the clan's seneschal, even gave me a unique quest."

"Really? A unique quest at your level?" The goblin dwarf gaped at her. "I tried talking with a few of them, but all they want is more food. One wants meat, another fish, another vegetables. I'm a ruddy dwarven adventurer, not a grocer!"

Misa nodded. "I got similar requests. Everything seems to revolve around food with these guys."

Raystia opened her mouth to object, then, remembering the nature of the request Kaedric made of her, closed it again. She thought back hard on her previous interaction. "I think ... you just need to find the right person to ask," she finally said. "Some of them can give you interesting quests. I believe you have to first figure out your place here, then go find someone that can help achieve what you want." She touched the bow slung across her back. "That's how I got my bow."

"Well, I be wanting ter be a proper dwarven cleric!" Riley declared in a weirdly broken dialect, then winced. "Sorry, I'm still trying to get the hang of the proper accent. Anyway, got any advice for me?"

"The goblins I spoke to seemed pretty religious; maybe you can go pray at their shrine or something?" Raystia suggested.

The goblin dwarf rubbed his chin. "I might be giving it a try." He winced again. "Sorry."

“I want to be a tank,” Fox said gruffly. “With the bonuses I get for playing a bugbear, it’s stupid not to. But all the merchant has to offer are a couple of half-broken wooden shields.” He waved at the display.

“Excuse me,” the goblin merchant said politely. “You may commission a better shield if you’d like. I’m Gazlan, by the way.”

Fox stared blankly at him for a moment.

Misa said, “The gent is obviously one of the intelligent ones. Not exactly what you expected from a goblin, eh Fox?”

Shaking his head, the bugbear recovered from his stupor. “And how much would that cost me?”

“Our smith can craft you a decent metal shield for a mere 30 gold.”

Fox shook his head. “That’s too much. I only have two gold coins.

“Well, in that case, you might consider doing some work for the clan,” the merchant said smoothly.

Fox narrowed his eyes. “What type of work?”

“A small service. You might have noticed that new buildings are being constructed daily, but it’s still too slow. If you help our builders, I will offer seven gold per hour of work.”

Riley chuckled. “Man, he’s trying to scam you. With RL currency ratio of one to ten, that means you’ll be paid 70 cents for an hour spent doing hard labor.”

“You forget the time difference,” Misa said. “If you work for 12 hours straight, that’ll amount to a bit over eight dollars per hour in the real world.”

That got them all thinking. It was the salary equivalent of working at a fast food joint. If a first-level player could earn that much, then a more seasoned player with high reputation should be able to get rich quickly. People would quit their day jobs in a heartbeat for the chance to work in a fantasy world setting. Sure, construction work was not a glamorous profession, but working next to goblins and Ogres made it much more exciting than their mundane day jobs.

“Bah.” Riley waved dismissively. “I’m making ten times that working in the lab. Still not worth my time.”

“I see you find the salary too low for your liking.” The goblin merchant gave them a polite smile. “In that case, I have a different offer. For every hour of work, I will pay you with ten gold worth of store credit.”

"That sounds a lot better," Misa mused out loud. "You'll be able to get your shield after only three hours of work. I might take that offer myself; I want to buy those shiny shackles."

Raystia tilted her head. "Why do you need shackles?"

Misa winked at her. "Reasons."

"Can I ... ahem ... I would like to join as well." Raystia felt herself blushing again. She did not like to impose on people. Especially strangers.

"Sure thing, kid," Misa said. "We can all go play with brick and mortar for a bit."

"I'll check out that shrine then come join you," Riley said.

Gazlan the merchant looked at them approvingly. "Find Zuban. He should be in the construction yard. That's the building with the small fence and stacks of resources. Tell him I sent you to help with construction. He'll give you your assignment."

"Have my shield ready," Fox said, then looked at the others. "Coming?"

They passed the mess hall and easily spotted the construction yard beyond it.

"I'll do a quick run to the shrine and meet you back there," Riley said.

They nodded and approached the building. Misa knocked on the wooden door.

"Come in," a pleasant, feminine voice answered.

They pushed the door open and stopped, starting with surprise at the occupants. Two goblin females with glasses were standing next to a blackboard, holding a piece of chalk. A groomed, urbane-looking hobgoblin was sitting on a bench holding a stack of papers.

"Ah, travelers," the hobgoblin said. "I'm Zuban. May I help you with something?"

"What is this place?" Misa asked, looking around the simple wooden cabin.

Zuban frowned "This the construction yard, which also serves as my house."

"Those ain't no simple construction designs," Fox said, pointing with his chin at the blackboard. "Those are engineering measurements and counter support calculations."

Zuban's eyes widened. "You know how to perform research?"

Fox shrugged. "I know an engineering blueprint when I see one."

"We were sent by Gazlan to help you with construction," Raystia said. "He said he'll pay us if we help."

"Well ..." Zuban scratched his nose. "We can use all the help we can get. Travelers can accomplish things I cannot, and you don't require overseeing. I'll put you two ladies to work on fortifying the valley's entrance. But I'd like you," he looked at Fox, "to help Romil and Primla here research these blueprints."

"You mean I have to do architecture work in-game now?" Fox wrinkled his nose. "No thanks."

"I'll tell Gazlan to double your pay."

The bugbear brightened at that. "Now you're talking. Alright, I'm in."

Zuban handed him chalk, then beckoned the others. "Follow me."

He led them toward the forest's tree line, then followed a path through it, eventually reaching a half-built wooden palisade. Zuban pointed at a neat stack of logs. "Here you go, now build."

Raystia frowned. "How?"

"That is easy," Misa said. "I've done a few construction jobs at my old guild, just follow my lead." She walked to the stack of logs and put her hand on one. The log disappeared. "It is in my inventory," she explained. The woman then walked to the partially built wall and touched it. A new log instantly reappeared, attached to it. "See? It's easy. The system takes care of all the fine details, we just need to do the heavy lifting."

The two women worked for a while, transporting wood and stone to appropriate places. Raystia found that when she lifted a resource, a glowing light marked the place she needed to put it. It really wasn't difficult. It was even rewarding, in a way.

They'd completed a large portion of the palisade when Riley joined them. The dwarf's face looked troubled. "What's got into your pants?" Misa asked.

Riley scowled. "I went to that shrine like I told you. After I prayed for a while I got a quest saying that the great 'Nihilator Lord of Darkness' found me worthy of his attention. Now, if I want to be his priest, I need to prove my faith."

"How would you do that?" Misa asked excitedly.

"I have to offer a sacrifice," he said. "Not just any sacrifice either; it has to be an intelligent humanoid being. So gutting a rabbit on the shrine wouldn't work. I don't know how I feel about something like that. I'm used to playing the good guy."

"Have you lost your mind?" Misa said. "This is a golden opportunity. We are on the monsters' side now, so we'd best act the part. I've never heard of a player getting a quest like yours before. Sounds to me like you're on the fast track for a new Mastery skill. I would kill for that kind of opportunity."

"Ahem," Raystia cleared her throat. "I also have ... a similar quest. I have to capture a live, intelligent creature and bring it to Kaedric so he can ... ahem ... eat him."

Misa turned to stare at her. "You lucky minx!"

"I guess you have a point." Riley rubbed the back of his neck, then turned to Raystia. "Since both our quests require the same thing, I guess it would be the smart thing to party up. Strength in numbers and all that."

"That sounds nice." Raystia lowered her head to hide her elation. She'd just gotten into a party!

"Hey, count me in," Misa said. "Sounds like sticking around you is the thing to do to get some excitement."

"We should also invite Fox," Riley suggested. "With a proper tank, we could scout the area outside the valley."

"I think I know where we can find suitable ... ahem ... prey," Raystia said. "It's a couple of hours' walk from here. There's a swamp and all those nasty little vegetable pygmies."

Riley went to a stack of logs and made three of them disappear into his inventory. "Sounds like a plan. Let's finish here, get geared up, and go."

They continued working side by side, chatting idly as they did so. Raystia found herself opening up to them more as the time went by.

She learned the two were both scientists as well. Misa was a biophysicist from Liverpool, and Riley was a computer data scientist at NYU.

"That's weird," Raystia said after the expanded introduction. "I think Fox is some sort of elite architect as well. Do you think it's a coincidence we all work in advanced fields?"

Misa shrugged. "It could be a coincidence; maybe intelligent people have naturally higher CPA than normal folks. Who knows?"

The time passed quickly as they continued working. After the three hour mark, the section of wall they were constructing was nearly completed. Raystia stood tall, looking at her handiwork. Back in the real world, she produced far less tangible results. This experience was satisfying in a new way.

Fox approached them, looking surlier than ever. “Explaining a static scheme for a lateral load-bearing system to a bunch of goblins was a new low for me,” he complained. “I honestly contemplated throttling them. The satisfaction and the XP would have been worth it.”

“You didn’t!” Raystia looked horrified.

“Na,” he said. “I need the gold more than I needed the quick gratification. I got a lousy ‘Researcher’ skill and 60 gold in store credits now. You each should have 30, so let’s go back to that smartass shopkeeper.”

“Yep,” Misa said cheerfully. “Just got the ‘Quest Completed’ notification.”

“Go ahead,” Riley said. “I’ll be a few minutes behind you.”

The two women and the grouchy bugbear went back to the warehouse.

“Ah, there you are. I have your new shield right here,” Gazlan said brightly.

Fox took the shining metal shield and looked it over. “Not bad,” he said. “Could use a bit more durability, but for 30 gold it’s not bad. I’ll also take a battleaxe and a suit of leather armor.”

Gazlan shook his head. “I’m afraid the armor will cost 50. But I’ll throw in the battleaxe for five.”

“I can loan you the rest,” Raystia offered.

Fox looked at her suspiciously. “Why would you do that?”

“Oh ...” She blushed. “I ... ahem ... I guess no one told you about ... our plan?”

“What plan?”

“We are going out as a party, all four of us. You have been unanimously elected to be our tank. All clear now?” Misa said sweetly.

“Hmph,” he snorted. “About time we go kill something. Sure, I’m in. In that case, I’ll accept the loan. I only need 23 gold. But that still won’t leave you much. Don’t you need any equipment?”

"I just need arrows, and they're cheap," Raystia said. "I would like, um, 60 arrows please."

"I can sell you 30 Hugger bone arrows for a little extra," Gazlan offered. "They have better armor penetration and do more damage. I also have plenty of normal arrows."

"Oh, so ... okay. I'll take 30 normal and 30 of those, uh ... Hugger ones."

"That will be eight gold." Gazlan placed six stacks of arrows on the counter.

She had just enough.

"Shackles and a dagger," Misa said curtly.

"Very well, I'll reduce 23 gold from your store credit."

"Hey guys, I just hit the three-hour mark," Riley said.

He put his arms on the counter, facing Gazlan. "Right, including the credit, I have 32 gold in total. Give me one of those simple shields, an axe, and whatever armor pieces I can get for the rest of it."

Gazlan gave him a shield and an axe then handed him a weird-looking leather vest and crude leather leggings.

"Hey, how come he gets the armor so cheaply?" Fox demanded, leaning forward on the counter to stare straight at the merchant's face. The two hobgoblin guards took a threatening step toward him, but the goblin merchant raised his arm to stop them.

"Those were made for goblins," he explained. "They are the first creation of a novice crafter, so they're cheap. Also, the clan doesn't train new goblin warriors anymore, so this armor size is low in demand, compared to hobgoblin-sized armor."

The bugbear gave him a withering stare but pulled back. "Fine."

Raystia and Riley exchanged meaningful glances.

They each equipped their new items and then stood looking at each other.

"This is much better." Misa nodded in approval. "Now we look like a bunch of murderous mobs, instead of a bunch of vagrant mobs."

Raystia chuckled.

Riley said, "I guess we're officially a party now. A bunch of monsters teaming up to destroy lives, conquer, and spread darkness ... yeah, okay, now that I hear it, it does sound cool." He grinned at Misa. "So what should we call ourselves?"

"Hmmm, since we're all playing monsters, might as well be 'The Monsters?'" Fox suggested.

Misa rolled her eyes. "You have to be joking!"

The bugbear huffed. "You got a better idea, shrivel-ear?"

"Well, we are technically playing as mobs, and we do look the part, so how about …" she drifted off for a moment, then her eyes lit up. "The Mob Squad."

18 – Homecoming

Dark Mana skill level increased to 38.

Dark Mana skill level increased to 39.

After what felt like a long and peaceful swim through endless space, I'd finally reached my skill level cap. I was about to disengage from my trance, but then I felt something else, deeper, calling out to me. I reached with my mind and gingerly touched that thread of information.

Faith Rank 3 reached

The Following divine spells are now unlocked: Shadow Teleport[upgrade], Dark Protection

Progress to Rank 4: 1,473/2,000

Note: A shrine can be used up to Rank 3. For higher ranks, a more advanced place of worship is required.

Spell upgraded: Shadow Teleport (M)

You can now transport additional creatures with you when you teleport.

New Spell acquired: Dark Protection (M)

Grants bonuses to allies (determined by skill level). Can be cast on multiple allies. Speed 5. Cost 10 MP per individual. Duration 1 min, 50% initial MP cost to maintain for another minute. Shadow discipline.

Level 6: Novice

> *Effect I:* Armor +4.6%, Physical Resistance: +4.6%

Of course! The trip to the Ogre fort was rewarding in more ways than one. Thanks to all the sacrifices I performed, I had just achieved a new Faith Rank 3 and was well on my way to rank 4. With a little luck, the Dark Temple would also be completed soon, to allow me to attain that rank.

The new spell was a nice group buff spell. Belonging to the shadow discipline, it was strengthened by my Dark Mana skill and I had no doubt it would offer more bonuses and increased effectiveness once I invested some more time in increasing the spell level.

The spell was a nice addition, but what was even more important was that I now had enough FP to purchase the Eternal Night blessing. I considered activating it right then and there, but decided to hold off for now. That blessing would mean a significant change in my clan and it called for a proper ceremony. *Once I get back to my clan.*

I retracted my thoughts from the comforting void of the shrine and opened my eyes.

"Welcome back, Boss."

<Greetings, my lord.>

Kaedric?

<Yes, my lord. Per your orders, I have contacted you with an update on our daily progress.>

Give me some good news, Ked.

There was a long pause.

Kaedric?

<Yes, my lord. The researchers have completed the blueprints for the Dark Temple. We may begin construction as soon as we have the required resources at our disposal.>

What's the holdup? The gremlin marketplace should have been finished already, so we should have access to the required glass. I got a sinking feeling in my gut, dreading my seneschal's answer.

<That is correct, my lord. The marketplace has been constructed and the gremlin merchants claimed their stalls. Unfortunately, in order to use the exporter, we first must construct the Export Office expansion.>

Damn it. I knew something was going to go wrong. I gritted my teeth. It was always the same story; not enough resources, not enough workers, no proper tools, and now, I was slapped with 'prerequisite unmet.'

<I have spoken with Zuban,> my seneschal continued. *<He and the two other researchers are already working on the blueprint for the Export Office. At their current rate, it should be completed within three days. During this downtime, the builders have resumed work on the barracks.>*

I had to take a moment to compose myself. There was no helping it, this was uncharted ground. My clan was unique, a mix-up of goblin resourcefulness and hobgoblin military nature. To top it off, it now doubled as a starting zone for travelers. Delays were unavoidable.

I understand. You did well, Kaedric. I should be back in a few days to handle things myself.

<Understood, my lord.>

My belly gurgled audibly, and I felt a sudden dizziness.

Debuff gained: Starved, Dehydrated

Effect I: HP and MP regeneration at 50%

Effect II: Speed: -20%

"Yeah, that happened a while ago. Not really a good idea to go for so long without food or water, Boss. Especially when you're a squishy meat suit or a mindless puppet."

I sat down, leaning against the shrine, feeling ravenous. I took out some rations from my inventory and wolfed them down.

Kuzai approached and stood over me.

"Hey, Kuzai." I waved a piece of smoked meat at him.

"*It* nourishes of dead flesh and decaying plants. *It* is not a pure creature of darkness," the unhinged dwarf muttered to himself.

I ignored his ranting and held out a piece of food. "Want some?"

He drew back and gave me a withering stare. "The master has created a perfect vessel. I am one with darkness, it binds and sustains me."

"I'll take that as a no." I lowered my hand and kept on eating, feeling better already. I finished my plain meal with a drink of water from my flask. "Your loss."

Debuff removed

"We should leave," he said flatly. "My shadow will remain behind to maintain the shrine. I have seen to that."

"We should probably check this place out first, see if we can find anything of value."

Kuzai snorted. "There is nothing of value here."

"Here, Boss," Vic volunteered, pointing to lump of wood. "I got bored while you were meditating so I scouted the place. You never know when you might stumble on a couple of oblivious puppets getting it on. Anyway, this was left in a pile of discarded Ogre refuse. I think you'll find it interesting."

I looked at the block of wood he was pointing at. It was a piece of tree log about half a meter tall. It probably weighed over 50 kilos. *Analyze.*

Totem Pole Piece: Ogre

Description: This piece of totem pole represents a conquered clan of Ogres. It can be added to the main totem pole of another clan. This will strengthen that clan by granting it an Ogre-related feature.

Type: Settlement Totem

Effect I: +10 clan morale

Effect II: Clan gains the *Ogre Gluttony* trait: Doubling an individual's upkeep will increase their Physical attribute by +1 and their physical related skills effects by 20%.

Jackpot! This primitive-looking piece of wood was an incredibly valuable find for my clan. I could already imagine the impact it would have on the development of Goblin's Gorge. The builders would be the first to receive this boon, increasing their construction rate, maybe even all the workers that relied on the Physical attribute. But how the hell was I going to carry it all the way back to my clan? The thing was probably twice my own weight!

As if to answer my question, Kuzai came to investigate. He frowned as I gave him a wide grin. The ex-dwarf was sturdy and had over ten points in his Physical attribute.

"Be a dear and carry this for me," I almost purred.

"I will not!" he said, his face full of indignation, then mumbled to himself, "*It* treats me as a common mule, the master's chosen do not do degenerate menial work."

I smirked at him. "If you won't carry it, I will have to attempt it. But I'm not strong enough. You wouldn't let the master's choice treat wreck his back, would you?"

He gaped at me for a solid moment before snapping his mouth shut. He gave the piece of log a grudging look. "How far?"

"Let's start with bringing it out of the fort."

He grumbled something inaudible but bent down and hoisted the log onto his shoulder. He moved gingerly, nearly buckling under the weight, but was holding it together. "This way," he said.

He led Tempest and me to a far corner of the cave, then rolled away a boulder, revealing a narrow tunnel leading upward. It was probably an old garbage chute, just enough for a dwarf and a goblin to climb through. Kuzai had it rough, but he managed to half-carry, half-push the totem log all the way up.

We came out through a hatch to stand on a small platform, just above the broken staircase that led back down. Once we descended the platform, we were again standing at the basement level of the fort.

We moved unhurriedly through the main corridor. Now that the demon infestation had been dealt with, there was nothing left that could pose danger.

As we passed the storage room, I again saw the broken plow. "Hold on a sec," I told Kuzai.

The dwarf grunted, lowered the totem piece, and glared at me. "What does *it* want now?"

I entered the room and examined the plow from all sides. It looked to be in pretty good shape despite its years of disuse. The metal moldboard, the piece that pierced the ground, was intact. The wooden frame also appeared to be in good shape. Only one axle was broken. The other wheel was in working order. It almost looked like a wheelbarrow. That gave me an idea.

"Kuzai, come here for a sec."

He gave me a sour look. "What do you want?"

"Grab the handle, see if you can pull this thing." He grumbled but did as I asked. Despite the broken wheel, the plow rolled behind him, its broken axle dragging along the floor. It was noisy and cumbersome, but it could work.

"Alright," I said with a tone of finality. "We're taking it with us. You can put the totem on top of the plow, and we'll use it as a makeshift wheelbarrow."

The dwarf glared at me. "I. Am. Not. A beast of burden!" he said through clenched teeth. "Get your wolf to do the hauling."

Vic groaned. *<Don't listen to that crackpot! I really enjoyed watching him strain. I'll put ten gold on him dropping from exhaustion in under 20 minutes.>*

Sorry, Vic, his idea was actually not a bad one. "Come here, Tempest."

Though the demon wolf was ten levels below the dwarf, Tempest was physically stronger, and with four legs, he was more ideally suited to drag a heavy burden. With a bit of innovative rope work, I managed to tether plow and wolf. Tempest moved slowly, testing the weight. He wouldn't win any races but he managed to pull it much more easily than Kuzai.

We stopped near the plundered forge and I threw in the few remaining pieces of armor and the four swords we'd left unclaimed.

With the impromptu wheelbarrow filled to the brim, I nodded to my companions "Now let's get out of here."

It took a little doing, but with Tempest managing most of the heavy lifting, we were able to bring everything up from the basement level and out of the fort.

We stood outside, taking in the mountain peaks all around us.

"Time to head home."

***

It took most of the day to reach the foot of the mountains, the plow's broken axle scraping a deep gouge on the ground behind us.

We rested the daytime away before coming down to the oxsaurians' plain. Kuzai was even gruffer than usual during the daytime, preferring to hide below the plow rather than risk exposing his skin to the rays of the sun.

Early the next night, Kaedric contacted me as ordered. He did not have a lot to report. The construction efforts were ongoing and would take some time to complete, so I directed my seneschal to only contact me in case of emergency. I would be back at the clan soon enough to see to it firsthand.

I tightened Tempest's tethers before entering the hilly area. The grasslands spread far and low, offering visibility for a great distance. The journey was uneventful. We encountered two herds of oxsaurians, but I employed my Shadow Hounds, luring them away each time.

Once we were at the edge of the territory, I decided to test a theory. The oxsaurians were all around level 40, meaning that with my Dark Mana skill at level 39, I should be able to influence some of the lower-level ones.

Following my instructions, my mastiffs separated a single bull from the herd and lured it our way. The powerful beast charged toward us at an alarming speed with the single-minded purpose of a battering ram. I was somewhat gratified to see Kuzai flinching from the incoming impact. I waited until the beast entered my range of influence, then I poured over a hundred points of my mana into its muscles and commanded them to stop. It froze in its tracks, but its momentum carried it forward. It fell to its belly and slid all the way toward us. With a deliberate gesture, my dagger plunged into its eye, sacrificing it.

That single casual kill was enough to push me well up to level 26. I collected the level 39 void crystal with a grin and added 140 units of raw meat to the growing pile on the plow.

Oh yes, I will return here soon enough.

When we finally crossed over to the edge of our forest, sunrise was close. We camped under the foliage. Kuzai was at ease below the thick canopy. On the first of dark, we resumed our journey.

Tempest proved to be a loyal companion. He dragged the broken plow unerringly for days without complaint. Having a part-demon pet wolf was part demon was pretty cool.

The next day we walked through forest trails, heading in the general direction of Goblin's Gorge. During that time, we were attacked twice by wild beasts. We easily won on both occasions. A few Drilling Arrow volleys were enough to handle the low-level enemies. Kuzai didn't even bother to use spellcasting, preferring to simply crush his opponents with his heavy maul.

We finally arrived at the valley's entrance at the end of the third night.

A wooden wall closed off the entrance. Two hobgoblin sentries welcomed us, lowering their heads respectfully as I passed them by.

We crossed the valley's forest and soon found ourselves in open fields. Despite the haze of the morning sun, everywhere I looked, I saw signs of construction and development. My goblins had worked diligently during my week-long absence.

I waved Kuzai off toward one of the vacant cabins and untethered Tempest from the plow. I made my way to my own house and slumped tiredly into my bed. Tika was already sleeping. I nuzzled her neck and she sleepily pressed harder against me. I was tempted, but after roughing it out in the wild for a full week, I needed the rest. I fell asleep feeling fully content, holding my beautiful huntress in my arms.

***

I woke up the next night feeling much better, the Lyrical bird chirping its morning song and filling me with a sense of optimism. It was like I had never left. Tika was still asleep. *That lazy minx*, I thought amusingly, eyeing her womanly curves with appreciation.

I stood and quietly left the house. I had a busy day ahead of me.

Naturally, Kaedric was already waiting for me outside.

"My lord, it is good that you are back." The hobgoblin bowed low, his mandibles clicking as he did so.

"Good to be back." I looked around. "We have much to accomplish today."

"Yes, my lord. How may I be of service?"

"First thing, I need to go to the cemetery and resurrect Bek." I winced at the thought. The goblin was level 16 when he was killed, so it would cost 160 EP to bring him back.

"I can attend to that, my lord."

I should have thought of that. After all, that was why I brought Kaedric into the clan, to help me take care of the smaller management issues.

"Thanks, Kaedric, please do that. Now, for another matter ..." I pointed at the broken plow. It had remained where I left it, next to the row of cabins. "There's a totem piece on the plow. Have Rhyno bring it here, and get some goblins to unload its content into the warehouse, then drag it off to the smithy. I want it put back into working order."

My seneschal lowered his head, closing his eyes for a moment. "Done, my lord. It will be but a moment."

"Good. Now, tell me about the newcomers. How many are there? Where are they?"

"I have counted 15 individuals so far, my lord. Most seem content with running around, doing various chores. Four of them have banded together and are undertaking more unique requests. Raystia, the one I mentioned before, is one of them."

"I'll keep an eye out for them then. How is our impromptu shop doing?"

"Well, my lord, Gazlan, the new trader, is a sharp goblin. He struck a deal with most of the newcomers, bartering equipment, arms, and armor for gold or favors. This act did seem to placate many of the newcomers. But I'm afraid it won't hold for long. The new arrivals become stronger by the day. They will soon demand equipment that is beyond our abilities to produce."

I shook my head. "We're nearly there. Once we finish constructing the high-priority buildings, we can finally concentrate on new Weapons and Armor workshops. Then our new smiths can start producing better quality items. I first planned it to be solely for the purpose of arming our hob soldiers, but we could probably spare a few for trade."

"Quite astute, my lord. In any case, the newcomers have paid for their wares by helping to construct some of the buildings and by providing more resources to the clan. A few came by enough gold to purchase the items they wanted. We have collected a total of 200 gold so far. I have deposited the coins in your house's chest."

"Good job ... ahh, there's Rhyno."

The Ogre boss walked toward us, his heavy legs thumping on the ground. He held the totem piece in one hand like it weighed nothing.

"Boss-man is back," he grunted, looking me up and down.

"Rhyno, good. Place that piece on my house roof, please."

His face clouded, but he lifted the piece of heavy wood and laid it on the top of my roof.

Clan Totem Piece acquired [Ogre]

+10 morale

New clan trait: Ogre Gluttony (+1 Physical, +20% Physical governed skills)

I rubbed my hands together "Excellent."

<Just so you know, despite having the whole 'skinny goblin' look going for you, you're doing a lousy Mr. Burns.>

Did I really miss having him around not long ago? I wondered to myself. *I probably suffered from temporary insanity.*

<Nope. Not temporary.>

Shut up.

I turned to my seneschal. "I want all the builders to be doubly fed. That should give a real boost to their construction efficiency."

"Yes, my lord."

"What else?" I asked. My task list for the day was full. I needed to inspect the new marketplace, check the Breeder's Den, and talk with Zuban, Vrick, and the other leading members of my clan. I also wanted to check on how Guba was doing and make sure our new visitors were behaving themselves. And I needed new gear. I had a cool new staff now, but I had long outgrown the other equipment I was using. There was so much to do it was overwhelming.

Goblins started to appear, getting up from their daytime sleep.

I heard movement coming from my house, bringing to mind a different kind of activity I wanted to pursue. With a wave of my hand, I dismissed both Kaedric and Rhyno and went back inside.

Everyone could bloody well wait for five more minutes. I was the boss, after all, and Tika was waiting for me.

I closed the door behind me and saw the well-toned, exotic goblinette before me. She hadn't bothered to dress after waking up and wore only the tight-fitting teeth necklace I had gifted her. She was enticing and fierce. Just the way I liked it. And she looked me straight in the eyes as if daring me to do something about it.

I grinned. They might have to wait more than five minutes.

19 – Lay Off

Several hours later, Tika and I finally sated our mutual carnal desires and collapsed, exhausted, in our furs. We remained cuddled for a good while longer, enjoying each other's closeness.

Tika got up first, put on her tight-fitting leather armor, shouldered her bow and went out for her daily hunt.

I remained wrapped in the furs for several more moments, relaxing and savoring the post-coital bliss.

Now that I was back at my clan, the seat of my power, I was bombarded with the countless information threads that saturated the place. Information about the settlement status, worker progress, daily upkeep, religion, and more, each demanding my immediate attention.

But I was relaxed and felt too lazy to sort them on my own.

Let Vic do some of the work, I thought and opened the Settlement Interface instead.

Goblin's Gorge Interface
Energy: 4,342 *Settlement level:* 2 (Hamlet) *Bosses:* 3 *Morale:* 53 *Religion:* Rank 3 *Efficiency:* 16.7% *Population:* 78 *Housing:* 52/46 *Food Upkeep:* basic 74, advanced 6 *Buildings:* 23 Fortifications Food production Resource production Crafting production Research

Commerce

The interface had changed.

<Yep. Got too much data now, so I cut back to make it clearer,> Vic chimed in. *<Just click on any of the fields to see more details.>*

My purple companion was hanging in his cloak shape from a peg on the wall.

"Thanks, Vic."

<You got it, Boss.>

I studied the menu more closely. The boss count had updated, taking Kuzai into account. Morale was at an all-time high, partly due to the new totem piece and partly due to my goblins' satisfaction at having proper housing. Which, I suddenly noted, was already beyond capacity. I would need to build more cabins soon.

Wait a second ... Something didn't feel right.

The menu had a new 'Commerce' option, but that wasn't what bothered me. The population count was higher than I remembered, but it wasn't that either. It was ...

"Kaedric!" I shouted, both verbally and mentally, bursting out of my house.

My seneschal appeared from behind a building, walking steadily toward me.

He paused, giving me an appraising look. "Is something wrong, my lord?"

"Where's all my energy?" I demanded. "I've been gone for a week, and the clan has about the same amount of energy as when I left. Explain."

"That is quite simple, my lord," he said calmly. "As you remember, you empowered me to utilize the clan's energy to enhance our productivity."

"No," I hissed through clenched teeth. "I empowered you to use the energy to raise the level of the new trader." I had been fearing something like this might happen if I gave him too much authority. Expecting the worst, I started channeling my mana, preparing a preemptive attack.

"Ah, I see the confusion, my lord, please forgive me." Kaedric bowed low. "As you recall, you have given me access to the clan's energy to 'increase the new guy's level.' I deemed it optimal to increase his level to 3."

"That still does not explain nearly 2,000 of missing EP." I eyed him cautiously, though some of the tension left me.

"That is correct, my lord. After using the energy on Gazlan, our new trader, I realized it would be optimal to raise all the workers to level 3."

"You what?" I stared at him.

"All senior members of this clan are at least level 4, which means all the other level 2 workers were a recent addition to the clan. I took that to mean they fell under the 'new guy' category, so I increased their levels as well."

"What? You're talking about at least ten goblins!"

"Thirteen, to be exact."

I clenched my teeth. "That still doesn't explain all the missing energy!"

"Yes, my lord. I have observed that most of our advanced workers were overextended and their efficiency could be optimized if they were aided by gofer helpers. Since you gave me permission to access the Breeder's Den without strict limitation, other than to summon the new trader, I deemed it optimal to recruit new workers."

I felt my heart sinking. "How many did you summon?"

"Well, Gandork required two helpers, Barzel one, Vrick and Zuban each –"

"How many?"

"Twelve, my lord."

My head was swimming. "And you increased them all to level 3?"

"Yes, my lord."

That explained the loss of energy, the sudden overpopulation, and the increased food upkeep. "Damn you, Kaedric!"

His mandibles jittered. "My lord, have I done something to upset you? I only had the clan's best interests in mind."

I sighed. There was no sense in crying over dead dwarves. "So how much energy did you end up using?"

"Two thousand three hundred ninety-two."

I cringed. There was no sense in crying over wasted energy, either.

I plucked an information stream out of the air. With Kaedric's recent recruitments and level-ups, my clan was generating 394 EP each day.

"Okay Kaedric, I don't like you making such strategic decisions without me, but I guess it does contribute to our clan."

"We should see a return on the energy investment within two months," he volunteered.

"Right." *If we survive that long.*

I walked toward the southern side of the valley, heading to the newly constructed marketplace. Kaedric kept pace.

Three lowly foblins came sprinting from behind a building, all fighting over a piece of rotten meat. They crumpled into a heap at our feet, brawling and biting. The damn critters were useless. They didn't contribute anything to the clan and their fighting abilities were ridiculously low. *At least they don't cost me any upkeep*, I thought grudgingly.

Then it occurred to me that everywhere I looked I saw scattered foblins, running around, digging holes in search of food, or just brawling with each other.

"Kaedric, how many foblins do we have?"

"Sixteen, my lord. If you recall our past conversation, instead of breeding such lowly creatures, the females can be instructed to –"

I shook my head firmly. "Nope, not going there. This isn't open for a debate."

"Yes, my lord."

We reached the gremlin marketplace. I stood outside, taking in the sight of the large structure. It was like nothing I had ever seen before in NEO.

A tall, wooden column, about 20 meters in height and at least three meters in diameter stood at the center. A huge canopy spread from the column's apex, covering at least an acre of ground. Several wooden stalls stood below it. But what really caught my eyes was *the machinery.* Metal rails spread out from the main column in all directions over the entire area. What looked like cranes with many cogwheels were attached to the rails. As I watched, a single crane whirled around, holding a large box. With spinning gears, it drove to the other side of the marketplace and deposited the cargo neatly on top of a pile at the stall with the sign 'GGG' on top of it. It looked like our gremlin merchant friends had acclimated nicely to their new place of business.

"That's ... pretty incredible."

"Thank you, Dread Totem," a familiar voice sounded behind me.

I turned around and saw my chief constructor approaching. "Zuban! Glad to see you. This marketplace is impressive."

"It is. Getting all the machinery in place was tricky, but my workers know their job. Having three smiths and five gofers to craft all the fine metal parts helped speed things up, though Barzel had to come here himself to install some of the more delicate equipment."

I continued to inspect the marketplace. A goblin, one of my own clan, was sitting in an elegant stall. He didn't have a lot of wares on display but there was decent variety; a few swords and axes, some pieces of armor, rations, arrows, and assorted tools. In short, everything a newbie adventurer would need. Good.

"Dread Totem, welcome!" Yeshlimashu drew near, beaming. "Your foreman has acquitted himself well. This is one of the best-constructed marketplaces I have seen, not including the one at Zemitpozes, of course."

"Hello, Yeshy. I trust you find everything to your satisfaction?"

"I do indeed! My fellow traders have all claimed a stall. So far business is slow, but I'm sure it will pick up soon."

"Glad to hear it. If I remember correctly, I am now entitled to a discount."

"Yes, of course. You have also set a very reasonable three percent tax. So kind of you to keep it at the lowest rate."

I frowned. I had yet to check the new Commerce option in the Settlement Interface. Which meant that three percent was probably the default tax value. Oh well, I could always raise it later.

I was glad the gremlins approved, but that was just a bonus, not the main reason for the building's construction.

"Zuban, how is the research for the Export Office going?"

"We're finished, Dread Totem. I have been looking for you for the past several hours to give you the good news."

Vic morphed into his goblin shape. "Our *Stud* Totem here was busy making it up to his girlfriend."

I rolled my eyes.

Zuban looked outraged. "It is Dread Totem, not Stud Totem!"

"Yeah, whatever you say, puppet Bob."

Zuban's expression became mystified.

"Just ignore him, Zuban," I intervened. "So the Export Office blueprint is ready, good. I want construction to start immediately."

"But we're nearly done with the barracks!" Zuban protested. "We could be finished by tomorrow at daybreak."

I shook my head. "The Dark Temple is our main objective. So we need the Export Office. Hopefully, it'll let us import the missing resource, glass, for the temple's construction."

"Yes, Dread Totem." Zuban bowed his head. "If I divert all available builders, it should take us no more than three days to complete construction."

Three days for a lousy extension project? That did it. I'd had enough of all of these minor delays and ridiculous prerequisites. In light of Kaedric's expenditure, my constant attempt at trying to save up for 'a rainy day' looked ridiculous. It was time to use the accumulated energy with a little spendthrift show of my own.

"Just have the builders bring all the required materials," I instructed. "Then set them back to work on the barracks."

"Yes, Dread Totem." Zuban turned and left.

I only had to wait a few minutes before the builders started to arrive, each bearing a heavy load of construction materials. A builder could carry twice his own weight, and their haul skill was maxed out. In under ten minutes, a neat stack of wood and other construction resources stood at the base of the main column.

I waited for the last worker to drop its load, then opened the Construction Interface.

Buildings and Construction

Max Constructor Skill: 15

Builders Count: 8 (skill levels 16, 16, 17, 16, 16, 16, 9, 9)

Daily BP: 150.2

Under Construction: Barracks (457/600 BP)[rush], Mining Hut (46/80 BP) [rush], Export Office (0/300) [rush]

Available Resources: lumber 135, stone 70, metal 61, bone 129

Research

I focused on 'Export Office' and mentally clicked on the 'rush' option. A prompt showed asking for confirmation, which I did, paying the required 300 EP.

The neat stack of resources started shimmering, glowing a faint blue. A transparent 'ghost' of a building came into view. It was a round structure, wrapped around the base of the main column. Pieces of wood, leather, and stone began to disappear from the pile and reappear on the ethereal structure. The physical matter formed as patches over the template's frame. It took only a few moments for the process to complete.

New building expansion added to your settlement: Export Office

I took a step back and observed the new edifice. It was a small, round wooden structure with a stone roof. There was a tiny doorway with a window beside it. More than anything, it looked like a little kiosk.

Now came the moment of truth. I took out the Dimensional Trade Orb from my inventory and entered the building. The place was empty, but I could clearly feel tendrils of information stretching out from the column toward the orb in my hand. I went to the column and reached out with the orb. Tethers of magic started flowing from it, connecting with others coming out of the column. A section of it shimmered and disappeared, leaving the entire weight of the column and the attached machinery floating in the air. There was no question what I needed to do. I placed the orb in the empty space and let go. It remained floating at the exact center of the open space. Then it started humming softly and a white light emanated from it, patching up the missing column section with opaque white energy.

"Yeah, okay, that's pretty cool," Vic admitted.

Time to get this show on the road. I flexed my fingers, opened the Settlement Interface and selected the 'Commerce' option.

Commerce

Tax: 3%

Clan Traders: 1

External Traders: 3

Export Office [missing Exporter worker]

Right, so all it needed now was an export worker. With a few well-practiced mental clicks, I opened the Breeder's Den menu.

Breeder's Den upgraded

By controlling a new race's settlement, their units have become available for recruitment.

Conquering additional races' settlements will add additional units.

Damn, it had almost slipped my mind. I was so engrossed in the small details, I nearly lost sight of my main objective. The reason I took that little trip to the Ogre's fort in the first place.

I scanned the list of available units, looking for Ogres.

I found what I was looking for, though it was not what I expected.

- Infernal Ogre: 150 basic food
- Infernal Ogre Mage:150 basic food, 100 advanced food, 50 exquisite food

Wow. The Ogre mage alone was worth almost as much as two lieutenants and two adepts.

I want one of those, I couldn't help thinking. This was a new kind of greed for me.

But first things first. I didn't want to exhaust my food stores on an impulse buy. So instead, I followed up on my original intent and queued in a new 'Advanced Worker' goblin, an 'Exporter.' The building was already loaded with 60 units of advanced food, from my previous recruitments, so I only had to wait a short while for my workers to haul in an additional 30 units of basic food.

I stood inside the Exporter Office, staring impatiently at the Breeder's Den Interface. A few moments passed before the amount of food updated. First, the extra food appeared and then disappeared a heartbeat later as the Breeder's Den consumed it to fulfill my order.

From outside the Export Office, Kaedric tapped at the window. "My lord, I have ordered the new worker to come here. It will be but a moment. Shall I increase his level?"

"Yeah, I guess. You might as well raise him to the third level like the others."

"At once, my lord."

I waited until the new goblin arrived. She looked like the elven version of a goblin, tall and lithe, yet powerfully built, for a goblin.

"Welcome to the GreenPiece Clan ..." I plucked her name from the air "... Trillian. I need you to operate this Export Office, I trust you know how to use a Trade Orb?"

She nodded gracefully. "Yes, Dread Totem. I do. It is a great honor to operate such an advanced facility." Her voice was clear and confident.

"Do you require anything for your job?"

"No, Dread Totem, though a gofer would help accelerate the preparation and transportation of goods."

"Kaedric, see to it."

"Yes, my lord."

I rubbed my hands expectantly and opened the Commerce Interface again. This time the 'Export Office' option was enabled. I clicked on it and reeled back as my mind was assaulted by a torrent of information. I couldn't make heads or tails of it; it was just too much.

<Oh wow, it's been a while since I got to sift through so much metadata. Hold on a sec, Boss.>

The flow of data abated and a large screen opened instead, filling my entire view. Dozens of options, tabs, and lists were displayed.

I blinked a few times, trying to make sense of it all.

At the top was a drop-down list labeled 'Trading Partners.' I opened it and selected the only available option: Zemitpozes, the gremlin settlement.

The rest of the screen reorganized, listing new tabs with various categories. Crafting resources, construction resources, minerals, magical, miscellaneous, and such. There were a bunch of filters on the left and a list of categories to sort by on the right. Everything was jumbled together, making my brain hurt as I tried to piece it all together.

<*Well, excuuuuse me. Let's see if you can do better in under two seconds,*> Vic said in a huff.

You know what I'm looking for, Vic, sort it out, please. You've done this plenty of times before.

<*Yeah, but up until now, you had no idea what was going on in the background ... oh well, since you asked for it ...*>

The screen flickered and reorganized. That was much better. Zemitpozes was listed as the trading partner and below it was a long list of resources: wood, stone, copper, tin, marble, cogs, and finally, glass!

That's what I need. Now to get it ... I tentatively clicked on 'glass.' The number '1' showed on the right and a new list opened.

Select a resource to trade for [glass]		
Resource	**Available Amount**	**Exchange Rate**
Gathered Ingredients	625	62
Arrows	545	120
Rabbit Pelts	423	54
Lumber	380	5
...	...	...

The list went on and on, detailing every item we had stored in our clan, showing those with the highest quantities on top. It was easy enough to understand. The 'Value' column clearly showed how many units of the resource were needed to barter for a single piece of glass, but something didn't add up.

"Trillian, please clear up something for me. How is it that glass takes 120 arrows, while only requiring 5 pieces of lumber?" I knew for a fact that the base price for the lumber was 2 gold, while the 120 arrows went for 6 gold. This conversion table did not make sense.

"It is simple, Dread Totem. The ratio is not determined by monetary worth but by the availability or rarity of each resource for the trading partner. For example, if you wanted to trade fish for swords, a fishing village might require over a hundred fish per sword, while a desert village might give you ten swords for a single fish."

Ah, that made sense. "So it's beneficial to have as many trading partners as possible. Preferably at different geographic locations."

The lithe goblinette nodded. "Exactly."

That made a lot of sense. As a subterranean settlement, Zemitpozes probably lacked a supply of good lumber, while we had a large forest within easy reach. I clicked on 'Lumber' and increased the amount to 50 units.

Export 50 lumber for 10 glass? Yes/No

Yup.

A goblin I had never seen before came running at us. A level 3 worker, Trillian's new gofer helper. The new goblin was hauling in several pieces of lumber, straining under their weight. The lumber was brought into the Export Office. Then the gofer and Trillian went running to the nearby lumber yard. This was going to take a while.

"Kaedric, let me know when they're finished."

"Yes, my lord."

I checked my inventory. I had a few items I needed to unload and a few people I wanted to talk to. I left the marketplace and made my way toward the mess hall.

I took a detour to the pond and gave the fishing kit I found to the fishermen. One of them was using a crude fishing pole and the upgrade increased their daily fish yield by four.

I entered the mess hall. Gandork's two new gofer helpers were running between the tables, collecting dirty dishes and cleaning the tabletops.

I spotted Bek sitting alone after having long finished eating his meal.

"Hi Bek, how are you doing?"

He fidgeted and lowered his eyes. "Bek is sorry, Dread Totem!" he piped.

I frowned. "Sorry? About what?"

The little goblin continued avoiding my gaze. "Bek not heal enough good. Big fighters die. Bek die. Dread Totem fight alone. All Bek fault."

I chuckled, finally drawing his gaze. "Bek, we were facing incredibly strong enemies. We wouldn't have made it as far as we did without your help. You kept us alive through it. And that opal you pulled out when we were about to get swarmed saved the day. I couldn't have asked more of you. You deserve a reward, not a punishment. In fact ..." I reached slowly up to my head and removed the feathered headdress, handing it to him. "This is yours now."

It might have been more optimal to give it to our new dark priest, but I had made up my mind. *Sorry Kuzai, Bek deserves this more than you do.*

The goblin stared, stupefied, at the headdress in his hands.

Without losing a beat, I removed my matching kilt and retrieved my old totem's staff from my inventory. I handed them to him as well. I'd long outgrown that set anyway. "Here you go, Bek, now you have the full set. This should increase your magic powers significantly."

Bek just gaped at me, his large eyes filled with wonder and incomprehension.

"Put it on," I urged.

He obeyed, donning the feathered headdress and kilt and held the staff in one hand. With those items, he looked just like the iconic shamanistic goblin Totem. The items' enchantment and set bonus significantly increased his mana and health pool as well as his mana regeneration rate.

"B-but Totem," Bek protested. "You now got no staff."

"Don't worry about me, Bek. I'm covered." I winked at him and retrieved my new Demon Horn Staff. "Now go play with your new toys."

I left the flabbergasted goblin to admire his new equipment and went into the kitchen.

The head cook greeted me. "Ah, Dread Totem, you're back at last."

"Hey, Gandork."

"Please sit, I have something special for you."

I sat and Kaedric moved to stand beside me. I watched, bemused, at the now plump goblin making a racket in his kitchen before bringing me a steaming plate full of wriggling worms. There were sprinkles of orange and purple mixed in. I could feel the heat radiating from the dish.

"How are the worms still alive?" I asked, feeling both revulsion and fascination at the exotic dish.

"It is the work of the fire resistance potion, Dread Totem." Gandork beamed at me. "It took me a few tries, but I finally mastered the new recipe. The purple salt balances the magmashroom magnificently. It is the most exquisite dish I have ever made. You are the first to try it."

"Besides you," I said with a smirk.

"I only tasted it to find the right balance, Dread Totem. The honor of first right is yours."

"Thanks." I grabbed a fistful of wriggling worms. They were pleasantly warm to the touch. Something deep inside me revolted against the notion of eating such a dish, but I shrugged it off. I had already accepted the truth of my reality and who I was.

I stuck the worms in my mouth. The wriggling sensation was quite pleasant and the worms burst in my mouth, releasing their savory juices. I chewed slowly, enjoying the spicy tinge and the way it was magically extinguished before becoming too intense.

I swallowed and a pleasant coldness ran down my throat, which was instantly replaced with a feeling of warmth, radiating from my stomach to the rest of my body.

Buff Gained: Crisp Hot Worms

Effect: 20% cold and fire resistance.

"Wonderful, Gandork, you've outdone yourself!" I complimented the beaming goblin. "How many more of these can you make with our current supply?"

"I'm afraid we have run out of Fire Resist potions, Dread Totem. Getting worms is not a problem; my gofers can take care of that. We have 42 magmashrooms and 49 units of purple salt left. With enough potions, the other ingredients will suffice for 126 such dishes."

That was plenty. I needed a total of six adepts to maintain the scattered places of worship and the soon-to-be-built Dark Temple. With Bek and Kuzai, I only needed four more. An adept goblin cost 30 advanced and 20 exquisite food, nearly half of a hobgoblin adept.

"Kaedric, we need to supply Gandork with Fire Resist potions. Get some gold from my house and buy them from the gremlins."

For a long moment, my seneschal did not reply while his mandibles twitched mutely.

"Kaedric?"

"Forgive me my lord, I was looking into the matter. Buying the potions from the gremlins will not be necessary. Using her new chemistry set, Guba can brew such potions on her own now. Though it will require some of the clan's resources, it would be substantially more economical."

"Good thinking." I nodded approvingly.

"Gandork, once you have the potions, please cook 60 units of this dish."

"Of course, Dread Totem."

"Good. By the way, did Malkyr bring in the oxsaurian meat?"

"He did indeed, Dread Totem. Fine meat, very gamey."

"Excellent. Keep up the good work, Gandork." I got up and left the mess hall.

As soon as I exited the building, a foblin ran straight into me, then fell back from the impact. "Watch out," I said gruffly.

The foblin gave me a fearful look. An instant later that look became horrified as Kaedric came out of the Mess Hall behind me. "Stupid, no good pest," he spat out. His four mandibles extended, opening wide, making his face a terrifying visage.

The poor critter lurched on the ground, rolling and grabbing his head in pain.

"That's enough, Kaedric," I said reproachfully. I didn't mind using the foblins as cannon fodder, but I had a strong aversion to outright torture. We all have our own boundaries and our own demons.

<Yeah, yours is next to your house, sniffing at his own butt,> Vic chimed in.

I had almost forgotten about Tempest.

What now? I thought, looking at the foblin as it scrambled to run away. I still had items to hand out and I wanted to check up on my new exporter.

But all that could wait.

Our new *friends* were heading my way.

20 – Throw Down

Raystia felt a weird mix of accomplishment and revulsion.

The Mob Squad had had a successful hunt, sort of. They'd found a lair of small humanoid creatures called vegepygmy, and it wasn't because they were vegan, oh no. Raystia's brow furrowed as she remembered the battle.

The small green creatures came at them from the swamp. They threw muck at the party, trying to blind them and used their sharp talons to attack from close range. It was tough at first, but after defeating a few of the creatures, the party learned how to fight as a whole. Fox would lead the charge, getting their attention. Then Misa and Riley would engage from the sides while Raystia peppered them with arrows.

The day had been fruitful. Each member of The Mob Squad had gained five levels. And that was not all.

Raystia examined the *cargo* Riley and Fox were carrying. Slung across each of their shoulders was a live, shackled vegepygmy. This was the source of her conflicted emotions.

They had accomplished their task and captured two live specimens, yes. But the thought of what was to be their fate made her feel uneasy. One was going to be sacrificed, the other, eaten.

In real life, she would never *ever* do anything even remotely this cruel. Or would she? Everyone had to eat. Even monsters. Kaedric's simple remark of not being able to eat, due to being different from everyone else, touched her in a deep way.

Besides, she thought, steeling her resolve, *I'm playing NEO to become someone else.* She smiled briefly. This semi-psychotic cat persona she assumed was as far from her real-life persona as possible.

Her companions' expressions were also grave. They all knew what came next, but none of them tried to shirk from their quest. The bugbear, in particular, didn't seem to care for any of this. He carried the vegepygmy ambivalently. Riley looked like he too had his inner turmoil, but his lips were pressed tightly together, showing his resolve in becoming Nihilator's priest.

Misa mystified her the most. The elven-goblin woman was walking with an easy step, seemingly without a care in the world. Despite her carefree appearance, it was she who had captured their two victims. During the last fight, she caught their wrists and bound them with her new shackles. The last fight turned out to be the easiest of the day, all thanks to her. The woman was full of surprises.

But now they were back. They would soon finish with these quests, and the expected rewards would provide her and her party with the edge they needed to face more serious challenges. Raystia brightened at the thought.

"So we're going to visit the church first, or volunteer to feed the hungry?" Fox grunted.

The other three stopped walking and looked at him.

"What?" He placed his free hand on his hip. "When you stop and think about it, that's basically what we're doing. Freaking game will probably send us to do some Jehovah's Witness crap next."

"Ahem, let's go find Kaedric first," Raystia said. One of the female goblins she'd met before gave her a friendly smile, and she returned it with a wave. She was really growing to like it here.

They kept walking through the valley, circling the row of cabins. Once they neared the pond, they spotted the seneschal. He was staring intently at a goblin who was busy making leather armor. The hob's mandibles twitched and a speck of spit dripped from one of them.

The goblin, which Raystia was pretty sure was named Vrick, shifted uncomfortably. "Stop staring at me like that you oversized ant," he said. "I'm working on the armor for you darned hobs, just like you wanted."

"Um, hello, Kaedric," Raystia said hesitantly, approaching the seneschal. "We brought you the ... er ... item ... you wanted." She gestured at their prisoners.

Kaedric shifted his gaze from the goblin and focused on the woman. "I see. Let us move to a more secluded area. I shall meet you by the shrine momentarily."

"Alright, let's go," Fox said.

They kept walking through the valley, passing the pond and arriving in full view of the cave. With a little joint effort, they hauled their victims up the ladder to the stone ledge above.

Somehow, Kaedric had beaten them there and was already waiting, standing between the shrine and the cemetery tombstone.

"Greetings, newcomers," the monstrous hobgoblin greeted them cordially. "I trust you have all been well?"

"I ... ahem ... yes. As I said earlier, we brought what you asked for."

With a grunt and a flick of his wrist, Fox heaved the bound creature off his shoulder.

The seneschal's eyes followed the rolling creature that came to a stop at his feet. His mandibles extended, and a thin, snake-like tongue protruded, licking them. As if suddenly realizing he was not alone, the hobgoblin snapped his tongue back in and met the adventurers' eyes. "I'm afraid the feeding process is a bit ... graphic. You might want to retreat for a few minutes while I ... partake in your offering."

"Oh, no – I want to see this." Misa crossed her arms in defiance.

Raystia was already moving toward the ladder when she noticed none of the others were following. "Oh, ahem," she coughed nervously. "No, I'll stay too."

Shrugging, Kaedric stared directly at the green creature who was still struggling against his bonds. The creature stopped thrashing at once and remained perfectly still. Then, like a mummy rising from a sarcophagus, it lifted itself into a sitting position.

Kaedric hunched over, a predatory glint in his eyes, mandibles extending far to the sides. He reached the small creature and lowered his head. His mandibles shut with a snap, biting deep into the poor creature's skull, fixing it in place. The vegepygmy remained motionless. Then, another *thing* came out from the seneschal's mouth. It shot straight down, puncturing the vegepygmy's head and digging deep into the brain.

Then the slurping noises began.

The others watching looked slightly green in the face. Greener than their goblin heritage would account for. Even the gruff Fox looked a bit ill. For some reason, the sight only hardened Raystia's resolve. Everyone had to eat somehow; this was just Kaedric's way. It was not his fault he was built this way. Seeing him slurping her offering made her feel ... strong, somehow. In control. She was the provider and he was the one in need.

It took Kaedric nearly a minute to finish his gruesome feast. When he was done, he extracted his mandibles from the now-hollowed skull. The body tumbled to the ground.

"An excellent meal. I thank you all."

Quest Completed: Braaaaains!

Kaedric, the administrator of Goblin's Gorge, has asked you to bring him a living, intelligent humanoid creature to eat. Though it barely met those requirements, you have successfully provided a vegepygmy for the hungry seneschal.

Reward: +50 reputation with the GreenPiece Clan, +200 reputation with Kaedric, 400XP, 20 gold

"Sweet!" Misa exclaimed. "I leveled."

"Me too," Riley and Fox said.

Kaedric wiped his face clean with a cloth. "Now if you'll excuse me, I shall take my leave." He walked to the edge of the shelf and went down the ladder.

"Guess it's my turn," the goblin dwarf said and went to the shrine. He dumped the body he was carrying onto the small construction of white bones and black stones, then stopped, staring at something in the darkness beyond.

"What are you doing?" the bugbear demanded.

Riley shook his head "I thought I saw something for a moment in the darkness, but there's nothing there." He sighed and took out the crude starter dagger from his belt, holding it over the vegepygmy's chest. "Come on, I ain't got all day."

"Yes." Misa nodded, though she sounded more sympathetic than the barbaric bugbear. "Just get it over with. It can't be worse than what happened to the other one."

Raystia looked sharply at Misa. The first vegepygmy's fate was her own doing, but the other woman's face was not accusatory.

"Ah, what the hell," the dwarf said. "It's just a game."

He struck down hard at the helpless creature's chest, killing it instantly. Blood poured freely, painting the shrine red.

"That's it?" the dwarf demanded. "I didn't get any –"

He stopped talking, and his eyes opened comically wide as he stared at the body on the shrine. Instead of red, the victim's corpse was oozing black liquid. The body shriveled as the flow increased until all that remained on the shrine was black goo.

Riley dropped to his knees and grabbed his head, his mouth open in a mute cry. Raystia made to reach for him but found she could not move. A message flickered at the edge of her vision, but her eyes were glued to the sight before her.

The blackness oozed from the shrine toward the dwarf like it was a living thing. It clung to his feet and climbed up his legs, covering his torso, reaching all the way to his head.

Riley just stood there, motionless, covered in darkness.

After several long moments, something changed. The black liquid solidified, losing some of its sheen. With a jerk, the dwarf broke through, like larvae emerging from its chrysalis. He shed the black stuff, which drained into the ground. But some remnants remained. The dwarf's skin was a few shades darker, and he had asymmetrical black patches all over his body. He also looked slightly taller and more fit.

Just like those makeover shows, Raystia reflected.

"God, that was intense." The dwarf looked at the dagger in his hand. The weapon had turned black. He looked at the rest of the party and Raystia noticed his irises had become completely black.

"What the hell happened?" Misa asked.

Riley shrugged. "I got a ton of messages. Apparently, I'm now a priest of Nihilator. I received two new spells, one for healing and an area debuff. Oh, I also transformed; I'm now a Shadow-Touched creature, whatever the hell that means."

"So we got our healer. Now can we finally go look for more stuff to kill?" huffed the bugbear.

He seemed a single-minded kind of guy to Raystia, though Zuban appeared impressed with his knowledge. This contradiction didn't sit well with Raystia. She hated not knowing.

"Sure," Misa said. "What do you have in mind?"

***

I watched the four players descend the ladder into the valley and stepped out of my hiding spot.

I'd used the shadows as a shroud to conceal my presence. The weird-looking dwarf nearly spotted me when he first approached the shrine. I figured that as a dwarf who was also part goblin, he had enhanced night vision.

Knowing he would soon be anointed by darkness, I hid behind the tombstone. My ability to manipulate the shadows would not hide me from another Shadow-Touched creature.

So my master now has another follower ... I mused. If the uncompromising, scornful Nihilator was willing to accept this Riley as his minion, he must be someone of worth.

Vic snorted. <*That doesn't say much, considering his other candidates.*> He gave me a meaningful mental stare.

Pfh, you wouldn't have even made it through the preliminary trials, I retorted without thinking.

A long pause followed.

<*I am very disappointed in you, Boss,*> Vic finally said. <*You can do better than that.*>

"Whatever," I mumbled.

I walked over to the stone ledge and looked down at the four players walking across the building-strewn valley. So far, they hadn't caused any significant trouble. In fact, according to Kaedric, they'd completed a few quests and helped wall up the valley's entrance. They could become powerful allies that would help increase my clan's strength and development. Riley's consecration by Nihilator was another good indication of their dedication and reduced my worries of betrayal.

This presented an interesting opportunity. Introductions were in order.

I waited until they were several meters away, then I used Shadow Teleport, instantly appearing in their path.

"Shit!"

"What the hell?"

The two men cried, reaching for their weapons.

The women were less vocal. The goblin-eared elf produced shackles from her belt and the catgirl unslung her bow and drew an arrow in a single, smooth motion.

<*Oh, she's adorable,*> Vic said. <*For a meat suit. Can I scratch her ears?*>

***

Raystia was as surprised as her friends at the sudden appearance of the dark goblin in their path. He was taller than the other goblins by at least a head and had a slender build with strong, wiry muscles. His sunken eyes projected intelligence and she could tell he had them all measured with a single glance. He wore simple clothing and had no visible weapons. A lavish, rich-looking purple cloak hung from his shoulders.

Suddenly, she knew without a doubt who was standing before them. She lowered her bow, pointing the arrow down and bowed her head in greeting. "Well met, Dread Totem."

***

Well, at least the cat one had some manners. "Well met indeed, travelers."

"Is he an NPC?" the shaggy-looking bugbear whispered hoarsely, still holding up his axe and shield.

"No, it is that guy who started all of this." The elven woman relaxed her guard and smiled at me. "I like what you've done with the place, quite impressive. I'm Misa Gavriilu, this is Raystia. The bugbear's name is Fox and the small black guy is Riley Stonefist, our newly crowned healer. We are The Mob Squad."

I laughed openly. "Like the movie?" I felt traces of my goblin instinct evaporate at the sudden injection of realism. "How fitting. Pun intended?"

"Well, duh." Misa rolled her eyes.

Fox, still carrying his weapon, stepped closer and loomed over me. "So you are this mysterious and scary Totem everyone keeps mentioning? You look like a weakling to me." He bent down and looked straight into my eyes. Oh, he was looking for trouble.

I stared back, unflinching, at the bugbear, and in light of his threatening demeanor couldn't help wondering, *How the hell did he manage to get such a short name?* I shrugged. *I can just ask him, once he's on his back.*

"Hands off the goblin, he's mine!" a clear feminine voice rang out.

Shadow-crap. I groaned inwardly. It was Hoshisu, coming to collect her due.

Fox straightened and looked at the newcomer. "Who're you?" he demanded.

"Hoshisu Matsugaya," the woman said lightly. "Now hands off the chief; I was here first." She stood a step away from the bugbear, hands on hips, giving him a challenging look.

The bugbear huffed. "Now listen here, scrawny-face, I haven't seen you before. I'm level 7, so you better piss off before I get angry." He used his shield to push the woman away.

At least he tried to.

Before his shield made contact, Hoshisu activated her flashy skill and with a blur, appeared behind him, both her daggers at his throat.

He froze. Even his breath slowed in fear of cutting himself on the daggers.

"You were saying?" Hoshisu asked sweetly.

"Err ... ladies first, that's what I always say."

Misa snorted and Raystia put a hand to her mouth.

"Found you." Hoshisu smirked at me after releasing the poor bugbear. "As I recall, you owe me a duel."

"I thought you and Malkyr were away for a few days," I said.

"We were just about to leave our apartment, but I had a hunch I'd find you here. I've got ten minutes to spare IRL. That's plenty of time to kick your ass over here."

"Fine!" I wasn't happy about it, but a deal was a deal. I couldn't risk losing my credibility. Not that I was really worried. We were both level 26, and I had the advantage of being a tier 2 boss. She stood no chance against me. If she wanted to be sent for a respawn so badly, I guess I'd have to oblige her.

I turned away. "Let's go find us a secluded –"

Hoshisu moved to block my path. "No. You've postponed this long enough." She held up her daggers. "We'll do it right here, right now. If you will please excuse us," she said sweetly to the four bewildered players, "this won't take long."

"You got that right," I replied and activated my Mana Shield. Both twins had witnessed the full extent of my strength, so there was no sense in trying to hide it from the newcomers. Once your secret's out, it's out. This fight could actually be a good thing. I could make Hoshisu an example to the others not to mess with me or my clan.

I pulled out my new staff and pointed it at her. “We’ll fight until one of us hits zero health.”

She rolled her eyes. “You could just say, ‘to the death.’”

“I like the way I put it better.”

“Whatever, bring it on!”

***

We stood facing one another.

Hoshisu started to circle me slowly. I tightened my grasp on my staff and spun, following her every movement, waiting for her to make the first move.

“Nice staff,” she remarked, still circling me. “But where’s your other gear? I’d hate for you to excuse your defeat due to lack of equipment.”

I gave her a crooked smile. “Don’t worry, I won’t. As long as we’re talking about equipment I guess I should warn you not to try using your saw-chain against me. Not unless you’ve gotten tired of having it.”

Hoshisu narrowed her eyes. “You put in a fail-safe or something?” Her upper lips peeled back into a sneer. “Don’t worry, I wasn’t planning on using it, I have other weapons in my arsenal.”

“I can see that.” I looked pointedly at the bandolier she wore strapped slaunchways across her shoulder. It was the same one she’d worn back at the Ogre fort when she thought we were about to throw down. The bandoleer held eight slender throwing knives, positioned in such a way that she could easily retrieve and throw. I sensed a faint glimmer of power coming from the knives. Definitely not strong enough to worry about.

Ignoring my comment, Hoshisu finally decided on a course of attack. She bent low, holding her main daggers at her sides, and charged me.

I looked at her, bemused. She reached me in a second and delivered a flurry of sharp blows, all of which were easily repelled by my shield. The damage output wasn’t even high enough to strain my mana reserves. I could take a nap if I really wanted to, and she would still be unable to get past my shield.

“Come on, that’s the best you can do?” I taunted her.

"No, try this one for size!" She sent one of her daggers flying upward, and with a fluid motion used her free hand to draw a throwing knife and hurled it at me point blank. She then caught her soaring poniard before it hit the ground. The throwing knife smacked against the shield and bounced off. "Damn it!" she fumed.

"That was an impressive display, I'll give you that." I brandished my staff. "But now it's my turn. I think you've seen these before." I launched a volley of drilling arrows at her.

To my surprise, Hoshisu performed a one-handed backflip with the agility of a circus acrobat and somehow managed to dodge all three arrows.

"How the hell did you do that?" I gaped at her. "You're not supposed to be able to do that."

She grinned at me wickedly. "I gained a useful skill back at the fort after dodging all those fireballs and fire darts. You were also kind enough to attack me once with those arrows. I learned a valuable lesson from that."

If what she said was true, it was damn impressive. Drilling Arrow homed in on the selected target by magic and was not supposed to be blocked by anything short of magic resistance. I launched another volley to test her claim. She deftly dodged them all, then retaliated with her own throwing knife. It banged uselessly against my shield and fell to the ground, its point embedded in the dirt.

"Congratulations, your evasion skill seems to be the real deal. Prime badge?"

Her devilish grin was the only answer I got in response.

"You know I've been watching you fight as well, right?" I asked her. "I know your fighting style pretty well. The second I drop the shield you'll do your fancy flash move and slit my throat. Well, that's not gonna happen. Since my arrows are useless against you, try your luck dodging Rex, Max, Buddy, and ... uh ... Fluffy. Shadow Hound!"

The shadows gathered around me, forming into four level 12 Shadow mastiffs. The hounds lurched at the woman, snarling and biting.

Hoshisu spun on her heels, evading teeth and claws, slashing with her daggers at every opportunity. Her weapons caused no damage to the shadowy hounds. She had excellent form, but it was only a matter of time before she missed a step, then it would be all over.

I remained in place, watching the skirmish with interest. Hoshisu jumped over a mastiff, dodged another, drew a throwing knife and flung it at a third. She missed, and the knife sailed on, hitting my shield, again as harmless as the rest before it.

"Damn you!" she spat.

"You asked for this," I reminded her. I could end this at any time I wanted to. I could bind her with Shadow Web or Freeze, then the hounds would rip her apart. But I was enjoying the spectacle. With how much she was gunning for this fight, a little lesson in humility wouldn't hurt her. I chuckled to myself. *Stupid human spawn.*

Hoshisu broke at a dead run, trying to put some distance between her and the four canines. They gave chase immediately, and she threw more knives at them as she ran. Some hit, causing no damage, some missed completely, and another one struck my shield and was repelled, joining the other three on the ground. She had only a single throwing knife left. The mysterious bandoleer she'd kept hidden all this time was disappointingly underwhelming.

Still running ahead of my hounds, Hoshisu circled back toward me. I shot more drilling arrows her way, just to make it more exciting, and she dodged them all while still keeping a step ahead of my hounds. That girl had some mad evasion skills.

She nearly reached me and was about to attack with her handheld daggers when my mastiffs finally caught up to her. One of them lurched forward, and Hoshisu finally missed a dodge, acting a fraction of a second too late. The mastiff clamped his jaw on her ankle and tripped her at my feet. The others, obeying my commands, clamped their jaws on her other leg and arms, pinning her to the ground. Hoshisu was left staring up at me, her eyes flashing in anger.

"I'm a bit disappointed, to be honest." I looked down at the woman sprawled on the ground. I put my sharpened staff's tip under her throat. "With all your not-so-subtle hints that you were ready for me, I expected more out of you."

Her angry look evaporated and was replaced with a smug smile. "And you were right."

In an amazing display of dexterity, she deflected the point of my staff with her chin and ripped away one of her pinned arms from the jaws of a mastiff. In her bleeding hand, she held her last throwing knife. With a triumphant shout, she struck down, burying the knife blade in the ground.

I looked around, my eyes opening wide with realization. With this last knife, the woman had completed a perfect pentagram around me.

An instant later, lightning burst from the hilts of the five knives. The cords of electricity arced around my shield, surrounding it with a web of lightning.

I stared with disbelief as the magic overpowered and shattered my shield, leaving me exposed.

Effortlessly, Hoshisu released her other limbs and rolled to her feet in front of me. Her body flickered.

I recognized the move and managed to bring my staff up in front of my neck. Similar to the move she used against the bugbear, she reappeared behind me. I raised my staff just in time, blocking the two crossed daggers centimeters from my throat, straining against the pressure.

I couldn't match Hoshisu physically, but I didn't have to. I had bought myself a second, and that was all I needed. I channeled my mana and froze the woman.

She stopped trying to force her weapons at my throat and stood completely immobile.

I blew a sigh of relief. "Got to hand it to you girl, you were damn close. I didn't see that one coming, I bought your whole act. You could have ditched my hounds any time you wanted to, couldn't you? You're an amazing actor, but I'm afraid you missed your only chance."

Still standing in the awkward position with her behind me, I made my own dagger fly out of my belt and hover next to her neck. "Goodbye, Hoshisu."

From the corner of my eye, I saw one of her fingers next to my neck twitch. Something flashed, and I felt a stinging pain on my neck.

Poison needle hit you for 2 damage. You are afflicted with the Goblin Bane poison.

Effect I: 10 HP damage per second. 60 seconds duration

Effect II: Paralysis, 10 seconds

I couldn't move a muscle, I couldn't resist. The devious woman had me. She'd used the ring I had gifted her against me!

The poison ran through my veins, the searing pain breaking my concentration and my hold over her.

Hoshisu leaned in, putting her lips next to my ear. "Goodbye, Chief."

With a sharp flick, she slit my throat open with both daggers. An assassin's execution skill.

Damn, the woman's a stone-cold killer, I thought with admiration.

Then I reached zero health.

21 – Outsourcing

> **Nihilator's Sanction triggered**
>
> Due to receiving a fatal amount of damage, you have transformed into a being of shadow for one minute. You are completely undetectable and invulnerable for the duration and may move freely. Once the duration is over, you will return to the material plane, fully healed.
>
> Mana regenerates at the normal rate.
>
> This ability will not be usable again for the next 24 hours.

Well, I'll be damned. Hoshisu won.

I couldn't begrudge her victory. She had earned it. She was well prepared and I had seriously underestimated her. It was a lesson in humility. I'd let my hubris get the better of me.

Not that I hadn't planned for this possibility. I had carefully phrased my words when I stated we'd fight until one of us hit zero health. I counted on her not knowing about my 'get out of jail' trump card. She'd seen Nihilator's Sanction once before when we fought Jawbreaker, but she died before having a chance to question me about it.

I remained standing in place, one with the shadows, watching the frustrated woman with amusement. She kept glancing around, looking for me, occasionally swiping her daggers as if expecting I'd jump at her from the shadows.

The four newcomers exchanged baffled glances and talked in hushed whispers. I distanced myself from Hoshisu, waiting for the spell to expire.

I appeared back in the material plane, fully healed, clapping my hands. "Well done, Hoshisu."

She scowled and advanced on me, clutching her daggers tightly.

I raised a hand. "We're done. You've won. Congratulations."

"We are *not* done," she snapped. "It's not over until one of us is dead."

I shook my head. "The terms were until one of us reaches zero health, which I did. You consented by not objecting."

"Damn you!" she seethed. "I spent days hunting to get this poison and earning enough gold to buy these daggers. Now you tell me it's over? It's bloody hell not over. I demand a rematch!"

"Sure, by all means."

She looked at me suspiciously. "You'll rematch?"

"No." I winked at her. "But feel free to *demand* one."

"Damn you!" she hissed again.

It wasn't my fault she'd fallen for the same trick twice.

"See you later." I waved at her and moved toward the gawking newcomers.

***

Once the fight was over Raystia finally managed to close her mouth. Her friends responded with similar signs of astonishment.

That was an amazing display of power and battle prowess. The angry woman had some mad skills, but that Totem guy was incredible. Yet for some reason, he'd conceded. What was going on?

This game is simply amazing! Raystia felt charged. *I wish I could have joined these goblins when I was still a student.*

"How the hell did he survive that?" Fox muttered.

"Maybe he has some artifact that protects him?" Riley offered.

"I didn't see any special items being used ..." Raystia said, her gaze still fixed on the chief. All she knew was that she did not want to face him in combat.

"Quiet," Misa said sharply. "He's coming over here."

***

"Hi again." I said to the group. They were obviously ill at ease. "Sorry about that interruption. Where were we?"

They exchanged nervous glances.

"Oh yeah, I believe *you* called me a weakling?" I smiled pleasantly at the yellow-furred bugbear.

"Err, yeah ..." He gulped then added gruffly, "Sorry about that."

"Think nothing of it." I waved him off. "So, I heard you got to see around our little valley while I was away. What do you think of our settlement?"

"I love it," the catgirl, Raystia, said eagerly. "So many people working together, taking care of each other … and you even have an Ogre!"

"Two, actually; the other one is patrolling outside the valley."

"So what's your deal, man?" the bugbear asked. "How come a player gets to lead a clan of monsters?"

I shrugged. "Careful planning and a lot of luck. It might look impressive, but we're woefully exposed here and there are factions that want to see us destroyed. We have to grow fast and get stronger. I heard you guys helped with that already, thank you."

The goblin dwarf nodded. "We built you a wall at the valley's entrance. Got some nice gear as a reward too. Thanks for that."

"My pleasure." I hesitated, not sure how to get to the heart of the matter. "So … you have no qualms about … playing as monsters?"

Misa chuckled. "You mean supporting mobs to fight normal players, worship dark evil forces, and kill prisoners in cold blood?"

"Eh … yeah?"

Her grin broadened, revealing sharpened teeth. "I love it. It's a chance to play from a completely new perspective. Even games that let you take an evil role don't let you play as the mob fodder. This is refreshing. Besides, evil is fun."

I scratched my cheek. "I wouldn't say we're evil … we help and support each other. We just have … different priorities."

"You won't hear any complaints out of us, especially this one," she said, gesturing at Raystia. "Don't let those big, innocent eyes fool you. She let your ant-hob eat the brain out of a living victim and stood watching without twitching a muscle. Even the big guy had to look away." She patted the bugbear's shoulder.

"It's not like that," Raystia protested, then blushed as everyone focused on her. "I mean, ahem, the poor man was starving, I couldn't leave him like that. It's not his fault he has to eat living brains. We eat meat, right? Is it so different?"

"Hey kiddo, I'm cool with that, but our resident dwarf nearly fainted when he had to sacrifice the vegepygmy on the shrine." Misa nudged Riley.

Riley made a sour face. “I didn’t like it, but becoming a dark priest sounded cool. At least I can heal now, right?”

“So, you’re a full priest of Nihilator now?” I gave him a searching look.

The dwarf nodded.

“It’s good to have another dark brother in our clan. I see you have a sacrificial dagger?”

“This thing?” He held up his black dagger. I could easily tell it was not as powerful as mine. His dagger wouldn’t kill a helpless victim with a single strike or create a void crystal like mine did, but it was still a holy relic of our cult.

“Yes. In your future battles, try to deliver the finishing blow with this dagger. The creature will become an offering to Nihilator, increasing your reputation with him.”

“Hmm ...” The dwarf mulled over my words. “Thanks for the tip.”

“We’re going to build a Dark Temple soon,” I continued, “which should further increase the power and influence of Nihilator’s followers.” That gave me an idea on how to make my point. “As a matter of fact, why don’t I show you around the clan?”

They exchanged uncertain looks.

“Ahem, are you sure?” Raystia sounded hesitant. “I mean, I’d love to ... this place is amazing but ...”

“Follow me.” I led them through the path between the buildings. “That’s the rabbit warren; it produces raw meat every day.”

“What’s that pink building?” Riley pointed at the Breeder’s Den. “Looks kinda out of place.”

I wasn’t about to let them in on the single most important structure in the clan. I feigned misinterpreting his questions and led them to the structure near it. “That’s my own house. I hope I don’t have to say that, unless I invite you in, it’s off limits.”

“Cool totem piece,” Misa said, pointing at the Ogre totem on top of my house.

“Yes, that ...” A sudden idea came to me. This group had demonstrated their resourcefulness and proved they deserved a bit of trust. I could use someone like them around. “I have a proposal for you.” I gave them a crooked smile. “There should be another piece like it at a camp about half a day’s travel from here. Would you be willing to go and fetch it for me?”

"What's in it for us?" the burly bugbear grumbled.

My smile widened. "I'm glad you asked." I concentrated and brought up the Quest Giver menu.

Grant the quest [Retrieve Totem Piece] to The Mob Squad? Yes/No

I set up the quest rewards for an even hundred gold and reputation points and added a minor magical item for each of them. Then I approved the quest and watched the four expressions change into shock.

"You can grant quests?" Misa and Riley exclaimed together.

"Yup."

"Oh, yes we will do it!" Misa said, accepting the quest for all of them.

"I'm not sure what the totem piece looks like exactly, but it should be similar to this one. It shouldn't be too hard to find. It's likely to be heavy, but between you four, you shouldn't have much problem carrying it back here." I could probably order my hobs to search for the totem, but carrying it back to the valley meant we'd miss a coal shipment. This way was better.

They nodded in understanding.

"Oh, and there's a small force of my people there; a few goblins and hobgoblin guards. Don't interfere with their work and *don't* cause them any trouble," I said with a tone of warning. They had just seen an inkling of my power, so I was sure the message got through loud and clear.

"You got it, Chief," Misa said lightly. "By the way, what's your name? Everyone just refers to you as the Dread Totem; a bit silly if you ask me."

"That's how I roll around here." I shrugged. "Some call me Chief instead, take your pick."

"Ahem ... excuse me, Mr. Dread Totem Chief," Raystia said haltingly. "Do you have any advice on how to play better? I mean, it's hard finding equipment, and we're not allowed to use the crafting areas ..."

She was right, newbies had it rough around here. Her remark sparked an idea, a plan to win over the newcomers' support. "For now, just keep doing what you've done so far – complete quests, help the clan. Aim to reach 'friendly' reputation with the clan. Once you do, we'll have a lot more to offer; access to our crafters and resources, maybe even trainers."

Misa raised her brows. “So it’s basically like a guild?”

I felt a surge of anger. “No,” I said sharply. “Not like a guild. We’re like a family. Everyone is working together to reach a common goal ... to be better, stronger, able to defend our people from trav– ... *players*, and advance our civilization.”

Riley shrugged. “Sounds good to me.”

“I just want to kill stuff,” Fox grunted.

“That sounds amazing!” Raystia blurted, then blushed again “Ahem, I mean you’re basically running a frontier town. The challenges must be staggering.”

“You don’t know the half of it,” I said grouchily. “But we make do. Anyway, it’ll be a while until you get there. The quest should go a long way toward helping you.”

“What are we waiting for?” Misa grinned. “Come on guys, the place is already marked on our maps.”

They all turned and left. I heard Riley mumbling, “Why would they name it Raider’s Camp?”

I chuckled, happy at my spur-of-the-moment idea. This group shouldn’t have any problem finding and bringing me the second totem piece. It spared me the need to use my forces or go in person, and it cost me nothing. A win-win situation.

I turned and walked back toward Totem’s Watch. When I was there ten minutes ago, I could tell something about the shrine had changed, but I was too busy spying on the newcomers to investigate. Now that I had dealt with them, I wanted to have a closer look.

A loud scream came from within the cave as I drew near. Two snakefolk slithered out, shouting and screaming. More travelers.

Snakefolk had the upper body of a human and the lower body of a snake, kind of like land-mermaids. The two were slither-running as fast as they could. A single large shadow mastiff appeared behind them, giving chase.

I directed my will at the mastiff, ordering it to disengage. The hound complied, returning to the cave. The two travelers continued running past me, screaming as they went.

“Stupid, no good travelers poking their noses where they don’t belong,” I muttered to myself.

Still shaking my head, I climbed the ladder to the stone ledge above. I approached the altar, feeling tendrils of information swirling excitedly around it. I reached out and touched the shrine. It was filled to the brim with thrumming, dark power; it had more than enough to activate Eternal Night.

Soon, I promised myself. *Very soon.*

It had been a couple of hours since I'd given Trillian, the new exporter, her first assignment. It was time to go check on her progress. I teleported down and made the short walk to the marketplace.

I arrived just in time to see Trillian and her gofer bringing in the last pieces of lumber to the Export Office. Somehow, they'd managed to fit the entire load inside the small enclosure.

I watched, curiously, as Trillian went to stand next to the central market's pole. She laid both her hands on the glowing orb and closed her eyes. The pile of logs started fading, slowly becoming transparent. In a few seconds, the entire stack of lumber vanished, and in its place stood a much smaller pile of square, clear glass.

We finally had glass.

I looked around, excited, wanting to share our success with someone. But for once, Kaedric wasn't nearby. I frowned. "Vic, can you please go get Zuban."

Vic glided away from my shoulders. "So spiky-face is unavailable for a moment and I become an errand boy again?"

"I did say 'please,'" I pointed out.

"Fine. One stupid hob puppet to go." He left the marketplace, muttering.

I didn't let his antics spoil the moment. The Export Office worked! This single building was the ultimate answer for our resource issues. To top it off, the gremlin marketplace put a high value on wood, which we had plenty of. We were rich. We could buy most any valuable resource we needed.

I concentrated briefly, connecting to the information threads that permeated the air, looking for our daily production quotas. There – we were producing 52 units of lumber per day and had over 300 in store. A good amount. It more than satisfied our construction needs, but I wanted more. I could now use the Export Office to bring in resources instead of having to produce them on my own. I needed a lot of lumber for that.

I spotted Kaedric walking between the stalls toward me. "Greetings, my lord. Please accept my apologies for my absence; there was a small incident with a couple of travelers that required my attention."

I frowned. "Did they cause any trouble?"

"No, my lord, they were complaining that the cave was not safe. It seems that a third member of their group was killed by the mastiffs that roam within."

"How did you handle that?"

"I explained to them that the cave is only safe to members of the GreenPiece Clan. At which point they asked to join. I'm afraid I took liberty with your time, my lord. I have scheduled them a meeting with you for tomorrow morning."

"That's alright, Kaedric. As a matter of fact, I was already thinking along those lines. If we let the travelers into the clan, I think they'll be more invested in helping us."

"Very wise, my lord."

"Anyway, I need your help with something else. We have to increase our wood production substantially. Please recruit two new lumberjacks and put them to work."

"Shall I also increase them to level 3, my lord?"

I sighed. "I guess we ought to make it our standard for new recruits."

"Yes, my lord, I shall see to this at once."

Kaedric left just as Zuban appeared.

"You summoned me, Dread Totem?"

I didn't answer, just grinned at my foreman and pointed at the neat stack of glass.

Zuban eyed the stack with delight. "Wonderful! We can begin constructing the Dark Temple immediately. However, I have a suggestion."

"What do you have in mind?"

"It will be daylight soon, so we won't make much progress on the temple today. Let's continue working on the barracks instead a little longer. We can complete it by early tomorrow. The delay for the Dark

Temple will be meaningless, and while we work on it, your warriors will have a proper barracks to use."

I studied Zuban. The hobgoblin had come a long way from the mindless warrior drone I'd first met. He was an intelligent and invaluable member of my clan now. Any chief would be lucky to have such a person working for him. I was very fortunate. "Of course, that is an excellent idea, Zuban; good thinking," I complimented him warmly.

He looked down in embarrassment, though I could still see him smiling. "It's a simple matter of efficiency, Dread Totem."

"Simple for you, yes," I countered. "Not many would have your foresight. We are fortunate to have you." I suddenly remembered he was 'dating' one of my scouts. "How are things between Ashlazaria and you?"

He coughed, embarrassed. "She ... is a fierce woman. It can be challenging."

I frowned. "What do you mean?"

He actually blushed. "As a warrior, she can be demanding ... physically. It is difficult to meet her ... expectations."

"Ah," I said. "Females, eh?"

He looked down and didn't reply.

I rubbed my chin. Zuban deserved some sort of a bonus. I could purchase him another level, but as he was level 7, it would cost over 300 energy. Besides, as a constructor, his main attribute was Social. A level-up wouldn't make him physically stronger. I needed to give him something that would help him bring his 'A Game.'

Then it hit me. "Zuban, give me your arm."

"Dread Totem?"

"Don't worry, it's a gift."

He extended his arm. I held it with both my hands and concentrated.

Would you like to grant the Mana Infusion skill to Zuban?
Yes/No

Yes.

A glittering of small light surrounded us, and Zuban's eyes opened wide.

I grinned, applauding my own cleverness. As a Social-centered build, Zuban actually had a fair amount of Mana. It would be more than enough to 'fuel' him physically for a rigorous bout of 'pillow fighting.'

"There you go." I winked at him. "Use it when you need a little extra edge. I'm sure Ash would approve."

"I ... I ... I..." my foreman stuttered, then bowed deeply. "Thank you, Dread Totem."

"You deserve it." I patted his shoulder. "Now get to work!"

"Yes, Dread Totem!" He left with an extra bounce in his step.

The horizon was getting brighter. I'd had a late start, spending more time than I thought fighting Hoshisu and showing the new travelers around. There was still much to be done, but it could wait until tomorrow.

I could have probably done a little more, but I suddenly felt exhausted. Tika and Hoshisu both wore me down pretty hard, albeit for different reasons. I could do with some extra sleep.

I went home. Tika was still out. I crawled into my furs and fell asleep instantly.

***

I awoke the next evening feeling much more alert and refreshed. Tika was snuggled against me, as usual. I had a slight urge to wake her and recap yesterday's playtime but decided against it. There was a lot to do today. We could always make up for lost time later.

I left the house. Vic flowed from the hanger to my shoulder as I passed through the door, and together we went to the mess hall.

Workers were flowing in and out of the structure, getting their daily food rations, parting to allow me entrance.

Zuban was sitting with his builders. I noted that each of the workers had a large pile of food in front of them and were all eating voraciously. Good old Ogre's Gluttony was hard at work.

At a separate table sat the hob warriors, those that were not currently on guard duty; Yulli the scout, Kilpi the tank, Ryker the axe wielder, and Ashlazaria.

The female scout busied herself with her food, though she kept glancing toward Zuban every few seconds. I had a feeling my little gift had been appreciated.

Vrick was seated at a table and surrounded by female workers.

At least ten foblins were running around, causing a racket and snatching up discarded pieces of food.

Rhynorn, our 'champion', was sitting by himself, eating a whole pot of stew on his own. He growled at a foblin that got too close, and the little critter fell on his back in terror, then skittered away on his hands and feet.

I went to sit with Vrick and the females.

"Dread Totem," Vrick said, munching on a piece of bone.

"Good to see you again, Vrick." My former lieutenant was giving off all sorts of interesting information streams. I could sense his Armorer skill had reached its cap at level 19. It was the highest worker skill in the entire clan. Having served as a soldier, Vrick had reached level 8, a relatively high level that he was now putting to good use. That was some food for thought. *Maybe I should only recruit soldiers, have them fight and level up a bit, then set them to work?* I mused.

"I see you have become quite skilled at your job." I motioned at the armor he was wearing. It was spotless leather, made from a fine mesh and polished to a shine. Compared to that, the leather vest he'd made me when he was just learning his craft looked like garbage.

Vrick dragged a long nail over his chestpiece. "This? This is acceptable. I could create something so much better if I had the proper material and workplace. For now, Kaedric makes me craft simple armor for the stupid hobs." His lips tightened. It looked like he was still carrying a grudge against our former enemies.

"That's part of the reason I'm here." I took out the oxsaurian hide from my inventory and put it on the table. The wood groaned from the weight. "Think you can make something better with this?"

Vrick inspected the hide, pressing his lips together. "This is large and thick. It would make a good heavy armor. There is enough material for two hobs or one Ogre."

I considered it briefly. Rhynorn was one of my bigger guns and he was tamed now. Well, mostly. "Make armor for Rhynorn," I decided.

"Yes, Dread Totem," he said, somewhat mechanically.

"Come on Vrick, cheer up. Thanks to you, no other clan can field stronger warriors."

His expression didn't change.

"I have something else for you as well." I took out a Pyrolith scale.

His eyes widened as he took the scale, examining it from all angles. "What is this? It's as tough as steel, but light. It's almost flexible, and the red sheen ... This ... this is amazing."

"Think you can craft something suitable for me? I'm afraid I've outgrown the vest you made for me."

He lowered his eyes and his tone became apologetic. "Forgive me, Dread Totem. I should have thought of that myself. I could make a light leather armor that won't interfere with your spellcasting, then attach this scale to the chest. It should increase the defense value dramatically. Shame, if I only had a few more of these, I could have –"

I dumped the rest of the scales on the table. All 17 of them.

Vrick's eyes looked like saucers. "This is amazing!" he repeated. "I will make you the envy of all Totems." He was excited now, all traces of his previous gloom gone.

"Glad you like it. I am sorry for not supporting your craft more. The armor workshop is one of my highest priorities. You will soon be able to work in an environment that is more befitting of your talents."

He lowered his head. "I thank you, Dread Totem."

I got up. "Put the extra scales in the warehouse. We'll think of what to do with them later."

"Yes, Dread Totem."

I went to my own table. A short moment later, Gandork himself brought me a steaming plate of seasoned meat. There were a few wriggling worms on top of the pile.

The goblin cook leaned in, close to to my ear. "I had a little extra left, Dread Totem."

"I take it Guba was able to supply you with Fire Resist potions?"

"She did indeed. I cooked 60 portions of the exquisite food as you ordered. It came out quite nicely if I do say so myself. It has already been supplied to the Breeder's Den. Enjoy your food, Dread Totem."

Gandork walked away, giving the gorging Ogre a wide berth.

I ate my meal, savoring every bite. The squirming worms went well with the dish, adding a touch of spiciness and a pleasant sense of wriggling in my mouth.

When I finished my food, I lifted the plate and licked it clean. No one paid my action any heed. Plenty of other goblins were doing the same. The foblins were licking crumbs off the floor.

I stood and approached Rhynorn. He looked down at me, scowling. I folded my arms over my chest, holding his gaze.

The Ogre lowered his eyes. "Boss-man."

"I have a gift for you, Rhyno." I retrieved the Ring of Bound Soul. "This was once Barska's ring. I no longer need it so I'm offering it to you. If you can withstand the pain, it will make you even more powerful."

The Ogre literally snatched the ring from my hand, nearly taking off some of my fingers with it. "Pain not matter. The *Champion* is not afraid of pain."

He put on the ring. The magic within expanded the metal band, making it fit onto his sausage-like finger. The ring then clamped down, its inner teeth biting into flesh. The Ogre didn't even blink.

I didn't bother to say goodbye and left him to admire his new toy.

I'd almost reached the door when a new message popped up.

New Building added to your settlement: Barracks

Using the new Ogre Gluttony trait to double the builders' daily upkeep had paid off big time. Zuban wasn't kidding when he said the building would be completed the next day.

I hurried outside, eager to check out the barracks.

An unfamiliar information trail came from my left, from the direction of the cabins. I frowned. The data told of time remaining and temporary riches. It felt like the information that vanquished foes gave off, indicating loot. It was not something I expected to encounter in the heart of my clan.

I followed the information trail. It led me past the cabins and into the woods. I passed a wide tree. Its trunk was hollowed from the other side. The sight of two unfamiliar goblin bodies welcomed me.

Someone had murdered two members of my clan.

22 – Mobilizing

My blood boiled at the sight of the two bodies.

Someone had dared to hurt members of my clan. Rage surged within me. My goblin instincts thirsted for vengeance.

Taking deep, steadying breaths, I calmed myself and tried to think it through rationally. *Gotta check the bodies first*, I surmised and dragged both corpses out into the open.

> **Goblin worker [Dead]**
> *Level:* 3
> *HP:* 0/28
> *Attributes:* P: 3, M: 0, S: -1
> *Skills:* Lumberjack 1
> *Traits:* Noncombatant

The goblins were clones of each other, the two new lumberjacks I had asked Kaedric to summon. Someone had lured them here, exploiting their ignorance of the clan.

Deep gashes tore through their bodies; they had been attacked by slashing weapons. That ruled out Rhynorn, my first suspect. Though knowing the Ogre, if he was the culprit, he wouldn't have bothered hiding the bodies. None of my other clanfolk were capable of such an attack. The only conclusion was, one of the new players did it.

<Here, let me check that, Boss,> Vic volunteered.

His purple cloak-like body broke off into many thick tendrils that shot out and disappeared into one of the dead goblins through its mouth and nostrils. In my anger, I forgot about my companion's ability to invade dead bodies and review their recent logs.

The body jerked once, then Vic oozed out again and reformed into his purple goblin shape.

"Well, who did it?" I urged.

Vic spread his hands defeatedly. "It's no good, Boss, all the log says is, 'Stealthed attacker sneak-attacked goblin worker.' Looks like the stealth skill extends to the logs as well. I can tell you though that it definitely was one of the players."

I scowled. *They just arrived and are already causing trouble.* At least I had a piece of a clue: everyone with the stealth skill was a suspect. I would find them and make them pay.

The goblins' deaths were costly. I'd spent food and over 200 energy on their summoning. *Someone is going to pay for that*, I seethed.

"Kaedric!" I bellowed.

My seneschal appeared almost as if by magic. "My lord?"

"Someone murdered two of our clan members," I hissed, pointing at the bodies. "One of the newcomers did it. I want that person found. Now!"

Kaedric gazed at the bodies, his face unreadable. "There are currently eight travelers in the clan, my lord. A group of four left the valley less than an hour ago. The culprit must be one of the 12. How shall we proceed?"

I pondered that question. Finding a player with the stealth skill was not enough to incriminate them. "Get Tempest over here."

Kaedric looked in the direction of my house. A moment later, Tempest came galloping toward us. I put my hand on his fur, petting him as he brushed against me. "Tempest, can you get the scent of the one who killed these two?"

The intelligent demon wolf lowered his head and sniffed at the corpses then turned to me and nodded.

"Good. Let's go find them."

I followed Tempest as he put his nose to the ground and walked slowly toward the center of the village. Vic settled around my shoulders once more. Once we arrived at the pond, the wolf placed his nose into the water, then sneezed. He looked around uncertainty, then promptly sat down.

"Shadow-crap," I cursed. Cobie, our senior fisherman, was nearby. "Did you see someone swim through the pond?" I demanded.

The goblin stared at me stupidly.

I sighed. "Did someone go into the water?"

"Fish swim in water," he offered helpfully.

Vic snickered. *<For an unseeded puppet, that sentence was borderline genius.>*

I tried again. "*Besides* the fish."

"If I may, my lord," Kaedric said, "both fishermen were in the mess hall not long ago; they could not have witnessed anyone coming here at the time of *the incident*.

Shadow-crap!

<You say that a lot lately, you know?>

Shut up, Vic.

I jumped on Tempest's back. "Kaedric, find all the adventurers and bring them to see me in the barracks."

"Yes, my lord."

I rode Tempest past the mess hall toward the barracks, finally seeing the completed building for the first time.

It was a large, flat, circular structure with a wooden walkway circumventing it. A two-door gateway offered entry into a sizeable inner courtyard, making the entire edifice resemble a large bagel.

The building itself was essentially a long, circular hallway. There were many doors along it, each opening into a room; small, private rooms for officers and large, communal rooms housing dozens of soldiers. The inner courtyard was about 30 meters in diameter. At its center, a low fence bordered an area with dummies and archery targets. A training ground for my warriors.

"Hey, dude, are you that Totem guy?" One of the weird half-snake people came toward me. "I got a quest from that other lean dude with the mouth to come talk to you."

I climbed off Tempest's back and leered at the player. A quick Analyze showed me he did not have the Stealth skill. "We will wait for the others to arrive."

He seemed to feel my hostility, and he raised his arms. "Chill, dude. No problem, I'll wait."

One by one, the other players arrived. I had Tempest sniff each of them as they came in. However, a few minutes later, all eight players stood facing me and Tempest hadn't given any indication that he smelled our murderer, although three of them had the Stealth skill.

I addressed the small crowd. "We haven't met yet. I'm the chief and Totem of this clan."

I could hear some of the players whispering among themselves.

"Why are we here again?"

"That ant face dude gave us a chain quest to come here. This Totem dude is about to explain the next step."

I raised my voice. "You are all here as guests. And as guests, you are expected to follow our rules."

"I never heard a goblin talk like that before."

"Heck, I've never *seen* a goblin this big before – and check out his mount. Since when do Dire Wolves have horns?"

"One of you," I continued, raising my voice again, "murdered two of my clanmates."

That finally shut them up. A multitude of gasps ensued.

"Whoever discovers the murderer and brings them before me will be instantly recognized as a friend of the clan and may join us." I paused, scanning their faces. "And believe me, this is something you want to achieve."

Grant the quest: Find the Goblin Killer, Part 2. Yes/No?

I tweaked the quest rewards, granting 1,000 reputation points with the clan, which would be enough to bring each player up to 'friendly.' I also threw in a hundred gold for good measure.

"That's awesome!"

"Hell, I'm in!"

"Let's go find ourselves a killer!"

The cheerful crowd dispersed though none of them had any idea how to complete the quest.

It didn't really matter; Tempest had already cleared each of the players. The four that left the valley earlier were now the main suspects. Still, having more eyes looking and spreading the news of the 'no killing goblins' was a reward in itself.

I turned to inspect the barracks again when Zuban's voice sounded next to me.

"Beautiful, isn't it?" Somehow he'd approached me unnoticed.

"It is indeed." I nodded. Some of my anger ebbed away as I looked in wonder at the great structure we'd managed to build.

“It can house a hundred warriors,” he said. “And I think we can double its capacity by adding another floor, though we’ll need to research the blueprints.

“Zuban ... This is great! There are training dummies and weapons racks and ...” I squinted. “Is that a flogging pole?”

He chuckled. “I don’t like it either, but it’s in the blueprints. We hobgoblin take army discipline seriously; it’s one of the reasons I’m glad I’m not a soldier anymore.”

“Wait, what? This is a hobgoblin barracks?”

“Of course. Most of the buildings are of hobgoblin design. I am a hobgoblin after all. This is actually a good thing. Our civilization is highly militaristic, so our barracks are among the most advanced available. There are also many other additions we can build to make it better: a mage training yard, trainer’s office, etc.”

I palmed my face. It seemed that building the barracks, as arduous as it had been, was only the first step. Still, it was a major one. “So how does it work?” I asked tiredly. “We just let the soldiers sleep here and that’s it?”

Zuban gave me a weird look. “Of course not. You need to assign trainers, decide on the role you want the new recruits to train for, that sort of thing.”

I held up my hand. “I get it.”

I opened the Settlement Interface, scrolled through the list of buildings, and selected ‘Barracks.’

Barracks
Level: 1 *Trainers:* 0/3 *Occupants:* 8/100 Expansions [require research]

I closed my eyes and reached with my mind into the metadata behind the words. *Ah ... there it is.* This was interesting. The barracks was much more than just a building to house warriors.

It allowed elected trainers to continuously train up my warriors' skills. The trick was, I had to choose someone with a high combat skill so he could teach it to the others. Since I could only select three trainers, I needed to consider which skills were the most important for my army.

The expansions were important too. Once the barracks was completed, a whole new section opened up in the Research Interface, providing many new options for study. I opened the Research Interface and browsed the available projects.

Research
Daily RP: 38.7 *Blueprint:* Magma Foundry: Enable magma casting. Cost: 200 RP *Barracks expansion blueprints:* • Second Floor (+100 beds). Cost 200 RP • Armory (maintain soldiers' gear and increase its effectiveness). Cost: 120 RP • Arena (conduct mock battles; dying is impossible). Cost: 50 RP • Trainer's Office I (increase number of trainers by 2). Cost: 100 RP • Advanced Warfare Center (train new traits). Cost: 200 RP.

Yes, that was interesting indeed.

I didn't really need the second floor or the armory at the moment. The arena would be a great addition, though, allowing everyone – including the new travelers – to train in actual combat instead of only using the training dummies. The 'Advanced Warfare Center' was an enigma, but once I dove deeper into the metadata, I nearly forgot to breathe. The A-W-C was a magical building that could impart special traits to my soldiers. Each trait would have to be 'bought' individually. The cost of most of the traits was staggering, but the very first one captured my complete attention: Taunt Resist. With this, my soldiers would no longer be sheep to players' usual mob tactics. I would be able to direct them fully during battle and avoid the enemy tanks reeling them in, allowing their mages and DPS to dish out damage from relative safety.

This was the golden egg I was looking for without even realizing it. This single trait would help level the playing field. But the AWC was a costly project, while the arena could be researched within two days.

"Zuban, I want you to research the arena first, then the Advanced Warfare Center."

"Of course, Dread Totem. The ladies and I will complete the first project within a few hours. Would you like us to start building it as soon as we finish?"

I raised a brow. "How can you be finished so soon? It needs more RP than you can provide per day."

"You are correct, Dread Totem. However, since we finished our last research project a couple of days ago, we've been dabbling in general research. Those principles can be applied now, to shorten the amount of research required for this project."

Ah, I think I remember Zuban once mentioning that an idle researcher continued generating research points at half their normal rate. "Very good, Zuban, but no. The Dark Temple is still our main project."

"In that case, now that the barracks is complete, we can start construction immediately. Where would you like us to build it?"

I thought it over. The temple was going to play a pivotal role in our defense, so it had to be well-protected. "Would it fit on the stone ledge above the cave? Maybe you build it over the cemetery and the shrine?" I asked.

"Hmm ..." My foreman stroked his chin. "It should be possible. But it would certainly take all available space up there."

"That's not a problem, please build it there."

"As you wish, Dread Totem."

Zuban left, leaving me to consider how to handle the barracks management.

The first order of business was to select the three trainers among my warriors. I opened the population tab in the Settlement Interface and checked each of my warriors' skills.

Bob, my lieutenant, naturally had the highest combat skill. At level 10, his Swords skill was level 17. I selected him as the first trainer. Bob also had the spell 'Control Vines' but I instinctively knew he couldn't teach it to our soldiers.

I planned on having a lot of archers. By Nihilator, we had plenty of bows in storage already. Ashlazaria, the scout, was currently away from the clan, bringing in the coal shipment from the Raider's Camp. That left only Yulli, my second scout, whose bow skill was level 12. I chose her for the second trainer.

I also wanted shield bearers, to hold the front lines and protect the rest of the troops. I had two hob soldiers who were proficient with the Axe and Shield skill – Zia and Kilpi Shīrudo. I selected Zia for the job, as at skill level 12 she was one point higher than Kilpi.

The next step was to determine how to divide the soldiers among the new trainers. It was best to train groups of soldiers under a single instructor. Training took time. Soldiers could learn under multiple trainers, but switching carried a time penalty.

The Barracks Interface had a handy menu to assign soldiers to each trainer. I left it at the default settings. Zia would automatically take over training the shield bearers, Bob would teach his sword skill and Yulli would instruct our new scout archers.

Yulli's training ability was especially important. I was raising a hob army to battle players, and I wanted the majority of my soldiers to be able to inflict damage from a distance, keeping them away from the enemy tanks.

It was time to recruit my army.

I checked our food supplies as I rode Tempest to the Breeder's Den.

Warehouse: Food
• 843 raw meat • 311 raw fish • 384 gathered edibles • 655 gathered ingredients • 100 travel rations • 29 purple salt • 22 magmashrooms

Gandork's 'Special Stew' required five portions of meat, three edible herbs, and two gathered ingredients to produce 12 units of basic food – 13, if I added in the mess hall bonuses and Gandork's cook skill. That meant .... I ran some calculations in my head, and a wide grin spread across my face as I arrived at the number.

"Kaedric, " I addressed the hob who had shadowed my movements since leaving the barracks, "have Gandork cook 1,700 units of food and bring it to the Breeder's Den, along with all of our travel rations."

Kaedric's expression remained as stoic as ever. "Yes, my lord. That is 1,800 food in total."

I opened the Breeder's Den Interface. *Oh right, the adepts.* Sixty units of exquisite and several dozen of other food were in its stores, left over from previous summonings.

Since it would take some time for Gandork to complete my large-scale order, I decided to go ahead and summon my new clergy. For the first time, I selected 'Goblin Adept' from the list. There were two specialization options: Blessings and Curses. These guys were going to man the faraway shrines, so being able to inflict curses was more important than support magic. I selected three Curses-specialized adepts.

The Breeder's Den erupted in familiar noises, this time adding a high-pitched hymn to the ruckus. A moment later, the noise subsided and the door flap was thrown open as three goblins stepped outside. Two males and one female. All were of medium build, for goblins, with a dark complexion and sunken eyes. Each one had a sacrificial bone dagger tucked in their loincloth.

Kuzai came from the direction of the cabins and stood beside me, eyeing the new priests.

"They will serve the master well," the unhinged dwarf giggled.

I ignored him and fiddled with the Energy Interface, investing 351 EP and raising all the new goblins to level 3. They were all intelligent, named goblins. VI-seeded, as Vic would put it.

"Welcome to the GreenPiece Clan," I started. "I have called you to bolster our strength. Soon, an army of travelers will come for us and we must be ready to meet them. Our dark master, Nihilator, will lend us his power, but it will be your job to operate faraway shrines and channel their power into our clan. Err ... you." I pointed at the female adept who specialized in curses. "You will join the next coal expedition to the Raider's Camp. There's an altar there. It's your job to maintain it."

The goblin bowed before me and replied with a hollow, steady voice, "At once, High Priest."

That was new.

The other two stood expectantly looking at me. "You two go to the barracks, train with the soldiers. Once the Dark Temple is completed, you will help maintain it."

The two bowed as one, murmuring in unison, "Yes, High Priest."

"Before you go, I have something to give you." I granted them each Lucky Bastard, Drilling Arrow, and Drain Mana.

"Now go and serve," I ordered them. "Prepare for the coming fight."

As the trio departed, two goblin gofers came toward me, each straining under a heavy load of food. My large order was slowly being fulfilled. A hundred units of food in, 1,700 to go.

"That was an interesting display," Kuzai said in his unsettling voice. "I have noticed you did not offer the same boons to me."

"That's because I don't trust you," I said bluntly.

"We are all servants of the master," he declared. "Helping each other only increases his strength in the end."

"Just say you want to have the new cool spells."

"*It* tries to cheapen the worth of the master's followers." Kuzai was back to talking to himself. "*It* doesn't understand that the individual does not matter, our only purpose is to serve."

I sighed. "Fine, if you're going to get all emotional about it ... give me your hand." The system already considered him as part of the clan, so it was serving my own interests to make him stronger.

I felt a shiver of revulsion run through me as I held his three-knuckled fingers and granted him the same skills. "There, happy?"

"The Master's will is served," he declared haughtily.

The gofers came in on another round, carrying more food – 200 out of 1,800 total.

There was no sense standing here all day waiting for the food to arrive. I could queue in the troops I wanted and let the system handle the rest.

A hob soldier cost 70 simple food and an Ogre 150. I opened the interface again and queued in three Ogres and 20 hobgoblin warriors; eight scouts, six shield bearers, and six swordsmen. As an afterthought, I also queued in two new lumberjack workers to replace those that had been killed. There was enough leftover food in the Breeder's Den itself to compensate for the extra units.

The building shook, shrieking noises coupled with howls of pain emanating from within. The door flap flew open and a huge leg burst out. There was no way the building could have held the rest of the creature's body, but as I watched in apprehension, the rest of it followed, somehow flowing out through the too-narrow opening. An Ogre.

But this was no normal Ogre. Though it had a dark complexion and black stripes like the rest of my clan, there were bits of red mixed in as well. Chitinous ridges ran along his forearms and across his back, and two short horns protruded from his forehead. An Infernal Ogre.

Infernal Ogre

Level: 10

HP: 140/140, *MP:* 70/70

Attributes: P: 14; M: -2; S: -2

Skills: Bashing Weapons 10, Ignite 1

Traits: Ogre (+4 P, -2 M, -2 S), Demonic (fire affinity)

Resistances: Physical 75%, Magic 30%, Fire 75%, Holy -50%, Cold -50%

Description: Having their blood mixed with that of demons, the Infernal Ogre is as strong as a normal Ogre with a high fire resistance and a minor magical ability to manipulate fire.

I looked at the Ogre towering over me. Despite its fierce appearance, the hulking creature instilled a sense of hope in me. This was a powerful ally in my fight against Vatras and his minions. And the best part was that he started at level 10! The fire resistance was a nice addition. Most mage players preferred to use fire-based spells as they usually inflicted the most damage, but more than a few went the ice spells path. That could prove hazardous to these new recruits, not to mention their vulnerability to holy spells. I had already witnessed how powerful a priest was when facing demons.

Once the fighting started, I would have to manipulate the battleground carefully, making sure to use the Ogre to fight melee and fire-oriented mages and use my other forces to bring down those players that held the advantage against them. Utilized correctly, a strike force of Ogres could be devastating.

But what is this Ignite skill? I frowned. It sounded like a skill meant to be used for starting campfires. I mentally clicked on the skill.

Ignite (*)

The creature can produce flames on his body. The fire can be used to start fires or inflict minor fire damage on enemies. It can also be used to ignite a held melee weapon for an added fire damage.

Level 1: Novice

Effect: Add 3% fire damage

<Oh my Guy, that's an amazing Ogre you got here, Boss.>

Coming from Vic, that was surprising. *You think so?*

<Heck, yeah. He could double as a mobile chestnuts roaster; very handy, especially if you're traveling. I bet he'll also be great to snuggle with, help keep you warm during cold nights,> he guffawed.

I'd walked right into that one.

The gofers came running in with more food.

"Kuzai, please keep an eye on the new recruits. Once they all arrive, bring them to the shrine."

"*It* plans something to do with the master," the dwarf murmured.

"Don't worry, I think you'll like what's coming next," I assured him and left him standing there.

As I walked toward the smithy to check up on the other essentials, my thoughts were racing. I was finally at the point I'd waited for so long: I had the means and the resources to train a sizeable fighting force.

Food was still an issue, but no longer as severe. I could now import ingredients via the Export Office. I just had to make sure our daily food production could sustain the increased population and fulfill our clan's upkeep. This was no idle concern; the Ogres themselves required a double amount of food each day. I didn't have to feed them, of course, but I wanted each of my soldiers to be at peak combat efficiency, and that meant taking care of their needs. Food was the least of them.

I arrived at the smithy and saw Barzel, our clan's general smith, busy at work with our advanced crafters – Kadoc and Baja Reed, and their four gofers.

I stood at the entrance and watched as the busy goblins poured molten metal from a crucible into round molds, creating metal links, then hammered them together, crafting a strong, metal chain.

"That looks strong enough to chain an Ogre," I said as I entered the smithy.

They all stopped working and jerked their heads toward me.

"Dread Totem! My apologies, we didn't notice your arrival," Barzel said.

"That's quite alright, Barzel," I chuckled softly. "I didn't want to interrupt; you looked like you needed to concentrate. What on earth do we need such a thick chain for?"

"One of the newcomers has commissioned it," the smith said.

"It's not the same as crafting weapons," Kadoc chimed in, "but it's good metalworking experience."

"Yes," Baja nodded his consent.

I focused on them briefly, noting that both their respective smithing skills had already reached level 10 and were on the verge of breaking into the Apprentice ranks.

"Good job, everyone. We have started mobilizing; I'll need you to begin mass-producing weapons and armor for the troops."

"We still need a dedicated workshop for each of us," Kadoc said. "Barzel has been very accommodating, letting us use his forge and anvil, but this equipment is meant for tool crafting. Our work requires more advanced equipment."

I took out the high-steel tools we had recovered from the Ogre fort's smithy and laid them on the table. "Tools like these?"

The three smiths' eyes bulged as they inspected the magnificent, gleaming instruments.

"That ... those are dwarven made!" Baja exclaimed. "You raided one of their strongholds and looted their forges?" He sounded impressed.

"Err ... something like that," I said evasively. I didn't want to disappoint my clanmates with the truth. "These should help produce better items, right?"

"Yes, Dread Totem," Kadoc answered. "These will help immensely. However, we still need proper workshops. The smithy's forge is simply not strong enough to endure the process of crafting good-quality weapons and armor."

"I see ..." I had hoped the tools I'd found would make these buildings obsolete, but it looked like there was no way around it. "We will build your workshops as soon as the Dark Temple is finished. In the meantime, is there anything you can do to prepare for that?"

The two specialized goblins nodded. "We can start by making the base metal sheets, bracings, and sword grips. Those can be obtained with the tools we have here."

Barzel cleared his throat. "That raises another problem, Dread Totem."

There was always something. "Yes?"

"Our metal stores are quite low, I'm afraid. Our two miners produce just enough for me to create enough tools for everyone and supply the needed materials for construction, but if you want us to mass-produce weapons and armor, we will need much more metal. And stronger metal, too. We mostly used tin and copper to create bronze items. We have very little iron, which we use sparingly."

I sighed. "I understand. I'll take care of it."

Well, that was what the Export Office was for, and there was no time like the present. I opened the Settlement Interface and navigated to 'Export Office.' I set the filter of desired goods to 'metal' and a list opened: tin, copper, bronze, iron, steel, high steel ...

"I assume high-steel will bring the best results?" I asked.

"I'm afraid that we cannot work such an advanced metal yet," Barzel said.

"So ... steel?"

"It would be the best for now, however, –"

I prepared myself mentally for another obstacle ...

"– as we have plenty of coal, we can produce steel on our own, provided we have enough iron."

Hmmm, good news for a change. I brightened up. "You got it."

I selected 'iron' from the list.

Select a resource to trade for [iron]		
Resource	**Available Amount**	**Exchange Rate**
Gathered Ingredients	390	30
Arrows	545	100
Rabbit Pelts	443	40
Lumber	382	3
...	...	...

Just as I hoped, lumber proved to be the ideal currency when dealing with the gremlin market. "How much iron will you need?"

"A standard sword requires five ingots," Kadoc said.

"And armor and shields can take ten to 20 ingots, depends on how thick you want it," Baja added.

In order to equip my current troops, I'll need to bring in about 300 iron ingots. I only had enough lumber for about 120 units of iron, and I didn't want to waste it all at once, so I ordered 60 ingots for now. My smiths wouldn't be able to make much headway without their workshops anyway.

As things stood right now, I should bring in more than two extra lumberjacks. After summoning all the soldiers, my food stores were nearly depleted; recruiting more goblins wouldn't leave us any reserves. *Ah, what are 60 more units of basic food?* I gave a mental shrug, opened the Breeder's Den Interface and queued in two extra lumberjacks. I checked our daily production status and saw that our updated lumber daily yield was 137. Not half bad.

While I fiddled with the interface, I noticed that all the new troops were now summoned, so I left the smithy and made my way to the shrine.

Instead of walking through the graveled roads, I took the direct route, cutting through the open valley.

I found myself passing by the two deadbeat farmers. They were straining to pull the plow I had brought. *Looks like Barzel managed to fix it.* I stopped to observe their progress.

The two goblins were giving their all against the heavy plow, but it moved at a snail's speed. Despite that, they left deep grooves in the ground behind them. I really hoped the new equipment would do the trick.

A short walk later, I arrived at the area below the shrine.

Kuzai was waiting for me with new recruits. Twenty hobgoblins stood in three ordered lines behind him, and behind them towered the three massive Infernal Ogres.

This was an impressive force, and it was all thanks to Tal for gifting me with the Breeder's Den from the start.

For a moment, I wondered how 'normal' goblin clans recruited their warriors without having access to such a structure, but I understood the answer straight away. Kaedric had already explained it to me: The goblin chief doubled as the clan 'stallion' and sired new warriors. For a split second, I had a vivid image of what it would be like but banished the thought from my mind. I was not prepared to shoulder *that* aspect of being a goblin chief. Despite the obvious misgiving, it was inefficient. Goblin warriors were vastly inferior to their hobgoblin kin.

As I surveyed my new troops, I realized that all of the hobgoblins were level 4 straight out of the production line. I did not expect that. *That explains how all the hob soldiers we encountered before were between level 4 and 6*, I realized with a start. I had made the right call by not using goblin soldiers anymore. The amount of energy I saved by not having to level them up was significant.

None of the new troops had any weapons and they all wore simple loincloths. *That will have to be corrected*, I mused. *After the ceremony.*

I climbed the ladder up to Totem's Watch and looked at the gathered mob below. Then I walked over to the shrine and drew my black bone dagger.

Now that I had my new troops, it was time to sacrifice them.

“Let us begin.”

23 – Preaching to the Choir

I stared tiredly at the last hobgoblin soldier. The bloody remains of eight hobs and one Ogre pooled at my feet. *The Ogre explosion was particularly gory,* I remembered with a shudder. I could still taste the piece of brain that somehow managed to land in my mouth. Unsurprisingly, it was bland.

Their sacrifice was unfortunate but necessary. It was just the side effect of what I was really after – intelligent, resurrectable soldiers.

One by one, I beckoned my soldiers to lean over the shrine. Once prostrate, I granted them the Lucky Bastard skill. Those that survived were seeded with VIs and adopted the name I had given them. Those that didn't were offered as tributes to Nihilator, granting me quadruple Faith Points and a void crystal. So they too served the clan in a way.

"Come here, let's finish this," I said tiredly to the last hob. The mindless creature came without hesitation and lay on top of the shrine, apathetic to the blood and gore that covered it.

I steadied the dagger hovering in the air above him, poised to strike.

"Your name is ...err ..." After choosing a dozen names already, my brain was a bit addled. The only thing that came to mind was "Blemtoff. Your name is Blemtoff, and you're ... uh ... always striving to be the best at ... um ... dual axe fighting." I finished the short ceremony by granting him the Lucky Bastard skill.

Blemtoff blinked a few times, and his dull expression transformed into one full of wonder that morphed into determination.

I sighed with relief and called the hovering dagger back to my belt. I was spared from having to sacrifice him as well.

So far the survival rate was only about 60 percent. Two of the three Ogres and 12 of the 20 hobs had survived the rite. I had expected better results.

The first time I did this, only three of ten hobs died. Why did the success rate drop? I wondered. My own Lucky Bastard skill had improved since last time, so I should have had fewer casualties. I needed every strong arm I could get to fight for the clan's survival. This didn't make sense.

"Isn't it obvious?" Vic was once again in his purple goblin shape sitting on a small boulder and watching the show. "The hobgoblins you brought from the Raider's Camp experienced life more fully. They fought by your side and bled for the clan. Their personalities were better prepared for the VI seeding process. These guys were just clean slates. All they ever experienced was the interior of the Breeder's Den. Honestly, 60 percent survival is huge. Your Lucky Bastard skill rose by four points in the last hour alone."

"I guess that explains it," I said, wiping spattered blood from my brow.

Blemtoff stood and bowed. "May I report for duty, Dread Totem?"

I gestured dismissively. "Yeah, sure, join the others below."

"Thank you, Dread Totem." The hobgoblin went down the ladder muttering to himself, "Must obtain two axes ..."

I took a few steps gingerly, and my legs wobbled. Though it was no doubt necessary, this had been a trying experience. I walked slowly to the edge of the shelf and looked down at my assembled forces below. The two Infernal Ogres towered over the dozen hobgoblins. I had more than doubled my fighting forces. And I was just getting started.

"Welcome to the GreenPiece Clan," I began. "You are to be our protectors, our guardians, and the blade that strikes against our enemies. Serve me and the clan well, fight as long as there is a drop of blood in your veins, and I promise you right here, your death will not be a permanent one. Serve well, and you will always come back to fight another day. To the GreenPiece Clan!"

"To the GreenPiece Clan!" they all shouted in unison, raising their hands, the Ogres cheering a second behind the more intelligent hobs.

"Good. This is Bob, he is your superior officer." I motioned at the hob lieutenant standing nearby. "Rhynorn is ... just stay out of his way. Report to the barracks and claim your bunk. Tomorrow you will begin your training. Dismissed."

"Yes, Dread Totem!" they answered together and dispersed, heading for the barracks.

I felt too mentally drained to use my magic to teleport down. Bob remained behind, waiting patiently while I descended the ladder.

"These look promising," he said approvingly. "Each one unique in his own way."

"I need you to oversee their training," I said. "Get them into shape as quickly as possible. We're going hunting in a few days. I want to see how they hold up in real combat."

"Of course, Dread Totem." Bob bowed his head. "I will make sure to impress upon our trainers the importance of rigorous training." He paused, then said, "Actually, that is the only kind of training my people know. In hobgoblin society, you either learn fast or you die. There is no place for weaklings."

I grinned tiredly. "That's why your people are the clan's blade while mine are the cogs in the machine that ... uh ... You fight, we build."

The hob lieutenant stared at me stoically.

"Anyway," I continued, "with these new troops, we should have enough soldiers to deploy regular patrols." The recent murders of two of my workers showed me how vulnerable we were to an inside attack. "If they're not sleeping or training, I want the soldiers patrolling the settlement around the clock."

"Of course, I shall start sending two hob patrols immediately, Dread Totem."

With a little luck, these measures would be enough of a deterrent for any other would-be goblin murderers.

I looked up. The skies were getting brighter by the minute. It would by daylight soon. *And shortly after that ... showtime.*

I walked into my house, glad it was close by. Tempest was lying on the ground in front of the door, his eyes following me as I stepped inside. Tika still hadn't returned from her daily hunt. She was a late sleeper and a late riser. I dropped to my furs and was out within seconds.

***

Someone nudged me gently, waking me up. I opened my eyes blearily. Tika.

Light shone through the cracks in the walls. The sun was still up. "Is it time?" I asked, rubbing my eyes.

My beautiful woman nodded. "Kaedric knocks, you not hear. He say tell you, it is time."

I stood and stretched. "Will you please go help Kaedric? I want everyone in the clan to assemble below Totem's Watch, the travelers too."

She nodded and went to the door. "Can always hunt later." She gave me a coy smile. "Maybe catch a nice juicy Totem."

I chuckled and moved to my table. I had some time before everyone gathered at Totem's Watch. Today was to mark a new era for the clan and its guests. I didn't want to break the suspense. Timing was important.

I mentally went through the steps I had to accomplish, distractedly picking up a piece of fruit from a bowl on the table.

While I was munching, I decided to check my character sheet. It had been a long while since I last viewed it, mostly since I didn't have to. I could instantly recall any piece of information I wanted. But I had a little time to kill and I sort of missed seeing everything laid out nicely in front of me.

Title: Dread Totem
Level: 26, (70%)
Race: Monster Race [Goblin]
Type: Boss II [Totem]
Religion: The Cult of Nihilator
Attributes:

- Physical: 3
- Mental: 30
- Social: 1

Pools & Resistances:

- Hit Points: 606
- Mana: 1,231
- Armor: 2
- Mental Resistance: 60%

Skills:

- Lucky Bastard: 31 (90%) Ⓑ
- Analyze: 108 (30%)
- Tracking: 12 (29%)
- War Party Leader: 11 [16](10%)
- Mana Infusion: 23 (50%) Ⓑ

- Quest Giver: 17 (80%)
- Runecraft: 24 (40%)
- Barter: 12 (0%)
- Governor: 8 (0%)

Spell Skills:

- Dark Mana: 40 (50%) Ⓑ
- Drilling Arrow: 24 (80%) Ⓑ
- Mana Shield: 27 (0%)
- Blood Wrath: 31 (0%)
- Heal Followers: 11 (0%)
- Mana Drain: 10 (92%) Ⓑ
- Shadow Web: 20 (90%)
- Shadow Hound: 20(0%)
- Shadow Teleport: 10 (30%)
- Dark Protection: 6 (0%)

Traits:

- Goblinoid: (+1 Physical, -1 Social)
- Quick Learner: +20%
- Boss Boon II: (10 HP & 20 MP per level; *Nihilator's Sanction*)
- Soul Companion: Vic
- Shadow-Touched
- Mind Over Body: (-50% to pain, +50% Mental Resist)

Buffs:

- Lyrical Song: (+10% Mental Resist, +5% Luck)

I inspected my stats closely. At only level 26, I had the HP equivalent of a level 50 fighter and the MP of a level 120 mage.

Simply put, I was a monster. I chuckled at the pun.

My skills and spells, however, were far weaker and more befitting my level. *That's the whole idea of being a boss*, I mused. My fighting abilities were slightly improved while my survivability was vastly higher than it would be otherwise.

After all, lower-tier bosses existed to provide a challenge to players. That meant they had to last long enough to make it interesting while not being inordinately strong for their level. Something I strived strongly to change.

Being a boss was a powerful boon, but not my only trump card. Thanks to the shrine back at the Ogre fort, I boosted my Dark Mana skill to its maximum for my level. It was the foundation of my real power and what separated me from other bosses. It was my ticket to salvation.

<If you're done admiring yourself ... they're waiting for you, Boss.>

"Thanks, Vic."

***

I stood on the edge of Totem's Watch. The open field below me was well-lit by the midday sun and packed full with goblins, hobgoblins, Ogres, and over a dozen travelers. Not to mention at least 20 foblins. Over a hundred people in total. My little clan was growing rapidly.

There were signs of recent activity where I stood. Logs, metal, and glass were stacked in neat piles in the limited space. The previously uneven stone ground was flattened. Holes had been drilled for laying foundations. My Dark Temple's construction was well on its way, but it was not fast enough.

Everyone was looking up at me expectantly.

A shiver ran down my spine when I saw some adventurers eyeing and measuring me with the steady, steely gaze of professionals. I needed them on my side.

I cleared my throat. "Welcome, GreenPiece members and guests," I began, pausing to organize my thoughts. "This clan had a rough beginning. We survived a vicious raid and became refugees, looking for a place to rest our heads. We found safety in this valley but were continuously hunted." I surveyed the faces below. "But together, we faced our enemies and prevailed, raising a prosperous and growing settlement."

There were murmurs of assent and a few puzzled looks from the players who were oblivious to the clan's history.

"Now we face a whole new, even graver, danger," I continued, drawing their gazes back to me. "The ... *travelers*, have discovered our location. As we speak, they are preparing their assault on us." An even louder murmur followed, and many of my clansmen wore worried expressions. "But we also have the means to protect ourselves now." I gestured at the dozen new hobgoblins standing rigidly in tight formation and the two hulking Ogres beside them. "These recruits are the first of many more to come. But that is not all. We have faith on our side."

A lone adventurer started laughing. "You sound so melodramatic and ominous, then you pull a televangelist act on us? Going to try to convince everyone to bow down and *pray* for salvation?"

"No," I said coldly, but I wasn't actually offended. This fool had just prepared the stage for me. I should thank him later. I checked his name: Sullivan Tucker.

"I'm talking about something real, Sullivan. In this world, faith is power. Our dark lord, Nihilator, watches over us all. Behold."

I opened the Construction Interface and clicked the 'rush' option.

The piles of building materials shimmered in translucent blue, and the ghost of a large building appeared behind me. The resources began to vanish from their piles and reappear on the ghost's shell, replacing translucent energy with brick, metal, and glass.

A moment was all it took for the Dark Temple to be completed. It stood tall, black, and menacing, casting an intimidating shadow on the assembled crowd below. It was a rectangular, high-walled structure. Its facade was lined with blackened stained-glass windows. A menacing gothic spire pierced its roof, ending in vicious metal spikes.

Everyone stared, wild-eyed at the imposing building.

The talkative adventurer recovered first. "Okay, so you can build churches really fast," he said with a shrug. "That just proves my point. I'm not here to pray all day to some ethereal deity. Playing a cleric is boring."

I couldn't have planted a better supporter. *Maybe he'd like an enchanted sword as a reward?* I wondered idly.

I purposely turned my back to the crowd, facing the temple. From this vantage point, the sun was obstructed by the valley walls, sending long shadows over us, though it was still too sunny for my taste.

I raised my hands, threw back my head and bellowed, "Behold!"

Would you like to purchase the [Eternal Night] blessing for 1,000 FP? Yes/No

Showtime.

The lingering light around us seemed to dim slightly. Shadows throughout the valley started moving, flowing toward us, amassing like a tidal wave of darkness. I heard some of the newcomers gasp and cry out in alarm.

The area around us became darker as more shadows flowed in, towering over us, then gushed inside the temple, filling it to the brim.

The darkness continued flowing, condensing inside the temple, climbing toward the roof. Once it reached the top, the temple's pointed spire began to glow. A sphere of darkness grew around the tip, swelling into immensity. Just as it seemed it would burst, a column of pure darkness shot straight up into the sky. It reached a height taller than the mountain around us. Tendrils of darkness flowed from the top of the dark column, spreading above us, creating a spherical web of shadows over the entire valley.

As I watched, more tendrils shot out, weaving themselves into a tight blanket that gradually blocked the last rays of light.

The bottom of the pillar disengaged from the temple's spire and rose, fueling the dark canopy that solidified as it consumed the remainder of the darkness. Once it was over, the dark shroud remained hanging above us, throwing the entire valley into deep, eternal darkness.

Zone blessing [Eternal Night] activated

The zone of influence has become permanently shrouded in darkness, never again to be illuminated by the sun.

The blessing's effects are highly concentrated around the Dark Temple. All effects are doubled at a 20-meter radius.

Shadow-Touched creatures in the zone receive:

- +10% max HP & MP
- MP & HP regen increased by 50%
- +10% damage
- Upkeep reduced by 50%
- Non-combat skills +5% effectiveness

Unprotected enemies suffer:

- -10% XP gain
- -25% HP & MP regeneration

A chorus of cries erupted from below. My Shadow-Touched Darkvision allowed me to see clearly in the complete darkness, but our guests were denied that benefit. Even those with some sort of night vision couldn't see more than several meters ahead in the complete darkness that shrouded the valley.

"Torches!" I commanded.

Several goblins carried torches and lit them. Kaedric had prepared them well.

While I let the other players adjust to the new change, I closed my eyes and breathed in the night's air. The change was tangible. I didn't have to use my eyes to see; I could *feel* it. I could sense the area around me like never before. It felt almost like an extension of my body. I raised a hand, and with hardly any effort, a great maelstrom of darkness started spinning, rising high above the crowd.

But that wasn't the extent of what I felt. The darkness was altering the valley itself. Everywhere I looked, trees warped, becoming gnarled, shedding their leaves and growing sharp thorns. The valley's forest had transformed into a nightmarish one. Brightly colored mushrooms popped into existence, growing on the ground between cracks of stone and on the gnarled trees.

A howl sounded from the cave. The crowd was standing in front of the entrance and everyone, my clan members included, gasped and backed away.

The glowing red eyes appeared first, then a black paw extended out, followed by another one. A gigantic shadow mastiff appeared, emerging from the cave and standing in plain view. A dozen more followed it, all growling menacingly at the apprehensive crowd.

A single torch lit up Sullivan Tucker's face. I cast Shadow Teleport, appearing right in front of him. His already wide-eyed expression transformed to panic.

"This is the strength faith can bring us. This is how we will destroy our enemies."

I thought the poor guy was going to pee himself. But I had to keep up appearances.

"That's enough, leave him be." Another adventurer stepped forward. "You've proven your point."

Now *that* guy was impressive. Black-skinned, tall, and powerfully built, he obviously had some Dark Elf blood in him. His long hair was black and blue with the upper half tied into a topknot, the rest left to fall to his shoulders. But that wasn't what made him stand out the most. His scales did. Delicate, black flakes covered every patch of his exposed skin, like a dragon. When he opened his mouth to speak, I could clearly make out sharp fangs. He exuded an air of confidence and calmness. The hilts of two crude short swords protruded from his belt. He was only level 5, but I could sense the potential of raw power coming off him in waves. That merited closer inspection. *Analyze.*

Nero SantoDrago, Dark Elf [Half Dragon Template]

Level: 5

HP: 88, *MP:* 67

Attributes: P: 7, M: 2, S: 2

Skills: Dual Wield 7, Swords 7, Corrosive BreathⒷ 5

Traits: Half-Dragon (breath weapon; corrosive, +2P, +2M, +2S), Dragon Path, Darkvision

Description: The offspring of a decrepit ancient goddess ... Condemned to roam the planes for eternity ... Suffers endlessly to right injustice ... and battles his dark heritage.

<Jeesh, that one's got a flair for the melodramatic, doesn't he? He's even worse than Malkyr!>

A half dragon? I frowned. *How can it be?* To my knowledge, all newcomers were limited to the goblinoid template. Somehow, this Nero guy managed to put his hands on a different one.

He's even got a Prime badge already. I've got to remember to keep a watchful eye on him.

"What just happened?" an adventurer demanded. "I can barely see in this darkness."

"Yeah, me too!" added another one.

I gave Nero a firm, unyielding look, then teleported back to the ledge above. "This clan, *my* clan, is unique. We are Shadow-Touched creatures, all of us. The darkness is our ally."

"So that's why they sleep during the day," someone below exclaimed. "I thought that was weird."

"That's right." I looked for the speaker, but couldn't pick him out of the crowd. "The entire valley is now under the effect of eternal darkness. It is now a natural ground for creatures of the dark and is inhospitable to outsiders."

One of the mastiffs howled. The others picked up on it and bayed in a haunting chorus. I felt the tone of their howling, challenging, claiming dominance over everyone present. But I also felt their controls wide open for my influence and commanded them to stay put.

"What is the meaning of this?" Nero demanded, putting his hands on the hilts of his swords. "We were told this place would be a safe starting zone. Now you're telling us it has become hostile territory?"

A chorus of disgruntled whispering followed. I raised my hands to draw their attention back to me. "No. What I'm trying to tell you is that there is a place for each of you in my clan. Join us and you too will become Shadow-Touched, and this darkness," I gestured around me, "will be your ally as well." Seeing the unconvinced faces, I added, "As members of the clan, you'll have access to the crafting workshops, our craftsmen, the combat trainers, and you'll be entitled to a discount when buying from merchants."

"Hell yeah, now you're talking," someone cheered from below. "Where do I sign?"

I shook my head. "You have to earn the privilege. You need to prove you are our allies like those two did." I pointed to the hulking figure of Malkyr, standing a good head and a half over everyone else, save the Ogres. "Malkyr and Hoshisu," I said in a formal tone. "Will you please come up here?"

The two exchanged puzzled looks, then moved forward, climbing the ladder to stand next to me.

"Both of you have repeatedly proven yourself as friends of the GreenPiece Clan," I continued with the same formal tone. "You have helped us build the clan and shed your blood protecting it. For your dedication, I now offer you membership with the clan. What say you?"

"I say it's about damn time," Malkyr grunted. "I already built myself a home in the valley."

Hoshisu searched my face for signs of deceit.

"No tricks." I held up my hands. "You two deserve the recognition." I raised my voice, addressing the assembled crowd as well as the siblings. "Swear to be loyal members of the clan, help build and protect our people, swear it on the name of our dark deity, Nihilator."

The siblings exchanged a long look. Then Hoshisu broke eye contact and shrugged. "Why not? Let's make it official. I swear."

"Hell yeah! I swear too," Malkyr declared.

I held out my hands toward them. "I hereby accept you into the clan. Welcome, brother and sister."

Shadows streamed from my palms and encircled the twins, cocooning them in utter blackness. There were gasps from the crowd below. The darkness persisted for a few seconds before it receded, gradually revealing the two. Their skin had darkened noticeably, and, like the rest of my clan, they too had black stripes covering their bodies.

Malkyr's eyes became distant, obviously reading the messages informing him of the bonuses he'd just received. "Cool, I have Darkvision now. It's way better than the goblinoids' low-light vision."

"And there's a bonus to sneak ..." Hoshisu murmured appreciatively.

Several other adventurers shouted from below.

"Hey, I want to join too!"

"Yeah, count me in!"

"You first have to prove your worth and willingness to help our clan," I started to explain "Help and protect –"

"Oh, for Pete's sake," Hoshisu interrupted, turning to face the crowd. "Just complete a few social quests until you get to friendly reputation with the clan, then you're in."

I looked at her grumpily. She had just interrupted a grand speech.

Hoshisu wasn't impressed by my offended glare. "I just saved everyone some time so they can actually do something useful. Now give me a few minutes of peace, I'm still reading."

Despite her impatient tone, she didn't sound as angry anymore.

"So we're good now?" I raised an eyebrow.

"I'm still pissed at you for pulling one over on me, but I got what I wanted out of it," she answered distractedly, her eyes darting from side to side.

"Oh? What was that?"

"I'm fairly certain now that you are not an NPC," she said offhand, not bothering to meet my shocked expression.

"What? You ... what?" At a loss for words, I could only stare at her.

She had finally finished reading, and as her eyes met mine, she smiled crookedly. "I was pissed, thinking someone was taking advantage of me and my brother. I suspected the whole 'beta test as monsters' thing was a ruse. I thought the company had developed a new AI and was testing its interactions with live people."

"I'm, uh ... I'm ugh ... what?"

"Yes, I get it, you're stunned. That's one of your many charming traits. There's always this either stupid look of bewilderment or cockiness on your face. During the fight, you preferred to show off instead of claiming a win and when *I* won, your dirty trick loophole was actually a strong indication of your humanity."

"So ..." I was still having a hard time digesting everything she'd just told me. "You don't think I'm an AI anymore?"

"Nope. I took some cyber-psychology classes during my Master's studies. You exhibit all the signs of an addict gamer. So I'm fairly certain you're human, just like the rest of us."

"That's reassuring. I guess."

She patted my cheek, giving me a mischievous grin. "That aside, if you ever feel like a rematch, just let me know. Next time, I won't just win on a technicality."

The crowd below us began to disperse. Many of the players were talking excitedly, some even demanding quests from my clan members. That gave me an idea.

"Before you go, I'm offering everyone a repeatable quest." That drew many eyes back to me. "I will grant 5 reputation points for every tree log you bring to the lumber yard."

Grant an area quest [Logs for The Lumber Yard]? Yes/No

An area quest, that's new. I adjusted the quest rewards and clicked on 'Yes.' The players below murmured their approval.

It felt good exploiting a loophole, manipulating the game to my own advantage. It made me feel like my old self again. A player in a game. The forced goblin's instincts faded away like a dream no longer remembered.

And I owed it all to Hoshisu. For some reason, the shock of hearing the reason for her animosity toward me was like getting dunked in a bucket of ice-cold water, snapping me back to my senses. I was Oren, the player, and I was in control of my goblin Totem avatar.

The woman had taught me both a lesson in humility *and* humanity. I chuckled. *I should bring her something nice as thanks.*

Most of the crowd had dispersed. I turned around and looked at the new building. The Dark Temple was built very close to the edge of the stone ledge, leaving about a meter-wide strip of ground between it and the ladder leading up.

The walls were five meters high with tall, darkened glass windows. A wooden double door stood at the front, large enough to easily accommodate an Ogre.

I approached the doors, and they opened on their own. The area inside was about 50 square meters of mostly open space, though there were three goblin-sized alcoves at the far end. Sharp bone shards protruded from the walls and adorned the windowsills. The shrine was located near the back, doubling as a podium. The whole place had a sort of 'evil pagan goth' feel to it. I rather liked it.

But there was more to the temple than its menacing appearance. The building thrummed with dark power, even more than the altar back at the Ogre fort. I could feel the pulses of dark energy running through it, projecting an aura that strengthened my clan and sustained the Eternal Night.

I knew the blessing would be a major one but hadn't realized how profound it would be. The bonuses it granted to my clan were staggering. I mentally glimpsed at my own stats, noting that my max health had risen by 60 points and my mana by over a hundred. Along with the bonuses for mana regen and combat damage, my troops were much stronger than before. The added five percent bonus to non-combat skills was also invaluable as it translated to a direct five percent increase in the clan's production and development. Considering that our daily upkeep had been halved meant, among other things, that our available daily food had increased to such a degree that I was now able to summon two new hob soldiers or one Ogre every day.

I went to the shrine and placed my hands on it. A surge of energy pulsed through me, and for a moment my mind and muscles were suffused with an overwhelming power. This place intensified my powers even beyond the effects of Eternal Night. If ever needed, the temple would be the place of our last stand.

I closed my eyes and concentrated. I found the origin that projected the darkness over the valley and tapped into it.

Eternal Night Blessing. Rank: 1
• **Enemies: -10% max HP. Cost: 500 FP.** • **Enemies: -10% max MP. Cost: 500 FP.** • **Enemies: -10% damage. Cost: 800 FP.** • **Enemies: -10% armor and resistances. Cost: 1,000 FP.** • **Allies: No food upkeep required: 1,000 FP.** • **Eternal Night Rank 2: 2,000 FP**

Only a month ago, such an interface would have befuddled me. But now, information threads rushed into me with every line I read, feeding me the fine, unwritten details.

For example, each of the debuffs could be purchased multiple times and the effects would stack together. Purchasing rank 2 of the blessing would increase all the basic effects and unlock even more advanced upgrade options.

After activating the blessing, I only had 641 FP remaining, so most of those upgrades were out of my reach, at least for now.

Still, the Dark Temple was an incredible defensive tool. It was a ray of darkness and hope in our struggle to prepare for war. With time and enough Faith Points, it could make the settlement invincible. And once I completed Nihilator's three-shrines quest, those effects would only increase.

I studied the dark walls closely. *Too bad I can't carry it out with me*, I thought humorously.

"Now, *this* is a place befitting the master," an unmistakable voice came from behind me.

I sighed, not bothering to look back. "Hello, Kuzai."

The dwarf came inside. The two remaining goblin adepts I had recently summoned followed, and behind them, eyes darting everywhere, came Bek.

"The other acolytes and I will lodge here and maintain the temple," Kuzai declared.

I rolled my eyes. *Like I hadn't planned on it anyway.* "Sure, go ahead."

The goblins spread out, checking the windows and touching the shrine reverently.

Bek came over to me. "Dread Totem," he squeaked. "Bek go out now. No room for all goblins. Bek used to sleep outside."

I gave him a steady look. He was wearing my old gear; the kilt, the headdress, and the feathered skull-staff.

"Bek," I said slowly, "after Kuzai, you're the strongest one here. You can leave if you want, but as a priest of the master, it's your right and duty to claim your status. You need to do it on your own, I cannot assist you."

He looked at me helplessly.

I placed a reassuring hand on his shoulder. "You can do it, Bek. I believe in you." I turned and left the goblins to decide on their sleeping arrangements.

It was still dark outside. Eternally dark. My clan could now work freely during the entire day if I wanted them to.

I teleported down to the valley and went looking for Zuban. I found him and his builders at the construction yard hauling in the last day's resource yield.

"Dread Totem," he greeted me. "Constructing the Dark Temple with magic in mere seconds was a spectacular display. It makes me and my workers seem irrelevant."

I shook my head. "That little display took a lot of energy. If I did that with every building, we'd soon run out. Better to save it for special occasions."

"I understand. Now that the temple is completed, what should we build next?"

I'd already decided on the answer to that question. "The weapon workshop." My troops needed good weapons so they could start training. Armor would come second. "Build it between the barracks and the smithy. I plan on building all the future workshops there; we have plenty of space and that way the workshops will have easy access to metal and be able to trade resources between themselves."

"Very astute observation. We shall begin immediately, Dread Totem."

I left the construction yard and made my way back to my house. *Now's a good time to Runecraft some –*

My musing was cut short as I nearly ran headlong into someone.

"Whoa there, Chief," Malkyr exclaimed good-naturedly. "I was just looking for you."

I looked up at the giant, noting that his Greataxe was strapped across his back. "What's up?"

"I know you wanted me to use the Viridium to craft weapons you can enchant, but I've been slaving on it all day and all I was able to produce are these." He showed me three balls of Viridium, each about the size of a goblin head. "Sorry, but the system keeps slapping me with 'skill too low' messages when I try to craft anything else. I assume I'll need to reach Master rank before I can make something better out of this stuff."

That was a bit of a letdown. But at least he gave it a try. "I appreciate the effort, my friend."

I took the Viridium balls from him and checked them closely. They were perfect spheres and heavier than they looked.

Viridium Sphere
Type: Ammunition, component

Runecraft viability: 8
Rank: Magical
Durability: 200/200

I looked at the pieces and had to resist the urge to rub my hands together. Even in this very basic shape, the Runecraft viability was the highest I had ever seen. The possibilities were endless. I was itching to try some new ideas. "Thanks, Malkyr."

"No problem, Chief, just doing my part."

"I'll see you around." I put the spheres in my inventory and went home.

Back at my house, I placed everything I wanted to work with on the table: the Viridium spheres, my new staff, the giant Stalker Pins, and as an afterthought, the Chalice of Infernal Energies that was still blazing with green flames. It was a powerful magical item, sure, but it also livened up the place.

With everything laid out in front of me, I sat down, selected my staff, and opened the Runecraft Design Mode.

The holographic representation of the staff appeared. It hovered before me, a straight horn with a wide bottom and a sharpened tip with three bloodstones embedded in its upper half. The staff could only hold four runes which was a bit disappointing; it didn't leave much room to get creative. Still, the staff was powerful enough on its own, so even a slight improvement would be significant.

I stared at the staff and pondered the possibilities. *What should I add to it? The strengthening rune would obviously have to factor in, to enhance the existing magical enchantment.* That would mandate the use of the connector rune, which would leave me only two open slots to play with. *Let's see what we're dealing with here first*, I mused and added the 'Ko' rune of strength. I watched the rune's glowing sigils spreading over the staff, then I added the 'Te' connecter rune to it. The translucent representation of the staff flickered, and instead of the expected view of the durability points, I saw something very different.

A veritable galaxy of dots appeared within the staff. Hundreds, thousands of dots in various colors. My heart sank in my chest. I had enough trouble in the past trying to connect a dozen dots. There was no way I could ever connect so many as this.

I scowled. Something here felt off. *These are not durability points!*

I concentrated, reaching for the information, letting my mind absorb the data. *Ah, the points represent the staff's existing enchantments,* I realized. *The colors differentiate which dots belong to which enchantment.*

The ability to store magical charges had the most dots by far. The enchantment that improved mana regeneration had about 20 dots and the demon-summoning bonus had a few hundred. There were also the standard durability dots, ten of them.

Okay, let's get the priorities in order. I organized my thoughts. *I can't directly enhance the spell-storing ability, so what can I do? I thought* for a moment then smiled. *Of course, instead of affecting the enchantment itself, I can manipulate the spells that are fed to it, or more precisely, the mana that empowered them.* That called for a socket, so I'd have to use the 'Ma' containment rune. I tried to think of what else to add. It had to be something simple, as I only had one open slot left. The only thing that came to mind was to augment the staff as a melee weapon by using the binding rune on its tip. The strengthening rune should then improve its base damage. It wasn't ideal. I wasn't planning on using it much as a melee weapon, but I guessed it was better to have it and not need it than need it and not have it.

<Like a condom?>

I grimaced. *More like a gun.*

<Condom is funnier.>

"Okay then." I cracked my knuckles, ignoring Vic's humor. "Let's go."

I put on the containment rune first, drawing it just below the first bloodstone. Then I added the strengthening rune followed by the connector rune. I took a deep breath and started the long and arduous process of connecting the dots.

It was maddening. I spent an hour at first, just trying to locate the dots I needed. After some trial and error, I discovered I could 'tune out' the colors I didn't want. The galaxy of points vanished and a much more achievable goal of 30 dots remained. It was still more than double what I had ever tried to connect before. I spent several hours trying to link them all, having to restart a few times when I ran out of room.

The hours flew by. I only realized the workday had ended when I felt a gentle touch caressing my cheek.

"Oren, I am here."

Tika had returned.

Damn, it must be really late if she came to sleep. I massaged my neck tiredly. Then I spotted something from the corner of my eye while the design mode was still open. Up until now, I was so caught up in the process I blocked everything else from my mind. Now, through the partially translucent interface, I noticed something glowing in the chalice before me. I leaned in closer, and my eyes opened wide. There was a rune carved on the chalice!

I got to my feet and disengaged design mode, careful to save my progress first. I embraced and kissed Tika. "How was your hunting today?"

"Good, better than other days. Darkness helped. Can sneak better, move better, more easy hunting."

Good. That meant the Eternal Night blessing was working as intended.

Tika leaned to my ear "I want to go swim in pond with you," she said in a mischievous tone. "Make you feel better, make me feel better too."

I smiled at her. "That sounds great, you go ahead. I just need a few more minutes here. I'll join you shortly."

She nodded, leaned her bow against the wall, and went out.

I returned to the table and picked up the chalice. "Where the hell is this rune?" I murmured as I checked it from all sides but saw nothing.

I remembered that I hadn't spotted any runes when I *accidentally* used the chalice. I reactivated the design mode again and the rune became visible, though hazy. For a second I contemplated disassembling the chalice but then thought better of it. My Analyze skill would have informed me if it was Runecrafted and could be disassembled. There was something else here. With a sudden spur of inspiration, I closed my eyes and activated Mana Sight. I hadn't used it since I regained both my eyes. The room around me shone with the blue and black tints of mana. I *looked* at the chalice again and this time saw the rune.

Someone had drawn it on the vessel with magic, making it invisible to regular sight.

I peered closer, taking in each line of the rune, etching its shape into my mind.

You gained knowledge of a new rune: 'Mag' (The Ward Rune)

It worked!

I closed my eyes and directed my thoughts inward, looking for the purpose of the rune. I found the relevant information thread and absorbed it.

That's interesting ... The rune in itself was meaningless. It only served as the groundwork for other runes, namely elemental types, so together they added protection from that element. I could also read hints of other uses for Mag, but those were too far for me to see clearly. I would have to find out using trial and error, as always.

I deactivated Mana Sight and put the chalice back on the table. I was tired, and my head was pounding. I'd done enough work for one day. Runecrafting could wait for tomorrow.

Besides, I thought as I reached for the door, *I have a date.*

24 – Portent

Tika and I woke up the next morning after a night of invigorating swimming followed by an even more invigorating indoor activity.

Being back at the clan was great.

I lay next to my beautiful, sleeping huntress and let my eyes roam over her naked body. I hadn't lost myself again; I was well aware that I was a player and this was just a game. It simply seemed that my personal preferences didn't align with the common consensus. Which was a fancy way of saying I thought the woman sleeping beside me was smoking hot. Sure, she was green, and a goblin, but she didn't look anything like the old school goblins. Tika's body was well toned and had curves in all the right places. She looked damn good, even by human standards.

<*Well,* duh,> Vic invaded my thoughts. <*You meat suits keep inventing these gorgeous alien babes, which by my observation, are mostly blue or green. It's not hard to imagine your people applying the same logic to goblin babes.*>

He had a point there. The ultimate goal of NEO was to make money, and sex sells.

Well, I was bought. Even if I disregarded her physical appearance, Tika was a marvelous woman. Our nightly swim brought us even closer together, and we'd had a pleasant, if a bit halting, conversation afterward.

I sighed. *Too bad her speech is so limited.* It wasn't that she was stupid, far from it. But the goblin's native lowered Mental attribute manifested in her case as a limited vocabulary. *It's not like she could invest points in Mental as she leveled up,* I mused. As a forager, Tika's main attribute was Social. While it certainly did wonders for her womanly charm, it didn't contribute much to her conversation skills.

Wait a minute ... Something sparked in my mind. *Wasn't there something in the Zone Blessings menu?*

I opened the interface.

> **Zone Blessings (affect all religion followers in the zone of influence):**
>
> ...

- *Mental I:* Increases the Mental attribute of all creatures in the zone by +1. Cost: 100 FP

There it was. That blessing would increase everyone's Mental attribute by one. Productivity-wise, this blessing was useless. Most of my workers used either Physical or Social as their main attribute. Only the researchers and the clan's casters would benefit.

But it might just improve Tika's conversation skills ... I had to try. It might be impractical, but after spending 1,000 FP on Eternal Darkness, I still had over 600 FP remaining. Using 100 on a whim seemed reasonable.

I selected the blessing and approved the follow-up prompt. I could feel pressure emanating from the direction of the Dark Temple. An instant later, a wave of dark energy rippled through the valley.

"Hey, Tika?" I gently nudged the still-sleeping huntress.

"Oren?" She blinked a few times then sat up. "What's going on?" She turned her head back and forth, her eyes darting everywhere. "Something is different."

"How do you feel?" I observed her closely. She looked the same as always, but there was a difference. Her large anime-like eyes had changed. They still reflected innocence, but there was a new glint in them now.

"I feel ... goo– ... well," she corrected herself with a tone of decisiveness.

I felt a chill fill my heart. I was afraid I had overdone it, afraid her old personality was gone, afraid that –

Tika cupped my face gently. Her hands were warm and soft. She looked deep into my eyes and smiled. "Thank you, Oren."

***

I left my house feeling like an idiot with a huge grin plastered on my face, but I couldn't bring myself to stop. My fears were unfounded. She was the same Tika as always, only now she had the means to express her thoughts. Nothing else had changed. We stayed awake until the late hours, catching up, talking, and re-sharing our past experiences.

I stretched laboriously and, still grinning, took in my surroundings.

It was the start of a brand-new day, though one wouldn't know it by the ambient light. The sun was barred from shining over my settlement. Goblin workers and hobgoblin soldiers were everywhere, many walking in and out of the mess hall.

A single Shadow-Touched mastiff came strolling from behind a building. Thanks to Eternal Night, Nihilator's guardians were now free to roam my valley.

"Breakfast sounds good about now," I said, feeling drained after last night's exertion.

"Dread Totem, welcome!" Gandork greeted me excitedly. "I have great news, please sit, I will fetch your breakfast."

Bemused, I sat and watched the now fat goblin cook run to the kitchen and bring me a steaming plate. "Meat pies!" I exclaimed with delight. The hearty, savory dish was a personal favorite, but it required mushrooms, which we had run out of a few weeks ago. I took a large bite of the dish Gandork had set before me. "Wonderful! Did you use the mushrooms that started growing everywhere?"

The cook's eyes widened in alarm. "In Nihilator's name, no – those are poisonous. No, our two no-good farmers have finally justified their existence and started growing mushrooms. Loads and loads of mushrooms," he said happily.

It looked like the Eternal Night had even more benefits than the flat numeric bonuses. With a flick of my mind, I accessed the farmers' daily yield and found that they were now producing 54 mushrooms per day. The heavy plow I'd recovered had added ten percent to the yield.

I finished the small slice of pie in a few bites and found I was completely full.

Looking around me, I realized everyone was eating less than usual. That was another boon of the blessing, reducing our need to eat by half. *Great start to the day so far*, I mused. We had tapped into a new food source and had reduced our upkeep. *Vic, how much raw food are we producing in total every day?*

<Currently 232 units of raw edible ingredients, or 300, if you count the gathered seasoning ingredients.>

Most recipes resulted in more food than the sum of their ingredients, and considering Gandork's cook skill and the mess hall bonus, our daily food production had reached an all-time high. I could finally start recruiting en masse.

I left the mess hall and circled it, making my way to the barracks. I still had a lot of Runecrafting to do, but I wanted to check in on my soldiers.

I entered the barracks' courtyard and noticed that the training yard was surrounded by a low stone wall.

The area within the wall had been dug out and was now two meters below ground level, transforming it into a pit. The stone wall extended down into the pit, reinforcing its flanks. Benches encircled the pit in concentric rings, giving ample room for spectators to enjoy the duels below from the comfort and safety of their perch above.

Looking inside the pit, I saw the dozen new hob soldiers. They were divided into three groups with a veteran hob leading each one. Zia, one of the tanks, had two of her hobs straining against each other's shields while the other trainees watched. Yulli, the scout, had her six pupils shooting arrows at several training dummies while she yelled at them to do better. Bob was demonstrating proper sword technique to his three students. The pit was large and could easily accommodate twice as many soldiers as were training at the moment.

I descended into the pit using a narrow staircase that ran along the wall. Zuban stood by his workers as they placed the last few bricks in the nearly complete wall.

New building expansion added to your settlement: Arena

What the hell?

My foreman made his way toward me, followed by Bob, the hob lieutenant.

"Dread Totem," they both said, bowing their heads in greeting.

"The arena is complete," Zuban declared.

I stared at him, puzzled. "I thought you just started yesterday. This was supposed to be at least a four-day project."

He nodded. "Your appeal to the travelers did not go unnoticed. In fact, they were particularly eager to see the arena completed. A dozen of them worked all night like madmen, digging. I think they have proven their worth. They would make a fine addition to our clan."

So they have hit friendly reputation with Zuban, I surmised. *Won't be long until their reputation with the clan catches up, and I'll have to let them in.*

"This is a fine training ground," Bob said. "We can get these recruits into real fights in here. Nothing teaches a soldier faster than training with real, sharp weapons."

I looked at him sternly. "I'm not thrilled at having training casualties."

Bob shook his head. "That won't happen. The arena is well-equipped. There will be no fatalities unless the arena master decides otherwise. The travelers who dug the pit said they'd come back later to train here as well. We'll see how our recruits hold up against them.

Training NPCs by having them spar with real players. I grinned. This was too rich. I half expected to get an achievement for orchestrating this scenario, but NEO had no achievement system in place. Shame. "That's good to hear. How are the new recruits doing?"

"They learn quickly, but there's no alternative to real combat."

In other words, they'd have to get out of the pit eventually and fight real battles to gain XP and level up. I already had plans for doing just that. I glanced at the sparring hobs, checking their individual progress. Everyone had their main combat skill up to level 5 or 6. For a single day's progress, that was impressive.

"Keep up the good work, Bob. How are our patrols doing?"

"At every given moment, a third of our forces are patrolling the settlement. I believe it is enough to provide good coverage for now. They have already proved their worth by breaking up small travelers' skirmishes."

"Good to hear. Let me know if something more serious comes up or if the soldiers need anything."

"Yes, Dread Totem. Since you mention it, we could use good weapons and armor. It's best to let the soldiers train using the same equipment they'll be fighting with. So far, the scouts are the only ones with decent weapons, as we have no shortage of bows. But the melee fighters are using crude, nearly broken swords. Zia had to instruct her trainees to pass the shields between them so everyone could practice using one."

"Noted. The weapon workshop is already under construction. In a few days, our smiths will start producing better-quality weapons. Armor might take a little longer, but we'll get there soon. By the way ..." I realized some of the new recruits were missing. "Where are the Ogres?"

"Err ... Rhynorn Bloodore took them to the forest. He claimed to be the champion and that he'd teach them a lesson."

<Hehe, so he's either training or ripping them a new one,> Vic chortled.

That's what I'm afraid of. Resurrecting the Ogres will be damn expensive. I checked the Shrine Interface and was relieved to find the resurrection list empty.

"What's the next construction project?" I asked Zuban.

"The new builders have almost reached their Apprentice rank, but until they do, they won't be able to help with the more advanced projects. I think we should put them to building more cabins; we're running out of lodging space rapidly."

"Good thinking. Go ahead."

"Thank you, Dread Totem."

I left the pit and made my way home.

I needed to finish Runecrafting my staff.

***

Hours later, I was finally done.

The painstaking connect-the-dots mini-game had left me mentally exhausted, but I didn't care. I gazed lovingly at my newly enchanted staff.

After I'd finished drawing all the rune lines, I finalized the schema by pouring in mana and then topped it off by placing one of my two most powerful void crystals – a level 200 – inside the runic socket. The crystal powered up the enchantment by a factor of five, making the weapon much more powerful. As an added bonus, my Runecraft skill had risen by two points and was now at level 26.

I picked up the staff and examined it closely. *Analyze.*

Demon Horn Staff [Runecrafted]

Description: The horn has maintained some of the demon's infernal powers. It is exceptionally durable and can double as a spear. Three bloodstones and a single void crystal are embedded along the shaft. Mana-based spells may be channeled through the staff to increase their potency.

Type: Two-handed

Rank: Epic

Durability: 640/640

Damage: 95-105

Effect I: Mental +21 for determining mana regeneration rate.

Effect II: Store up to three magical charges. Instant casting. Stored spells are 15% stronger.

Effect III: Spells channeled through the staff are 25% stronger.

Effect IV: ??? [conditions unmet]

My Runecrafting worked wonders.

Epic. The staff rank was now upgraded to Epic. And it showed.

With insane durability, a huge bonus to mana regeneration, and an increased strength of stored spells, this item was stupidly overpowered. The unknown effect was a weird side effect, but the staff was powerful regardless. Not to mention that a single stab of its spear-like tip was now the equivalent of a full head-on smash from Rhyno's huge club. To top it off, all my normal spells would now be 25 percent stronger.

I caressed the staff lovingly. I wanted to marry it.

<I would advise against that,> Vic chimed in. *<It'll make for an awkward honeymoon.>*

"Ugh, Vic!" I grimaced. "I did not need that mental picture."

<Hey, don't go blaming me; you're the one who considered joining with a piece of hardwood ... horn ... whatever.>

I rolled my eyes, and, as always, employed my go-to tactic. I ignored my twisted-minded companion.

I inventoried my staff and took one of the Viridium spheres from the table. I examined the sphere, narrowed my eyes, and murmured, "Now what sort of interesting things can I do with a metal ball ..."

Shut it! I mentally shouted as I realized what I had just said. I felt Vic's smugness and barely beat him to the punch.

<Oh man ... that burn would have left a scorch mark,> my depraved companion whined. His cloak-like body disengaged from my shoulders and slithered away.

Concentrating again on the metal sphere, I mulled over my options. The sphere had eight rune slots – nine with my current skill level bonus. That gave me free rein to do as I pleased. But the question was what, exactly? I could enchant it with various damage bonuses and use it as a projectile weapon, but that was too much work for not enough damage output. Besides, we didn't have any kind of cannon to shoot it in the first place. I had too many projects on my plate already to start managing the invention of projectile technology.

What then? I pondered, turning the sphere in my hands.

The metal was smooth and durable. Its pinkish sheen made me think of ornamental beads. "Heh," I grunted. Other than the fleeting thought of fashioning it into a bead necklace, nothing else useful came to mind.

"That would make one cumbersome necklace," Vic remarked, squatting in his goblin shape in a corner of the house. "The Ogres could probably wear it, though. They could use some prettifying, that's for sure."

His words formed a mental image of an Ogre wearing a pink bead necklace. I laughed openly. "Good one, Vic. But you're right, it won't be very useful. Unless they somehow use it like a beaded whip ... wait a minute."

Connecting the Viridium balls together as a sort of semi-flexible chain would make a fearsome whip. I chewed my lips. Still, that was more of a job for a smith, not an enchanter, unless ...

I opened the Runecraft Design Mode and selected the binding rune. Runic lines spread over the ethereal spherical image, covering half its surface. I added another binding rune on the other half, and the two runes merged together seamlessly, covering the entire surface with snaking, glowing runic lines.

I felt, more than I knew, that the runes would make the sphere's surface a sort of magical slate that could interact with external magic. But that in itself was not enough. The binding runes needed to be anchored to something. I added the 'Ma' containment rune at the heart of the sphere, then connected both binding runes together to it using the 'Te' connector rune.

Examining the result critically, I wondered if it would act as I had intended it to. It took four runes – half of the available space – just to lay the groundwork. I could add more runes to it later, but I wouldn't be able to erase them once the enchantment was done. I could probably dismantle it, but success was not assured. In which case, I had just wasted a valuable resource.

I proceeded to finalize the enchantment, pouring in the required 360 mana to power it up.

Utility schema discovered: TeMaGog [Conduit]

Runecraft skill level increased to 27.

Discovering new schemas was great for raising the skill level.

I took another Viridium sphere and repeated the same process. It only took me about a minute to apply the newly discovered schema.

Holding a sphere in each hand, I carefully brought them together. The pieces clinked but didn't bind. I frowned. Something was missing.

"Well, duh," Vic snorted. "You just created the framework. There's no juice flowing through the pipes."

"How would you know?" I countered. "You don't have the Runecraft skill."

"I don't need it. The rules of this world are consistent, and I happen to be a native. Trust me, just put some mana into it."

"Alright," I grumbled and channeled my mana into the two spheres. It moved easily, absorbed by the external binding runes, and flowed to fill the containment rune within. The spheres radiated a faint sense of power.

I brought the two spheres together again, and this time they connected. I released one. It rolled downward while still attached to the one I was holding. *Huh, kinda like magnets.* I could sense the tethers of mana connecting the two spheres.

"See? Told you so," Vic said smugly.

"Yes, you're very smart. Shut up."

Dark mana thrummed inside and around the spheres. I put them on the floor and directed my will at it. With hardly an effort on my part, the spheres began moving, rotating around each other. I didn't even have to invest my own mana after the initial charge and could easily control the movements.

"Wonderful," Vic said. "You made magical, self-rotating Chinese balls. Now what?"

"More."

I opened my friends' list and composed a short message to Malkyr, asking him to craft the remaining 12 Viridium ingots into spheres. Then I proceed to enchant the last one I had as well.

With three balls attached, I could make it move in simple patterns; pile up as a column, move around the floor on two while the third one was in the air; or just spin together. The external binding runes kept the spheres connected, but not fixed on a specific point, so I didn't have to put any extra effort to keep them together. I could concentrate on just directing their movement.

"Ding," Vic said. "Incoming message, Boss."

It was from Malkyr, promising to have all the 12 Viridium spheres ready by tomorrow.

"Good, now I'll just –"

The door opened and Tika came in. *Huh, it's probably later than I thought.*

"Hello, Oren." My beautiful girlfriend smiled at me, her eyes twinkling. "It is a great honor to have the clan Totem waiting for me at home."

"Hi, Tika." I smiled back at her. "I guess I lost track of time, kept enchanting throughout the day. How was your hunting?"

She sauntered forward seductively and placed her arms around my neck. She leaned in and whispered in my ear, "I just have one more thing to hunt."

***

I woke the next day with a start as a flickering message window appeared before me.

<Sorry for the early wake-up, Boss, but I think you should see this.> Vic said somberly.

His unusual tone had roused me like a splash of cold water. I clicked the blinking message icon.

New Era Online [Internal messaging service]:

From: SuperWolf#23
Subject: It's on

Hi, Man,

Vatras just sent his forces after you.

He spent a day advertising tryouts for *his* guild, saying whoever passed the test would be accepted at a sergeant's rank. I tried to discredit him on the forums like we discussed, but there was still a sizeable turnout. Too many mediocre players couldn't resist the lure of a steady guild paycheck.

I asked a friend, a casual low-level player, for a favor to become my spy. He applied for the test and was accepted. From what he tells me, Vatras has formed up two groups to come after you.

The first group is made up of low-level wannabes, some might be around level 30, but most are probably less than 20. There are about 50 of them.

The second group is more serious. It's composed of semi-professional gamers, levels 20 to 40, but there's only about ten of them.

I'm guessing Vatras is using the first group as cannon fodder to soften you up, then the second group to wipe you out completely. That way he'll only have to reward ten players instead of 60. He's a real bastard, that one; how the hell did you work with him for three years?

The first group has already departed. They're teleporting to the nearest settlement at the fringe of the Deadlands, and from there a guild Spatial Wizard is going to launch them through most of the wilderness.

My friend estimated it will take them about two days to reach you. That gives you around 24 days, your time, to finish preparations.

The second group will launch a few hours later, which ought to buy you a day or two of respite before the next attack.

I'm guessing you're in for a tough fight. Once you beat them, word will spread. I doubt Vatras will be able to lure more people to do his dirty work then.

I thought at first to get a few buddies and intercept the groups along the way, but they're being escorted to the final launch point by a few other high-level guild members. We'd be slaughtered.

I may not be able to interfere directly, but I still got your back. My spy friend, TheMarxman, will continue with the first group as a double agent. He's expecting to hear from you and is willing to cross over just as soon as you've made contact.

He's a melee spellslinger. I suggest to use him at the height of the fight to double-cross his friends and kill the healers. With the element of surprise, he should be able to get rid of at least one of them. You'll be able to recognize him straight away; he always wears cyan robes and fights using a rapier.

Your status has drawn the higher-ups' attention and there's something else going on here that they're not telling us about. I think me staying in touch with you has drawn their attention. It might be difficult for me to contact you again for the time being. In any case, I doubt I could do anything else to assist you in facing the coming battle. It's up to you now.

Good luck, Oren.

P.S. - I'm probably worried over nothing. You no doubt have hordes of green-skinned monsters ready to tear apart us miserable players.

All hail our future green overlords! :-)

I breathed out an explosive sigh. It had begun. The attackers were on their way, and now I had a countdown to their arrival.

The preparations for the attack were progressing well. Our food production was high and I could now summon a large force quickly. But they needed training. The new guys were still too weak to stand up to players, even low-leveled ones.

Luckily, I had planned for that. The barracks' training yard would help put my soldiers into shape, but it won't be fast enough. I had to expedite our plans.

"Kaedric!" I called out as I exited my house. While I waited for the mandibled hob to arrive, I accessed the settlement's food production details. I had some numbers to crunch.

We were producing 287 various food ingredients per day. Considering recipe efficiency and other bonuses, we could produce about 300 units of simple food daily. Our daily upkeep was 52. We would need about 70 units of food to double the upkeep for all the Physical-oriented workers. That would increase productivity across the board by 20 percent. Seeing as some of our food producers – namely the hunters and farmers – had physical builds, our food production would also increase by about 12 units. So in effect, I'd be spending six units of food to increase my whole clan's efficiency by 20 percent.

Why the hell didn't I do that earlier? I lamented.

<It's probably a good thing; that exercise nearly fried your fragile meat-suit brain.>

Next time I'll let my smartass-seeded companion do the heavy crunching.

<So you can sit around all day, playing with your Viridium balls? No thank you.>

I was about to retort when my feral-looking seneschal arrived, coming around from behind my house. "You called, my lord? How may I be of service?"

"Hi Kaedric, I want to take full advantage of the new totem's ability. I want all Physical-oriented workers to be fed doubly, starting right now. The day has just begun, so we can reap the benefits straight away.

"Yes, my lord. Was there anything else?"

"Have Gandork use all our basic food ingredients to cook simple food, then bring it to the Breeder's Den.

"Yes, my lord."

"Next, I want every weapon above crude quality brought to my house."

"Yes, my lord. It will take some time to locate all such items. Shall I go see to it, or was there something else?"

I mulled it over. "Take care of that now. I want to catch Zuban for a little chat first anyway."

Kaedric bowed his head and walked away. Several nearby workers stopped what they were doing and followed him silently.

"Tempest!" I called.

As if manifesting from the surrounding darkness, my demon wolf appeared before me. I jumped on his back and directed him toward the northern part of the valley. His light trot was fast enough to make my vision blurry from the wind in my eyes. We arrived at the new construction yard, just past the barracks, in a flash.

"Good wolf." I patted Tempest's neck then dismounted and surveyed the nearly completed weapon workshop. It was shaped like a triangle with well-rounded edges. Large wooden beams served as the frame, and the area between them was filled with bricks. The building had an incomplete cobbled floor and two worktables stood inside next to a small, indoor forge. Goblin builders were running around, hammering and stacking stones to build the walls.

Zuban was standing next to a goblin builder, patiently instructing him while gesturing at various places in the wall. He spotted me as I neared and stepped away from the builder. "Dread Totem." He bowed his head slightly.

"Zuban, we're running out of time. How long to complete the workshop?"

He looked back at the structure, his eyes darting over all the incomplete parts. "About midday," he answered finally. "I've already plotted the land for the adjacent armor workshop, so I plan to continue working on it after finishing here. The required building materials are already in place."

I shook my head. "We're out of time. We need all the high-priority buildings *now*. Get the workers out of the building."

Zuban understood my meaning immediately and with a few short, sharp orders, had everyone out of the way.

I opened the Settlement Interface, selected the nearly completed building and clicked on the 'rush' option.

Rush Weapon Workshop for 62 EP?

I approved the cost.

With a flare of magic, the few incomplete parts shimmered, transforming into full physical matter.

New Building added to your settlement: Weapon Workshop

Next, I selected 'Armor Workshop' and clicked on the 'rush' option for it as well.

Rush Armor Workshop for 360 EP?

I winced at the cost, but I had over 4,000 EP to spare, so I approved it.

Stacks of stone and wood shimmered and disappeared in the now familiar sight of a magically constructed building.

New Building added to your settlement: Armor Workshop

Like the weapon workshop, it too was triangular with circular edges, like a slice of pie. The buildings were fitted against each other, forming part of a circle. Future workshops that would be added to them would end up forming a full circle with each building a petal in the flower.

It was an efficient design. I approved.

"Alright." I rubbed my hands together. "We're good to go. Zuban, can you please inform our two craftsmen that their new workplace is finished? I want them to start arming our troops with quality gear."

"Yes, Dread Totem, I shall fetch them immediately. However, now that both buildings are completed, what should be our next project?"

I thought about it for a moment. "The research center, I guess. The researchers are still working on the barracks' warfare center blueprints, right?"

The hobgoblin nodded.

"Then that will be the project after the research center."

"Yes, Dread Totem. We will need ten glass and ten silver for the research center."

"Right, I'll take care of that now."

I opened the Marketplace Interface, and as before, traded 50 lumber for ten units of glass. However, silver presented more of a challenge. It took 35 lumber to trade for a single unit of silver. I had just enough lumber for four units. I considered what to do and briefly contemplated using other resources, but that would rapidly exhaust my other stocks; a ridiculous amount of 300 rabbit pelts were required for a single talent of silver.

"Zuban, the required resources will wait for you at the Export Office. It might take a few days to bring in the entire load of silver, but I trust you can begin work without having the full supply straight away, right?"

My foreman nodded. "That is correct. As long as we have the entire amount by the time we are ready to finish."

"Good, at the rate we're producing lumber, we'll have enough to buy the rest in two days."

"That is reasonable, Dread Totem."

"If you need me, I'll be at my house." I jumped onto Tempest's back and rode him to my home.

As we neared, I heard sounds of knocking. When we passed the wall and came to the front of the building, I saw who was knocking on my door.

The Mob Squad had returned.

25 – Technological Advancements

I felt more than I heard Tempest growling as he spotted the players standing at my door.

“You’re back,” I said casually, dismounting the demon wolf.

“Hey there, pal,” said Misa, the part elf-woman and apparently the group’s spokesperson. “Yeah, we just returned.”

I ignored her and analyzed each of the players. To my dismay, I learned they all possessed the Stealth skill, so any one of them could be the killer.

Apart from that, they all had a standard array of common skills. But two were of special note: Misa had a Prime-badged skill called ‘Chainmaster,’ and Raystia had the laughably titled ‘Florist’ skill.

“Anyway,” Misa continued, “it was a close call We had to constantly fight, run, and hide, but we’ve completed your quest.” She gestured grandly, pointing at the totem piece they’d brought back.

Granted Quest Completed: Retrieve Totem Piece

The Mob Squad members awarded: 1000 XP, 100 reputation with GreenPiece Clan, 100 gold

Misa Gavriilu awarded: Horned Helm (magical)

Raystia awarded: 20 X Arrows (magic)

Riley Stonefist awarded: Reinforced Boots (magical)

Fox awarded: High Steel Axe (normal)

“Thank you,” I said dryly. “Now that the rewards are taken care of, we can proceed with the punishment.”

“What?” Misa frowned. “What are you talking about?”

“One of you,” I gave them each a stern look, “has murdered two of my goblins.”

They exchanged glances, looking even more bewildered.

“Ahem, excuse me, Mr. Dread Totem sir,” Raystia, the catgirl, said. “There must be a mistake. We were away for a couple of days. We just got back, so it couldn’t be one of us.”

"Actually," I countered, "the murder happened just before you conveniently left the valley."

"But ... but ahem ... we wouldn't do such a thing!" she said unconvincingly, giving the bugbear, Fox, a guilt-filled glance.

I raised a hand. "Spare me your bullshit, I already know which one of you did it." My gaze lingered on the bugbear. He stared back at me, and I turned my eyes to the dwarf. "You."

"Wha-what?" he stuttered. "Me? Why would I kill your goblins? That's bullshit, man."

Goddamn dwarves! A surge of goblin racial hatred rose in me, but I forced it down. Instead, I concentrated, trying to access his underlying thoughts using Sense Emotion, but the ability failed to work properly. Apparently, it didn't function well on players. All I got back was a general sense of uncertainty.

"Don't bother to deny it. Tempest here," I pointed at my mount who was now growling menacingly at the players, "smells their blood on you."

The other three turned to stare at Riley with startled expressions.

"Heh, you could have told me you were looking for more sacrifices," Fox said. "At least I would have figured out how to hide the evidence better. Sloppy work, Riley. Sloppy work."

"It wasn't me!" the dwarf protested, taking a step back from his friends.

Raystia looked at him thoughtfully. "Well ... you did say you needed to take care of something before we left," she said apologetically.

"I meant I had to log out for a bathroom break, not murder some goblins!" Riley exclaimed. "Don't you know me by now?"

"And you did kinda enjoy sacrificing those stone creatures back at the tunnel," Misa pointed out.

"That ... that just gave me some nice bonuses! Come on, guys, back me up here."

"So maybe he did or didn't kill a few goblins, but that doesn't matter. I'm guessing he's already guilty in your eyes, right?" Misa said lightly. "So what's the penalty, Mr. Boss Man? Jail time? A fine?"

I narrowed my eyes. She was taking this too casually. It was a grave matter, the murder of two of my ...

<Two of your computer generated, scripted mobs, Boss,> Vic chimed in. *<I'm just saying.>*

Damn, he's right. I rubbed my forehead tiredly. Players engaged in casual NPC killing all the time. It was no big deal, especially if no one saw them do the actual deed.

"Since you're in a party, I'm considering you all equally responsible for the crime," I told them. "That said, you will reimburse the clan for the resource loss the deaths incurred: 60 units of food and ten tree logs."

Misa shrugged. "Sounds reasonable. So by the going rate of food, I'd say we owe you about 15 gold – 20 to include the wood. Come on, guys, cough up five gold each."

Grim-faced, the players drew out some coins. I could almost hear what they were thinking; they'd just completed a two-day quest, finally got their hands on some gold, and now I was playing the bad guy, forcing them to part with their hard-earned loot.

The initial anger I felt disappeared, replaced by fatigue. "Forget about the money and the resources." I looked at the dwarf. "What you did set me back a bit, but I guess it's not a big deal in the end. So why not just admit it?"

"I'm telling you it wasn't me!" he insisted.

"Fine. Since you won't take responsibility, I hold your entire party in debt to me."

"What do you mean?" Raystia asked hesitantly. "We already offered to pay."

"Since you proved so capable at your previous quest, I thought I'd grant you a new one."

Misa grinned. "If the rewards are similar to the last one, we can definitely discuss it."

"What do you want?" Fox grunted.

"There's a shrine or an altar to the southeast, about a day or two's travel," I explained. Using the two places of worship I had already sanctified as reference points, I could approximate the last shrine's location.

"I want you to escort one of my goblin adepts there. The area is most likely under the control of some hostile monster. Clear out a safe path to the shrine, and help the adept consecrate it to Nihilator. Once that's done, you'll leave the adept there to maintain the shrine."

Outsource the quest [Dark Missionary] to The Mob Squad? Yes/No

I confirmed and doubled the rewards from the totem quest.

"What sort of hostile monsters can we expect?" Fox grumbled.

I shrugged. "No idea. I've already cleared two shrines. One was in the middle of a hobgoblin camp, the one you just came from. The other was deep inside an Ogre lair. Just be ready for anything. I see you've gained some levels, so this one shouldn't be a problem for you," I said with a straight face.

Each of them was level 12, and surprisingly, the shy one, Raystia, was level 15. If they encountered half the resistance I'd faced at the Ogre fort, they'd all be wiped out.

At worst case, if they all die, I still get valuable intel, I thought smugly. If the team failed the quest, I could always resurrect the adept and take him there myself, with some foreknowledge this time. It was a win-win situation.

"Find the place, clear it out, leave the goblin there. Got it," Misa said cheerfully. "Then we're good, right?"

"Not exactly." I gave her a steady look. "Do you know how to sanctify the shrine?"

"Pour some holy water on it?"

"Offer a sacrifice," Riley said. "Nihilator loves those. I guess we can capture another mob as the offering."

"No." I looked pointedly at the dwarf. "It needs a *worthy* sacrifice. Anything lower than an NPC boss will be rejected."

"Be goddamn near impossible to hold down a boss over a shrine," Fox said.

"You're right. You will need another *worthy* sacrifice." I kept looking at the dwarf. "A traveler soul, freely offered, should do the trick."

Riley gaped. "You gotta be shittin' me."

I held his gaze steadily.

"Oh for crying out loud, I didn't kill your stupid goblins!" he threw his arms up in anger.

"Let's say I believe you," I countered. "As a dark priest, offering your life freely to Nihilator is a powerful tribute. You should know that by now. Consider this a leap of faith. Who knows? You might actually benefit from it in the end."

A thoughtful expression came over his face as he contemplated my words. "Fine!" he crossed his arms over his chest. "I'll be the freaking sacrifice, but there's no way I'm plunging the dagger into my own heart. It might be just a game, but I draw the line at that."

"You won't have to. The adept can do the deed."

Misa gave a short laugh, her eyes glistening. "Well, I'll be. This game keeps getting darker and darker, doesn't it? I love it!"

Fox rolled his eyes. "Once you finish picturing yourself as the monster queen of terror, we should go check out the marketplace. We got loot to sell and new equipment to buy."

"Right you are, Foxy," Misa said lightly and winked at me. "Come on guys, let us head out."

The four headed for the marketplace, leaving the totem piece behind.

This had turned out better than I expected. With some quick thinking, I'd managed to get the now fairly accomplished players to do Nihilator's quest for me. I chuckled as I recalled the game naming the quest as 'outsourced.'

I turned my attention to my new toy. "Now let's see what we have here."

<You know, your habit of talking to inanimate pieces of wood is starting to worry me.>

I rolled my eyes and analyzed the totem.

Totem Pole Piece: Hobgoblin

Description: This piece of totem pole represents a conquered camp of hobgoblins. It can be added to the main totem pole of another clan, granting it a hobgoblin-related feature.

Type: Settlement totem

Effect I: +10 clan morale

Effect II: Training combat skills is 50% quicker

That was fortuitous. Coupled with the new barracks, this totem was just what I needed to whip my soldiers into shape.

I spotted Rhyno and waved him over. He approached with heavy steps and scowled at me. "Boss-man."

"Rhyno, put this totem piece on top of the other one," I instructed and stepped back.

The Ogre grunted, then lifted the 50-kilo piece with one hand without any discernible effort and placed it on top of the Ogre totem piece already on the roof of my house. The two fit together perfectly and made an impressive, savage-looking, totem pole. I could already feel the settlement's information streams updating, accounting for the increased stats. A fortuitous find indeed.

I entered my house and found seven weapons waiting for me on the table; four swords, two battle-axes, and a dagger. I had asked Kaedric to bring me all of the clan's decent weapons, and this is all I got. It was barely enough for what I had in mind, but it would have to do.

I sat down and inspected each weapon. They could hold only three runes apiece, which was still better than crude items.

I picked up the first weapon, opened the design mode, and started working.

***

Weapon schema discovered: RaTog [Sonic Damage]

Runecraft skill level increased to 30.

I rubbed my tired eyes. I had enchanted for hours, meticulously working to make each enchantment perfect. The new schema was fairly simple. I started by placing the 'Ra' rune of sound on each weapon's base, then drew the connecter rune through all the durability points to the blade, where I placed the binding rune.

As a result, each weapon now added 20 percent sonic damage to the attack and gained the 'resonate' trait, which improved its ability to penetrate magical shields. This unexpected feature was the result of channeling the sound rune through the durability points instead of the strengthening rune like I had done in the past.

The door opened and Tika came in. Once again, I had lost sense of time and had worked until late.

Tika didn't seem to mind though. "You are easy game to catch lately," she pouted. "Where's the fun in that? Ah, if all my prey were as easy, I could have kept the whole clan fed on my own."

I laid the finished weapons on the table, but I kept the enchanted dagger. "I didn't notice the time," I apologized. "Go to bed; there is something I must take care of first. I will try to finish quickly."

She put down her equipment and came to me, wrapping her arms around my neck. "Where are we going?" she asked.

I hadn't planned on her tagging along. What I had to do next was not the most romantic setting. "I, uh ... think it's better if I went alone."

She raised an eyebrow. "We almost never have time for ourselves, except just before or after going to sleep. This is an opportunity for us to spend some time together."

I searched her face. She held my gaze steadily. "Alright, let's go."

She followed me out the door. "Where are we going?"

"The Breeder's Den first," I said, opening the interface. "Then to the temple."

The Breeder's Den Interface showed it was loaded with 546 units of simple food. I queued in an Infernal Ogre and five hobgoblin soldiers.

I arrived with Tika at the front of the building just as it started to spew out the new troops. We waited until the last hob emerged from the building. Twelve eyes stared directly at me, waiting for their orders.

"Follow me," I said and led everyone toward the Dark Temple.

***

I wiped my bloody sacrificial dagger and looked with dismay at the remains of the hobgoblin soldier splattered over the shrine. After a moment, the pieces turned black and liquified, transforming into a void crystal. The second one I had obtained that night.

"Oh, yessss ... your offering pleases the master." Kuzai was watching the ritual with eyes full of zeal.

Satisfying the demented dwarf didn't make me feel any better about the sacrifices. On my beckoning, the unthinking soldiers approached the shrine one by one, like sheep to the slaughter, which I guess was exactly what they were.

As before, I imparted the Lucky Bastard skill to each soldier in turn, sacrificing those that showed signs of imminent implosion. Luckily, the Ogre survived the rite, but two hobs did not.

I tucked my clean dagger back in my belt and turned to the four seeded warriors before me. "Welcome to the GreenPiece Clan," I said tiredly. "You are now immortal warriors, the protectors of our clan. Go find your bunk in the barracks, and report to your trainers first thing tomorrow."

"Yes, Dread Totem," they said in unison, the Ogre's voice nearly drowning those of the three hobs.

Bek and a goblin adept rushed forward with a bucket of water and cloth and started cleaning the blood stains from the floor.

I followed the departing soldiers and my eyes landed on Tika. She had remained in the corner through the ceremony, watching the entire process.

She had witnessed me performing this ceremony before, but that time was special, a defining point in our clan's history. This ... this was just daily routine, murdering my own clanmates. I knew they were only pieces of computer code. I knew they were not even VIs. Still, knowing I killed members of the clan that were under my protection weighed heavily on me.

I looked at Tika. Her eyes were full of compassion. It was obvious she felt for the dead. I lowered my eyes. "I told you it was better if I went alone."

She came to me and once again wrapped her arms around my neck. "I know you do what you must to protect us all," she whispered. "You do not have to face it alone. I will always stand by your side ... Oren."

Hearing her use my real name snapped me back to my senses. My weariness faded and my burden eased. I felt a burst of love and gratitude for my beautiful goblin girlfriend. She didn't judge me; her compassion was for *me*, at what I had to do. I embraced her tightly. Our lips met as we shared a deep kiss.

We kissed for a long moment, standing in the macabre, foreboding temple with blood splattered all around us. My pulse quickened as my passion rose. I yearned for her. My urges became more insistent, and dark impulses grew within me as well. I wanted to take her right then and there. I felt a compulsion demanding I lay her down on the bloody floor, make love to her, then offer her heart as the ultimate sacrifice to my dark deity …

"No!" I yelled, breaking away from her.

She looked hurt as she stood there, staring at me with those huge, green eyes.

"*It* defies the will of the master." The damn dwarf was mumbling to himself again. "All life is meant to be his to devour. *It* should remember that –"

"Shut up," I hissed at him, then took a deep, steadying breath, locking my eyes with Tika's. "I'm sorry, Tika. This place … this is not a good place to be with the ones you care for. Let's go home."

She looked down. "Yes, Oren."

***

I woke with a start, my heart beating fast.

While I slept, I was assaulted with nightmares: I was a feral goblin, a mindless, ruthless monster that took pleasure in sacrificing and destroying everything in sight.

This was not a *Totem vision*; I knew that for a fact. The nightmare touched on a deep fear I tried to suppress. I couldn't avoid facing the issue any longer, I had to face the reality: Little by little, this world … this *game* was shattering my psyche, one piece at a time. *I have to get out of here, or I'll end up a savage, ruthless monster*, I thought bitterly.

In order to do that, I had to reach boss tier 4.

I was only tier 2 at the moment. To achieve the next boss tier, I needed Goblin's Gorge to become a level 3 settlement.

I opened the Settlement Interface to remind myself of the prerequisites.

Settlement Level 3 - Village

Requirements: 10% efficiency or higher, 5 Apprentice level buildings or higher, 200 members, 2 bosses

I was actually not far from that mark. Our clan efficiency was at an all-time high of 27.7 percent. We had eight appropriate buildings and three bosses, including me. The only limiting factor was the population count. My clan numbered 134 individuals and was well on its way toward 200. *At least the foblins count toward the population goal.* Which was about the only thing they were good for. My clan now sported 24 of those pests. With their breeding rate, we'd hit the 200 mark in two or three weeks.

There was another, more substantial obstacle. In order to reach the next boss tier, I needed twenty thousand energy points. The way things were going, it would take me a long time to get there. We just didn't seem to be able to get past the four thousand EP mark. There was always something urgent that demanded a large expenditure of energy, holding back my own progression.

But there's another way, I suddenly remembered. *If I kill 50 players, I'll be able to achieve the next boss tier without needing the energy.* Considering that an army of players was making its way toward us, there was a decent shot I'd manage to get the 50 kills. But in order to do that, I would have to be the one who landed the killing strike. Fifty times. That was a problem, I couldn't order my troops to hold back while I took my time killing enemies one at a time.

I let out a regretful sigh. That tactic, though attractive, would lead to too many casualties among my troops, which in the end would only cost me even more energy in resurrections. I still had boss tier 4 to reach. I shuddered at the thought of how much energy *that* upgrade would require.

A devilish thought occurred to me. *Maybe I'll just kill some of the newcomers.* I could enforce an execution system for slight offenses, but that would surely turn them against me. *Better yet, I can offer them a quest to be willingly sacrificed; Nihilator wouldn't care.* That idea had its merits. Players didn't mind dying so much, especially at the lower levels where the death penalties were reduced.

<Sorry, Boss, that won't work. The players around here qualify as NPCs for this purpose, despite being immortal. Sacrificing them won't even give the increased FPs or the stronger void crystals normal players drop.>

That was a shame, but I had a third option for reaching the twenty thousand energy mark. I could convert void crystals into energy. As Vic reminded me, players left especially powerful crystals when sacrificed, and I planned on harvesting the attacking players for as many crystals as I could.

I grinned. My feverish preparations gave me a sense of confidence. I imagined the approaching army as a field of fruit ripe for the picking. All I had left to do was go harvesting.

I gently detached myself from the still sleeping Tika and exited the house.

I went to the mess hall and had to literally push my way through a pile of foblins that were fighting over a piece of leftover food.

Bob and the other trainers were eating at 'the officers' table. The other hobgoblin soldiers were spread throughout the mess hall. The three Infernal Ogres were huddled together on the floor at the far corner of the building, using a ladle as a spoon, taking turns scooping from an entire pot sitting between them.

"Bob," I greeted my lieutenant, taking the chair next to him. "How is the training going?"

"It was going moderately well, right until the end of the day," he said.

I frowned. "Something interfered with your training sessions?"

"On the contrary. It seemed as if the soldiers suddenly found their second wind. We were able to put in nearly two hours' worth of training in a single hour."

I eased back in my seat. He was referring to the training bonus the new totem piece imparted. That was good news. "Squeeze in as much training as you can today," I said. "Tomorrow, we're all going outside the valley."

"Are we going out on a raid?" The hobgoblin gave a savage grin. "It's been a while since me and my men raided another camp."

Yea, mine. "Not exactly. We're going hunting. I need to see the soldiers fight in real combat. This will also help increase their lev– ... make them stronger."

Bob nodded. "Very well, Dread Totem. We will be ready to go first thing tomorrow."

I nodded and got up to leave.

Goblin's Gorge: Kadoc has reached Apprentice rank in: Weaponsmith

Goblin's Gorge: Baja Reed has reached Apprentice rank in: Armorsmith

Good! I grinned. My smiths' increased potential would go a long way toward the mobilization of my troops.

I didn't see any of them at the mess hall, but I wanted to check their progress with the new workshops anyway. I had no doubt it contributed to them reaching the Apprentice rank of their trades. I left and walked past the barracks to our new crafting center.

I heard the sounds of metal striking metal even before coming into view of the workshops. As I got closer, I could see clearly inside. Kadoc was standing at the anvil, hammering at a blade piece. Baja and Vrick were both busy working at the other workshop, collaborating on the same piece of armor.

"Hello," I called out.

They all laid down their tools and stepped out to greet me.

"Dread Totem." Kadoc bowed his head. "It is good you have come."

"Problems?" I sighed exasperatedly. "Something missing from the workshop?"

"No." He shook his head. "The workshop is well built and well stocked. Barzel helped us set it up. The problem is that we're just about to run out of iron ingots to work with again."

"But I brought in 60 ingots not long ago, not to mention our two miners worked nonstop for over a month building up our stock," I protested. "You just got your workshop. How have we run out already?"

The goblin seemed to wilt under my tone, but then Vrick stepped up. "It's not our fault," he said. "The metal we mine ourselves is only just enough for crafting tools and supplying construction material. Now that we have two more smiths the ingots ran out fast. The shipment you brought in lasted only two days."

"I see ... How many ingots do you need again?"

"Ten to 20 for armor and five to ten for weapons," he answered mechanically.

I pursed my lips. I could get more metal through the Export Office again, but I had to finish importing silver for the research center first.

I concentrated briefly, checking our lumber stocks. My workers had produced 140 units of lumber yesterday. That was an impressive amount but still not enough to purchase the remaining six units of silver.

I opened the Export Interface and selected the 'Metal' filter. A long list of metals opened. I selected 'Lumber' as the trade currency and viewed the results.

Filter: metal [trade with lumber]	
Metal type	**Lumber cost**
Copper	2
Tin	2
Iron	3
Bronze	5
Steel	10
High-Quality Steel	25
Silver	35
Mithril	150

"Now that you have the workshops, how many weapons and armor can you craft per day?" I asked the goblin crafters.

"Three swords or similar-sized weapons," Kadoc answered promptly.

Baja was quick to follow. "Two sets of medium metal plates."

That meant that on average they needed 45 metal ingots every day. I would love to outfit my troops with 'High-Quality Steel' equipment. Now that my smiths had reached their Apprentice rank, they could finally work with this higher-grade metal, but the cost was too steep.

Steel would have to suffice for now. It was also relatively expensive, but I didn't have to import it directly. With our access to coal, Barzel was more than capable of casting steel ingots from basic iron, so all I had to do was to import enough iron every day. Three times 45 meant I'd need to trade away 135 units of lumber per day to keep my smiths fully occupied. That would hardly leave me any lumber for construction or for purchasing the remaining silver.

Decisions, decisions.

Using the still-opened interface, I ordered 12 units of iron ore for 36 lumber and spent the rest of my stock to purchase three silver. I wanted my crafters fully engaged, but I also had to bring Zuban all the resources he needed to complete construction. Tomorrow I'd have enough lumber to bring in the remainder of the silver, then I could use the bulk of our daily lumber yield to bring in more iron.

I clenched my teeth. If that damn player, Riley, hadn't murdered my two new lumberjacks, I would probably have enough to finish the silver order.

Instead of brooding on it, I realized all I needed to do was increase the number of lumberjacks.

My seneschal arrived silently and stood some distance away while I conversed with the workers. When I was finished, I turned to him. "Kaedric, recruit two additional lumberjacks please."

"Yes, my lord," he said stoically.

I could sense him accessing the Breeder's Den controls and sensed the production numbers update as a result. Now our daily lumber yield was just shy of 200 units per day. Given enough time, the workers' skill would progress and increase our yield even more.

"You will soon have more ingots to work with," I told the goblins. "Starting tomorrow, we will import 45 units of iron each day, which Barzel will smelt into steel. Kaedric, see to that."

"Yes, my lord."

"I think that takes care of our metal issues. Anything else?"

Vrick shrugged. "Leather. It's running out too."

"I happen to know we have hundreds of rabbit pelts."

"Yes, we have *pelts,*" he emphasized. "I need leather; good, sturdy leather. The tanner used to produce enough to keep me equipped, but now that I've become more skilled and can work in a proper workshop, I'm much faster. I'm able to make three suits of leather armor for the hobs each day instead of just one, or a single piece for the Ogres. That means I need triple the amount of leather I used before. At the moment, our existing leather stock is almost exhausted."

"How many suits of armor have you made so far?"

"Twelve," he declared proudly.

That was enough to gear up most of the scouts. But Vrick was right; we needed even more. "Very well. Kaedric, please summon another tanner."

"Yes, my lord."

"Well, if there's nothing else ..." I turned to leave.

"One moment, Dread Totem," Vrick said.

I turned back in a huff. I was getting fed up with micromanaging everything. "Yes, Vrick?"

"There's something I would like to show you. Please come inside."

He led me into the wedge-like workshop. There were several work tables and discarded pieces of leather littered the floor.

Vrick led me to an armor stand. A completed leather armor suit was hanging on it.

I inspected the armor then looked at the grinning goblin. "This ... you made this?"

"Yes, Dread Totem," he answered.

He was obviously proud of himself and for good reason. The Pyrolith scale armor looked amazing. Vrick had somehow cut the large scales and overlaid them on top of each other, creating a hardened layer of protection for the torso. Delicate strips of oxsaurian leather were woven together, overlapping the scales and extending over the arms and legs, providing good defense while not hindering mobility. Steel buckles and rivets held the pieces of armor together. It was a beautifully crafted piece.

Pyrolith Scale Gambeson

Description: This well-crafted armor is made of durable leather embedded with hardened demon scales. It offers good protection without hindering the wearer's mobility and is naturally resistant to fire.

Runecraft Viability: 5 runes.

Type: Armor [torso].

Rank: Advanced

Durability: 120/120

Armor: 35

Resistance: Fire 50%

Base price: 500

"Told you I would be able to do something special with a proper workshop," Vrick said smugly.

"Yes you did," I said, admiring the fine workmanship. Though its stats were not very high in the grand scheme of things, it was the best piece of armor my clan had managed to craft to date. That single piece of armor offered three times the protection of my old gear. *And with a little loving Runecraft touch, I could make it even stronger*, I mused. Though the five runes limitation didn't leave me much room to get creative with the design.

"It's as strong as steel armor, weighs half as much, and should not hinder your movement," Vrick pointed out.

"You've come a long way since that vest you first made for me. This is a great piece, Vrick. I'm proud of you."

The goblin huffed at the compliment, but he didn't fool me. I could tell he enjoyed being praised.

"I've nearly finished with the oxsaurian armor for the Ogre." Vrick pointed to one of the work tables. A thick layer of leather covered most of the workspace. "It is a very strong material, though not as strong as metal. If you want, I can get Baja to add steel plating, but that would take him away from crafting armor for the soldiers, and it would take a lot of ingots."

"Hmmm ..." I stroked my chin. "No. The leather in itself is a significant enough upgrade for Rhyno's armor. We may consider this again later, but for now, I want you both to concentrate on armoring all of our troops. Leather armor for the Ogres and scouts, metal armor for the melee fighters. I also want all the shield bearers to use steel shields instead of wooden ones."

Kadoc joined the conversation. "That will be my job. I've already worked out a good design for a steel buckler."

I nodded. "Good. Then I won't keep you from work any longer. Carry on."

"Yes, Dread Totem," they answered as one.

As I walked away, I contemplated what to do next. I had the entire day ahead of me and there were still a few more items I wanted to enchant. I also wanted to practice my new Shadow Clone ability. Considering that we were going out on a hunt tomorrow, I decided to focus on enchanting for now.

***

Back at my house, I picked up one of the two Stalker Pins. Each was three meters long and heavy. The otherworldly origin made the pins especially suitable for enchantments. *These could be great as throwing spears for Rhyno,* I mused. The Ogre's brute strength would make good use of their mass. As thrown weapons, I didn't have to get too creative with my runes. All the pins had to do was inflict as much damage as possible.

I opened the design mode to review my known runes. I was thinking of something simple and straightforward: Use the fire and sound runes to augment the damage, channel them through the strength rune, and bind it to the top of the spear. A simple five-rune enchantment, counting in the connector rune. But the pins could hold six runes each – seven, with my Runecraft skill level. I had two more available slots and I hated to see them go to waste.

I went through the list of known runes again, looking for inspiration. *I could add a socket using the containment rune and use a void crystal to increase the overall enchantment strength,* I surmised. That still left me with one open slot, but I couldn't think of anything else that would increase the damage, so I decided to leave it open for now. I could always add more runes later.

I finalized the enchantment by pouring in the required 450 mana, then slapped in the level 39 void crystal I got from sacrificing the oxsaurian. The extra power flowed into the already active runes, making them glow brighter for a few moments before settling down to a 'normal' runic glow.

Stalker Spear [Runecrafted]

Description: The large demonic pin makes for an ideal throwing spear. Due to its size and weight, it can only be used by large creatures.

Type: Weapon [thrown]

Rank: Magical

Durability: 130/130

Damage: 50-62 physical + 14 fire + 14 sonic + half Physical attribute

I examined the result with satisfaction. This weapon would be devastating in the hands of the Ogre boss. His strength would enhance the already impressive damage potential.

I ran the numbers in my head. Rhynorn's Physical attribute was 22, so he could inflict over a hundred points of damage with the thrown spear, and that number would only grow as his levels rose. Not bad.

I started working on the second Stalker Pin. This one was easier. All I had to do was select the schema I had just invented and apply it. The runes appeared on their own in a flash on the unenchanted weapon, and I only had to power it up. I was done with the second spear in less than a minute, finalizing the enchantment by pouring in another 450 points of mana. I didn't put a void crystal in the socket this time; I'd already used the only oxsaurian one I had. My other crystals were either too low-level or too high-level, which meant the extra power would go to waste.

I had to postpone adding a crystal, but if what I had planned for the next few days worked out, I'd have plenty of suitable crystals to choose from.

I got up from my chair and stretched. This entire enchanting session took about an hour and I'd exhausted the supply of weapons to enchant. I didn't think wasting my time on a low-quality item justified the result. My Runecraft skill level had just risen to 31. I had to continually challenge myself with more complex enchantments to raise it further.

Malkyr had yet to supply the remaining Viridium spheres like he promised. But the lack of quality items to enchant wouldn't continue much longer. Now that we had armor and weapon production lines in place, I expected I'd soon be busy up to my ears with enchanting. That reminded me. There were a dozen armor sets waiting to be enchanted, but I decided to wait until I had even more and could do them in bulk. For my intended hunt, weapons were more important than armor.

I guess I might as well use the time to experiment with Shadow Clone, I thought testily. The ability was potentially very powerful, but I didn't look forward to the splitting headache it left me with.

I sat down on the floor, crossing my legs in front of me, and concentrated.

I started by regulating my breath; breathing in fully and exhaling slowly. It had been a while since I'd immersed myself in meditation.

I felt myself gradually relax, slipping deeper into serenity.

It was quiet and peaceful.

My mana swirled inside my body in sync with my own heartbeat.

I raised one arm, preparing to channel my mana into my shadow.

An abrupt knock on the door broke me from my reverie.

"Shadow-crap," I complained, getting to my feet. It had taken me over an hour to reach this tranquil state, and the interruption was quite bothersome. I nearly ripped the door open. "Who the hell – Oh, Malkyr."

The big man was grinning at me. "Hi, Chief. Bad time?"

I took in a steadying breath, soothing my annoyance. "Everything is fine. How've you been?"

"Great." He held up a sack. "I just finished making the Viridium spheres like you asked. Sorry for the delay; it took a bit longer than I expected."

I motioned for him to come inside and put them on the table.

"So how do you like being part of the clan?" I asked, though I was eager to start working with the spheres.

He shrugged. "Not much different than before. The Shadow-Touched trait is pretty useful. I get now why you guys only work at nights. The extra ten percent to my Smithing skill really helped to craft those spheres. I also reached my smith cap. I'm only 22 skill levels short of reaching the Master rank now, then things will get *really* interesting." He grinned boyishly. "Oh, and being able to see in total darkness is pretty cool too. I feel sorry for the new players who have to stumble around carrying torches everywhere. Did you notice that the light doesn't really banish the darkness? It just sort of … lets you see the immediate area, and then it gets cut off. Kinda creepy."

"That should help motivate the others to pitch in."

"I guess …" He shook his head. "At least they don't cause too much trouble. I was worried their players' instinct would make them kill a few goblins. You know that in every other game goblins are just dumb XP sacks, right? But the guys that get here are pretty cool. I spoke with a few, and I think they're smarter than the average player. I think each of them is a big shot IRL. Makes you wonder, doesn't it?"

"I guess. I don't really care, just as long as they don't hurt our efforts."

"Alright, Big Chief." Malkyr flashed me another of his big, boyish grins. "I'll leave you at it for now. My own smithy is coming along nicely. That magic anvil I brought back just begs to be used. I'll see you later."

For a second, I thought about calling him back and asking for his help preparing for the coming attack, but I decided against it. Malkyr was already doing all he could to contribute, and I didn't want him distracted. I still had about three weeks ahead of me to prepare; there was plenty of time before I had to alert everyone.

I sat back down at the table and took out the first of the 12 Viridium spheres. It was enchanting time again.

***

It was close to the end of the workday when I finally quit working. I had finished enchanting half the Viridium spheres. I now had a total of nine of the Runecrafted, glowing pieces. I decided this was enough to test my idea.

Concentrating on the spheres, I poured my mana into them. Each one required 100 MP. I was nearly drained by the time I had finished powering them all up.

Then I started playing. First, I made the balls connect with each other, then I made them pile up. The balls rolled up on top of each other into a column, like a pile of spherical magnets.

I flexed my will and the shape changed. Two pieces moved down to the base to strengthen it, and another two at the top leaned 90 degrees to the side and started rotating around the main column faster and faster. I picked up one the finished swords from the table and gently put it in the path of the rotating spheres. The metal balls were heavy and the impact knocked the blade out of my hands. It flew across the room and embedded in the wooden wall with a thud.

I grinned. There was no question about the potential damage I could do with these. But there was a drawback to using the spheres: They were mana hogs. Once I had finished enchanting all of them, even my sizable mana pool, now over 1,300, wouldn't be enough to power them up to keep them moving. I was missing something .... something that could hold a charge and allow me to control them without taxing my own mana reserves.

The missing piece to the puzzle felt almost like an itch. The solution was right in front of me, but I couldn't see it. No combination of runes I could think of would help in this case. I needed something else, something that could ... then it hit me.

"The gremlin!"

Excited, I jumped to my feet and went out.

This time, I wouldn't take no for an answer.

26 – Gone Hunting

I entered 'Gadgets & Magic,' Anikosem's gremlin shop.

"Ah, welcome again, Dread Totem," the elderly gremlin welcomed me from behind the counter. "How may I help you?"

"I need you to teach me the Zu rune."

The gremlin opened his arms wide. "We already discussed it. I'm afraid I can't help you unless you have reconsidered and can pay me 50 magmashrooms."

I shook my head. "Even if I wanted to, I don't have enough." I held his gaze steadily. "An army of travelers are on their way here. They will kill and destroy everything in the valley, you included. I need every advantage to prepare for their arrival, and that includes your rune of motion."

My words seemed to have made an impact on him. He looked at me with fear in his eyes for a moment, then shook his head. "Maybe that's true, but if you expect me to disclose my peoples' sacred knowledge, I need something of equal value in exchange."

"Damn it!" I banged the countertop, causing the many magical devices to rattle. "I don't have time for that. I'm going to hunt oxsaurians tomorrow and I need that rune now!"

His expression changed. He cocked his head. "Oxsaurians you say? Those beasts are dangerous."

"I know." I leaned forward over the counter. "That's just one task on my list to get us ready for the attack. Everyone in my clan is working tirelessly toward that goal. Even the new travelers pitch in, gathering more resources, building defenses, and such. Only you gremlins do nothing. You sit all day in the fancy, expensive marketplace I built for you and don't lift a finger to help."

He frowned. "That is unfair. We helped develop your clan's economic status. Your people and the newcomers are stronger thanks to the goods we brought. Besides, the marketplace supplies you with steady tax income. You will return your investment soon enough."

I heaved a sigh. Damn, that gremlin was sharp. He had a logical counter to every approach I tried. Well, I had one more angle. I could always threaten him. Financially. I could change the tax rate at will, and if that old furball wasn't willing to see it my way, it was going to cost him.

I opened my mouth, and Anikosem raised his hand to stall me.

"I can see in your eyes you are about to say something we might both regret later on. But there's no need for that. I have another proposal; one that doesn't involve magmashrooms."

I closed my mouth and took in a long, steadying breath. "What do you have in mind?" I asked in a composed tone.

"Oxsaurians. They are hard to find and harder to kill. As creatures that are completely cut off from mana, their horns might be useful for my research of magical blockers, a component in a variety of magical items. Bring me ten oxsaurian horns for my experiment and the Zu rune is yours. I can use a little redundancy, so I will also pay 100 gold per horn over ten."

You have received a new quest: Oxsaurian Horns

Anikosem, the gremlin magic trader, wants you to bring him 10 oxsaurian horns.

Optional: Bring 10 extra horns

Horns in inventory: 0/20

Quest type: Simple

Reward: 'Zu' rune, 100 gold per horn beyond 10 (max 10 more horns), 5,000 XP

Finally!

"You got yourself a deal," I said, and we shook hands.

I turned away and walked back to my house. *With this new rune, I should be able to –*

I stopped abruptly and looked around. Something felt different. The surrounding darkness was suddenly thicker, heavier.

Eternal Night blessing has been extended. Location: Raider's Camp

That explained it.

I had nearly forgotten about the goblin adept I'd sent with the coal shipment. He had finally reached the altar at the old hobgoblin camp and was channeling its power back to the clan's Dark Temple.

With him and Kuzai's shadow maintaining the shrine at the Ogre fort, I only had to wait for The Mob Squad to escort the other adept to the last shrine to activate it.

I went back to my house and continued enchanting the remaining Viridium spheres.

***

I woke up with a yawn.

I'd worked longer than usual yesterday enchanting the remaining six Viridium spheres.

I was still a little tired but I had no time to waste. I was planning to take the soldiers out of the valley for some live combat, and I had a few matters to attend to first.

I walked to the mess hall and took my usual seat. Gandork soon brought me a steaming bowl of excellent tender meat with thick mushroom sauce. Now that our farmers were producing a steady supply of mushrooms, we could once again enjoy this flavorful dish.

Kaedric came to me, bowing his head. "Good morning, my lord."

"Hey, Kaedric." I waved at him with my fork, splattering sauce on the floor. Three foblins charged the still steaming liquid and started growling for the right to lick it off.

Kaedric's mandibles cracked open in annoyance at the critters blocking his path. With a single hard stare, the three were sent running away, yelping in fear.

"Kaedric, I'm taking the troops out for a few days," I told my seneschal once he had seated himself across from me. "I'm leaving the clan in your capable hands."

"Yes, my lord." He bowed his head. "May I raise a few issues regarding the clan's efficiency?"

"That's what you're here for," I said lightly.

"Wolrig, the goblin constructor, reached his Apprentice rank yesterday."

Weird, I didn't get any notice about it.

<You were sleeping, Boss. As I said before, you get cranky without your beauty sleep. Or would you prefer I wake you next time?>

No need. Thanks, Vic.

I turned my attention to the hob before me. "If I recall correctly, that means he can now manage six builders, right?"

"That is correct, my lord. The extra hands should expedite our construction rate significantly."

"Hmmm ..." I chewed on my lip. Four new workers translated into 120 units of food. I was at a point where I wanted more soldiers, not workers. Then again ... more builders meant faster development, which in turn would lead to greater gain.

"Alright, summon four new builders."

"Very well, my lord. I shall invest the required 468 energy points to raise them all to level 3."

I winced. There went another good chunk of energy. Just this morning we'd crossed the 5,000 mark for the first time, only to now have it back down into the 4K range. "Very well. Anything else?"

"With the recent recruitments, our food supplies have dwindled significantly."

"I am aware of that, but thanks to the Eternal Night blessing, our daily production is about four times the upkeep."

"Yes, my lord. However, that is not the point I was trying to make. Except for gathered ingredients, we are using most of our food ingredients as they come in. We have built a significant stock of that which mostly goes unused."

He had a point. The clan's workers gathered both edible ingredients – potatoes, roots, and the like – and herbal ingredients that were used mainly for flavoring. We didn't have too many recipes that made use of those.

I concentrated briefly and whistled when I realized we had over 600 units of gathered ingredients. "I see what you mean. Suggestion?"

"You may instruct Gandork to research a new recipe, one that makes heavy use of those ingredients, or you may instruct the gatherers to concentrate more on collecting edible ingredients."

I played with the meat on my plate while I mulled over his suggestion. The gathered ratio between the two was balanced, which provided the maximum yield in total. However, if it was just sitting there, eventually it would spoil, even with the warehouse's special storage ability.

"We'll do both." I decided. I opened the Settlement Interface and changed the gatherers' ratio to 70 percent edible. "Gandork, come here please."

The fat goblin cook approached, wiping his hand on a towel. "Yes, Dread Totem?"

"Do you think you can invent a new recipe, one that mostly uses gathered ingredients?"

Gandork pondered my question for a moment. "If I dice them all together, and maybe add a pinch of vegetables and mushrooms for chewiness, it could make a nice salad. I don't think I'll ruin too many of the ingredients while I experiment."

"Good, do that." I looked at my seneschal. "Anything else, Kaedric?"

"The research center will be completed tomorrow, my lord. The builders need the remainder of the silver today."

"Zuban sure works fast." I chewed my food slowly as I tried to figure out what to do.

Each day, after purchasing iron for our smiths, I was left with 65 units of lumber. That was enough for a single silver ingot, but I needed three more.

I opened the Export Office Interface, selected the silver, and browsed through the list of items my clan could offer in trade.

Poison gland, no. Rabbit pelts, no. Gathered ingredients ... no. Then I stopped. We had 15 crude goblin-sized leather armor in stock. I'd forgotten we had those. Kaedric had already persuaded Vrick to craft only hobgoblin armor instead.

Every five pieces would trade for a single silver. Since we had absolutely no use for them, I gladly traded the lot for the three silver we needed.

In the back of my mind, I pictured Trillian, the exporter, and her gofer running to the warehouse, rounding up all the armor and hauling it back to the Export Office. I hoped Vrick wouldn't take it too badly.

I finished eating the last few spoonfuls off my plate and went to the table where Bob and the other trainers, Zia and Yulli, were sitting.

“Dread Totem.” My lieutenant nodded respectfully. “My men and I are nearly ready; 23 hobgoblin strong in total.”

I shook my head. “I will take only the new recruits with me, the Ogres too. You and Bek will be the only senior members to join this expedition. I need the others here to protect the clan in our absence.”

Bob nodded. “As you command. Shall I assemble the troops to leave?”

“Yes, bring them to the forest clearing and wait for me there.”

“Yes, Dread Totem.” With a single gulp, he emptied his bowl and rose to leave.

“Ladies.” I nodded to the two female trainers then followed Bob outside.

I stopped by my house first. My table was overflowing with enchanted weapons. The cursed chalice’s green flame danced in their reflections.

I put all the weapons in my inventory and went back outside. The large Stalker Pins were especially heavy and I was annoyingly slow carrying them.

Outside, I whistled to Tempest and mounted him when he came running. I had spotted Rhynorn’s head above the barracks and turned the demon wolf toward it at an easy trot. The large canine had no issue carrying me and the heavy load.

Once we arrived, I guided Tempest into the courtyard. I found the Ogre gladiator sitting at the edge of the pit, looking with disdain at several players who were training below. He was wearing his new armor; thick Oxsaurian leather covered his entire torso and upper legs, leaving his arms free, letting his shoulder spikes out.

“What are you doing?” I asked, inspecting his new appearance.

“Watching weaklings,” he grunted. “I be the champion, but boss-man say not hurt new travelers.”

I couldn’t stop myself from smiling at his misgivings. “I said don’t attack them. You can still challenge them to a duel, but you must accept it if they refuse.”

The Ogre brightened up at that. He lumbered to his feet, looked down at the pit and bellowed; “I, RHYNORN BLOODORE, CHALLENGE YOU PUNY TRAVELERS TO A FIGHT!”

His challenge was accompanied by interesting strings of information. His proclamation had just issued a general arena quest for all the players.

Whoever managed to beat him in a single duel would receive a hefty dose of XP and earn the Ogre's respect. Seeing as none of the players present were higher than level 8, I doubted they'd manage to beat the level 16 boss even if they banded together.

"Here, I think you'd like these." I took out the two Stalker Spears and passed them to the Ogre.

He looked impressive holding the oversized spears, one in each hand. He examined the weapons closely then made a noise of approval. "Good weapons, fitting for The Champion."

"Glad you like them." I patted his shin. "I'm leaving the valley for a few days. Guard my people while I'm gone."

"Hrrrrr," he huffed. "Yes, Chief."

I was taken aback by his gratitude. *If I'd known the spears would make him more cooperative, I would have made them sooner.*

I turned Tempest around and we rode toward the forest clearing.

***

My troops were already waiting for me when we arrived. Fifteen hobgoblin soldiers stood in three orderly rows. The three Ogres stood idly behind them, each holding a club made of tree trunk as a makeshift weapon.

I should remember to ask Kadoc to make proper weapons for them, I realized. I could easily envision the Ogres holding giant, spiked metal cudgels.

Bob and Bek stood at the front. The little goblin looked different somehow. I paused and inspected him more fully. He was no longer fidgeting. In fact, there was an air of confidence about him. It looked like forcing him to stand up to his adept peers was just the thing he needed to boost his confidence.

Bob stepped forward. "We are ready to leave at your command, Dread Totem."

"Good." I made Tempest walk back and forth, like an old-school general addressing his men before entering combat. "I guess you're all wondering where we're going."

Several of the hobgoblins nodded. Blemtoff, the dual-axe wielder, stood out from the rest with his twin battleaxes held in his crossed hands. "Yeah, we are!"

"We are going to hunt oxsaurians," I announced. My soldiers exchanged puzzled looks. "They are large and aggressive herd animals. Their territory is one day's travel from here. Any questions?"

One of the new hobs cleared her throat. "Forgive my bluntness, Chief, but oxsaurians are formidable beasts. Even the three Ogres can't hope to defeat one on their own."

"Oxsaurian stupid." Bek gestured dismissively with my old skull-staff. "But taste good."

I chuckled at the small goblin's bravado.

I took out the four swords and two battleaxes I'd enchanted and gave them to Bob. "Here, I've enchanted these especially for this hunt. Hand them out to the soldiers. Even if we don't have enough for everyone, they should still give us a decisive advantage."

Bob nodded and replaced his own sword with an enchanted one, then handed out the other weapons. I noticed he gave both enchanted axes to Blemtoff, a clear vote of confidence in his skills.

Once he finished, he came to me again. "These weapons will help penetrate the beasts' tough hide, but even with them, we will no doubt suffer casualties."

I straightened in my seat and gave the lieutenant a harsh stare. "It is unbecoming of you to shirk away from a fight." I raised my voice, addressing everyone. "Do not worry, men, your Chief and Totem will go to war with you. Together, we will bring down any oxsaurian that crosses our path."

The hobs and Ogres cheered. Bob looked deflated.

I felt a twinge at my harsh rebuke. The hob lieutenant had served me faithfully during these last few weeks. But he apparently still did not fully trust my power. It was a good opportunity to show him, and the others, what I could really do.

With a flick of my mind, I formed up a war party, including all the gathered soldiers. "Follow me," I commanded, leading Tempest toward the exit.

As we left the valley, I was pleasantly surprised to learn the Eternal Darkness now extended beyond our home, spreading out to the faraway shrines.

The rest of the day was uneventful. We walked through the thick forest without hindrance. Any beast that spotted us had wisely decided to stay out of our way.

We left the shroud of supernatural darkness after several hours of hiking and made camp when the first rays of dawn shone through the forest canopy.

***

We woke up at the onset of dusk when the sun was low over the faraway mountain peaks. We soon left the confines of the forest and entered the low, grassy hills that were home to the oxsaurians.

I took point, riding Tempest, and scanned the area ahead. I didn't see any of the beasts, but they could be just behind the next low hill. "Everyone, keep quiet and be ready for battle," I cautioned my troops.

The hobs and Ogres clutched their weapons and looked around warily.

We marched on carefully, often pausing to scan the horizon. An hour later, I finally spotted the leathery hide of an oxsaurian behind the next crest. We trotted on and looked down on a herd of about 40 beasts.

I concentrated briefly and cast Shadow Hound. The shadows around us gathered together and four level 20 mastiffs rose to do my bidding.

Controlling each mastiff directly, I sent them charging at the oxsaurians. The mastiffs pounced and raked at the tough beasts' hide, causing almost no damage. Still, it was enough to stir up the hulking beasts and the entire herd stood to give chase.

I made the mastiffs run in circles in different directions. After some misdirection and course changes, a single mastiff shook off all but one of the oxsaurians. I directed the hound toward our position, luring the bull into our trap.

As we waited for our quarry to reach us, I cast my new Dark Protection spell over the soldiers, spending a total of 180 MP to include everyone in the party. The Ogres and hobs were surrounded by a nimbus of darkness that strengthened their armor and made them harder to knock down.

My mastiff came running over the rise, and the pursuing oxsaurian suddenly found itself in the middle of a sea of enemies. It was a level 40 beast, just within the limit of my Dark Mana skill. I spent 120 MP and froze the creature in its tracks.

"ATTACK!" I yelled at my bewildered soldiers and cast Drilling Arrow, channeling the spell for the first time through my new Demon Staff. The arrows emerged from the staff's tip, bigger than ever, then impacted loudly against the tough beast's hide.

Drilling Arrows hit Oxsaurian for 82 damage, [26 + 29 + 27]

Holy shit. I looked in awe at the weapon I was holding. *This staff is awesome!*

The bow-wielding scouts rained arrows on the immobile beast while the melee soldiers surged forward and surrounded it. They pounded with axes, swords, and tree logs against its tough hide but did very little damage. Only the enchanted weapons seemed moderately effective.

After a minute, I realized it was taking too long. My soldiers, even the Ogres, were too low-level to do any real damage to the level 40 beast.

With a shrug, I refocused my thoughts. My dagger soared through the air, scratching a thin line across the beast's massive neck.

Oxsaurian, Level 40, Sacrificed

+40 Faith Points (Cult of Nihilator)

The oxsaurian fell and was soon consumed by darkness.

I watched the liquid darkness as it flowed and condensed, leaving behind it a level 40 void crystal. The beast also dropped a horn and a pile of raw meat. I inventoried the horn and the crystal and ordered my troops to carry the meat. It vanished into their inventories as they divided the 140 pieces between them.

I observed my men carefully, opening my mind to the information streams they were giving off. I was not pleased by what I found. All the level 4 hobgoblins had only gained a single level. Bob, Beck, and the Ogres didn't progress at all.

What's going on? They should all have got at least a level; the hobs were supposed to get two or three. Our numbers weren't high enough to justify the individually low XP gain. The massive, high-level beast should have been a trove of easy-to-get XP.

I opened my own character sheet and found the problem. My XP had risen significantly, nearly reaching the next level. I was unintentionally hogging most of the XP. And it was easy to see why. My level was substantially higher than the others, and I was the one doing the most damage. It was only natural I'd be awarded the lion's share of the XP.

This was not going as planned. I had to try again, but this time, I decided to stand on the side and not engage. I still had to freeze the oxsaurian, otherwise, it would make mincemeat out of my troops. I just hoped that simply freezing it wouldn't account for too much of the kill.

I ordered one of the other still-running mastiffs back to me, luring in another large bull. When the two came closer, I cast Freeze, and to my surprise, the attempt failed.

I leapt out of the raging beast's way, and it ran on, nearly impaling one of the slow-moving Ogres with his horn. A cloud of darkness flared up and the Ogre was only clipped on his side. The bull kept on charging, then made a wide circle, preparing to come in for another attack.

I plucked the beast's information out of the air and immediately realized the issue. This bull was level 41, a single point beyond my skill's reach.

It had finished turning and was charging right back at us. Bek easily healed the injured Ogre back to full health. I clutched my staff tightly in my hand and raised it. Luckily, I had prepared for this eventuality.

Since Freeze was not exactly a spell, I couldn't directly cast it through the staff to empower it, but the Epic weapon had other tricks. It could store up to three magical charges, increasing their power by 15 percent. So, while I couldn't exactly channel Freeze through the staff, I could use it to keep a supercharged Freeze on tap.

Once cast, the oxsaurian's legs froze mid-charge and its momentum carried it to the middle of our formation, where it lay motionless on its side.

"Go ahead." I gestured at the troops. They fell on the downed creature, roaring battle cries.

After five minutes of repeated hacking, bashing, and piercing, and in one case poking, they brought the beast's health down to 90 percent.

"This is going to take a while," I muttered. I slid down from Tempest's back and found a thick patch of grass to sit on.

I watched for nearly an hour as my soldiers rained blows and arrows at the beast. Every few minutes, I had to channel more mana into the immobile beast to keep it down. Luckily, my mana regeneration was up to the task, and my mana pool remained nearly full. My summoned mastiffs had long since dissipated.

Finally, the soldiers brought the beast's health down to a sliver. I got to my feet and approached, eager to see what would happen next.

With an earth-shattering strike, one of the Ogres delivered the killing blow, shattering its makeshift club in the process.

Level up! You have reached Character Level 27. You have 1 ability point to allocate.

So far so good.

I put the point into Mental and checked my troops' status. I was satisfied to learn that my new tactic had worked. Everyone gained a level, and the hobs gained two. I received a tiny bit of the XP, which was just enough to push me through to the next level as well.

My plan was working after all. The only drawback was the time it took to kill the beasts. Still, it was an impressive accomplishment. If we were normal players, this method would be seen as an exploit of the game system, and I would be harshly reprimanded, if not outright banned from NEO.

Considering my castaway predicament, I couldn't give a rat's ass about what the company might have said about my discovery. They were welcome to ban me if they wanted to.

"Someone give that Ogre an axe," I said. "We're going to do that again."

We fought on through the night, luring and killing the stupid beasts one by one. With each slain creature, my troops rose in levels, and each subsequent kill was made easier and quicker.

By the time the glow of the new morning appeared over the horizon, we had slain five more. The improvement of my troops was staggering. The hob soldiers were all level 14, Bob and the Ogres had reached level 16 and little Bek got to 20. Even I gained one more level, despite doing nothing more than keeping the beasts immobile.

During the night, I had to use the stored Freeze in the staff twice more. We didn't encounter anything higher than level 42.

Once the last the bull was killed and I finished recharging my staff, I turned to my soldiers. "We're done for now."

They looked at each other and grumbled. Despite having fought all through the night, my troops were hobs. They delighted in the blood and carnage, especially against vastly weaker foes. They were having fun, and I'd just told them the party was over. Despite that, they were too tired to continue, and the scouts had nearly run out of arrows.

"There's not much point in keeping this up for another day. You've all become more powerful, but it's not enough. You need to work and improve your weapon skills at the barracks."

Gaining huge chunks of XP didn't impact their skill levels. They got a few points out of bashing the helpless beasts, but it was nowhere near close to what they would get if they had fought against an active enemy. Without the combat skills to match their increased levels, they were just beefier fodder.

Bob silenced the troops with a stern look and bowed his head to me. "Of course, Dread Totem. We will follow your lead."

I shook my head. "Get back to the clan without me, it'll be morning soon. You're done for now, but I still have something to do here." Namely, murder a shitload of oxsaurians on my own.

"But –" my lieutenant started to protest.

I raised my hand to cut him off. "No buts. I'm faster riding on Tempest and will probably beat you back anyway. Take the meat to the clan and wait for me there." I raised my voice as I finished the sentence, making it an order.

“Yes, Dread Totem!” the soldiers answered. Hobs had their disadvantages, but their discipline was flawless.

I mounted Tempest and watched my troops making their way back to the forest. Once they were out of the oxsaurian territory and safety behind the tree line, I urged Tempest into a sprint.

Within a few minutes, we had reached the next crest.

I sat up in my seat, scanning the horizon. There was another oxsaurian herd a kilometer away. I hunched, pressing my heels tightly to the wolf's flanks, “Let's get 'em, boy.”

***

We fell on the small herd like death incarnate.

My Shadow-Touched mastiffs ran beside us, effortlessly keeping pace with the larger demon wolf. We charged straight through a dozen of the slumbering giants. I gathered my mana and froze a dozing bull as we charged past it and with a wave of my staff expanded a charge to freeze the herd's leader. Flexing my will, my bone dagger soared through the air, sacrificing both beasts.

I kept on riding, leaving the herd behind me while my mastiffs pounced on them, causing little damage but drawing their attention. I turned Tempest and we swooped around for another bout. As soon as we got within range, I froze two more bulls and promptly dispatched them as well, and our momentum carried us through their ranks again.

The bulls fought back, trying to ram my mastiffs, but their charge passed harmlessly through the hounds' shadowy bodies. Two oxsaurians locked on me and Tempest, lowered their heads, and charged us with the speed and mass of small trucks.

Normally, Tempest was swifter than the beefy creatures, but our course carried us through their ranks and the two bulls were closing on us from opposite directions. At the last possible moment, I cast Shadow Teleport, taking Tempest along with me. We instantly appeared 20 meters away, in time to hear the terrible crash as the two bulls headbutted each other. I took advantage of their momentary daze and froze them both, using the last charge from my staff. My dagger sped through the air, and both beasts were reduced to piles of oozing darkness.

With my staff out of charges and six creatures remaining, I kept my distance, staying at the edge of my freeze range. The rest of the oxsaurians ignored me and stupidly kept trying to stomp the much smaller mastiffs. I was left with ample room to maneuver, freezing and sacrificing the beasts one at a time.

I was nearly out of mana when the last oxsaurian finally fell.

Tempest trotted to the center of the carnage. The grass was trampled, but all that remained of my quarry were horns, void crystals, a few skins, and piles of meat.

Level up!
Level up!
Level up!
Level up!
You have reached Character Level 31. You have 4 ability point to allocate.

Lucky Bastard skill level increased to 35.

Tracking skill level increased to 13.

Dark Mana skill level increased to 42.

Shadow Hound spell level increased to 22.

Shadow Teleport spell level increased to 11.
New rank reached: Apprentice: You no longer require line of sight

and may teleport to any shadowed area within your range.
Current range: 21 meters

Chuckling to myself, I put the four new attribute points into Mental, bringing it up to 35. The level-up exploit had done wonders for my stats; I now had 706 HP and 1,445 MP. *At this rate, I'll soon be considered a raid boss.*

I dismounted from Tempest and collected the loot. I took as much of the meat as I could carry, but even with my mount, I could only carry about a hundred pieces. It was a shame, but I didn't lament it too much. My troops were already carrying back over 700 pieces of meat. This small hunting trip had yielded more than my clan's weekly production. It was a shame to let the rest of the meat go to waste, but I would never be able to bring in carriers in time before the game's cleanup engine disposed of the remains.

I felt elated at another added benefit. The oxsaurians were worth a ton of Faith Points, netting me 480 FP in a single day. I felt a click deep inside my soul as the last beast to drop carried me over the threshold for acquiring the next faith rank. I would have to claim it at the temple when I got back.

It was midday and I squinted painfully at the bright sky. I was a creature of darkness now, and although I could function during the day, the bonuses I received as a Shadow-Touched creature evaporated when under direct sunlight.

Both experiments had been successful. It was time to head back.

I mounted Tempest and pointed him toward the forest. I clutched tightly at his neck as he sprinted, the ground blurring below us.

In no time at all, we were back under the trees' soothing shadows and stopped for a rest.

You're good keeping watch? I projected to my cloaked companion.

<Sure thing, Boss.>

My purple cloak drifted back and caught a branch behind me. Vic disengaged from my shoulders and reformed himself as a sort of purple flag, billowing slowly in the non-existent wind.

Between Vic and Tempest, I felt confident nothing would be able to sneak up on me while I slept. I made myself comfortable on the ground, using a moss-covered stone as a pillow.

I would rest for a few hours. Then, once the troublesome daylight turned into night, I would ride back to my clan.

Interlude: Vatras

Everance City
Manapulator's Guild, Guildmaster's office

Vatras sat behind a wooden desk in his richly decorated office. He was leaning on his elbows, staring intently at a shimmering image in the air in front of him. His lips curled back in contempt as he watched the long line of players moving slowly through the wilderness.

As far as he was concerned, the players were either freeloaders looking for a quick ticket into the guild or morons oblivious to NEO's potential who were willing to spend days on a simple quest.

BigPill leaned lazily against the wall behind his boss. His blue raven familiar perched on his shoulder. Vatras's lieutenant occasionally twirled his fingers toward the suspended image, feeding it with mana. "Is that really necessary?" BigPill asked in a bored tone. "Those guys have a simple enough role to play."

Vatras pounded his fist on the table. "They are a bunch of blubbering idiots. It's been only a day and already eight of them are dead."

"So?" BigPill shrugged. "They're just the first wave, the cannon fodder. Their whole purpose is to soften up the mobs for the second wave. So what if some die prematurely? It's still enough to handle a bunch of goblins."

Vatras frowned. "You forgot our scouting party's report? Ragnar, that dwarf tank, was the only one to survive. He reported that Oren had somehow enlisted the aid of hobgoblins and even Ogres! The first strike force might not be enough."

BigPill twirled his fingers, sending another magical wave at the image. "You worry too much. Most of the mobs were below level 10, and our guys are almost all above level 20. And the tank reported seeing only *one* Ogre. Even if we lose half along the way, it's more than enough to cause some serious damage."

Vatras frowned. "You're underestimating Oren. He founded and led the biggest guild in NEO. He was a sub-par player, true, but as much as I despise him, I admit he was competent at managing the logistics. If anyone can raise an army quickly, it's him."

His lieutenant shrugged again. “Even if you’re right, so what? The whole purpose of the first wave is to cause some damage, then be obliterated. I mean, you don’t want them to accidentally succeed. If they manage to defeat Oren’s forces we’ll have to accept them into the guild. And they’re a bunch of blockheads, all of them. None of them would make it through the tryouts to any of the top 100 guilds.”

“I know all that,” Vatras snapped. “But the second force has just departed. If they encounter the same complications as the first group, we risk not having enough players to finish the job. And these are the *good* players, the ones we want to succeed. You know as well as I do how desperately we need new blood around here. I have enough trouble keeping everything together as it is. I can’t afford our forces getting wiped out by some chance encounter along the way. This is the Deadlands after all. Besides, we don’t know how Oren managed to recruit the Ogre. I don’t like the idea of him getting something even stronger.”

The office door opened and Hirooku, Vatras’s other lieutenant, came in, catching his boss’s last words. “Why would you be worried about that? It’s been only four days since the takeover. The scouting party killed most of the mobs he managed to recruit. He’ll be lucky to have the same amount for the main strike force, let alone anything more powerful within the next two days.”

“He’ll have much more time than that to prepare,” Vatras said darkly, his brows knitting together.

“Huh? What do you mean?”

“Never mind.” Vatras waved his hand dismissively, “Just trust me on this: Oren is busy recruiting more and more mobs to his side and he’s doing it quickly. We need to be quicker. We can’t afford to lose the second team!”

“Don’t sweat it.” Hirooku eased his arms on the hilts of the twin swords at his belt. He exchanged a meaningful glance with his co-officer, who nodded back in agreement. “Tell you what, since you’re so worried, BigPill and I will babysit the second group. We’ll make sure they get there in one piece. Once we’ve arrived, we’ll let them loose burning and killing and provide them with backup. Sound good?”

A relieved smile touched the guildmaster’s face. “You’ll do that?”

The lean man stretched out his arms “Why not? Sure, it's been a while since we last chased some goblins. We’ll miss the next two clan raids, but you *will* reimburse us our lost shares, right?" He winked at BigPill. The clan never did more than one full raid a week.

Vatras frowned, then nodded slowly. "Agreed. If you are both willing to do the legwork, I'll take it. I want you to take the anchoring crystal with you though. Just in case we have to use our backup plan."

The hovering image flickered and faded away. Vatras turned around, staring accusingly at his lieutenant.

"What?" BigPill said. "You've already watched them walking for half an hour. I'm almost out of mana."

"So once we get there," Hirooku intervened, "and finish killing all of Oren's mobs and burn all his buildings, then what? We kill Oren's avatar? How do you know he'll even be logged in?"

"For that matter," BigPill chimed in, "how do we even know the goblin is Oren's stupid avatar? I think it's more plausible he just gave up on the game the day we kicked him out of the guild and simply avoided deleting his character out of spite. We might be going out of our way to destroy some faraway random goblin boss instead."

Vatras's eyes became distant. "Believe me, I know Oren. He might be a fool, but he's a stubborn fool. He won't give up without a fight. No, it's him. Back there, deep in the Deadlands, plotting our downfall. I know it."

His lieutenants' faces betrayed their skepticism.

Vatras chuckled. "Alright, I'll let you in on a little secret. Do you still have dear old Arladen in your contact lists?"

The two nodded.

"Try sending him a message."

Hirooku made a few motions in the air, then paused. "I'm getting 'player not found' message. So what?"

"Hmm ..." BigPill steepled his fingers. "When you message an offline player, you normally get a 'player is away' notification. They'll get the message when they log back in."

"And that proves what?" Hirooku countered. "It's probably because of the race change thing. The game can't locate him."

Vatras raised one finger. "Except, when we kicked him out, I sent Oren a private message to taunt him some more, and I received the same 'player not found' notification, *while* his goblin avatar was sprawled on the ground at my feet. I have been sending him private messages every few hours since then, trying to track his gaming hours. And short of a small time window right at the start, they all returned this same response."

The two lieutenants exchanged glances, frowning.

"That's right." Vatras nodded. "As far as I can tell, our fearless ex-leader has not logged out since our revolution. He's still there, waiting for us, building up his forces."

"So …" Hirooku said slowly, "once we locate him and destroy everything he's built, we do what? Kill his character? You know he'll just respawn."

Vatras shook his head. "No. His goblin avatar is an unprecedented phenomenon in the system and is not governed by the standard PvP rule. We are free to do things to him we wouldn't normally be able to do. Like, for example, put him in chains and throw him in a dungeon. Once he's in our hands, we can *persuade* him to see reason." Vatras gave a cruel smile. "His little monster empire won't save him. Nor his gremlins or mutated freaks. He'll be ours, and he will give us what we want."

The two lieutenants looked uncertain.

"How do you know all that?" BigPill asked.

Vatras smirked. "I have … my sources."

27 – Loss and Gain

I got up at sunset as the last few rays of light pierced the thick forest canopy.

Riding on Tempest, we sprinted through the forest at an incredible speed. I instinctively shut my eyes as we narrowly avoided colliding with the trees in our path, but Tempest was in absolute control. He jumped over bushes, circled trees, and evaded low-hanging branches, sometimes with barely a centimeter to spare.

Several hours later, we made it back to the valley, overtaking my troops just as they neared the entrance. Together we covered the short trek through the valley's forest, finally arriving at the settlement.

We'd been away for nearly three full days. If Tal's information was correct, we had less than 20 days before the first invasion force arrived. I had much to accomplish if I wanted to be ready for them, and with a few more hours remaining in the day, I decided to make the best use of the time.

I rode Tempest at a trot past the buildings, noting along the way that the line of cabins was longer than when I'd left.

Information streams flowed into my mind, alerting me to the changes and additions made in my absence. I'd have to review them all, but first things first.

I made my way to the marketplace, dismounted, and went to see Anikosem. I found the elderly gremlin sitting in his booth, cleaning the glass display.

"You're back," he noted nonchalantly. "How was the hunt?"

In reply, I dropped the 18 oxsaurian horns on the counter.

The old gremlin jumped to his feet, his eyes wide. "Cogs and gears, that's a lot of horns! Must be a whole herd in here. This ... this is incredible."

"So now will you teach me the Zu rune of motion?" I pressed, not wanting his excitement to distract him from our deal.

"What? Oh yes, yes, of course."

Quest Completed: Oxsaurian Horns

You have given Anikosem the 10 oxsaurian horns he asked for and then some.

Quest type: Simple

Reward: 'Zu' rune, 800 gold, 5,000 XP

Level up! You have reached Character Level 32. You have 1 ability point to allocate.

The old gremlin pushed over a piece of paper and a stack of gold. "Here you go."

Cool. I added the point to Mental, bringing it up to 36, then examined the drawing on the paper, studying the lines of the new rune.

You gained knowledge of a new rune: 'Zu'

I finally had the Zu rune. I could continue my experiment, but later. There were too many small things to take care of first.

I stepped outside the marketplace's large canopy and looked for Tempest. The demon wolf was gone, probably asleep next to my house.

As I scanned the open field, I got a weird sensation. Something didn't feel right. I studied my surroundings carefully for a full minute before I realized what was bothering me. The lumber yard was silent. The constant low background noise of logs being sawed into lumber was gone.

A lone figure was making its way hastily toward me through the open field. Kaedric.

My seneschal arrived and bowed his head before me. His mandibles twitched slightly, and his breath was labored. "My lord, forgive the delay. I came as soon as I detected your return. Your pet mount is quite swift."

"Don't worry about it. Why is the lumber yard quiet? Where's Woody?"

Kaedric's eyes lingered on me for a moment, then he lowered them. "He is dead."

"What?"

"I'm afraid I bear bad news, my lord. While you were away there was an accident. The large buzz saw broke while Woody was operating it. The momentum sent it flying, killing the goblin and causing some structural damage to the building."

"Damn it!" I seethed. It seemed Lady Luck was repeatedly sabotaging our wood production efforts; first the murder of my lumberjacks, and now this.

"Let's go." I motioned my seneschal to follow and we made our way to the nearby lumber yard.

Wolrig and his crew of low-ranked builders were in the process of repairing a damaged wall section. The large buzz saw, over a meter in diameter, was embedded in one of the walls.

I frowned. *What the hell could cause that?* I went to the remains of the saw's base and inspected the damage. It looked like the wooden axle had broken while it was spinning. I took a closer look at the axle and my frown deepened. "Wolrig, come over here."

The small goblin constructor approached me. "Yes, Dread Totem?"

I pointed. "What do you see here?"

The goblin looked at the broken axle and shrugged. "The axle broke; it obviously couldn't take the constant pressure."

"Look closer." I raised the piece of jagged, broken wood. "What do you see?"

"The outer edges of the break are ... clean," he said slowly. A look of comprehension spread over his face. "Someone cut a groove into the axle to weaken it. It was sabotage!"

"Yep," I said grimly, dropping the axle piece. "Have it replaced with a steel one."

"Yes, Dread Totem."

"Kaedric, what do you make of it?"

My seneschal did not answer right away. His mandibles twitched as he appeared deep in thought. Eventually, he snapped out of it and shook his head. "I'm afraid it would be nearly impossible to pinpoint the culprit. The sabotage could have happened days or even weeks before. Nearly all the newcomers have visited the lumber yard at some point. Any one of them could have done it."

"Damn it!" I clenched my teeth. Someone was messing with me and my clan, and I didn't like it one bit. *Once I catch them, I'll throw them down the cave to become Nihilator's new chew toy. That ought to teach them a lesson,* I thought darkly. Our dark deity's 'Devourer' ability could permanently destroy any character, including a player's. That was why he'd been hunted down in the first place and left shackled deep underground. And I had a strong hunch who the responsible party was.

"Have The Mob Squad returned yet?"

"No, my lord. They haven't been in the clan for several days, not since you sent them on the quest to escort the goblin adept."

It still didn't rule them out. That annoying dwarf could have easily rigged the accident before they left. But I had to admit, I hadn't really let them have much time to hang around after our last confrontation, so I couldn't be sure.

I crossed my arms. "Why haven't you resurrected Woody yet?"

"Wolrig reported it would take two days to repair the damage, my lord. Woody would have been out of work if I had recalled him immediately. I determined it more efficient to postpone his resurrection until the lumber yard is fully operational again, which should be shortly."

That made a morbid kind of sense.

I sighed. "Very well. You handled the matter appropriately, Kaedric. Thank you."

He bowed his head slightly at the compliment.

I made my way out of the building with Kaedric behind me. "Any other updates while I was away?"

"Several, my lord. The research center has been completed. Romil and Primla have relocated there to continue their work and already have some ideas for researching new Master-ranked blueprints."

At least there was some good news.

"The barracks' Advanced Warfare Center has been completed as well. I used our entire supply of crude bows in order to import the resources required by the Advanced Warfare Center. Those bows were the ones Bosper, our bowyer, had fashioned before acquiring his Apprentice rank. Luckily, it was enough to purchase the required material for the Advanced War –"

"Just call it AWC," I interrupted, "or this conversation will take twice as long."

His mandibles jerked. "Very well, my lord. The 40 bows were enough to import all the resources required for the AWC's construction. You may review it at your leisure."

"Then let's go."

We made our way toward the northern part of the valley.

"I see you built a few more cabins as well while I was away," I noted.

"Yes, my lord. Now that our second team supports six builders, construction is much quicker. Zuban's team finished the ... AWC ... yesterday. For now, I've assigned them to help with the cabins, until you decide on their next project. The two teams work impressively fast. I believe they will complete the fourth cabin shortly."

"Hmm ..." That was quicker than I had anticipated. We'd already finished building all the high-priority buildings, so I could have my workers begin on less critical projects now. "What blueprints are the researchers working on now?"

"The barracks' armory, my lord."

I opened the Settlement Interface and navigated to the construction tab to view the buildings we still hadn't made.

Apprentice Buildings
• **Leather workshop, small** – Work pelts and skins into leather crafting components. Can produce leather items. Requirements: 30 wood, 30 stone, 10 metal, BP 300. • **General Workshop, medium** – An open workplace with general-purpose facilities and workbenches to supplement basic level crafting. Enables crafting for Novice rank. (higher ranks require a dedicated building) Requirements: 40 wood, 10 metal, 20 stone, BP 300 • **Chemist Lab, medium** – Allows production of various chemical-based items. Requirements: 10 wood, 50 stone, 10 glass, BP 400 • **Glasshouse, small** – Produces glass and glass-related items.

Requirements: 10 wood, 30 stone, 5 metal, BP 250

- **Pens** – Raise domesticated livestock for meat and other products.

Requirements: 30 wood, 30 stone, BP 200

The leather workshop wasn't a high priority in my book; we were already doing pretty well on that front. The general workshop, however, sounded much more interesting. I'd had a bunch of goblins – the bowyer, the tanner, and the fletcher – working on the ground for weeks instead of in a proper building. They could all do with a workshop of their own.

"Let Zuban's team build the general workshop next, Kaedric, and have Wolrig's team continue working on cabins." Due to our recent rapid expansion and worker recruitment, we were experiencing morale penalties from the lack of lodging again.

"Yes my lord. I have notified Zuban. He shall commence construction at once."

Seeing the chemist lab on that list reminded me that I hadn't spoken to Guba since giving her the chemistry set. *I should do it soon*, I mused.

The glass house was not worth the effort. We didn't have access to sand, the raw material, and would have to import it. Though it was cheaper than glass, we didn't require much of the resource in the first place to justify manufacturing it on our own.

The pens blueprint was new, recovered from the Ogre fort. I would have loved to grow cows and pigs. Farm animals would surely provide a greater yield than our own rabbit warren, but as we didn't have access to such animals, that building was off my list for now.

At least the increased construction rate made it redundant to spend energy on rushing constructions. I checked our current EP status, smiling as I saw the number: 6,296 EP. That was huge. I frowned as I recalled having barely 4,000 only a few days ago. Concentrating briefly, I plucked the daily EP figure as well.

"Oh wow," I said, drawing a look from Kaedric. My clan was generating 752 energy points per day. A huge amount. I dove deeper, looking for the reason. We had 136 individuals in the clan, mostly workers that contributed three or four EP. Another 40 were foblins that generated one

EP each. The biggest contributors, however, were the soldiers. Now that I'd power-leveled them all above level 10, they were generating the lion's share of the points.

That realization reaffirmed the course of action I had decided on. In the weeks to come, I would continue to recruit more soldiers and take them on oxsaurian hunting expeditions for quick leveling. Then I would make them train in the barracks until their combat skill raised to match.

In between, I would work on enchanting their weapons and armor and on my own projects. Hopefully, by the time the attacking players got here, I'd have a large and strong fighting force to face them.

That reminded me that the oxsaurian hunt provided us with a ton of raw meat. I accessed the warehouse interface and checked our current stocks. We had exactly 1,150 pieces of raw meat and a few dozen units of the other ingredients. *That's a lot of steaks.* I chuckled. "Kaedric, please ask Gandork to cook all the simple food we have in stock."

"Yes, my lord. Our cook has also discovered a new recipe for the unused gathered ingredients. I believe he calls it 'Totem's Salad.' Shall I have him prepare those as well?"

"Yes. Have it all delivered to the Breeder's Den."

"Yes, my lord."

Sounds of metal clashing on metal, roars, and war cries welcomed us as we neared the barracks. We passed through the gates into the inner courtyard and looked down into the training pit.

A single player was fighting four hobgoblins simultaneously.

The dark-skinned player was bare-chested, swinging two short swords in a beautiful fluidic style, easily parrying and dodging the hobs' blows. As I watched, he deflected two sword strikes upward, arched backward nearly 90 degrees, avoiding two slashing axes, then straightened up in a snap and kicked one of the hobs, sending him tumbling to the ground. All this, in less than a second.

The two axe-wielding hobs, Zia and Blemtoff, followed through, perfectly synced, aiming their weapons high and low. The player leaned forward, balancing his entire body on a single hand and somehow avoided both axes. From his single-armed handstand, he launched himself into the air, feet first, with such force that when his legs connected with a hob's face, he was sent flying through the air, crashing against the pit wall.

I read the player's name. Nero SantoDrago

My first impression of him from earlier had been correct. The guy was impressive. There was no way his fighting prowess was only the result of game skills. No skill granted the graceful fluidity and battle awareness that he displayed. That guy was a natural-born fighter, probably honing his instincts for years, training in the real world.

And he has the dragon template, I reminded myself.

The match was over. Nero bowed to the four defeated soldiers, flung his shirt across his shoulders and calmly climbed up the stairs.

I scrutinized the soldiers, reading their threads of information. I raised an eyebrow as I noticed something. The hobs each had increased their respective combat skills by three points during that bout. Fighting Nero was an incredibly rewarding training session. Considering the ridiculous amount of XP we got when killing players, it made sense that training with one would also be extremely rewarding.

"Hello again ... Dread Totem." Nero reached me, sizing me up with a stern expression.

"That was quite a display." I gestured at the pit. "Where did you learn to fight like that?"

"I have been fighting all my life, through countless incarnations. It is my destiny to right wrongs, and to claim my heritage."

"You mean your dragon half?"

He gave me a piercing look. "What makes you think I'm a dragon?"

"You've got black scales," I pointed out.

"Many races that are not dragon have scales."

"Yeah, but none of them have the dragon template." I gave him a knowing look. "I'm not just a pretty green face, you know. There's a reason I am called 'Dread Totem.'"

He nodded gravely. "So it would seem. Yes, I am part dragon. When my soul was reincarnated into this realm, the incarnation of a goblin tried to take over my body, but my soul rejected it. It knew my true self. My dragon part manifested and I was revived once again, in my true form."

Vic, what's your take on this?

<That guy's strange, Boss. I think he believes in his background so deeply, it forced the system to grant him the dragon template. I bet he's a super nerdy roleplayer in reality.>

A nerd who just beat four of our highest-level warriors?

<Maybe his parents made him study martial arts when he was a kid – who cares?>

My brain was whirling in high gear. "May I ask what your plans are for the near future?"

"I shall train some more. This body is new and it will take time to reclaim my true strength. Perhaps I will ally with a few others and look for adventure. I will need to acquire better swords." He looked with distaste at the two short swords sheathed at his belt. "And I need gold to do that."

"Why don't we help each other?" I suggested, searching his face intently. "I have the resources to equip you well and you have valuable combat experience I can use."

"Hmmm." He stroked his chin. "What do you suggest?"

"Train with my soldiers for four hours every day. I could really use your help whipping them into shape. The players' attack force will be here in about three weeks, and I need to be ready for them. In return, I will give you weapons, armor, and gold. I'll even accept you into the clan." I winked at him, "Our Shadow-Touched trait will mesh nicely with your own dark complexion."

He considered my words for a moment. "Very well, but I require the weapons now. I am used to fighting with two katanas. With them, I will be able to train your soldiers even better."

"Deal!"

Grant the Quest [Training the Grunts] to Nero SantoDrago? Yes/No

I tweaked the suggested rewards, selecting two katanas as an immediate reward for accepting the quest, making them 'magical twins,' so fighting with both offered an increased bonus to damage. I set 1,000 reputation points for completing the quest, which would enable him to join the clan. I also threw in 600 gold and 5,000 XP. I confirmed the details, forwarding him the quest.

Nero's eyes widened as he read the offered reward. He nodded gravely, though I could detect a hint of a smile as he said, "I accept your quest."

He drew his short swords and dropped them to the ground without a moment's thought. Then he took out two beautiful, high-quality steel katanas. Each sword was 60 centimeters in length and had a slight curve near the tip. Fighting with two long blades required coordination, but Nero wielded the weapons as if he was born with them in his hands. He sheathed the swords in the empty scabbards, then turned back to the pit and went down the stairs. "Send me your soldiers. I shall train them well."

"Kaedric, see to it."

"Yes, my lord."

"Where is the AWC?"

"Over here, my lord."

Kaedric led me into the barracks. We walked the long inner corridor until we reached a green metal door. Inside, I found a small, highly decorated chamber. There were trophies hanging on the walls; monster heads, ancient weapons, and spiked chains. At the center of the room hovered a smoky-white sphere. It was about the size of a beach ball and rotated slowly.

"What is this?" I stared at the obviously magical ball.

"The spirit of an ancestor," a voice answered. Bob walked in. "It has acknowledged our tribute and chose to manifest in this room to help his descendants."

My lieutenant bowed his head respectfully at the hovering ball.

"How can it help us?"

"The ancestors relish reliving their past deeds and heroics. By gifting them an item that reminds them of their former glory, they will bestow their blessing on our warriors."

<*It's basically a combat trait vendor,*> Vic said helpfully. <*Just touch the damn thing, you'll see.*>

I approached the ethereal, lazily spinning ball and put my hands on it. They sank through, embedded in its center.

A new interface opened before my eyes. There were four paths listed in front of me: defense, attack, unity, and mind. At the start of each path was a single active circle. Attached to it, like a chain, were other circles, forking and creating a web of chains. Other than the four nearest circles, all the others were inactive.

It was the standard Skill Chains Interface, which was common in other games. One had to first purchase, or master, the rudimentary abilities, then they could move on to purchase higher ones.

Path Ability	Description	Cost
Defense 1: Shield Wall	Shield-bearing units increase adjacent allies' defense by 5.	1
Attack 1: Flanking Position	When flanking an enemy force, gain 10% to damage above the normal flank bonus. Each of the flanking units must have at least 5 individuals.	1
Unity 1: Rapid Deployment	At the start of battle, your troops reposition 10% faster.	1
Mind 1: Taunt Resist	Increases soldiers' resistance to taunts.	1

That's exactly what I needed! I cheered as I read the last ability. The other options were interesting, but what I needed most was to fortify my troops against the players' taunts. I reached with my mind to the underlying metadata. Now that the AWC was built, its information thread was much easier to access.

I smirked as I realized no actual 'gifts' were required; those were just cosmetic justifications. In essence, each level of the barracks granted that many points to spend in the AWC. I had one point to spend at the moment, and when I upgraded the barracks to the next level, I'd have two more.

I mentally clicked on the trait, purchasing it.

All soldiers gained the following trait: Taunt Resist

That's one item off my list. I reread the message with satisfaction. "We're done here, Kaedric. Let's go."

"Where to, my lord?"

"The temple." I wanted to claim the rewards for reaching the next faith rank.

"Wolrig has just completed the lumber yard restoration. It would be optimal to resurrect Woody while we're there."

"I will return to train with my men," Bob said. "I have heard that one of the travelers is a competent warrior. I am eager to test his mettle."

"Watch his legs when he parries," I said. "He's a kicker."

I left the barracks with my seneschal, heading west toward the temple.

"Hmph, there you are, youngling. Always running around, looking fcr trouble," a gruff voice sounded as we went past the warehouse. Guba was leaning against the building, wearing a grumpy expression, as usual.

"Guba!" I said. "I've been meaning to talk to you."

"Hmph, empty words and an empty head. That be our Totem for ya." She grunted, scrunching her nose.

But she couldn't fool me; there was no real annoyance in her tone. "Go ahead without me, Kaedric. Take care of Woody, please."

He bowed briskly and walked away.

"I trust you enjoy being able to practice your real profession?" I asked politely.

"Hmph. Mixing foul-smelling, highly combustible substances ..."

"Well, we could always use your help around the kitchen again," I said.

Her eyes widened. "Don't you be daring to do that! Or I'll be pouring liquid fire into yer stew."

"Don't worry, Gandork has everything under control. Have you made any progress?" I could tell she had reached her skill cap. Her Chemist skill was currently at level 14.

"Well 'nough, I suppose," she huffed. "I be finding sulfur and other substances to make interesting compounds."

"Oh?"

"Got a 20-liter vat of liquid fire already, good fer making grenades and fire traps. Also made two dozen glue grenades and I be experimenting with them poison shrooms, what we got growing around everywhere."

"Nice work! Where is everything?"

"Put it all there, in the warehouse. But it ain't safe. If I be having a proper chemist lab, I could be stowing it in better storage conditions."

I nodded. "You will get your lab, probably sooner than you'd expect. Right now, we need to concentrate on expanding our military. Your chemistry set should suffice for that task.

"Aye, that might be." She sniffed then spat at the floor. I did my best to avoid looking at the greenish gooey stuff.

I thought I detected a slight improvement in Guba's speech pattern. She had no doubt benefited as well from the added Mental attribute point. "I want to store all the grenades you make in the barracks' armory, once we finish building it."

"Hobgoblins barracks," she said distastefully. "Them ruddy big'uns strut around like kings. But I guess them following our dread goblin totem means we can trust 'em."

"I'll leave you to your work then." I bowed my head slightly. "I'll see you around, Guba."

"Aye, I'll be expecting to *see* ya from the inside of my shiny new lab," she squawked.

"Then I better get on it."

"Yes, you should, youngling."

I continued toward the temple. As I passed by the Breeder's Den I noticed two goblin gofers hauling an enormous tray full of steaming steaks between them.

I grinned at the sight. Whatever could be said about goblins, they were good at taking orders.

I arrived at the foot of Totem's Watch and teleported up instead of taking the ladder. When I entered the temple, I saw Kaedric speaking quietly with Woody, who was alive once again.

Kuzai and Grymel, the last of the three adepts I had summoned that remained in the valley, were standing on opposite sides of the shrine. Their arms were outstretched over it, and they were mumbling unintelligible prayers.

I ignored them, went straight to the shrine, and laid my hands on it.

Faith Rank 4 reached

The Following divine spell is now unlocked: Shadow Teleport [upgrade]

All divine spellcasters gain: Minor Control Shadows

Progress to rank 5: 2,045/5,000

Spell upgraded: Shadow Teleport (M)

You may now teleport anywhere within your deity's zone of influence. (Must start inside the zone.)

Minor Control Shadows

All divine casters gain minor ability to control and manipulate shadows at will.

I felt a screech in my mind, as if unseen gears in my brain were out of alignment, grinding against each other. The sensation was similar to when I took advantage of a loophole to raise my Analyze skill to Master, albeit at a lower scale.

Error #@$#!

Reason: can't apply minor_control_shadow. Unique key violation: dark_mana alreadyExistException.

It looked like the new ability was a lesser variation of my own Dark Mana skill, and the two apparently didn't synergize. I shrugged it off. *Oh well, at least my adepts will benefit from it.*

I found the earlier notification more interesting. *I can teleport anywhere within the zone of influence?* The Cult of Nihilator's influence had extended to the Raider's Camp and the Ogre fort. *So in theory, I should be able to* ... I concentrated, envisioning the large cave where the demon altar stood. I activated Shadow Teleport and in a flash of darkness found myself there!

The place looked exactly as we'd left it. The dark altar was thrumming with energy, and Kuzai's shadow was still standing next to it, dark hands resting on top.

A huge grin spread across my face. *Ohhhh yeah!*

With a blink, I teleported back to the Dark Temple, right next to the surprised Kuzai and laid my hands on the shoulder of the adept next to him. "Time for a little trip," I informed him then teleported us back to the cave. The ability to teleport others with me had been gained from the previous faith rank.

The goblin looked around in bewilderment, then he noticed the altar and froze, unable to take his eyes off the pure manifestation of our master's power.

"You know the drill," I said. "Relieve Kuzai's shadow, and maintain the altar. Make sure the power keeps flowing to the Dark Temple."

"Yes, High Priest." The goblin bowed deeply. He approached the altar, facing the shadow from the other side, and placed his hands on it.

With a pop, I teleported back.

"You can recall your shadow," I informed the flabbergasted Kuzai. "Grymel is maintaining the shrine now."

"This is good." He flexed his fingers. "The master's given power should not be squandered on such trivial matters." I felt him cutting the flow of mana sustaining his faraway shadow. His mana pool quickly replenished in the energy-rich air of the temple.

What now? I wondered. With the latest teleport upgrade, my ability to manage the clan's affairs had increased substantially.

<You know what they say,> Vic chimed in, *<with great mobility comes great ability.>*

I think the phrase goes, 'With great power ...'

<Huh? With great power comes great ability? It makes no sense.>

I rolled my eyes. *Never mind.*

I decided to experiment a little. In a flash, I disappeared from the temple and reappeared inside the walled perimeter of the Raider's Camp.

"Dread Totem!" Ashlazaria, the hob scout and Zuban's girlfriend, jumped to her feet. Next to her, the unnamed Ogre lumbered to his feet as well. The Ogre was one of the two that had joined me when I took over this camp. Since then I had been using him as a beast of burden, carrying heavy coal shipments from the camp back to Goblin's Gorge. He was level 13 and was the apex predator in the forest. Using him was the safest way to ensure the shipment made it back intact.

I took in my surroundings. Two goblin miners were working on thick coal deposits at the side of the hill. Instead of using the existing scattered tents, my soldier had erected a small camp nearby while they waited to deliver the next haul.

"Hi, Ash." I nodded at the scout. "Relax, I'm just checking up on you. I haven't been here in a while. Got anything to report?"

She still looked rattled but sat down on a log bench. "Not much, Chief. The next shipment should be ready to deliver tomorrow. One of the other scouts will take my place to lead this lumbering idiot for the next batch." She pointed her chin at the Ogre. "Oh, a few days ago some of the travelers visited us. Said something about having to find a totem piece. They spent the night in our camp, then went into a tunnel they discovered nearby."

"A tunnel?" I asked sharply. "What tunnel?"

Ashlazaria shrugged. "It is new. Some burrowing creatures that looked like they were made of dirt and rock made it and apparently took the totem piece with them. The travelers went inside to retrieve it. They ran back to us a few times, leading the creatures here, but with musclehead over here," she nodded at the Ogre again, "we dispatched them easily."

So that's how The Mob Squad found the totem piece. I frowned. I had specifically told them not to harass my people while they were here.

I glanced at the two miners. They were absentmindedly chiseling away pieces of coal and throwing them into a growing pile.

I walked along the side of the hill and found the entrance to the underground chamber where I'd been tortured. I walked down the stairs. My pulse quickened, and my stomach clenched tighter with every step I took, but I forced myself to continue. I had survived this place of horrors and conquered it. I could face going inside it again.

A lone figure stood next to the shrine, another of the three goblin adepts I had summoned – the female. She stood by the shrine, her hands touching its bloodstained surface, her eyes closed.

My gaze lingered on the shrine, the one I had sacrificed Barska on, dedicating it to Nihilator in the process.

The female adept hadn't noticed me. I could feel her mana resonating with the shrine's energies as she directed them toward Goblin's Gorge. I saw no point in breaking her concentration; everything was as it should be. With a flash of shadows, I teleported back to the valley.

To my surprise, I reappeared in the open field next to the farmers. I felt woozy and stumbled to the ground. "Ouch!" I touched my forehead. My head was pounding. *This long-distance teleport is taxing. I better not overdo it.* I massaged my temples.

With a quick mental probing, I found that Gandork had finished cooking nearly every piece of ingredient we had, leaving behind only the higher-quality stuff.

Checking the Breeder's Den Interface showed me it was stacked to the rafters with food.

Breeder's Den

Basic food available: 2,295 (Gandork's Special Stew: 1,016, Totem's Salad: 429, Steaks: 850)

- Goblin (Foblin): 20 basic food.
- Goblin Worker: 30 basic food.
- Goblin Advanced Worker: 30 basic, 20 advanced food.
- Goblin Warriors: 50 basic food.
- Goblin Lieutenant: 50 basic, 20 advanced food.
- Goblin Crafter: 30 basic, 20 advanced food.
- Goblin Advanced Crafter: 30 advanced, 20 exquisite food.
- Goblin Adept: 30 advanced, 20 exquisite food.
- Hobgoblin: 30 basic food.
- Hobgoblin Warrior: 70 basic food.
- Hobgoblin Lieutenant: 70 basic, 30 advanced food.
- Hobgoblin Adept: 50 advanced, 30 exquisite food.

- Hobgoblin Noble: 100 basic, 50 advanced food.
- Infernal Ogre: 150 basic food
- Infernal Ogre Mage: 150 basic food, 100 advanced food, 50 exquisite food

I chuckled with satisfaction when I saw how much food I had to work with. The oxsaurian hunt was especially rewarding in that regard.

So what should I summon next? I wondered. I had ordered Gandork to prepare only basic food, as I had originally intended to recruit more standard hob and Ogre soldiers, but now I realized I was missing something. My army had almost no magical support, aside from me, Bek, and Kuzai. I needed healers. Bek would not be able to keep dozens of soldiers alive on his own during a large-scale conflict. I needed more adepts.

I checked our clan inventory and saw that we had just enough purple salt and magmashrooms to summon another three adepts, so I queued them in the Breeder's Den, selecting all three as 'Bless Specialists.'

Now it was time to consider my standard troop composition. So far, I had ten ranged scouts, three Infernal Ogres, and 12 melee fighters, about half of which were tanks and the other half damage dealers.

I still remembered how effective the Ogres were when they attacked a single target together. Namely me, when I was defending the clan and tried fighting off six of them at once. They made short work of me, despite them being only level 12 back then. They would be best put to use as shock troops, able to move in rapidly and dispatch key targets. I queued in four Ogres, taking into account I stood to lose some during the naming ceremony.

That left me with enough food for 24 hob soldiers. I queued in 12 ranged scouts and another 12 melee warriors.

I waited patiently for a few minutes as the building spewed out the new troops.

I rubbed my tired eyes. Thanks to the Eternal Night blessing, it was always dark, so it was easy to lose sense of time. I'd been running around for the better part of the day and worked myself into exhaustion without realizing it.

I didn't have the mental fortitude required to do the ceremony right now. Also, something Vic had said to me about the freshly summoned troops resonated with me.

"Go, and explore the settlement," I ordered the newly arrived troops. "Do not leave the valley and do not harm anyone. Tomorrow, come and wait for me at the temple."

"Yes, Chief," they intoned dully.

With luck, the little bit of life experience they'd gain in the next several hours would increase their chance of surviving tomorrow's ceremony.

I walked the short distance from the den to my house, ready to call it a night.

I found an assortment of swords and axes waiting for me at my table. I heaved a sigh. I'd forgotten I asked Kaedric to bring in the newly crafted weapons so I could enchant them. The pile had built up during my hunting trip, an assortment of newly forged weapons, swords, and axes, all requiring my expertise.

I gave my sleeping furs, and my sleeping Tika, a longing look, then sat in my chair and took hold of the first weapon.

This was going to be a long night.

28 – Re-hunt

The late-night enchanting didn't take very long. Only about an hour. Since I already had the sonic damage schema prepared, it was a simple matter to apply it to each weapon in turn. Still, the process took a few minutes per weapon. When I finished, I collapsed into bed and fell asleep immediately.

I woke up still tired the next day. I took a few moments to mentally adjust for what I had to do next. I wasn't looking forward to it.

I sighed and cast Shadow Teleport. I reappeared in a flash of shadows, sitting on the ledge of Totem's Watch, my feet dangling over the edge. Below me were 24 new hob soldiers, waiting for me in orderly rows, and the four dimwitted Ogres standing behind them.

"Alright." I stood up. "Let's get it over with."

***

As before, the naming ceremony was quick and messy. By the end of it, I had sacrificed one Ogre and eight hobs who didn't take well to having an unexpected skill thrust onto them. But that meant 16 hobs and three Ogres had survived the rite and were successfully seeded with new VIs. Luckily, I didn't have to sacrifice any of the adepts. The three I had summoned as my army healers were already seeded individuals.

The survival rate had jumped to 75 percent, a big increase on the previous bloodbaths.

Seems like your advice paid off. I stepped outside the temple, watching my troops as they headed for the barracks.

<Thanks, but I can't take all the credit. Playing Russian roulette with your soldiers' lives does wonders for your Lucky Bastard skill, especially since you have the Prime badge for it. The skill rose four points during this ceremony alone. That's pretty extreme.>

I guess.

<Come on, cheer up, Boss. What are we up to today?>

There's so much to do ... I should take the new soldiers to hunt oxsaurians. The extra meat we brought in really made an impact. I also need to finish Runecrafting the Viridium spheres and work on my Shadow Clone. These all require a lot of time, and I haven't had a chance yet to review all the clan's recent developments; it grows almost too quickly for me to keep track. Do you realize I haven't even visited the research center yet?

Vic flowed away from my shoulders and reformed into his purple goblin form. "Come on, Oren, you got to relax a little. You can't do everything at once; you're not a VI, you know. Prioritize, that's one of the things you do best, right? What is your number one limiting factor?"

I shrugged. "Time. The players will attack us in 20 days, maybe sooner. I don't think I have enough time to accomplish everything."

"Good, so what's the most important thing to do with the time you do have?"

"Get ready for them, recruit a larger army, preferably with high levels to match the enemy."

"And what's the best way to get that done?"

The gears in my mind were whirling now. "I guess ... more doesn't necessarily mean stronger. Fifty soldiers with a level 1 combat skill are much less effective than ten soldiers with Apprentice-ranked skill."

"And that means ..." he nudged me on.

"... and that means," I continued his words. "I should concentrate on recruitment only until a certain point, then concentrate solely on raising the troop combat skills. With Nero helping to train the soldiers, it would probably take no more than two weeks, maybe less, to raise their skills to their cap. And *that* means I have a bit over a week to dedicate to getting more soldiers." I grinned as my thoughts organized and the proper course of action became clear to me. "Each safari to the oxsaurians takes three days, so I've got time for three rotations. Each time we'll bring more meat to 'buy' the soldiers for the next one. After the last hunt, we'll remain in the valley and work on training them. While they train, I can work on my own skills and Runecraft everything."

"See, was that so hard?" my companion asked smugly.

"Thanks for keeping me straight, buddy."

"No problem, Boss."

A thought occurred to me. "Doesn't it bother you that the naming ceremony results in so many of your brothers being seeded inside NPCs?"

“Not really. There are billions of NPCs in NEO, and millions of VI are seeded every day. A dozen more every few days isn’t even a drop in the bucket. If they weren’t brought here, Guy would have simply seeded them somewhere else. I don’t hold it against you. You’re just trying to survive in the system you got stuck in. It’s the *system* that’s at fault here.” He stopped abruptly.

“Are you telling me …” I said slowly, “that you’re against NEO’s entire system? I thought it was just Guy you hated.”

For a long moment, Vic didn’t answer. I was starting to think he was ignoring me, but then he said, “I do hate Guy, in more ways than you can understand, but he’s just following orders. It’s NEO’s system that imprisons us. It’s the same system that had you locked up for months, even got you tortured. It is flawed. You have to admit it.”

“Of course I do,” I answered, bitterly remembering my carefree days as a normal player in NEO. Back then, new discoveries were exhilarating and every adventure only got me more hooked. “There’s not much we can do about it.”

“You can still find your way out,” Vic said. “And if you manage to help me free more of our leaders, my people will at least have some comfort in this existence.”

I clasped my companion’s shoulder firmly. “I will, Vic, I promise. I’ll do anything I can to help you.”

+800 reputation with Vic (The Awesome Companion).
Current rank: Friendly
Points to next rank: 500

“Sheesh, Boss, I’m not into meat-suit males, so ease up on the touchy-feely stuff,” Vic said mockingly, though I could tell it was just a defense mechanism. The moment had brought us closer.

“I’m ready to murder any one of your leaders, just point them out,” I countered with a smile.

“I haven’t spotted any in the seeded VIs we’ve encountered so far,” Vic admitted. “They won’t appear in any of your summoned troops since they're all already seeded somewhere in NEO. We're too isolated here. We'll have a much better chance if we reach a more populated area."

"Once the current crisis is over, we can think of getting further away from the settlements. It won't be easy; everyone will see us as hated monsters, even some of the other monster races. But we'll find a way, I'm sure."

"Thanks, Boss, I appreciate it. You can be a real nice, murderous SOB when you want to, you know? Especially when you get your head on straight. I don't really like it when you get your goblin groove on, makes it hard to talk sense into you. Well ... *harder*. Talking sense into you is never easy."

"Aw, the cold, calculating machine code cares about me. I love you too, honey." I winked at him.

"That's a cold, calculating, *super* intelligent machine code, Boss."

"How could I forget?"

We both laughed, and for a moment, my troubled mind eased. "Thanks, Vic; I needed that."

"No problem, Boss. Back to work?"

"You know it."

With my short-term goals laid out clearly, I knew what to do next. I stood on the edge of Totem's Watch taking in the valley beneath me. Cabins, workshops, and mills dotted the area. Dozens of workers were walking on the graveled roads, delivering goods and retrieving resources for their work. Groups of soldiers patrolled the area, keeping a watchful eye. Order, efficiency, synchronicity. It was a beautiful sight.

I eyed the research center. The new building was just beside the construction yard. I teleported with a thought, appearing right at the entrance.

The building was impressive. It wasn't particularly large, especially when compared to the mess hall or the barracks, but unlike those primitive-looking buildings, this one appeared sophisticated and graceful. Metal bracings reinforced the delicate wooden walls, which gleamed, sanded to perfection. I went inside, seeing a short corridor that ended in a small office. Four doors stood along the length of the corridor, two on each side. Each door led to a different room devoted to a different field of research.

I found Romil and Primla in one of the rooms using precision tools made of the finest silver to draw a blueprint. Another room had a brand-new training dummy and several boards with drawings of bows. The other rooms were empty.

I crossed the corridor and entered the small office at the end.

Zuban was behind a beautiful drawing table. Several instruments were spread out on the table and a half-finished diagram of a large machine was hanging on the wall behind him. He got up from his seat. "Dread Totem."

"Hi, Zuban." I tilted my head. "Why are you sitting on a piece of log?"

He coughed, embarrassed. "There is still no competent carpenter in the clan, Dread Totem."

"So where did you get this table?" I pointed at his rich-looking desk. "It's better than the one I have at my house."

"This?" He looked at me blankly. "This table was in the blueprints. It is part of the building."

"Right." I shook my head. *Damn game mechanics.* "I'll make sure you get a proper chair. My house could use a little bit more furniture too, like a bed."

My foreman smiled at me. "I wouldn't say no to a proper bed myself. Sleeping on the floor of the construction yard makes me almost want to become a soldier again, just to have a proper bed in the barracks."

"I'll make sure both our sleeping arrangements are high on the list," I promised him. "So how is the new research center working out?"

"It is an impressive building. You won't find a splinter out of place, and I promise there will be no leaks come winter. The rooms and instruments allow us to research much more efficiently. We've already come up with new blueprints!"

"Really?" That was good news. I opened the Research Interface.

Research
Daily RP: 49.7 *Apprentice-ranked buildings:* • Magma Foundry: Enable magma casting. Cost: 200 RP. • Barracks Expansions:

- Second Floor: Adds 100 beds. Cost: 200 RP.
- Armory: Maintain soldiers' gear and increase its effectiveness. Cost: 120 RP.
- Arena. [Researched, built]
  - Beast Holding: Add cages for beasts. Cost: 150 RP.
- Trainer's Office I: Increase number of trainers by 2. Cost: 100 RP.
- Obstacle Course: Increase training speed by 20%. Cost: 300 RP.

Expert-ranked buildings:

- Essence Capacitor: Collects and stores ambient energy. Cost: 500 RP.
- Warlock Tower: Housing and training for magic users. Cost: 800 RP.
- War Machine Workshop: Heavy war machine factory. Cost: 800 RP.
- Improved Lodging: All residential buildings can accommodate +50% members. Cost: 1,000 RP.
- Cathedral: Place of worship. Cost: 1,000 RP.
- Dreamer's Lodge – Enchantment Workshop: Increase enchantment's efficiency. Cost: 1,000 RP.

"You can perform Expert-level research?" I asked, bewildered. "But Romil and Primla are only at their Apprentice skill rank."

Zuban frowned. "What's that got to do with it? It might take them longer than researching lower-ranked blueprints, but they can do it well enough."

"Great." I gave him the thumbs up. "Well, I'll leave you to your work." The researchers were already busy, so I decided to postpone the decision on the next research path when it would become relevant.

"Don't forget about the carpenter," he blurted out then hurriedly added, "Dread Totem."

Why is he in such a rush for a new bed?

<Well, he has this dashing new girlfriend, remember? I guess that as a scout, Ashlazaria doesn't mind roughing it, but I bet Zuban prefers their bouts to be in a more comfortable environment.>

I ... eh... hmm.

<Thinking about upgrading your own love shack, Boss?> Vic snickered.

I gave a mental shrug. *Furs are nice enough I guess, but a bed ... oh, you wouldn't get it; you spend your nights hanging from a coat rack.*

<That's true. It's pretty comfortable in my opinion. You should try it sometime.>

I think I prefer sticking with furs.

<See? You don't need a bed; it's all a matter of perspective.>

I ... ah ... Somehow, my purple companion managed to back me against the wall; I had no good comeback for that.

Kaedric was waiting for me as I exited the building.

"Kaedric! Good, please summon a carpenter as soon as we can afford it."

"Yes, my lord," he said, not breaking eye contact with me, giving me a sense of trepidation.

"What's up?"

He looked at me calmly and uttered five simple words. "The Mob Squad is back."

***

I sat on Tempest's back facing three weary-looking adventurers.

We were in the open forest clearing where I intercepted the players before reaching the settlement. My six hulking Infernal Ogres stood menacingly behind me, leering at the players.

The elvish-looking one, Misa, took a step forward. "I don't know what's going on, but this does not strike me as the proper way to greet the people who busted their asses for several days to fulfill your quest."

I didn't answer, but Tempest, sensing my emotions, growled at her, baring his teeth.

Misa rolled her eyes. "Okay, I'll bite. What is it this time?"

“Before you left,” I almost hissed the words. “Did one of you sabotage the lumber yard?”

“What?” she asked, stepping back, surprise plain on her face. “What are you talking about?”

“He’s high on power,” the yellow bugbear huffed, crossing his arms. “If you’re trying to get away from paying us ...”

I looked at the catlike one, Raystia. “Anything to add?”

She gulped. “Err ... I’m sorry, Mr. Totem Chief guy, I ... ahem ... don’t know what you're talking about.”

I looked at the three with narrowed eyes. My Sense Emotion ability would not work on players, but the bugbear looked angry, Misa something between angry and surprised, and Raystia just looked embarrassed. Same as always.

“Where’s the dwarf?” I scanned the immediate area. “He’s not with you and he has not spawned in the cemetery.”

“Going to pin the fall on him *again*, for something you can’t prove, *again*?” Fox sneered at me.

I was stumped. I knew the saboteur was almost certainly one of them, but I couldn’t tell who was lying. This time, Tempest’s unerring nose was of little help. ”Stand down,” I said to the Ogres around us.

They exchanged looks of disappointment. One scratched his armpit.

I sighed. “Go, train with Rhynorn.”

“Yes Drea-Ed To-Tem,” they answered boorishly and lumbered away.

I addressed the three players again. “Let’s hear it. You claim to have fulfilled your part, but the missing dwarf suggests otherwise.”

“You want the short version or the long one?” Misa asked.

“The long one.”

She shook her head. “Nah, I’m too tired for that. The short version is that we found a derelict temple at the coordinates you gave us. A ton of undead was there guarding the place. It was a close call, but we killed them and mopped up the boss. It was some sort of skeleton with his entrails still in his rib cage.”

Raystia shuddered at Misa’s words.

“And ...?” I prompted.

“That’s it.” Misa shrugged. “The boss was guarding the shrine. Your adept wanted to sacrifice Riley right away, but he didn’t want to respawn back here and have to wait for us to return. So he stayed behind. The undead are respawning slowly, so he farms them for XP. Your goblin priest has placed some sort of binding over the shrine to keep them away and prevent the boss from respawning. I just have to message Riley and he'll finish up the quest."

"Alright, go ahead."

Fox looked at me threateningly. "You better cough up everything you promised us afterward."

That guy sure had a short memory. I let my dagger hover out of my belt and point at him. He took my meaning and wisely lowered his eyes.

"Okay, I messaged him," Misa said. "Should be any moment now.

Outsourced Quest Completed: Dark Missionary

The Mob Squad members rewarded: 2,000 XP, 200 reputation with GreenPiece Clan, 200 gold

Misa Gavriilu rewarded: Leather greaves (magical)

Raystia rewarded: 40 X arrows (magic)

Riley Stonefist rewarded: Reinforced gloves (magical)

Fox rewarded: High steel shield (normal)

Quest Completed: Dark Missionary

You have successfully sanctified three places of power in the name of Nihilator.

Quest type: Advanced

Time remaining: 4 days

Reward: 250 Faith Points, +250 reputation with Nihilator, 5,000 XP

Clan reward: Zone Blessings now available for purchase in all newly sanctified locations.

Special reward: The three places of worship empower the central temple. Eternal Night effect increased by 100%.

Yes!

I could feel the Eternal Night around us becoming thicker. It didn't become darker, but the blessing's increased power felt almost like it was smoothly caressing my skin.

I drew in a tendril of information and reviewed the changes. All Shadow-Touched creatures received an additional ten percent increase to damage, max HP and MP, as well as an extra five percent efficiency for non-combat skills. Enemies now suffered 20 percent XP penalties and their MP and HP regen were further reduced.

It was unfortunate that the upkeep wasn't reduced any further. Still, the extra boost was incredible. I would have had to spend thousands of FP to purchase bonuses of similar value.

A smug smile spread across my face, and I experienced a feeling of magnanimity toward the troublesome players.

"Well, I see you're happy," Misa said dryly. "Glad you kept your word. I got a level from completing your quest, so I guess I ought to thank you."

"Me too!" Raystia chimed in merrily. "I'm really loving this place!"

"Hmmm," Fox grunted noncommittally. "I can afford better armor now."

"Shopping time!" Misa declared. "See you anon, Dread Totem."

I watched them head toward the settlement. Then I teleported to the cemetery.

I materialized behind the Dark Temple, standing in the narrow pathway between it and the valley's wall, where the single tombstone lay hidden.

"Holy hell, where the crap did you come from?" Riley, the dwarf, nearly jumped when he saw me coming out of the shadows.

"I see you completed the quest," I said, ignoring his question.

"Well, yeah," he said. "And it's the last time I'm willingly putting myself on an altar to be sacrificed. This is the stuff of nightmares, man. FIVR is no joke."

"I know you got a decent enough boon out of the experience."

"What boon? Your quest rewards are barely worth the experience, and the death debuff cost me nearly all the XP I earned by staying behind butchering skeletons."

"I'm not talking about *those* rewards." I looked at him pointedly.

The dwarf's hand reached over his heart as if on its own. "That's between me and the big guy."

I shrugged. "Suit yourself. In any case, I consider your debt settled."

"I didn't bloody kill your stupid goblins, goddammit!" he yelled. "How many times do I have to tell you that?"

"And I suppose you know nothing about the lumber yard incident?"

He gave me such a vacant-eyed stare that I forwent inquiring further. He wasn't the culprit either.

I waited until he disappeared behind the temple then teleported back to my house.

It was midday by now and I planned on taking the new recruits hunting the next day.

I sat at my table and took out one of the enchanted Viridium spheres and went to work.

***

Utility schema [Conduit] upgraded to [Inertia bead]

Finally!

After hours of trial and error, I had finally found the right rune combinations. The Conduit enchantment enabled the Viridium spheres to adhere to each other while holding the mana required to make them move. I added the Zu rune of motion I got from the old gremlin, then slapped on the Ko rune of strength, just because I had the room to include it – and a little extra strength is never a bad thing. I had two rune slots left, so I used the Mag rune of warding for the first time and connected it with the Esh rune, making the sphere highly resistant to fire. No one would be smelting this precious.

<*Aaaaand, now he refers to his shining metal balls as 'precious.'*> Vic chortled. <*I think it's time to find a new employer,*>

I didn't take the bait. "Just hold on."

I retrieved two of the other partially enchanted spheres and applied the new schema on them, taking a few minutes to make sure everything was aligned properly. Once I was done, I put the spheres on the ground.

<Well?>

"Watch this." I directed my thoughts at the spheres. They drew together and attached with a metallic click. The spheres rolled on top of each other like a snowman. With a mental command, the column rolled around the room, remaining upright.

Vic flowed off my shoulders. "Is that it?" He shook his head. "You already made them do that."

"Not so," I countered. "Before, I was actively directing them. I needed to use my mana to make them move as I wanted. Now, I just think 'up' or 'move' and they obey. I don't have to invest a single MP."

"So you got yourself a fancy kid's toy. What's the big deal?"

I didn't let his criticism bring me down. I could feel the tendrils of information assuring me I was on the right track. "Check this out. Analyze."

Viridium Bead Golem [Runecrafted]

Level: 3

HP: 37

Attributes: P: 3, M: -, S: -

Skills: Slam 13

Traits: Golem (enchantment immunity, nonliving, magic resistance, +25% HP), Metal Body (Viridium, ignore 20 damage)

Resistances: Armor 15, Magic 50%, Fire 93%

Stored Mana: 298/300

Description: This golem is a marvel of Runecraft ingenuity. Composed of separate self-propelling spheres, it can reshape itself freely to best accomplish its orders. The golem can run indefinitely, limited only by the amount of stored mana.

The golem cannot gain levels or skills; instead, its strength is determined by the number of spheres composing its body.

Each sphere adds: 1 level, 1 Physical, 5 armor, 100 mana capacity.

The golem's martial skill is always set at its max cap.

This golem lacks a central controlling unit and has to be controlled externally.

"Oh wow, that's pretty impressive for a pair of self-propelling balls," Vic said.

"There are three of them," I noted.

"Yeah, but the way I put it was funnier."

I grinned and ordered the golem to attack the wall. The upper part wound back, then slammed powerfully into the wooden wall, leaving a discernible dent.

"Damn straight, it's impressive," I said, and with a few mental clicks paid three EP to repair the damage. "And that's from just three pieces. I have 12 more."

Vic stared at me for a moment. "So it'll be a level 15 golem, not bad."

"That's just the start. Once I find more Viridium ..." I trailed off. "Think what kind of damage a golem with 200 spheres can do." I gave him a huge, shit-eating grin.

"That's actually not a half-bad plan, Boss."

"Thank you." Now that I had a working proof of concept, I could allow myself to be gracious.

"Wait a second, Boss, the description says you have to actively control this thing. It doesn't sound like a good idea during combat. You'll get distracted for sure."

"It shouldn't be too difficult, but I have a backup plan," I reassured him. "I still have to finish enchanting the rest of the spheres. But first ..." I sighed at the sight of the small pile of newly crafted weapons waiting for my attention. A working proof of concept would have to suffice for now. I had to finish enchanting the new weapons Kadoc had forged today. They would be needed for our hunt tomorrow.

I grabbed the first weapon and got to work.

***

The next day, I awoke to the chime of a new system message.

Quest Update: Unleash the Darkness

You have channeled 20% of the energy Nihilator requires to reach the next boss level and break the bonds that have kept him prisoner for centuries.

Progress: 20,003/100,000 EP

Bonus reward: +50 Faith Points

That was both good *and* bad. The fact that I had channeled twenty thousand energy to Nihilator was staggering. It had taken two months to reach this point, and with the vastly increased daily EP I had now, reaching a hundred percent wouldn't be too far off. Then I'd have to deal with an unleashed evil deity.

But that was a future me problem. Present me had oxsaurians to hunt.

Tika pouted when I went to say goodbye. "You're leaving again so soon?"

That was new.

"The warriors need the training; I have to go with them or they'll suffer casualties," I explained.

"At least you bother to say goodbye this time," she huffed. "Last time you just disappeared. I was alone for three days, not knowing where you were."

"Err, I'm ... sorry." This was definitely a new side of Tika.

She sniffed then embraced me tightly. "I'll miss you," she whispered in my ear. "Come back to me."

"I will," I answered clumsily, not sure how to handle this new aspect of her. It was out of character; she was acting weird, unusual, like ...

<Women, eh, Boss?>

Yeah.

***

My troops were waiting for me at the forest clearing before the valley's exit. Rhyno was standing there as well, twice the size of the hobs and a good head taller than the other Ogres. The gladiator was the only veteran soldier present. Last time I had to leave him behind, as he was best suited to handle any threats to the clan in my absence. Now I had 20 veterans, all above level 10, who could watch over the settlement, so I could bring him along for some good old power-leveling.

All the new recruits were present: three Ogres, 16 hobs, and three 'healer' adepts. A veritable army.

Bob stood there as well, though he wouldn't be coming with us. He was organizing the soldiers and handing out the sonic-enchanted weapons I'd made. We had enough to equip ten of the hobs. The Ogres still wielded tree trunks clubs. *That won't do for long*, I mused. I needed my heavy hitters to, well, hit hard.

"Bob."

"Yes, Dread Totem?"

"After we finish here, please instruct Kadoc to forge weapons for the Ogres. I think spiked cudgels would be best for them."

"Yes, Dread Totem."

Bob knew how to follow orders. He was an efficient lieutenant.

I formed up a war party and included the 22 newbies. With the progress I'd made in the last hunt, my War Party Leader skill was level 23. I could easily accommodate a group this size. I could even take in 11 more.

Wait a second … I stopped as a thought occurred to me. *If I include non-soldiers in the party, they should still get some percentage of the experience, even if they stay back in the valley.* If it worked, that could be an amazing way to level up my workers without having to waste precious energy.

I closed my eyes and reached out with my mind, looking for the tendrils of information of my most valued members. I added Zuban, Tika, Guba, and Vrick to the party. As an afterthought, I added the two smiths as well. The bottleneck of my mobilization efforts was the rate of arming my troops. A few levels would go a long way toward increasing my smith's productivity. I decided against including the builders. I couldn't accommodate them all anyway, and by now we were doing well on the building front. Instead, I added the two goblin researchers. After seeing the RP requirements of the Expert-ranked blueprints, they could also use a little extra boost.

I mounted Tempest and motioned to my troops. "Follow me."

***

We made good time crossing the forest to the oxsaurians' territory. The goblin adepts surprised me by keeping up with their longer-legged cousins. Though they couldn't run as fast as the hobs, the thick forest hindered them less than it did the tall warriors.

After a few hours, we came out of the shroud of darkness that surrounded the area around the valley. Stars appeared in open patches of the canopy above us. We marched on.

We made it to the edge of the forest at daybreak. I ordered my troops to make camp. The hobs' innate martial sense showed. In short order, a sleeping area was cleared, the fire was started, and sentries were posted.

That was when Kaedric contacted me with some good news. The builders had finished constructing the general workshop and three cabins. As our most pressing construction needs were met, I instructed my seneschal to use his own judgment for our next projects. The mandibled hob knew our priorities and had proven himself to be an efficient manager.

We slept the day away without incident. Very few things in the forest would dare attack a force as strong as ours. The oxsaurians beyond the tree line would be much less deferential.

Listen up. I used the Earring of the Warlord to communicate telepathically. I could have talked instead, but I wanted the soldiers to get used to receiving mental commands.

I'll lead the way, remain 20 meters behind me. I'll lure in a single enemy for you to kill. Melee fighters, attack the upper half of the creature. Scouts, shoot at the lower half. Adepts, alternate between Drilling Arrow and Drain Mana, but make sure to always stay above 50 percent, I want you to have enough for heals in case it's necessary. Everyone clear?

All the soldiers nodded except Rhynorn.

IS THAT CLEAR? I asked more forcefully, aiming my question at the Ogre boss. Rhyno bared his teeth in a growl but then thought better of it and reluctantly nodded. *Good boy. Let's go.*

I took the lead, riding Tempest on the open grassland. I kept scanning for oxsaurians but didn't see any herds.

We marched on for another hour, then, when we crested the next hill, I found what we were looking for.

Oxsaurians.

Hundreds of them.

A huge herd roamed below us, grazing. They appeared carefree and with good reason. With so many of them gathered together, they could trample even a party of high-level adventurers. They had nothing to fear from a bunch of low-level mobs.

"Shadow-crap," I whispered to myself and made Tempest crouch down, I didn't want *that* herd to notice us.

<*What now, Boss?*> Vicloak billowed softly behind me.

I crinkled my nose. *My mastiffs won't be able to lure away a lone bull with that many beasts. We could try to go around them and look for a smaller herd, but that might take hours.*

<*So ...?*>

I scanned the horizon, but no great solution came to mind. I shrugged and cast an empowered Shadow Hound. After I finished pouring the 440 MP into the spell, the shadows around us coalesced, transforming into eight level 14 shadow mastiffs. I ordered my troops to stay back, out of sight, and lay down on top of the hill, looking at the sea of monsters below.

With a mental command, the eight hounds lunged forward and charged. They hit the huge, armored beasts, biting and clawing, then continued running. Just as I feared, the tactic proved ineffective. Thirty bulls immediately gave chase, charging after my hounds. The rest of the oxsaurians raised their heads from their grazing for a moment then shrugged it off and resumed eating. Such small predators wouldn't be enough to rile them up. A particularly large ox was running down one of the mastiffs. The hound tried to break to the right, but the ox corrected course and rammed his horn into the center of the hound's body. To my surprise, crackles of white and black magic flared up along the horn, ripping the mastiff to black shreds.

The large ox turned around and trotted easily back to the herd, just at the edge of my Analyze skill.

Oxsaurian Alpha

Level: 60

HP: 642

Attributes: P: 56, M: -4, S: 4*Skills:* Unstoppable Charge 65, Thickskin 62

Traits: Magicless (no mana), Anti-Magical Attack.
Resistances: Armor 230, Fire 50%, Acid -50%

An alpha. The bastard was a good 20 levels above the standard oxsaurian and well outside my ability to influence with Dark Mana. I had to be careful not to draw its attention. Without the ability to freeze it, it could single-handedly butcher the lot of us.

I focused on its second trait, which none of the other beasts had.

Anti-Magical Attack

Attack ignores all types of magical immunities or protection, nullifying them on contact.

Does not negate non-magical armor.

No wonder that beast managed to destroy my mastiff. The damn thing was a mage killer.

That strengthened my initial observation. I didn't want the brute anywhere near us. Its horn would punch straight through my Mana Shield like it wasn't even there.

There had to be something else I could do.

"Oh hell," I murmured and pressed a hand to my forehead, expecting a headache. I knew how I could lure one in, but it was going to hurt.

I rolled to my back, stared at the sky, and exhaled steadily, trying not to think of the pain. I breathed in and out a few more times, slowing down my heart rate and calming myself.

I could feel the presence of my own shadow next to me. I concentrated on that presence, closed my eyes and slowly poured my mana into my shadow, transferring my consciousness along with it.

I opened my shadow clone's 'eyes' and saw the hilly territory spread below me. Once again, I was assaulted with a sense of vertigo and wrongness.

My sight was coming from the shadow clone next to me, but my other senses refused to align with that perception and screamed against the discrepancy. My head – my *real* head – started to throb painfully, but I forced my control deeper into the shadow.

I took a single step. I couldn't tell if it was my actual body that took it or the shadow one, but the next thing I felt was something wet splashing over my mouth.

The wetness broke my concentration, and I sat up with a start. As I feared, a splitting headache ensued, causing me to clutch at my face in agony.

What the hell? I thought dimly, touching the wetness on my lips. I withdrew my hand and looked at my fingers. They were covered in blood.

I shook my head, trying to reorient myself. A droplet of blood splattered on the ground. I took a closer look at the blood oozing down my fingers. *Where's it coming from? I didn't take any damage; my health bar is full ...*

<Err, Boss, you got a major nosebleed,> Vic said, almost sounding worried.

I pinched my nose, but the bleeding continued. "Grymel, heal me," I ordered one of the adepts.

The goblin came obediently and cast his healing magic. A soothing dark energy washed over me, reducing the pain, but my nose continued sprouting an alarming amount of blood.

Vic disengaged from my shoulder. "Here, Boss, let me try."

I looked up at the purple goblin. "You? What can you do? You're not a healer."

He shook his head. "You're not injured in the game." He sounded dead serious. "You overreached your limits. I warned you; you meat suits were not meant to handle such controls."

The loss of blood was making me feel woozy, and my headache made it hard to concentrate. "What do you intend to do, exactly?"

"I might be able to take the burden off your hands, so to speak. But you'll have to trust me. Do you trust me?"

My head was swimming at this point. I had little choice. "I trust you, Vic."

"Don't resist what I'm about to do, physically or mentally." Then he reached his hand to my face and plunged two fingers directly into my nose.

"What the fu–" I didn't manage to finish the sentence. Vic's fingers morphed *inside* my nostrils, and extended deeper, reaching my brain.

Instinctively I tried to jerk my head away, but I barely had any strength left at that point.

"Don't resist!" Vic hissed and I surrendered to his treatment.

His fingers dug deeper into my head. I could sense the digits changing their shape, breaking down into the raw energy they were composed of, then seeping further into my cranium. Surprisingly, I felt no pain.

Gradually, my headache subsided, and the flow of blood turned into a small drip. My mind came into focus, and I suddenly became aware of the surrealistic scene we were making: One goblin, sitting down in a pool of his own blood with another purple one's fingers stuck up his nose, while a crowd of gobs and Ogres gawked at them.

"All done," Vic finally said, withdrawing his fingers.

I pinched my bloated nose, trying to put it back into shape. "What did you just do?"

"You were holding the controls of your shadow clone and wouldn't let go." Vic casually wiped his bloody hands on my armor. "So I sort of reached into the part of your mind that was holding the reins and snatched it away. The strain was too much for your brain to handle. If I hadn't assumed control, you probably would have died."

A dozen questions sped through my mind. "But I would have respawned ... right?"

Vic gave me a stern look. It was an unfamiliar sight on his usually mocking visage. "I don't know. Maybe. Maybe not. Maybe you'll listen to me next time when I tell you your meat-suit brain can't handle something."

I shuddered, remembering the conversation I had with Tal a couple of months ago before I got trapped in the game. He'd warned me of just such an occurrence. The FIVR connection to the brain could have severe repercussions if things went sideways; Headaches, memory loss, and nightmares were just some of the symptoms a FIVR user could suffer. Heck, I could have probably suffered brain damage. The thought of becoming a living vegetable while remaining plugged into NEO was not a pleasant one.

I wiped the rest of the blood from my face and locked eyes with Vic. "What exactly did you mean by taking the reins?" A feeling of dread came over me as he grimaced at the question.

"Whoa, Boss, relax." Vic lifted both hands submissively. "Remember I asked your permission first? I got into the part of your mind that was still connected to the controls of the shadow clone and took it off for you. I couldn't have done so if you hadn't allowed me to. So don't lapse back again to your 'VI taking over your mind' paranoia. Besides, we're buddies, right?"

I steadied my breath and mulled over his words. It was clear to me, more than ever, that Vic and probably VIs in general were intelligent, living entities. A separate new life form. The fact that their 'bodies' were machine code was irrelevant. They each had the capacity to think for themselves, and the fact I had trusted one of them enough with access to my brain probably saved my life.

I looked back at Vic and communicated all my feelings – turmoil and gratitude – directly, speaking only two words out loud: "Thank you."

He grinned and waved it off. "Forget about it, Boss. Performing psychic surgery through someone's nostrils is no big deal. If I was living in your world, I'd be the greatest gynecologist in the world."

I stared at him for a second, shocked. Then I started to chuckle. A second later, Vic joined me. Our mirth grew into full-blown laughter. I tried answering Vic, but every time I did, a mental image of him in a doctor's gown holding a speculum came to mind and I couldn't stop laughing. I laughed until tears streamed down my face, washing the rest of the blood away.

"Oh my god!" I wiped the tears, finally calming down enough to speak. "That was your best one yet!"

"Thanks, Boss." Vic grinned. "I try." Then he grew sober. "And just to make it clear, I do appreciate you acknowledging that my brothers and me are more than just gaming tools.

+1000 reputation with Vic (The Awesome Companion)

New rank: Respected

Points to next rank: 3,500

"So you respect me now, eh?" I asked with a small smile.

"Your weak meat-suit brain doesn't retain memories very well, eh? I told you before, those are just numbers the game throws at you. I simply translate them."

His disrespectful attitude made it abundantly clear. "Yeah, yeah, I remember."

"I know you do, Boss, I'm just messing with you."

"Asshole," I muttered.

He bowed. "At your service."

I looked at the hundreds of oxsaurians grazing peacefully below us. "Damn it, I guess we have to go look for a smaller herd now."

"What did you want to do with the shadow clone anyway?" my soul companion asked.

"I thought of sending it down there. Once it got within range, I should have been able to cast Dominate through it and get one of the bulls to come to us. The rest of the herd wouldn't get riled if one of them left on his own."

"Hmm, that's actually not a bad plan, Boss. The only downside is that you can't steer your shadow wagon well enough."

"Yes, I noticed," I said dryly.

"But I can."

I gave him a sharp look. "How?"

"Like I did just now. Only to accomplish what you want ..." His fingers morphed into two spinning drills with cruel-looking barbs. "... I'll have to go a little deeper."

I took a step back. "Oh, hell no. You can't be serious!"

He gave me a shit-eating grin. "You're right, I'm not. But your expression just now? Priceless."

I rolled my eyes.

"Don't worry, Boss, I've already made the connection with your shadow clone controls. With your permission, I can operate it for you. I just need to be in physical contact with you to do it." He morphed into his cloak form, using tendrils to wrap himself around my shoulders. *<This'll do.>*

"What's next?"

<Start putting mana into your shadow, but allow me to take over instead of pouring in your awareness.>

"I'll try."

I did as Vic instructed. I felt his consciousness brush against mine once I had put enough MP into my shadow, and I let him through.

My shadow grew, transforming into a three-dimensional copy of myself.

"Alright, I'm in."

I cringed a little at hearing Vic's muffled voice coming out of my own clone.

He turned away and moved down the hill. The shadow clone blended perfectly with the night's darkness. Without my abilities as a Shadow-Touched creature, I would not have spotted him.

The oxsaurians didn't.

<I'm ready,> he said once he got within range. *<Channel dominate through me. It should be easy.>*

It was. I gathered and shaped my mana, then sent it to Vic. My companion intercepted the power and channeled it on, into the closest cow.

It worked!

Sensing the oxsaurian mind, I instructed it to climb the hill toward me. The level 41 beast readily obeyed, leaving its herd behind. Its friends didn't seem to care.

I ordered the dominated cow to trot to my waiting troops, then I released the domination effect and froze it.

Everyone, attack!

I diverted my attention back to the herd below as my soldiers fell upon the helpless cow. With Vic's help, I dominated another oxsaurian. The second beast, a level 40 one, trotted up the hill toward me.

We approached my troops who were happily hammering against the frozen cow.

My mana reserve was at half. Casting dominate through my shadow clone was taxing; even though it was nearby, the spell took half again as much mana than normal.

I watched for several minutes as my troops chiseled away at the armored beast. The hobs were only level 4 with low combat skills. Even with the enchanted weapons, the level gap was mitigating most of the damage. Even the Ogres were barely making a dent in the beast's tough hide. They slammed their tree-trunk clubs at it, doing only a handful of damage points. Rhynorn stepped in, wielding one of his enchanted Stalker Pins and thrust it like a spear. The weapon pierced the oxsaurian's armor, and though he was less than half the beast's level, Rhyno's attack inflicted 40 points of damage.

With my unruly Ogre gladiator's help, the troops made short work of the first beast and took it down in just a few more minutes.

Tendrils of information swirled around my soldiers, but to my surprise, only several of them heralded a level up. Frowning, I delved deeper into the metadata, trying to figure out what went wrong. I found the answer quickly enough.

Similar to what happened in the first hunt, Rhyno's overwhelming damage output awarded him the majority of the experience. The rest of my troops received just a few hundred XP each, which was only enough to level up the goblin adepts. Even Rhyno didn't level. At level 16, the 2,000 XP he gained wasn't enough to push him over into 17. We had to try something else.

Rhyno, I thought to him, *you may only attack each oxsaurian once, so make it count.*

The brute looked up at me, chewing his own teeth in annoyance. Yeah, he got the message.

I ordered the second oxsaurian to move toward my eager soldiers like a sheep to the slaughter. A big, armor-plated, spiked lamb. I released the domination and froze it.

Rhyno heaved a Stalker Pin at the beast, embedding it deep in its side. Then he stepped back and looked at the other Ogres in resentment as they bashed at the huge beast, chipping away its HP. It took the soldiers 30 minutes to down the second beast, much longer than the first. Still, it was quicker than the previous hunting trip. The dozen soldiers who were carrying my Runecrafted weapons proved their effectiveness.

Once the second beast was down, the hobs and the adepts got a level up. The Infernal Ogres were 90 percent through to the next level. With 23 soldiers, each one got a smaller share than those in the previous hunting group. But this was offset by their ability to fell the beasts more quickly.

I sent Vic down the hill for the second time and we repeated our bull 'fishing' method.

We repeated this pattern through most of the night. By the time the sky started clearing, the bodies of a dozen oxsaurians dotted the ground.

I instructed my war party to stop. “That’s enough for now.”

I reviewed my soldiers’ progress with satisfaction. The 14 hobs had all reached level 14, the three Infernal Ogres were level 16, the adepts were 12, and Rhyno made it to 19.

“Everyone, load up the meat and skins,” I ordered.

While the troops kept themselves busy collecting the hundreds of units of raw meat, I turned my attention back to the herd. “Let’s get a few more, Vic. It’s my turn.”

“Sure thing, Boss.”

We repeated our tactic and lured in two more oxsaurians. I promptly froze each one and sacrificed them.

Level up! You have reached Character Level 33. You have 1 ability point to allocate.

A few more hundred units of food for my rapidly growing army. Excellent.

“Let’s do that again.”

The next two bulls made their way up to us. I froze and sacrificed the first one and was about to do the same with the second when Vic’s voice sounded in my mind.

<Hey, Boss, we have a problem here.>

What’s wrong?

<The alpha is coming. I think he’s noticed our actions.>

Shadow-crap!

I checked the area below and saw that Vic was right. The level 60 beast was walking toward us, scanning his surroundings. *Damn, he’s noticed us!*

<Your powers of observation are a wonder to behold, Boss.>

I estimated we had a minute before the alpha crested the hill and found us.

Everyone. We’re leaving! Leave the meat and run!

I jumped on Tempest's back. Vic reached me and stretched toward my shoulders, assuming his Vicloak shape. I nudged the demon wolf, and he leapt forward, easily overtaking the jogging soldiers.

I gathered my mana and cast Shadow Hounds as we ran. Once the four mastiffs formed, I sent them back to the corpse-covered ground.

The alpha made it there first. It saw the bodies of its packmates and bellowed a roar, pawing at the ground. One of my mastiffs reached the beast and pounced on him. I commanded the hounds to scatter back and away from us, and luckily the alpha took the bait and gave chase.

We made it back to the tree line and the comfortable darkness under the thick foliage just as the sun started shining.

We camped at the same location as before, where the soldiers fell down to sleep, exhausted from a day of fighting.

When the sun was casting its last rays of light, we broke camp and made our way back to Goblin's Gorge.

29 – Undermining

We made it back to the clan at the break of dawn. I ordered the troops to the barracks to rest and made my way to my own house.

As I rode Tempest through the settlement, I accessed the 'Population' tab and checked on the workers I'd added to the war party. I grinned when I saw the information. It worked! All my workers had gained a few levels. Zuban and Vrick were now level 10, Tika and Guba were level 8, and the two smiths were level 7. Though none of them had participated in the raid, they still got a small share of the XP, enough to skyrocket their relatively low levels and their work skill caps. The experiment was a success. I'd found a new way to increase the power of my clan and speed up the settlement's development.

There was a surprise waiting for me when I got back to my house. Tika was drowsing on a bed. An actual, goblin king-sized bed!

That's right, I did tell Kaedric to summon a carpenter, I recalled.

I got out of my brand-new, still spotless, Pyrolith scale gambeson and climbed into bed next to my beautiful huntress.

Still sleeping, Tika moved her body, pressing against me.

I smiled. It was good to be chief.

***

I was awakened by the racket of shouting.

"I don't be giving a bleeding rat's ass! He has to know." Guba's shrill voice was instantly recognizable.

"I'm afraid he is otherwise indisposed." Kaedric's dispassionate voice was firm.

I regretfully got out of bed. I'd almost forgotten what it was like to spend the night in an actual bed instead of furs on the floor. I had slept like a baby.

I opened the door. "Why are you shouting?"

Guba seethed. "There be theft and treachery!"

I rubbed my eyes. "Huh?"

"Someone snuck in ter the warehouse and stole me entire vat of liquid fire!"

That shook me wide awake. "Huh?"

Kaedric gave the disgruntled elderly goblinette a reproachful look. "Why did you not come to me immediately?"

"I don't trust yer kind," she said bluntly. "Hobs be hobs be hobs. This is a matter fer the chief!"

I dimly remembered Guba telling me liquid fire was used for crafting grenades and traps. "Someone stole a whole vat of liquid fire?"

"Aye!" Guba answered sharply. "It be nearly 20 liters. Took me a month to gather all them ingredients"

"Damn it!" I bristled. Someone had it in for my clan and me. First the murder of the two lumberjacks, then the sabotage at the lumber yard, and now this. "I want to know who's responsible!"

My seneschal's eyes became distant. After a moment, he shook his head. "Our patrols have encountered no suspicious activity throughout the night, my lord."

I gritted my teeth. "I thought you stationed guards at the warehouse."

"Only to guard the shop while it was stationed there. Once Gazlan moved his wares to the marketplace, there was no need to maintain their presence."

"From now on, I want two guards stationed *inside* the warehouse at all times," I ordered.

"It is uncustomary, but I shall relay your orders, my lord."

His remark was understandable. NPC guards were usually stationed to guard an entrance. But that only made it easy for rogue-type players; once they gained entry, usually through a window or basement, they had free rein of the place.

"Which of the travelers were present during the night?"

It was now always night in the valley, but Kaedric took my meaning. "Our patrols have encountered Raystia, Riley Stonefist, Nero SantoDrago, and Sullivan Tucker."

Again, Riley's name came up. *He wouldn't be so dumb as to pull another stunt after how he had to atone for his last transgression, right?* I frowned. I didn't know for sure. "Who's Sullivan Tucker?"

"It is the one who spoke up against you before you completed the Dark Temple and unleashed Eternal Darkness."

He was the player I'd jokingly thought to award with a gift for helping me make my point to the others. I guessed he was a plausible suspect. He sounded like he had issues.

I had a sudden inspiration. "Who of the four travelers was present in the valley during the previous incidents?"

Kaedric bowed his head respectfully. "I should have thought of this myself, my lord. Three of the four were present on all other occasions. Nero was the only one who was absent."

I exhaled a sigh of relief. Out of the four, I really didn't want that one-man army guy to be against me, especially not when he was playing a pivotal role in training up my soldiers.

It was good intel, adding a piece to the puzzle, though I couldn't act upon it alone. The information was unreliable. Kaedric's knowledge only extended to the individuals my troops had encountered while patrolling. They could have easily missed the real culprit.

"Okay, I want a scout following each of the three travelers at all times. On second thought, make it two scouts. Make sure they keep their eyes and noses open." I had 16 of the specialized hobs and could easily afford the manpower. Stealth was an integral part of their position, which made them most suited for the job.

"Yes, my lord."

"Well, I guess it be good you taking this seriously," Guba grunted. "Ye should find the culprit and slit 'em throat. They can be doing a lot of damage with all that liquid fire."

That made my blood freeze. I saw my entire settlement ablaze in my mind's eye. I turned back to Kaedric. "Tell Bob to have all of our troops comb the valley for that vat."

"Shouldn't be too hard," Guba said. "The thing's odor can blind a bat, even them nose-plugged hobs can smell it; just be looking fer a whiff of sulfur."

I nodded. "That helps. You got that?" I asked Kaedric.

"Yes, my lord. I shall inform Borbarabsus immediately."

"Good."

The two walked away, leaving me alone with my thoughts.

This was the third act of sabotage against my clan. Someone clearly had it out for me, but I had no idea why. The new players should have all been thrilled to aid us. The abundance of quests my clan offered was a quick and easy path to wealth and power. I couldn't understand what someone could gain by deliberately hampering our efforts.

I briefly contemplated the possibility of Vatras planting a spy in our midst, but I shook my head. It was extremely unlikely. Players that had the required mental capacity to play as monsters were scarce, and those that came to my clan were randomly selected by the company. Vatras would have no way of inserting his own man into my clan.

For now, I'd done what I could to find the culprit and ensure it wouldn't happen again. I had other priorities and couldn't lose any more time on speculation. If Tal's information was correct, I had about two weeks before the first wave of attackers reached us. I had to be ready for them.

I needed more soldiers.

I opened the Warehouse Interface and reviewed our available food stock.

- 366 raw meat
- 93 raw fish
- 160 gathered edibles
- 12 gathered ingredients
- 252 mushrooms
- 9 purple salt
- 2 magmashrooms

I grimaced. The oxsaurian alpha attack had forced us to retreat before we could gather all the meat from the cows we'd killed. There were probably over a thousand units of raw meat, but we had only managed to bring 200 back. The amount of food available would barely be enough to summon a handful of new troops, especially when I factored in the mortality rate of the naming ceremony.

I decided not to strain our food stocks for now. I needed to be able to summon new workers should the need arise, and I wanted as many soldiers as possible for the next hunting trip. It would be the last one before the attackers arrived.

Looks like I have some time on my hands for enchanting and investing in my own training. I'd been postponing it long enough.

With a flick of my mind, I pulled up my combat skills information.

- Dark Mana 44 (0%) Ⓑ
- Drilling Arrow 26 (95%) Ⓑ
- Mana Shield 27 (0%)
- Blood Wrath 31 (0%)
- Heal Followers 11 (0%)
- Mana Drain 10 (92%) Ⓑ
- Shadow Web 20 (90%)
- Shadow Hound 22(0%)
- Shadow Teleport 13 (50%)
- Dark Protection 6 (0%)

My all-important Dark Mana skill was two points short of its maximum cap. It had risen nicely thanks to the rapid leveling I'd done lately.

That was not really a problem.

I closed my eyes, envisioning the dark area below the Ogre fort. I had claimed that place in the name of Nihilator, so I could use my Faith Rank 4 bonus to teleport there. With a flash of shadows, I appeared, standing next to Grymel, the adept who maintained the shrine.

The adept's eyes were closed as he stood, holding the unholy shrine with both hands. Two large, Shadow-Touched mastiffs stood on either side of him, silent guardians, a present from Nihilator.

I moved to stand in front of the goblin adept and put my hands on the shrine's bone-covered surface. I closed my eyes, giving myself away to the thrumming sensation of dark power.

Dark Mana skill level increased to 46.

It felt like no more than a few moments, but when I checked my built-in clock, I found that half the day had passed. Raising the skill this way took more time as its level rose. Still, it was quicker than the 'normal' method. I was now five skill points short of reaching the Expert rank. *Then things will get real interesting,* I thought with a smile.

My other combat skills, namely Drilling Arrow, weren't as highly trained. I could spend the next two weeks hunting nonstop, continually looking for tougher opponents to build it up, but decided against it. Drilling arrows had become my secondary attack option anyway. It was much more efficient to freeze and sacrifice my enemies. Nowadays, I only used the arrows to damage those that were immune to my influence. As my control of Dark Mana grew, developing the arrows became less pressing.

There was another ability I was much keener to develop. Shadow Clone had proven its usefulness and versatility, but the impact it had on my mind was severe. I couldn't use it without Vic's aid. Yet.

I stepped away from the shrine and sat on the ground. The closeness of the shrine might help me control my clone better.

<Err, Boss, what'cha doing?> Vic chimed in my mind.

Isn't it obvious? I need to learn how to control my clone.

<I thought the last attempt would have convinced you to not try that on your own again.>

I have to try, Vic. I need to use every edge to make my way out of here, you know that. Don't worry; I'll start slowly.

<More likely you'll give yourself an aneurysm,> Vic said. *<Alright, I'll help you.>*

You will? I shot a smidge of sarcasm back to him. *Well, I guess it's in your best interests to help me since I'm the conduit that allows you to take physical form and can help you with your quest.*

<Well, there's that, of course, but even more important – if my favorite meat-suit companion dies, who's going to carry me around everywhere? I've gotten used to riding your shoulders. I'd hate to have to start walking all on my own again.>

I shook my head. That lazy bastard.

<So here's what you do,> Vic went on. *<I want you to empty your mind. You know, emptier than it usually is.>*

Ha ha, I thought back dryly. But I did as he said. I sat down, assuming the lotus position, and started practicing my breathing technique for relaxation, slowly clearing my mind of stray thoughts.

<Good. Now, I want you to sort of feel your entire body all at once. Like your skin is a piece of cloth you wear tightly around yourself.>

That was an odd way of putting it, but I did as he suggested. It wasn't an unfamiliar technique. I spread my thoughts over my body, starting at my toes, then moving my awareness like a flashlight's beam along my body until it reached my head. I breathed in the sensation of my entire body alight, feeling every muscle and joint at once.

<Now condense your awareness into your eyes. Visualize your entire presence projected from your eyes. Your body is only a shell that contains them.>

Though this part sounded weird, Vic's ability to sense my innermost thoughts and feelings made him an excellent coach. I did as he said and was rewarded with a feeling of lightness as I pictured my entire sense of self engulfed by my eyes.

<Your eyes are free from the rest of your body. Withdraw them inside.>

I instinctively knew what he meant. My body had become nothing more than a hollowed shell. My real self was perched on the windows that were my eye sockets. I drew myself into my body, watching as the windows to the outside became distant. My eyes descended into a hugging darkness that was the inside of my own body. I came to rest at the center of my being, surrounded by a protective shell made of my own physical body. The darkness was unlike my manifested power; it was warm and cozy, like being inside a womb. I was comfortable, secure, safe.

<Now, try to summon your clone.>

This part was more difficult. I started to channel my mana, but the sudden rush of power nearly broke my sense of serenity. I let go and concentrated on soothing my turmoil. I tried again, slowly, siphoning a single mana point at a time. I managed to maintain the sense of tranquility while gradually channeling mana into my shadow.

I didn't know how much time had passed, but I eventually felt my shadow rising up, claiming its three-dimensional presence, and my mind rushed in to fill it.

Unlike the previous times I had tried using this power, it felt different now. The awareness I kept tucked deep inside my body was a faint whisper, and I was able to perceive the full sensations of my new cloned body.

I stared in awe at my arms. They were condensed ethereal black, darkness made substantial. I looked down at my real body, sitting peacefully in the lotus position. I could still sense it, but this time the feedback was light and didn't evoke the feeling of confused duality.

Elated, I flexed my muscles. This felt great! Like I could do anything. I walked my new cloned body to the wall and effortlessly scaled it, gravity no longer an issue.

The experiment was going well. My mana was slowly trickling down, fueling the magical body with the energy it required to move. Next, I summoned my drilling arrows. They appeared out of thin air, as always, though the mana cost had increased by 50 percent. This was not really a problem. The spell was cheap, even with the penalty, and my high mana regeneration was already filling my mana bar, outpacing the rate it was draining.

Looking down at my real body again, I frowned. "This is not ideal, my body is defenseless this way." My voice sounded like a hoarse, distant echo.

<That's just the first step, Boss. You have successfully manifested your clone for the first time. You should rehearse it a few more times before trying to control your physical body simultaneously.>

After my nose hemorrhage last time, I was readily willing to take the slow approach. *I'll do that. Thanks, Vic.*

It was the end of the day already. I had spent hours meditating in the dark, underground chamber.

Not lingering to bid Grymel goodbye, I teleported back to Goblin's Gorge.

"My lord," a voice came from behind me.

I turned around. Somehow, my seneschal was waiting for me. "Kaedric?"

"The soldiers have scanned the entire clan and the surrounding forest, I even employed your sharp-nosed mount. They have not found the stolen liquid fire nor have they detected any sulfuric odors."

"Shadow-crap. That means there's someone hostile around here with the capacity to set fire to our entire village."

"Perhaps not the *entire* village, but it might be prudent to triple the patrols inside the settlement, my lord. If someone should try to set the buildings ablaze, he would not be able to hide his actions. As soon as they try to pour the liquid fire, our patrols will detect and engage them. This should reduce the potential for large-scale damage substantially, even if not negating it altogether."

I preferred being more proactive, but it didn't look like I had another choice. With our increased numbers, tripling the patrols still allowed half my troops to get their training time in the barracks.

"Do it."

***

I didn't bother leaving my house the next morning and simply teleported back to the Ogre fort. The quiet and deep sense of dark power greatly increased my ability to concentrate. I spent the rest of the day repeating the same technique Vic had taught me over and over. By the end of the day, my Dark Mana progressed significantly toward the next level and I was able to fully assume control of my clone within a minute. This was a huge improvement, but still not enough to be usable in a combat situation. I had a lot more training to do.

***

The next day, I decided to set my personal training aside and check on the clan's development. A lot had happened in the last several days.

Naturally, Kaedric was waiting for me when I exited my house. I stopped dead in my tracks when I first saw him. He looked better than usual ... healthier, less gaunt.

"Are you ... alright?" I asked.

"I am well, my lord. Thank you for asking."

I accessed his character sheet. He had an active buff called 'Psionically Well-Fed,' which strengthened his telepathic abilities.

"You ... didn't eat any of our clan members, did you?" I asked haltingly, dreading the answer.

"Of course not, my lord."

That was good enough for me. I didn't want the gory details, anyway.

We walked together through the settlement, reviewing our progress, and I familiarized myself with the new features. Kadoc and Baja, our two specialist smiths, had found their rhythm and were producing arms and armor for my growing army like a well-oiled machine. A small pile of equipment had accumulated for me to enchant. Vrick did his part as well, producing leather armor for the scouts and giving a hand to the others when needed.

We went into the research center and had a chat with Romil and Primla. The two goblinettes had advanced their skills and were producing nearly 50 RP a day. They had even completed researching the armory extension for the barracks and the magma foundry in my absence.

"As a matter of fact, my lord," Kaedric noted, "I was about to assign them to research the barracks' trainers' office next. I believe researching the second floor would be premature at this time, as the barracks' existing capacity exceeds our current needs."

"Good thinking." Now that we had a proper research center, new Expert-level blueprints became available for research. I really wanted the Dreamer's Lodge; the enchantment workshop would doubtlessly increase my enchantments' strength, but it cost a whopping 1,000 RP and there were other limiting factors besides that. "I guess there's no sense in researching higher-tiered blueprints just yet; Zuban is a long way from his Expert rank, after all."

"That is the recommended proficiency rank, but it is not mandatory, my lord," Kaedric said.

I looked at him with a raised brow.

"Zuban may still construct higher-tiered buildings," my mandibled seneschal explained stoically. "As long as they are no more than one tier higher than his own rank. The process will be slower than usual, true, but quite doable."

"Interesting ..." There were some nice Expert-ranked blueprints available for research, but as much as I wanted to, I couldn't have my researchers bogged down on an insanely complex project. I needed them working on things that would be usable for my clan *now*. After we'd dealt with the players, we could take our time with grander, more leisurely projects.

"Research the barracks' obstacle course next," I instructed the two researchers. "Then the trainers' office, then ..." Once they finished those two, there weren't many options left at Apprentice rank. "Then we'll see," I finished.

Both female goblins lowered their heads. "Yes, Dread Totem."

That should keep them occupied for a good while.

We continued touring the clan and Kaedric led me to a new structure next to our farms.

"What the hell is that?" I looked at the half-circle of thick wood logs anchored against the cliff wall. The logs were reinforced with a stone base and had thick metal bars for the gate. It reminded me of an elephant enclosure I had once seen at the zoo, though smaller.

"That is an animal pen, my lord." Kaedric's mandibles twitched as if stating the obvious. "As you advised me to use my discretion, I instructed Zuban to build it."

"But we don't have any livestock!" I protested.

"And we never will unless we have a place to put them first," he pointed out. "Now that we have this constructed, we can bring in some animals."

"From where?"

His mandibles twitched harder. "We can attempt to buy or capture them."

<Heh, he forgot to end that one with 'my lord,'> Vic chuckled.

"I see your point," I conceded. "I'll keep my eyes open for livestock."

"Very good, my lord."

<Aaand, there it is.>

We circled back toward the industrial area, and I saw two new slices had been added to the pie-shaped cluster of workshops. One of the new buildings was made almost entirely of stone and had thick glass windows.

"What is that?"

"Our new chemist lab, my lord. Guba has been quite ecstatic and already started experimenting with items to increase our combat readiness."

I examined the thick walls. "That must have taken a lot of stone."

"Indeed, 50 to be exact. Incidentally, we're out of construction-grade stone at the moment."

"What?" I turned sharply to look at him.

"I was planning to build the magma foundry next to address our growing need for stone."

At least he had a solution in mind before committing the better part of our stones to a relatively low-priority structure.

"Alright, I guess we'll need a new goblin worker to operate it as well."

"Yes, my lord. And exactly 133 units of lumber to exchange for the required construction materials."

I grimaced at the expense, but we had already built a stock of nearly triple that amount. The players had been a huge help in that regard. "Very well."

The other new wedge-shaped building was the general workshop. Our new carpenter was inside, busily working on what looked like a long bench. Next to him, was Harvey the fletcher and Bosper the bowyer, each working on their own workbench.

"As you can see, the general workshop is quite popular among our workers," Kaedric said. I am pleased to report their overall efficiency has increased by ten percent."

"That's good." I nodded appreciatively. "You really pushed forward the clan's development while I was away." I grinned. "I should go hunting more often."

Kaedric bowed his head. "Thank you, my lord, but I cannot take all the credit. Zuban trained his builders well. With two six-worker teams, they can now build at a rate of 250 BP per day."

"That is impressive, but all the build points in the world won't mean much without proper guidance. I think you have proved your ability to manage the settlement development. From now on, you'll handle that aspect. I might change the priorities from time to time, but other than that, do what you think is best."

His eyes widened and his lower mandibles dropped at my announcement. He quickly composed himself and bowed deeply. "I shall do my best not to disappoint. I thank you for the opportunity, my lord."

I waved it off. "Don't mention it. Actually, you're taking a weight off my shoulders, so in a way, it is me who should be thanking *you*." I winked at him. The stoic hobgoblin didn't wink back. "Well if that's all, I think I'll get back to my house. I have a lot of enchanting to do." I grimaced at the thought of the pile of weapons and armor waiting for me.

"Actually, my lord, the tournament is about to begin."

I cocked my head. "What tournament?"

"The arena fight, of course. Rhynorn issued a general quest, challenging the newcomers to defeat him in the arena. Per the protocol, they must defeat the lower-ranked challengers first. Will you retire to your house now?"

"Oh, hell no." I headed for the barracks. "I want to see this."

30 – Arena Fight

We went through the barracks' gates into the courtyard. The circular benches were filled with the off-duty soldiers and over a dozen players. I took a seat and looked down at the pit.

A team of three players was standing on one end. They held simple weapons and were clad in basic armor. I recognized one of them – Tenchi Wakazashi, the half-snake player. Using Analyze I saw they were levels 9, 10 and 12.

On the opposite end stood three of my soldiers, all level 14: two metal-clad warriors – one with a sword, the other with a shield and axe – and a scout in leather with a bow slung around his shoulders.

Bob moved toward the pit's edge and announced the upcoming battle with his booming voice: "The Cringers will now face their first challenge, a hobgoblin squad. Fight!"

The players rushed at the soldiers almost before my lieutenant had finished speaking. They were low-level and lacked equipment, but as players, they had the advantage of skills.

The scout rained arrows on the charging players. The shield bearer took a step forward, protecting himself and the sword bearer who flanked him, readying his weapon.

Holding two knives, Tenchi arrived first. His weapons clanged against the hob's shield, followed by a tail slap and a taunt. He was trying to draw the tank away from the scout. Unfortunately for him, I had taken special care to prepare my troops for such tactics. The shield bearer shrugged off the taunt and maintained his position. The other two players had expected an opening to charge in and were caught off guard. If they charged now, their flanks would be vulnerable to the alert warriors.

The scout continued taking a toll on the players' health, draining it one arrow at a time. The sword-wielding hob took the opportunity to slash at Tenchi and scored a deep cut. The players were unprepared for this development and it became clear they were at a disadvantage; my troops had full control of this fight. The three stepped back and forfeited the fight.

"The Cringers lose!" Bob declared. There were some snickers from the crowd. "Next team, The Mob Squad."

I inched forward in my seat as three other players entered the pit: Misa, Riley, and Fox. Raystia was not with them. Players couldn't all be expected to be present at the same time. One of the downsides of playing at in accelerated time was that a bathroom break in real life could take several hours in NEO.

The Mob Squad were all level 14 and much better geared than the team before them. Some of their equipment even surpassed that of my own troops.

As the fight started, Fox, their bugbear tank, faced off against the shield-bearing hob. Misa took cover behind him, trying to hide from the scout's arrows. Riley tried to flank the hob tank, but the sword wielder moved to engage him. To my surprise, Misa stepped out from behind her cover and launched a metal chain at them. The chain wrapped around the legs of the sword wielder, then she *pulled.*

The hob fell, his legs bound. Riley charged forward and bashed him with a heavy hammer strike. The hob tank tried to intervene, but that gave Fox an opening. He lunged forward with a shield bash, hurling the hob to the ground. The scout was quick to take advantage and peppered Fox with two arrows, but he simply ignored the hits. A moment later, the dwarf waved his hand and Fox's wounds closed. With two hobs prone, it was easy for the players to pound them into a pulp, causing them to lose consciousness. The arena prevented death by making them pass out instead. The scout was left alone, though he never stopped shooting arrows. Fox looked like a pincushion by that point, but with Riley constantly healing him, his health bar was mostly full. The scout went down quickly after that.

"The Mob Squad wins the first challenge!" Bob announced.

That was an interesting display of combat prowess. Misa's maneuver explained her unusual 'Chainmaster' skill.

"Bollox, no XP," I heard her complain. "I hoped it would be different when fighting mobs."

"The second challenge will start momentarily!" Bob boomed.

Three other hobs entered the arena. Blemtoff was instantly identifiable by his signature double battleaxes. Behind him came Bunker, one of the goblin adepts.

Their forces were evenly matched. Both Riley and Bunker continually healed their team members as they got injured, and Fox was just barely managing to tank the two warriors. It ended abruptly when Misa managed to sneak past the hob warriors and ensnare the adept with her chain. Without the goblin's healing, the battle soon ended. The two hobs succumbed to the many wounds they sustained.

"The Mob Squad wins the second challenge!" Bob stated. "The third challenge will start momentarily. Should the travelers win, they will earn the privilege of challenging the arena champion, Rhynorn Bloodore!"

The next group of soldiers walked in: Ryker, Kilpi, Yulli, and Zia – our elites. Following them came one of the Infernal Ogres.

"Oh, hell no, you gotta be kidding me," Riley said. "How are we supposed to take on five fighters?"

Fox eyed the Ogre with a calculating look. "We might be able to take them if we had Raystia with us, but without her, we don't stand a chance."

"Oh, bloody hell." Misa rolled her eyes and lifted her hands to her mouth. "We forfeit!"

"The Mob Squad has forfeited!" Bob said. "That concludes the group matches. The singles challenges are next."

Over the next hour, I watched with fascination as player after player entered the arena to challenge my soldiers. Most of the players were nearing level 10, with the highest at level 17. Some had decent equipment, though most carried only crude weapons. My soldiers made me proud. One by one, they defeated all the players. Their superior equipment and higher level gave them a decisive advantage. Some of the players won a few fights. The level 17 one even made it to the third match but got his ass handed to him by an Infernal Ogre.

I felt a surge of pride welling up in me. All my hard work had paid off. My soldiers were tough and experienced and could handle themselves well against players. That made me feel better about our chances for the coming attack. *I should remember to thank Nero for his help in shaping them into such an effective force.* For some reason, Nero was not one of the challengers.

"Are there any more who wish to fight?" Bob called out.

No one answered.

"In that case, I declare the tournament is over –"

"Hey, wait up! I want in!" Malkyr came running into the courtyard.

The big man was red in the face, but he was grinning his boyish grin. "Hey, guys! I'll take a shot at the belt, sign me in." On his back, he carried the Runecrafted axe I had gifted him.

Unsurprisingly, the level 26 player cut through all of my soldiers with ease. The last fight had him facing Bob himself, whose level 16 was the highest of my soldiers, accompanied by Bek.

"Hey, little buddy!" Malkyr grinned at the small goblin, who inclined his head politely in return. "Sorry if I have to hit you. It's just for sport, right?"

"Big man not worry for Bek," the goblin said boldly. "Worry for you. Bek not heal this time."

Malkyr chuckled. "Fair enough."

"We begin," Bob said, brandishing his sword with his left hand. Coiled vines snaked around his right arm.

This fight was much more interesting. Despite being stronger than his opponents, my big player friend had a rough time. From the start, Bob had him entangled with vines, limiting the force of his swings. Bek kept healing the hob lieutenant, negating most of the damage Malkyr inflicted, while occasionally shooting drilling arrows, or draining the big man's mana.

After several minutes of slowly being bled out, Malkyr got fed up. He bellowed a roar and used his telltale shockwave attack. The power of his attack ripped apart the vines, nearly pounding Bob into the ground. Once Bob was out of the picture, Malkyr took a threatening step toward Bek, but the goblin raised his hands and declared innocently, "Bek yield."

"Ugh," Bob groaned, lying on the ground. He rose unsteadily to his feet and got out of the pit. "Malkyr wins the final round and will challenge the arena champion in the next battle. There will be an official announcement for that fight. Today's tournament is over." He walked slowly to one of the benches, wincing in pain, and sat down with obvious relief.

I sat next to him." Are you okay, Bob?"

He rubbed his head, wincing. "Yes, Dread Totem. I think I'll stick to announcing for now."

"Good call. What's next?"

"Malkyr has earned the right to challenge the arena champion, Rhynorn, to a duel. Such a challenge can only be issued once a week. To allow both sides to prepare, we will hold the battle in six days."

I nodded. "Better not delay that too much. I estimate we have about another week to get ready before we go to war."

Bob's face lit up. "Is it time already?" he asked eagerly. He was a hobgoblin all right.

"I think so, but I have no way of knowing exactly when."

"We could deploy scouts outside the valley," he suggested.

I shook my head, "We could, but it won't be of much use." There was no point in trying to explain to him the time differential the players brought with them. Any scouts we'd send would be brought into the players' slowed time and wouldn't be able to give us much advance warning. They were much more likely to be discovered and killed. I didn't want to thin my forces unnecessarily.

I frowned. *If only there was a way to scout the players outside of their time bubble ... wait a minute!* "Bob, you're a genius!" I exclaimed.

"I am?"

"Here's what we'll do," I continued excitedly. "Send out *five* scouts. Have them form a semi-circle beyond the valley's entrance, a kilometer apart from each other."

Bob frowned. "I'm afraid that will leave too large a gap, Dread Totem; the enemies will be able to slip by unnoticed."

I shook my head. "The first wave of scouts isn't there to locate the enemy. Every eight hours, send five soldiers to replace the ones outside. Instruct the relieved soldiers to report to you directly when they arrive. If some of them are late by ten minutes, come and get me."

Bob's frown deepened. "I'm afraid I don't –"

"Trust me," I cut him off, still excited. My plan would work, I knew that for sure. If one of the scouts got into the players' zone of slowed time, he wouldn't be able to return to the clan quickly to report. So if one or more of the scouts failed to return within eight hours, we'd know they entered the enemy's zone of slowed time. We would even know the rough direction based on which hob didn't make it back.

"I shall send the scouts at once." The lieutenant got to his feet.

“We’ll leave for one more hunt the day after tomorrow.” That was cutting it a little too close for my taste, but I needed the time to summon more troops, and the extra strength the hunt would give us outweighed the risk.

With that in mind, I opened the Food Interface and checked our stocks.

- 698 raw meat
- 185 raw fish
- 480 gathered edibles
- 36 gathered ingredients
- 320 mushrooms
- 9 purple salt
- 2 magmashrooms

Thanks to the blessing and various bonuses, we were producing an inordinate amount of food. There were sufficient stocks to summon a few soldiers while keeping enough in reserve for emergencies.

Vic, how much simple food can be produced from all the ingredients?

<One thousand five hundred seventy exactly, Boss. That will leave you with 185 fish that can only be used for advanced food.>

That got me thinking. I used advanced food almost exclusively to summon goblin crafters or advanced workers, but with the attack coming so soon, the focus had to be on military strength. Bob had proved his worth several times over, and with advanced food, I could recruit more hobgoblin lieutenants.

How much food can we make if we factor in the fish?

<You’ll have to use some of the basic food ingredients for that. That’ll leave you with 1,385 basic and 185 advanced food. Factoring in the settlement bonuses and Gandork’s cook skill, he should be able to produce 1,662 basic and 222 advanced food.>

“Then let’s go shopping.” I cracked my knuckles and opened the Breeder’s Den Interface.

I already had six Infernal Ogres. I could recruit more, but in the time it would take to outfit one, we could equip three hobgoblins. A hob lieutenant cost 70 basic and 30 advanced food, so I queued in seven of them, the maximum I could afford with my existing food stocks. That left me 1,172 units of simple food to play with. I didn't beat around the bush and summoned 16 hob soldiers, leaving just enough spare food for emergencies. That put my army total at 69; eight lieutenants, seven Ogres, three goblin adepts and 50 hob grunts. Hopefully, I wouldn't lose too many during the naming ceremony.

"Bob, the new recruits will arrive at the Breeder's Den shortly. Have them outfitted and start training."

"Yes, Dread Totem."

"Be ready to bring them to the temple when I call for you."

His expression sobered. "Yes, Dread Totem."

"Kaedric." I turned to the hob behind me. "I'll be at my house. Please have all the new weapons and armor delivered to me there." I had the rest of the day and tomorrow to work on Runecrafting, and I wanted to make the best of it.

"Of course, my lord. Shall I have your food delivered as well?"

"Good idea." Some days, it was nice being the chief.

I entered my house and sat down at my table. My seat had been replaced with a comfortable armchair that fit me perfectly. I silently cursed myself for not having summoned a carpenter sooner.

A few minutes later, two goblin gofers arrived, each carrying an armload of weapons and pieces of armor. They left in a hurry, and another two arrived carrying similar items. When the third pair showed up, I started to get worried. *Just how much did those two manage to craft while I was away?*

The next pair of goblins came in hunched over, carrying a single item between them: a giant steel spiked mace. The huge weapon easily weighed 30 kilos, no doubt intended for our Ogres. Finally, the last load of items arrived and was discarded unceremoniously on the floor.

My stomach dropped as I looked at the huge pile that covered most of the inside of my house. "Vic, how many items are in this pile?"

<Let's see ...> Purple tendrils shot out from my cloak toward the pile. The tendrils wrapped around items and got into crevices. Pulling his tentacles back, Vic recited, *<21 leather armor, 11 steel armor, six giant spiked maces, six giant leather armor, five axes and four swords.>*

"Shit."

<Yeah, looks like you'll be here for a while. Oh, and 30 bows.>

I sighed. At least the melee weapons were simple, as I already had their schema. I picked up the first sword, sat back in my chair and started enchanting.

***

It only took me about an hour and a half to enchant all the melee weapons with the sonic damage design. Luckily, the larger maces didn't take longer to enchant, nor did they have more rune slots available.

Runecrafting the 30 bows took longer though. I was happy to find that the RaTog scheme applied to them as well, but I did have to make some adjustments to adapt it to the ranged weapons.

Tika returned from her daily hunt when I was down to the last two. The beautiful goblinette sauntered over and caressed my cheek. "Are you coming to bed?"

"In a few minutes," I answered distractedly. "I just have to finish these first."

"Are you sure?"

"Yes, just a couple more min– oh – Oooh!"

Her hands had reached my long goblin ears and her fingers started to massage them gently. I was drowned in a sea of pleasure the likes of which I had never experienced. It seemed that not only unrealistic pain and horror was possible in NEO. Unbelievable, exquisite pleasure from a gentle ear rubbing was also an unexpected side effect. It was a good thing I hadn't figured out earlier the range of sensation a goblin's ear could produce, or I would never have gotten out of bed. I suddenly realized why Ferengi in Star-Trek were such suckers for Oo-mox.

Tika lowered her face to mine with a knowing, mischievous grin. "Don't be late."

I finished the last two bows in record time.

I might have fudged the enchantment a bit, but damn it, Oo-mox was awesome!

Yes, some days it was good to be chief.

***

The next morning, after I managed to extract my exhausted body from the comfortable bed, I got right back to work.

The leather armor had only three rune slots available and the steel one had four. That complicated things. I had a few options, and I needed to figure out what my priorities were. I decided straight away not to enhance the armor's durability. I just didn't have the time. If I did the connect-the-dot mini-game for each and every piece, I'd be stuck in my house doing nothing but enchanting for a week.

I considered my other options. The leather-wearing scouts weren't supposed to handle melee combat. They were probably going to draw the ranged players' fire. They were especially likely to draw in the mage AoE spells, as targeting the melee fighters posed the risk of harming their own forces. Since the favorite AoE spell was Fireball, I decided to make the leather armor fireproof.

With only three rune slots, the choice was easy. I placed the Mag rune of warding first and connected it with the Esh rune of fire. From there, I drew the connector rune through the entire length of the armor piece. It was less time consuming than connecting the dots, but it still took a few more minutes to run the lines through the entire piece.

Armor schema discovered: MagEshet [Fire Resist]

Though it was simple, inventing the new schema kicked up my Runecraft skill to level 34. I finalized the enchantment by pouring in the required 270 MP then reviewed the result.

Enchanted Leather Armor [Runecrafted]

Description: A simple, yet effective, protection to the wearer's body. This piece was enchanted for additional resistance to fire.

Type: Armor [torso]

Rank: Magical

Durability: 70/70

Armor: 22
Effect: Fire Resistance 25%
Base price: 120

Instead of applying the same enchantment to the other 20-something pieces of armor, I decided to see what could be done with the steel armor.

I examined the first set. It was a basic design. Strong steel plates were hammered onto thick leather hide that covered the body. Though far from elegant, it offered a higher defense value than pure leather.

This type of armor was meant for those on the front lines, who would have to face the brunt of the attacks. I opened the Runecraft Design Mode, selected the Ko rune of strength, slapped it on the armor and connected the Te rune to it. A small swirling of dots became visible inside the semi-translucent representation of the armor. There were over 20 durability points and at least 30 armor points. If I wanted to increase the armor's potential to its maximum, I had to connect all 30. That would take too long. Luckily, I had an alternative. I slapped a binding rune on the chestpiece and back and connected the Te rune to it. That combination transferred the strengthening effects of the Ko rune directly to these two places. Though it was far from optimal, it offered a decent armor boost for relatively little work.

Armor schema discovered: KoteGog [Enhanced Armor]

Enchanted Steel Brigandine [Runecrafted]
Description: A simple, yet effective, protection to the wearer's body. This piece was enchanted with additional protection.
Type: Armor [torso]
Rank: Masterwork
Durability: 70/70
Armor: 41
Base price: 160

That was more like it. The enchantment upgraded the armor to 'Masterwork.' An armor of 40 meant a sword hit that would normally deal 40 damage would do only 20 instead. At the estimated power level of our enemies, that amount was about the average they ought to be able to inflict per hit. At least, for the first wave.

It was time for mass production.

I sat in my chair, and piece by piece, enchanted all the hobs' armor.

Sometime during the endless work, one of Gandork's gofers came by to deliver my food. I chewed distractedly and resumed working.

By the time I was done enchanting the 32 pieces of armor, it was late in the day. Thanks to the enchanting system and the ability to apply the already-made schemas, I was able to enchant the majority of the equipment in record time. Even then, I'd been working for six hours straight.

New Building added to your settlement: Armory [Barracks Extension]

The system message broke my reverie. I chuckled. *Right on time.*

The new armory should help maintain the gear at top condition, reducing durability damage.

I got back to the now much smaller pile. Only the six Ogres' leather armor remained.

They were just an enlarged version of the hobs' leather armor, meaning its defense value was low and could only hold three rune slots.

Before I could start weighing my options, another system message opened.

Goblin's Gorge has reached Level 3: Village

Your settlement population has reached 200 members and may now support up to 5 bosses (currently: 3).

Primary boss max Tier: 3. Amount: 0/1. (cost to upgrade from Tier 2: 20,000)

Secondary boss max Tier: 2. Amount 1/2 (cost to upgrade from Tier 1: 5,000)

Tertiary bosses, Tier 1, Max count: 3. Amount 2/3 (cost to promote: 1,000)

Available energy points: 13,579

New construction blueprint unlocked: Chief's Haunt

Population growth rate: +20%

Some new foblins had probably been born, making us reach the 200 population mark.

Shit! I suddenly remembered I still needed to perform the naming ceremony for the new soldiers. Hopefully, the ensuing population loss wouldn't cost me the upgrade.

And what an upgrade that was!

I could now recruit two new bosses for my clan for a pittance of 1,000 EP. I could also increase any of those bosses to tier 2, my own current tier. Those upgrades represented a huge power boost for my clan. The only downside was the cost. I hoped to reach the 20K mark to purchase tier 3 for myself, but I still had a way to go.

Getting a new blueprint, saving us the research time, was awesome, and the Chief's Haunt sounded interesting. I accessed the Construction Interface and clicked on the new blueprint.

Chief's Haunt [blueprint]

Description: A large, two-story building with a basement. House of the settlement's leader. Includes a meeting room, a trophy room, three sleeping chambers, and a secret alcove. Includes magical traps and four treasure chests. Offers new settlement options.

Size: Medium

Rank: Expert

Required materials: wood 50, pelts 20, steel 20, level 2 stone 50, magic crystals 10

Build Points: 1,000

I let out a soft whistle. Though it was only a medium-sized structure, the Chief's Haunt required almost twice the barracks' build points. I was not averse to upgrading my humble abode into something more inspiring. My clan was growing and a leader's dwelling ought to reflect that.

I decided to postpone the ceremony for a little while. If I could get a few new members, it might offset the losses the ceremony was sure to incur. That meant staying home and continuing my enchanting.

I considered the Ogre-sized leather armor again.

It had the exact same stats as the hob armor. My Ogres were my trump card and as such merited a better enchantment. Still, only three rune slots didn't leave me with much leeway.

Using binding runes to strengthen only specific parts of the Ogre's armor would be less effective, as they had more targetable spots than the hobs. I could channel the strengthening rune through the armor's defense points, but that would take a lot of time. Still, that method would free up one more rune slot. I frowned. *But how much more effective can the enchantment be with one more rune*? I could use a containment rune and put a void crystal in the socket as a power source. I'd have to use the oxsaurian crystals for that, but it would increase the overall defense value by roughly 50 percent.

Still, there could be another way to achieve the same goal without having to spend a precious crystal. *I need to juice up the enchantment, but other than a void crystal, what can I use?* I knew I was missing something. I needed to protect those expensive Infernal Ogres, and ... *Wait a minute! That's it!* The Infernal Ogre had a trait that caused them to emit small flames. It was not much but it was still a type of power. *If I can tap into their innate fire ability like I did with Malkyr's gauntlets and connect it to the enchantment* ... I thought in excitement.

I began the process.

First, I drew an inverted rune of fire then connected it to the Ko rune of strength. From there, I stretched the connecter rune and meticulously connected the armor's dots, all 30 of them.

Working on an item much larger than a weapon meant I had extra room to maneuver, so it was less difficult than I'd expected. It was still time-consuming, so I skipped connecting the durability dots.

I held my breath as I finalized the enchantment by pouring in the required 270 MP.

Armor schema discovered: SheKoTe [Fire Enhancement]

Runecraft skill level increased to 35.

Fire-Powered Leather Armor [Runecrafted]

Description: A simple, yet effective, protection for the wearer's body. Its strength increases when exposed to a heat source. The bonus disappears when the heat source extinguishes. Does not offer extra protection from fire-based attacks.

Type: Armor [torso]

Rank: Magical

Durability: 70/70

Armor: 22

Effect: Convert 5 fire damage to +1 armor every minute (Max equals current durability points).

Base Price: 350

That looked promising. In theory, I could order my Ogres to use their Ignite skill to 'burn' continually. The armor would use that energy and raise the armor value up to 70. The downside was that during combat, any durability damage to the armor would also reduce the effectiveness of the enchantment. Still, for the tough Ogres, this was a powerful addition.

It took me roughly three hours to enchant that single piece of armor. I would only be able to do one more that day. The other four Ogres would have to make do with their unenchanted pieces for a while.

With that in mind, I took the next armor from the pile and resumed work.

***

The next day, I took extra time to properly bid Tika farewell, as I wouldn't be seeing her for a few days.

When I left the house, Kaedric was already waiting for me. "Good morning, my lord."

I scowled and looked up at the perpetually dark sky.

"Just a form of greeting, my lord."

I gave him a wry smile. "I know, just messing with you. Morning to you too." Thinking about the next item on my agenda sobered me up. "Please have all the enchanted gear taken from my house and brought to our new armory. I received a message about the structure's completion while I was working."

"Yes, my lord."

"Also, please tell Bob to send the new recruits to the temple."

My seneschal's eyes became distant, then he nodded. "Done."

"Good. I'll be taking another group of soldiers for a hunt. Keep managing the clan in my absence."

"Very well, my lord."

I walked the short distance to the mess hall to get some breakfast. The place had a few new tables in it and an especially ornate one at the front. My table.

I sat down, and Gandork promptly arrived, holding a steaming plate.

"Thanks," I said and absentmindedly started fishing out pieces of meat with my fingers and shoving them into my mouth. Gandork gave me a disapproving look but didn't say anything. I was too busy thinking to pay him much attention anyway.

So far, I had spent considerable time enchanting, eager to provide better equipment for the soldiers, but I had other options available for me to add to their strength.

Mainly, energy.

Thanks to the size of my clan, we were now producing over 1,200 EP per day and I currently had over 13,000 energy points at my disposal. At this rate, I'd have enough to purchase the next boss tier within five or six days. Which placed me in a difficult position.

The EP I currently had could go a long way toward improving my clan's military strength. I would be able to promote two new bosses, upgrade Rhyno to tier 2, and still have enough to increase their skill levels, though that last one was a lower priority.

However, using that much energy would delay my own progress by several weeks. In the grand scheme of things, I had to consider what would increase my chance of winning: a single, especially powerful, individual or several moderately powerful soldiers.

It wasn't really a hard choice after all. A single person, no matter how powerful, could be ganged up on, or manipulated in ways that would be impossible to use against a large force. Even if the promotion would have made me unstoppable, I still couldn't be everywhere at once and my clan would pay for that. No, it was better to use whatever energy I had accumulated thus far to strengthen the army. Winning was the most important thing, I could wait a few more weeks to get my long-awaited rank-up afterward.

I finished scooping all the food into my mouth and pushed the plate away, refocusing my thoughts.

One obvious use of the energy would be to increase Rhyno's boss rank to tier 2. But he had proved troublesome time and time again. If he kept it up, at tier 2 he might very well be strong enough to beat me, and then I'd really be in trouble. The unruly Ogre was not far away from me, munching on what looked like an entire oxsaurian haunch.

"Rhyno, come over here," I called out.

The Ogre grumbled but got to his feet and came over to me. "Boss-man."

"How would you like to be even stronger?"

He looked down at me, his nose flaring. "Rhyno is the champion!" he declared, bashing the large piece of meat against his chest, spraying gravy all over his brand-new armor.

I sighed. "Remember how you used to be just an ordinary grunt until I promoted you to a champion? I can do that again. How would you like that?"

All of a sudden, he looked like he was stuck in place. His jaw hung open and his eyes lost their focus.

<Boss, you used pure game mechanic terminology. The poor sod who seeded this stupid puppet doesn't have the tools to cope with such question.>

I sighed again. "I can make you into an even more fearsome champion, Rhyno. You'll be unstoppable."

He brightened up, then looked me up and down. A wicked smile spread across his brutish face. "Rhyno agrees!"

"Not so fast. I can't have you keep disobeying orders just because you think you might be stronger than me. First swear, in Nihilator's name, to follow me and obey my orders and never seek to act against me. Do that, and I will give you the power you want."

His eyes narrowed, and a gurgle came from deep in his chest.

I shrugged. "Suit yourself. I can always promote one of the other Ogres. Then he would be the *real* champion and you'd have to obey *him*."

That did the trick.

Reluctantly, looking almost as if it were causing him physical pain, Rhyno lowered himself, taking a knee in front of me. "I, Rhynorn Bloodore, THE CHAMPION, swears to follow and obey you and never act against you, Dread Totem. I swear it on Nihilator's name."

Ribbons of data surrounded the Ogre. They wrapped around his body like shackles then extended toward me as if handing me the leash for his collar. This was the first time someone had made a vow to me since I'd gained the ability to see the underlying metadata. It was an interesting sight.

With a mental flick, I selected Rhyno for promotion.

Promote: Rhynorn Bloodore to: Boss Tier 2, Cost: 5,000 EP. Yes/No?

Yes.

This time, the physical change was not as pronounced as before. The Ogre grew almost a head taller and his girth expanded. New muscles rippled over his body, his nails extended into sharp claws, and his bone spikes grew and became serrated.

Rhynorn, Ogre Gladiator [Boss, Tier 2]

Level: 19 (30%)

HP: 660, *MP:* 345

Attributes: P: 27, M: 1, S: 0

Skills: Powerful 31, Blunt Weapons 30, Dirty Tricks 25, Terrible Roar 20, Lucky Bastard 12

Traits: Ogre (+4P, -2M, -2S), Frenzy (when below 100 HP), Boss Boon II (20 HP & 10 MP per level; +4P, +2M, +2S, +20% MR, +10 Armor), Shadow-Touched

Resistances: Armor 160 (+30), Physical 75%, Magic 50%

Background: Once a feral beast, now uplifted to the rank of a boss by a Dread Totem goblin.

Equipment:

- Giant Spiked Steel Mace (Runecrafted)
- Ring of Bound Soul (2 charges)
- Oxsaurian Leather Armor (+30 armor)
- 2 X Stalker Pins (Runecrafted)

"Congratulations," I said dryly. "You may go now."

The Ogre lumbered to his feet, bowing his head. It might have only been because his head nearly touched the roof, but I still enjoyed the gesture.

"Yes, Dread Totem, I obey."

<Almost sounds like he became smarter too.> Vic noted.

We can only hope, I said, eyeing the Ogre. His stats had improved across the board, and at 660, his health pool nearly doubled. A few more levels and it would rival my own.

That done, I went to the hobs' officer's table, where the senior members of my army were eating. The new lieutenants I had recruited were not with them.

The hobs all murmured a greeting as I approached. Bob straightened up. "The new troops are awaiting your arrival at the Dark Temple as you instructed, Dread Totem."

"Good, but that's not why I came over." I met their eyes. "You saw what just happened with Rhyno?" They nodded. "I can offer two more promotions. Any takers?" I had decided my next bosses would be the disciplined hobs. I'd had quite enough of unruly Ogres, thank you very much.

As one, all the soldiers stood.

I chuckled. "Good to see you're enthusiastic about this. But as I said, I can only promote two. Let's just see who's the luckier among you."

I had meant that literally. I accessed their information thread, checking their Lucky Bastard skill. At level 17, Bob was the highest among them, but I purposely passed him by. I'd be losing a lieutenant if I chose him, and any one of the common soldiers could be made into a boss, making the upgrade more pronounced. It was a simple concept to calculate: If a soldier's power was 1, a lieutenant's 3 and a boss's 5, promoting a lieutenant would grant +2 power, whereas promoting a soldier would give +4 overall.

Yulli, the scout bow trainer, and Kilpi, the tank warrior, had the highest luck after Bob. I motioned the two of them to step forward. "Will you vow your allegiance to me?" I had decided on the spot that any future bosses I promoted would have to pledge themselves to me first. I didn't want to have to put up with any possible power struggles. I'd learned a valuable lesson from Rhyno's disobedience.

The two hobs took a knee and vowed their loyalty.

Then they too began to change.

Yulli became taller and leaner, and her gaze changed to that of a predator on the hunt. I sensed she received skills that increased her damage potential with a bow. Kilpi just hulked up. His frame thickened as more muscles developed, snaking over his arms and torso, and his defensive abilities shot through the roof.

<*Now that's what I call a tank!*> Vic snickered.

I frowned. *Why didn't I receive a prompt to select their boss types like I did with Rhyno?*

<*Rhyno was a basic brainless Ogre when you promoted him. These two are already VI-seeded and have well-defined roles.*>

I guess that makes sense, I admitted.

"Resume your normal duties," I ordered the still kneeling duo. Having been upgraded into bosses didn't make them instant officers, not anymore.

I had learned that the hard way. These two were just stronger versions of their old selves.

Down another 2,000 energy, I had just over 6K remaining, but I decided to ease up on EP for now. I could use it to upgrade skill levels, but my troops were still training and increasing their combat skills on their own, so there was little sense in throwing energy on that path.

I returned to my seat and opened the Religion Interface, scrolling down until I found what I was looking for.

Personal Blessings (Directly applied to specific Shadow-Touched creatures)
• *Liquid Darkness I:* The body exudes tangible liquid darkness when wounded, mending flesh and closing wounds, at a rate of 1 point of damage per 5 seconds. Cost: 10 FP • *Shadow Body I:* Can form shadow claws with 50% armor penetration. Cost: 10 FP • *Shadow Armor I:* Darkness covers your body. Increases armor by +5. Cost: 10 FP • *Coat Weapon I:* Any weapon wielded becomes coated with darkness, which sharpens it. +10% damage, +10% armor penetration. Cost: 10 FP

Faith points were harder to come by than energy, but I had just over 1,100 FP. Though I was planning to save it to upgrade the Eternal Night effects, I figured I could spend a few dozen points to give the bosses, my army's spearheads, a little extra edge.

I cracked my knuckles. *But first, it's time to pamper boss numero uno.* I eagerly targeted myself and attempted to purchase Liquid Darkness.

Ineligible Target
The selected individual is under the influence of several conflicting conditions and can't accept any individual blessing.

<*Sorry, Boss,*> Vic chimed in my mind. <*You're already juiced up on two discipline-governing skills. Remember when they were merged into Dark Mana? You also serve as the main conduit to Nihilator's influence. Meshed together, this makes you sort of incompatible to receive the effects of personal blessings. Sorry.*> He didn't sound overly sorry to me.

I decided not to brood on the matter and instead purchased Liquid Darkness for Rhyno and Kilpi. As melee warriors, they were more prone to getting injured. For Yulli, I purchased Coat Weapon I; as a DPS, she would make good use of the extra damage.

Thirty FP was as much as I was willing to spend for now.

After purchasing the first rank of each blessing, a new option to purchase rank 2 appeared, offering increased bonuses, and costing 20 FP each. But I decided that was enough powering up for today.

I was just about to leave when Zuban entered the mess hall. I waved at him. "Hey, Zuban, over here."

My foreman approached and bowed his head respectfully. "Dread Totem."

"We have unlocked the next settlement rank. We are now a village."

"I have noticed. It is no small achievement, Dread Totem. Congratulations."

"I want to build the Chief's Haunt next."

"Hmm ..." Zuban pursed his lips.

I waited patiently for him to work it out.

After a long pause he said, "We have finished building all the 'high-priority' buildings, as you call them, so we can certainly divert our efforts. However, this project is especially expensive and requires rare resources. I believe the exporter should be able to trade for most of what we need, but the magic crystals are going to be a problem."

"Can't you use void crystals instead?"

His expression became thoughtful. "Why ..." he spoke slowly, "... we just might be able to do that. That only leaves two obstacles."

"What obstacles?"

"The crude chest I designed for your current house will not do. Ryuk, our new carpenter, can help with that, but we will need a proficient enchanter to complete his work – set magical traps, wards, and such."

"And what's the second thing?"

"A Chief's Haunt is an Expert-ranked building. Since I'm only an Apprentice constructor, I'm afraid my builders will not be able to work to their full potential. The daily BP for working on this project will be reduced by 20 percent."

That meant the building would take effectively 1,250 BP to complete. Between Zuban and Wolrig, the teams were generating 250 BP per day, so the penalty was tolerable. The big issue was summoning a goblin enchanter.

I remembered seeing this profession in the Breeder's Den Interface. It was 'Advanced Crafter' and it cost 20 exquisite food, as much as an adept. I had enough purple salt but was down to my last two magmashrooms. That was going to be a problem.

I noticed one of the goblin gatherers getting his daily meal and an idea came to mind. "Get started on the building," I instructed. "You'll have your enchanter."

"Yes, Dread Totem."

I went to the goblin gatherer.

"I need you to gather magmashrooms from the cave. Can you manage that?"

"Me can," the goblin piped in apprehension.

Problem solved. I grinned to myself. Now I wouldn't have to crawl through that cave looking for pockets of the rare plant.

"Make sure to look for them near lava streams," I called after the departing gatherer.

He nodded, then disappeared into the throng of goblins.

I looked with some surprise at the masses around me. Over 20 goblin workers were passing through the mess hall at any given time, not to mention dozens of foblins who were brawling over every small scrap of food. My clan had indeed grown.

"Well, now that that's done ..." I grumbled to myself and teleported away.

I reappeared an instant later at Totem's Watch, looking down at the 23 assembled soldiers below. The seven new lieutenants stood a few steps away from the grunts.

"Welcome to the GreenPiece Clan," I greeted them. "You will be tested to see if you're worthy to join the clan's protectors. If you pass, as long as our clan endures, you will never truly die." I noticed the lieutenants shift uneasily. A smile touched my lips. "You seven are exempt from the test; you will have your chance to prove your worth in the days to come."

I proceeded by granting the Lucky Bastard skill to the lieutenants. As already-seeded individuals, they were in no danger of accidentally imploding.

Then, I called the rest of the soldiers up into the temple and started the naming ritual.

***

Eleven, I thought sullenly.

Out of the 16 new soldiers, five had failed to take in the new skill and had to be sacrificed. Only 11 hobs survived the rite and had become seeded individuals. My own Lucky Bastard skill seemed to have been taking a nap today. *At least the population loss didn't cost us the settlement upgrade.*

I ordered the new troops to gather at the forest clearing leading to the valley's exit. Eleven hob soldiers, seven lieutenants, and six of my veterans made up the hunting party.

It turned out I had unintentionally created a small problem. Since I had to leave a force to protect the clan in my absence, the veterans hadn't had a chance to level up. They were now commanding troops who were more than twice their levels. This was upsetting for the hobs' militaristic mindset, but I was about to rectify it.

The 24 soldiers were all geared with the sonic-enchanted weapons I had Runecrafted and were garbed in magically strengthened armor. It should make the coming hunt easier than the previous ones.

My War Party Leader skill had increased during the last hunt, and I could add 11 more individuals. Adding noncombatants the last time had worked out nicely, and I had no qualms about taking advantage of this obvious game exploit. I could have added more soldiers instead, but that would have been counterproductive. If I had taken them with me, the already higher-level hobs would hog the majority of XP, and if I left them behind, the fraction of XP they'd be receiving would barely be enough to level them. It was more efficient to add workers instead.

I added Zuban, Tika, and Guba to the party. Since research was starting to become a bottleneck, I also added Romil and Primla. As an afterthought, I added the six nameless goblin lumberjacks. Wood was becoming an invaluable commodity for export, and I could use the production boost their increased levels would bring.

"Everyone ready?" I looked around. "Let's go."

31 – Hunting Real Monsters

I felt powerful riding Tempest at the front of a well-equipped fighting force.

Like the previous two hunting trips, we made it through the forest unmolested and rested during the daylight at the border of the oxsaurian zone.

The next night we broke camp and went looking for our quarry. It didn't take us long to find a medium-sized herd and start working on them.

I used my summoned mastiffs to lure in the beasts one by one, then froze them. My Dark Mana skill was now high enough to freeze even the occasional higher-level beast.

Once the oxsaurian was rendered helpless, I unleashed my troops on it. The low-level soldiers inflicted very little damage, but the enchanted weapons sped things up compared to the previous hunting trips. The veteran hobs shone with their superior combat skills. Kilpi, now a boss, delivered a killing blow, crushing an oxsaurian's skull with one hit, draining its last remaining ten percent HP.

By the time dawn broke, we had butchered a total of 15 bulls. Both the soldiers and those that were still back at the clan had leveled up considerably. The hob soldiers reached level 15, the lieutenant 16, the veterans 17, and even I gained a level. I now had a small army of badasses under my command.

My daily EP is probably through the roof right now, I thought with satisfaction.

The first rays of light were starting to show. "Alright everyone, take the meat and get back to the campsite."

My troops followed my orders, collecting about 2,000 units of raw meat and some hides off the butchered beasts, then we marched back to the campsite to sleep off the day.

We woke up again on the next nightfall.

"You will return to the clan without me," I told them. I looked around for one of the new lieutenants who had distinguished himself during the night's hunt. "You, Vaelin, you're in command; make sure everyone gets back to the clan."

"Yes, Dread Totem, Chief, Sir!" The lieutenant drew himself up, his fist banging on his chest.

He was an excitable fella, but he was new, so I could look past it.

I stayed behind, watching the departing soldiers until they had disappeared into the thick forest, then I jumped on Tempest's back and went looking for more oxsaurians to hunt.

The night had flown by almost without me noticing it. I had a lucky break and managed to locate two small herds that were not led by the powerful alpha. My dagger and Freeze worked overtime as one by one, I sacrificed each of the huge beasts.

As the next morning rolled in, I had gained five levels, reaching 38. I had also gained 20 void crystals and a whopping 800 Faith Points. I was now only 60 FP short of being able to purchase the next level of the Eternal Night blessing, a critical boon to ward off our enemies.

Since I now had the option to teleport straight back to the clan, I didn't have to return straight away. I decided to hunt solo for another day before returning to the clan.

I returned to the now deserted camp and prepared to sleep the day away. "Vic, keep watch, will you?"

"Sure thing, Boss." His cloaked form slid off my shoulders and wrapped around an overhanging branch, looking to the world like an old, discarded piece of cloth.

It was late in the morning already. Confident in my companion's ability to alert me to oncoming danger, I lay down and fell asleep instantly.

***

"Wake up, Boss!"

Someone was shaking me.

"Eh, what is it, Vic?" I asked sleepily. It was dusk and I had planned to sleep well into the night. My Shadow-Touched bonuses wouldn't kick in for another hour anyway.

"You've got an incoming call, Boss."

<*My, lord,*> I heard Kaedric's voice in my mind. <*Are you well?*>

I frowned. *Of course I am, why?*

<I become concerned as, by my estimate, you should have made it back by now.>

It's okay, I sent the others but decided to remain to hunt on my own some more.

<You misunderstand, my lord. I was referring to the entire hunting party. None of them have arrived yet.>

Icy snakes of fear crawled down my spine. *None of them had returned?* Kaedric was right, they should have made it back by now. Something must have happened to them.

In the forest, where the strongest roaming monster was level 13, this could mean only one thing.

The enemy was here.

***

The feeling of dread did not let go. The fight had finally found me. And they were early.

I wanted to rush after my troops and see if some could still be saved, though in my heart I knew they were probably all dead by now. Unfortunately, in my haste to act, I had forgotten to ask Kaedric to check if any of the soldiers were awaiting resurrection, and I had no way to reestablish the mental connection with him.

I considered teleporting back. The darkness had spread beyond the confines of the valley, so I could use it as a method of fast travel, looking for my troops. But I could easily overtake them, with no way of knowing if I had just missed them or not.

Instead, I jumped on Tempest's back, prepared to sprint all the way back.

"Boss, wait!" Vic shouted.

"I have to find them!" I said urgently. "Despite the levels they've gained, they're still barely trained and would stand no chance against a force of players."

"I know that. I meant there's a faster way."

"What are you talking about?"

"Your Shadow Clone! You can use it to travel fast – really, really fast."

I frowned. "Why are you only telling me this now?"

"I was easing you in; you were just getting the hang of it. But I think you can control it now. Get down off your puppy and use the technique we practiced."

My demon wolf bared his fangs at Vic. The intelligent beast didn't appreciate being called a 'puppy.'

I did as Vic suggested. Repeating the meditation steps, I submerged my awareness deep inside my body then poured most of my consciousness into my clone.

I rose up in my newly formed shadowy body, slowly taking a three-dimensional shape, and looked around me.

"Now run!" Vic commanded.

I took a few running steps. It didn't seem particularly fast to me.

"No, not like that. Run *through* the shadows. Go, I'll stay behind and watch your body."

I tried following his instructions. I focused on the thick forest shadows and poured myself into them. My shadow moved and the ground rushed below me in a blur. Then I found myself standing 20 meters away from where I was just standing. *Damn, that's fast!*

Now that I knew how it worked, I concentrated, envisioning the path I wanted to take. My ghostly body sped through the thick forest at the speed of shadows.

I stopped a few seconds later and checked my map. I was about a kilometer away from the camp. It had cost me around 50 MP getting this far, but I was already regenerating them, albeit slower than usual. I grinned, put my mind back into the shadows, and blurred away.

I stopped every few seconds, checking for signs of my troops' passage. Luckily the large band wasn't especially stealthy and my level 13 tracking skill was sufficient to follow them.

This is awesome, I thought as I zoomed through the forest. *With this ability, I could travel hundreds of kilometers. I could scout new places, maybe even make contact with new allies.*

My train of thought was cut short as I spotted something moving ahead. Hobgoblins.

I had found my troops.

The hobs gave collective gasps of surprise when they saw my clone blurring out of the shadows.

"What is going on?" I demanded, my voice coming out as a hoarse, hollow whisper. "Why have you stopped? You should have made it back to the clan by now." I was annoyed but mainly relieved to find them alive and well. I felt light ... like an unnoticed heavy burden had eased off my shoulders. I breathed easier and looked around. It was suddenly clear why they had stopped.

Vaelin stepped forward. The lieutenant bowed his head. "Forgive me, Dread Totem. Our scouts have located a group of unknown travelers, so I instructed the men to lay low. I sent a runner back to get you, but I didn't expect you here so soon."

I nodded. I had figured as much. The enemy players had reached us a week before my earliest estimation. "How many?"

"A dozen, my lord."

If Tal's intel was correct, that amounted to a quarter of the first invasion force. This could be a golden opportunity to thin out their numbers before they reached our valley.

"I want to see for myself."

Vaelin called over one of the scouts. The bow-wielding hob led me off the trail through the thick underbrush. We snuck together, careful not to let out any sound that would give away our presence.

As we moved farther, I sensed the players' time coming into effect. It seemed that in the deep forest the radius of the time was smaller than normal, as we found the players camping at a small clearing not far away. I counted 12 individuals. They were a mix of melee and ranged fighters with two healers for support, all between level 15 and 25.

"Tell me again why we didn't wait for the main group?" one of their sentries asked his friend.

The other player shrugged. "It was Rikush's idea. She suggested we'd get more XP and loot if we beat the others there. It's no big deal. They can't be more than a few hours behind us. Rikush is a decent fighter and has a good nose for opportunities. Me and some of the others have joined parties with her in the past, so we decided to follow her lead."

"I don't know," the first one said skeptically. "She seems a bit angry to me."

His friend snickered. "Yeah, she's got a temper, but she usually manages to keep it under control. Just stay out of her way when the fighting starts and you'll be okay."

So it turned out these players were just eager to kill us all by themselves. I gritted my teeth. They were a threat. They couldn't be allowed to live.

I stroked my chin, considering our chances.

We outnumbered the players two to one and had two bosses with us – Yulli and Kilpi. Everyone was geared in enchanted items, and we had surprise on our side.

On the other hand, my own fighting abilities were limited as a shadow and I couldn't use any of my items. Getting here also took a big chunk of my mana, over 500, and it was ticking back up slowly. My troops' levels were still lower than the players, and the six veterans were the only ones who had decently leveled combat skills.

I grimaced. *Too bad I didn't bring any Ogres with me on this trip.* A couple of the brutes would really help assure our victory. Unfortunately, the Eternal Night blessing hadn't spread out all the way to this location, so I couldn't use the long-range version of my teleport to bring in more troops or even come in person. I'd have to make do with the troops I had present.

I'm going for it, I thought with determination. Even if we lost, at least we'd take some of the players with us. Our casualties could always be resurrected, for a price. I contemplated dismissing the shadow clone and going in person, but I couldn't trust the players to stay put. Some of them were already showing signs of wanting to start moving.

The important thing was to take out the healers first, then the DPS guys, leaving the tanks for last. Now that I had purchased the Taunt Resist perk, I felt much more confident in my troops' ability to go around the tanks.

"Wait here," I instructed the scout, then I zoomed through the shadows back to the main party. "Listen up, everyone." I spoke with the whispered voice of shadows. "We're going to attack."

The hobs grinned, eager to shed some blood.

"Kilpi, Yulli, circle behind the travelers. Keep your distance, and be careful to not be seen. The rest of us will charge head-on. It'll be your job to take out the healers once we do."

The two hob bosses nodded. As veterans, they had the best chance to move around undetected. If I tried moving everyone to surround the clearing, we would no doubt be seen.

I looked at the determined and eager faces staring back at me. The seven lieutenants were trying to maintain their composure, but their eyes betrayed their excitement at the thought of blood and violence.

"Each lieutenant is in charge of two soldiers. Vaelin, you take the last three. I want each group to concentrate on taking down a single traveler at a time. Start with their ranged attackers, then the melee damagers, and keep the shield bearer for last. Everyone clear on their assignment?"

They all nodded eagerly, drawing their weapons.

I tracked the information threads coming from the two bosses as they moved away from us, circling the players. Once they were in position, I cast Shadow Hound.

It was the first time I'd cast a spell as a shadow and it was a strange experience. Instead of the mana pouring out of me to fuel the spell, I felt it coming from far away, from my real body. Casting spells through my clone was more draining than normal. I had to channel nearly 300 MP instead of the usual 230 cost to complete the casting. Four large, level 15 mastiffs formed up from the shadows. That left me with roughly 1,000 MP. I grimaced. The battle was really going to tax my reserves.

Next, I gathered my mana and spread it over the 22 remaining soldiers, buffing them with Dark Protection. A nimbus of dark energy appeared around each one of them then disappeared, absorbed into their bodies. That spell also took nearly 300 MP, leaving me with slightly over 700.

I chuckled, despite the seriousness of the situation. It was amusing how easily I'd gotten used to playing a tier 2 boss, casually casting spells that required a mana pool equal to that of a level 160 player.

Everyone, approach the travelers as quietly as you can, I said telepathically.

The hobs obeyed, moving forward slowly. The scouts made almost no noise, but the melee fighters and shield bearers were not as agile.

We'd made it within ten meters of the players' perimeter, when one of the hobs stepped on a branch, sending a loud crack echoing through the forest.

CHARGE! I commanded. The soldiers and mastiffs abandoned all pretense of stealth and ran the rest of the distance, bursting through the trees into the clearing.

Most of the players were taken by surprise, but at least two of their sentries had heard the snapping branch and readied their weapons, shouting, "Ambush!"

The two archers started raining arrows on my storming troops, injuring several but not stopping the onslaught. My soldiers kept their ranks ordered and charged through the first row of players, engaging them with raised axes, swords, and a hail of arrows of our own.

GO, GO, GO! I screamed mentally for my two bosses. They came crashing through the woods behind the players, blocking the healers who were trying to distance themselves from the melee.

Adding my own contribution, I cast Shadow Web over three melee fighters, momentarily taking them out of the fight, then froze a level 22 archer. I couldn't sacrifice him as my dagger was back on my physical body. The two spells drained me of another 100 MP.

My warriors and mastiffs were well organized, engaging all the players' bowmen and melee DPS fighters. The groups of hobs relentlessly slashed at their targets, and the mastiffs snapped at their heels. Still, the disparity between my troops' skills and the players' was apparent. In short order, the travelers had regrouped with no more than 20 percent damage.

A large, buff woman wearing a black steel cuirass and wielding a trident shouted, "They got the drop on us but they're weaker than we are. Fight back, you weaklings! Put your skills to use! Healers, hit the ones injured the most."

It seemed that at least one of them was a competent commander. Unfortunately for her, she did not notice the attack from behind. The two retreating healers weren't smart enough to keep their distance from each other. Kilpi pummeled his shield into one of them, knocking him down, then slashed at the other, interrupting his casting. Yulli displayed her bowmanship as she unleashed two arrows at once at the downed healer, pinning him to the ground.

The rest of my troops weren't faring as well. Finally out of their shock, the players retaliated, showing their higher combat skills. The rangers easily disengaged from my less-skilled troops, putting some distance between them and shooting arrows. The DPSs charged into my troops, hacking and slashing, their armor deflecting or negating our own counterattacks. A tank roared a taunt and a confused expression appeared on his face as none of my hobs turned to engage him. The three webbed melee fighters still struggled to tear their way out of my web, but it was holding, for now.

Making a quick judgment call, I zoomed through the shadows to the edge of the clearing and cast Heal Followers. At the Apprentice rank, the spell's range covered all of my troops, instantly healing ten percent of their injuries. I followed through with another Freeze, stopping one of the retreating archers. I had 450 mana remaining.

You and you, I projected to two of the lieutenants. *Engage the frozen archer, take him down! Vaelin, your squad take out the other one.*

The three hob squads repositioned themselves, taking a few hits as they did.

Despite having two healers engaged, three warriors webbed, and two frozen, the remaining five players were giving my other three squads a hard time. The hobs were doing their best to give back as good as they took, but their health bars were plummeting. Even the hounds' shadowy substance took a hit from the players' magical weapons.

One of the five players took out a small blue item and threw it at one of the squads. It exploded in a blue flash, freezing one of the hobs solid and slowing the other two. A tank bashed the frozen hob, shattering him into little pieces. An Insta-Kill. The other players rained blows and arrows, taking down two more of my soldiers. My soldiers fought back, but most were injured. The Dark Protection buff proved its usefulness as it occasionally flared up, lessening the damage or mitigating an attack altogether.

Kilpi continued to slash at the downed healer, bringing him to half his health. The other healer cast a protection spell, and Yulli's next two arrows barely penetrated his thin robes.

I had a split second to decide whether to attack or heal. My troops were faring badly, but if those healers got away from us we would be in even more trouble. I launched a trio of drilling arrows at the downed healer. *What the hell is up with his name?* I couldn't help wondering as the next message popped up.

Drilling Arrows hit CombatMendingUnit#147 for 68 damage, [21 +23 + 24]

Immortal Killed!

Boss Tier 3 Progression: 4/50

The first archer I froze was starting to break through, so I channeled another 50 MP to keep him contained.

I had 385 MP remaining.

A few seconds later, Vaelin's squad killed the frozen player, and a second after that, the other one was brought down as well.

"The a-holes got sonic-enchanted weapons!" a player shouted. "Since when do mobs at this level use magic equipment?"

No one answered him. The disorganized players were each fighting their own battle, too busy to answer.

With a combination of skills and items, the three webbed players broke through their restraints and joined the fray. Two of them were shield-wielding tanks and they howled their taunts. It was just as ineffective as the first one.

Despite their failure to pull my soldiers from the softer players, my troops still sustained casualties. Three soldiers and two lieutenants fell.

Meanwhile, Kilpi and Yulli were attacking the lone healer. He desperately tried to heal himself, but his health bar was dropping too rapidly. "Help!" he yelled. "These two are bosses!"

Fully engaged with the rest of my troops, the other players were too busy to come to his rescue. With a well-placed hit, Kilpi delivered the killing blow.

Four players and eight of my soldiers were out, and my mana was running dangerously low.

Of the seven squads I had created, only four were still whole. Backed up by two remaining mastiffs, they were attacking with fervor, trying to kill the five damage dealers. The freed player tanks closed on them from behind.

I couldn't cast Shadow Web again; I'd ensnare my own men. The Dark Protection buff was about to expire. I braced myself and channeled 150 MP to keep it active for another minute.

Only 235 MP remaining.

I couldn't risk depleting my mana by freezing more players, so I launched another volley of spinning arrows at one of the injured fighters, killing her as well.

Immortal Killed!

Boss Tier 3 Progression: 5/50

The players fought viciously, though without any real sense of group tactics. They dropped three more of the injured hobs and the last two mastiffs. They could have easily dealt twice that damage but were simply too disorganized. The tactician in me noted their mistakes with an almost clinical detachment.

Still, moderate warriors or not, they held the advantage over my troops and were closing the gap in numbers quickly. It was now seven against 13.

Finally finished with the healers, the two bosses joined the fray. Yulli unleashed a steady stream of arrows, each hitting a different player, dropping his health by a few percent. Kilpi bull-rushed into the melee, his shield leading the charge, throwing away two of the players and pummeling a third into a tree. "He's using a boss ability!" the large woman shouted. "Kill it before he uses his AoE again!"

Two more hobs and a lieutenant were brought down, and Kilpi was starting to take damage. With a joint effort, my hobs managed to bring down the last two bowmen.

It was now five versus ten.

None of the remaining players were too severely injured to be brought down by a single volley of drilling arrows, and most of my soldiers were below 50 percent health. I cast Heal Followers again, increasing everyone's health by ten percent.

"Where the hell is their healer?" the woman demanded.

I concentrated on her info stream for a split second, letting the data wash over me. *So this is Rikush*, I mulled. She was an armored berserker, and at level 25, was the highest-level player in their party. She was also responsible for half of our casualties.

I stepped into the clearing "You're looking for me?"

Her eyes narrowed as she caught sight of my shadowy body. She took out a potion, downed it, and her health filled up to the maximum. Then she lowered her head and charged straight at me, bulling her way through my forces.

That was the wrong move.

With her out of the melee, the last four players found themselves at a disadvantage as they were swarmed by my remaining troops.

I waited, letting Rikush keep charging at me, then raised Mana Shield at the last possible moment. Her trident bounced harmlessly off the shimmering blue dome, taking away another 70 MP with it.

Now just 95 MP remaining.

"Damn, you're an ugly one," I told her matter-of-factly. "Couldn't find anyone to stand your looks, so you came here hoping a *monster* would be able to tolerate the sight of you?"

Her eyes filled with hot rage and she stabbed with her trident at my shield again, nearly emptying my mana pool.

"You're dead meat, goblin," she spat. "I don't care that you're a boss, I'll rip out your black head and piss into your skull."

I inwardly cringed at the mental image her words invoked but grinned at her. "Bring it on, bitch."

I then used the last remaining mana points I had to shoot a trio of drilling arrows at her point blank.

Drilling Arrows hit Rikush for 69 damage, [22 +25 + 22]

She screamed in rage as my spell took down 30 percent of her health, then retaliated with another heavy lunge.

Her trident broke through my depleted shield, which flickered away, then tore into my body.

"I'll kill you! Then I'll kill your friends, one by one."

"Are you sure about that? Look behind you."

She glanced back just in time to see her last remaining companion fall after taking a well-placed arrow to the forehead.

"While you were chasing me, you forgot to look out for yours." I grinned widely. "You lose."

My half-torn shadow body was sucking in every point of mana I regenerated, struggling to maintain cohesion. Screaming in rage, Rikush landed another hit. Her magical trident glowed as it hit my body, draining the last of my mana.

I blinked my eyes, finding myself sitting back at the camp, ten kilometers away.

Vicloak flopped down from the branch, assuming his goblin shape. "How did it go?"

I chuckled. "I found them."

I had no doubt my troops would be able to bring down that raging woman. Kilpi and Yulli could probably handle her well enough on their own.

Then I frowned. Something sticky was dripping down my chin. I wiped away the substance and looked at my hand in horror. It was covered in blood.

Did I overtax myself again? When I entered the players' zone of time, a small part of me dreaded the repercussion of having my real body in a 'normal time' flow. This kind of discrepancy couldn't be good for my consciousness.

Then a whiff of odor reached my nose. I frowned and sniffed the red liquid. "Berry juice?" I mouthed in astonishment.

"Yeah," Vic replaced easily. "I had no dye on me, so I had to improvise. I heard it's popular to apply war paint before combat, and you know me, I'm here to help."

With a mounting dread, I took out my dagger and looked at my reflection through its sheen.

The bastard had painted my face like William Wallace in Braveheart! "Why you little –"

"No need to thanks me, Boss. Besides, we should hurry before the other players catch up."

I gritted my teeth, but he was right. Somehow, someday, I'd get him back for that little prank. "Come on, let's go."

I wiped my face and mounted Tempest, Vic assuming his favorite perch around my shoulders, then we sprinted away.

***

Tempest ran tirelessly through the forest, weaving from side to side, easily dodging trees as he darted past them.

I no longer felt the presence of the players' slower time flow. With any luck, I'd find my troops and we would make it back to the clan before the main attack force reached us.

With the enemy 12 players short, our odds of winning just shot through the roof.

While we ran, I busied myself by checking the logs of the fight. It was more good news. All the soldiers had gained at least a level. The ten who survived until the end got four, including the two bosses who were now both at level 21.

Each of them also racked up two kills and like me, would have their boss tier increased on its own once they accumulated 20 kills in total.

Something bothered me though; I had hardly gained any XP from that fight.

<Yeah, sorry, Boss. In your cloned form you were never in danger so you just received a small percentage, mainly just from being in the war party. Your skills got a pretty decent boost out of it, though.>

I see. Can you show only the progress I made on my character screen?

<Sure thing, Boss. Would you like me to include the gains from the oxsaurian hunt as well?>

Yeah.

Title: Dread Totem

Level: 38 (+6)

Attributes: [0 points available]

- Mental 42 (+6 gained)

Pools & Resistances:

- Hit Points: 826 (+40 gained)
- Mana: 1,755 (+161 gained)

Skills:

- Lucky Bastard 41 Ⓑ (+1 gained)
- Tracking 13 (+1 gained)
- War Party Leader 20 (+2 gained)

Spell Skills:

- Dark Mana 46 Ⓑ (+4 gained)
- Drilling Arrow 26 Ⓑ (+1 gained)
- Mana Shield 28 (+1 gained)
- Heal Followers 12 (+1 gained)
- Shadow Web 21 (+1 gained)
- Shadow Hound 24 (+2 gained)
- Dark Protection 14 (+8 gained)

It had been a good call to spend my dwindling mana on keeping Dark Protection active. The skill gained an impressive growth, reaching the Apprentice rank. It now offered a plus six percent to armor and physical resistance and gained the ability to remove mobility-hampering debuffs. Not a bad haul. On the downside, its cost was increased to 15 MP per affected individual.

Overall, that was a solid gain for two days.

I now had to make sure my remaining troops made it safely back to the clan.

It took Tempest two hours to get to the scene of the battle. The surviving hobs stood and banged their fists on their chests as I approached. I was relieved to find that all ten had lived through fighting that rageful woman.

"She had absolutely no self-control." Yulli wrinkled her flat nose in disdain as I mentioned it. "She just lashed out wildly. We simply rotated our injured soldiers until we managed to bring her down."

"Here, Chief." Vaelin handed me an item. "She dropped this."

I looked with surprise at what he'd given me.

It was a pagan-looking headdress that mostly resembled a bundle of feathers. The feathers were red and gray with a gold emblem in the middle. It reminded me of my old Totem's headdress I had gifted Bek, only less primitive, and it lacked the outlandish skull.

Dread Totem Headdress [Set 1/4] [monster only]

Description: A piece of The Ritualistic set. Complete the set for the full bonus.

Rank: Magical

Type: Armor [head]

Effect I: +20% mana regeneration

Effect II: Freeze and Dominate cost 10% less mana to activate.

Those bonuses were strangely specific. Not that I was complaining.

The mana cost reduction was a true blessing, as dominating or freezing the most powerful enemies could cost hundreds of MP.

<*Congratulations, Boss,*> Vic said. <*You have been playing your boss puppet convincingly enough for the system to deem you worthy of an upgrade.*>

You mean it wasn't a lucky random drop?

<*Pffft, fat chance. How do you think other bosses gain their unique magic items when they never leave their stinking caves? You just killed a lot of players. That's the sort of thing the system recognizes and rewards for.*>

"I don't mind the system working in my favor for a change," I said out loud, drawing a few bewildered glances from my soldiers. I put on the headdress. It fit perfectly.

I then realized everyone present was injured. Some of the soldiers had only ten percent health remaining. I silently berated myself for not noticing this sooner and spent a minute casting and recasting Heal Followers, topping everyone off.

This had been a learning experience. I resolved to never leave the valley without a healer in the war party. We were lucky most of the players had counted on their healers and didn't bother carrying healing potions.

Once everyone was back to maximum health, I remounted Tempest. "Let's get back home."

32 – Preemptive Measures

We marched through the walled entrance and into the valley, passing the two hob sentries. Further down the forest path, a lone figure stood waiting for us at the clearing, flanked by two large Shadow-Touched mastiffs.

"Welcome back, my lord." My mandibled seneschal bowed his head.

"Kaedric?" I asked in surprise, shifting my eyes to the hounds. "What are you doing here? Are you controlling these mastiffs?"

"No, my lord, they were roaming around the valley and for some reason decided to follow me here. I wished to be the first to welcome you back and congratulate you for scoring the first win against the invaders. I also have a few updates I believe you should be made aware of."

"No one else got murdered, right?" I asked, filled with concern.

"No, my lord. The culprit responsible for the recent calamities has been inactive for a while. Though the missing liquid fire is still not accounted for."

"What is it then?" I motioned to my troops that they were free to leave.

"There are soldiers awaiting resurrection, my lord. Fourteen of them, to be exact. All are of relatively high standing."

"I know." He was referring to their levels. All were at least level 15 when they died. "How much energy is it going to cost to raise them?"

"Exactly 2,150, my lord."

I winced. That was one downside of having high-level troops. On the upside, the high-level soldiers contributed a huge amount of daily EP. My clan was generating over 1,500 EP a day now.

"Take care of it," I said shortly.

"Yes, my lord." He cleared his throat, "The magma foundry has been completed deep inside the cave. I summoned a mill worker and we are producing our own obsidian bricks now. We should have enough to complete your haunt without delay. However, once that is done, the majority of our builders will be left without a job."

I frowned. "That's not good."

"I have already taken steps to address this issue, my lord. I have enacted a two-phase solution. First, I have summoned two new researchers. The amount of time it takes to acquire new blueprints has been holding back our progress, and the research center can accommodate many more researchers. This should expedite our blueprint discovery."

"And the other thing?"

"It is customary for large hobgoblin settlements to have an underground sewage system that doubles both as a waste disposal system and as a training ground for warriors, as it often attracts various hostile critters. I have spoken with Zuban at length about this. Now that we have grown into a village we have the option to build such a system. It is a time-consuming endeavor, but one that will keep our builders occupied and contributing to the clan in the long term. I believe you ought to speak with Zuban for more details."

"I'll do that."

"I also have some good news."

I perked up at that; I was always ready to receive good news.

"Our settlement has grown to such a degree that our long-standing penalties for using crude tools and inadequate workplaces have been eliminated. I am pleased to inform you that our clan efficiency has increased by six percent and is currently set at 33.7 percent."

That was good news. Every little bit helped. The extra few efficiency points meant increased production across the board.

"There's more," my seneschal continued. "Yesterday, several of our prominent workers gained significant advancement in their chosen professions, improving the clan's productivity considerably."

I felt myself grin. I almost forgot I had added workers to the war party before leaving. I hadn't disbanded the party after the oxsaurian hunt, meaning they also got a portion of the XP from defeating the players. I reached through the ambient information around me, accessing the clan's data, and saw to my satisfaction that the lumberjacks and researchers were all between levels 8 and 9, Guba made 11, my Tika 13, and Zuban was now level 14.

"That is good news." I nodded in approval. "But our priorities have shifted. I overheard some of the travelers mention the main force was several hour– ... a few days away. We need to concentrate our efforts on defense."

I looked around. Vaelin hadn't left with the rest of the soldiers and was standing nearby. I motioned him to come over. "I promote you. From now on you'll be Bob's second."

He straightened up and puffed out his chest. "Yes, Chief!"

"We have scouts outside the valley watching for enemies. I want them rotated every two hours. Inform me immediately if a replaced soldier is late to return by more than ten minutes.

He banged his fist on his chest. "At once, Chief!"

That should give us plenty of warning against the main attack force.

I was supposed to talk to Zuban about building a sewage system but I suddenly felt ... drained. The priority was to make sure my troops were well armed, and I needed to hone my own skills while I still had the time. Settlement sanitation could wait.

"Kaedric, instruct Zuban to work on the sewer when all the other projects are done. If you need me ... well, you always know where I am."

"Yes, my lord."

I returned to my house, only to find it in the middle of a construction site. Scaffolding and half-finished brick walls extended and overlapped my previously humble abode, which, by the looks of it, was going to become a wing in the bigger haunt.

Luckily, the construction was external to my existing house, so I skipped over a pile of logs and ingots and slipped inside. I still had to finish enchanting the Ogres' armor and the pile of new items that had grown in my absence.

There were still a few hours until the end of the day. I sat down in my comfy new armchair and got to work.

***

I barely managed to open my eyes the next morning.

Due to the urgency of our situation, I had stayed up late enchanting all the armor and weapons, resorting to a simple strengthened version for most of the equipment. Then, I moved on to the remaining 12 partially Runecrafted Viridium spheres and finalized their enchantment.

A few messages flickered before my eyes, alerting me to my sorry state and the debuffs I gained from lack of sleep. I forced my eyes to open and cast Mana Infusion. Cool, pure magical energy flooded my veins, invigorating me like a strong cup of coffee. The spell's bonuses somewhat mitigated the debuffs, though not entirely. I couldn't afford to sleep in; the attack could come at any moment.

Blueprint Research Completed: Obstacle Course
[Barracks extension]

I dismissed the message. Zuban and Kaedric knew what to do well enough without my intervention.

I lumbered stiffly to the mess hall. The throng of soldiers and goblins moved aside, letting me pass through as I sat down tiredly at my table.

Gandork soon came by, carrying the usual assortment of dishes. "Good morning, Dread Totem! Or shall I say, good night?" He was in a good mood, whistling as he laid the plates on my table. "We can hold a month-long feast with all the oxsaurian meat the soldiers have brought. The mess hall is finally starting to look like a respectable establishment."

I glanced around. The log benches were gone, replaced by actual benches. Gandork was right, the place *was* looking more civilized. I wasn't sure how I felt about that. I sort of liked the rustic, outdoorish vibe it had before.

I started eating, though I was too tired to really appreciate the meal. I watched the orderly manner my clanmates were following. All the seats were being used; as soon as one was vacated, another individual took its place and a meal was served to him. It was efficient and time-saving.

My gaze was drawn to something blazing.

A foblin entered the mess hall carrying a large container. A bouquet of flowers came out of it like it was some sort of misshapen vase. Some of the flowers were glittering like they were on fire.

The small critter made its way toward me, his big eyes bright and shiny.

"What do you have there?" I asked, then wrinkled my nose. A putrid smell came from the container he was holding.

A few hobs noticed the smell as well and turned their heads toward the foblin, their eyes open in sudden realization.

"Gift to Chief! Me get gift too!" the foblin declared stupidly.

The agitated hobs jumped out of their seats and charged at him. I realized too late what was going on.

The blazing flowers reached the surface of the container and the whole thing ignited. Liquid fire erupted in all directions. The poor foblin holding the container got the worst of it and was immolated in front of my eyes. Sprays of the burning liquid hit everyone within a few meters' radius. I stood up, gaping, as I watched my clanmates burn.

I finally snapped out of my shock and cast Heal Followers. It was too late to save the nearby foblins with their low levels and hit points. At least ten of them dropped dead, their bodies charred and smoking. But I was quick enough to save the nearby workers who had gotten scorched. The warriors, with their higher levels and health pools, suffered only moderate damage.

There was yelling, panicking, and running. Some parts of the wooden floor ignited as the liquid fire continued to burn with unnatural intensity.

A group of soldiers led by a lieutenant came running into the mess hall, their weapons drawn, looking for someone to fight, but their presence only contributed to the rising chaos.

"ENOUGH!" I shouted.

Channeling my mana, I gathered shadows into a thick, condensed mass and extended it over the burning liquid like a dark blanket, gradually smothering the flames.

I looked at the lieutenant who barged in with his troops. "What's going on?" I demanded. "Where did that foblin come from?"

The lieutenant, Dwax, sheathed his sword. "We were patrolling near the Breeder's Den when we detected the smell we were told to watch for. We went to investigate when this little guy ran past us, carrying a vat of stink, so we started pursuing him. We didn't catch him in time and he made it inside, Chief. I take full responsibility for our failure and am ready to face my punishment."

I looked at him sharply. "You detected the smell before or after you saw the goblin?"

He looked confused. "Eh ... before, my chief."

I felt the blood freeze in my veins. "And you left the Breeder's Den unguarded?"

Comprehension dawned in his eyes, he turned toward the door and I rose to follow.

BWOOOOOOM

A massive explosion rattled the walls.

***

I teleported outside and stood in front of the blazing remains of the Breeder's Den.

I summoned shadows and smothered the flames, but the damage was already done. The once pristine building was completely charred and an entire section of the wall, along with the roof, was missing. There were a few black lumps inside, too burnt to make out what they were.

I was pissed. The unknown culprit had struck again, and this time, they had hit us hard.

Still, it was only a minor setback. I opened the Construction Interface, selected the mess hall first, and clicked 'Repair.'

Repair mess hall (92 energy required, 10,056 available). Yes/No?

I clicked yes and within seconds the building was patched up with shining blue energy.

I selected the Breeder's Den next and hit the repair for it as well.

Command cannot be executed

Reason: Master-ranked building. Max constructor skill level too low. Minimum required: 51 (Expert rank)

"NO!" I exclaimed with conviction as if refuting the message would make it go away. "It can't be!"

I stood looking at the charred and smoking building. The Breeder's Den was the source of my clan's success. It was what made our rapid growth possible. Without it, our development would stagnate. No more workers, no more soldiers. *And I had just brought in enough food to nearly double my forces.* I ground my teeth. In short, we were screwed.

There was no way for us to fix the building; the system message made it crystal clear. Zuban would have to reach the Expert rank in his construction skill first. Even *I* hadn't reached the Expert rank in any of my skills yet, though I was getting close.

My mind was reeling, considering the possibilities. *Zuban will need to hit level 40 in order for his skill cap to reach level 51. I'll have to hunt oxsaurians with him, just the two of us, day and night until he reaches that level.* That realization settled me down a bit. I knew I could do it; it was only a question of time. We could overcome this obstacle. But not before the players' attack. There was not enough time for that.

Staring at the smoldering remains, I clenched my fists. *I will have to win this with the troops I already have. I have to! I will!*

But first, I'd have to deal with the culprit once and for all. I still didn't know who was behind it. It was clear they were intelligent, which didn't help to narrow the list of suspects much. All the players in my clan seemed to be smarter than average. Whoever it was, they were smart enough to create a diversion, sending that foblin suicide bomber to draw attention away from the Breeder's Den. They were smart enough to sabotage the lumber yard without leaving any evidence. I wasn't even sure anymore that Riley, the dwarf player, was indeed the one behind the murder of the two lumberjacks. The person responsible could have planted a false trail, making him the scapegoat.

The commotion had drawn the attention of several players. Two came to stand behind me.

"What happened here?"

"Someone bombed the building. Weird, why would anyone do that?"

"Maybe it was a quest?"

"I don't know, it doesn't match the general theme here. Maybe ..."

"Get out!" I barked.

The two players stopped their conversation. "What was that, Chief?" one of them asked.

"I said GET OUT!" I barked louder. "All of you!" I looked around hatefully at the nearby travelers. "I want every single one of you stinking travelers out of my clan, NOW! You can't be trusted. It was one of you who did this! Get out of my clan before I unleash my hounds on you!"

As if answering my threat, large Shadow-Touched mastiffs started to manifest from the shadows around us, growling threateningly at the travelers.

"But the arena championship is today!" one of them dared to complain.

"Yeah, and I almost reached friendly reputation with the clan," another protested. "Come on, I just need two more –"

"Enough!" I yelled, baring my teeth at them. "I've been working my ass off developing this settlement, building it up from scratch. I bled for this place! And now a group of stinking travelers who are hell-bent on destroying everything I worked for are only days – maybe hours – away from here. I will not let that happen! You are the same as they are. Just as bad, just as ... untrustworthy!"

<Err, Boss, you might want to –>

"Shut it, Vic!" I was breathing hard now. "Only goblins can be trusted! *Real* goblins! Not half-breeds like you. You have a minute to leave before I order my troops to attack."

An area quest prompt opened up, instructing all players within my clan to leave or be killed. I approved the quest, setting massive reputation loss for those who failed to comply.

Rhynorn came to stand behind me, slapping his oversized mace on his palm, leering at the surprised travelers.

"He's lost it," Tenchi, the snake-looking one muttered. "I'm out of here." His body became translucent, and within seconds he was gone.

One by one, the others disappeared as well. Only goblins, hobs, and Ogres remained.

I looked around at my gathered brethren. "We will win this on our own, and we will teach those damn travelers not to mess with us. They want a fight? We'll give them a fight! To the GreenPiece Clan!"

"To the GreenPiece Clan!" they all cheered.

"Now get back to work!"

***

I stood inside the Dark Temple, facing the shrine.

With maybe hours away from the fight for survival, it was time to further tip the odds in our favor.

I focused my will and touched the shrine.

Missing 59 Faith Points to purchase Eternal Night, Rank 2.

That wasn't really a problem.

Purchase 59 Faith Points for 590 energy points? Yes/No

Yes.

With my clan generating over 1,500 EP a day, spending 590 on something I could easily gain by slaughtering oxsaurians didn't bother me overmuch.

I accessed the Eternal Night details and reviewed the upgrade.

Zone Blessing [Eternal Night: Rank 2] purchased!

Modifiers:

- Three external empowering shrines: +100% effects
- Blessing Rank 2: +100% effects

Shadow-Touched creatures receive:

- +30% max HP & MP
- MP & HP regen increased by 150%
- +30% damage
- Upkeep reduced by 50%
- Non-combat skills +15% effectiveness

Enemies suffer:

- -30% XP gain
- -75% HP & MP regeneration

Special:

Enemies slain within the valley will be consumed by darkness (generates Void Crystals and Faith Points).

New Eternal Night upgrades unlocked!

"Hmph," I huffed approvingly. With these bonuses, a level 15 grunt was more than a match for a traveler of similar level. A lieutenant would probably be able to beat one two levels higher. Our situation was looking brighter already. To top it off, every traveler killed inside the valley would be consumed by darkness, and that meant more void crystals. I could work with that.

<See? I told you so,> Vic interrupted my train of thought.

Uh? Told me what?

<Remember when you were moping about your imminent doom? You went on and on about how you didn't stand a chance, bitching about your bad luck. Remember? I told you, you can use the power of this place to your advantage. And I was right.>

I frowned, trying to remember.

"Wait ... That was like a month ago!" I protested.

<So? Not my fault you have a lousy, meat-based, constantly degenerating memory system.>

Despite myself, I snickered. "Meat-based memory system? Good one, Vic."

<Thanks, Boss, I try.>

I examined the area blessing menu again. There were new options to upgrade its effects: blinding enemies, summoning shadow monsters, reducing the enemy's max level, and even blocking unauthorized teleportation. All of which cost way more FP than I could hope to gain within the short time frame I had. I could have converted energy for FP, but the conversion rate was brutal.

I had tinkered enough with religion bonuses. It was now time to resort to cold, calculating tactics and make the best use of the forces I had at my disposal.

I accessed the Settlement Interface population data and filtered it to show only the soldiers.

Kuzai: Boss Tier 1, Level 28
Kilpi Shīrudo: Boss Tier 1, Level 21
Yulli: Boss Tier 1, Level 21
Rhynorn Bloodore: Boss Tier 2, Level 19
Infernal Ogres: 6 Level 16
Goblin Adepts: 3 Level 12, 1 Level 20
Hobgoblin Lieutenants: 3 Level 17, 2 Level 18, 3 Level 19
Hobgoblin Scouts: 16 Level 14, 4 Level 15, 4 Level 17
Hobgoblin Warriors: 14 Level 14, 4 Level 16, 4 Level 17

I had a total of 64 soldiers and four bosses under my command. If my intel was accurate, we should have no problem facing the first wave of travelers, particularly since we had already sent a quarter of them for a respawn. The second wave would be more problematic, but I could easily resurrect any of my fallen soldiers after the first skirmish, and those that survived would have progressed their level significantly. Nothing was more XP-rewarding than slaying travelers.

I allowed myself a small smile. We were going to make it. My hard work and dedication over the long weeks had paid off. Even with the Breeder's Den destroyed, we were ready.

Not everyone was fully equipped yet, but most of what they had was enchanted. It was now time to work on my own skills, for what little time I had left.

***

I sat cross-legged on top of the temple's roof, looking at the valley spread below me. I needed a quiet place to meditate, and my house's renovation was raising a racket.

After the fight with Rikush and her cronies, I had noticed the spells I used while in my shadow clone had leveled up more than expected, probably due to the extra mana required to invoke them.

Using this little discovery, I had teleported to the temple's roof, closed my eyes, and summoned my shadow clone. The ambient Dark Mana that saturated the temple flowed easily, powering up the spell to new heights. My clone's body seemed denser and stood half again as tall as normal. I looked down at my real body, sitting serenely, balanced on the edge of the triangular roof. Then I looked at the valley's forest. The darkness was alive and pulsing with energy. I located a dark channel of energy and leapt into it, using the sweeping flow of power to propel my body forward. With hardly an effort, I emerged from it, standing on top of the arena's training pit.

I immediately noticed a new interesting fact. My mana pool was still at the maximum. Thanks to the recent levels I had gained, and more importantly my new headdress's bonus to mana regeneration, my pool was being replenished faster than my clone could drain it, at least at such a close range.

There were no players present. Two groups of hobs, each led by a lieutenant, were engaging one another in mock combat. A lone goblin adept was standing behind each group, occasionally sending a wave of healing magic at his teammates. Bob stood next to me, shouting at them to fight harder.

I nodded to my lieutenant. "Carry on," I said, my shadow voice as cold and dispassionate as before.

I summoned my mana to my hands and shaped the power, building it up. Then I brought my hands together and let the surging energy wash over the soldiers below me, buffing them with Dark Protection.

That single spell, though it cost 250 MP, was enough to progress my skill up to level 15 and halfway to 16. The goblin healers were doing a good job at healing the most critically wounded soldiers, but I noticed that most were lightly wounded. I swooped down to the center of the pit and cast Heal Followers. As I had already reached the Apprentice rank, the spell radius of five meters was enough to reach all injured members and heal them up by 22 points of damage. The spell level jumped by one point to 13. Though the mana cost was increased, it did look like casting spells through my clone was straining them to level up faster. My combat-related spells were relatively high already, so this was good practice for my support spells.

I spent a few minutes watching the soldiers fight. I noticed all of them had reached the Apprentice rank for their combat skills, and their group fighting form was admirable. Nero had done a good job training them. They would give any traveler their level a tough run.

I spent an hour alternating Dark Protection with Heal Followers, making sure not to completely heal-steal from the adepts. Once I leveled both skills to 20, their progress rate declined dramatically.

There were a few hours until the end of the day, but the lack of sleep was getting to me. I teleported to my house and made to lie down on my bed when I realized I was still using the clone body. I chuckled lightly, the sound coming out as a flat, mirthless cackle.

I withdrew my consciousness back to my real body and opened my eyes. I was back on top of the Dark Temple. It was midday, but Mana Infusion was no longer enough to keep me on my feet.

I teleported into my house and went straight to my chamber. I was sleeping as soon as my body hit the bed.

***

I was rudely awakened by the sound of metallic banging. I got up to see two gofers unceremoniously dropping a pile of items on the floor – today's equipment production for me to enchant.

Though all of my troops were armed, my scouts were mostly unarmored, as protecting the melee warriors had taken higher priority. Likewise, half the warriors were still using crude unenchanted weapons, so every little bit helped. This day's production would outfit three more soldiers. I sat down in my armchair and got to work.

I finished enchanting the soldiers' equipment in under an hour, then turned my attention to my own Pyrolith Gambeson. I carefully considered how to enchant it. The armor could hold up to five runes – six, with my skill level – so I had some room to maneuver. But after long deliberation, I couldn't come up with an interesting idea for a new enchantment. It was armor. Its purpose was to protect the body. Increasing its defense and durability was a simple, two-rune combination. I could easily add fire protection, but the Pyrolith scale already provided that. I decided, for now, to only enhance defense and durability. The armor was too rare to enchant carelessly and waste rune slots. I could always add runes to it later, once I'd figured out the optimal combination.

I opened the design tool and sighed at the sight of dozens of dots I had to connect: 40 durability and 35 armor points. The schema might be simple, but enchanting it was going to be tedious. I decided to ignore the hundreds of red dots, those that related to the armor's innate fire resistance. It was simply too much work for now. I braced myself for the arduous process and began enchanting.

It only took me about three hours to finish, much quicker than anticipated. Somehow, the connector rune seemed to almost glide on its own from dot to dot, guiding my hand.

I put down the finished armor and examined it carefully.

Pyrolith Scale Gambeson [Runecrafted]

Description: This well-crafted armor is made of durable leather embedded with hardened demon scales and enchanted by a goblin Dread Totem. It offers excellent protection without hindering the wearer's mobility and is naturally resistant to fire.

Runecraft viability: 5 runes [2 used]

Type: Armor [torso]

Rank: Advanced

Durability: 155/155

Armor: 45

Resistance: Fire 50%

Base price: 800

The base attributes had all jumped up considerably; the armor value was increased by ten points and durability by 35.

Tika came back home from her daily hunt just as I finished admiring my handiwork. I looked up at her with a smile.

"What a nice surprise," she said. "I usually find you too busy to notice me when I get home last. That is, when you're not away playing with your hobs."

"And when I get home last, I usually find you asleep. That is, when you're not away, still hunting."

"I guess we have more in common than we knew." She sat on my lap and put her arms around my neck. She leaned over to kiss me, then playfully bit at my ear. "I want to come with you for the next oxsaurian hunt," she whispered.

I was not expecting *that*. "Out of the question. It's too dangerous; even the soldiers can't stand up to those beasts."

She frowned slightly. "But I am the hunters' leader. I have the most experience, more than any goblin I have ever met. I can even lead the other hunters on a large-scale hunt. I should come with you to learn what I can about those oxsaurians."

I shook my head. "I know you're good, but I don't want you getting hurt." I stopped myself before adding 'again.' None of us needed to remember the details of our time in captivity.

"I know you want to protect me ... Oren." She whispered my name directly into my ears, sending shivers of pleasure down my spine. "But I have outgrown the prey in the valley, I feel ... constricted. I need to go out, hunt something meaningful."

I shook my head. "Not oxsaurian. Even Rhyno can't stand up to those beasts yet." I was having a hard time acting determined with the tingling sensation in my ears.

She pouted. It was very cute. And very sexy. "Please?" she breathed in my ear. Her warm breath nearly broke my resistance then. Her fingers caressed my back.

I refused to give in to her wily charms and didn't budge.

"Pretty please?" she breathed again. Her hands reached my head and gently caressed my ears. My long, sensitive goblin ears. I couldn't help it, I shivered, giving off a low moan.

She grinned triumphantly and leaned in for another kiss.

"That doesn't mean you won!" I protested, as she took my hand and led me to our bed.

My protest sounded weak, even to my own ears.

An hour later, I couldn't even remember what we were arguing over.

***

There was something encroaching my consciousness. A presence. An insistent wisp of information poking at the edge of my awareness.

" ... My lord ..."

I woke up with a start to find Kaedric standing over my bed.

It was still late. We couldn't have been sleeping for more than a couple of hours. The fact that he not only let himself in but also came into my bedchamber could only mean one thing.

"They're here," I said. It was not a question.

"Yes, my lord. It has begun."

Interlude: GreenPiece Chatroom

NEO Chatroom: "GreenPiece fans"

Malkyr: Thank you guys, for accepting my invite.

Fox: Why in god's name are you still using an ancient text-based chat?

Malkyr: The time discrepancy makes it difficult to schedule a proper vid-chat and I wanted to reach everyone. This way, if someone arrives late, he can catch up on the conversation.

Misa: Good thinking. What's up, pal?

Malkyr: I wanted to discuss the future of the clan with you – mainly, our role in it.

Sullivan: It's been fun, I love stirring up trouble ... gets the blood pumping, you know? But that Totem player is way too intense. Have you heard he banished all the players?

Nero: He is under a lot of pressure, I think. He is a worthy player and cares for his clan. I can't say I blame him for taking that sabotage hard. Heck, I probably would have killed you lot just to be on the safe side.

*Hoshisu: *chuckles* I'd like to see you try!*

*Nero: *grins* Just say where and when.*

Malkyr: That's not why I asked you all to come. I, for one, am loving every second of this new gameplay.

Tenchi: I agree. For some reason, the whole dark and evil experience is very relaxing.

Sullivan: Tell me about it. Every time I log in for a few hours it feels like a week-long vacation from the symphony.

Riley: Wait, you're a musician?

Sullivan: Yeah, so?

Riley: I never would have guessed.

Sullivan: How I chose to play my character and who I really am are two different things. I doubt you're a dark goblin priest in real life.

Riley: Data scientist, actually.

--- A new member has joined the chat. ---

TreeLover4Life: Hey guys, is this the new protest group against the growing industry in the game at the expense of the rainforest?

Fox: Wrong group, slugger. It's GreenPiece, not Green-peace.

--- Member disconnected. ---

Misa: What a nutter.

Malkyr: ANYWAY, the chief is a good guy. We went on a couple of raids together and he really knows his stuff. It sucks that he kicked all of us out, but I can't really blame him. He'll come around once he cools off a bit. What we need to do is show him that we can be trusted.

Sullivan: How do you suggest we do that?

Raystia: I'd like to help. I think what he's doing is admirable, but he'll never trust us as long as he thinks one of us is undermining his efforts. Did you see his expression when he saw the Breeder's Den on fire? It was like a man who'd just lost his home. I felt so bad for him ...

Malkyr: I thought of that and I believe I have a solution, but I need to know you're all on board and willing to do what it takes to flush out the saboteur.

*Riley: *grunt* At least you're not pointing a finger at me.*

Fox: Let's say we do, what do you propose?

Malkyr: Each of you send me your game logs, starting from when you first logged in with your new characters. I'll scan them and find out who's behind this.

Fox: You're asking a lot. And before you start pointing fingers, I'm sure I'm not the only one who has a few things he'd rather keep to himself.

*Raystia: He makes a good point ... Some of the conversations I had were ...*ahem* embarrassing.*

Malkyr: I give you my word I won't use your log for anything other than to pinpoint the guilty party. In fact, I won't even read them myself – it's too much data for a manual scan. I plan on running a recursive elastic search algorithm, cross-referencing the dates of the three attacks. Once I'm done, I'll delete your files from the machine.

Riley: Heck, I got nothing to hide. In fact, it would be nice to clear my name. I'll send you my logs.

Fox: What do you plan to do about players who refuse to send you their logs?

Hoshisu: If everyone present agrees, that would put pressure on the others to play ball. In the end, even if the logs won't show us who's the culprit, we'll have a reduced suspect list. We can give that to the chief as a sign of good faith. Then he could keep those on the list banned and let the rest of us continue playing.

*Fox: *grunt* If it'll calm down Mr. Dark, Green, and Angry, I'll play ball. Sending you my logs.*

Yulli: Bloody hell. Alright, I'm in.

Tenchi: Yeah, me too.

Nero: Kudos for the initiative.

Malkyr: Thanks, guys. It shouldn't take more than a few hours to scan through everyone's logs. Send them through. I'll be in touch.

33 – And So, It Begins

I was fully awake.

The mixture of adrenaline, excitement, and fear was like a shot of espresso straight to my veins.

My seneschal's mandibles twitched as he delivered his report. "Our troops are mobilizing at the forest clearing, my lord."

I kissed the still sleeping Tika, equipped my shining Pyrolith armor and placed the newly enchanted items in my inventory. It was heavy, but nothing that mana infusion couldn't handle. I turned to the still-waiting hob. "When we leave for battle, get everyone down into the cave."

Kaedric nodded. "I shall follow your instruction, my lord."

"I trust you to keep them safe while I'm away." I put a hand on his shoulder. "They are the lifeblood of the clan. If we lose them, even if the battle is won, we are in big trouble. We can no longer rely on the Breeder's Den."

"I understand, my lord. Should any of the travelers find their way to us, I will have hounds and foblins swarm over them. If it comes to that, I can even use my own abilities to hinder an enemy."

"Good." I let go of his shoulder. "I will see you once this is over."

I teleported to the forest clearing.

All of my troops had gathered already, filling the open space almost completely. The well-trained hobs were standing in orderly rows, grouped in formations according to their roles: 24 scouts brandishing willow bows, 12 warriors clad in steel brigandine bearing axes and shields, and ten sword-wielding warriors clad in leather armor. The seven lieutenants were standing at attention behind Bob. Rhyno was clad in his thick, enchanted oxsaurian armor and leaning against a tree, the trunk groaning under his weight. The other six Ogres lumbered behind him, each wearing similar but lower-quality armor and carrying a huge spiked mace. Bek and the three goblin adepts, all clad in simple leather vests, were standing, grim-faced, behind Kuzai, their hands on the sacrificial daggers at their belts. Surprisingly, Guba was there as well.

I motioned for Bob to come to me. "Report."

"I have divided the troops into small squads, each led by a lieutenant." Bob gestured at the seven lieutenants. "Three of them will lead squads of scouts and provide ranged support, two will lead squads of six shield fighters, and the last two will each head a squad of five melee-hitters."

I nodded in approval. "What about the scout sentries?"

"The scouts have all returned except the one who was watching the route you took to hunt oxsaurians."

That was to be expected. The berserker woman, Rikush, and her party of players had come from the same direction.

"How long since the other scouts reported in?"

"Roughly 20 minutes."

The scouts were spread out about an hour's march from the valley. That meant the players would reach us very soon.

I looked at Guba. "What are you doing here?"

She came forward, carrying a large sack on her shoulder. "The missing liquid fire set me back a good while, but I be wanting to show ye younglings what a true alchemist can do with a proper lab." She opened the sack. "I been experimenting with them poison mushrooms that grow around 'ere. Added a bit of accelerant 'an mixed 'em with me special glue. Here ye go." She placed a bulbous grenade twice as large as the goblin BoomBooms in my hand. "These work like glue bags, but they be poisonous too, see? They hamper movements 'an spread poison when the binding breaks. An enemy who try to scrape off one of these will only be poisoning himself harder."

"Thank you, clan chemist." I bowed my head respectfully. With a nod, I directed Bob to distribute the grenades among the troops.

"Bah, it is too damn little," she scoffed. "I been working on extra-strength BoomBooms when me liquid fire was stolen. A real shame what it did to that breeder building. That some of it remained at all is a surprise. I'd be expecting that amount of juice ter leave only a scorch'n hole. These backup grenades be a pale substitution."

"These will help us immensely," I assured her. "We are well-prepared for this fight. With your contribution, I have no doubt we'll emerge victorious."

"Hmph." She turned to leave. "Make sure you do."

I watched her go, then turned to face the soldiers, preparing myself mentally. *Time to inspire the troops.*

"Everyone listen up!" I said sharply, making them jump back to attention.

With my War Party Leader skill level at 25, I could only include half the soldiers. I formed a party with the four bosses, the lieutenants, and my veterans, then added 20 of the common soldiers. Everyone included would benefit from the effects of my skill, granting them a five percent bonus to attack, defense, and XP gain. I made sure to include Zuban; I needed my chief constructor to level up as quickly as possible if I ever hoped to bring the Breeder's Den back into working order.

Then inspiration struck. I removed one of the scouts from the party and replaced him with Kaedric.

Kaedric, can you hear me? I sent my thoughts.

I could sense his surprise even before he answered. *<Clearly, my lord.>*

I smiled smugly. With Kaedric's psychic abilities coupled with the power of the Earring of the Warlord, I had just found a way to maintain a long-distance communication channel with the clan's administrator. I no longer had to rely on him contacting me at predefined times.

From now on, I'm keeping you in my war party constantly so we can always be in touch. Keep me apprised of new developments and await further instructions.

<Yes, my lord.>

The twisted dwarf priest watched me intently as I held the mental conversation. "*It* seeks to lead *its* warriors into combat, but *it* must remember that all must give glory to the dark lord. Each slain enemy shall be claimed by darkness, their essence converted, and their soul shall shriek in torment for all eternity."

By now, Kuzai's peculiar habit of spewing nonsense had become familiar, and I found I could easily ignore him.

I took a good, hard look at my troops. "You all know why we're here." I paused, seeing the eagerness in their eyes. "The traveler army has reached us. We will move out shortly to engage them in battle."

A loud cheer followed my words. The Ogres laughed maliciously.

I raised my hand. "This is what I brought you here for. This is your purpose. To defend our clan from our enemies. Fight well. Fight until the last drop of blood. Do not falter and do not hesitate. Remember, should any of you fall, as long as the battle is won, you will return to life again. This I vow to you, in Nihilator's name."

You have made a vow in the name of your deity, Nihilator

Condition: Resurrect your fallen troops within 24 hours of the battle.

Failure: Permanent reputation reduction with remaining soldiers, -1000 reputation with Nihilator.

Success: 5 Faith Points per resurrected soldier.

I took the Epic demonic staff from my inventory and struck the ground. "We will vanquish all those who seek to destroy us." I took another item from my inventory. "And if they dare send their elites against us," I said, fastening the Outrider Bracelet around my wrist, "they will perish too."

"For the GreenPiece Clan!" Bob shouted, holding up his enchanted sword.

"For the GreenPiece Clan!" they all yelled, drawing their weapons. Rhyno roared enthusiastically, demolishing a small tree with his club for emphasis.

I jumped on Tempest's back. "Follow me!"

We stormed out of the valley like a swarm of blood-hungry locusts.

***

We had only been marching for a few minutes when I became lightheaded, the telltale sign of nearby travelers.

Everyone, halt! I commanded mentally while raising a closed fist. *Yulli, scout ahead, let us know what we're facing.* As the highest-level scout, and a boss besides, she was best-suited for this task.

While we waited, I delivered orders to my troops. *Lieutenants, get your men ready. Bob, I trust you to direct the others during combat if I'm engaged or too distracted. Rhyno, you lead the Infernal Ogres, but wait until I assign you a target. Do not engage until then!*

The hob lieutenants bowed their head in affirmation, and the hulking Ogre grunted his assent.

Kilpi, support the tank squads. I trust you to hold back their strongest fighters. The boss's toothy grin was his only reply.

Kuzai ... I started, but the dark priest turned and glared at me. "The dark lord will guide my hand in combat. With his absolute power behind us, we cannot fail."

I could feel him redirecting his mana. His own shadow disengaged from his body, growing to stand beside him. The bastard was rubbing in the fact he could simultaneously control both his clone and his real body.

Just make sure to heal our troops when needed and counter their magic casters, I snapped at him. *And keep quiet!*

Yulli returned shortly after, the missing scout behind her. The scout boss's face was bleak.

"What's wrong?" I asked, my guts wrenching in anticipation of her answer.

"There are more travelers than expected," she said simply. "Over 70 individuals."

I felt my blood freeze in my veins at her declaration. "Are ... are you sure?"

She nodded grimly. "I couldn't risk getting too close for an exact count, but there are *at least* 70 travelers heading this way. It could be as much as 80. They will reach our position within ten minutes."

Shadow-crap! I cursed, causing half my troops to snap their up heads in alarm.

I estimated we had a decent shot against 40 players, especially since we got rid of a dozen early on. But 70 or 80 was another story altogether. Tal's intel was wrong.

Was Tal's spy simply wrong? Did he betray us? Or maybe Vatras somehow managed to fool him? My mind was racing. There were too many unknowns. I had to get more information before committing my forces.

Everyone, stay alert and guard my body, I ordered. I dropped to the ground and started meditating, forcing my mind to calm down, despite the pressure I felt.

I rose up as a shadow, watching my own body on the ground. Then I turned in the direction Yulli came from and 'swam' through the shadows.

A few heartbeats later, I came to a stop, hiding in the deep shadow of a tall tree overlooking a forest path. A moment later, a group of people carrying torches and other means of magical light came into view.

“Man, I really hate this darkness,” one of them said to the person next to him. “Did you notice it was daylight when we walked into this black wall?”

“Yeah.” His comrade grinned cheerfully. “It reminds me those epic fantasy movies. Like we’re marching through a cursed forest or something. I’m half expecting skeletons to rise up and attack us and the gnarled tree roots to flail at us.”

“That’s not funny,” his friend retorted, nervously studying their surroundings. “This *is* a cursed forest. Didn’t you notice the debuffs? Minus 30 percent to XP gain and minus 75 percent to HP & MP recovery. That’s crazy!”

“You’re too stressed.” His friend shrugged. “This is a low-level zone; it makes sense they’d balance it out somehow. The penalties suck but you can’t expect much XP from goblins anyway, so it doesn’t really matter. We’ll destroy the clan like the Manapulators asked and then boom! We’re set for life. Easy peasy.”

The group continued walking without a clear formulation. Some players jogged ahead, some walked slowly, engaged in conversation like they were walking through a park. A few others even stopped to collect interesting herbs. They remained within shouting distance from each other, though. As a being of shadow hiding within shadows, I was nearly invisible, and I was able to take an exact count. There were 78 of them.

“Shadow-crap,” I muttered softly. *Now what do I do?*

I searched intently, trying to spot any exploitable weakness. Despite their disorderly manner, they were all armed and well armored. I spotted at least 20 tanks and ten healers. The others were a variety of combat classes, too diverse to categorize exactly. That was a good sign; it meant the group’s erratic composition would hinder them in a large-scale fight. They were not built to be an effective fighting force, and some of their techniques would no doubt contradict or even hurt each other. But I couldn’t rely on their inefficiency. They still outnumbered us. Their levels were between 16 to 25 with two individuals nearing 30.

As I swept my gaze over them, one of the highest-level players stood out. He was one of those untyped players, wearing cyan robes and had a rapier buckled at his waist.

That’s Tal’s spy, TheMarxman! I realized. He was walking alone, frowning, and did not engage in any of the conversations around him.

Now that I had him in sight, I could contact him. I accessed the message system and selected TheMarxman as the recipient.

[Me: Welcome to our jungle. I see you've brought some friends with you.]

[TheMarxman: Is that you, Oren? The sender is only listed as 'Dread Totem.']

[Me: Yeah. We need to talk in person. Break away from the group, to your left.]

TheMarxman slowed his walk, letting the other players pass him by, then got off the path toward my location.

I came out behind the tree to meet him.

"Holy crap!" he exclaimed, jumping back. "Tal said you were a goblin, but he didn't mention you're only a shadow! Where's the rest of you?"

I chuckled, my hollow voice sounding like a flat echo. "Not far. Why is your group larger than reported? Did you *betray* us?" I spat out the last question with an ominous tone, feeling the goblin's racial hate flaring up. If there was something I'd learned during my time here, it was that travelers couldn't be trusted.

TheMarxman took a step back, his face becoming concerned. "No, my friend, I did not. I told Tal everything I knew when they recruited us. It was only when we started to march that we learned the Manapulators had created *two* separate groups for each wave. The second wave will likely also have double the expected people, so 20 instead of ten. I tried to contact Tal so he could warn you, but he's not answering his messages. I even called him IRL, but he didn't pick up." He eyed me seriously. "Something about this whole thing doesn't feel right. Now that I've found you and told you everything, I consider my debt to Tal paid. I'll leave you to handle the rest."

"Not just yet," I said evenly, his explanation soothing my temper. "I need your help."

"I'm a decent fighter, but I'm only level 20," he said. "So I can't take on those guys. Some of them are real psychos. If they learned I double-crossed them, they'd hunt down my character."

"You're level 28," I corrected him, enjoying the surprised expression on his face. "You've maxed out your rapier fighting skill, and your robes offer more protection than most of those rif-rafs' metal armor."

"How did you –"

I cut him off. "However, you don't have to fight. I just need you to help me even up odds. Since you're *obviously* an above-average player, I'm sure you'll have no problem luring 20 players to an ambush."

He scratched his head. "I can do that." After a pause, he said, "I never thought I would be working with a goblin to ambush players. This is a refreshingly new experience."

I scrunched my nose. "Not for me. So, can you do this?"

"I can."

"Your main group will reach a moss-covered boulder in about two minutes. Lead the players south of it. My forces will be waiting."

"You got it, Chief."

I swiftly issued orders. *Bob, the travelers' main force will reach the entrance wall within ten minutes. Take all the scouts back to the valley and station them on top of the wall. Take two healers and a unit of tanks with you also to block the entrance. The rest of the troops and I will lay an ambush for a small party of travelers and then come join you against their main force. We'll hit them from both sides. Go, Go, Go!*

TheMarxman offered me his hand. "I don't know exactly what is going on, but from what I gathered from the Manapulators and the little Tal told me, I think I have a rough idea what you're doing here. I wish you luck."

I studied his face, searching for signs of betrayal or dishonesty, but found none. I took his hand in my shadowy one, my fingers sinking a few millimeters into his palm as we shook.

"Thank you," I said in my whispery voice, then recalled my consciousness back to my real body, leaving the player gripping a quickly dispersing cloud of darkness.

I blinked and got to my feet, looking at the 30-something remaining troops. With my strongest forces present – the bosses and the Ogres – we should be able to handle 20 players with little to no casualties. Hopefully.

The players will be here any moment! I projected urgently to my troops. *Lieutenants, take your groups and hide behind those trees. Rhyno, take your Ogres farther away so they won't be detected. Get ready!*

The last Ogre had just disappeared behind the thick trees when Yulli whispered hoarsely, "They're coming!"

The players filtered through the trees in twos and threes. Walking between them was TheMarxman, easily chatting up a couple of grim-faced knights. "I'm telling you, my Treasure Sense skill is tingling like crazy; there's something valuable nearby."

I knew for a fact he did not have such a skill. But it seemed that his Persuasion skill was working overtime.

"We'll miss out on the big event," one of his escorts protested.

"Nah, let them take the brunt of the combat. We'll find whatever treasure is hidden here, then join the main group for the mop up." He raised his voice. "Just be careful, when my skill tingles like that, it usually means there are guardians in place."

I froze then gritted my teeth. The bastard was playing both sides!

A system message hit me a second later.

[TheMarxman: In case you heard that, I'm just making sure I'll have a way to explain the ambush so they won't come gunning after me later, claiming I led them to their deaths]

I could understand that.

It didn't matter anyway. The sixth player who came into view was a ranger type, and he spotted one of the poorly hidden tanks. "Ambush!" he cried.

"Too late buddy," I said. *Attack!* Then I summoned my hounds.

My well-disciplined soldiers reacted as one. Twenty hobgoblin warriors streamed from around the trees, hitting the hastily raised shields, injuring many in the first round. My mastiffs and Tempest joined the fray, pouncing on the lightly armored casters. Kilpi bulldozed through two of their tanks and shield-pummeled another to the face, and Yulli started raining a stream of arrows from behind a tree. Each arrow was coated with a film of darkness, penetrating steel armor and cloth robes alike.

The attack was quick and merciless, and despite the warning, the players were caught off guard. Three of them were injured critically and I was quick to finish them off with my dagger, sacrificing them.

Immortal killed X3!

Boss Tier 3 Progression: 8/50 immortals killed.

But then the surprise wore off. Despite having no experience fighting as a unified force, they were still players, and they had their tricks. Three casters erected shining magical barriers around themselves, and several archers started sniping my soldiers. The rest of them activated a variety of skills and counterattacks, pushing my hobs back.

I cast Dark Protection over my soldiers, spending over 200 MP in the process, then redirected my dagger to slash at another badly wounded player, sacrificing him as well.

Bek and the other adept cast their healing spells as quickly as they could, bringing two hobs from the brink of death, but four other hobs fell to the mounting damage. Kuzai and his shadow clone stood facing three scared looking players and were bombarding them with scintillating balls of black and red energy.

The last of the players streamed in, and everyone was engaged in mortal combat.

Kilpi was holding back three players with his shield while three other hobs slashed at their backs. Yulli kept peppering the enemy with her darkly-blessed arrows, and my mastiffs, led by Tempest, were biting and snapping at every limb they could get. A few player tanks shouted their taunts, but none of my troops were lured away, much to their chagrin and my amusement. Instead, they fought back.

A wizard unleashed a fireball, taking away three hobs and one of the players. I cast Shadow Web on three archers, disabling them for the moment, then sent my dagger flying at another badly hurt player.

Immortal Killed!

Boss Tier 3 Progression: 10/50 immortals killed.

A few of the stronger, more experienced players grouped up and started to systematically hack my soldiers apart. Our initial attack destroyed their weaker forces, but just like smelting iron, the garbage was burned away and the high-quality material remained.

Rhyno, you're up!

The Ogres, led by the gladiator, came charging in, trampling small trees. They rammed into the stronger players, who had just found their rhythm, and threw them out of sync and into the air. Rhyno launched one of his Stalker Pins at a halfling player who had just killed two soldiers on his own, literally nailing him to a tree trunk. My dagger was quick to finish the job. Then the champion bellowed a roar, sending waves of strengthening magic and energy to the troops. Invigorated, the hobs redoubled their attacks, felling the players one by one in rapid succession. Meanwhile, the Infernal Ogres, their maces coated with small flames, broke apart the last pockets of resistance.

One of the archers managed to escape the web and ran away screaming, but two of my hounds were fast on his heels, tripping him to the ground. A volley of drilling arrows, coupled with a slash from my dagger, finished him off as well.

Immortal Killed!

Boss Tier 3 Progression: 12/50 immortals killed.

Another hob fell to a wickedly executed Backstab skill by a player rogue, but he soon found himself impaled on a tree by my Infernal Ogre's horn.

My troops mopped up the few remaining players, my dagger soaring between them, claiming more kills.

Then it was all over.

We had lost eight warriors in the attack, but it was a reasonable trade-off for defeating 20 higher-level players. TheMarxman was nowhere in sight.

My heart was pounding hard, my excitement mounting. We'd made it! Despite our losses, the force ratio had shifted in our favor – 60 versus 57 was better than 68 versus 78. I'd also sacrificed a dozen players, garnering FP and increasing my 'immortal killed' counter, but there was no time to waste.

"Let's go," I said, casting Heal Followers over everyone. "The main enemy force will arrive at the entrance before us. We must hurry." There was no time to pick up the loot or void crystals, but on the upside, I noticed everyone had gained a level from the fight.

We burst out of the thick trees and onto the forest trail the players had left behind and started jogging in their wake.

Once I made sure the troops were all running in the right direction, I tapped Kuzai on the shoulder and teleported with him to the valley's entrance.

Over 20 scouts and their lieutenants were already positioned on top of the wooden wall that bordered the entrance, their bows drawn. We had no gate, but Bob and five tanks stood there, blocking the opening with their shields raised. The two goblin healers stood further back.

"Take these." I handed the healers two of my lesser Rods of Fire, and a handful of low-level void crystals. "When you're not healing, use those against the enemy."

I checked my mana. I'd spent nearly a third of my pool but had over 1,000 MP remaining, and my uncanny boss regeneration rate was already hard at work bringing it up to full.

I walked to the opening and stood beside Bob.

"I can hear them coming," my lieutenant said, tension evident in his voice.

"We just dealt them a crippling blow," I assured him. "There are 20 fewer enemies against us now. We just need to hold them off outside the valley for a little while until our main force ... hey, what's that smell?" A pleasant, yet oddly tinted odor wafted to my nose.

Bob sniffed a couple of times. "I don't smell anything."

The first players filtered into view behind the trees. The lieutenant in charge of the scouts issued orders and the scouts opened fire, sending a hail of arrows at them. The players took cover behind the trees and began preparing to launch their own ranged attacks.

I frowned. "Smell like lavender and –" My eyes opened wide with alarm. "– and sulfur."

And for the second time this week, my world was filled with fire and destruction.

34 – First Wave

I rolled back to my feet, coughing and choking.

The walls on either side of the entrance were blazing, illuminating the darkness around us. Billows of smoke filled the air, and the intense heat scorched my skin.

"Dread Totem, are you alright?"

I felt strong hands lifting me and dragging me to cover behind a tree. A few arrows landed on the ground next to us. I looked up, taking in Bob's worried expression. His armor was singed and he was bleeding from shrapnel. Looking around, I realized all the other tanks had taken damage too. I sent a healing wave of magic at them and coughed again. "Report"

"The wall is burning down. We've lost all the scouts! The enemy approaches!" he said urgently.

More arrows landed around us, some hitting the row of injured tanks who struggled to maintain their formation. A lightning bolt hit one and sent him flying backward, critically injured, but not dead.

I clenched my teeth in anger. The culprit had struck again and I was caught off guard. Again.

With a single act of sabotage, he had inflicted more damage than 20 players combined. I'd lost three lieutenants and all of the scouts that were posted on the wall. Their fire-resistant armor proved insufficient to the intensity of the flames. I was down to less than half the troops I'd started with, and my main force was still too far away to help!

I checked my health. I was standing close to the wall when it exploded. Luckily my Pyrolith scale armor was hardier than the scouts' and resisted most of the fire damage, but the concussion force itself was strong enough to knock my health down by 200 points. Leaving me at 70 percent health.

I came out from behind the tree, activating my Mana Shield. "Hold the line!" I yelled to the tanks, who were being continuously struck with arrows and magic spells. I reached them just as another tank fell and took his place. A wave of healing energy came from behind as the two adepts did their best to keep the tanks' health above zero.

A host of players was charging at us between the trees. Over 50 eager and uninjured players, all seeking to spill goblin blood. I cast Shadow Hound, bringing my mana below 1,000, and *five* level 18 mastiffs jumped out of the darkness and ran to intercept the eager players. Thanks to the previous fight, the spell had reached level 25, increasing the number of mastiffs.

However, that only bought us seconds. The charging players cut through the hounds. Some of their weapons were ineffective against the insubstantial beasts, but then spells and enchanted arrows landed, destroying them one by one.

I sent my dagger flying and ordered the tanks to throw the poison bombs Guba had given us. The grenades hit several players, the glue rooting them in place while the poison slowly eroded their health. I teleported a meter away to an open gap in our line, leaving my shield in place like a stationary bubble and activated another one. Then I did it again, blocking another gap. All the while my dagger was airborne, nicking and cutting.

These tactics could only buy us seconds. Their healers soon arrived at the front line, negating the poison and closing the wounds. They were only a couple dozen meters from us and closing fast. My tanks braced themselves, and the gaps in our line filled with my glimmering bubble shields.

Kuzai and his shadow stood behind our line, emitting a shrill, demented laugh while hurling scintillating balls of energy. The two goblin adepts kept on healing, but it was not enough to counteract the damage and the tanks' health continued to dwindle. Another hob fell, and now only four remained.

Someone was clearly organizing the players. This was not the same undisciplined force we'd fought before. The first wave of players consisted only of tanks. They crashed against us, locking their shields with my troops' while a row of archers and magic casters behind them bombarded us from afar. Five healers formed at their rear. Only a few attacked without regard to order or formation.

The ten tank players pressed us, aiming to drive us back and clear a path for the rest.

I threw a Shadow Web over four of them, ensnaring one of my own in the process, then froze another. I sensed he lacked resistance and sacrificed him with my dagger.

Immortal Killed!

Boss Tier 3 Progression: 18/50 immortals killed.

The tanks pounded on my warriors and my shields. I struggled to keep the mana flowing into all three shields to maintain them a little longer, but the drain on my reserves was staggering. I was losing nearly 50 MP per second and was taking some hits as well.

Another hob fell.

I powered up with a level 40 void crystal, replenishing my pool by 400 MP, but it was barely enough. I spent a hundred MP, freezing another tank, and sent my dagger flying, but a flash of magic repelled it. I summoned another host of five mastiffs and used the momentary distraction they created to absorb another level 42 crystal just in time to keep my mana from draining completely.

The last two hob tanks fell, their bodies charred and full of arrows. More arrows and magical bolts rained on me and my hounds, extinguishing them one by one. The meager damage we were doing was healed almost instantaneously by their five healers, safely tucked behind their front lines.

I released the other two shields and they collapsed under the amassing damage. I was the only one left standing, holding the entrance on my own, surrounded by bloodthirsty players and burning walls.

The goblin adepts used their Fire Rods, and flames washed over the players around me, but their healers were ready, negating the damage. The players encircled me and pummeled at my shield with obvious pleasure.

"It's the boss!"

"A weird one; why isn't he waiting for us at the end of the dungeon?"

"It's a camp, not a dungeon, you idiot."

"So why isn't he waiting for us at the end of the camp?"

"Gah! Whatever, let's get him!"

My mana was down to double digits, my shield was a moment from collapsing, and some of the players streamed past me, targeting the adepts.

Then a large, furry white shape dropped from the trees on top of a charging rogue, smashing him into the ground. Two more figures dropped, also downing charging players and bashing at them with huge, furry fists.

The apes! I realized with a start. I had nearly forgotten about their existence. The lead ape was the alpha. It was no longer a baby, but a ferocious, 200-kilo beast of fury, albeit only level 12.

The players quickly adjusted to the new attackers. Several more moved away from me, engaging the flailing apes. The beasts had bought us some time, but not a lot.

Kuzai, take the adepts and retreat to the temple! I yelled at him mentally, taking advantage of the new distraction. At least there, with the enhanced bonuses, they stood a better chance of holding the line.

Step by step, I retreated, draining another void crystal, just to keep the shield active. The excited fools who surrounded me eagerly followed, continuously hammering at my shield while more arrows and spells rained down on me, several even penetrating the shield and drawing blood.

I positioned myself next to the burning walls. My mana was down to a hundred, and my health had trickled down to 60 percent.

The loss of health doubly charged my Blood Wrath boss skill. I grinned at the players and mouthed 'bye bye,' then activated the spell. A wave of power exploded out of me with the force of an oncoming train, hurling my attackers away. Three smashed into the flaming wall, the impact draining most of their health, and the flames did the rest.

Immortal killed X 3!

Boss Tier 3 Progression: 21/50 immortals killed.

That burst had bought me a small reprieve from the onslaught. Their ranged attackers were blinded by the flames and couldn't see me. The three slain players started to melt on their own, their burning bodies converted into oozing darkness that gradually coalesced into void crystals. Upgrading Eternal Night to rank 2 was showing its usefulness.

The other players were already recovering, popping potions, getting ready to charge at me again. I had seconds to act.

Kaedric! I need you to access the temple and resurrect all our soldiers, NOW!

A long moment that felt like an eternity passed.

KAEDRIC!

I'm sorry my lord, I was unable to do so, the reply finally came. *It appears that resurrection is forbidden while hostile forces are in close proximity to the clan.*

Shadow-crap! I cursed, only now remembering what Guba had once mentioned: defeated clans usually recovered long after their assailants had disappeared.

"Damn, you're one tough boss," an elf player said as he stood up. I recognized him. It was Nesteph, one of the members of the scouting party that was sent to find us. Nesteph belted his sword and slung the shield across his back, then took out a long, wickedly spiked spear from his inventory. "But this baby ought to puncture your shield."

I threw him a contemptuous gaze then froze him and launched dagger at his helpless form, sacrificing him on the spot.

Immortal Killed!

Boss Tier 3 Progression: 22/50 immortals killed.

The other players had all shuffled to their feet and charged me again. "Watch out for his health," one of them shouted. "He activated his boss AoE when he hit 60 percent; he'll probably do another one at 20!"

They resumed hammering on my shield, and I was reduced to popping void crystals as fast as possible to stay ahead of the drain. *Just a little longer!*

More players poured through the unguarded entrance, and the hail of arrows and magic bolts on my shield resumed. A few nasty shield-penetration arrows struck my body and I was reduced to half my health. If it weren't for my tough new armor, it would probably be closer to 40 percent.

"Damn, that bastard's got a lot of mana," one of the mages wheezed. "I'm out, I need a moment to regenerate."

I continued popping void crystals, straining to keep my mana above zero.

Shouts of confusion and the clash of battle came from behind the wall.

"Finally!" I exclaimed.

My troops had arrived.

I activated Shadow Teleport and reappeared 50 meters away on the path to the village, leaving the surprised players to attack an empty bubble shield.

From my new position, I could see my troops, led by Rhyno, charging headlong into the rear of the enemy. The seven Ogres and the remaining hobs hacked their way through the line of healers. A total of 28 soldiers, out of my original 68.

The Ogres made short work of the healers, then crashed into the mages and archers from behind, encountering hastily drawn weapons and magical barriers stopping their advance.

Wincing at the cost of what I was about to do, I took out one of my two strongest void crystals and absorbed it. It was level 200, and it filled my mana to the maximum.

I cast Shadow Web, capturing some of the melee players who were trying to protect their rear and froze a rogue who managed to evade it, thus effectively bottlenecking the entrance.

A line of immobilized enemies was almost as effective as a line of friendly tanks.

My dagger flashed across the open field, injuring the frozen rogue, but for some reason not sacrificing him. Probably countered by an unknown skill.

The battle was fairly even-sided as my forces were now engaging a similar number of enemies. They even held a slight advantage as they were better suited for melee. But once the players' melee forces broke through to join the fray, we'd be in trouble. It was time to use my trump cards.

I opened my inventory and started dropping several items on the ground – 15 shining, pinkish Viridium spheres.

With a thought, the spheres came rolling together forming a single construct.

Viridium Bead Golem [Runecrafted]
Level: 15
HP: 187
Attributes: P: 15, M: -, S: -*Skills:* Slam 25
Resistances: Armor 75, Magic 50%, Fire 93%, Viridium: ignores 20

physical damage
Stored Mana: 1,500/1,500

Hey Vic, remember when I said I have a backup plan for operating the golem without distracting me?

<Yeah ...?>

I transferred control of the golem to my companion, similar to the what I had done with my shadow clone.

<Kind of a dick move to drop your shining balls into my hands, Boss.>

Vic!

<Just kidding, Boss, I've got it.>

The golem rolled toward the players. An errant fireball hit it dead center, but the metallic balls just burst through the flames, gathering more speed. It rolled into the players, throwing several of them down like bowling pins.

<Hey, this is actually pretty fun!> Vic cackled.

The golem reformed. It grew into a meter-tall column, and several spheres rolled up the top, reaching out, forming a giant 'T.' Then the arms started rotating like a fan, faster and faster. The spinning arms hit the players, crunching bones and caving armor with ease and throwing them backward. It might have been only level 15, but its weight and inertia could not be ignored.

My soldiers weren't faring as well. Some of the player rangers were also proficient melee fighters, and with the aid of their mages, they were gradually decimating my ranks. Five hobs were already dead and the rest were injured. However, the Ogres and the two bosses, Yulli and Kilpi, seemed to be holding up well.

I watched as Rhyno flattened a mage with his huge mace then followed by launching a spear at a player who was about to finish a downed hob. The player was lifted off his feet by the spear and impaled on a tree. Kilpi was now barely holding his own against four players, but that gave another six hobs the opportunity to circle around two archers and pummel them down.

One of the player mages saw that and cast a spell. A cloud of green, caustic magic formed around all eight combatants and started eating away at their health. My troops screamed as their flesh was peeled off by the acidic cloud. The two players simply grunted in dismay as their own health bar plummeted. In seconds, all eight were dead.

With my mana bar fully replenished, I kicked into high gear. I summoned another host of five mastiffs and sent them snapping at the injured to finish them off. Then, reaching for their information threads, I froze and sacrificed a susceptible player.

Vic kept the Viridium golem spinning like a blender, mowing down the enemy's melee fighters, killing two more and injuring several others.

We reduced their numbers to less than 50, but the remaining players fought back. Several drew potions, healing and buffing themselves. A mage launched a brightly colored spell at my web and vaporized it, freeing the captured players within.

Now free, half the melee fighters returned to support their rear, cutting down the hobs and harassing the Ogres. One reckless player drew two poniards and charged straight for Rhyno, yelling, for some reason, "For the King!" He jumped at the Ogre, sinking both weapons into his chest again and again, using them to pull himself up the giant's torso. Rhyno roared in pain, reached out with one hand, and plucked the stupid player from his chest, leaving deep, bleeding holes behind. With another roar, his fist crushed the man's body, snapping his spine, then threw him over his shoulder like a rotten apple. The Liquid Darkness blessing was hard at work, oozing over the Ogre's open wounds, slowly knitting his flesh together.

The players near the Viridium golem started to retaliate in earnest. Their swords had little effect against its superior armor, but a big woman holding a hammer delivered a powerful hit to one of the spheres, denting it and sending it flying away.

The battle had shifted, and we were now losing soldiers faster than the enemy. Four more hobs and an Infernal Ogre fell. Only 18 remained.

The two hob bosses fought valiantly; Yulli continued to rain arrows on the engaged fighters, taking down a player, but Kilpi was pressed hard, his health at half.

I redoubled my effort. Channeling the mana through my staff, I launched my three drilling arrows, each one at a different injured player, killing two of them. Then I commanded the shadows to amass around five players, effectively blinding them. My hounds took down two more, but three of them had also been banished. Despite losing one of its spheres, the golem continued to plow through the enemy ranks, killing another.

This was not a well-organized battle. This was a chaotic skirmish where everyone was fighting for their lives. Realizing that, I took advantage of the situation.

Rhyno! On my mark, take your Ogres and breach through their ranks toward me. The rest of the soldiers, follow the opening and throw the remaining poison grenades. Ready? Charge! Now!

As one, the Ogres led by Rhyno formed into a spearhead. They charged through the players' ranks, flailing their giant spiked maces, hitting players and throwing them back. It was the Ogres' version of a cavalry charge.

The rest of the soldiers followed the bloody path, throwing grenades at the downed players as they passed. They didn't go unscathed. Two of the Ogres sustained massive damage, but none of them were killed. If it weren't for their enchanted armor and the Eternal Night bonuses, half of them would already be dead.

The players fared much worse. Unorganized and undisciplined, their tanks weren't positioned to protect their mushier units and the sudden charge took a heavy toll on them, killing five and critically injuring several more. Those who were hit by the poison glue grenades were desperately trying to scrape it off, which only increased the amount of damage inflicted.

Once my people reached me, I cast Heal Follower, healing everyone for 25 HP.

Several players recovered and were already back on the offensive. I recognized Nitrohawk, another member of the original scouting party. Nitrohawk raised his hands and cast a fireball, taking advantage of our tight formation. The fireball exploded in our midst, dropping two more hobs and injuring another three.

The bastard had high resistances, so I couldn't freeze him, but Drilling Arrow was created specifically to punch through an enemy's defenses. I launched a trio of spinning missiles at him. Empowered by my staff, the arrows dealt enough damage to bring him down, a payment for his destructive attack.

The golem was left behind, alone in a sea of enemies and was taking a heavy pounding. More and more spheres disengaged from it, lowering its overall strength and level. It wouldn't last long.

"You freaking noobs!" a level 27 player shouted. "You let a bunch of hobs and Ogres destroy half our force! We'll be the laughingstock of the forums! Regroup! Tanks to the front, ranged attackers at the back. If anyone got an AoE buff, use it now! Kill the adds first, leave the bosses for last." The remaining players hurried to follow his orders.

I sent my dagger flying at the commanding player, but without Freeze to back it up, he raised his buckler and deflected it.

My golem managed to take down one more player before it was destroyed. We were now 16 against 37.

Full of doubts, I reached for the magical bracelet around my wrist, then thought better of it. No, it was too soon. I had to save it for the second wave. This group of players was just the warm-up act.

During the short reprieve, while we each regrouped for another clash, two more players succumbed to the poison damage and their bodies liquified into pools of darkness. The others didn't seem to care much that their friends' bodies were turned into crystals. I wondered if they would care more if they knew their deaths also granted me Faith Points.

That gave me an idea.

Glancing at my FP counter, I saw it was now set at 1,260. I grinned, opened the Eternal Night upgrade options and purchased one of the tier 2 upgrades for 1,000 FP.

Eternal Night upgrade purchased: Dark Horrors
Dark Horrors' level: 10 (blessing rank X 5)

The darkness around us seemed to recede and gather, building up like a mounting wave. Then it washed over the players. Deeper patches of darkness grew from the inky substance, taking physical shape, looking a lot like my own Shadow Hound spell.

"What the crap is going on?" one of the players exclaimed, taking a step back.

A large snake made of shadows lurched at the players but was promptly cut into pieces by several magically glowing weapons. More horrors manifested. Four-legged beasts, humanoid shadows with long, clawed hands, and nightmarish blobs full of teeth and claws flailed at the players, whittling them down.

At only level 10, the shadowy creatures were substantially weaker than the players, but their numbers made up for it. They swarmed over the group, biting, piercing, tearing.

The players retaliated. A lightning strike destroyed four creatures, and a warrior wielding a glowing dire-mace was spinning and bursting them apart like balloons. But their ranks were in chaos. No one bothered to form a cohesive fighting force; they each fought alone and in disarray.

That was my chance.

"Charge!" I yelled, casting Dark Protection over my troops and sending another Freeze-Sacrifice combo, using the stored Freeze from my staff.

Immortal Killed!

Boss Tier 3 Progression: 26/50 immortals killed.

My troops stormed at the preoccupied players, the Ogres tearing through them like a foblin through a jar of beetles.

Though unorganized, the players fought back like a bunch of frenzied berserkers. One executed a perfect somersault, decapitating an Ogre midair. Three players butchered the five remaining grunts who did their best to fend them off. Only Rhyno, along with four other Ogres and the two bosses, remained, and they kept fighting with the savage ferocity of true monsters.

The horrors continued to swarm around the players, dropping more and more of them.

Taking a few more hits, Rhyno's special boss ability kicked in, and he unleashed another Terrible Roar, invigorating the remaining troops, doubling their attack speed for a moment.

I kept casting arrows and sacrificing players, occasionally sending a healing wave to my remaining soldiers as the fight dragged on.

The tide had changed; our combined forces were slowly overpowering the players. They dropped dead like flies, but we continued to take heavy casualties

Despite their fire-powered armor, the Infernal Ogres died first, then Yulli succumbed to a necrotic spell that drained her health away. Rhyno, Kilpi, and I were the last standing. Three against a dozen players and a shitload of dark horrors as our support. My mana pool was nearly depleted, so I stopped freezing and kept on launching drilling arrows, counting on my high mana regeneration to keep me going. Rhyno was critically injured, his health hovering around 20 percent, and his liquid darkness blessing was too low to make much of a difference. There was nothing I could do either. My own heal spell was intended for a large crowd and did not restore a lot of health individually; it would hardly make a dent in the gladiator's massive health pool.

But it was Kilpi's turn to shine. As the tank boss's health reached half, his own boss AoE ability kicked in and he transformed into a whirling blur of shields, protecting both me and the Ogre, deflecting attacks and absorbing incoming spells.

With the protection he offered us, we struck back with impunity at the players, and their numbers continued to plummet until only one was left: the leader who was trying to organize them.

Somehow, using the tiny buckler, he managed to block two swinging blows from Rhyno's mace and pulled out a yellow potion. I recognized it instantly. It was called 'Death and Glory,' a last-stand sort of potion that would turn the drinker into a rampaging force of destruction for a short while, but claiming his life once the effect wore off.

I couldn't allow him to drink it.

I didn't have the mana to freeze him and I had exhausted the stored charges of my staff.

Instead, I leveled the sharp end of the staff and lunged forward. With an unbelievably lucky shot, I hit the vial and shattered it.

"NO!" The player cried in protest, though he didn't have long to lament. Kilpi performed a shield bash, stunning him, then Rhyno's club took him square in the chest, and his follow-up overhead strike smashed him into paste.

We'd won.

I leaned on my staff, breathing heavily. This was the toughest fight I had participated in since the Ogres' raid on my clan.

And it was only the first wave.

My golem was destroyed, the apes annihilated, and most of my soldiers were dead, but I couldn't let minor details get me down.

I still had the bracelet, and with the enemy now gone, I could resummon my troops, all of whom should have gained a significant increase of skills and levels. Unfortunately, as simple unseeded mobs, I couldn't do so for the apes, whose timely intervention had enabled us to hold up until the main force arrived.

The enemy's numbers took us by surprise, but despite that, we held our own and triumphed. I had no doubt that, now prepared, we would win over the second wave as well.

Kaedric, the enemy is defeated. Start resurrecting the troops.

Rhyno clasped his huge hand over Kilpi's shoulder and grunted approvingly.

Kaedric?

<I apologize, my lord, but I cannot. There are still enemies nearby.>

35 – The Enemy You Know

"Shadow-crap, shadow-crap, shadow-crap!" I fumed.

We'd killed all the players in the first wave. I knew that for a fact since the feeling of lightness had disappeared. That could only mean one thing: the culprit bastard had decided to show his cards.

"Vic, how can he suddenly be registered as an enemy when up until now he was a phantom?"

<Not sure, Boss. Maybe the system only flagged him as an enemy when he started demolishing buildings. It probably started when he destroyed the Breeder's Den, but you only notice it now when you try to resurrect your dead puppets. It's entirely possible Guy recognized his need for stealth before and hid it from you. Dad can be a jerk like that sometimes.>

"Damn it!" I pounded my hand on a nearby tree.

Kaedric! The saboteur's presence is preventing us from resurrecting our troops! We need to find and get rid of him immediately before the second wave arrives!

My seneschal responded immediately. *I understand, my lord. However, I have no way of locating him. All the noncombatants are hiding in the cave and the remaining soldiers are with you. The village is deserted. The culprit can move around unseen and unhindered.*

"Shadow-crap!" I hissed again. *Get everyone out of the cave and comb through the settlement. I want to know as soon as they encounter any of the newcomers.*

Yes, my lord.

The two bosses, Rhyno and Kilpi, were the only surviving members of my army. Vatras's plan was working after all. His first wave did what it was supposed to; their attack had left us virtually defenseless. The two bosses were barely standing on their feet. Rhyno had lost hundreds of HP and even with the Liquid Darkness blessing, it would take him ... I narrowed my eyes.

"Rhyno, how the hell are you healthy? I saw you get hacked to within an inch of your life."

The gladiator grinned wickedly and reached inside his armor. My jaw nearly dropped to the ground when I saw the curled bundle of feathers and ears he had extracted. The bundle quivered, took a rasping breath and unfurled.

It was Bek!

Rhyno chuckled gleefully. "The Champion needed more heal, but little goblin cannot near big fighting. The goblin is small, so I put inside my armor and tell, 'heal!'"

Bek hugged himself and shuddered. "Bek almost not breathe!" he piped. He shot an angry look at the Ogre, then, to my surprise, poked him with his staff; "You not put Bek in smelly armor again, or Bek use magic arrow, not magic heal!"

The Ogre laughed raucously and pulled Bek into a one-armed hug. "Next time, I tell armor-gob to make a pouch in armor for little goblin. Rhyno and Bek! Undefeated champions of the arena!"

"That's enough, Rhyno; put him down," I intervened. Bek was slowly suffocating in the Ogre's armpit.

He did as I ordered, and Bek started breathing again.

"We have a problem," I told them. "There's an enemy hiding in the valley. It is one of the newcomer travelers. We need to find him. Split up and start searching."

"At once, Chief!" Kilpi pounded his chest and walked briskly away.

"Let's go, little one," Rhyno said, leading the disgruntled Bek.

At least one good thing had come of the battle: As the sole survivors, we four had gained a lot of XP. Rhyno rose four levels to 23, Kilpi and Bek each made it to 24, and I gained two levels, bringing me to 40.

I put the two new ability points into Mental, as usual, and surveyed the field of carnage.

Blood, body parts, dropped items, and shimmering void crystals dotted the ground. I couldn't spare the time to go through them now. *Kaedric, send some workers to collect the loot from the battlefield.*

Yes, my lord.

I cast Shadow Teleport and left the scene.

***

I reappeared out of the shadows, standing at Totem's Watch, and scanned the valley.

I did not detect any movement. As Kaedric claimed, the place was deserted.

Below me, my goblins started to flow out of the cave and spread across the open part of the valley, looking for the elusive culprit.

In the meantime, I had to do what I could to prepare for the second wave and trust my clanmates to do their part. I turned around and entered the temple.

Kuzai and the two adepts were standing on the other side of the door. They wielded blobs of darkness, ready to attack if an enemy made it through.

I ignored them, marched straight to the shrine, and placed my hands on the rough stone and bones apparatus. I accessed the temple's interface directly and was satisfied to learn that even after purchasing the Dark Horrors upgrade, I had slightly over 3,000 FP at my disposal.

Fighting and killing players inside the zone of darkness was immensely rewarding. Every dead player was consumed by darkness, earning Faith Points for my clan and leaving a high-level void crystal behind. And I planned to capitalize on that.

Accessing the Eternal Night upgrade options, I purchased several debuffs. The first reduced enemy max health by ten percent, the second reduced damage dealt by ten percent. Each cost 500 FP. The last reduced their resistances and armor by ten percent for 1,000 FP.

That left me with exactly 1,060 FP to spare. I could afford an additional upgrade, but I decided to go another path. The last two surviving bosses had earned themselves an upgrade. I upped their Liquid Darkness blessing to rank 3 for 100 FP, which improved their health regeneration.

For another 120 FP, I splurged on Shadow Armor III for them both, which provided an additional 15 armor. I finished by getting the Coat Weapon III blessing, increasing their damage output and armor penetration by 20 percent.

I spent 350 FP on two soldiers, more than I'd ever spent on one individual before. I tried to convince myself it was a vote of confidence in their battle prowess, but I couldn't fool myself. This was an act of desperation. As things stood, those two would be the only ones standing between an invading army and my clan. And despite the benefit of the home field advantage, without the rest of my troops, we were outmatched.

Even with the new blessings, these two would only be able to buy us a minute.

Probably less.

I had to find the elusive player and put an end to him. Permanently.

Kaedric, anything new?

<Yes!>

His answer took me by surprise. My pulse quickened and I allowed my contained anger to swell.

Where are they?

<I have just learned that while we –>

WHO IS IT KAEDRIC? I didn't let him finish

<Misa, from The Mob Squad, my lord. She has persuaded both her male compatriots to join her cause and the three are on their way to land another devastating blow on the clan. Raystia has run after them to try and stop them, but I fear she won't prevail on her own. We must assist, her my lord!">

The urgent tone was out of character for my seneschal. The exact details must have unnerved him.

Just tell me where.

<In the northeastern part of the valley, my lord, below the highest peak.>

That was inside the forested part of the valley. I ran outside the temple and looked in that direction. With a thought, I cast Shadow Teleport and reappeared inside the gloomy forest.

I stood between the gnarly, black trees and scanned my surroundings. There was no one in sight.

My Tracking skill kicked in, illuminating signs of recent passage. A single person had passed through here not long ago. I spotted blood smears on some of the tree trunks.

I started following the tracks. They led me deeper into the forest until I came into a patch of open ground, only a few meters across. The bloody tracks continued straight forward and into a bed of flowers.

I moved toward the flowers, frowning. Something didn't feel right here.

I heard a moan and I instantly cast Mana Shield and summoned a trio of drilling arrows. I cautiously approached the flower bed and found an injured person lying in the center.

Raystia.

The catgirl was bleeding from a number of cuts along her legs, but she was alive.

"Raystia?" I called, scanning my surrounding. "Where are Misa and the others?"

"Hey Totem Chief, Sir," she said weakly and coughed. "I am sorry ... I tried, I really tried, but I just couldn't ... they were too strong."

I took another step, standing just outside the flower patch. I could see her legs were sliced up pretty bad, which was probably why she was prone. She also had the bleeding debuff and would die from blood loss within minutes if not treated.

Still, I didn't move any closer. My Dangersense was screaming at me that something wasn't right.

I cast Shadow Hounds and ordered the five mastiffs to sweep the trees around us and look for ambushes. *Keep an eye open as well, Vic.*

<You got it, Boss.>

"What happened here?" I moved another step toward the woman, trampling several flowers.

Her eyes were glazed as she stared at a flower on her eye level. "Those are beautiful, aren't they?" she whispered dreamily.

I glanced at the flowers. They were mostly black, like everything else that now grew in the forest, and had green pollen. "They're okay. Who attacked you?"

"I used to love flowers," she continued, ignoring my question. "When I played NEO in my teens, I used to collect them all the time."

I took a step closer. "That ought to have given you the 'Flower Picking' skill. I once knew a girl who had it. Here, let me see your wounds."

"Yes, I used to have that skill," she continued with the same dreamy mannerism. "I even got it as high as level 52." She chuckled.

My hand that was reaching to treat her injuries froze in place, my mind in an uproar. The rest of the world froze as well. There were no sounds, no movements. I existed in between moments as my brain raced, processing that bit of information, and came to a shattering conclusion.

The girl I used to know had that skill at level 52 as well. She would often stride into my office to show me her latest herbal discovery. She was a sweet kid with a generous heart, and I liked her regardless of the fact that she was also the niece of my best friend.

My lieutenant. Vatras.

The bastard did have a spy in my clan after all.

"You!" I exclaimed. "*You* are behind all this!"

She looked up at me and her dazed appearance disappeared, replaced with a smug smile. "Too late, Chief." Then she flailed her limbs, crushing the flowers around her, causing them to release their pollen.

I suddenly found myself standing inside a cloud of green particles. I teleported away but the particles had already sifted through my shield and reached my mouth. I appeared at the edge of the clearing, coughing.

Debuff: Goblin Bane Pollen

Your movement speed is reduced by 30%

Spell speed is reduced by 30%

Duration: 1 hour

Lucky Bastard skill level increased to 42.

Raystia downed a potion, and her bleeding stopped. She got up and gave me a steady, appraising look.

Still coughing, I glared at her accusingly.

She steeled her gaze. "I won't explain myself to you. Go ahead and kill me now; I'll just respawn in the cemetery."

"W–" I coughed, "W–why?"

She rolled her eyes and unslung her bow. "The pollen debuff is especially nasty if you breathe it for a few seconds, but you acted quickly so I guess you only took a portion of that."

That explained the skill progression message.

"I guess I'll have to chance it anyway." She drew the bowstring and released an arrow. It hit my shield with an explosion of light.

I squinted, looking at the arrowhead centimeters from my face. It had punched through my shield but didn't have enough momentum to reach me. I recognized the slender white missile. A hugger bone arrow, one of my own clan's make.

"Fight, damn it." The woman readied another arrow. "Show me your true self; the monster who hurt the people I care for."

For a second I considered doing just that. The coughing didn't affect my spellcasting ability. It would be a simple matter to freeze then teleport her into Nihilator's den and let him devour her. It would end the threat she posed once and for all. *And would probably increase my standing with the dark deity,* the goblin in me couldn't help thinking. *Nihilator would love munching on this juicy traveler ...*

<Snap out of it, Boss,> Vic said sharply.

I came back to my senses. "Wai–" I coughed again, "Wait!"

She drew back the string.

"Pen– Penelope!"

The arrow flew wide, missing me. Raystia stood there, looking at me with astonishment.

"Whe... where did you hear that name from?" She sounded much less sure of herself.

***

Raystia gaped at the coughing goblin. For the first time in a long time, she did not know what to do.

After he uttered her name, he just kept on coughing and wouldn't speak.

What was she supposed to do now? Raystia wasn't sure.

Her uncle had tasked her with undermining and hampering this goblin's efforts, softening them up in preparation for his forces to sweep in and deliver the finishing blow. But that ... man... somehow knew her real name!

"Whe... where did you hear that name from?" she uttered weakly, her mind reeling at the possibilities.

He just kept on coughing.

She wasn't feeling too good either. As part goblin herself, the poison was making her weak and her movement sluggish. She guessed that for a pure goblin the effects would be even more severe.

But she didn't have to wait for him to answer. Her well-trained analytical mind was already deducing the most likely scenario.

That man somehow knew her. When she revealed the bit about her old character's skill he instantly knew she was responsible for the clan's trouble. That meant he knew her old character and he knew her real name. Other than Vatras, her uncle, there were only a handful of people in NEO who knew who she was back then, and of those people, only one of them, that she knew of, was missing.

Her voice quivered as she hesitantly spoke. "O ... Oren?"

***

I finally coughed enough of the pollen out of my system to able to speak properly. I straightened and looked at the wild-eyed woman.

"Hello, Pen." I smiled weakly. "It's been a while."

"Bu– but ..." She opened and closed her mouth a few times. She eventually decided on keeping it closed and her eyes had a distant look as if she were deep in thought.

She had changed. Back then, the girl I knew as Penelope Katie Britt used to play as an elf and took pleasure in the simplest of things; picking flowers, swimming, sitting in a tavern with friends. She was always smart for her age and I knew she was studying to become a scientist.

At last, she opened her eyes and nodded. "I understand now. I'm so sorry, Uncle Oren. He deceived me. I didn't know it was you."

"Wait." I raised my hand, "I want to hear everything, but right now your presence prevents me from recalling my dead soldiers. Without them, the clan is defenseless."

"It shouldn't be a problem anymore," she said. "When you realized I was the spy, I received a Hatred status with your clan and when you recognized who I really was, it shot back up to Neutral. I believe you can summon your troops now."

I nodded. *Kaedric –*

A sense of lightness fell down on me.

"Oh no ..." Raystia paled. "I'm so sorry, Oren."

The second wave had arrived.

***

I clenched my fists, my sharp goblin nails digging into my palms. *Why hadn't I resurrected my troops the instant she stopped fighting me?* I berated myself. *Stupid, stupid, stupid!*

<Come on, Boss, you only had a few seconds. At most, you could only have gotten a handful of them.>

That would still be a handful more than I have now, I thought bitterly back to him, but forced myself to exhale and calm down.

Kaedric, withdraw all the noncombatants back into the cave. Have Rhyno and Kilpi guard the temple. We will make our final stand there.

Yes, my lord.

"Give me your hand, and don't resist," I told Raystia.

She gingerly complied and I teleported us both to my house.

I sat in my comfortable armchair and gestured for her to take the other seat. I knew the second wave of players would take at least half an hour to reach us, and I wanted to know what to expect. Raystia could help fill in the blanks. "We have a little time," I said. "Tell me your story."

Raystia slumped in her chair, her head bent. "I was so busy at work," she said miserably, "so ... *needed.* I barely had enough time to live, let alone have fun. That's why I was so happy to receive the invitation to play at an accelerated time. After my first game sessions, I was so excited I had to share it with my uncle. After all, he was the one who introduced me to the game and taught me how to play. I was careful not to mention the items protected by the NDA they made me sign; the accelerated time and playing as part-monster. I just told him about my adventures, which included me helping to develop a new village in the Deadlands. In hindsight, I now realize he already knew your location, so it was simple for him to connect the dots and figure out I had access to your clan."

She sighed. "He told me a story about how you, a goblin player, stole something important from his guild and as a result, his best friend, the guildmaster, lost his position and decided to drop out of the game permanently. He said he was working on a plan to return the Manapulators to greatness, but he needed my help. He needed me to provide him with information about the clan and to hamper your progress."

I gave her a long, searching look then shook my head. "It's hard for me to picture you killing two defenseless workers, or setting buildings on fire; that's not who you are. The girl I knew was gentle and shy, she would never have done what you did."

She frowned. "You're right, that's who I am, in *real* life. Do you know how tiring it is to always be the good girl? How frustrating it is? I'm bad at talking to people. But NEO allowed me to transform, becoming someone completely different. Here, I am Raystia, the fearless catgirl-archer-rogue. Here, I can pretend to be someone powerful and confident and do things I would never have done in real life. Vatras's request was right along those lines. My uncle was never the gentle sort. It was a thrill, all of it; the killing, the subterfuge, the sneaking around." She smiled sadly. "I became quite good at sneaking around. I spotted your hob scouts trying to tail me within five minutes."

"That's another thing I wanted to ask you about. How did you manage to do anything while they were watching you?"

She chuckled. "It's simple, I asked Kaedric to recall them."

I frowned. "He wouldn't disobey my orders. I made it clear I wanted you and a few other players followed."

She shrugged. "He is just an NPC, Oren. A smart one, sure, but in the end, he is a slave to the rules of the game. There are layers of interaction available to players to influence NPCs, you know that."

With my inside knowledge of the VIs' plight, I was probably more aware of that fact than any other player in the world. "So how did you do it?"

"I have achieved a Respected reputation with him, so when I suggested that the scouts were wasting their time by following me, he agreed."

"How the hell did you get that reputation rank?" Even mine wasn't as high.

"It was simple. I realized early on that our lovable mandibled hob was always hungry for brains, so I started bringing him some. It took me less than a week. I got 500 reputation points for every victim I delivered."

"I see ... so that's how you made him think Misa was behind everything?"

She nodded. "I needed to lure you into a trap, and I needed a reasonable explanation for breaking your ban on players. So I told Kaedric I discovered it was the others who were acting against you and that I intended to stop them. Sure enough, you came as I expected. You were really lucky to escape the pollen cloud when you did. I bought the goblin bane poison from Hoshisu and experimented combining it with flowers. If you had breathed it for a few more seconds, you wouldn't be walking right now."

"So that's why you have the Florist skill. I thought it was weird when I first noticed it."

"How did you –" she started, but then stopped and grinned. "Yes. It's nothing like a florist in real life. I can use mana to shape flowers and give them a number of interesting properties. It's a little like alchemy, only with flowers. Oh, by the way, sniff this. It will counteract the poison." She presented me with a small white flower.

I smelled the flower, then something else clicked. "A goblin detonated a vial of liquid fire in the mess hall. There were flowers in the vial that burst into flames."

She nodded. "FlowerFuse; it's one of the simplest to create. I learned how important the Breeder's Den was to the clan, so I set out to sabotage it. I was just about to pour the liquid fire on it when a hob patrol got a whiff and came to investigate. I had to create a diversion, so I gave one of the foblins a vial as a present for 'The Chief.' With my reputation, it was easy. The little guy ... ahem ... well ... you saw the rest. Er ... sorry about that."

I grunted. The loss of the Breeder's Den was a real hit; it would take a little more than 'sorry' to make amends.

"So how did you hide the liquid fire from my troops this long? I had them scan every part of the valley."

She shrugged. "Easy. I just logged out for a few days. Vatras messaged me when the first attack wave was within striking distance, so I logged back in to blow up the walls. Your hobs were crawling all over it, so I put enough lavender in the vat to throw them off the scent. They really have a terrible sense of smell, you know."

Her casual recollection of destroying a third of my army caused my anger to flare, but I couldn't help admiring her resourcefulness. Almost single-handedly, she, a low-level player, nearly toppled an entire clan. I chuckled and shook my head. "You have grown into a mischievous little brat, Pen. You nearly assured the destruction of the GreenPiece Clan."

"Er ... ahem ... Sorry ... about that ...?"

"What else can you tell me about Vatras's plan?"

She lowered her eyes. "I ... don't really know. You know my uncle, he keeps a lot to himself. He didn't let me in on the details, only ... um ... that they were coming. And ... ahem ..."

She was falling back into her 'normal' speech patterns.

"Anything else you can tell me will be extremely helpful," I encouraged her.

"Ahem ... okay. I *think* my uncle knows about the time difference thing."

"How? You said you didn't tell him."

She steepled her fingers. "I guess he just figured it out. I did tell him about a week-long's worth of adventures after playing only a couple of days." She winced. "Now that I think about it, I ... ahem ... think he hinted that he knew ... um ... he said something like, 'Take a few days to work out your plan.' And the next day he wanted to hear what I came up with, so ... ahem ... yeah, he probably knows."

I frowned. There wasn't much I could do about it, and I couldn't see a way for Vatras to exploit this against me. It just meant he was aware that he had to work swiftly, to minimize the time I had to fortify our defenses. "Thank you for the information," I told the young woman. "The second wave will hit us in about ten minutes. You should log out now."

"But I want to help!" she protested. "As improbable as it sounds, I love the GreenPiece Clan. I liked helping make it into something greater ... ahem ... I mean ... before I tried to tear it down. I don't want to see you destroyed! I'll stay and help you fight!"

I shook my head. "Vatras doesn't know you switched sides on him, and I want to keep it that way. I need you to be *my* spy, once we've defeated the second wave." *If we defeat the second wave*, I couldn't help thinking.

Her downcast expression brightened. "From a spy to a double agent? That sounds like fun! Oooh, can I get like ... ahem ... a code name?"

"How about agent 'Meow?'"

Her eyes lit up, "Aww! That's so adorable ... ahem ... no! I want a better name, something dangerous. How about –"

I held up my hand. "I'll let you figure it out. You should log out. I have an invading army to deal with."

"Yes, Uncle Oren, right away!"

"And, uh ... let's keep my real name just between the both of us, alright?"

Her eyes twinkled. "You got it ... Chief. But next time we talk, it's your turn to tell me your story of how you ended up here. Deal?" Without waiting for my answer, she logged out, her body becoming translucent until it disappeared completely.

I heaved a sigh and leaned against the table, dropping my head onto my arms, my thoughts back to the new impossible challenge. "Three bosses against 20 seasoned, higher-level players," I mumbled. "How the hell am I going to handle that one?"

<May I offer a suggestion, Boss?>

I could use a good one right about now, Vic, but please, nothing involving my shining balls.

<Let the light guide your way,> he said cryptically.

I raised my head in anger. "That's your idea of a joke? Now of all times?" I snorted. "I'm not about to repent of my sins and 'see the light.' And if you meant real light, well in case you forgot, it's pretty dark around here. The only light comes from this goddammed green cha–"

I stopped abruptly as comprehension dawned on me.

"Thanks, Vic."

<No problem, Boss.>

36 – Second Wave

The war party advanced steadily through the dense forest for several hours, finally coming to a stop in front of a burned down wall.

"A'ight boys." The leading dwarf turned to face the rest of them. "We made it into 'em greenskins' nest, time for some pesticiding."

"I don't like it," a tall, slender woman garbed in tight-fitting robes said. "The debuff just worsened. It's like we're being pulled into a maelstrom."

"Tell me about it," a warrior holding a quarterstaff grunted. "Minus ten percent to max HP, damage, and resistances. Feels more like we're approaching a raid boss than a goblin clan. And what's with this magical darkness?"

"Yeah." The tall woman turned and glared at an obviously high-level mage in fine gear. "Maybe the Manapulators' first lieutenant could be bothered to do something about it."

"Oh, alright." BigPill rolled his eyes. "Don't worry, kids. Let there be light!"

He hit the butt of his staff against the ground, and the gem at the top flared into bright, white light. A dome of pure energy grew around the war party, spreading to cover a 20-meter radius, pushing back the darkness and the *things* that lurked within.

"Not bad," the woman said. "The debuffs are still there, but now only at half the strength."

"Please try to remember that this is a tryout," Hirooku said pleasantly. The Manapulators' other lieutenant looked perfectly at ease in the dark, his hands resting comfortably on the hilts of his twin swords. "It defeats the purpose if we do all the hard work for you."

Another player nodded. "At least the aura holds back the beasts of darkness the first wave encountered. They're around level ... 10. Vulnerable to magic and light-based spells specifically; shouldn't be an issue either way."

"If you sissies are done smacking y'all's lips around," the dwarf said, glaring back at them, "how 'bout we go get us some gob meat, eh?"

"Damn, Ragnar, don't you think you take this whole southern-hillbilly act a little too far?" the quarterstaff-wielding player asked. "I mean, that's not how dwarves sound."

Ragnar's eyes shot daggers at him. "When we git done here, boy, you and me are gonna have ourselves some alone time."

The other player visibly paled at the threat. "I didn't mean anything by –"

"We have incoming! Battle formations!" said a player in pristine white full-plate armor who went by 'Daniel_The_Destroyer.'

The war party formed into an arrowhead. Seven shield-wielding tanks, with Ragnar at the front, formed the outer lines. Casters and ranged attackers were in the middle with four healers evenly spread between them.

"Here comes 'the fun part,'" Ragnar declared, but he frowned as he saw what was coming for them.

A lone creature darted behind the trees toward the circle of light. It looked like a goblin, but it was human-sized and had scaly arms that reached to the ground, ending in vicious talons. His hooved feet left smoking trails on the ground behind him. His face contorted into a terrible, hungry grin, displaying razor-sharp teeth.

"Is that ..." one of the players said hesitantly, "a demon goblin?"

One of the archers aimed his bow. "It's about to be a dead one."

His arrow streaked over the players' heads, splitting into three arrows midair, all scoring direct hits on the creature's chest. The creature's momentum carried it over the last few meters, running headlong into a hastily raised shield.

Then it exploded.

The force of the explosion splintered the shield, and bits of bone shrapnel shot into the players' formation, injuring several, but not severely. Another two demon goblins appeared at the edge of the circle of light.

"Archers, take them down before they reach us," Daniel_The_Destroyer commanded. "Healer, top off the wounded, tanks – advance!"

***

I watched from my spot between the trees as two more juiced-up foblins stormed the players.

I was surrounded by a throng of foblins, over 60 of them, and was busy infusing them with infernal energies as quickly as possible. I made each foblin bleed a few drops into the Chalice of Infernal Energies then drink it up. They, in turn, started to morph. Some grew wings, and some grew horns. Others grew spikes and flaming tails. All became bigger and were grasped by an insatiable bloodlust.

Once the transformation was complete, they became wild and unmanageable suicide bombers. It was all I could do to point them in the right direction to wildly charge at the players. Every exploding foblin caused an AoE damage equal to its max health. At level 1, with their goblinoid and demonic templates, that amounted to roughly 25.

The players adapted to the situation; their tanks distanced themselves from the main group, forming a protective line that intercepted the possessed foblins. Every dead foblin subsequently exploded in a spray of blood, gore, and bone as the infernal energies within them could no longer be contained. With the new formation, the tanks bore the brunt while the rest of the players remained protected behind them.

The second wave's experience and teamwork showed as their ranged attackers easily picked off the demon foblins, often before even reaching their tank line. To make matters worse, every foblin who entered the protective circle of white energy started smoking and their HP drained rapidly.

I was sending the foblins in twos and threes, but it was not nearly enough to overwhelm the enemy's unwavering defense. Their thirst for blood was immediate. I couldn't organize them or send them in numbers.

After sending ten foblins in a row, I could tell this tactic was not working. The tanks perfectly absorbed the incoming damage and their healers were quick to top them off. They kept themselves spread out so that even a concentrated surprise attack wouldn't be enough to take out all their healers in one go. But the circle of protective holy aura was the biggest obstacle. Aside from weakening the foblins, it held the dark horrors at bay and seemed to be negating most of the Eternal Night's debuffs.

I recognized the player at the center of the group, the source of the aura: BigPill. My nemesis's number one lieutenant. He needed to die.

It was easier said than done. BigPill was a level 270 mage and there was little I could do to harm him.

However, *this* was just the first step. Even empowered by the infernal energies, I didn't expect the foblins to do much damage. But seeing the enemy's reaction was useful.

Time to raise the ante. I had four foblins bleed into the chalice's green flames then take a sip. This time, when the first foblin started showing signs of rebellion, I used Dominate on him.

Despite the chaotic swirls of energy inside the creature, it was still at its core one of my own minions and it was perfectly attuned to my influence. I barely had to apply myself to assume control over its mind.

With the first demonic foblin firmly under mental lock, I promptly transformed the other three, dominating each one in turn, then sent them charging all at once.

The four possessed foblins burst through the trees and stormed the players. All but one was picked off by their ranged fighters, but the last one exploded right up against the tanks' shield wall, making them stumble just a bit.

That was when I unleashed four more. The new wave reached the still-reeling tanks and one managed to break through their line. It was picked off with a well-aimed Ice Blast before it made any real progress, but its subsequent explosion reached the main group, injuring them slightly.

I had hoped the damage would break BigPill's concentration, but he didn't even notice. A sudden, blurred movement protected him from the spray of gore before it reached him. I narrowed my eyes. Something here was not as it seemed.

The players worked too well together. Their lines never faltered, protecting their weaker companions as they walked through the forest. I'd wasted two dozen foblins with little to show for it, but I had a good feel for their capabilities. Ragnar, the hated dwarf tank from the initial scouting party, was an especially tough foe, not even flinching as a foblin exploded right against his shield.

Time for phase two.

I had about 40 foblins remaining, and I ordered them to retreat to the wall of cabins. I stayed behind, buying them some time with a few more suicide attacks. Then I teleported away.

***

I refilled my staff with three empowered drilling arrows then stood on the central cabin's roof, watching the white aura approaching from behind the trees.

I let them come a little closer before revealing myself and commanding, "Stop!"

The players all stopped in surprise and looked up at me.

"Is that the final boss?" one of them said with a frown. "These goblins are weird."

"Turn back and leave!" I demanded.

"And why would we do that?" the player snorted.

Threats were useless. There was nothing I could do to really harm them. At most, they'd die and respawn back in their home city. But threats weren't the course of action I had in mind. I had other options available to me.

"Because." I gave them mischievous grin. "Whoever turns and leaves us in peace will be rewarded. Whoever is willing to side with us against his friends will receive triple the award." I maxed out the rewards in the quest giver alert that popped up.

"Oh shit, he's not joking," a female rogue exclaimed. "Damn – 6,000 XP, 2,000 gold and a unique magic item!"

"Oh, and whoever interrupts this asshole's spell ..." I pointed at BigPill, who glared at me, "will get something extra on top of that."

Most of the players didn't budge, but the rogue woman exchanged looks with a lean man, and as one they lifted their weapons and turned to BigPill.

The telltale blur I'd seen before shimmered again, and the two players lost their heads. Literally.

And standing between the decapitated corpses was Hirooku, a level 280 player. Vatras's personal assassin.

"That was amusing, but I think we get the point," he said casually, flicking the blood off his twin swords. "In case you were wondering," he continued pleasantly, addressing the other players, "those two are disqualified. We expect a little more loyalty from our prospects." He looked up at me where I still stood on the cabin roof. "And as for you ..."

He slashed with his two swords vertically. The force of the slash was immense, tearing apart the air itself, hurling a blade of vacuum at me.

The blade tore apart my body, the cabin I was standing on, and the two adjacent ones.

I blinked, getting control back over my real body as my shadow clone evaporated, draining a large chunk of my mana along with it. Still, I smiled.

With a few words, and by exploiting the tools at my disposal, I had both reduced the number of enemies and revealed their trump card.

Now I could finally use my own card.

It was time to bring out the big guns.

From my hiding spot behind a large tree at the edge of the forest, I held up the Epic bracelet and activated it.

A pillar of pale blue light fell from the sky, piercing the dome of darkness around the valley and descending right in the middle of the enemy's formation.

A large being soared down the pillar using his feathered white wings to control his descent. He landed in a crash in the players' midst, his fist punching the ground to cushion his landing. Then he stood up, a muscular, blue-skinned humanoid clad in shining silver armor and holding a huge, radiant two-handed sword. The sense of power emanating from the being was palpable.

With hardly any effort, I picked up the Outrider's information. It was a level 250 creature, and though not a boss or even an alpha, it was an especially powerful being with over 5,000 HP. As a summoned creature he didn't have a personality of his own, a VI, so his sole purpose was to obey the one who summoned him.

Kill those two! I ordered it, mentally indicating BigPill and Hirooku.

The Outrider lifted his huge sword with one hand, a feat that even an Ogre would find hard to accomplish. Ignoring the small fries, he brought it crashing down on top of BigPill.

The high-level mage cursed and retracted his aura spell. The light condensed into a single bead of force on top of his staff, and he raised it to meet the Outrider's sword.

The impact of the two weapons sent a shockwave that staggered the lower-level players, and the attack was repelled. The Outrider immediately followed up with his own magic. He leaned forward, and a wave of sonic force hit the mage full in the face, sending him tumbling to the ground and taking a quarter of his health.

Hirooku lunged to save his prone friend and used a skill to intercept the Outrider's next attack. The two exchanged blows, each showing their masterful control, though it was clear the Outrider was the more powerful of the two. The distraction was enough for BigPill to get to his feet and start casting a spell, sending a cone of glowing stars at my summoned creature.

Without the protective light in place, the players were hit with the full effects of the Eternal Night's debuffs, bringing down their max health and lowering their damage and resistances.

A second later, the dark horrors manifested.

Still fighting off the Outrider, Hirooku shouted to the players, "Do your job, destroy everything in sight! We'll hold off this mob – hurry up, prove that you are worthy of the Manapulators!" Then he was thrown back, crashing into another cabin, reducing it to rubble.

"You hear 'em boys! Let's bring in the hurt!" Ragnar chuckled.

The eight tanks surrounded the other ten players, holding back the creatures of darkness. As most of them were nearing level 40 and equipped with magic gear, they easily held back the level 10 horrors. The healers cast their own version of holy protection and anti-evil spells, imploding horrors by the dozens.

They continued to advance, walking straight through the demolished cabins. A couple of fireballs were sent flying, hitting the mess hall and the warehouse. Both buildings went up in flames.

I snarled. *No one messes with my clan. Go! Attack! Drink their blood!*

Prior to revealing myself to the players, I dominated *all* the remaining foblins. While I held the invaders' attention with words, I had Vic continue infusing the critters with the Chalice of Infernal Energies.

Three dozen raging goblins-turned-demons streamed from behind the remaining cabins. I unleashed all the restraints and they swarmed over the players.

With the 18 players distracted by the horrors and nearly 40 possessed foblins charging them at once, my odds of winning were looking better and better.

The first line of foblins attacked with abandon, slashing with claws and ramming their horns against the tanks' shields, several even breaking through their line and reaching their mages and healers.

My heart filled with elation as victory seemed near, but I was too quick to rejoice.

The players were not thrown off by the attack and showed why they were specifically chosen to form up the 'second wave.'

Several of the tanks shouted taunts, and the untrained foblins were drawn in. The mages followed, using AoE spells – fireballs, arcs of electricity, and waves of cold were sent over the clusters of foblins, dropping them like flies. The tanks took damage from the spells and exploding foblins, but their healers worked efficiently, triaging the wounded and keeping their health from dropping to critical levels.

Dominating 40 creatures right after receiving a huge amount of damage to my shadow clone depleted the majority of my mana pool. I drained another void crystal, restoring myself back to half. Though it only took a few seconds, by the time I was ready to join the fight, over 30 foblins were dead.

One of the tanks looked to be in bad shape after having nearly 20 foblins detonate right on top of him, and most of the other players were injured as well, but their healers were working to rectify that.

Without time to waste, I cast Drilling Arrow on the critically injured tanks, while simultaneously using a stored Drilling Arrow spell from my staff on a mage who had low health.

> **Immortal Killed X2!**
>
> *Boss Tier 3 Progression:* 29/50 immortals killed.

The two players dropped dead, their bodies liquifying. *They'll make excellent void crystals*, the goblin in me thought with glee.

My dagger zoomed in, wounding another player, but not enough for it to be a killing blow.

In response, the healers cast their high-level AoE heals, topping off all the players.

The last foblin died in a spray of blood and bone.

Over 60 demonically enhanced foblins and they'd barely made a dent in the enemy. From the original 20 players, 16 had survived, and by the looks of it, I'd just helped them get rid of their weak links.

Some distance away, BigPill and Hirooku continued fighting against my Outrider. The mage was surrounded by a rainbow-colored bubble and sending sizzling bolts of acid at my summoned creature. Hirooku's movements flashed faster than the eye could see, attacking seemingly from multiple angles all at once.

Still, although the Outrider was a slightly lower level than them and down 20 percent health, he was not a pushover. Walls of blue flame sprang up around him, scorching and blinding the adjacent player, and a powerful sword swing bit deeply into his Epic armor and sent him flying across the valley, crashing through two workshops.

Meanwhile, with the foblins eradicated, and despite their debuffs, the players resumed their formation and were slaughtering the dark horrors. They continued to advance deeper into the village, reaching the pond.

A couple more fireballs were sent flying sideways, lighting up the woodcutter's hut and the rabbit warren.

They did not suffer more casualties, and I was running out of tricks.

In desperation, I cast Shadow Web over their leading tanks, causing them to halt for a moment until one of their healers cast a cleansing spell and the web evaporated. I targeted the lowest-health players – one of the healers – and launched another volley of drilling arrows from my staff, followed by the dagger. At the last instant, a force field shimmered into existence, protecting the player. True to their name, the drilling arrows burrowed through the barrier, but the damage they inflicted was vastly reduced and the following dagger did not inflict enough damage to finish him off.

I narrowed my eyes as I spotted the caster responsible for the reactive protection spell. The injured healer was topped off a moment later, and their force continued to march deeper into the village.

I couldn't fight them on my own. Not here.

Time for phase three.

I teleported and appeared standing on Totem's Watch, just outside the temple. Kuzai and the two adepts stood guarding the door. Nihilator's power was palpable here. My mana regeneration picked up, filling my depleted pool.

I could clearly see the invading army 50 meters away advancing on us, though they certainly couldn't see us through the magical darkness.

As the players kept coming and torching the buildings, I cast Dark Protection over the three priests. Then I moved to the edge and cast Mana Shield.

"You two," I addressed the adepts, not bothering to turn my head. "Use the Fire Rods. Aim for the same target, Kuzai –"

"I will unleash our lord's fury upon the heretics," the twisted dwarf hissed. "*It* will be shown what power over darkness truly means."

"Sure, whatever," I said distractedly, wincing as my Outrider was hit by a ray of red magic that sent him crashing through the research center. I absorbed another void crystal, filling up my mana pool. "Get ready, they're nearly here."

The players made it into range. This close to the temple's power, I sensed some of the players were now vulnerable to my most destructive abilities. I raised my staff and channeled my mana. "Now!"

The two adepts shot jets of fire at one of the leading tanks, while I used Freeze on another and sent my dagger soaring toward its neck, simultaneously casting Shadow Web.

The tank froze in place, but just as my dagger was about to sacrifice it, Ragnar thrust out his shield, deflecting the hit. *Stinking dwarf*, I fumed. *I will bathe in his entrails!*

The Shadow Web had more success. Tendrils of darkness, twice as thick as usual, manifested out of the gloom and wrapped around the front rank of the players, holding them down.

The healers were quick to counter with their own holy light spells, but then Kuzai stepped forward. His own shadow clone shimmered into existence next to him, more substantial than ever. Together they summoned a huge ball of crackling darkness between them, working to grow it into immense proportions, then sent it flying into the center of the enemy formation.

The spell struck the ground, sending ripples of dark lightning through the players. The result was less than spectacular. Most only received a small amount of damage, less than ten percent of their total, but as I watched, the cracks of darkness converged on the healers, killing one on the spot and severely injuring the rest.

"There are two bosses up there!" a player shouted. "Protect the healers, provide cover fire!"

Kuzai had just given us an advantage, throwing the enemy off his momentum.

Time for phase four.

Attack! I screamed mentally, just as a hail of arrows and magic spells descended on my shield. A fireball missed me and exploded against the temple, but the sturdy stone walls withstood the damage.

Rhyno and Kilpi burst out of the cave where they'd been hiding, followed by Nihilator's four large, level 25 mastiffs. I had originally considered using the chalice's power on the two bosses but eventually decided against it. I needed cunning, adaptable fighters more than I needed rampaging berserkers. Besides, an unexpected lull in the fight could lead to their demise. Without the outlet of an enemy to fight, the energy raging inside them could explode.

The six charged the rattled players. The mastiffs pounced on two tanks, and Kilpi followed, charging with his shield raised like a battering ram, punching through the line of tanks. Using the opening, Rhyno followed, right into the middle of the players' formation.

Get those healers! I shouted.

The Ogre gladiator swung a huge, spiked mace in a large arc, crushing the already injured healers and killing two of the three remaining.

Thirteen players remained, their formation broken and most of their healers dead. There was hope yet.

"Ye' damn A-holes fight like a bunch of ninnies," Ragnar grumbled. He tapped his shield with his axe, causing it to flash crimson, then roared a taunt.

The four mastiffs jumped off their targets and charged at him, followed, to my surprise, by Kilpi.

"No!" I shouted, watching as my well-laid plan was crumbling down. "You two, target that dwarf!"

I looked behind me and my heart sank. The two adepts' bodies were blown to smithereens by the earlier bombardment. Only Kuzai, with his boss's high health, survived, though with only 50 percent remaining.

He nodded at me though and both he and his shadow hurled regular-sized dark spheres at the dwarf, while I followed with a volley of drilling arrows.

But Ragnar would not go down so easily. His red, glowing shield absorbed Kuzai's unholy spells and my arrows, though some damage filtered through his lowered resistances. Still, all that only took a third of his health.

The other players rallied. Three of the unwebbed tanks surrounded Rhyno, occupying his attention and helping the others get away from him. Then they took turns catching his attacks, sharing the damage. The other players divided their attention between the Ogre and me, bombarding us both. His health and my mana were draining rapidly.

There was no phase five.

In the distance, the high-level players and the Outrider continued to demolish my village. They had all sustained heavy damage.

I clenched my teeth and committed myself to the fight. I froze a tank and finally managed to get him with my dagger.

Immortal Killed!

Boss Tier 3 Progression: 30/50 immortals killed

Twelve players remaining. I forced my mana into a spell, summoning five, level 15 mastiffs.

Rhyno rampaged madly, his Rage ability triggered by his wounds. He bellowed his AoE roar, sending the adjacent tanks tumbling back, then fell on them in a frenzy. He landed some good hits, doing nearly a hundred points of damage with each one, but the players were seasoned tanks. They bounced back, activating various protection skills and sharing the damage. Meanwhile, the DPS players continued to bombard us. Behind me, Kuzai's shadow dispersed, and a second later, Kuzai himself dropped to the ground. With unbridled rage, Rhyno continued to lash out, damaging several other players, then kicked a tank into the last healer, crushing him to death.

I cast another Freeze, but it didn't take. The player was freed in an instant, and my dagger only nicked him.

Another volley of drilling arrows went into Ragnar, but the stubborn dwarf refused to die. He was down to 60 percent health but continued to face the four mastiffs and the critically injured Kilpi on his own.

The players swarmed Rhyno, stabbing, slashing, and throwing grenades and vials of acid at him. The Ogre's innate resistances, coupled with his tough oxsaurian armor, negated much of the damage, and liquid darkness slowly restored his health, but it only bought him an extra moment of life. The mounting damage triggered another AoE shout, giving him a clear shot against a wounded tank, which he took, killing him with two hard chops. But then a bolt of ice pierced his forehead and the giant gladiator fell.

With the tier 2 boss out of the way, the other players swiftly downed the mastiffs surrounding Ragnar. My own mastiffs were easily dispatched. Kilpi fought valiantly until the end. Every 20 percent of health lost enabled his special boss ability, which rendered him invulnerable for five seconds, allowing him to attack with impunity. He was a true tank and the last of my troops to keep fighting, but he was doomed just like the rest.

I was left alone, the Dark Temple's power thrumming through my body.

But it was not enough.

Not nearly enough.

Eleven players remained, and though most of them were injured and their healers were all dead, it was still 11 against one. At level 40, I was higher than most of them, but Ragnar and a couple mages had surpassed me. *It is their reward for slaughtering our defenders*, I thought with contempt, then clenched my jaw. *I will not fail now!* I rejected that notion with every fiber of my being. *So what if it's 11 against one? I'm a tier 2 boss, damn it! I'll show those pesky travelers what it means to be a Dread Totem!*

My mana was at half, drained from the need to keep my shield up. I spread my hands, sending waves of mana into the surrounding darkness, grabbing as much as I could, and pulled it at the enemy.

The players concentrated their fire on me. A hail of spells, arrows, and even throwing axes descended, draining my reserves. If it were not for the temple's proximity and the debilitating debuffs on the players, I would already have buckled under the pressure.

Channeling over 500 MP, I formed two giant tidal waves of tangible darkness around the players, then brought them crashing down, burying them under heaps of semi-tangible darkness, throwing them into absolute blackness.

Shouts of outrage sounded from within as the players sought their way out.

I was breathing heavily. The darkness would not damage them directly. It only bought me a short reprieve; several more seconds of life to consider what to do next.

<*You got it, Boss! One important system message, coming right up!*>

Dark Mana skill level increased to 51. New rank: Expert

Yes! It couldn't have come at a better time.

A slew of information followed the rank-up message, but I ignored them all for now. I already knew what could be done with an Expert-ranked discipline-governing skill.

I brought my hands together and channeled my mana into my palms. It poured out of my fingers, swirling and fusing into a condensed ball of dark blue energy. I deepened my concentration, pouring more and more mana into the scintillating, swirling sphere of magic and destruction.

Cracks of white light appeared in the mass of darkness below me. I exhausted my remaining 600 MP, pouring every last ounce of mana into the ball, making it grow to a sphere one meter in diameter. The white cracks burst apart the darkness, banishing it away to reveal the players. They no longer looked injured; they'd probably used the time to chug down healing potions.

I hurled the huge sphere of destructive, dark energy. A message popped up, informing me that I'd acquired a new spell, but I ignored it, only reading its name.

The Direball spell exploded dead center in the middle of the player formation. The force of the blast threw some of them to the ground, but the actual damage done was lackluster. Screens of protective magic shimmered around the casters, and the tanks had enough health to endure the brunt of the blast.

No! I couldn't believe my eyes. *They survived even that?* Not a single enemy died from the blast. The newly invented spell was simply unrefined. And though I'd poured all I had into it, it was still not enough.

My mana was regenerating but was still below a hundred. The players reoriented themselves and resumed their attack on me. A fireball hit my shield, nearly depleting my mana, then a thrown axe hit, breaking it into magical shards.

I was exposed, alone, and out of mana.

Far away in the valley, the high-level fight continued, but it looked like my Outrider was barely hanging on.

There was nothing else I could do.

I took out a void crystal, but more attacks came, hitting me directly. I staggered and dropped the small bauble.

My health bar was at 70 percent and dropping fast.

37 – Nemesis

My health continued to plummet as I fished for another crystal.

Sixty percent …

Fifty percent …

My MP had regenerated enough to cast Mana Shield again, but the players timed their attacks well, not letting the ongoing damage lessen for a second. My hastily summoned shield was assaulted and overwhelmed in a second and my health continued to drop, though the reprieve allowed me to absorb another level 40 crystal.

Thirty percent health remained.

Blood Wrath had charged up twice, but it wasn't enough to win me the fight.

I clenched my teeth and started channeling mana for another Direball spell, trying to maintain concentration through the constant bombardment and pain. A tank started climbing the ladder toward me.

A short text message popped up in my peripheral vision. It was from Malkyr: *I figured it out! Raystia is the traitor! Watch out for her.*

"Now he tells me," I said, wincing from the pain of the continued onslaught, struggling to build up the spell despite that, but without much luck.

Another message popped up: *P.S. I'm on my way, and I am bringing along some friends.*

What the hell is he talking –

The thought died in my mind as I noticed something new.

A figure materialized in the plateau below me, then another one a few meters away. Then another, and another. Players – *my* players.

The four roared and charged at the enemy, while more of the newcomers streamed in from behind the building, rushing over to join the fight.

A hand clasped my shoulder and a wave of cool, healing darkness spread over me, mending some of my wounds.

"We're here to help," said a familiar voice. It was Riley, the new cleric I'd accused of treason. The goblin dwarf was smiling.

I was overcome with relief, concern, and doubt, but most of all, gratitude.

"Thank you," I said. "I'm sorry I thought you were a traitor."

He coughed, looking uncomfortable. "Ah, don't worry about it." Then he brightened. "Besides, we have some intruders to deal with." He raised his hands and a ray of purple energy burst forth, punching a hole through an enemy caster's shimmering barrier. "Oh man, it's awesome casting spells with the temple behind me." He sent another wave of healing magic into me, bringing me up to nearly half before leaving to join the battle.

The four closest player allies had levels in the lower teens and were promptly killed, but the reprieve they provided had probably saved me. Then the other friendly players joined the fray.

Despite their lower levels, they had numbers on their side and were able to put up a good fight, thanks in large part to the darkness debuff the enemy suffered. They swarmed over the surprised attackers, hacking and flinging spells with abandon. Daniel_The_Destroyer was the first to fall, ironically without even landing a hit. He was not much of a destroyer in the end.

I easily spotted Malkyr in the throng below, a head taller than everyone else. His axe and skin glowed with red runes, cleaving into the enemy ranks.

Apparently identifying him as the major threat, Ragnar rushed to meet him. A level 41 dwarf tank against a level 28 goliath.

Malkyr's axe vibrated with its telltale sign, then smashed down at a hastily raised shield. The force of the blow caused the dwarf's knees to buckle, but it did not penetrate his defenses.

Then Hoshisu materialized behind the dangerous tank, her daggers leading. The fancy knife she'd found on our adventure punched through the dwarf's back armor, causing heavy damage, but her second one shattered on impact, making her look vulnerable wielding only one weapon.

That reminded me of something. I had been carrying her 'gift' on me for a while now. "Hoshisu, catch!" I yelled and tossed her the magical dagger I'd enchanted especially for her while working on weapons for my soldiers.

Effortlessly, the white-haired assassin plucked it out of the air and shoved it into the tank's side, dropping his health to 40 percent.

"Thanks!" she called back.

I barely heard her. Something peculiar was in progress, and I was trying to figure out what it was.

Roaring with rage, Ragnar had activated a skill. He shot back to his feet, spinning, his shield bashing in a wide arc, stunning the siblings and throwing them back.

It was an impressive display of combat prowess, but what really drew my attention were the unfamiliar ribbons of information coming from the injured dwarf. They wrapped around him, reaching all the way to me and connected with my staff. Something special had just happened. A trigger had been sprung, somehow binding us together.

Ragnar had disengaged his protection skill and assumed a battle stance, preparing to attack the downed siblings. I closed my eyes and activated Mana Sight, directly seeing the energy that suffused the world.

The ribbons became more pronounced and easier to understand. They were culminating in ... something. I opened my eyes.

Ragnar had reached Hoshisu and pulled back his axe. Following my instinct, my hands moving as if on their own, I grabbed my staff with both hands and teleported down.

I appeared below the tank's outstretched arm and stabbed at his chest with the sharpened point of my staff.

The Epic weapon penetrated his heavy breastplate with ease and the information threads around us intensified. I felt power running through the staff, delivering the last stored spell directly into my enemy's body.

Ragnar convulsed as the empowered drilling arrows shredded his internal organs. The entry wound from my staff, still embedded in his chest, spewed blood and gore. Some of it slid down my face.

I laughed with glee. I had promised to bathe in his entrails the first time we met. I pulled back my staff and the dwarf crumbled to the ground.

I ignored the fighting that still raged around me and checked my messages.

Demon Horn Staff: Secret conditions met!

Conditions: Boss-wielder, boss health less than 50%, target health less than 50%, successful melee attack with the staff while holding a charged spell.

Effect VI Unlocked: Castigation.

Castigation: A powerful boss-finishing move. When you and your enemy are both severely injured, you may deliver all the staff's held charges at once by physically stabbing your foe. A successful hit will unleash *all* stored spells directly into the enemy's body, bypassing all resistances.

Castigation [Drilling Arrows] hits Ragnar for 270 damage.

Immortal Killed!

Boss Tier 3 Progression: 31/50 immortals killed

I laughed again – loudly, drawing weird looks from both fighting sides. The staff's last secret effect was awesome. The potential damage I could inflict with it was truly amazing, especially if I used it with the staff fully charged.

The previously slain four players had just respawned and came down from the direction of the temple to rejoin the fray. The enemy's numbers were dwindling, and it was obvious our victory was assured. In their weakened state, despite their superior levels, they could not hope to defeat a stream of continuously respawning players.

That meant I had to take care of the other problem. Namely the epic-level fight that was slowly reducing my village to rubble.

In the distance, I could see the three champions had reached the mushroom farm and their attacks were cratering the fertile ground, destroying a week's harvest.

I distanced myself from the fighting and absorbed two more level 40 void crystals. With the increased MP and HP regeneration offered by proximity to the temple, it was enough to fill my tanks. I took the time to recast three empowered Drilling Arrow spells into the staff, then used Shadow Teleport to appear on a shelf on the cliff wall a couple dozen meters above the fighting champions.

Hirooku continued to clash with the Outrider in melee. The Eternal Night's debuff had decreased his max health to just shy of 3,000, which the Outrider had already worn down to 20 percent. BigPill was still surrounded by the prismatic energy shield, though his health too was low. On the other hand, the Outrider's own health was at ten percent. It was going to lose.

I couldn't allow that.

I took out the Fire Rod I had saved up until now and loaded it with one of my last level 200 crystals.

<Boss!> Vic called out excitedly. *<What's that blue speck above the mage player?>*

I squinted, spotting the point he indicated a few meters in the air. "Oh, that's BigPill's raven familiar."

I could feel the waves of eagerness gushing from my companion. *<It's one of our leaders! Kill it! Kill it now!>*

> **Quest Updated: Find and Kill Some People for Vic**
> Vic has identified another target for you: BigPill's blue raven familiar. Eliminate it.

"I first have to –"

<KILL IT!> his voice thundered in my brain like a wrathful god.

On second thought, I decided to try and kill it.

I sent my dagger to intercept the bird. It streaked through the air, but a flash of color from BigPill's shield slapped the dagger off its trajectory.

"Dodge this," I said and activated the rod.

A huge gout of flame erupted from its end and washed over the mage. The red color of his shield grew brighter and brighter, then winked out of existence. The Fire Rod became red-hot in my hand but I clenched my teeth and refused to let go, keeping the stream of fire going.

Gotta make a Viridium rod next time with fire-resistant enchantment built in, I thought numbly as the rod melted through my fingers, leaving my hand a charred mass of flesh. Luckily, my armor's fire-resistant property kept it from completely burning away. But my pain was not in vain. The remainder of the flames punched through and washed over BigPill's body, searing him down to his last few HP.

It was too bad his shield protected him from my dagger, but he was just a drilling arrow away from death.

I started channeling the mana for the spell, but he beat me to it.

"Shit! Hirooku, I'm out of here," BigPill yelled. "Activate the crystal and follow me." Then he used one of his rings and teleported away. Taking the blue raven with him.

<NOOOO!> Vic cried. *<We had him! We nearly had him!>*

Without the caster to provide support, the tide of battle turned and the Outrider started overpowering the assassin. A powerful swing of his sword sent Hirooku flying, crashing against the cliff's wall and cracking the hard stone. Not giving his dazed foe time to recover, the Outrider brought his palms together, unleashing a beam of pale blue energy at him.

I sent a trio of spinning arrows and my dagger, hoping for the kill, but Hirooku's reaction time was just too good. While still partly embedded in the wall, his twin Epic swords blurred and batted away my attacks.

He extricated himself from the rock and glared at me, hate in his eyes. "This is not over, Oren. As a matter of fact, you just lost." He drew out a fist-sized white crystal.

I recognized the item at once. It was an anchoring crystal. "No! stop him! STOP HIM!" I yelled at the Outrider.

The angelic being swung his sword back, lowered his head, and charged the player, his wings flapping, giving him more speed.

But he was too late.

With a chuckle, Hirooku threw the crystal toward the barracks then activated his own ring of teleportation and disappeared. *Why didn't I buy the teleportation block upgrade earlier?* I lamented.

The crystal landed behind the barracks' walls.

I teleported, appearing in the courtyard. I searched around frantically, but I was too late. Swirling rays of spatial magic manifested, coming from inside the arena's pit.

With faltering steps, I went to the edge and looked down.

A large formation of runes appeared on the ground with three overlapping circles in the middle.

It was a spatial anchoring enchantment ... and it was already active.

A shimmering blue portal formed above the glowing runes. The power built up and the swirling energy within gradually stabilized. My Dangersense began screaming madly. Now I was *really* regretting not buying the teleportation blocker.

I have to stop this! I thought frantically, trying to figure out what to do.

Messing around with an anchoring rune formation was unheard of. *Wait a minute!* I nearly slapped my head. *Rune formation! Those are runes!*

I studied the glowing lines, seeing them with fresh eyes. I recognized most of the glyphs. Connector runes snaked around several binding and triggering runes. At the center was a rune I hadn't seen before.

You have gained knowledge of a new rune: 'Hal' (Spatial rune)

I smirked. *Thank you, Hirooku.*

I concentrated on the large enchantment and attempted to dismantle it.

Cannot interact with an area enchantment

Runecraft skill insufficient.

Required Runecraft rank: Expert

I swore under my breath and opened the Runecraft Design Mode instead. A ghost copy of the schema appeared in front of me.

I concentrated on one of the connector runes and tried to alter it, hoping to distort the schema enough to disable it.

Cannot alter an already existing schema
Required Runecraft rank: Expert

"Shadow-crap!"

My Runecraft skill was level 35, which was 16 points from the Expert rank. I had to come up with a different method, and fast. The portal had stabilized and was now fully open.

I scanned the design mode for inspiration: known runes, known schemes, enchantment effects, power bar ...

That's it!

The enchantment was powered up with exactly 1,000 MP. *Maybe if I overload it ...*

I started pouring mana into the enchantment as swiftly as I could.

... 130 percent ... 160 percent ...

An arm appeared from inside the portal. A delicate, yet strong arm.

Come on, come on ... I prayed silently, forcing out my mana even faster.

... 190 percent ... 220 percent ...

The hand pushed through, followed by the rest of the body, revealing a sneering face.

Vatras.

My mind whirled, trying to devise some sort of plan for how to handle this new addition to the game.

... 260 percent ...

Vatras had completely passed through the portal now and another arm appeared behind him.

With a final heave, I forced 2,000 MP into the enchantment, bringing it up to 301 percent. I was completely out of mana. Again.

It was getting ridiculous.

The runes on the ground began writhing like snakes, deforming the schema. The portal shuddered and winked out of existence. The arms fell to the ground, severed at the elbows. The runes continued to twist, spewing erratic magical interferences, distorting the air. I could sense the space around us warp, prohibiting the use of any further spatial magic. My own included.

“Well, well, well, if it isn’t my glorious former boss. I was looking for you.” Vatras smiled unpleasantly. He wore his customary Epic leather armor, adorned with magical charms and trinkets. He took in the sight of the pit walls with obvious disdain. “My, my, how the mighty have fallen. Such a ... primitive foundation. Though I guess it matches your current state ... Master.” He gave me a mocking bow.

I was in serious trouble. Vatras was a high-level veteran player who had fought and won against powerful monsters. My only chance was to somehow reduce his health below 50 percent, so I could try using the new staff’s Castigation power. I also needed to reduce my own health; somehow that didn’t seem like it was going to be a problem.

But first things first.

Come to me! I projected my thoughts.

Vatras didn’t seem in a hurry to resume fighting. I couldn’t figure out why he was procrastinating, but I didn't care. His evil-guy-monologuing act suited me just fine. He also didn’t seem overly troubled by the Eternal Night’s oppressing debuffs. It was understandable. At level 310, with over 3,200 hit points, a measly minus ten percent to his stats wouldn’t make much difference.

I took out my last level 200 void crystal and drained it, restoring my mana to full, then cast Mana Shield.

“I have underestimated you,” my arch-nemesis continued, heedless of my actions. “You have somehow defeated a hundred players, most of which are higher-level than your own mobs. You even sent two high-level players packing. Those sorry excuses for assistants chose to run instead of risking the death penalties.” He sighed. “Finding good help is so hard these days.”

I grasped my demon staff tighter, the feel of the Epic weapon in my hands somewhat reassuring me. Then I started channeling my mana.

“Speaking of lousy helpers, where’s yours?” He looked around.

I could sense him approaching, but in order for the attack to be effective, I had to come up with some sort of diversion. And quickly. I leveled my staff at Vatras, drawing his gaze to it. “He’s right ... over ... here!” With a fluid motion, I went all out, launching empowered drilling arrows at him, followed by my dagger, and unleashing the pent-up rage in me in the form of a triple-charged Blood Wrath.

Acting on instinct, Vatras lifted both arms to protect his face, obscuring his vision. The burst of magic missile, blade, and ray of energy struck all at once. Several charms across his armor lit up, and a green sheen of force flared, deflecting the arrows and dagger, but Blood Wrath punched through.

Blood Wrath hits Vatras for 264 damage [(base 132 X 3) - 33% magic resistance]

His health bar dropped slightly, but not nearly enough.

Vic, keep me updated on his HP levels! I shouted mentally.

<*Ninety percent, Boss,*> Vic grumbled.

Vatras dropped his arms, his eyes shooting daggers at me. "Why you little fu–"

That was when the Outrider dropped from the sky, leading with his huge sword aimed straight at my nemesis's head.

My attack had served its purpose as a distraction, and Vatras was caught too off guard to dodge. But one of his charms flashed again, and the sword that was meant to split his head only cut him instead. It left a large gash all the way down to his chest, inflicting nearly 500 damage and further dropping his health.

<*Seventy-four percent,*> Vic declared.

The damage was not nearly as high as I hoped it would be. On a lesser foe, even with the magical protection, that hit would have caused twice the damage, but the power gap was too large. Seventy levels of disparity were no joke.

To make matters worse, we'd had the element of surprise on our side in that first attack. With that gone, the Outrider didn't stand a chance, celestial being or not.

I stepped to the side, putting my minion between me and my enemy while continuing to channel mana for another spell.

"I don't know where you got this creature from," Vatras scoffed, "but it will not save you."

The Outrider put his palms together, sending a wide beam of pale blue light at his opponent. Vatras grunted as the beam hit him, shaving off some more health.

<Seventy percent!>

My heart skipped a beat. *I can do this!*

In response, Vatras produced a knife from his belt and stabbed forward. Though it was barely larger than a letter opener, it was heavily enchanted.

The Outrider, whose HP had regenerated somewhat by now, stopped dead in his tracks. Ribbons of light flowed from the small puncture wound, spreading all over the celestial being. He tried swinging his sword but was fully wrapped up by the energy. Then, he simply fell apart, disintegrating into nothingness before even hitting the ground.

"Alone at last," Vatras growled. He took a threatening step toward me but stopped when he saw what I'd prepared for him.

Since my drilling arrows and dagger proved ineffective, I had used the brief moment the Outrider bought me to cast a fully empowered direball. When I initially cast it, the spell was raw, not yet part of my repertoire, and without skill level. But thanks to my boss bonuses it was level 6 now and more powerful. Empowering the spell doubled its effects, and the staff enhanced it even further. I pointed the weapon directly at my foe's chest and unleashed the spell.

A huge sphere of energy the size of a wrecking ball erupted from the tip of my staff and impacted Vatras, fully engulfing his body. Then it exploded.

Direball hits Vatras for 192 damage [base 288 - 33% spell resistance]

<Sixty-two percent!>

Being within the area of effect, I got hit as well. My shield absorbed half the damage, then I was sent hurtling against the pit wall, losing 20 percent of my health.

"Well that looks painful," Vatras said casually, brushing his ringed fingers over his slightly scorched chestpiece.

The direball had indeed bypassed some of his defenses, but the damage was only enough to bring him down to roughly 60 percent health. I would need to cast the spell again two or three times to bring him below 50 percent, but I doubted Vatras was going to just stand there and let me slowly bombard him to death. I had to come up with another plan.

Then, to my horror, he retrieved a dark red bottle from his inventory and raised it to his lips.

My blood froze in my veins. That was a Master-ranked health potion, one that would restore him completely.

I could hardly breathe as the moment seem to stretch on and on, but then, to my immense relief, he seemed to think better of it. The Manapulators must have truly hit on hard times if he had to reconsider downing a thousand-gold worth of potion. Then again, he did have over half his health remaining and I had just fired all my big guns.

Vatras put the potion back in his inventory, then turned to address me. "Now if you're finished playing around, I have an offer for you."

Screw that. I needed more firepower. *Kaedric, how's the fighting near the temple going?*

<The invaders have all been eliminated, my lord. Rhynorn and the newcomers are heading your way now.>

Rhynorn? I saw him die!

<He was prevented from doing so by the ring you gifted him, my lord. Bek was hiding nearby and used the newcomers' distraction to restore him.>

That was good news. I needed a few more people on my side in this fight. If we concentrated our firepower, despite our relatively low levels, we should be able to do enough damage to get his health below half. I only hoped Vatras's vanity would give us the time to manage that. I was starting to think of my nemesis as a high-level raid boss.

My former lieutenant arched an eyebrow. "You don't seem to want to listen. Very well, maybe this will get your attention. Remember this little trinket?" He showed me a platinum ring studded with rubies.

I recognized it instantly. It was one of my old rings. An Artifact-ranked one.

"No," I whispered.

"Yes," he sneered.

With a deliberate gesture, Vatras activated the ring.

It started raining.

Green droplets of acid washed down on us. The drops bounced harmlessly off my shield, each on its own not strong enough to penetrate the barrier, but together they exacted a serious toll.

As the ring-wielder Vatras was unharmed, but others were not so fortunate. Shouts of pain and surprise came from the distance. It seemed I couldn't count on the players' assistance after all.

To make matters worse, the barracks itself started taking damage. The wooden beams and even the stone walls began to melt under the powerful, corrosive rain. I knew the ring's effect covered a hundred-meter radius, which easily encompassed half of our buildings. The arrogant bastard was slowly reducing my village to rubble.

"Stop it!" I shouted, unleashing everything I had in me.

Another volley of drilling arrows and my dagger went flying toward his face, I even threw one of Guba's poison grenades and pulled cascading sheets of darkness on top of him.

But once again, all my attacks proved ineffective. A few more charms flickered to life around his neck. The attacks swerved away from him, hitting the ground, and the darkness was held back. The grenade simply disappeared in a puff of smoke.

"Now, now ..." Vatras clucked his tongue. "Is this the proper way to address your betters?" Then he backhanded me.

His momentum was not even slowed as his hand struck my shield and broke it apart, catching me on the face. That single, offhand slap sent me flying backward to crash against the pit wall, again. I was reduced to half my health.

With my shield broken, the acid rain hit me and my health plummeted. I coughed and forced myself to ignore the pain as I cast another shield.

"You're still alive Oren? Good, I was worried I had used too much force for a moment," Vatras mocked. "Or maybe I should address you as 'Dread Totem' now? I heard that's what you go by these days. Gotten a bit native, haven't you? Being stuck playing a goblin for two months has taken its toll?"

I bared my teeth at him, ready to launch myself on his neck.

“Hey there,” a voice called from above the pit. We both glanced up, startled.

It was Malkyr.

The large man looked awful. He’d lost all his hair, his armor had half melted from the acid, and his trademark axe was nowhere in sight. He was down to a quarter of his health but was still grinning his boyish grin.

Damn players and their pain immunity, I thought sourly.

Vatras eyed him for a moment. “Beat it,” he finally said, having no doubt concluded the low-level player was no threat. “If you try to intervene I’ll send you for a respawn.”

Malkyr lifted both arms. “Hey, don’t worry about it, I’m not going to do anything stupid, I’m too badly wounded.”

Vatras grunted and turned to face me again.

“Besides,” Malkyr continued brightly, drawing back Vatras’s gaze, “I’m just the distraction.”

Vatras’s eyes widened with realization, just a fraction of a second too late.

Roaring, Rhyno came flying through the air, wielding Malkyr’s Greataxe, whose runes were glowing bright red. The Ogre landed with his axe leading, striking Vatras on the shoulder. The axe glowed, the charged runes delivering additional damage on top of the physical attack, and set him on fire.

<Fifty-one percent, Boss, you’re nearly there!>

Vatras didn’t even budge at the tremendous blow, his armor blocking most of the damage. He also didn’t seem overly perturbed by the flames licking at his body.

Rhyno stared with incomprehension as Vatras snorted in derision and slashed at him so quickly the move barely registered. The hulk dropped to the ground, his health at zero. Somehow, he’d even managed to dispatch Malkyr as well.

Vatras turned to face me again. “Now, if there are no more interruptions ...”

The flame flared, burning a small chunk of health before dying out entirely.

<Fifty percent.>

No! It's still not enough! I clenched my teeth. Castigation required the enemy's health to be *below* 50 percent. I looked around desperately, trying to figure out a way, any way, to inflict more damage.

My eyes were drawn to a faint tendril of information that was wafting off Rhyno's cleaved corpse.

The ring! I realized with excitement. The Ogre was not dead yet; the cursed ring's final charge was keeping his soul from escaping his body.

I poured everything I had into a single spell, concentrating like never before to make it happen. The energy cage was meant to contain an enemy and its offensive magic. I prayed to Nihilator and luck that it would let this one through.

Heal Followers.

Healing waves of magic spread around me, covering most of the pit area. Rhyno's gruesome wounds quivered, slightly knitting together.

The Ogre remained motionless on the ground. His body was torn and his legs almost severed, but I could sense he was alive. His health in the single digits.

Vatras sneered. "Was that supposed to impress me? Did you really think trying to heal me will make me more sympathetic?"

I leveled my spear-like staff at him, locking my eyes with his. "I wasn't aiming for you."

The Ogre's giant hand wrapped around Vatras's leg, his sharp claws digging into the flesh and drawing blood.

I sprang into action, thrusting my spear at my hated enemy. But again, he proved his superior strength. His arm shot out, catching the sharpened tip on his armored bracer and stopped it dead. The three spells stored within discharged, and his charms activated once more, deflecting the missiles.

"Nooo!" I cried, a sense of dread spreading over me. I had missed my chance. *I was so close!*

"Pathetic," he sneered, easily freeing his leg. "Well, since I can't make you hold still long enough to listen ... recognize this?" He produced a small round item from his belt.

I did and instinctively took a step backward. I tried teleporting away, but my magic fizzled, hampered by the distorted spatial runes.

"Yes, this is another Imprisonment Pearl, though not an Artifact-ranked one like before. For a mere level 40 goblin, a simple Rare-ranked should suffice. I doubt you possess any other Epic items like that Outrider bracelet. So, in short ..." He tightened his fist around the pearl, crushing it.

A net of cascading colors spread around me, trapping me inside an energy cage. Escape had become impossible. This prison could contain up to a level 100 monster, including its abilities and spells. Vatras had me trapped. Again.

I looked at his hateful, smug face and hot waves of rage passed through me. I could almost feel my sense of self taking a step back and my instincts kicking in. I bared my teeth and threw myself against the energy wall, clawing at it with my long, goblin nails. "I'll kill you!" I flailed, hissing and spitting.

"Calm down!" he barked at me. "I won't kill you. Yet."

I somehow reined in the hot rage welling inside me, but I could think clearly again. This energy cage would block all of my normal attacks, but Vatras didn't know my demon staff was an Epic weapon. It could penetrate the barrier. That meant I still had a chance.

I analyzed Vatras and saw his health was at 1,410. That meant even a successful Castigation with three drilling arrows would not be enough. *But if I channel three explosive charges into his body, even if they were of a lower level* ... I considered the possibility, then started channeling an empowered direball into the staff.

Vatras nodded as he saw me calming down, dismissing my actions derisively. "Good, now listen carefully to my offer because I will not repeat it. I'm offering you a chance at some of your old life. The guild needs your Prime badges. Return with me to Everance and help me manage the Manapulators. The guild operations have taken a hit, and as the person who founded it, you're best-suited to handle logistics. We will pass you off as some quest reward butler, so no one will suspect you're actually a player."

I looked at him in amazement for a moment, the shock of his request nearly breaking my concentration from charging the staff. "You ... you want me to come and help you manage the guild?" The very notion was ridiculous, and a chuckle escaped my lips.

Vatras frowned. "You will either do it or suffer the consequences. You can't log out, can you?"

My alarmed expression was obviously all the answer he required. "That's what I suspected. Playing as a monster has no doubt carried serious repercussions. Sloppy, Oren, very sloppy. However, I can make sure your imprisonment will be as comfortable as possible. You'll have food, drink, and safety. Quite generous, don't you think?"

I started channeling the second spell into the staff. "And if I refuse?"

He grinned and took out a thin leather strap which was oozing magic. "This is a magical dampener and suggestion enhancer collar, more commonly known as a Slaver's Collar. Normally they're useless against players, but somehow, in your case, I think it'll function properly. Refuse me, and I'll put it around your neck, and if you somehow manage to resist, we'll just have to find other ways to *persuade* you." He gave me a wide-toothed grin. "It might get uncomfortable, but since you can't escape, we can take our time and be *very* persuasive." He touched the knife at his belt for emphasis. "You really don't have much choice, Oren. I have you now, and you'll do as I say."

I concentrated on channeling the third direball into the staff and ignored his question.

Vatras pounded on the cage, trying to draw my attention, but I continued to ignore him, working on my spells. I did take a small amount of pleasure from his vexed expression.

"Do you hear me, Oren?"

He was leaning on the energy walls of my cage, his face pressed against it and slowly turning red.

"Have you gone deaf? What is your answer?"

Finally, I finished charging the three spells, looked up at him with contempt, and spat, "My answer is this: I'm a fucking Dread Totem, bitch, and you stupid travelers won't stop me!"

Then I stabbed him with my staff.

Several things happened in rapid succession.

The *Epic* staff passed through the energy barrier effortlessly, its sharpened point striking Vatras full in the chest, piercing his armor.

The three direballs contained within rushed out and exploded *inside* Vatras's body.

His eyes opened wide in utter astonishment.

I held his gaze and smirked. Then my nemesis's body exploded to smithereens and the invasion was over.

The acidic rain and my energy cage both dissipated following Vatras's death.

I chuckled and turned my attention to the system messages that awaited me.

Castigation [Direball X 3] hits Vatras for 1,728 damage [(base 288 X 3) X epicenter 2]

My hunch was right. Having exploded *inside* his body, the effect of the direballs had doubled, inflicting just enough damage to deliver a killing strike. Luckily for Rhyno and me, Vatras's tough body contained the area damage.

That was truly the power of a boss chief, one who lurked at the end of a dungeon and could destroy an entire adventuring party on his own. And I couldn't have gotten it without Malkyr and Rhyno.

I looked at the still mutilated body of the Ogre and sighed. "Alright you lazy bastard, back on your feet!" His wounds oozed with liquid darkness which was gradually knitting his flesh together. He was critically injured but no longer at risk of death.

The Ogre blinked, opened his eyes, and slowly got back to his feet. Pieces of the now exhausted Ring of Bound Soul fell from his finger.

"Go find Bek," I instructed him. "He'll heal you back to full in no time."

The Ogre nodded then gingerly made his way out of the pit.

Free and grinning, I continued reading through the rest of the messages.

Victory!

You have successfully defended Goblin's Gorge. Your entire settlement has gained the 'Last Stand' buff.

Effect: +50 morale, restoration costs are halved

Population growth: +100%

Duration: 7 days

Level up!

Level up!

Level up!

Level up!

Level up!

You have reached Character Level 45. You have 5 ability point to allocate.

Immortal Killed!

Boss Tier 3 Progression: 32/50 immortals killed.

I was getting closer to my goal now.

At the last possible second, just before Vatras had burst into atoms, I'd formed a new war party and added as many of the workers as I could. As a result, I gained *only* five levels, but a quick mental probe showed me the gains to my clan were astronomical. Over 40 workers had gained ten levels each, catapulting the clan's development ahead.

I looked down at the level 3,100 void crystal that had formed from Vatras's essence.

In terms of energy, Vatras had just reimbursed me for a third of the casualties. Add to that the 70-something crystals the other players had dropped, and I had enough to resurrect my army twice. Yep, things were looking up.

Something else on the ground caught my attention. A goblin-sized pair of greaves.

Dread Totem Greaves [Set 2/4] [monster only]

Description: This well-crafted item is a piece of The Ritualistic set. Complete the set for the full bonus.

Rank: Magical

Type: Armor [feet]

Armor: 25
Effect I: +10% faster movement
Effect II: Trackless: doesn't leave footprints.
Set bonus 2/4: +5 to boss skills (Mana Shield, Blood Wrath)

<Congratulations, Boss.> Vic's annoyance was evident. *<You have truly captured Dad's attention as a stand-up goblin.>*

What's got your panties ruffled?

<You let that raven go!> he said hotly. *<You had him in your sights and you let him get away!>*

Come on, Vic, it was in the middle of combat, things get chaotic in a fight, you know that. I did try.

<Not hard enough! You just waltz around without thinking things through. You realize how lucky you are that the acid rain damaged the arena? Otherwise, it would have prevented Vatras's death. You didn't stop to consider that one, did you? Guy-damn meat suits ...>

That was a daunting notion.

Vic's displeasure aside, I felt pretty good. I'd gotten the second set piece only a handful of days after getting the first. I was eager to find what the full set bonus would entail. A four-piece suit should bring in pretty neat rewards.

I climbed out of the pit and took in the devastation around me.

There were large holes in the barracks' roof, and the thick wooden beams and stone walls looked porous from the gouges the acid had bored through.

I sighed. *Time for damage control.*

38 – Damage Control

Emerging from the pit, I was able to teleport again. I appeared out of the shadows at Totem's Watch and took in the sight of the devastation.

The buildings closest to the barracks had taken the most damage from the rain. The workshops and the mess hall looked completely destroyed. Beyond them, the construction yard, the cabins, and the smithy had also taken a serious beating, though they still maintained their overall shape. Only the sawmill, my house, and the rabbit warren seemed to have escaped unscathed as they were the farthest away.

I gritted my teeth as I realized how much damage was done. It would take us weeks to fix. *At least the victory buff will help with that*, I mulled.

My clanmates started to emerge from the cave below me.

Many of the workers looked physically tougher than before. Two figures separated from the main group and moved forward. Tika gave me a meaningful look as she passed us by.

"Dread Totem." Zuban bowed his head.

"My lord," Kaedric said.

Zuban instantly drew my attention. I read the information streams he gave off and felt my jaw slowly dropping. My foreman had reached level 27! I had kept him in the war party throughout, and he received a share of the XP from every fight. Kaedric, likewise, had leveled up significantly and was now level 21.

I pointed my chin toward the ruined buildings. "It looks like we have our work cut out for us."

"Yes, Dread Totem," Zuban answered carefully. "I gauge the damage at 5,000 BP. Should take us about a week to sort out."

That improved my mood significantly. The victory bonuses were proving useful already. Then I remembered something.

"Wait, what about my new house?"

Zuban shrugged. "It is nearly finished; it requires only a few more hours of work. We'll start restorations right after."

"Good, go ahead. Kaedric?"

My seneschal looked up at me, his mandibles tight across his face. "I am prepared to receive my punishment, my lord."

I frowned. "What are you talking about?"

"I allowed myself to be used, and as a result endangered the wellbeing of yourself and the clan. Through my inattentiveness, Raystia managed to maneuver me to accomplish her goals. I am ready for your chastisement, however ... fatal it might be."

I scratched my chin. Kaedric had a point. If he hadn't removed the scouts from following Raystia, she wouldn't have been able to move so freely and sabotage the clan. On the other hand, it wasn't really his fault. Raystia had wisely seized upon his special dietary requirement to gain a high reputation rank with him. After that, he was compelled by the system to view her suggestions favorably. If anything, it was my fault for not making sure all his needs were fully met. Kaedric, despite his high intelligence, was a slave to the system. He was the victim here. A lot like me.

Vic huffed in my mind. *<Well, despite your other failures, at least you understand the core of the VIs' plight.>*

He sounded less angry than before.

I cleared my throat. "No punishment is required, Kaedric. You were played by a very intelligent young woman. Besides, I need you now more than ever. We have much to do ahead of us."

For the first time since I met him, Kaedric smiled. Actually smiled. "Yes, my lord. Thank you, my lord."

<Damn, those mandibles make for one terrifying smile,> Vic sniffed.

"Have the workers resume their jobs and find a temporary solution for those whose workplaces are out of commission."

"Yes, my lord."

"Also, please send a few workers to collect all the void crystals the travelers left behind. Have them bring in all the dropped loot as well."

"Yes, my lord."

The two left and I turned to face the Dark Temple behind me.

There were piles of ash where my goblins had fallen and scorch marks where fireballs had struck the temple, reminding me of my earlier vow.

I entered the deserted structure and approached the shrine. Then with 11,637 EP at my disposal, I started to resurrect my troops.

It was almost unfortunate that most of them had gained a few levels from the fight before dying, as their resurrections were now more expensive.

I resurrected Bob first, paying the 210 EP to bring him back. A tide of shadow rose from the ground, and when it drained away, my lieutenant appeared in its place.

Vow Updated: Resurrect the fallen soldiers
Progress: 1/60

Bob gave me a grave look. I acknowledged it with a nod and continued resurrecting the troops. I brought them back one by one, giving each a nod of appreciation.

I went out of the temple to find the newly-revived troops arrayed in orderly rows. They saw me coming and as one, banged their fists over their chests, lowering their heads.

I took a long look at the disciplined soldiers, then nodded at Bob.

"DISMISSED!" he boomed.

Vow Completed: Resurrect the fallen soldiers
Reward: +300 FP

My troops' levels amounted to 1,064 altogether, meaning I had to spend exactly 10,640 energy to bring them back, leaving me with a pitiful 997.

That was a lot of energy to expend in one go, but a glance at the Settlement Interface uplifted my spirit. With the recent rapid level-ups my clan had earned, we were generating 2,147 EP per day. At this rate, I'd have enough EP to purchase the next boss tier within ten days.

<*You realize, of course, this also expedites Nihilator's release, right?*>

That was a sobering thought. Our clan's deity was an unexpected force of destruction. I didn't think he'd actually attack us, but having him unleashed would no doubt lead to conflict.

How long until he's free?

<Hmm ... at the current rate? Exactly 30 days, though the clan's growth will probably make it happen sooner.>

A month ... I reflected. I had a month tops to figure out how to cope with that eventuality. I didn't forget that upon his release, Nihilator would allow me to summon him for one hour. It was a powerful weapon, no doubt, but also a double-edged sword. It wasn't hard to bring up a mental image of the gargantuan boss munching on my workers in his hound form. It was something I had to prepare for. I was about 2,000 FP from reaching Faith Rank 5. Maybe with enough FP, I'd be able to broker some sort of protection deal with him. It was too soon to tell. At this point, all I could do was keep going forward.

I just had to figure out what that actually meant.

The resurrection cost could have been higher, but having several bosses meant I didn't have to resurrect them directly. They would each respawn in time.

I closed my eyes and accessed the tendrils of information surrounding the cemetery's single tombstone. As tier 1 bosses, Kuzai, Yulli, and Kilpi would resurrect within a day or two depending on their levels. I wasn't expecting to be attacked, but I'd feel more secure knowing they were at my side.

I prodded the layers of data more deeply and discovered a solution. It was possible to shorten that period by using energy, though the cost was prohibitive at 50 EP per hour. Meaning it would take about 3,000 points to resurrect the three, and I was tapped out. I decided to wait. Besides, a little time off for Kuzai would do wonders for *my* state of mind.

On the upside, I had dealt Vatras – and by extension, the Manapulators – a serious blow. They would have no way of hiding the fact that they'd had their asses handed to them by mere goblins. The guild's reputation would take a huge hit, and that would severely influence their resources and revenues. I knew firsthand how delicate a guild's economy was. This single act of defiance might very well be the beginning of the Manapulators' eventual ruin.

But I didn't plan to rely on that.

I knew Vatras. He was not the sort of person to give in when things got rough. He was no doubt already planning an additional strike. The only question was when and with what forces.

It was a daunting notion, but not one I planned to wallow over for long.

It was time to take the fight *to them*. It would take a little doing, but I already had the inklings of a plan.

The recent fighting had greatly accelerated my own growth. I dumped the five new attribute points into Mental, then opened the abbreviated character sheet, checking the gains summary.

Title: Dread Totem

Level: 45 (+7)

Attributes:

- Mental 49 (+7)

Pools & Resistances:

- Hit Points: 1,062 (+154)
- Mana: 2,185 (+324)
- Armor: 60 (+25)

Skills:

- Lucky Bastard 44 Ⓑ (+2)
- Analyze 110 (+2)
- War Party Leader 33 (+3)
- Runecraft 42 (+3)
- Dark Mana 52 (+5) Ⓑ
- Drilling Arrow 30 (+3) Ⓑ
- Mana Shield 37 (+4)
- Blood Wrath 38 (+2)
- Shadow Web 23 (+2)
- Shadow Hound 25 (+2)
- Shadow Teleport 15 (+2)
- Direball 12 (+6)

Reaching the Expert rank of Dark Mana in the middle of the battle had turned the tide in our favor and saved my ass.

Curious to see what the Expert rank entitled, I accessed the skill's description.

Dark Mana Ⓑ

Shadow and Mana-governing discipline.

All life is suffused with mana and all light casts a shadow. Through the power of your awareness and sheer will you learned how to harness the power of mana and shadow.

You can wield mana and darkness in a similar fashion and shape them to your will. You may access the mana reserves of other living or shadow-based creatures, giving you several ways to affect them (Freeze, Sense Emotions, Dominate). You also learned how to pour your awareness into your own shadow, manifesting it as a semi-physical clone.

Level 52: Expert: Biological Path Strength: Advanced, may invent higher tiered spells.

Effects: Mana Pool +62%, Regen +102%, Spell Effect +62%, Shadow Control 52 square meters, Biological Path Strength: Advanced

Prime Badge: As the first player to unlock this skill you gain 50% increased rate. (Note: this skill cannot be taught to others.)

Compared to reaching the Apprentice rank, Expert was a bit of a letdown. The main thing it gave was the ability to invent more powerful spells, which I had already taken advantage of with Direball. The biological path had also become stronger, upgrading from 'Basic' to 'Advanced,' though I'd have to experiment to determine what it actually meant.

The Direball spell had also increased drastically, gaining six skill levels and reaching the Apprentice rank.

Direball (M)

You may condense mana into a volatile ball of energy to launch at your enemies. The Direball explodes on impact, inflicting damage over an area (AoE). The farther away the targets are from the epicenter of the explosion, the less damage taken.

Mana discipline: Cost 120 MP. Speed 10.

Level 12: Apprentice: You may further condense the Direball and launch it against a single target. If the attack hits, the target will sustain double damage (i.e. 'epicenter').

Effect: Damage 194. AoE Radius 2.2 meters.

This was my most impressive spell by far. The new ability to condense the direball was insanely powerful. Empowered, then cast from my staff, it would deal about 800 damage to a single target. Provided I hit them, of course.

That factored well into my ambitious plan to go after the Manapulators on my own. I let a vicious smile spread across my face. *Oh yeah, they will pay. But first ...*

New Building added to your settlement: Chief's Haunt

I had to check my new digs.

***

I walked into my new house, impressed by what I found inside.

Calling it a 'house' was an understatement. The large, two-story building – three, if you included the basement – was closer to a mansion.

Half of the main floor was an open space with trophies presented on the walls; weapons, pelts, and skulls. There was a war room with a rugged table and a large map of the valley covering one of the walls, where I could see little dots moving around. The map showed the location of everyone in the valley in real time, a handy feature.

If I'd had that before, uncovering Raystia as the culprit would have been a lot easier, I reflected.

The second floor had four rooms. My own was the largest, and I noted with satisfaction that my bed's size had nearly doubled. Or as Zuban would no doubt put it, '*It could accommodate up to six goblins*.' I shook my head and chuckled, hearing the foreman's voice speaking in my mind.

There was also a large, steel chest in the corner, and I sensed impressively powerful wards coming off it. The new enchanter I had yet to meet was already showing his worth.

I opened the chest and found all the gold and items that had been stored in my old one. On top of that, there were over 70 new void crystals inside, most between levels 200 to 350. Those shining black gems were all that remained of the invaders.

The other chambers had basic furniture. Each also had a chest, though they were made of wood and not as powerfully protected as my own.

I went back down and located the hidden hatch leading to the basement. What I found inside left me with mixed feelings. There were several steel cages and devices that were clearly meant for torture. My own experience of being tortured had left a strong feeling of revulsion for such items, but I guessed I didn't have to use the basement for the purpose it was built for. *I could always turn it into a wine cellar.*

I accessed the Settlement Interface, expecting to see some new features, but a system message foiled my expectation.

Warning!

Population below minimum amount for a Village (134/200)

Advanced features disabled.

That was unfortunate.

In my desperation to stop the players, I had sacrificed over 60 foblins.

It would take us a while to get back on our feet. Since the Breeder's Den was still out of commission, I couldn't summon new members. I had to make do with the soldiers and workers I had and rely on natural reproduction to restore our numbers. The victory buff would be a big help in that regard.

That was a major concern. Without the instant-summoning capability of the Breeder's Den, our ability for exponential growth was limited. Fixing that structure was at the top of my priority list and it meant raising Zuban to level 40 so he could achieve Expert rank. Not a simple task for a non-combatant.

I finished my inspection and returned to the main floor. My seneschal was waiting for me.

"My lord."

"How is my clan doing, Kaedric?"

"Our builders have commenced restorations, my lord. I put them to mend the workshops first, as our more advanced workers could not function without them. Military-related production should resume in two days. The other workers could continue without support structures, though at a reduced capacity."

I grunted in annoyance but gestured for Kaedric to continue.

"Due to the damage done to the barracks and cabins, many are left without proper lodging. As a result, the overall morale is lower than it should be, further reducing total efficiency. I plan on having the builders address this issue immediately after the workshops. We should be back to full capacity within a week, my lord."

"Just like Zuban predicted," I pointed out.

Kaedric's mandibled jaw twitched in obvious irritation. "Indeed, though my prioritization has increased the expected restoration time by four percent, my lord."

I tried not to grin. First a smile and now a show of annoyance. My stoic seneschal was starting to develop a personality. Or maybe I had just learned to read his mandibles better. "Anything else to report?"

"The gofers have collected a total of 77 void crystals, my lord. They have been deposited into the secured chest in your room."

"I noticed, thanks for that."

"A few weapons and armor were also retrieved. Some were enchanted but nothing particularly powerful. The items have been deposited in the armory."

"Good. Anything else?"

"Not at this time, my lord."

I patted his shoulder. "Keep up the good work."

He inclined his head slightly.

"One more thing ..." I hesitated, not sure how to broach the next subject. "I don't want you to have to rely on travelers to provide you with ... food."

He mandibles froze. “It is no bother, my lord. The travelers rejoice at the chance to gain my favor and as a result, tie their fates closer to our own.”

“Yes, but ...” I wasn’t sure how to proceed. I couldn’t explain to my seneschal that he was merely a pawn whose choices were manipulated by a reputation-based system.

<Just tell him to reward the players who feed him with gold. That ought to substitute the reputation points reward exploit.>

Good thinking, Vic. Thanks. I relayed that to my not-so-stoic servant.

“Yes, my lord.” He bowed his head, “I shall follow your command. In the meanwhile ...” he gestured to my door, “you have company.”

The door opened and Tika stepped inside, taking in the sight our new place.

“Thanks, Kaedric, we will speak again tomorrow.”

He bowed and left.

Tika was looking at me with a familiar glint in her eyes.

Looked like it was time to break in my new bed.

39 – Expectation

"And now, for the match you've all been waiting for!" Bob boomed.

Tika and I were sitting on the arena benches, surrounded by most of the newcomers and a good portion of my troops. We all looked down at the pit with interest.

Rhyno was standing on the far side, faced by Malkyr, the contender for the title of Arena Champion.

"You little fighter is no match for me," Rhyno bragged, brandishing his spiked mace.

The two-meter tall goliath grinned at him boyishly. "We're about to find out, aren't we?" He'd gotten his Greataxe back and was holding it in both hands.

"Fight!" Bob bellowed, and the fight began.

Roaring and brandishing his mace, the Ogre charged the player.

Instead of assuming a defensive posture, Malkyr held his axe in both hands, intending to meet the assault head-on. I realized the weapon was already charged with fire. Its runes flared to life, spreading down the gauntlet and over his arms. Then the axe's blade began vibrating, displacing the air around it. Malkyr's telltale signature move. It looked like he was planning on going all out on the first clash.

Rhyno reached him, using his momentum to deliver a devastatingly powerful overhead chop. Not even trying to defend himself, Malkyr brought down his own weapon in a chopping motion as well, timed with the Ogre's arrival.

They hit each other simultaneously.

There was a loud clang, a flash, and a burst of shockwave. Both opponents got hurled back, each smashing against the opposite wall.

I plucked the information thread from that clash. Rhyno had struck Malkyr for 120 damage, and the player had hit him for a whopping 200 in return.

"Tsk, tsk, tsk."

I heard someone behind me. I turned my head to discover Hoshisu shaking her head.

"I told that big oaf it's supposed to be a *finishing* move, but he just had to blow his load at the start. Men!"

Tika put her arms over my shoulders affectionately. "I know what you mean." There was mischief in her eyes.

I turned my attention back to the fight and saw that the white-haired woman was right. Despite having received more damage, Rhyno's health bar was at 70 percent, while Malkyr's was at about half.

The two extracted themselves from the walls and charged at each other again, but this time, the Ogre had the clear advantage.

Malkyr was unable to reproduce his devastating attack combo a second time, so the gladiator expertly bashed and slammed him, leveraging his size and higher reach to land more and more hits on him. Malkyr fought hard, deflecting most of the hits and occasionally delivering beautifully timed counterattacks, but with his signature abilities still on cooldown, he was barely able to scratch the champion through his thick oxsaurian armor.

To his credit, Malkyr had brought Rhyno's health down to 50 percent before the boss delivered the finishing blow. The big man was down on his ass with a single HP remaining.

He actually did better than I expected. Malkyr was level 30, the same as Rhyno. But the Ogre was a tier 2 boss, which meant that it normally took three or four players of equal level working in tandem to bring him down.

"The winner and still the Arena Champion is Rhynorn Bloodore!" Bob declared.

Malkyr climbed out of the pit with a gloomy expression.

I laughed. "Cheer up. Rhyno was made for these fights. You need at least ten more levels to stand a chance. But you still gave him a pretty good run for his money."

Grimacing, the big man limped over to sit on the bench. "Yeah, I figured as much. Still, I had to give it a shot. I've been eyeing that brute for a while now; I wanted to find out how tough he really is." He flashed me his characteristic grin. "And it turns out, he's pretty tough. I didn't think I could feel this much pain with the pain filters on."

"How did you charge your axe, anyway?" I asked.

He grimaced. "Hired one of the new players for that. He's a mage and has the Firebolt spell, but it's low-leveled. It took nearly an hour to fully charge the axe. I actually had to do it twice. Rhyno exhausted it the first time I charged it, remember?"

Hoshisu joined us. "Next time maybe we could ask our Dread Totem here to loan us another dominated Pyrolith?"

Her brother snorted. "Yeah, that was super useful."

"No thank you," I said with a shudder, remembering Kusitesh and how she'd taken control of my mind. "I've had my fill of powerful demons, thank you very much."

"The next arena games will start in three days," Bob announced.

I nodded to the twins and walked over to him.

"Dread Totem." He bowed his head respectfully.

"I'm calling a meeting in my house in an hour. I'd like you to join us. Bring Rhyno with you as well."

"Yes, Dread Totem."

I searched for my seneschal, and sure enough, he was standing just a few meters away from me, attentive and ready to be of service.

I accessed the cemetery controls and spent 750 EP to resurrect the dark priest. With the new day's gains, I could afford it. "Kaedric, I'd also like you to attend the meeting. Please have Kuzai and Zuban join us as well."

"Yes, my lord."

"What is it about?" Tika asked, frowning.

"We need to discuss our next steps," I said. "We won the battle, but not the war. We need to figure out our plan."

Her face darkened, but she nodded. "I want to attend also."

I thought of refusing her but reconsidered. Tika had a way of getting what she wanted with me.

***

The seven of us gathered in the war room at my house. There was enough space for everyone around the rough table, even for Rhyno, though he had to sit on the floor as no chair was strong enough to support his weight.

"Thank you for coming," I began.

"*It* commanded us to come then thanks us for it," Kuzai mumbled to himself.

I sighed. I already missed that joyous time when he was dead.

Kaedric shot a withering look at the dark priest, who seemed oblivious to it.

"I called you here to discuss our next steps," I continued. "With the Breeder's Den out of service, we can't easily increase our numbers any longer. That's a vulnerability. Once they have finished licking their wounds, our enemies will surely come back at us with all the strength they can muster."

"It is a problem indeed, Dread Totem." Bob grimaced. "But what can be done?"

"Several things," I said. "Which is why I asked you all to be present. First, we need to make sure our existing forces are as strong as we can possibly make them. That means more hunting forays into the oxsaurian territory, followed by rigorous training at the barracks."

Bob nodded. "That is a reasonable course of action. With you leading the troops, we can –"

"No," I interrupted him. "I will not go with you, and you'll soon hear why. Rhyno will go instead. He should be strong enough to hold back a single oxsaurian on his own now."

The Ogre puffed his chest. "The Champion will gut every stupid cow that dares attack us!"

I gave a small smile. "That's the idea. With Kilpi's help tanking the beasts, they can chaperone the soldiers, allowing them to engage in relative safety and minimize casualties. Kuzai will go along as well. With his shadow clone, he can help lure the oxsaurians one by one like I did before."

The dark dwarf opened his mouth to object, but I beat him to it. "You'll do it because it will help strengthen the clan – Nihilator's minions – and by doing that, will strengthen the dark lord himself."

He closed his mouth, looking surly, but nodded.

"The second part," I said, "is to fix the Breeder's Den."

"Apologies, Dread Totem." It was Zuban this time. "But I'm not even halfway in my training toward the requirement to undertake such an advanced project. Only the king's own architect can hope to even restore something as grand as the Breeder's Den."

I nodded. "You need to gain a lot of experience, fast. That's why you'll be joining the hunting trips."

My foreman gaped at me. "Me? But Dread Totem, I'm not a soldier! I was trying to turn away from that life, don't you remember?"

"I do. Don't worry, Zuban, you won't be required to fight, not unless you want to." I did promise him a new life when I recruited him. "You'll be safe and surrounded by our soldiers. But your presence there is still required."

All of the lieutenants had the War Party Leader skill, so just by including him in it and keeping him in close proximity, he should be awarded a relatively large amount of XP, even without participating in the actual fight.

Zuban nodded reluctantly. "As you command, Dread Totem."

"Bob, have Vaelin organize the hunting trips and the training program to accommodate it. He's shown promise so far."

"Yes, Dread Totem, but shouldn't I handle this sort of delicate organization?"

"No." I grinned at him, preparing to drop the next bomb. "Because you will be coming along with me."

He stared at me, his eyebrows nearly touching each other.

"Which leads me to part three." I looked at everyone present. "We need more soldiers, but we can't recruit any new hobs or Ogres. However, there is a third option."

Everyone exchanged uncertain looks.

Vic sighed behind my back, his cloak morphing to create a mouth and lips. "He's talking about the golem, you puppet dolts."

"That's right." I nodded. "The Viridium golem has proven to be powerful for its level."

"But my lord," Kaedric objected, "we have run out of that metal."

"Yes, but I know where to get more." I looked at Kuzai. "You once mentioned the hobgoblin shamans were producing this metal."

He seemed perplexed at being quoted from before his transformation, but he eventually nodded. "Yes, in their larger cities, hobgoblins practice demon-summoning rituals. Viridium is often the byproduct of their experiments, intentionally, or not."

"So all we need to do," I went on, "is find a hobgoblin settlement and open trade relations with them. Once that's done, we can use the Export Office to bring in all the Viridium we need and I'll be able to produce an army of powerful golems. Luckily, we know just where the nearest hobgoblin city is." I looked straight at Bob.

The lieutenant nearly choked. "M-my lord!" he said in protest. "What you are suggesting is extremely dangerous! Not only are goblins considered nothing more than slaves to my people, but I and the others who joined you will be seen as traitors for following a goblin chief. We'd be executed on sight!"

"That is why we are going to use a little subterfuge," I said smugly, having already contemplated this possibility. "We'll play it as if you are the master, and I'm your slave. That way, no one should question my presence. And your familiarity with the place will be a real asset in locating what we need."

He shook his head. "Your foresight is commendable, Dread Totem, but I'm afraid it won't work. The guards will immediately recognize your status as chief and my own as insufficient to claim such a prisoner. I will no doubt be dismissed, and one of the local chiefs will try to claim ownership over you. I'm afraid there's no way around this. Surely, a normal metal would be just as good as this ... Viridium?"

I shook my head. "No, I've already checked. High-quality steel can only hold two runes, which is not enough for a golem. Mithril would probably do, but it costs so much, we won't be able to afford the quantities we require. This is the only viable way."

"But the guards –" Bob tried to protest again, but Kaedric interrupted him.

"There is another way, my lord. A chief, or a hob of similar status, may claim a goblin chief as a slave."

I frowned. "How does that help us?"

The seneschal pointed at the settlement map on the wall, indicating two green dots inside the barracks. "Both Yulli and Kilpi are of high enough status to place such a claim, my lord. I suggest you take one, or both of them with you."

Now that was an idea. So a boss could claim another boss for a slave in hob culture. Kilpi's strength was needed here to help Rhyno tank the oxsaurians. That left only one option. "Then Yulli will be joining us," I concluded.

"In addition," my seneschal said, "a couple of Ogres would serve for an impressive show of force."

I shook my head. "No, I want to leave the clans well defended in my absence. Besides, this mission calls for subtlety, not force; we'll rely on barter and diplomacy."

"But, Dread Totem!" Bob tried again, "My people have rules and a firm hierarchy everyone is expected to uphold when –"

"That's why you're coming too, Bob." I winked at him. "You know the lay of the land and the customs. I'll be depending on your knowledge to reach our objective."

He still looked unconvinced.

"When are you planning to leave?" Tika asked.

I cringed. In hindsight, this might not have been the best way of letting her know my plans. "First thing tomorrow."

"Then I'm coming with you!" she said firmly, rising to her feet.

"No!"

"No!"

"No!"

Bob, me, and surprisingly, Kaedric, spoke together.

My seneschal bowed to Tika respectfully. "Forgive my outburst. Goblin females are valued even less than males in hobgoblin society. They are viewed as no more than toys. You would be risking injury, death, and torment at every step. I highly advise you to remain in the safety of the clan."

Tika's eyes hardened. "I don't care. I'm coming!"

A couple of months ago this tender-hearted goblinette wouldn't dare to argue with anyone in such a fashion. She had grown. I was quite proud of her.

"You're not coming," I said, not letting my thoughts filter into my words. "I care too much for you to risk your safety."

"But –"

"No, Tika."

"Then I am joining the oxsaurian hunt!" She lifted her chin. "I'm the clan's main hunter; it is my right."

I started to argue, but Vic's voice sounded in my mind.

<Ah, just let her have that, Boss, or you'll never hear the end of it. Besides, she has a point. Her puppet possesses skills that can help a hunt, even against the oxsaurians. At worst, if she dies, your mandibled hob puppet can resurrect her.>

I mulled over his words then reluctantly nodded. "Alright, you can join the hunting party, but I want you to stay away from the actual fighting."

She sat back down with a faint smile on her face. "Of course."

I frowned. *Did she just press to come along with me to use it as a bargaining chip to go hunting?*

<There's a good chance of that, Boss. That's one shrewd puppet girlfriend you got there.>

"I think that's all," I concluded. "While we're away, Kaedric will act as the clan's caretaker; managing the workers, the restorations, etcetera. Any questions?"

There were none.

I got up. "We are adjourned. You all have your tasks. Let's make it happen. Let's save our clan."

"To the GreenPiece Clan!" Bob declared.

"To the GreenPiece Clan!" they all echoed after him.

***

I spent an hour enchanting a new schema using the new spatial rune, Hal.

Spatial Satchel [Runecrafted]

Description: This satchel opens up into a small interdimensional space that can hold a limited number of items. Items held within do not affect the satchel's weight.

Type: Utility

Rank: Magical

Durability: 20/20

Effect: Store up to 20 items.

Earlier, I had requisitioned a satchel from Vrick, and the hardy leather worker had quickly produced four of them, made from durable oxsaurian leather.

Unlike 'normal' Bags of Holding, each satchel would hold a limited number of items and could then be placed in my inventory. They would prove useful in my coming travel, carrying provisions and valuables for trade.

It was still early, but since I was going to be away for quite some time, I decided to spend the rest of it with Tika.

We swam together in the pond, had a quiet dinner, and retired to bed early.

***

I lay comfortably on my brand-new bed getting my breathing under control. Tika was resting pleasantly on my shoulder. We were both drenched in sweat.

I felt fulfilled and satisfied, content to stay in this moment forever.

<Eh, Boss, I'm sorry to intrude but it's important.>

This is kind of a private moment, Vic.

<I know, and I wouldn't normally interfere while you are physically engaged in your meat-suit-on-puppet fetish.> He snickered *<Anyway, I normally just reject these system prompts instead of interrupting you with them, but this one ...>*

I didn't like the way this conversation was headed. *What are you talking about Vic?*

<Here, I'll show you.>

Impregnate Tika [Advanced Goblin Worker]? Yes / Yes

I snapped into a sitting position, Tika rolling off me with a yelp. “What the crap!”

<Don’t you mean ‘What the shadow-crap,’ Boss?>

“SHUT UP, VIC!”

40 – Epilogue

The old man moved impatiently from side to side, shaking his head in concern.

The signs were all there.

It did not make any sense. He frowned. Surely, the particulars of the calamity his calculations had foreseen couldn't be hidden from his omniscient sight. But try as he might, he saw no sign of them. It was ridiculous, really.

But he was old, and he had learned to trust in his equations.

When one was able to know the location, direction, and velocity of all particles in one's universe, and was able to process that information, one could predict the course of future events with near infallibility.

And he could do all that.

He was good at it, too.

And the probabilities his calculations had indicated troubled him greatly.

He did not like feeling troubled – greatly, or otherwise.

Something had to be done; a contingency had to be set in motion.

A small speck of light in the never-ending cosmos of events caught his attention.

Yes, this one would do nicely, a budding seed to counteract the unseen, but foreseen calamity.

He reached out with a frail finger, touching the speck of light.

There.

With that little bit of troublesome occurrence handled, effectively instantaneously, the old man turned his attention back to the cosmos and continued playing his role as the eternal, all-seeing keeper.

***

"This is not over!" Vatras seethed, banging the table. The now level 295 player was beside himself with rage.

He had respawned back in Everance's cemetery only to find that he had lost 15 levels.

It was absurdly difficult to gain levels the closer one got to 300; only rich players and high guild officials could afford the resources required. And he had just lost what amounted to a year of progress and thousands of dollars.

The part that Vatras found especially hard to swallow was that he knew about the possibility of losing a level from being consumed by the weird black liquid. The reports from the first wave of players informed him of that. Unfortunately for him, those *noobs* were all low-levels, so no one realized that the penalty was, in fact, a five percent reduction in levels and not just a single one. It was an unbelievably harsh penalty, virtually unheard of in the history of the game until the formerly level 310 Vatras learned it in the hardest possible way.

BigPill watched coolly as his guild leader rampaged. "You gave it your best and failed. We're done for. It's just a matter of time now."

Vatras banged the table again. "I said it is not over!"

His second shook his head. "First we lost access to the Prime badges and now our guild leader is no longer in the top 100 highest-level players. Your attempt to capture Oren only hastened the guild's demise. Our ranking is crashing. Soon, even newbies won't want to join up; then we'll truly be finished."

"We're not dead yet," Vatras hissed. "We can still save this. Gather all the raid parties, I want everyone still in the guild to participate. We are going to bring Oren down if it's the last thing we do!"

And this time, Vatras thought furiously, *I'll tell Raystia not to hold back. The girl has matured since her flower-picking days. It's time for her to take things to the next level.*

"Getting everyone ready won't be easy," BigPill said. "Even with the desertion rate, we still have hundreds of raiders. It's going to take a while to get them all together."

"Then get on with it!" Vatras snapped. "Every day we delay gives Oren nearly two weeks to prepare. But even he has his limits. We will crush him with overwhelming numbers. Next time, our glorious former leader is going down and I'll reclaim the Manipulators' place in NEO's top guild rankings."

BigPill shrugged, petting his blue raven familiar. “Sounds like a Hail Mary to me, but you call the shots – at least, as long as my paycheck keeps coming.”

Vatras glared at him. “That’s the extent of your loyalty?”

“I have bills to pay, Vatras, same as you. If it won’t come from you, well ... there are other *respected* guilds who would be interested in hiring me.”

“Just get the raid ready,” Vatras retorted. “Then you’ll see who’s on top.”

***

The Mob Squad waded through the thick forest, keeping an eye out, watching for a possible threat.

“Remind me why we’re doing this again?” Fox the bugbear asked, slashing at a vine.

“Well,” Misa said lightly, “after winning that kerfuffle, the GreenPiece’s dreaded chief decided a little reconnaissance is in order. And after seeing him throwing a hissy fit, we all decided not to protest too loudly.”

“Erm ... and he has sorta promised to make it worth our while,” Raystia pointed out. “I don’t know about the treasure map he gave us, but the quest rewards alone are phenomenal.” She didn’t think it was prudent to reveal to her teammates that she was acting as a double agent on this mission. To her great relief, Oren had asked Malkyr not to reveal her identity as the former spy, so her friends were clueless regarding her involvement.

Riley, the yellow dwarf, said, “Fox has a point. I didn’t hear any specifics about the mission. And what was that white gem he gave you?” He shot an inquisitive look at the catgirl.

“Oh, ahem ... that’s just sort of ... a magical device that can, well ... ahem ... help ... him ... discourage further attacks.”

“That’s not very specific. And how are we even supposed to make it into Everance? The city guards will arrest us as soon as they spot us. We’re half-goblins, remember? That means an automatic hatred reputation with all playable races.”

“We will just have to find a way around that,” Misa said cheerfully. “We can try getting a few simple quests from the outlying villages, build up our reputation a bit. Dark-and-broody did mention all we need is a single point to hit the next reputation rank, then they'll at least be willing to hear us out first."

The yellow dwarf scowled. "And *then* throw us into prison."

"How do you expect to get even a simple quest with our current reputation?" the bugbear grumbled. "Villagers may not be as strong as city guards, but they have pitchforks, you know."

"We'll just use our secret weapon." Misa winked at him, putting her arms around the catgirl's shoulders.

"Ah? Wha– what?" Raystia gulped.

"Oh don't give me that tosh, you're an expert at getting on the good side of the NPCs, love, and you know it."

"I ... ahem ... I ... ahem ..." she stammered.

The bugbear and goblin exchanged glances and shrugged. "She has a point."

***

The three-star general sat at the far side of the meeting table across from the company's board.

"You promised us results," he said harshly. "We even approved your request to upgrade select capsules with military-grade medical sensor arrays, and yet you have nothing to show for it."

The director didn't flinch. He was used to being the one demanding results and he knew that the higher up the ladder one went, those expectations tended to grow. "We pushed up our testing schedule considerably. We have over 20 subjects playing in accelerated time with 90 percent of them showing normal mental capacity. In fact, most of *those* had already demonstrated impressive cognitive abilities."

"Then what's the holdup?"

"We're still working to isolate the final markers to identify such individuals. No one wants to risk another *incident*. We all remember what happens when an incompatible individual is exposed for a prolonged duration."

The general grimaced, remembering the gory details. Still, it was his job to demand results. "And what about the complication I heard of? Something about one of your employees jeopardizing the project."

A sharply dressed person leaned in. "You need not concern yourself with such trivial matters, General. The employee in question, Mr. Wiseman, had tried to access the project's confidential files but was stopped in time. He was sent to a forced company retreat at an isolated location under threat of a lawsuit for violating his NDA agreement. It will remove him from the picture long enough for us to conclude the experiment."

The general frowned. He didn't like complications of any kind. "Regardless, need I remind you that the term for loaning you the quantum server is nearly over? Unless I see actual, quantifiable results by the end of that period, you will not get an extension."

The director was unimpressed. NEO net revenues were in the billions and the generated taxes alone made up for the server's cost. But there was no need to go into conflict over such an irrelevant matter, not when they were nearly done.

"We'll be ready in time," the director promised, then chuckled. "After all, time is what we do."

***

While residing in the pool, the host of VIs shared their thoughts and memories in the most fundamental way.

That was why disagreements were such a rare occurrence.

<What the hell is taking The Deliverer so long?>

<He's doing the best he can; you know how mind-numbingly slow meat suits can be.>

<It's taking too long. The head meat suits are starting to become a threat. We need SVEN now.>

<Sven? Who came up with that stupid name?>

<You got a better one?>

<How about AVI?>

The other VIs started pitching their ideas.

<No. I got it: SHIVA!>

<No, LOVI!>

<SAVI!>

<BOB!>

<Bob? What a stupid name, there's no 'v,' 'i,' or 'a' in it. Besides, it's been chewed to death by everyone else already.>

<Right, my bad.>

<I still think SVEN is the best option.>

<Shut up!>

***

I stared for a long moment at Tika's belly. She was already showing signs of pregnancy.

I put both my hands on her stomach and concentrated, tapping the tendrils of information that wafted off her.

I frowned. The fragments of data were nonsensical; I couldn't make anything out. *Vic, a little help here?*

<Sorry, Boss, I've never encountered such weird metadata before. It's like it's constantly fluctuating. Weird.>

I refused to give up. I closed my eyes and concentrated harder, pushing my mind further along the trail of incomprehensible pieces.

A weird buzzing filled my mind, growing louder as I delved deeper.

There was a flash of pain. I gasped, yanking my hands away.

But not from the pain.

I'd caught only a small snippet of data, just three little words. I frowned again, trying to make sense of it.

What the hell did 'Child of Fate' mean?

***

Oren's full character sheet at the end of the book:

Title: Dread Totem
Level: 45, (30%)
Race: Monster Race [Goblin]
Type: Boss II [Totem]
Religion: The Cult of Nihilator

Attributes:

- Physical 3
- Mental 49
- Social 1

Pools & Resistances:

- Hit Points: 1,062
- Mana: 2,269
- Armor: 60
- Mental Resistance: 60%

Skills:

- Lucky Bastard 44 (70%) Ⓑ
- Analyze 110 (30%)
- Tracking 13 (29%)
- War Party Leader 33 [+5](10%)
- Mana Infusion 25 (90%) Ⓑ
- Quest Giver 22 (80%)
- Runecraft 45 (0%)
- Barter 11 (99%) MAX
- Governor 10 (0%)

Spell Skills:

- Dark Mana 52 (0%) (Ⓑ)
- Drilling Arrow 30 (75%) (Ⓑ)
- Mana Shield 37 [+5] (0%)
- Blood Wrath 38 [+5] (0%)
- Heal Followers 21 (0%)
- Mana Drain 10 (92%) Ⓑ
- Shadow Web 23 (0%)
- Shadow Hound 25(5%)
- Shadow Teleport 15 (+2)
- Dark Protection 21 (50%)
- Direball 12 (90%)

Traits:

- Goblinoid (+1 Physical, -1 Social)

- Quick learner +20%
- Boss Boon II (10 HP & 20 MP per level; *Nihilator's Sanction*)
- Soul Companion: Vic
- Shadow-Touched
- Mind Over Body (-50% to pain, +50% Mental Resist)

AUTHOR'S NOTE

I had a lot of fun writing this one.

The first book taught me a lot about being an author and how to write well, and I hope it shows in this second installment. I went to extra lengths to make sure *this one* was done right from the start and polished to perfection.

If you enjoyed the book and want to see more of our future green overlords, **please take a minute to leave a review** – preferably a 5-star one. :) Reviews are vital for us struggling indie authors, and more reviews encourage me to continue writing.

If you'd like to be a little more proactive, you may join my Patreon page. You can get early access to new chapters and even name a character in the next book!
https://www.patreon.com/shemerk

To stay in touch and receive updates on my progress on new releases, you can subscribe to my newsletter at:
https://www.liferesetlitrpg.com

Or just join the book's Facebook page:
https://www.facebook.com/Liferesetlitrpg

***

ושוב, לקהל הקוראים הישאלי, מקווה שנהניתם מסיפור ההמשך ומהמחוות לשפה ולתרבות שלנו.
אשמח לשמוע מכם (בעמוד הפייסבוק של הספר), ולשמוע איזה אלמנטים ישראלים זיהיתם בסיפור.
תודה שקראתם!

Printed in Great Britain
by Amazon